HEARTS AND FLOWERS

Though her former partner is completely uninterested in his unborn child, heavily pregnant Jess can't wait to meet her new baby. However, she hadn't planned on going into early labour at the local garden centre! After baby Poppy arrives, the manager Ed visits the pair in hospital, and they strike up a friendship. Ed finds himself falling for Jess — but can't quite bring himself to tell her. Will the seeds of their chance encounter eventually blossom into love between them?

VIVIEN HAMPSHIRE

HEARTS AND FLOWERS

Complete and Unabridged

LINFORD
Leicester

First published in Great Britain in 2018

First Linford Edition
published 2020

A catalogue record for this book is available
from the British Library.

ISBN 978–1–4448–4516–7

1

*Mind your own business —
Otherwise known as Baby's Tears, it
forms dense carpets of tiny green leaves
and is often used as ground cover or for
edging pathways. It will not tolerate
overly wet, soggy conditions.*

'Mel, where are you?' Jess Markham
screwed her eyes up tightly as another
intense pain squeezed its way through
her and threatened to double her over.
'You have to come right now, Mel. I've
started.'

'Started what?' Mel's voice down the
phone sounded sleepy and very far
away.

'The baby, of course! I'm in labour,
and I need you — now!'

'Labour? But you've got ages to go
yet. You're not due until the twenty-
eighth of June. Are you sure it's not just

a false alarm? Those Braxton-Hicks thingies?'

'Of course I'm sure. This is the real thing all right — and I do not have ages to go. The twenty-eighth is next week, not that this one is going to wait that long.'

'Is it? Oh, Jess, I've been so busy lately I must have lost track.'

'Doesn't matter. What matters is where you are now, and how long it's going to take you to get here.'

'Ah, well . . . '

'Ah, well? What do you mean by that exactly?'

'Could be a problem there . . . I'm on a train, you see. Somewhere between Newcastle and York, I think. I can't tell you exactly where because I've been asleep for a while, and at the moment all I can see outside are fields and trees.'

'York? But that's miles away! By the time you get back into London, and get the Tube, and then the walk at this end . . . oh, it could be hours! I don't know if I can wait that long. How could you

do this to me? You're meant to be my birthing partner, remember? You're supposed to be here — now! You promised.'

'I know I did, but . . . '

'What on earth are you doing on some train anyway? And on a Thursday, when you should be at work?' Jess could feel her voice rising at pretty much the same rate as her panic. 'Oh, hang on. Don't tell me you've been with that bloke? The one you met at my thirtieth. What's his name again — Steve? He was from up north somewhere, wasn't he?'

'He was, and he still is, and yes, I am with him, actually. Not that it's any of your business, Miss Jessica Noseypants, but it's a long story, and not one I want to tell you right now. Anyway, we're on our way back, so we're heading in the right direction. Look, if you really can't cross your legs or something to hold things up a bit, why don't you get down to the hospital and I'll meet you there as soon as I can?'

'Cross my legs? You must be joking! If only it was that simple!'

Now the pain was building up again, but much stronger this time. *Think, Jess, think. Do what they told you. Breathe? Pant? Scream? Oh, no, I can't remember. Can't think. Can't talk.*

'Aaaaa . . . '

'Jess! Jess? Are you OK?' Mel sounded anxious now. 'What was that all about? I lost you for a minute there. Where did you go?'

Jess waited until her breathing had returned to as near normal as it was going to get.

'That was . . . well, a contraction, I think.'

'You think?'

'OK, yes, it definitely was. Baby Markham is trying to say she's ready, even if I'm not. Why didn't someone tell me how much this was going to hurt?'

'They did, but you chose not to listen. You weren't going to worry about it until it happened, you said. And now it has happened. The usual Jess-Markham-can't-be-bothered-to-prepare-properly-for-anything attitude to life. How you ever decided to be a teacher I will never know! All those lesson plans surely don't write themselves. So, how far apart are they, anyway? The contractions, I mean?'

'I don't know. I've only had three so far, and holding the watch was meant to be your job, remember? Five minutes, maybe . . . ?'

'Five? Already? Isn't it meant to start off a lot slower than that? For heaven's sake, Jess, get off the phone and hotfoot it down to that maternity ward before you have the baby on the hall floor or something! You are at home, I assume?'

'I only wish I was, but no. I'm hiding in the loo at the garden centre . . . '

'You're *what*?'

'Look, I came here to buy a gardenia for my nan's birthday, OK? And I'd just picked out a really nice one, with loads of buds on it, when I suddenly felt a bit funny. A bit sort of . . . wet. I looked down, and guess what? It turns out it was my waters breaking. Luckily I was in the outside bit, on the path behind the hydrangeas, so it only hit gravel and not carpet, but it just came in a sort of whoosh ... like pouring a bucket of water out, all in one go. There's hardly anyone about, so I don't think I was spotted, but I'm soaked, it's gone all down my legs and into my shoes, and there isn't even any toilet paper in here.'

'See what I mean? What nine-months-gone woman of sound mind goes off to the garden centre by herself to lug plants about when she's due to drop at any minute? And what good is toilet paper going to be? You need help, you dimwit! Proper help. You shouldn't be doing this on your own. Find a member of staff, call a taxi or an ambulance or something. Better still, call Gary. It's him who should be with you really, not me.'

'No way! I am not having that rat anywhere near me, or my baby ... '

'It *is* his baby too.'

'Huh! Since when has he cared about the baby? Or me, for that matter!'

'OK, OK, no ranting. It's bad for your blood pressure. Save it for another day, eh? Gary's the least of your problems right now, and it's not as if I haven't heard it all before, a thousand times. Now, get off this phone and get some help, before you give birth sitting on some tatty public toilet. Just think how that will look in the Place of Birth column on the birth certificate.'

'Right. OK, I will. But be as quick as you can, won't you?'

'Of course.'

'And come by yourself, right? No Steve. I really don't want some man I don't even know waltzing in while my legs are hooked up in the air and I'm dripping in sweat, or worse.'

'Right, boss. Whatever you say.'

'And can you bring me some stuff? My hospital bag's all packed but it's still at my place, in the hall . . . which is no use at all as you don't have a key . . . just improvise, OK? Run into the supermarket or something. Get me a cheap nightie if you can, and some knickers, nappies . . . and drinks. I can't be doing with those plastic water jugs full of salmonella or MRSI or whatever it is you get in hospitals these days.

'Oh, and have you got your camera with you? If not, your phone will have to do . . . '

'Stop panicking, Jess. Just leave it with me and I'll sort it, OK. Now go. Just go!'

Then, just as Jess was shoving her mobile back into the bag she'd stupidly put down on the suspiciously mucky-looking floor, and was trying to heave herself upright and back onto her feet, someone started banging on the door and an irate voice shouted at her.

'You going to be much longer? There's a queue, you know. What you doing in there, anyway? Laying an egg or something?'

Oh, how I wish I was, Jess thought. *An egg would be a lot easier than what I'm about to lay . . .*

She pulled back the bolt and eased the old wooden door towards her, only just finding enough room to squeeze her enormous belly out through the gap.

As toilets went, it was not one of the best. More like a small shed tucked away in the corner near the exit, right next to the racks piled high with bags of compost and the dead-looking plants they were trying to get rid of at knock-down prices.

As Mel had so rightly said, not the ideal place to give birth at all. She gulped in a big dollop of fresh air and took a couple of faltering steps before the pain started to build up again.

'You all right, love?' An elderly woman, presumably the one who had been banging on the door, was now reaching out a hand to steady Jess as she scrunched up her face and tried to remember how to breathe. 'Only, you don't look too good.'

Behind her, a girl, probably no older than about fourteen or so, stood open-mouthed with a wriggling toddler in her arms. 'Oh,' she said, almost excitedly, 'you're not actually having a baby, are you?'

'Yes.' Jess clutched at the nearest metal rack, her fingers sinking into a layer of grimy soil.

'What? Now?'

'I certainly hope not. Well, not right this minute, but pretty soon, I think. Look, it's not easy for me to even think straight at the moment, let alone talk. Have you got a phone? Do you think you could phone for an ambulance for me?'

'Yeah. Yeah, of course.' The girl pulled her phone from her jeans pocket, shifting the toddler onto her other hip. 'What's the number?'

'Oh, for heaven's sake. Don't they teach you anything in schools these days?' The older woman snatched the phone from the girl's hand and pressed her bony finger three times on the keypad. 'Why don't you make yourself useful and go and find help? A manager or somebody. And get them to bring a chair . . . '

Jess mouthed a silent, 'Thank you' and stood listening as the woman proceeded to explain what was happening and give the address of the garden centre to the operator.

The pain had stopped again and she felt remarkably and embarrassingly normal.

What if she was making a fuss about nothing? What if it was still way too early to be going to the hospital? She probably still had hours left before her baby decided it was time to make an appearance. Days, even. They might not even let her in yet, what with bed shortages and all that. No, she should have just got back into her car, driven herself home, and waited for Mel to get there. She could have made her way to the ward later, when the contractions were the right distance apart, and arrived with dignity, with her carefully packed bag and her birth plan.

She looked up as the teenager came

running back towards her, followed after a few moments by two members of staff, both looking flustered, one of them carrying a bottle of water and some sort of cloth, the other lugging a big cane chair.

Oh, no! Everybody was going to be looking at her now!

She really shouldn't have even left the house today. She should have been lying down on the sofa now, with her feet up and a cup of tea, not about to provide an impromptu centre-of-attention floor show for curious shoppers.

She should have done things properly, by the book — and she probably would have done, if only she'd bothered to read the book in the first place!

* * *

Ed Burton was on his knees, trimming the dead leaves from a begonia, when a young girl came tearing up to him, a baby in her arms and a wild gleam in her eyes.

'D'you work here?' she said, grabbing impatiently for his arm.

Ed smiled. He was wearing wellies and a pair of green overalls with the words 'Blooming Marvellous' embroidered right across the front, so he would have thought it fairly obvious. Even so, it wasn't right to be rude to a customer, so he simply nodded and answered, 'Yes, I do. I'm the manager, in fact. Can I help you at all?'

'It's not me what needs the help,' she spluttered. 'There's a woman about to give birth out there.'

She pointed through the sliding glass doors in the vague direction of the outdoor plant area.

'Like, right now. And she needs a chair.'

Ed stood up quickly.

'A chair? Right . . . and has anyone called an ambulance?'

'Yeah, that's being sorted. Some old lady's doing it. Unless it's all a scam, of course, and they're in it together. Flipping 'eck, they could be making it all up just to steal my phone . . . '

Before he could stop her, she was off again, running back outside. Still, he'd better check it out. Whichever it was — either a baby being born or some kind of attempted robbery — he should get out there and do something about it.

A baby? That would be a first!

They'd had a broken wrist before — luckily not as a result of a slippery floor or anything like that, so at least they weren't sued — and a couple of women having fainting fits on a hot day. But there had never been a birth before.

Well, it wasn't that sort of a place really. Not like Sainsbury's or Mother-care, where heavily pregnant women might get caught short buying up their last-minute emergency supplies. It wasn't as if plants were so essential they couldn't wait a while, even though he said it himself — and he'd spent more or less the whole twenty-five years of his life surrounded by the things.

'Carol!'

He called the nearest assistant over with a frantic wave of his hand, whispering in her ear when she reached his side, so as not to alert the customers to what was going on. She quickly grabbed a bottle of mineral water, and the biggest blanket she could find in the pet section, and followed him outside.

There was already a small gathering around the compost racks.

The teenaged girl who'd come to get him had clearly been reunited with her phone and was now taking pictures with it, the toddler she'd been carrying finally released from her grasp and crawling happily about in the dirt at her feet.

An elderly woman was bending, as far as she was able, over someone sitting on the ground, and gently patting her on the head as if she was a good dog.

'There, there . . . ' she was saying, over and over again, but otherwise didn't seem to be offering a lot in the way of help.

At least four or five others were just standing around gawping — among them an old man shaking his head and tutting in disgust and a child peering curiously around his mother's legs while sucking loudly on an ice lolly.

'The mother-to-be, I assume?' Ed said, edging his way through the spectators and holding out his hand.

'However did you guess?' the woman on the ground replied, a tad sarcastically, staring at his hand but choosing not to take it.

'Oh, I don't know. Just a hunch.'

He almost laughed, but somehow managed to hold it back. Despite her hands being firmly locked together over a belly as big as a balloon about to burst, and a mop of ridiculously wild red hair splayed out around her, she didn't look like someone who'd be in the mood for humour.

'Sorry . . . Ed Burton, garden centre manager, at your service. Here, let me help you up. I've brought the chair you asked for.'

'And a blanket,' Carol added, from somewhere behind him. 'You can put it over you and it might give you a bit of privacy, in case . . . well, you know, if the ambulance doesn't get here in time . . . and some water.'

'And what's that for, exactly? To wet the baby's head?' the woman demanded, wincing in pain as she tried to pull herself up. 'Or were you thinking of boiling it and bringing me a heap of towels as well? I've seen those old movies too, and I've never understood what they do with that stuff . . . '

Ed heaved her all the way to her feet, hoping she wasn't about to deposit a load of slime or blood, or whatever came out of women at a time like this, all over one of the centre's most expensive top-of-the-range conservatory armchairs.

He noticed her reach round and slip

the blanket underneath her bottom as she dropped down into the chair, so she must have been thinking much the same thing. That was a relief! As stock went, he'd rather sacrifice a pet blanket than an expensive chair.

'I think it's time everybody moved away now,' he said, putting on his best voice of authority, which wasn't easy when he was wearing the kind of green overalls that made him look like Kermit the Frog. 'Show's over.'

Gradually, they all wandered off, the boy who'd been eating the lolly dropping the wooden stick behind him on the path and the old woman retreating to the toilet so rapidly he thought she might be about to wet herself.

'Thanks,' the pregnant woman said, smiling at him at last. 'I don't think I could have coped with an audience.'

'It's fine, um . . . ' He suddenly realised he didn't know her name. 'Mrs . . . ?'

'Jess. Just call me Jess.'

'Right, Jess. Do you want me to go away, too? Perhaps leave you here with Carol, until the ambulance arrives? She's had two children of her own.'

'Three,' Carol corrected him. 'But that doesn't make me an expert. Or a midwife, for that matter.'

'Of course not. I just thought . . . '

'That's the trouble with you men. You never do think, do you? Go on, off with you. I'll sit with her. But don't you go docking my wages if I'm not there opening my till when I'm supposed to.'

'As if I would!'

Ed started to walk away.

Best leave them to it. Perhaps he'd go out onto the street and wait for the ambulance, make sure they found the place all right. It could be tricky, spotting the entrance from the dual carriageway, and it wouldn't be the first time someone had driven past and had to go all the way to the roundabout and back again to find their way into the car park.

He glanced at his watch. Five to two.

He should have taken his lunch break by now but, as usual, he had got distracted. There always seemed to be something needing his attention. A stroppy customer, an order nobody could find, something spilled or broken, and now this.

Come to think of it, his stomach was feeling a bit on the empty side, and it had been hours since he'd even stopped for a cup of tea. He might as well make one now, and eat the sandwich from his packed lunch while he waited outside for help to arrive.

The little boy in him was quite looking forward to the flashing blue lights and wailing siren of an ambulance screeching up to the doors in a flurry of dust.

The man in him, however — the grown-up responsible businessman that he was supposed to be these days — knew that there were far more important things to think about. And a baby being born right here at Blooming Marvellous — blooming marvellous though it undoubtedly would be — was suddenly right up there at the very top of that list.

2

Speedwell —
A common and troublesome rock
plant, with small blue flowers and hairy
stems. It's highly invasive, stubborn,
and spreads rapidly.

'Can you manage to walk? It's not far from here to the car park.'

The girl from the ambulance crew, who had introduced herself as Sally, had a hand under Jess's armpit and was already easing her out of the cane chair without waiting for an answer.

'I think so.'

Jess took a big breath as she straightened up, hauling her bag onto her shoulder, and hoping that sitting on the blanket had saved the seat from whatever liquid was still seeping through the rear of her soggy elastic-waisted skirt. Still, that wasn't really her problem. It was that manager, Ed's, and his assistant's. They'd brought her the stupid chair, after all.

'In fact, I feel fine now . . . all this fuss! And I do have my own car here, so I probably should have just gone home . . . '

'I don't think driving right now would be a very good idea, Jess. Not while you're having contractions. And, besides, we're here now, so why not make the most of it, eh? Comfy bed, door to door service, even a hand to hold if you should feel the need . . . '

Jess shook her head. 'I don't think . . . '

But then another pain washed over her just as she was climbing up the step into the back of the ambulance, and she didn't get to finish what she was about to say, or even to remember what it was. *Ow, that hurt!*

'Another contraction?' Sally put a dark green uniformed arm around her to steady her. 'OK, breathe . . . that's it

. . . it will soon pass. Right, only three minutes that time, so things are certainly speeding up. Now, you come and lie down here, and we'll soon have you safely delivered.'

'What?' Jess could feel the panic welling up inside her, her hands shaking uncontrollably. 'Delivered? I'm not going to have the baby here, am I? Now? In the back of an ambulance?'

'Well, what I actually meant was delivered to the maternity ward,' Sally laughed. 'Don't worry, we should have plenty of time to get you there — in theory, anyway — but if things should change, we can deliver babies. We're fully equipped.'

She nodded towards her colleague, John, a strapping great bear of a man with enormously wide shoulders that looked like they belonged to a prop forward, and who was now climbing into the driving seat.

'We've both done it before,' she added.

'Oh, wow! You were right about me

not driving, weren't you? Imagine trying to steer a car in the middle of all that pain. I had no idea how bad it was going to be, and it's going to get worse, I bet? It's all I can do to keep my eyes open, let alone my legs! Like it's spreading everywhere, from top to toe. Or is it the other way around?'

'That's all perfectly normal. And why we've got John here, to battle the traffic for you, and to get you there safely. Now, is anyone coming with you, Jess?' She peered out through the open doors. 'Is this your partner?'

Jess hadn't noticed him before, but Ed was hovering just outside. She couldn't decide from his pale face and open-mouthed expression if he was showing genuine concern or was more like someone watching *One Born Every Minute* on TV, appalled by it all but strangely unable to look away. Had the man never seen a woman giving birth before? Well, probably not, actually.

'Oh, no. We're not . . . I mean, no, I only met him for the first time about fifteen minutes ago!'

'Right. Just us then. Ready?'

Jess nodded. 'As I'll ever be.'

'Good luck!' Ed called, waving her off with a half-eaten sandwich in his hand, as the doors closed and the ambulance moved away.

Jess tried to relax. Luck? Was that what it came down to? Like watching the lottery balls chucking themselves around in their big glass bowl as you clutched your ticket and waited for the result? Whatever she said or did now would make no difference. It was happening, really happening. She was in the hands of luck, and Nature, and the NHS. This baby was really coming, and soon by the feel of it, whether Mel turned up or not.

She half sat, half lay on the narrow bed, gazing down at her own legs, white, shaking and far too hairy. When had she last shaved them? Or the bikini area everyone was going to be looking so closely at pretty soon now. Since when had she stopped caring about things like that? Since she'd put on two-and-a-half stone and couldn't even see her own feet, probably.

'How are you feeling?' Sally asked, holding her hand just as she'd promised and wincing as Jess dug her nails in just a tad too hard.

'Yeah, OK, I suppose. Well, I've been better, to be honest!'

As they whizzed along the streets, taking corners as if they were on some frantic fairground ride, she wasn't at all sure what she was feeling. Scared? Excited? Sick? All of the above.

Strangely, none of that worried her. Even as John switched on the siren and the blue flashing light, and guided them swiftly and safely through a traffic jam at high speed, a gap between the cars miraculously opening up before them like the parting of the Red Sea, only three things did seem to matter. Stupid things, that kept popping to the front of her mind as if they were trying to keep the really important stuff at bay. Things like, why was she still clutching a bottle of water she hadn't asked for and definitely hadn't paid for? What would happen to Georgina, her poor little Mini, left by itself at the garden centre with the keys still somewhere at the bottom of her bag? And where on earth had she put her nan's gardenia plant?

★ ★ ★

There was one good thing about giving birth alone, and that was that there was nobody there to hear her scream like a banshee or swear like a trooper, both of which she was doing in abundance! Nor was there anybody there to witness that mortifying moment when her bowels came out in some sort of unplanned sympathy with her womb and expelled a little something she'd rather have kept inside.

Of course, she wasn't totally alone. From the moment she had arrived, the system had swung effortlessly into auto mode.

Sally and John had wheeled her in,

28

reeled off her name and a load of numbers Jess couldn't even begin to understand, and left her to her fate, dashing off out to deal with their next car crash or heart attack or whatever. Jess didn't know how anyone would choose a job like that, let alone stick at it and still keep a smile on their face, but she was glad they did.

Now in their place at her side was Nancy.

Nancy was big, bouncy and black, a middle-aged midwife with a no-nonsense attitude that spoke of years of experience and an aura of utter confidence, which seemed thankfully to be mixed with a good dollop of compassion.

'Not long now, my lovely.'

Nancy bent to take another close-up look at Jess's nether regions and came up smiling.

'We should see the crown at the next push.'

Jess grinned. The gas and air were taking the edge off the pain and making her almost euphorically light-headed, and a vision of a tiny princess popping out, already wearing a tiny golden crown, suddenly seemed like the funniest thing she could ever imagine.

When the baby finally came, slithering out like a little fish and uttering the strangest but most wonderful of *Here I am!* cries, Jess was amazed to find that all the pain just stopped.

Everything stopped, as if time had stalled and something momentous and incredible had happened. Which, of course, it had.

In an instant, the world felt like a different place. She was a mother. She, Jess Markham, was a mother.

There was a lot of action going on somewhere at the bottom end of the bed, a feeling of wetness, anonymous hands swooping and scooping, and someone talking about stitches.

None of that mattered. She was a mother now. A real-life, living, breathing mother.

After a moment or two, Nancy

wrapped a pink blanket around the little girl, still smeared in goo, pronounced her perfect and gently laid her in Jess's arms.

'Here we are, my lovely,' she said. 'Meet your daughter. Placenta still to come, but you've done pretty much all of it in three hours flat, start to finish. That's some speed, I can tell you. Well done. We'll make a marathon runner of you yet!'

* * *

Mel came bursting in at visiting time, bumping several huge carrier bags along beside her.

'About time, too!' Jess sat up in bed and made a point of looking at the watch that wasn't actually there on her wrist. 'I can't bear wearing this hospital gown thing a moment longer.'

'I got here as soon as I could. You wouldn't believe the trouble I've had, what with trying to charge up my phone for the photos, and the rush hour crowds on the tube, and the supermarket not having any newborn nappies, and . . . '

'OK, OK, I get it, but, Mel, today is not about you.' Jess giggled, to let her friend know she was only joking.

'Of course not . . . oh, Jess, I'm so sorry I wasn't here at the time.'

She dumped all the bags on the end of the bed, only just missing Jess's feet, and dived in for a hug, her hands meeting bare flesh where the sides of the stiff white gown didn't quite meet up properly at the back.

'What sort of a birthing partner doesn't even get to be there at the birth? And when I did get here, they said I was too late and had to wait for visiting times like every other Tom, Dick or Harry!'

'Which is exactly what you are, as far as they're concerned.' Jess laughed and turned towards the little crib next to the bed. 'But now you *are* here, don't you want to meet her?'

'Yes — more than anything!'

Mel tiptoed the few short paces around the bed and gazed down at the baby, now sound asleep and making little snuffly noises, a pink knitted teddy propped up beside her. Jess's nan had made it, and she'd been carrying it around in her bag for ages. It had looked quite small before, but now, next to her tiny baby, it looked enormous.

'Oh, just look at her,' Mel cooed, gently looping her fingers around the baby's hand. 'She's absolutely adorable.'

'Of course she is. She's mine!'

'And Gary's.'

'No swear words allowed. Baby present.'

'Oh, stop it. You know you don't mean that. But she does look a bit like him, doesn't she? Don't you think so? She's got his chin, and his cheekbones . . . '

'I can't see it myself.'

'Well, you wouldn't, would you? Because you don't want to. I don't suppose you've rung him to tell him, have you?'

'No, I haven't. Not yet. I've told my mum and dad, and they're driving up from Devon in the morning. And you. And my nan, naturally. And I'll ring the girls at work later, and see who's won the sweepstake. Date, weight, sex . . . they've been making their picks for weeks . . . '

She paused and gave Mel a stern look.

'Oh, don't look at me like that. Gary can wait his turn. There's a pecking order for these things, you know. Family and friends first, and Gary's way down the list. Maybe I'll tell him when I'm out of here and back home. I don't think I could face him turning up here just yet.'

'You sure?'

'Yes, I am. We split up months ago, Mel. He made his feelings totally clear, and I somehow don't think he's going to come running back now, baby or no baby.'

She put on a brave smile and brazenly changed the subject.

'Now, come on, you've been here all of three minutes and you haven't taken a single photo yet. I've done a few of her on my phone, but I want mother and baby together, so I can be all proud and smug, and show her off all over Facebook — with privacy settings on, naturally. I can't have just any old body gawping at her. So I hope you've brought me a half-decent nightie in one of those bags. There's no way I'm being photographed in this thing!'

'Well, it'll do. Plain blue with a bit of lace around the neck, and buttons up the front in case you . . . you know, have to open them.'

'To feed her, you mean? Yeah, I suppose that will make it a bit easier — the access part of it anyway — but as for the rest . . . I've had my first try, and I swear she's got teeth! Now, just pull the curtain round the bed for a tick and I can wriggle out of this awful gown . . .'

'Ooh, Jess,' Mel squealed, only seconds later. 'Hurry up in there. I think she's waking up. Oh, just look at those eyes! They're so blue. They're exactly like yours.'

Jess leaned across and swished the edge of the curtain back just enough to peer out, as she wriggled the nightie downwards over what was left of her baby bump — which felt like most of it, despite the sudden removal of a seven-pound baby and all that came with it. She winced as she lifted her sore rear end, stitches and all, from the bed, and tried not to think about what she must look like down there, all ripped apart like a badly opened parcel someone had tried to tie back together with string. She could already imagine the look of horror on Gary's face if he were to come anywhere near her, and felt immensely glad that that was no longer going to happen.

'All babies have blue eyes, Mel.'

Jess tore her thoughts away from her ex, made the final adjustments to her clothing, and reached into the little see-through cot to lift the baby out, burying her nose in her warm skin and breathing her in. What was a bit of soreness, when this beautiful baby was the result? She could hardly believe this perfect little thing was hers, really hers. To keep and to take home.

'But I think I can detect a tiny bit of Markham red in her hair.'

'What hair?' Mel giggled, easing the curtain all the way back around its rail. 'She's as bald as a coot!'

'She is not!' Jess said, defensively, although secretly she had to admit to herself that it was true. 'And what's wrong with coots anyway? They're lovely little birds.'

'Yes, they are. Just like her. Totally, scrummily lovely. Oh, she's going to break some hearts!'

Mel reached over and tentatively touched the baby's soft cheek, then rummaged in her pocket and pulled out her phone.

'Right. That's enough adoration for

now. She'll be getting all big-headed. Time for some photos.'

'Hang on a minute. There's one very important thing you haven't asked me yet.'

'Which is?'

'Her name, of course,' Jess grinned.

'Oh, yeah. Silly me. After all those baby name books and endless lists you made, you never did come to a decision, did you? I knew you'd have to actually see her before you knew what fitted. So, what have you decided to call her, in the end?'

'Poppy.' Jess gazed at her daughter and gently kissed her on the forehead. 'I'm calling her Poppy. A flowery name, because she was very nearly born among the flowers.'

'Poppy . . . ' Mel pondered for a few moments. 'Yes, I like it, I really do. Poppies for remembrance and for peace. It suits her, and it's very *you*, if you know what I mean. Come on then, pretty Poppy.'

She held her phone out in front of

her and pointed it at the two of them, snuggled closely together.

'Pose with your mummy and give us a big smile, Poppy, because you are about to become a Facebook sensation!'

★   ★   ★

Ed hovered in the reception area, his face almost hidden behind the enormous bouquet of flowers he was clutching, along with a shiny silver 'New Baby' balloon that bounced about on its over-long ribbon and kept bopping him on the cheek and only just missing his eye.

If there was one big advantage to owning and running a garden centre, it was the easy availability of flowers, whatever the time of year, and an abundant array of cards and gifts suitable for any occasion.

He had no idea if the baby was a boy or a girl — so pink or blue were out of the question — or even whether it had actually been born yet. From what he'd heard, they could pop out in a sudden rush or hang about biding their time for days. But either way it was only right and proper that he should turn up at the hospital and pay his respects, if that was the right phrase to use.

The near-birth of a baby on the premises had certainly been a first for Blooming Marvellous, and he felt it should be marked in some way. Perhaps he could put a plaque up, on a bench or a greenhouse, or name one of the planted areas after the child — depending on what name it had been given, of course. He really couldn't face having to call something the Horace House or the Kylie Rose Garden forever more!

Now, what had the woman said she was called? Jess. Yes, that was it. But did she mention what her surname was? If she had, he'd either not been listening or he'd already forgotten it.

He approached the desk with caution, not sure what he was actually going to say that didn't make him come across as some kind of weirdo. This was going to sound very odd, he knew; asking if he could pop in and visit a patient whose name he didn't even know.

'Um . . . I'm here to see Jess. She was brought in this afternoon, by ambulance.'

The girl looked up from her computer, taking in the floral vision before her, and grinned as the balloon slipped from Ed's hand and bobbed upwards towards the ceiling.

'Ah, yes. Jess and baby are in bed three, down there on the right.'

Well, that was easy enough!

'What a shame you missed the birth, but I'm sure she'll be pleased to see you now.' She gave him a big smile. 'Congratulations, Daddy!'

What? That was twice today he'd been mistaken for the expectant father! Or the new actual father now, he supposed. He must have that look about him, whatever that look was. Stressed and scared to death, probably.

He hesitated, grabbing for the ribbon on the balloon and reining it back in. Should he try to explain? Best not, in case she changed her mind and refused to let him in. It wasn't as if he intended to stop long anyway.

Right. Bed three, here I come . . .

'Oh,' the girl called after him. 'I should also tell you that no flowers are allowed on the ward. Health and Safety . . . germs, pollen, that sort of thing. If you'd like to leave them with me, you can pick them up again on your way out. Pop them in a vase at home and they'll be ready to welcome her when she comes out. A nice surprise for her.'

Oh, that would be a surprise all right! he thought, handing them over quickly and heading through the glass door and into the ward in search of bed three. *Not just the flowers, but finding me waiting for her at home!*

The ward was busy, every bed surrounded by exhausted-looking fathers and over-excited grandparents, but he found the right one easily enough. And there was Jess, surrounded by plastic carrier bags and grinning as a tall dark-haired girl, who had her back towards him, was busily snapping away from just about every conceivable angle on her phone.

'Oh . . . hello.' Jess had taken her eyes away from the camera lens for a second or two and had spotted him hovering.

'Hello. Remember me? Sorry if this isn't a good time, but I . . . well, I . . . just wanted to see that you were all right.'

Ed didn't usually stutter like that but suddenly he felt very nervous, out of place, as if coming here just might have been a mistake.

'How things turned out, you know . . . '

'Of course I remember you. Ed, right?'

'That's right. Ed Burton.'

He took a tentative step nearer to the bed. At least she knew who he was.

'As you can see, things turned out very well, thank you.' She looked down

43

at the bundle in her arms and smiled. 'Mother and baby doing well.'

'That's good. Look, I won't stop. I really don't want to intrude, but Carol and the rest of the staff were wondering ... and so was I, I have to admit. It's not every day something like this happens at work, and I'd have hated not knowing ...'

'It's kind of you to be concerned.' Jess smiled up at him. 'And I'm happy to report, to Carol and to anyone else who might want to know, that I have a beautiful healthy daughter. I've called her Poppy. Come a bit closer, and meet her. Oh, and this is my friend, Mel, by the way.'

'Hello, Mel.'

He nodded to Jess's friend and smiled to himself as he got his first close-up glimpse of the cutest little baby he had ever seen.

'And hello, Poppy.'

'Ed sort of came to my rescue earlier,' Jess said, as Mel dropped the phone back down on the edge of the bed and plonked herself beside it. 'At the garden centre.'

'Well, someone had to.' The girl was shaking her head, a mane of dark hair flicking from side to side across her forehead. 'I told you that you were an idiot for even being out in a place like that, on your own, and in your condition.'

'Well, I was, and there's nothing we can do to change that now, is there?' Jess turned back to Ed. 'I feel I must owe you something for the bottle of water you gave me, and for messing up that blanket, and the chair . . . '

'The chair survived. The blanket not so good, but who cares? As for the water, it was hardly a gin and tonic, was it? Just cheap and cheerful, and cold. You looked like you needed it.'

'I think I probably needed a gin and tonic more, to be honest!'

'Maybe another time?'

Oh, no. Had he really just said that? He'd made it sound like he was asking her out on a date! When she'd just given birth. And she must be a good three or four years older than him too, if not more. And married? He had no idea.

'Like I said, I'm not stopping,' he went on, feeling suddenly and stupidly embarrassed. 'This is a special time for you. Family time. And now I have something positive to report back, I'll get out of your hair. Oh, and I brought flowers, by the way. I wasn't allowed to bring them in, so they're at the desk out there. Maybe your friend . . . Mel could pick them up when she leaves and look after them until you go home.'

'Thanks. That's very kind of you, but there was no need.'

'No, really. My pleasure.'

His cheeks were burning now. Definitely time to leave. Should he shake Jess's hand, kiss her cheek, kiss the baby, or stand well back and just wave? Knowing how to say goodbye was proving almost as hard as knowing how to say hello had been just minutes earlier.

'And the balloon?' Jess was looking upwards, her eyes following the ribbon all the way up, almost to the ceiling, her mouth clearly trying to suppress a giggle. 'Is that for me too?'

Ed had completely forgotten he was still clutching it.

'Of course! Well, I suppose it's for little Poppy really, isn't it? Not that's she old enough to play with it. Here, I'll tie the ribbon in half. Heaven knows why Carol cut it so long.'

He looped the ribbon and knotted it, then tied it loosely to the end of the bedframe and started to back away.

'Oh, and Ed . . . ' Jess was calling him back. 'My car — it's still in your car park. A red Mini. I don't know when . . . '

'Oh, that's OK. It can stay as long as it likes. I promise I will guard it with my life.'

'No need to go quite *that* far.'

'Maybe not. But please . . . when you come to collect it, you will come inside and find me, won't you? There's something I'd like to show you. If it's ready by then.'

'That sounds mysterious.'

'All will be revealed. See you soon, I hope. And little Poppy.'

Then he left, walking away quickly before he outstayed his welcome, plans for the little brass plaque with the baby's name on it — and where to put it — already forming in his head.

3

Orchid —
A widespread family of flowering
plants, with blooms that are colourful
and fragrant, but often need support.
They are generally heavy feeders.

Ed hung around for a while after leaving the ward, not yet feeling quite ready to go home. It had been a strange, unsettling sort of day, and he already knew how his mother would react, with squeals of excitement and far too many questions, when he got back and told her what had happened.

He found a seat by the window in the small coffee shop in the lobby downstairs and, clutching a large Americano, sat and watched the world go by. Or one small corner of it, anyway.

Various nurses and porters popped in and out to buy takeaway drinks and

49

pastries, or sit down for a few minutes and close their eyes. When the evening visitors started to trickle out of the lifts soon after eight o'clock, several patients came down with them, dressed in pyjamas and dressing gowns, kissing goodbye, ordering hot drinks or just wandering about, apparently aimlessly, as if reluctant to return to their beds.

Through the glass he could see at least three men and one woman, obviously patients, standing outside in the dark, pulling dressing gowns or anoraks tightly around them, their bare feet pushed into slippers or trainers, having sneaky cigarettes, seemingly oblivious to the cold. He wondered which would get them first — pneumonia or lung cancer.

Ed downed the last mouthful of his coffee, stepped through the big glass sliding doors and headed back to the car. He slid his ticket into the machine at the barrier and paid the hospital's extortionate parking fee, then took a left turn out onto the main road.

Aware that he hadn't eaten anything since the sandwich at lunchtime and remembering that it was his mum's bingo night so she wouldn't actually be there after all, he thought he'd treat himself to fish and chips. Heavy on the salt and vinegar, and with a portion of mushy peas on the side. Hardly a healthy meal, but not one he indulged in too often, and the peas would probably count as one of his five a day.

'Hiya, Ed. How are you?'

The girl behind the counter was called Leanne. He'd known her at school, and had quite fancied her back then, before she went down the pierced nose and tattoos route.

'Not so bad, Lee. Usual, please.'

He hadn't been in for at least a month, but she would remember his regular order, he knew. He wondered if she remembered everybody's, or was it only his? It was fairly obvious that she was interested in him as more than just a customer.

He watched her pick up her tongs

and choose the biggest piece of cod from the glass cabinet, shovel a mound of chips on top and spoon a big dollop of peas into a tub, before wrapping the whole lot up tightly in several layers of paper. He was sure she gave him bigger portions than anyone else, but if he couldn't manage it all, the dog could always help him finish it up.

Old Rex had never been known to refuse a scrap, or leave so much as a crumb behind on the carpet when he'd finished. Who needed a Hoover when they had a spaniel with a bottomless pit of a stomach and eyes as big as its belly?

'That'll be six pounds fifty please.'

Leanne took his ten-pound note and rang it through the till, her hands greasy and warm and lingering over his as she handed him his change.

'Off anywhere at the weekend? There's a gig on at The Feathers on Saturday night, I think. Some new comedian, and a band after. I've got the night off for a change.'

It was starting to sound very much as if she was hinting for a date, but he really didn't want to encourage her. She wasn't his type, and getting tangled up with the wrong person only ever led to trouble it wasn't always easy to get away from.

He'd seen enough of that with his mate Rich and that fruit-loop girlfriend of his, who seemed to have got her long purple claws into him and was rushing him towards the aisle like a lamb to the slaughter.

No — Leanne was a nice enough girl, but it was best to let her down gently and steer clear.

'Sounds good,' he said, 'but Saturdays are always really busy for me at work. By the time I get home, I'm usually too worn out to do anything much except flop in front of Ant and Dec. And then I'm up early to do it all again on Sundays. We sell an awful lot of plants on Sundays. You have fun, though.'

'Another time, maybe?'

Oh, boy. She sounded just like he had earlier, saying pretty much the same thing to that Jess girl about the gin and tonic. Clumsy and pushy, and downright embarrassing. Whatever must she have thought of him?

Luckily, there was a queue building up behind him and Leanne's attention had already turned to the next customer by the time he reached the door, so he was able to make his escape before things got any worse.

Oh, he liked girls all right, liked them a lot, but it was true what he'd told her about being busy, about just not having the time. Work had taken over his life lately, and if he was ever, somehow, going to make the time to let a girl into his life, then it would have to be the right girl. And he knew that wasn't Leanne.

Ed climbed back into the car and headed for home, dipping his gaze as he passed his grandparents' house. He was still finding it difficult to look at its little front garden and know that he'd never again see Grandad out there waving to him as he mowed the lawn, or the hanging baskets tumbling with a mass of bright fuchsias he'd helped him to grow.

Ever since the old man had died, just eight months earlier, Ed had been struggling.

At twenty-five, he'd suddenly found himself not only the manager of Blooming Marvellous, but the owner too. It was a huge responsibility, and he still wasn't sure that a good head for figures and an inside-out knowledge of plants really were quite enough.

In the normal course of events, the business would have gone to his dad, but they'd lost him first — to cancer, when Ed was just twelve and his sister Kate only eighteen months older. In the years that followed he didn't know what any of them would have done without Gran and Grandad. He was sure his mum would have gone to pieces if left to her own devices. They had provided the always-there support that had held her up, taking both children off her hands whenever she needed the time to herself, Gran dishing up apple pies and games of Scrabble and oodles of tea and sympathy, while Grandad took care of all the practical stuff involving screwdrivers and paintbrushes and engine oil that a woman on her own had never had to deal with before.

Grandad Burton had not been the sort of man who talked about his emotions, not the sort to wallow in his misery when times got tough. Not even when his only son had died in the most cruel of ways, too young and much too soon.

In all the years he'd known him, Ed couldn't remember ever seeing his grandad cry. Instead, he would walk purposefully down the garden to his greenhouse, to spend time alone and take care of his plants. Quietly, tenderly, watering and nurturing, potting seeds or taking cuttings, all the while whistling tunelessly to himself or muttering under his breath as if he was talking to each tiny shoot and willing it on.

It hadn't come as a surprise when the will had been read and Ed had been told that Blooming Marvellous was now his.

For as long as he could remember he had been his grandad's unofficial apprentice, his shadow, following him around after school and in the holidays, learning all he could about the flowers and plants, digging and pruning, copying what he saw. His fingernails were rarely clean, constantly edged with a layer of ingrained dirt.

If he was honest there was nowhere else he would rather be, no other job he could ever imagine himself doing but, still, it was hard. There was so much more to it than flowers. There were the accounts to keep on top of, the ordering, the maintenance and cleaning to worry about, plus the staff to manage.

As well as all that, pretty soon the lease would be up for renewal and the council who owned the land would no doubt be trying to put up the rent.

He had never realised just how much was involved, or given much thought to the garden centre's future, but now it was what he thought about more than anything else. Keeping the business going, thriving, moving forward, not letting his grandad down.

He pulled into the drive, opened the front door, and took his bundle of fish and chips through to the kitchen, giving it a quick re-heat in the microwave while he found himself a plate and some cutlery.

There was a scribbled note stuck to the fridge with a magnet: *Left you a ham salad if you want it. Back by eleven. Mum xxx*

Ed grinned to himself. One of these days she would remember he was twenty-five years old and capable of feeding himself, even if his choices were occasionally of the takeaway variety. But that's what mothers did, he supposed . . . cared about you, fussed over you, fed you, no matter how old you were.

For a fleeting second an image jumped into his head of Jess and her new baby, of a new maternal bond being formed right now, magically and pretty much instantly, one that he was sure would last for a lifetime.

As he tucked into his meal, he let his mind run through some ideas for the baby's bench — a bench with a little brass plaque commemorating her arrival in the world and Blooming Marvellous's part in it certainly felt like the most appropriate and lasting choice.

He'd place it on one of the pathways, somewhere with a nice view of the roses, where customers could take a breather while they browsed and take in the scents of the flowers around them. Not in the actual place where he had found Jess, as that was most definitely too near to the toilets!

★ ★ ★

'Sorry about running off and leaving you at the station like that.'

Mel flopped down heavily into the big squishy sofa in the quietest corner of the pub, laid Jess's huge bouquet down on the seat beside her and gratefully picked up the glass of red wine that was already waiting for her on the table.

Steve put an arm along the back of the rather worn upholstery and rubbed his fingers up and down her neck until she shivered.

He was wearing a bright green and white striped rugby shirt that he must have pulled out of his travel bag, because she was sure she hadn't seen it earlier. It seemed to swamp his skinny frame, but she liked the rugged masculine look of it, even though it was clear it had never met an iron in its life. She was definitely going to have to take his domestic arrangements in hand if she was ever going to present him to her mum and dad as a serious long-term prospect.

'I'm just glad you came back,' he said, looking at his watch. 'I wasn't sure you would.'

'Missed me, did you?

She kissed him on the cheek, breathing in the fading musky scent of the aftershave he had put on after shaving that morning, although she could already feel the beginnings of bristle bursting out again against her skin.

'I was only going to the maternity ward, not Outer Mongolia! Of course I was coming back. I might have been a bit longer than I expected to be, but I'm here now.' She nuzzled her face into the crinkled collar of his shirt, his musky aftershave making her insides do that little flip she still hadn't quite got used to. 'And all yours.'

'That's what I like to hear. And you didn't have to buy me flowers, by the way. A simple sorry would have done!'

'Idiot! These are for Jess, not you. And what am I meant to be sorry about?'

'Abandoning me for hours on end? No, not really, I'm only joking. So, tell me what happened. Did you make it in time to hold her hand and help cut the cord and all that?'

Mel pulled a face. 'Yuck! No, I didn't. To be honest, I didn't mind the idea of just being there, you know, telling her to breathe and pant, and mopping her brow, but I was never really sure about getting involved at the gory end. Still, it was all done and dusted by the time I arrived, so no need. Jess did pretty well on her own, by the sound of it. She had a little girl, by the way. Poppy. Oh, Steve, she is so sweet!'

'Don't you start getting all broody on me.'

'Oh, heavens no! She's a little darling, but she's most definitely someone else's little darling. I'm sure I'm going to love her, and I'll probably end up spoiling her rotten, but I can always hand her back afterwards, can't I? As soon as the wailing starts and the smelly nappies kick in. Just the way I like it. No, I'm nowhere near ready for having babies myself just yet.'

Steve took a gulp of his pint and took her hand.

'Me neither. Been there, done that,' he said, and she half expected him to finish the sentence with something about having got the T-shirt too, but he didn't. It was pretty obvious though, from the look on his face, that the two children he had already fathered were quite enough, and he was in absolutely no hurry to do it again.

Mel hadn't mentioned anything to Jess about Steve or their recent trip to Scotland and, with the baby clearly the only thing in her thoughts right now, Jess hadn't asked either. Maybe it was best that way. Despite Jess's own chequered history with the opposite sex, Mel felt sure her friend would not approve. She wasn't even a hundred per cent sure how she felt about it all herself at the moment, so not having to try justifying her actions to anyone else for now was a blessing.

What they were doing wasn't wrong — not something to feel ashamed of. OK, so he was married — technically. His divorce hadn't actually been finalised yet, but they weren't sneaking around behind anyone's back or hurting anyone, were they?

Stella, Steve's wife — almost ex-wife — had taken the children back up north to live with her parents and didn't want to know what he got up to any more, and it seemed she didn't care much either. She was the one who had ended things between them and, from what Mel could gather, had already moved on to someone else.

Still, there was something about their situation that made her feel a bit uneasy. Married men were somewhere she had always told herself she would never go, and married men with kids were even more of a concern.

Theory was one thing. Real life was quite another, but she was in too deep to back out now. Not that she wanted to. She already knew that she loved Steve and, although neither of them had yet said it out loud, she was sure he felt the same way. Why else would he have asked her to travel all those miles with him this week to meet his children, Harry and Josh?

They had turned out to be wonderfully bright and happy eight-year-old twins, who had held her hands, one on each side, as they strolled along the beach in the wind, and chatted away as if they had known her all their lives.

'Do you want to get some food?'

Steve's voice cut into her thoughts as he picked up the menu and ran a finger down it. 'Only they stop taking orders at nine, and I could do with a sandwich at least, if only to soak up the beer.'

'Nine? We've got ages yet.'

'Er, no, we haven't, Mel. It's ten to.'

'Is it?' Mel looked at her watch. 'Where on earth did today go?'

'Well, I'd say a fair bit of it went on your friend Jess and her baby. Now, I'm having a toasted ham and cheese and another pint, so make up your mind quickly before they shut the kitchen, or it'll have to be back to mine and take pot luck what's in the fridge . . . beans on toast, if you don't mind scraping the green bits off the bread.'

Mel wrinkled her nose and quickly chose the bangers and mash with onion gravy and another glass of wine, knocking back what was left of the first one while Steve queued at the bar.

Did they have wi-fi in this place? She opened her phone and flipped through the photos she'd just taken at the hospital. The quicker she got them up onto Facebook so Jess could start sharing them with all and sundry, the better.

4

Poppy —
Bringing beauty back to the fields after
battle, and seen as a symbol of peace
and sleep. It's ideal for creating a bright
splash of colour in a sunny corner.

Jess's dad was sitting awkwardly at the
end of her hospital bed, idly crunching
his way through a packet of mints he'd
found in his pocket.

'So, how long are they keeping you
in, love?'

'I should be going home tomorrow, I
hope.'

'Are you sure you'll be able to
manage?' her mum said, worried. 'On
your own, I mean.'

'Mum, you're not at it again, are you?
Look, Gary's gone. For good, as far as
I'm concerned, so I don't have a lot of
choice, do I? I've been on my own, as

you call it, for months already, but now I have Poppy, so I'm not on my own any more, am I?'

'You know what your mother means, love. Will you be able to manage her by yourself? The nappies, and the feeding, and the sleepless nights, and all that.' Her dad laid a hand over hers. 'You can always come home with us, you know, Jessie. Get some sea air into your lungs, have a bit of a rest. For a while at least, until you find your feet.'

'This is the first time in weeks I've actually been able to see my feet without having to peer round my bump! Seriously, Dad, I'll be OK. I've still got at least another six months off work, more if I need it, and full pay coming in for a bit longer yet, and all the time in the world to spend with her. So stop worrying about me. I'm really pleased you're going to be staying for a few days, but after that, I'll cope. Remember, I'm used to dealing with a whole class of thirty five-year-olds, so how hard can one child be? As for rest, what new mother gets much of that, wherever she's living? I can rest when she rests. Let the ironing wait.'

'That's the spirit, Jessie! Oh, she is such a sweet little darling.'

Her mum was clucking over the baby again, like a grandmother hen, itching for her to wake up so she could lift her out of her cot and cuddle her.

'She has your nan's nose, don't you think?'

'What? Long and pointy, with warts on the end?' her dad chuckled, just as his mother-in-law came rushing along the ward towards them, as if on cue. 'I swear that woman's a witch,' he muttered, turning to greet her with a smile. 'Hello, Doreen. I was just talking about you!'

'Nan!' Jess sat up straight and held out her arms for a lavender-scented hug. 'I'm so glad you're here. And happy birthday.'

'Thank you, duck. Not that I want to be reminded at my age. If you'd held off for one more day, we could have shared a birthday, couldn't we? Same day, but seventy-eight years apart! I'd never forget to get her a present or a card every year then, would I? Not that I will anyway.'

She grinned as she leaned carefully over the cot, lowering her voice to a whisper so as not to wake the baby.

'Ah, here she is. My new great-granddaughter. My *only* great granddaughter. Oooh, that makes me sound so old! And you've called her Poppy. Such a pretty name. What a little angel she is. Can I hold her first, when she wakes up? Seeing as it's my birthday.'

Jess sank back into the pillows and closed her eyes, letting her family chat and chirp all around her, like a flock of eager birds all waiting for someone to throw them a scrap so they could race to pounce on the prize.

Her dad was right, of course. Coping on her own, day after day, night after night, with everything a helpless new baby needed, when she'd barely even held one before, was not going to be plain sailing. What if Poppy wouldn't stop crying? What if she fell ill? Or if Jess herself fell ill? What would she do then?

She'd have Mel, of course, some of the time, and Nan nearby, but it wasn't quite the same, was it? Not like having someone there, under the same roof, all the time, someone to share the burden and the work, and all the good bits too. The cuddles, the bath times, that first smile . . .

She shook her thoughts away and looked around the ward, at the other mothers, in the beds nearest to hers. At the fathers, all gooey-eyed over their new offspring, cack-handedly trying to cradle them in big, inexperienced arms, clicking camera shutters and beaming with pride.

She really would have to tell Gary before he found out second-hand, confronted with Facebook images of the daughter he didn't yet know had been born. If only she could trust him.

If only he'd actually wanted a baby — their baby — then everything could have been so different.

* * *

When Jess had first set eyes on Gary Roche she had been instantly smitten. He had that chiselled, handsome sort of face that you usually only see on cartoon heroes. High cheekbones, straight nose, dark hair that curled, sexily, tantalisingly, about his ears. Like the prince in *Beauty and the Beast* — but the way he appeared at the end of the film, after he'd turned back from being the hulking great beast, obviously.

Gary was a whizz with computers. Installing software, sorting out internet problems, all that turning them off and on again to unfreeze the screen. It was what he did. When the laptop she used in her classroom had started to play up, Gary was the man sent to fix it.

They had been a couple for less than

a year when Jess had fallen pregnant. It hadn't been what either of them had planned or even talked about, but there had been plenty of talk once she had taken the pregnancy test and laid it in front of him, that was for sure!

'How could you have been so irresponsible?' he asked, anger and fear melding together in his eyes as he glared at her.

As far as she knew, it took two to make a baby, but suddenly all the blame was being laid at her door. How did she expect them to manage financially? They weren't living together, had no plans to be, and certainly not to get married, and he needed all his cash to lead his own life, not have to plough it all into buying nappies and who knew what else. He wasn't ready for fatherhood, he told her, most emphatically, and wasn't sure he ever would be.

After a lot of arguments and tears, he had finally suggested she have an abortion. Jess had put her hands protectively over her still-invisible bump and flatly refused. The baby may have been a surprise, but she loved it already, and nobody was going to take it away from her. In the end, the baby had meant a lot more to her than Gary did.

So that was that. If she insisted on going ahead with this 'thing' as Gary called it, she'd have to do it alone. He wanted no part in any of it. *A bit late for that,* she remembered thinking, because he was a part of this baby whether he wanted to be or not.

Now, Poppy's beautiful cheekbones and sweet little chin, shaped quite uncannily just like his, were lasting evidence of that.

She decided to wait until she was back at home before ringing him. Somewhere with a lot more privacy than a hospital ward, in case their conversation turned nasty, somewhere she felt safe and could refuse him entry if he decided to turn up making trouble.

Her dad drove her home from the hospital the following morning, Jess enjoying the trickle of fresh non-antiseptic air coming in through the open window, and little Poppy looking so tiny bundled up in her brand new car seat in the back. He'd promised to get a bus down to the garden centre later to pick up her Mini for her, and bring it back to the flat, and to stop off for some bread and milk on his way back.

As soon as he'd set off, Jess took a deep breath and dialled. Her mum was fussing about in the kitchen, cleaning everything in sight, and Poppy was sound asleep. Now was as good a time as any.

Gary answered on the second ring.

'Jess? That you? What's up?'

He sounded busy, distracted, presumably in the middle of a job somewhere. It didn't really surprise her that he hadn't a clue why she was calling. She doubted he had even put her due date in his diary.

'She's here, Gary. I thought you should know.'

'Here? Who's here?' he asked airily.

'The baby, of course. Your daughter. I had her yesterday.'

There was a stony silence down the phone.

For a moment or two, Jess wondered if he was even still there or had hung up on her, but then he let out a long low whistle.

'Oh,' he said, slowly and carefully. 'I see.'

'So you're a father now, Gary, like it or not.'

'Right. I suppose you'll be chasing me for money now, won't you? All that CSA business you hear so much about.'

'I think it only right that you contribute, yes, but that's not why I called. I thought . . . well, I thought you should know . . . hoped you'd want to know.'

'Right,' he said again. 'Look, Jess, I'm working. It's a lot to take in. Maybe we can talk about this another time?'

'Fine.'

Jess closed her eyes and took a deep breath, not sure what she had expected, but not altogether surprised by his lack of enthusiasm.

'If you want to see her . . . '

Gary grunted. 'Not sure that's a good idea, Jess. Best I stay out of her life, I reckon.'

She swallowed hard. How could a father be so lacking in interest in his own child?

'Well, you know where we are if you ever change your mind.'

He disconnected the call before she had even had the chance to tell him their baby's name.

★　★　★

Saturdays were always busy.

Ed ran his hands under the tap in the small staff room, dislodged just enough soil to feel able to hold his sandwich without catching anything nasty, then wandered back outside to eat it.

He had decided on exactly the right spot for Poppy's bench, as he was already calling it in his mind, and had moved the best one he could find from his limited stock into position earlier that morning. Now he settled himself on it and gave his thoughts over to what colour he should stain the wood and what wording he should use for the plaque.

These things were so often in memory of someone who had died, but he wanted to make sure that Poppy's bench was different, and very clearly a celebration of life — new life. Poppy had not actually been born here, but it had been a close thing, and nothing quite like it would probably ever happen here again. It needed jolly words, joyous optimistic words — in rhyme maybe? Perhaps he could ask the engraver to add some little balloons or teddies? Or poppies . . .

'You all right out here?'

Carol had come outside to join him, vigorously shaking her shoulders free after a long stint on the tills, and slopping drops of some sort of red juice from the open bottle clutched in her hand.

'Still thinking about that woman and her baby?'

'How did you guess?'

'Well, because of where you're sitting, mainly. It's not every day, is it? That something like that happens. Hard to forget.'

'Just what I was thinking.'

'Her car's gone, you know. The Mini, in the car park. It was there this morning when I opened up, but it's not there now.'

'Oh.'

Ed felt unexpectedly disappointed. He had been looking forward to seeing Jess again when she came to pick it up, maybe meeting little Poppy properly, and being able to tell them about his plans for the bench, inviting them to be the first to sit on it once the plaque was in place.

'Never mind. I expect she'll be back

sooner or later. For a plant or something,' Carol said.

'I expect you're right.'

Ed bit into his sandwich and threw a few crumbs down onto the gravel for the tiny sparrow that had been waiting patiently at his feet.

He hoped Carol was right, and that Jess would reappear soon, because he had no way of contacting her to tell her about the bench, or just to ask how she — they — were getting on. Apart from her name, he knew nothing about her. Where she lived, how old she was, what she did for a living, if she had a partner . . .

With a jolt, he realised he would really like to know the answer to all those questions.

Especially the last one.

5

Dahlia —
Few plants flower so generously, with
a wealth of variety in form and colour.
It's bold, showy, and likely to
attract pests.

Mel bumped into Jess's nan the following Sunday morning on the pavement outside Jess's flat. Poppy was ten days old already, and with Jess's parents now on their way back to Devon and Jess facing her first day completely alone with the baby, it was obvious that both visitors had decided on a similar course of action — to turn up, offer help, and bring cake.

'Hello, Mrs Barker. How are you?'

'I've told you before, Melanie, call me Doreen. And I'm fine, thanks. Looking forward to another cuddle from my dear little great-granddaughter. Actually, that's a bit of a mouthful, isn't it? I've been thinking I might cut it down to GG, or Gigi, for short. What do you think?'

'I think it's lovely. Your own special name for her. But best see what Jess thinks. She might not want her daughter saddled with nicknames. She never really got over being called Jammy when we were at primary school!'

'Jammy?'

'It was because of her initials, I think. You know, J M. Hard to remember really, once a name has stuck, where it first came from, but she wasn't keen, I do know that! Good job she lost it when we moved schools. Although having Markham as a surname usually caused a few laughs at exam time. I often wonder if that's why she decided to become a teacher, with all that homework to mark, just to live up to her own name!'

'There's not a lot of marking for five-year-olds though, I suppose. Except their names on their lunchboxes and pegs, maybe.'

They walked up the one flight of stairs together, still chuckling, and arrived side by side at Jess's door, behind which Mel could distinctly hear the sound of a baby crying, very loudly.

Jess was still in her pyjamas, with a trickle of what looked like baby sick on one shoulder, and Poppy clutched to the other. She ushered her visitors inside and quickly closed the door.

'Oh, I do hope you've brought chocolate,' she said, slumping down on the sofa. 'I need something to perk me up a bit!'

'Will chocolate cake do?' her nan asked, reaching over and taking the baby from her arms. 'Home-made, covered in butter cream, and with a whole packet of buttons sprinkled on the top?'

'Perfect!'

'Difficult morning?' Mel asked, reaching for the bag Doreen had carried in and was now signalling for her to open.

'You could say that. Just look at me. I

haven't even had time to comb my hair!'

'You look fine, duck. And who's going to be looking anyway?'

Doreen had slipped her finger into Poppy's tiny hand and was rocking her back and forth. Miraculously the crying had stopped and the baby's eyes were closing.

'She comes first now. Everything else can take a back seat.'

'I'll put the kettle on,' Mel said, lifting out the plastic box containing the cake and heading for the small adjoining kitchen.

'We'll have our tea,' Doreen said, 'and then, much as I hate housework, I am at your disposal. For a bit of vacuuming or ironing, or whatever needs doing.'

'But you haven't come round to work.'

'No protests. We insist, don't we, Melanie?' Doreen said, raising her voice to include Mel in the conversation, before carefully laying a sleeping Poppy in her wicker basket and patting her granddaughter on the knee. 'But cake first.'

Mel came back in and the three of them sat with their tea and cake, enjoying the silence.

'Oooh, I've brought a little something,' Mel said then, suddenly remembering the cute little pink dress and knickers set she'd found in Mothercare a few days earlier, and pulling it out of her handbag. 'Sorry I haven't wrapped it. They don't even give you a carrier bag these days.'

'Oh, Mel. It's lovely. Thank you so much. She'll look adorable in it.'

'She'd look adorable if you dressed her in a sack!' Doreen laughed. 'And here's a little gift from me. No need to wrap this one.'

She delved into her purse and handed over a small white envelope containing a bundle of ten pound notes.

'Now, I know there are probably lots of things she'll need over the next few months, and of course I'll help you in any way I can, but this money isn't for any of that. I don't want it spent on clothes or nappies. I want you to start a little savings scheme for her future, for her university fees, or her wedding.'

'But, Nan, all that's years away!'

'The sooner she starts saving, the sooner it will grow. You'd be surprised how much you can put away in eighteen years. So, open a bank account, or buy her some Premium Bonds, however you want to do it. I tried to get the ball rolling myself, but everyone says a parent has to sign the forms, and so many of these things are done online these days, and you know I'm not good with all this interwebby stuff.'

'Nan, I can't accept all this. It's too much. There must be — what? A couple of hundred pounds here, at least — and you're on a pension.'

'Nonsense. If I couldn't afford it, I wouldn't be doing it.'

Doreen licked the last traces of

chocolate butter cream from her fingers and stood up.

'Anyway, it's not for you, Jessica, it's for Poppy. And I insist. Now, you put your feet up for a while and have a snooze, or go and wash your hair or whatever you need to do, while Melanie and I tackle this mess.' She waved her arms around to indicate the general untidiness surrounding them. 'Show us where you keep the polish and the iron, and we'll get started.'

★   ★   ★

Ed stood back and admired the plaque he had just screwed onto the back of Poppy's bench. Lovely though it looked, with her name and birth date in curly letters across the middle, the inscription he had agonised over underneath, and the little poppies etched into the corners, the whole thing felt like a bit of an anticlimax now that Jess and her baby weren't here to see it.

He'd had visions of some sort of

unveiling ceremony, with a glass or two of bubbly, a speech, and someone taking photographs, maybe even a small piece about it in the local paper, but none of that was possible since he had no idea how to track Jess down or how she would feel if he did.

It was a sunny afternoon, but the garden centre was quiet, which was not that surprising for a Monday. He stretched his aching back, the result of too much uninterrupted bending and planting, lowered himself onto the bench, and tipped his face up to catch the rays of the sun.

With his eyes closed, he let his thoughts run back to the letter he had opened that morning. Its distinctive brown envelope had made it obvious it was from the council, even before he'd torn it open, and he had half expected to find that they were intending to increase his rent. He'd been expecting it for a while now. Money was tight, and he had already started juggling figures about on a spreadsheet on his computer to figure out how he would be able to afford a rent rise without letting at least one member of staff go.

What would Grandad have done? he had asked himself, just as he so often did when faced with a problem, but this time he was far from sure of the answer.

As it turned out, the problem that faced him now was a far greater one than having to find a few extra pounds in rent, and it looked horribly like he might have to let *all* of his staff go, himself included.

Ed had always known that Grandad did not own the land the garden centre was built on, but the lease from the local council had been granted many years ago, and it had never occurred to him, and probably not to Grandad either, that anything would ever happen to change things.

How wrong he had been!

It seemed that the council had plans for the future of this area of town, and the land the garden centre occupied. Big plans for redevelopment, including a huge new housing estate, and those plans certainly did not appear to include Blooming Marvellous. He had been given a year's notice but, after that, the land would be reclaimed and the garden centre would have to close.

Ed took a deep breath and tried to think beyond the worst case scenario that, ever since he'd read the letter, had eclipsed everything else.

Maybe he could try to negotiate some kind of deal, keeping the business going with the new houses built all around it? People would still need plants, after all, to fill their brand new empty gardens?

Perhaps if he was to open a little farm shop and sell milk and eggs too, he could prove that his was a business the residents actually needed? Or maybe he should just try to find new premises, move everything, lock, stock and barrel, and carry on as usual, somewhere else?

Whatever ideas his jumbled mind came up with, a host of objections came just as instantly into his head.

He could never win against an organisation as big and powerful as the council, he would never be able to convince them that his little garden centre was important enough to be saved, and as for new premises . . . finding anything nearby, of the right size and at the right price, was nigh on impossible. Plots of land like that were like gold dust, and no doubt the council would have got there first and snapped them up as well.

'You OK out here?'

Ed hadn't heard Carol come up behind him. His eyes flew open as he felt her hand on his shoulder. He turned and forced a smile.

'The bench looks good. You should be proud of it,' she said, sitting down beside him and running her fingers over the shiny new plaque. 'Just think, this could be standing here for years, with people stopping to take the weight off their feet, and to read all about the baby who inspired it. It's a day I'll never forget, that's for sure! Maybe little Poppy will come and sit here herself as she gets bigger, and bring her friends . . . '

That's never going to happen now, Ed thought, but what good would it do explaining that to Carol? It would only worry her, and for now it felt like a worry he had to carry by himself.

At least until he had had time to work out what to do.

6

Rambling rose —
Usually seen rambling through bushes
and trees, or it can be trained to cover
unsightly objects.

Jess stepped out of her pyjamas and took a good close look at herself in the full-length bedroom mirror.

It had been more than a month now since she had given birth, but her stomach still looked far too big and round, little silvery lines running across it like the trails a snail might leave behind. And her breasts resembled a pair of big white balloons about to pop at any moment.

Of course, it didn't really matter. Everyone knew that getting a pre-baby body back took time. It wasn't as if anyone was likely to see it except her, but still it bothered her.

Jess had always prided herself on being slim and fit. She'd visited the gym at least twice a week before her pregnancy, joining in spinning and aerobics classes and swimming up and down in the pool. The larger and more tired she had become, the less she had felt able, or inclined, to do, and now the nearest she got to exercise was climbing the stairs to the flat or a slow stroll to the shops pushing Poppy's buggy. It wouldn't do!

Jess rummaged in the bottom drawer and dug out a pair of grey jogging trousers and one of her old baggy T-shirts, and pulled them on. The looseness of the material did a good job of hiding her shape and, looking in the mirror again, she could almost believe that nothing had changed.

A wail from the carrycot beside her bed soon brought her back to reality. Something — no, everything — had definitely changed.

As soon as Poppy had been fed and her nappy changed, Jess slipped her trainers on and carried the baby down the stairs to the lobby, lay her in the buggy she had taken to leaving down there, the stairs presenting too big a challenge, and opened the door to the street.

It was a nice day, with just a light breeze and no sign of rain, so she kept the buggy's hood pushed down out of the way, popped a little white cotton hat on Poppy's head in case the sun came out too brightly, and set off at a swift pace. Strolling was all well and good, but she needed to feel her heart pumping and break out in a sweat if she was ever going to get fit again.

Where she was going she had no idea, but the thought of just heading off into the world and ending up wherever fate took her was appealing after weeks of mind-numbing baby-led routine.

She missed going to work, the planning and paperwork (she never would have believed she would ever say that!), and the buzz of all those lively and inquisitive little children entrusted to her care. Most of all, she missed being with other adults, the interaction, the conversation in the staff room, someone to talk to who actually talked back. She certainly wasn't going to find that sitting at home alone, with only her laptop and the TV for company.

Within ten minutes, Jess was leaving the rows of houses and shops behind. The yellow-lined and litter-strewn streets and wide pavements slowly gave way to trees and pathways and the scents of country air. She felt her spirits lift as she walked, her hair blowing across her face, her lungs starting to struggle satisfyingly as she pushed the buggy up a steep incline and stopped for a moment to get her breath back at the top.

Below her, the town spread out in all its brown-roofed splendour, the little square gardens dotted in splodges of green behind the rows of houses. She searched among them for her own flat, trying to get her bearings and have something she could point out to Poppy just as soon as she woke up.

Across to the right was the hospital where Poppy had been born. It looked particularly ugly from this angle, with its flat grey roof and mass of masts and aerials. She should show her that too.

What about the garden centre where she had so nearly given birth on a cane chair with nothing but a pet blanket to cover her modesty? She followed the road with her eyes, trying to locate it among the bunch of trees that seemed to shroud it from view.

Ed Burton! With all the upheaval since she'd been home, she had forgotten all about Ed. He had been so caring, trying to look after her in his own inexpert way, seeing her into the ambulance, and then coming to the ward with flowers and a balloon. She hadn't even been to thank him.

She glanced at her watch. It was only mid-afternoon, and it wasn't as if she had anywhere else she needed to be. If she set off back down the hill now she could easily call in and see if he was there, and still make it back to the flat before Poppy's next feed was due.

* * *

Ed felt an unexpected churning in his stomach when he saw her walking towards him, but he knew it wasn't anything to do with the rumblings of hunger. He'd already had his lunch, and finished it off with an ice-cream and two cups of coffee, so this had to be something else entirely.

She was pushing a small buggy with muddy pink wheels across the gravel, and smiling at him as if they were old friends.

'Hi,' she said, stopping beside him and waiting for him to stand up from his weeding. She was wearing a loose T-shirt with the outline of a big red heart on the front and a slogan advertising a charity run with a date that had already passed two years before, and there were grass stains on her once-white trainers. But none of that, he couldn't help but notice, stopped her from looking like a very attractive woman.

Stop it now, Ed! he thought, wiping his mucky hands down the side of his overalls and wishing he'd been wearing something a bit more flattering. *She's older than you, she's just had a baby, and she's probably married, or at least spoken for . . .*

'Well, hello!'

He stood up and took a step forward, then stopped, not sure of the right etiquette here at all. Should he shake her hand, give her a hug, a peck on the cheek? As it turned out, the decision was made for him as Jess let go of the buggy and reached for his hands, clasping them both together and giving them a squeeze.

'I'm so glad you've come back,' he said. 'I was hoping you would. And little . . . '

'Poppy.'

'Of course. I hadn't forgotten. Just wasn't expecting to see you. My mind's a bit slow today, that's all. Too full of other stuff.'

'Good stuff, I hope.'

'Not entirely, to be honest, but you don't want to hear about it. How are you? And how is Poppy?'

He bent down and peered into the buggy, pleased to see the baby's eyes were not only open but staring straight at him — and she hadn't decided to start screaming at the sight of him.

'We're good, thanks. And we thought it was about time we paid you a visit to say thank you for everything you did for us. Maybe buy you a coffee or something?'

'It was nothing, Jess. I can call you Jess, can't I? Only I never actually caught your other name.'

'Markham. Jess Markham. And of course you can call me Jess. Now, if you can spare us a few minutes, how about that coffee? You do have a little cafe area here, don't you?'

'We do, and I'd love to, but there's something I want to show you first.

Come on, follow me . . . '

It was only a short walk to the bench. He could hear the wheels of the buggy churning up the gravel as Jess followed him along a path too narrow for them to navigate it side by side.

'This rose is lovely,' she said, stopping beside a pot containing a particularly fragrant velvety deep red rose that was one of his own favourites.

'Take it,' he said, turning to face her. 'As a gift. You can plant it in your garden, and Poppy can help you water it. When she's older, obviously.'

'Ed, that's too generous of you. And we came here to treat *you*, not the other way around. Besides, I'm sorry to say I don't have a garden.'

'That's a shame. Everyone deserves a garden! Never mind, we'll find you a nice indoor plant before you leave. Believe me, I have hundreds, so I won't miss one . . . '

'Thank you. And I bet you know them all by name, don't you?'

'Well, I don't call them Marjorie or

Gladys, if that's what you mean.'

Jess's eyes sparkled, her shoulders rising and falling as she laughed.

'But I do know all their botanical names,' he went on. 'Even the Latin ones. Now, look, just over here is what I wanted you to see . . .'

He stood back so he wouldn't block her line of vision, and pointed at the little brass plaque on the back of the bench.

'It's for Poppy,' he said, watching her closely and trying to figure out if she liked it or would find the whole idea ridiculous, or embarrassing, or maybe even hate it on sight. 'And for you.'

Jess didn't speak at all for a few moments. She just stood and stared ahead of her, silently reading her daughter's name and the inscription beneath: *This bud of love, by summer's ripening breath, may prove a beauteous flower when next we meet.*

He saw a small tear emerge from the corner of Jess's eye and run slowly and smoothly down the side of her face.

'Oh, Ed. I love it!' she murmured.

'Not my words, of course. Shakespeare's. Romeo and Juliet. But I thought they fitted somehow. You know, what with Poppy so nearly starting her life here, like a tiny bud, and then opening out and blossoming into . . . well, a beautiful little girl.'

'And you did this for us? It's just so thoughtful, so special. But why? You hardly know us.'

Oh, but I'd like to, I really would, Ed thought. But he didn't say it out loud.

'You don't think the poppies in the corners are a bit over the top? Morbid? I wasn't sure if people would associate them more with death, war . . . '

'Ed, it's perfect. The poppies are perfect. And they're symbols of peace, aren't they? Not war. I love them. I love all of it. The whole thing. Oh, I don't know what else to say! Can we sit on it?'

'Of course you can. Anytime you like. In fact, I could go and fetch the coffees and bring them out here so you can sit for as long as you like.'

'That would be really lovely — but I'm supposed to be buying them.'

'Nonsense. I'm the boss, with coffee on tap, whenever I want it. Although I have had rather a lot of it already today, so I'll think I'll stick to tea, if that's OK. Do you take sugar? And what do you say to a bun?'

'One please, and I'd love a bun.'

'Coming up. You wait here, and I'll be right back.'

He started to walk away but, as a silly thought flew into his head, he stopped and looked back, grinning at her.

'Oh, and if you need to feed the baby, I can probably find you a nice dog blanket and show you our outdoor toilet, if you need a private moment!'

She reached out and tried to swipe at his arm, but he managed to dodge her and walked off, smiling to himself. He could still hear her laughing all the way to the sliding doors.

Inside, he studied his face in the mirrored steel of the coffee machine as

Andy, his newest young recruit, poured their drinks and put two iced buns on a tray. Was he looking a bit flustered? Was that a speck of soil on his cheek, and a twig caught in his hair? Quickly he did his best to neaten himself up before manoeuvring the tray past a couple of elderly customers and rejoining Jess on the bench outside.

'So,' he said, balancing the tray on the seat between them. 'How's mother-hood?'

'It's lovely. Busy, tiring, every day something new to learn . . . but definitely lovely. Do you have any yourself? Kids, I mean. A wife, family . . . ?'

'Me? Gracious, no! Not that I wouldn't love to, one day, but work keeps me pretty much fully occupied, so kids are way down the list. No, for now I am very much single.'

Jess's expression clouded for a moment. 'Me too, I'm afraid.' She looked up at him. He was a good six inches taller than her, even when they were sitting down. She shook her head.

'Sorry, forget I said that. Over-sharing, as usual.'

'Not at all. Say what you like. We gardeners are like priests, you know. We spend half our lives on our knees, and the other half praying for rain! Everything you tell us is in the strictest confidence. We know how to keep a secret. How else would I know that old Mr Phipps has a problem with his corms, or Mrs Barrett likes her bushes well-trimmed?'

Jess giggled. 'Well, so much for keeping secrets. You've just told me!'

'True, but I trust you. And, as I'm sure you well know, I just made those up. Seriously though, Jess, you're on your own? No Mr Markham?'

'Well, there is a Mr Markham, but he's my dad.' Jess grinned. 'It's just me and Poppy, but I'm not complaining. Her father isn't on the scene any more, but it's OK, we're happy that way.'

'His loss.'

'Thank you.' Jess took a bite out of her bun. 'Mmm, delicious. Thanks for this too. If this is the welcome we can expect, we'll come again.'

'Yes — please do.'

Poppy was starting to stir, and Jess rocked the buggy backwards and forwards with one hand as she quickly finished her bun and took a final swig of her coffee.

'I think I'd better get her home. We've been out much longer than I expected to be, and she's going to need a feed soon. I'm still a bit unsure about doing it in public. No dog blanket please!'

'Of course.'

'But how does sometime next week sound? Monday? Assuming it's not pouring with rain.'

'I'd like that.'

Ed stood up and picked up the tray, so at least he didn't have that awful dilemma again of what to do with his hands. Handshake? Hug? He felt a warm glow rush over him as Jess leaned forward and kissed him very lightly on the cheek, taking all his feelings of indecision away.

'The bench,' she said, taking a last look at it. 'Poppy's bench. It's the nicest thing anyone has ever done for me. And it'll make a lovely meeting place, so I'll see you right here next week, for another chat and another coffee. OK?'

'OK. And I promise I'll look after it — for as long as it's here.'

The thought of the day when it wouldn't be here — when none of this would be here — flashed uninvited through his mind.

'No graffiti, no litter, and that plaque will be so polished you can see your face in it! Oh, and, Jess . . . ?'

'Yes?'

'If you come a bit earlier, say around one-ish,' he said, swallowing hard to keep his nerves in check, 'perhaps you'd let me buy you lunch. There's a nice pub just over the road.'

★　★　★

'So, what's he like, then?'

Mel had listened to Jess's account of

108

her afternoon and was eager to know more about the mysterious but apparently charming Ed Burton.

'You met him, remember? At the hospital. The guy with the flowers and the balloon.'

'There was a lot going on that day, Jess. Like me rushing off a train, and having to buy nappies for the first time in my life, and meeting little Poppy here. The finer details of your visitor didn't really register. So, come on, tell all. Tall, dark and handsome? Short, ginger, and fat?'

'What does it matter what he looks like? I'm trying to tell you what a nice person he is. Thoughtful. Kind. Look at this sweet little plant he made me take. And the bench . . . '

'Yes, I know all that, but do you fancy him? That's what I really want to know. Perhaps even more importantly, does he fancy you?'

'Mel, stop it! I've only just had a baby, wobbly belly and leaky boobs and all, so I hardly think I'm fanciable material at the moment. Besides, he must be at least five years younger than me. And I am not, repeat not, looking to start any sort of new relationship right now, OK? With him, or anyone else. I've only just got over the last one.'

'Aha! Gary! I wondered when you'd get around to talking about him. Has he been yet? To see how you are? To see Poppy?'

'He says he's busy.'

'Too busy to come and visit his own daughter?'

'I'm not bothered. Not any more. Not really. Yes, it would have been good to raise her as a couple. A family. In an ideal world, I like to think we'd have got married and had a little house with a picket fence and roses round the door, and that we'd have grown old together. But the world isn't ideal, is it? Still, I would have liked him to get to know his daughter at least. It won't be nice for her growing up without knowing her own dad. But if he's not interested, there's not a lot I can do about it, is there?'

Mel tutted, not even trying to disguise her utter disgust.

'You're better off without him, Jess, if that's how he's going to be. Fathers are important, though, aren't they? I mean, look at yours, fussing about that first week or so after you came home, driving you about, getting your shopping in and everything. And mine, love him! He still thinks I'm his little girl, checking his watch when I come in at night, and vetting all my boyfriends.'

'Well, if you will still live at home with your parents, that's what you're going to get. Whether you're nine or twenty-nine, it makes no difference! So, what does your dad make of this latest one?'

'Steve?'

'Well, unless you've dumped him already and have taken up with someone else without telling me, then, yes, of course I mean Steve.'

'Dad hasn't met him yet.'

'And neither have I. So, what's going

on? It's not like you to be so secretive. Hang on . . . oh, he's not married, is he?'

Mel's silence said it all.

'Oh, Mel. He is, isn't he? You always said . . . '

'Yes, I know. I always said I wouldn't do it. No married men. Ever. But he's not actually living with his wife any more. Or his kids.'

'Kids? He's got kids?'

'Yes. Kids that he makes the effort to see. Unlike your Gary, so don't go all judgemental on me. Besides, married or not, I love him, Jess. So, like you just said yourself, there really isn't a lot I can do about it, is there?'

7

Antirrhinum —
Commonly known as Dragonflower or
Snapdragon because of its resemblance
to the face of a dragon that opens and
closes its mouth when squeezed.

'Did I tell you I ran into Margaret in town this morning?' Doreen put down her mug of tea and held out her arms, signalling that it was now her turn to hold the baby.

'Margaret?' Jess said, kissing Poppy and passing her across. 'Gary's mum, do you mean?'

'Yes, and this little one's other granny.'

'Are you trying to make some sort of point, Nan? Because Mrs Roche is very welcome to come and see Poppy if she'd like to, but she hasn't even rung. No card. Nothing.'

'Well, maybe that's because she had absolutely no idea that Poppy even existed.' Doreen's voice had risen a little, and she gazed defiantly at Jess, waiting for her answer.

'I assumed Gary would have told her. I didn't think it was up to me.'

'Well, he hasn't. Not a word. And, believe me, Jessica, the woman was shocked to the core. I can only imagine how I would feel, or your mother, if it was one of us. To find out, in the street, that she has a six-week-old grand-daughter and that nobody — nobody — had thought to tell her. She looked devastated.'

'Nan, I haven't set eyes on Gary for months, nor on any of his family. He didn't want anything to do with the baby. I assumed they didn't either.'

'Margaret not want to know her own grandchild? Can you imagine that? What sort of woman would that make her? No, she says she had no idea, Jess. Not only that you'd had the baby, but that you were even pregnant at all.'

'He hadn't even told her that?' Jess was shocked, and sounded it.

'Obviously not. Turn his back if he must, pretend it's not happening, probably even try to say the baby might not even be his, knowing what he can be like, but to deny his own mother the chance to be a granny! Unforgivable, that's what I call it.'

'Oh.' Jess didn't know what else to say.

'Anyway, I've told her to call you, but I do think you should have done that yourself, Jess. Called her, I mean. And sent her a photo, at least.'

'OK, OK, you're right. I'll call her.'

'Today?'

'Yes, OK.'

Her nan was giving her one of her stern looks, the kind she had always used when Jess had stepped out of line as a child. It was a look she had learned never to ignore. Like a dragon, saying little but threatening fire.

'Look after Poppy for a minute, will

you? I'll go and do it now, if I can find her number.'

'Invite her over, Jess.'

Doreen pulled a slip of paper from her pocket, with a phone number scribbled on it in pencil.

'For a cup of tea, and some cake. I've brought a Swiss roll.' Doreen's expression softened. 'I like Margaret. No airs and graces about her. No nonsense. Unlike that son of hers. This will be a special moment for her, meeting little Gigi for the first time. And she likes a nice slice of Swiss roll, does Margaret.'

'Gigi?' Jess said. 'Since when . . . ?' But her nan had turned away. She was cooing over the baby and rattling a jangly toy rabbit at her, and it was clear she was no longer listening.

* * *

Ed sat on his mum's settee and lowered his head into his hands. All around him, on the cushions beside him, on the coffee table, on the carpet, were piles of

116

paper. He had been at it for hours, reading all his grandad's old letters and files, poring over bank statements and adding up the bills.

One year. That was all he had left before the lease came to an end and the whole business his grandad had built up, had loved so much, and had entrusted to him, would be gone. And nothing here, among all these papers, gave him any clue at all about how to stop it.

'But they'll have to pay you something, won't they, love?' His mum was doing her best to be sympathetic. 'Some kind of compensation. I mean, they can't just take everything away from you, your livelihood, your future . . . '

'I don't know, Mum. But even if they do pay me something, what am I supposed to do with it? Pack up all the stock, and the staff, and move off down the road, find a plot of land and start again? It would be a huge undertaking, and the chances of me finding a place that's halfway suitable are virtually nil.

I'll be finished. Blooming Marvellous will be finished, and I will have let him down, won't I?'

'Your grandad, you mean? Of course not! You could never let him down. You mustn't think that. Ever. He idolised you, just as you did him. Like his little shadow, you were, from as soon as you could walk. None of this is your fault, love. It could just as easily have happened while he was still in charge.'

'Well, thank God it didn't. It would have broken his heart to see it all taken away like this. It's not doing a lot for mine, either. I have no idea how I'm going to tell the staff. Carol especially. She's been with us for twenty-odd years.'

'Is there really no other way? Nothing that could persuade them to change their minds? Perhaps if we started a petition . . . '

'Or stage a protest with all the customers lying in the road and blocking the bulldozers? I wish it was that easy, Mum, but I think we just have to accept it. Face it head-on and deal with it as best we can. We'll have to start selling off as much stock as possible, give the staff plenty of notice so they have a fair chance of finding new jobs, and decide what I'm going to do with myself for the next forty years.'

* * *

'I'm so sorry, Margaret.' Jess smiled apologetically at the woman she had once hoped would be her mother-in-law. 'I had no idea Gary had kept you so much in the dark.'

'It's what he does, I'm afraid. If something bad happens he tends to bury his head in the sand.' Margaret gasped and brought her hand up to cover her mouth. 'Oh, not that you having little Poppy is a bad thing. Far from it! I didn't mean . . . '

'It's OK. I know what you meant. I think he went into denial from the moment I told him. A baby was the last thing he expected. Or wanted. He really didn't know how to deal with it.'

'So he walked away. Oh, Jess, I could thump him, I really could!'

'It wouldn't do any good, and it wouldn't change his mind.'

'Maybe meeting her might, though? Whose heart couldn't melt at the sight of her? She's such a sweetie.'

'He knows where she is, but he's not been near. I couldn't even put his name on the birth certificate. The father has to be there, apparently, if you're not married. I suppose that's so I can't just pluck the name of any old person out of the air and register him as the dad. I might have been tempted to put George Clooney or Johnny Depp otherwise. Then imagine the hoo-hah if I'd tried claiming child support!'

'Such a shame,' Margaret said, slowly shaking her head. 'He could have made such a great dad, if he'd put his mind to it. Gary, I mean. Not George Clooney.'

'I don't suppose we'll ever know now, will we?'

'I'll talk to him, Jess, I promise. Make

him see sense. He should meet her at least, before he turns his back. And you'll be needing money. It's only right, after all.'

'Maybe. We'll see. But you're welcome to visit any time, Margaret, whatever Gary decides to do. Or not do. Children need their grandparents. My life certainly wouldn't have been the same if I didn't have Nan.'

Doreen patted Jess on the hand, her face suddenly flushed pink.

'Ah, thanks, duck. I've always tried to do my best. And, look at us, sitting here putting the world to rights, like three old witches round a cauldron. Hubble, bubble . . . '

'Speak for yourself. Witches indeed!' Jess laughed. 'Now who wants another cup of frog slime? Oh, sorry, I mean tea!'

★　★　★

Ed wasn't much of a drinker. His long working hours and the need to get up early with a clear head for work tended to put paid to too much time hanging around in pubs in the evenings and, since his mate Rich had hooked up with that girlfriend of his, Cheyenne, their old lads' nights had more or less died a natural death.

A quiet lunchtime drink, with a nice meal, and in the right company, was a different prospect altogether, however.

The Gardener's Arms was the sort of place that attracted couples and young families rather than gangs of teenagers or stag night drinkers. It had an old-fashioned, traditional feel, an open fireplace surrounded by piles of logs, and a garden with plenty of seating and a kids' slide. Not a juke box or a gaming machine in sight. And the food was good too.

'Poppy's first visit to a pub,' Jess said as she eased the buggy over the grass and parked it beside a wooden table in the shade. 'Not that she's actually going inside, so I suppose this is pretty similar to just sitting in the park.'

'Parks may have trees and the occasional ice-cream seller, but they're usually pretty poor on facilities, aren't they?' Ed spread his arms out to indicate their surroundings. 'This has the added benefit of a meal, a drink in a proper glass, sun umbrellas, and a decent loo. For her mum, I mean. I guess it's all milk and peeing into her nappy for Poppy for a while yet!'

'True,' Jess said with a giggle.

'So, what can I get you to drink? I'll find a food menu while I'm inside.'

'Sorry to sound like a wimp, but could I just have an orange juice and lemonade? I'm a bit wary of alcohol while I'm still . . . '

She pointed vaguely in the direction of her breasts, which gave Ed the perfect opportunity to glance at them too.

'Oh. Breastfeeding. Of course . . . sorry, I hadn't thought . . . ' He quickly averted his gaze and stood up. 'I think I'll stick to a soft drink too, as I have to run a business and drive myself home later this afternoon.' He dug his wallet out from his trouser pocket. 'I'll be right back.'

Inside, Ed leaned on the polished bar and waited his turn to be served.

Jess looked great today. Although she'd walked here again, saying how much she needed the fresh air and exercise, she had ditched the baggy T-shirt and joggers this time and was dressed in jeans and a lovely pale blue lacy jumper that perfectly matched the colour of her eyes.

He was aware of just how much he was attracted to her. Well, how could he not be? She was beautiful in that pale and natural way he had always found so appealing and, in the normal course of things, he would be plucking up his courage to tell her that, and to ask her out.

However, he also knew that a woman who had not long ago had a baby, and whose ex was suddenly no longer around, was probably not ready to think of him — or anyone — in that way right now. Best just stick to being friends. To start off with, anyway.

The sun was shining as he carried their drinks back out to the garden. Jess had tipped the umbrella over their table into a position that covered the buggy in a cooling puddle of shade, and had slipped her feet out of her trainers and was wiggling her bare toes in the grass.

'Feeling hot?'

'Just a bit. It's quite a long walk, you know, and a fair bit of it uphill.'

'I could always drive you back, if you like.'

'It's a nice thought, but Poppy would need her car seat, and that's at home in the Mini.'

'Of course. Sorry, I didn't think. I'm not really used to babies and all the things they need.'

'Believe me, neither was I until she came along! You wouldn't believe the amount of stuff I've had to buy, and how much of it I have to carry about with me.' She pointed to the enormous bag stashed on the tray beneath the buggy. 'It's like packing supplies for a trek to the South Pole.'

'But without the snow suit and ear muffs?'

Jess laughed. 'You can joke, but I bet she'll need those too, come winter.'

'Well, what do you fancy?'

'Apart from a double vodka, a long hot uninterrupted bath and Johnny Depp to scrub my back, do you mean?'

Ed grinned. 'I meant what do you fancy to eat, but you knew that, didn't you?'

'Only teasing. The lasagne sounds good. With salad, not chips. I really do have to do something about losing this excess baby weight.'

'You look fine to me.'

'Fine? What sort of a word is that? I want to look sensational, thank you very much!'

Oh, you already do look sensational, but it wouldn't be right to say it, he thought.

'Lasagne it is then,' he said out loud instead. 'And, if you're serious about losing weight, there will be no pudding, even if you beg me!'

With that he stood and went inside to place their food order, wondering if Jess could tell that he was swaggering just a little inside his head!

★ ★ ★

It was lovely to see her mum and dad again, and they were thrilled to spend time with their granddaughter. Jess had dreaded the drive down to Devon, the first long journey she had attempted with just her and the baby, the boot packed with so many nappies, clothes, toys and a fold-down travel cot, she was surprised the car hadn't tipped over backwards from the weight.

Setting off early in the morning and choosing mid-week made all the difference though, and the roads were remarkably empty, so she had only had to stop once, to use a service station loo, grab a quick coffee, and manage a discreet breastfeed as soon as she was back in the car.

A few days by the sea were just what she needed, and her mum made sure she had lots of time to relax, taking over most of the cuddle duties and fighting with her dad over who was going to push the buggy along the prom.

'So, what's happening about Gary then?' her dad asked over dinner the first evening. 'Is he going to step up and be a proper dad, or what?'

Jess could see her mum trying to shush him but he was not to be stopped.

'It doesn't look like it, and now he's shown so little interest, I'm not sure I want him to any more. And, honestly, we're doing OK on our own.'

'Disgusting behaviour!' Her dad laid down his knife and fork and turned to look at her. 'How you ever got mixed up with a man like that in the first place I'll never know.'

'He's not a bad man, Dad, and I did love him. I think he was just . . . well, unprepared, you know. Not ready for the commitment. It wasn't as if we'd planned to have a baby.'

'Defending him now? It takes two to make a baby, even if by some so-called accident. He needs to play his part. Financially, if nothing else.'

'Ken . . . ' Her mum had her hand on his arm. 'Leave it, eh? Our Jess came for a holiday, not a lecture. She's old enough to make her own decisions.'

'I suppose so. Sorry, love. Give it time, eh? Hopefully you'll meet someone else, someone who deserves you.'

'Thanks, Dad, but Poppy's all I need right now.'

'But what about when you go back to work? I'm assuming you will.'

'Of course. I'm not sure I could afford to be a stay-at-home mum, even if I wanted to. Which I don't, not really. I love my job. And there are childminders, nurseries . . . '

'Oh, I do wish you'd consider moving down here, love, so we could help you more,' her mum said. 'You wouldn't have to live here with us, if you want your independence. Get a little place of your own. We'd love to have little Poppy with us while you're at work. Just think, you'd have all those long school holidays with her, in the sunshine, down on the beach, and country walks, and there's the zoo . . . It's a lovely life for a child. There are lots of schools in Devon, you know, and some of them must be in need of staff. After all, it's not as if you need to stay where you are, now that you and Gary are . . . '

Jess sighed. It wasn't the first time since her parents had retired to Devon that they had tried to persuade her to follow them there, but she had to admit it was the first time she could actually see the positives in the idea.

Her mum was right. She had no ties any more. She did love her job, but the children came and went, with a new class to get to know every year. She could do that anywhere, couldn't she? Gary didn't want to know. Mel's time was taken up with her new boyfriend.

Nan had her own life and friends, and she could still go back for visits. She'd only be a few hours away.

'I'll think about it,' she said, smiling up at her mum who was bustling about clearing plates.

'Really? That's wonderful.'

'There are some nice young men around these parts, too,' her dad said, winking at her.

'Dad! When I'm ready for that, I will find my own man, thanks very much!'

'Well, don't take too long about it, Jess. Poppy needs a father.'

'She has a father.'

'That waste of space? Where is he, then? I bet you've not seen hide nor hair of him! No, what this little one needs is a real father. Someone who will love her for the long haul, think the sun rises just to shine on her, and be ready and willing to always put her first. The way I've always felt about you . . . '

Jess could have sworn there were tears in his eyes as he lay a big, wide, suntanned hand on her shoulder and gave it a squeeze.

'But, from where I'm standing, love, just sharing the same genetics is clearly no guarantee of that, is it?'

8

Heather —
Symbolising admiration and good luck,
and believed to have protective powers.
Often synonymous with Scotland,
its scientific name means 'to brush',
as heather twigs were once used
for making brooms.

Mel sat on the train, reading a magazine. Beside her, Steve was snoozing, his knees spread apart, his head lolling against the window, and the remains of a sandwich packet crumpled on the small table in front of them.

They had both managed to get two days off work, meaning that they could stretch their weekend to a four-day visit and see more of the twins than usual. With a hotel room booked, it would mean being able to spend more time with each other too, once the boys had been returned to their mother in the evenings.

Mel thought back to the weekend before, when she had finally found the courage to take Steve home to meet her parents. Her mum had fussed, as expected, offering home-made cake and constantly refilling the teapot. Her dad had been more wary, sitting back, watching and listening, taking his time to make up his mind.

'Do you follow football, Steve?' he'd said at last, latching on to a safe topic.

'Newcastle,' Steve replied. 'Man and boy.'

'I'm a Chelsea man myself.'

'They're doing well . . . '

'They are that.' Both men fell silent as they drank their tea. 'Don't suppose you fancy a drop of something stronger? I've got a good bottle of single malt tucked away.'

'Don't mind if I do, Mr Black.'

'Just call me Robert. Or Bob. Everyone does. Come on, let's leave the girls to their chat and go into the back room, shall we? I don't suppose you smoke? I've got a couple of cigars going begging.'

'Trying to ease up a bit, actually. For my health, you know . . . '

'Ah, one won't hurt.'

'I suppose not.'

Mel watched them get up and leave the room. Her dad wanted one of his little chats, she was sure, and had no intention of doing it here in front of her and her mum. Still, there was nothing she could do about it. Steve would have to get through the interrogation as best he could. But a cigar? Really? She had half expected to hear the coughing and spluttering sounds through the adjoining wall.

Steve had not told her exactly what was said, but the two men had emerged half an hour later, seemingly the best of friends — and just too late to help with the washing-up.

She put her magazine down now, finding it hard to give it her full concentration.

She knew her parents would have had their doubts about her seeing someone like Steve. A little older than her, with an estranged wife and two absent kids, sharing his time and his income between two women, two parts of the country miles apart, two very different lives.

Of course they wanted the best for her, and she hoped that, in meeting Steve, they could now see that he was OK, that he made her happy and that, although not ideal, everything else in his life could be managed and dealt with.

Mel liked looking for the positives in life, not dwelling on the negatives — and children could only ever be regarded as positives, whoever their mother might be.

Steve gave a little grunt and jerked awake, blinking in the light that streamed in through the glass.

'Sorry. Was I asleep? I wasn't snoring, was I?'

She laughed. 'Only a bit. Not enough

to disturb anyone but me.'

'Where are we?'

'Coming in to Berwick any time now, I'd say.'

'Great. We'll get a taxi from there. I can't be bothered waiting about for buses. It'll be good to see the boys. Spend time with them. Maybe we can all get down to the beach this afternoon. Buy some chips and an ice cream.'

'You sound like a big kid yourself. Have you brought your bucket and spade?'

'They'll be easy to get once we're there.'

'I was joking.'

'I wasn't! Let's have fun while the sun shines. They'll be back at school next week, and then it will be all homework and getting uniforms and packed lunches ready, early nights and all. Let's all enjoy their last days of freedom while we can.'

The train pulled into the station and Steve lifted their bags down onto the platform.

'Mel?' he said, plonking the bags at his feet and reaching for her hand. 'I am glad you're here with me, you know. Coming up here like this, it's not just about the kids. It's about us too. Time we had a holiday. Some fun of our own.' He kissed her on the nose, then slid his lips down to meet hers. 'So, if there's anything you'd like to do, with or without the boys, just say.'

'I will.'

'You know I love you, don't you?'

His face was still close to hers, and she nodded, looping her arms around his neck.

'And I love you too . . . warts and all!'

'Warts? I don't have any warts. A few moles maybe, and the odd hair growing out of my ears.'

'And out of your nose.' Mel giggled.

'Really?' His hand flew up to his face to check.

'Don't worry. I'm only teasing!'

She lifted the smaller of the bags, leaving Steve to carry the heavier one, and headed for the exit.

'And, besides, I like a bit of hair on a man. It's a sign of strength.'

'I'll probably need plenty of that over the next few days.'

'And nights?' Mel put on her best seductive look and gave him an exaggerated wink.

'I actually meant all the running about with the boys. Chucking them into the sea, carrying them home when they get shattered, that sort of thing. Why, whatever did you mean, little miss hussy?'

'Just that being here with you offers certain opportunities. Living at home with my parents does cramp my style a bit.'

'And you'd like it uncramped?'

'Well, I wouldn't say no. If you're offering . . .'

* * *

Ed munched his way through yet another take-away fish supper, straight out of the paper, trying to ignore the piles of paper scattered over the kitchen table that he had spent the past two hours working his way through with the proverbial fine toothed comb.

He knew he had come to the end of the road now. He had read every piece of paper, every letter and deed and document his grandad had meticulously filed away, and quite a few he had found stuffed into boxes in the attic.

The council's decision to reclaim the land hadn't been quite so out of the blue as Ed had assumed. Grandad had known this was coming, had known for a long time, but he hadn't said a word. There were letters he'd hidden away, as if by turning a blind eye to them the whole sorry business would just go away. But it hadn't, of course. And one thing was clear. There was no loophole, no magic clause that was going to save him. The land was not his and never had been, and the council had the law on its side.

Leanne had been there again, in the chip shop, giving him the eye, not to mention extra chips and a free pickled egg he really hadn't needed. She had dyed her hair jet black, and he could have sworn she had added a new tattoo to the already large collection that seemed to be growing slowly up her arms. It was a bird, some sort of eagle with its wings opened out, that he didn't think he had seen before. Why did she do that? Why did any girl do that? Still, each to their own, he supposed, a mental image of Jess's pale, undecorated skin and shiny red-brown hair flashing into his head.

'You all right in here, love?' His mum appeared at the kitchen door. She had her coat on and her handbag slung over her arm. 'I'm just off out to the bingo. Won't be late back.'

'Fine. Have a good time.' He looked up and gave her his best attempt at a carefree smile.

'Anything I can bring you back? I'll

be passing the late-night shop on my way home.'

'No thanks, Mum. Unless you could bring back a bundle of cash, of course. A big win at the bingo tonight would be great. Enough to buy us a lovely new garden centre in the country, and a huge house to go with it. Do you think you might manage that?'

'I'll do my best, son.' She patted her pocket. 'I've got my lucky shamrock right here. The one your dad had with him the night he met me, so it must be lucky, mustn't it? And I'll buy an extra card tonight, just for you. You never know . . .'

He was still smiling after she had gone.

*　*　*

September seemed to come around all too quickly. Jess's colleagues would be preparing for the start of a new term, planning lessons, looking ahead to the reinstatement of the daily routines with the usual mixture of excitement and dread.

As the final days of summer settled into the beginnings of autumn, so Jess and Poppy settled into a new routine too. One that seemed to work for both of them.

Poppy always woke early, so Jess had found it necessary to do the same, and they were usually both fed and dressed well before eight o'clock. It was at that time of the day that Jess had the most energy, before the rigours of childcare and household chores wore her out and sent her to an early bed — sometimes even before the evening news had come on the TV.

Although the morning streets were busy and noisy with rush-hour traffic, the paths out of town proved remarkably empty and Jess would often take the buggy out for long walks, giving Poppy plenty of fresh air and herself the exercise she so badly needed.

Once or twice a week, her walks would lead her to the garden centre and to Poppy's bench, where she would sit with a coffee in a polystyrene cup and watch Carol or one of the other staff watering the plants or raking the gravel, which had been churned up by passing feet and wheelbarrows, back into line.

Ed was usually there before her, beavering away in the greenhouse or head down at his desk, but he'd usually spot her through the window and give her a wave. Sometimes he would come out and sit beside her for a while, lifting Poppy out of the buggy if she was awake and jiggling her on his knee, something he was doing with increasing confidence each time he tried it.

However, there were always things he had to attend to in the office — paperwork, bills, phone calls — and he couldn't sit for long.

'You work too hard,' Jess said one morning, when he had gulped his coffee quickly and was about to head back to work. 'You're the boss. Chill for a bit longer. The place won't fall apart without you.'

She had only been joking, but the cloudy look that flashed across his face took her by surprise.

'Ah, but it might,' he said, standing up to go. 'And it very likely will, whether I'm here or not.'

For a moment it looked as if he was about to say something more, but he held back and forced a smile, picking a small sprig of white heather from a nearby pot and bending over the buggy to tuck it beneath the covers.

'For luck,' he said, by way of explanation. 'Gypsies swear by it.'

'Ed? Is there something the matter? What do you mean about being here or not? You're not thinking of leaving, are you?'

'Not exactly. Look, let me buy you lunch later, and I'll explain, OK?'

'No, let me buy you lunch. It's my turn.'

'Well, OK, thank you. Gardener's Arms? About one o'clock?'

'Here.' She pulled her mobile phone out from her bag. 'I think it's time we swapped numbers, don't you? In case anything were to happen and you can't make it. Or I can't. You know, Poppy might . . . '

'Of course. Good idea.'

They quickly tapped their numbers into each other's phones and handed them back, their hands brushing in passing.

'One o'clock then?' Ed looked awkward, a bit embarrassed. 'Unless something . . . '

'In which case I'll call you. I promise.'

Jess watched him walk away and pick up a broom, his shoulders a lot more hunched than they usually were as he brushed it haphazardly through the gravel, its handle barging into the rose bushes as he passed and knocking a few petals to the ground.

Something wasn't right. She'd had her suspicions the last couple of times they'd talked, a feeling that he wasn't telling her something, but she didn't know him that well, and she knew she had no right to ask. He had never seemed so down as he did today. She couldn't help but wonder what was troubling him and why he felt luck was needed. Family problems? Girl trouble? Money? He said he would explain later, so at least she wouldn't have long to wait to find out.

Jess took the long way back, in no rush to get home. She might as well make the most of the great outdoors before winter came along and forced her back inside. Birds were fluttering about up above, a mix of different calls filling the air. Some of the leaves were already starting to change colour, small green conkers were appearing among the branches of the chestnut trees, and there were all sorts of patterns in the clouds if she stopped long enough to look.

'Look, Pop,' she said, spotting movement on the path ahead, and pointing the buggy the right way round, hoping her daughter would see what she could see. 'A squirrel!'

Poppy just gazed straight up at the sky and gurgled, and the squirrel darted away, his tail swishing as he ran almost vertically straight to the top of the nearest tree.

Jess ran her hand over her tummy. It was definitely getting flatter. The walking was doing her good, and being out here, just walking about and enjoying nature, was good for her mind. It kept her thoughts from straying back to Gary and his betrayal, because the more she thought about it the more she knew that was what it was. He had led her on, made her believe he loved her, and then let her down, at the very time she had needed him the most. And now she was on her own, doing what must be the hardest and most important job in the world. Bringing up a child.

There was no doubt about it. She missed him. Or the idea of him, at least. Yes, she had her parents, her nan, and Mel. All of them had been incredible these last months, bringing gifts, giving up their time to visit and to help out when they could, but it wasn't the same, was it? Not the same as having someone there all the time, someone to share it all with, and to curl up with at night, when Poppy was asleep. When had she last felt a man's arms around her, last been properly kissed? Being a mum was lovely, and she wouldn't change it for the world, but it would be nice just to feel like a woman too.

When she got back to the flat, the postman had just been and was walking back down the path towards the street.

She stopped the buggy to let him pass, then bumped it over the step and parked it in the downstairs hall as usual as she picked up the letters from the mat.

One for Mrs Cooper in the ground floor flat, which she popped through the old woman's letterbox, two for Bob up on the top floor, which she propped up on the narrow hall table for him to find next time he passed through, and three for herself.

Slinging Poppy's enormous bag of

bits and pieces over one shoulder and holding Poppy, still wrapped in her blanket against the other, she climbed the thirteen stairs to her own door, the heather dropping onto the floor at somewhere around stair seven. It would be far too tricky to bend down and retrieve it with her arms so full, and who believed in all that nonsense anyway? Luck! As if a bit of plant could have any influence on a person's luck!

Laying Poppy down on her activity mat on the lounge carpet for a moment, she sank into an armchair and studied her letters.

Electricity bill . . . she pushed that one aside. The summer quarter was always the cheapest, and she paid by monthly direct debit anyway, so it wasn't as if it was likely to be a final demand.

Her payslip from the school. Well, she knew exactly how much she was getting paid this month, as she'd already checked her bank account online and knew the money had safely arrived yesterday.

That just left envelope number three. Standard white, with a window, and her name and address neatly lined up behind it, computer generated. Glasgow. Who did she know that could be writing to her from Glasgow?

She tore the envelope open, unfolded and read the letter inside.

Then, open-mouthed and not quite sure she wasn't dreaming, she read it again.

It was from the National Savings and Investment people, telling her that Poppy's premium bonds had won a prize — and there was a cheque attached at the bottom . . . a cheque for one hundred thousand pounds!

9

Money plant —
A popular and rewarding indoor plant
with great longevity, said to have the
power to increase your bank balance
and help your savings grow.

Jess leaned against the cool tiles of the
kitchen wall, breathing deeply and
waiting for the kettle to boil. Tea, the
answer to everything. All through her
life, at times of stress or happiness or
grief, her mum had turned to tea, and
now here she was doing exactly the
same.

The letter lay beside her on the
worktop.

She kept coming back to it, reassur-
ing herself that it wasn't just ten
pounds Poppy had won, or a hundred.
But all those noughts kept staring right
back at her, and she knew it was real. A

hundred thousand! It was more money than she had ever owned, or ever seen before. Of course, it wasn't hers; it was Poppy's, and she was going to have to think long and hard about what to do with it. So much for her nan's plan to start a small savings account and watch it grow over the next eighteen years! Suddenly it had grown beyond all expectations.

Jess's hands shook as she sipped her tea, but it was still too hot to drink.

Nan! She had to phone her and tell her, before she breathed a word to anyone else.

Then she had to get ready to meet Ed for the pub lunch they had arranged. He had said he had something to tell her, and it hadn't looked as if it was anything good. Should she tell him her own news, or would that be rubbing his nose in it? To be honest, it was going to be hard hiding something so earth-shattering. She had a feeling the huge smile on her face would give her away.

She shook her head and tried to clear her thoughts. Why on earth was she worrying about Ed? She needed to call Nan, and her parents, and then Mel. She needed to shout her excitement from the rooftops and celebrate with something a lot stronger than tea. Break out the champers, her baby was rich!

Just as she went to pick up the phone, Poppy started to cry. She recognised that sound now, could distinguish it from the other cries that meant pain or cold, the arrival of another poo, or just the sheer need for attention. This was the Feed Me Now cry she knew so well.

Poppy didn't understand about money, and wouldn't do so for some years yet. All Poppy needed was a dry bottom and a full tummy, and a mummy who loved her. As she lifted the hem of her top and pulled her breast out of its enormous and rather damp bra, Jess realised that Poppy being happy and healthy and never wanting for anything meant more to her right now than just about anything else too. And this money could help her to secure that for her daughter.

A celebratory glass of champagne was out of the question while she was breastfeeding, anyway. Tea it would have to be, for now — and maybe a giant bar of Cadbury's. Well, a girl had to have some pleasures in life.

* * *

'I hope you don't mind,' Jess said, lifting Poppy's seat from the back of the Mini, as Ed came strolling up to her across the pub car park. 'But I've asked my friend Mel to meet us here. You remember Mel? You met briefly at the hospital. And her boyfriend, Steve, who I haven't actually met yet, but I'm sure he'll be OK. They work together. Accountancy. Boring, I know. Oh, and I invited my nan along too . . . '

'Is something up?' Ed took the usual enormous bag of stuff from her shoulder as she hooked the baby seat over her elbow and locked the car door. 'Only, you do seem to be babbling a bit, if you don't mind me saying so.'

'Am I?'

'Come on. Let's grab our usual table in the garden, shall we? Then you can tell me all about it. Unless you want to sit inside, for a change?'

'No, let's make the most of the weather. Who knows how much longer it will last? And Mel will spot us more easily out here, when she arrives. They won't be able to stay long. She and Steve are just on their lunch break from work. And I've asked them to pick Nan up on the way. I can drop her back later.'

'So, why the group lunch?' Ed asked, once they were settled. 'Afraid I might bite if I'm left alone with you?'

'Of course not, Ed! It's just that I have some news. Some very good news. And I fancied sharing it with some of my favourite people, that's all. So, you can put that wallet away, for a start. I'm buying, remember?'

'Your wish is my command!'

'Ah, here they are now.'

Jess stood up and waved her arms wildly until they spotted her, the three of them making their way into the garden, her nan already grinning like the Cheshire cat from Alice.

Jess made the introductions, fussing everyone into seats, and made sure she got a good look at Steve as Mel thrust him forward for inspection. He wasn't quite what she'd expected, not that she could have said exactly what she had expected. Two heads? A big Married Man sign flashing over them? He was a bit on the thin side, but he looked at least presentable in his work suit, if not exactly smart.

'Pleased to meet you at last,' he said, pushing his floppy hair back and bending over the car seat which Jess had placed on top of the wooden table, next to her bag. 'And to meet Poppy, of course.'

Jess could tell he was a dad by the way he instantly reached for the baby's dummy when it slipped from her mouth and popped it back in, at the same time pulling the corner of her blanket back up to keep her warm. If only Gary . . .

'Right!' Jess said, focussing her thoughts back on the here and now, and drumming her hands on the wooden table top to get everyone's attention. 'Nan already knows why we're here, but for everyone else . . . '

All eyes were on her now.

'Get on with it, Jess,' Mel said, pretending to droop. 'Some of us are dying for a drink here!'

'And drink you shall have. Plenty of it. Just as soon as I show you all this.'

She withdrew the letter from her pocket with a flourish and held it aloft.

'What is it, Jess?' Mel's curiosity was kicking in.

'This,' she said, beaming from ear to ear, 'is probably the most important letter I have ever received. This letter, and the cheque that came with it, will secure Poppy's financial future for the next . . . well, quite possibly forever.'

'Don't tell me Gary's coughed up some maintenance money!' Mel joked, snorting.

'Oh, look, I think I just saw a pig fly past!' Jess quipped back. 'No, this is a cheque for — wait for it — one hundred thousand pounds! Yes, you heard correctly. And it's all Poppy's, nothing to do with Gary. This is all down to my wonderful Nan.'

Mel turned to Doreen, sitting opposite her. 'What? I didn't know you had that sort of money, Mrs Black.'

'I don't, but little Poppy does now she's had a win from those premium bonds I bought for her. Who'd have thought it, eh? From two hundred quid to a small fortune in just a couple of months. Now, that's what I call an investment!'

'Champagne?' Jess said, trying to make herself heard above the sudden din as everyone started clapping and cheering and patting each other on the back. 'I called ahead to ask them to put a bottle on ice.'

'Well, that won't be cheap, Jessica. Is that what our Poppy's going to spend her newfound wealth on?' Doreen said, tutting loudly and trying not to laugh. 'Alcohol? Whatever next? A designer wardrobe? A sports car?'

'Nan! I wouldn't dream of using any of Poppy's money. These drinks are on me.'

'Well, in that case, make mine a gin and tonic, duck. I never could abide that fizzy stuff!'

Over the next hour or so, as the drinks flowed and everyone chipped in with more and more ridiculous ideas about how Poppy might spend her windfall, Jess looked across at Ed every now and then and worried that she had taken away his chance to talk to her about whatever it was that was bothering him.

Somehow he had ended up sitting at the other side of the table, between Steve and Nan, and it wouldn't be easy to say anything to him that couldn't be overheard by everyone else.

He looked happy enough though, engrossed in some garbled conversation with her nan that she could only hear snippets of — something about the best way to look after dahlias — and munching his way through a plate of cottage pie.

If there really was something on his mind it can't have been too terrible, and she felt sure he would tell her soon enough. Wasn't that what friends were for?

⋆　⋆　⋆

Ed waved goodbye and walked slowly back along the road to work, feeling as if a lead weight had settled on his heart.

He wasn't jealous. Far from it, even though a sum like that would have been the answer to all his prayers. No, it was wonderful that little Poppy had won such a fantastic prize, but how could he ever tell Jess about losing the garden centre now? All he had wanted was a friendly ear, the chance to unburden himself, and to share his problems with someone who cared. But not now. The timing was all wrong. If he told her now, it would just sound as if he was after her money.

As the sliding doors opened and swallowed him up, he went straight to his office and pulled on his green Blooming Marvellous overalls.

This business was his now, and he still felt a great pride in it and in what he and his grandad before him had achieved. But Grandad wasn't here any more to help him out, to tell him what to do. Ed had to make the decisions by himself.

The time had come to make plans. And to talk, but not to Jess. Not yet, anyway. No, he had to talk to his staff and break the news that it was all over, that he had no choice but to close, and that their jobs were on the line.

There was no point in putting it off any longer.

There were five of them, not including himself. Carol and Sandra were working the tills this afternoon. He'd passed them on his way in, busily chatting and smiling, wrapping assorted plants in sheets of paper and dishing out advice on how to care for them. Ben, his part-time trainee, a young university student who was showing real promise and hoped to make his future career in horticulture, was outside watering and sweeping, and young Andy, fitting work around his A-level college course, was manning the café area.

That just left Trish, who wasn't working today. All the staff took time off during the week to compensate for working weekends, so it was rare to have everyone in at the same time.

Yet he felt it only right to tell them all together. He'd have to call a staff meeting after hours, or perhaps invite them all out somewhere neutral where he wouldn't be faced with looking at his grandad's dream as he told them all it was soon to be shattered.

He leafed through his diary, trying to pick a suitable day and time that wouldn't put any of them to too much inconvenience. They were busy people, with lives of their own outside the garden centre. Kids, in Carol's case, studying for Ben and Andy, a disabled husband for Trish, and Sandra had a second job cutting people's hair in the evenings and on her days off. She fitted it all in, she said, because she loved both jobs equally and, besides, she needed the money.

It wasn't going to be easy, breaking the news, or saying goodbye.

Ed ran his thumb down the page, and settled on Thursday evening. Only Ben would be missing then, but he would probably be happy enough to pop in at closing time if Ed promised him an hour's overtime.

Oh, no! He gasped as he spotted today's date. It was Grandad's birthday. Or it would have been if he'd still been here. Why hadn't his mum said anything — unless she'd forgotten too?

He ran a quick calculation through his head. Grandad would have been sixty-seven today. He should have been enjoying his retirement, like other men of his age, with a pie and a pint, opening gift-wrapped socks and blowing out the candles on one of Gran's home-made cakes. Not that he had retired, of course, or shown any signs of being about to, right up to the day he died.

Suddenly, Ed realised exactly why that might have been. Grandad hadn't told a soul but he'd known the garden centre's days were numbered and he'd wanted — and expected — to be there, right to the end. He would have been, if the stroke hadn't taken him so suddenly. Whether he had intended to fight the council, or bow out gracefully, Ed would never know, but he certainly hadn't expected to die before having to do either. He never would have left Ed in a mess like this, with such big decisions to face, had he known he wouldn't be right here beside him.

Quickly, Ed went in search of the best blooms he could find, cutting a rose here and a hydrangea there, encasing them in ferns and sprigs of lavender, carefully bundling them together and tying them with a Cellophane wrapper and a length of thin white ribbon.

'I'm popping out,' he said, having slipped out of his overalls again, nodding to the girls at the tills as he headed for his car. 'Won't be long.'

The cemetery lay behind the church at the edge of town. Its oldest parts looked unkempt and overgrown, some of the gravestones tilting slightly, much of their weathered wording almost unreadable, encrusted with lichen and splattered by bird droppings, all having been there too long to still have regular visitors, their incumbents no longer mourned, nor remembered. There was a stillness hanging over the place, one corner shadowed by an overhanging tree, a solitary pigeon pecking around in the grass.

Ed hung his head as he made his way towards Grandad's grave on the far edge of the churchyard. It was one of several newly erected in recent months, all still white and with small vases of flowers propped up in front of them.

It was ages since he'd last been here. He'd found the burial traumatic, upsetting, and somehow unreal, all the while telling himself it was just a dream and he would soon wake up and Grandad would still be there, helping him mend his bike or testing him on his spellings for school, showing him how to take cuttings and talking him through the accounts, just as he always had. It was real enough, though, and his own mixture of fear and grief was no excuse for staying away.

There was a bunch of carnations in the vase — pink ones, freshly laid. He knelt down in the damp grass and lifted the small card attached to the stems. It was from Gran.

To my darling Peter. Always in my heart.

Ed should have come with her. The first birthday she'd had to deal with since Grandad had died, and she should not have had to do it alone.

He would call round there, right now, have a cup of tea, maybe fetch out the old photo albums and let her have a bit of a cry on his shoulder.

He laid his own bouquet on the grass, not wanting to disturb Gran's carnations, and stayed on his knees for a while, staring at the headstone.

'What shall I do, Grandad?' he said, knowing full well he would not be getting a reply, but asking anyway. 'About the lease? About the staff? Should I look for another job, or try to start Blooming Marvellous again, somewhere else? I'm not like you. I'm not sure I have the expertise, the energy, the courage . . . '

'Of course you do,' said a voice from behind him, making him jump.

'Gran?'

She held out her wrinkly hand and helped him to his feet, throwing her arms around him in a warm hug. 'You're every bit as strong as he was, you know.'

She let him out of her embrace, but kept hold of his hand as they stood side by side, gazing at the grave of the man they both loved so much.

'Your grandad started with nothing, built up the business from scratch. I know about the lease, Ed. Oh, I didn't before, he kept it to himself, but I've been speaking to your mum. She came over to see me this morning, and we talked about . . . well, your grandad, and your dad — and you, because she's worried about you. We both are. He had absolute faith in you, Ed, your grandad did. He trained you well. You know everything he knew about plants, about being courteous to the customers and good to your staff, about the way the place is run. He knew he was leaving the future of Blooming Marvellous in safe hands . . . '

'But what if it doesn't have a future?'

'Well, that's up to you, lad. The future is what you make it, isn't it?'

Ed had no idea what to say. Standing there, deep in thought, he so wanted to believe what his gran was saying, and to share her faith in him. He saw her take a folded hankie out of her coat pocket and wipe it across her eyes.

He tightened his grip on her hand.

'I'll do my best, Gran.'

'That's all any of us can do, Edward. Nobody can ask for more.'

They walked back together towards the gate, his gran insisting she did not need a lift home but was happy to stay a while longer, to be close to her husband in the only way that was possible now, and enjoy the peace.

'I come quite often, and I'm happy enough to sit here on a bench by myself, alone with my thoughts, as they say, and my memories. I'll be fine, don't you worry,' she added, making Ed feel more guilty that he had visited the grave so rarely.

That would change from now on. Like so many other things in his life, it would have to.

★ ★ ★

It was pouring with rain on Thursday evening as the staff gathered in the saloon bar of The Chequers Inn in the centre of town. For some strange reason he could not explain to himself, he had not wanted to meet at The Gardener's Arms, which reminded him of happy times and of Jess, things he had no wish to taint with what he was about to do now.

Trish was the last to arrive, apologising profusely as she took off her mac and hung it over the back of the last empty chair.

'I had to dash home to sort out my Rodney's tea. Hope you weren't waiting too long.'

'It's fine, Trish. No rush. I'm just glad you could come at all. Now, what's everyone having to drink?'

Ed pulled a small notebook out of his trouser pocket and started scribbling down their orders before heading towards the bar.

Behind him, they were already starting to whisper among themselves. Well, they were bound to be curious, and he'd been careful to give no hint of what was about to come.

With all the drinks delivered, Ed sat back down and took a deep breath.

'Right,' he said, straightening his back and looking around the table at each of them in turn. 'There's no easy way to say this, so I'll just cut to the chase. Blooming Marvellous stands on ground we've always leased from the council, and usually that lease is renewed year after year pretty much automatically. A bit of a rent rise from time to time, but that's all. But this time . . . '

All eyes were suddenly upon him.

'This time, they're not going to renew. They want the land back to build houses on, and our little garden centre doesn't figure in their plans.'

'They're closing us down?' Carol gasped.

'As good as, I'm afraid. What they're doing isn't very nice, but it is legal. We never owned the land, and while they had no other use for it, they were happy to let us carry on, but now . . . Well, we've got about another nine months, that's all, and then it's all over.'

'But surely they can't just . . . '

'Unfortunately they can, and they will. So, what I'm telling you all — reluctantly, believe me — is that I'm going to have to let you go. Stay for a while if you want to, but if any of you prefer to go sooner, to look for other jobs right away, that's absolutely fine. Girls, you've all been with us a long time, so I will do my best to give you the best possible redundancy deal. Ben and Andy, I know for you it's only been a few months and just a way of earning while you study, and you probably had bigger plans long-term anyway, but I will make sure you get the best references, I promise you.'

'But what will you do, Ed?' Sandra asked. 'I can always cut hair for a living, and that's probably exactly what I will do, but that place is your inheritance, your life . . . '

'I've no option but to pack up and move on. There must be other jobs out there working with plants, a nursery, or a park somewhere. I probably won't be the boss any more, but at least I should have some money, once the stock is sold.'

A shocked hush fell around the table as they tried to take it all in.

'You don't get rid of me that easily, young man,' Carol said, as if suddenly pulling herself together, and laying an arm across his slumped shoulders. 'I'm sticking around to the bitter end. We'll be packing up the last pot and closing those gates for the last time, side by side, you and me. I owe you that much. And your grandad. Did he . . . ?'

'Know? Seems he did, but he didn't say a word. I just hope it wasn't the shock of it all, bottling it all up, that led to his stroke.'

'You can't think that way.'

'I know. And nothing's going to bring him back, I know that, too. So, onwards and upwards, eh?'

'That's the spirit!'

Ed took a big swig of his beer. 'So, that's the news, I'm afraid, everyone. Any questions?'

'Yes.' It was the first time Trish had spoken since her flustered entrance. 'Can I buy you another drink? You look like you need it.'

10

Geranium —
There is no plant in the garden more
useful, more dependable, or more of a
thoroughly all-round 'good egg' than
the hardy geranium.

The more Jess saw of Mel's new boyfriend, the more she liked him. Getting out and about, especially in the evenings, was nowhere near as easy as it had been before Poppy had come along, so it just seemed easier to invite her friends over to the flat, throw a pizza in the oven and open a bottle or two, even if hers was only cola.

Now that Poppy was four months old, she had decided to try weaning her, so she could have a little more freedom and accept help from others from time to time. It was good to know she would, hopefully, be able to

176

enjoy the occasional glass of wine again one day soon.

For now, the transition would be in easy stages, and she'd started to express milk and use bottles as a forerunner to trying Poppy on formula.

Steve was clearly a natural when it came to babies. Jess watched in awe as he held the teat at exactly the right angle, knowing just when to tip the bottle a little more, and when to stop and pat Poppy's back, invariably being rewarded with the most perfect burp before she settled back comfortably in the crook of his arm and drifted into a contented sleep.

'Do you want me to take her?' Jess asked now, moving towards him with her arms open.

'Ah, no, she's just fine where she is. Why disturb the sweet wee thing?'

'Well, if you're sure. She certainly looks comfortable there.'

'Comfortable's right!' Mel said. 'Comfortably off! She must be the richest baby in town. Have you decided what to do with the money yet?'

'It's not mine to spend, it's hers.'

'Yeah, but she's going to need a bit of help with the big decisions, and the signing her name and stuff. Is the cheque in her name or yours?'

'Mine. I've put some of it straight back into more premium bonds for her. I know lightning's not meant to strike twice, but you never know, she might just win again. And I've been to the bank and sorted out a savings account with the rest of it. Terrible rate of interest, but at least it's somewhere safe while I think about what to do.'

'You could buy a house. Or put down a massive deposit for one. Get yourself out of this flat and onto the property ladder. And don't say you can't because it's Poppy's money. You'd be using it to provide a home for her. A proper home, with her own bedroom, and a garden and everything.'

'Mel . . .' Steve cut in. 'Let Jess make up her own mind. I know it's all very exciting, but keep your voice down. You'll wake Poppy.'

'Yes, Dad!' Mel laughed. She was sitting on the carpet with her back against his knees. 'You're good at this baby stuff, aren't you?' she said, turning to smile up at him.

'Well, it's been a while since mine were this small, but you don't forget. I do miss my two, being with them every day, and they grow up so fast. You have to make the most of every minute, enjoy them while you can.'

'Would you like more children, Steve?' Jess asked. 'One day, I mean. Not right now, obviously.'

She saw a look pass between him and Mel before he answered. 'I didn't think so. I always thought two was enough, but being apart from them so much, and spending time with little Poppy here, I may be starting to change my mind. Maybe one day. But that will rather depend on my lovely fiancée here, and how she feels about it.'

'Fiancée?' Jess's voice rose at least an

179

octave. Mel giggled and held out her hand. Why hadn't Jess noticed that she'd had it hidden in her lap all this time?

'Do you like it?' she said, wriggling her finger so her new diamond ring sparkled under the light.

'Oh, I love it! Come here for a group hug, you pair of dark horses, you! Oh, Steve, you've got Poppy so you can't, can you? Sorry about that.'

Jess and Mel threw themselves at each other, then stood up and danced around the room.

'And the divorce?'

'All sorted,' Mel said, excitedly. 'The nisi was issued last week, finances and access to the kids all agreed, so in another five weeks or so, he'll be a free man.'

'Free? More like out of the frying pan and into the fire!' Steve joked, grinning into Poppy's wisps of hair as he shifted her across to his other side without a murmur from her.

'Well, we should be celebrating.' Jess

lifted the near-empty bottle from the coffee table and held it up. 'Or you two should. But we appear to have run out of wine.'

'Shall I pop out to the offie and get another?' Mel jumped up and grabbed for her purse.

'I would go myself,' Steve said, peering down into Poppy's face, 'but as you can see, I am otherwise engaged!'

'I think you'll find that we both are — to each other!' Mel said, kissing him on the top of his head and gazing longingly at her ring again.

'OK, won't be long. You three behave yourselves while I'm gone.'

★ ★ ★

Ed sat in the corner of The Feathers and watched his mate Rich slip his hand into the back pocket of Cheyenne's jeans, as they stood side by side up at the bar, and sneakily squeeze her bottom. The girl squealed in surprise, then clasped her hand over Rich's to make sure it stayed exactly where it was.

Ed envied them their togetherness, their obvious attraction. She wasn't the sort of girl he went for himself, but each to their own, and she certainly seemed to make Rich happy.

As they came wandering back to the table, giggling over some private joke, lager slopping over the edges of the glasses they were trying to carry through the crowd, Ed couldn't stop his mind drifting towards Jess. He fancied her, he couldn't pretend otherwise, and it would be nice to have her here, to spend a carefree evening together, away from babies and from work worries, and not to feel like the saddo mate with no girlfriend who had a habit of playing gooseberry and feeling decidedly like the third and totally unnecessary wheel of a perfectly well-oiled bike.

The band had been taking a short break but started up again now, noisily and not quite in tune, just as Rich and Cheyenne sat down, making any attempt at conversation pretty much impossible. As the others turned away from him to watch what was happening on stage, Ed was happy enough to be ignored for a while and turn his thoughts back to Jess.

Jess was nearly thirty-one, a primary school teacher, and she lived in a flat just a mile or two from him, quite close to his gran's place. He knew because he had asked her one morning, sitting on Poppy's bench, in a sudden fit of 'Let's get to know each other better', each of them sharing a fact in turn. Because of that, he also knew that her favourite colour was blue, that she'd once had a childhood pet tortoise called Speedy Gonzalez, that she liked rom-com movies and Disney cartoons, and ate far too much chocolate, preferably milk with nuts, but anything — even the white stuff — if she was desperate.

How could anyone ever get desperate for chocolate? He was a cheese man himself, but as he'd said to himself not five minutes ago, each to their own.

Ed smiled.

He liked Jess. He liked her very much, but he had no idea how she felt about him. Just someone to chat to, probably, although their meetings at the bench were now a regular event, and they'd had lunch together a few times too, so she must like him or she wouldn't keep coming back.

The age gap didn't bother him at all, but it might well matter to her.

He knew it couldn't be easy for her, bringing up a child alone. He would bet that she didn't get out much in the evenings, not with Poppy to care for, and no man at home to help her.

The chocolate and rom-com DVDs were probably playing an even more prominent part in her life these days. Maybe she would appreciate some adult company. Male company. *His* company. There had to be someone who could babysit from time to time, so she could come out in the evening, surely? To somewhere like this, maybe, to meet his friends, and have a laugh.

For a drink, some music, maybe a meal? Not on a date, obviously. It would be wrong to call it that and risk frightening her off, but it would be a start, wouldn't it?

He would so like to kiss her. To properly kiss her, and feel her kiss him back . . .

'You all right, mate? You've gone very quiet. Fancy another?' Rich mouthed at him, in a brief lull between songs, lifting his own empty glass and tilting it towards Ed's still full one.

'No, I'm fine. No more for me.'

'Right. If you're sure. Oh, look. Friend of yours, I believe.' He was winking, and pointing at someone approaching their table. 'Good luck with that one, mate!'

Ed turned to see Leanne heading straight towards him, the little gold stud through her nose twinkling as it caught the light from one of the tall red candles that stood on every table — presumably to provide atmosphere, but which seemed to do nothing but drip wax in great gloopy piles onto their mismatched saucers.

'Hiya, stranger,' she said, plonking herself down on the edge of the bench seat and giving Ed no option but to make room for her. He was painfully aware of her naked thigh pressed against his trouser leg as her way-too-short skirt rode up, and of the fact that he was now trapped between her and the wall with no escape route that wouldn't involve looking incredibly rude and going straight home.

'So . . . ' he said, trying hard to make some sort of conversation that wouldn't give her the idea he was chatting her up. 'How's the chip business?'

'Busy. Hot. Same old, same old . . . My dad's thinking of selling the shop, actually.'

'Your dad owns it?' Ed raised his voice and moved nearer to her, so she could hear him above the music. 'I didn't realise.'

'Oh, yeah, it's a family business.' Leanne grabbed her chance to press even closer, and Ed caught the faint whiff of vinegar. 'He wants to find a bigger place. Room for tables and chairs, make it more of a fish restaurant, you know? Add a few extras to the menu. He's going to buy us all proper uniforms. Posh ones, like real waitresses wear. A step up from a greasy apron, I suppose!'

'Sounds good. Staying local?'

'Hope so. We'll do a take-away service, and we don't want to lose regular customers. Like you!'

Ed inched away and pretended to listen to the band. She was right, of course. If a business was to carry on, even from a new location, it was vital to hang on to as many of its existing customers as possible. He had plenty of those — people who had bought their plants and compost, and their pet food, from Blooming Marvellous for years — and who would definitely miss the place when it went. Maybe he could sign them up for some kind of loyalty scheme? It would be a way of getting hold of their names and email addresses, keeping them up to date with what was happening, offering discounts or vouchers to keep them coming and entice them back.

It was only later, as he walked home alone in the dark, that he realised what he had been doing. He'd been thinking of the future. Of Blooming Marvellous rising from the ashes somehow, moving premises and starting up somewhere new, and taking as much of its existing business — and maybe even some of its staff — along with it. For the first time in weeks, he felt a wave of optimism wash over him.

Change wasn't always bad. There was no need to fear it or back away. No, he had to meet it head on and find a way to carry on, to keep his grandad's business alive and kicking, with the same name but just in a different place. It might have to be on a much smaller scale, but he felt sure it could be done.

As a rush of plans started forming in

his head, he knew without doubt that it could be done.

★   ★   ★

The loud ringing of the doorbell almost woke Poppy from her contented milky sleep, but Steve quickly settled her back down with a series of soft and obviously well-practised shushing noises.

'Wow! Mel was quick. She must have run all the way there and back!' Jess said, easing herself up from the armchair to head for the door.

'Missing me, I expect,' Steve joked. 'Or gasping for more booze, one or the other.'

Jess pulled on the latch and opened the door with an exaggerated flourish.

'If you're bearing wine, you can come in . . . ' she began, her words stopping abruptly in her throat as her hand flew up to her mouth.

It wasn't Mel. It was Gary.

'Oh. It's you.'

'Of course it's me, you daft thing.

Surely you haven't forgotten what I look like already? And, sorry, no wine. Will these do?'

He brought his hand out from behind his back and held out a bunch of supermarket roses, wrapped in Cellophane, the price label still attached.

'What do you want, Gary? I have company . . . '

'To see you and the baby. Mum told me about her. She thought I should . . . well, you know . . . come and see her. Little Polly. So, here I am.'

'Poppy. Her name's Poppy.'

'Of course. Slip of the tongue, that's all. So, can I then? Come in, I mean?'

'I suppose you'd better.'

Jess stood aside and ushered him in, taking the flowers from his hand and dropping them on the shelf in the hallway.

Gary strode straight into the small lounge as if he owned the place, then stopped dead in his tracks.

'Who's this?' He stared menacingly at Steve, and then at the baby lying asleep in his arms. 'God, Jess, it didn't take you long, did it? A new bloke already? And sitting there, bold as brass, holding my baby.'

'This is Steve, and he is not — '

'Yeah, well, whoever he is, I think it's time he left, don't you?' Gary interrupted. 'You and me have things to talk about.'

'Do we?' Jess stood her ground, blocking the way between Gary and Steve, not quite sure what he might do next.

'Well, you said we should, didn't you? When you called me after she was born, and you're right. I've stayed away long enough, and it's time I got to know her. So, if your friend here could just make himself scarce . . . '

Steve's arm was curled around Poppy, as if he was protecting her from what was starting to look like trouble.

'Jess, are you OK? Do you want me to leave? I will if it's what you want me to do, but not because this thug tells me to.'

'Who are you calling a thug?'

'Right, stop it, both of you. You're upsetting Poppy.' She bent down and lifted the grizzling baby from Steve's arms. 'I think I would rather deal with this on my own, Steve, but thank you. Go and find Mel, and tell her I'll call her tomorrow. I'll be fine, really. Gary may have forgotten his manners, but he's not a threat. Honestly.'

'If you're sure . . . '

'I am. Really.'

'Well, call us if you need us, and we'll be straight back, OK?'

Steve pulled on his jacket and opened the door.

'Bye, Poppy,' he whispered, blowing a little kiss towards the baby. 'See you soon, sweetheart.'

'Can I look at her properly then?' Gary said as soon as Steve had gone. 'My daughter. Mum seems to think she looks like me.'

'She does — a bit. Well, her chin and maybe her cheeks, but the eyes are definitely mine.' Jess pulled the shawl back from Poppy's face to show him. 'Why are you so inquisitive about her looks all of a sudden, anyway? Are you trying to prove to yourself that she's yours?'

'Well, the speed you've got someone else in here, perhaps she's not. There are always tests, aren't there? One of those DNA swab things.'

'Why would we need one of those? You know full well there was nobody else while we were together. Or since, actually. She's yours, all right.'

'I suppose,' he said, reluctantly, picking up the wine bottle from the table and quickly replacing it once he saw it was empty.

'Would you like a drink?' Jess asked. 'It will have to be tea or coffee. The wine was Mel's. I'm off alcohol at the moment.'

'Not pregnant again already, surely?'

'It's called breastfeeding, Gary. Heard of that?'

'Oh, yeah. I didn't think . . . '

'You rarely do. Dive in feet first, and

think later. And Steve is not my boyfriend. He's Mel's, OK? Now, would you like to hold Poppy, while I put the kettle on? Then we can sit down in a civilised way and start this conversation over again.'

'No. You hang on to her for now. I'm not used to holding babies.'

'Then it's time you got used to it. Sit there and hold out your arms. That's it . . . support her head. See, that wasn't so hard, was it?'

Leaving Gary looking very awkward and more than a little terrified, Jess went out to the kitchen, leaned against the cool tiled wall and finally let herself breathe.

11

Forget-me-not —
Often grows near water, spreads easily
and blooms in shady spots wherever
the seeds may fall. It is petite, beautiful
and considered a symbol of true love.

Ed hadn't seen Jess for more than two weeks. It wasn't like her not to pop into the garden centre every few days or so, usually after one of her long walks, and she hadn't called or texted.

Perhaps it was the change in the weather, the early November evenings drawing in rapidly, the heavy clouds that had produced several thunderstorms lately, and the constant chill in the air that meant winter was on its way. Who would want to drag a baby out in that? But she had the car, so the weather was not really a valid excuse.

Of course, she was rich now. Or

Poppy was. Jess might be out spending some of their prize money. For a girl with no garden and no dog, there had to be a lot more enticing shops to visit than his — ones with more than just plants and pet food and garden furniture on offer.

He had decided to confide in her about having to close the place down. Well, she had told him her big news, so it seemed only fair to do the same, despite the fact that hers had been good and his far less so.

Of course, she wouldn't think he was after Poppy's money. It was ridiculous when he thought about it now for anything like that to have even crossed his mind.

The fate of the garden centre would be common knowledge soon enough anyway, when he put up the Closing Down Sale signs, which he planned to do straight after Christmas.

Now he had started looking at the property websites and commercial premises available, he was feeling more positive about the future every day. Starting again was do-able. It really was.

However, just as he was ready to share some of his tentative ideas for the future, Jess had disappeared. The thought that perhaps she wouldn't be coming back kept niggling at the back of his brain. She might have decided to take up her parents' offer and move down to Devon, or she had gone back to work earlier than planned, or she might have met someone . . . a man . . .

Of course it was none of his business what she did. He had no claim on her, other than that of friendship, but he knew he would like more, if only things were different. If he was a little older maybe, or she was younger. If she hadn't so recently had a baby, or been let down by the father. If she had shown even a hint that she felt about him the way he felt about her.

The truth was that Jess had started to mean a lot more to him than just a friend. He cared about her, and he cared about Poppy, but this didn't feel like the right time to do anything about it. He sensed she needed time, that there were just too many things in the way right now. After all, the best things in life were worth waiting for, weren't they?

'Ed? Can I have a word?'

Young Ben was standing right behind him on the gravel path, a broom in his hands, yet Ed hadn't heard him approach.

'Oh, yeah, sure.'

'Only, you did say you'd be OK with us looking for other jobs, what with the place closing, and I've been offered something. In the uni shop.'

'That's great, Ben.'

'It's a bit boring, compared with here, and all indoors, but that's probably not a bad thing with the colder weather coming in. It's easy to get to, while I'm living on campus.'

'Sounds perfect. When would you like to go?'

'End of the week? I could probably

stall them for a bit longer if I have to . . . '

'End of the week's fine. Come into the office before you go home and we'll sort out the paperwork and your pay. I'll be sorry to lose you, Ben. You've a real feel for plants and you're a hard worker, but good luck with the new job, and the rest of your degree. We'll have a bit of a leaving do for you on Friday, if you're up for it? Over at The Gardener's Arms, after work? Drinks are on me.'

'Sounds great. I'll bring my girlfriend Ellie, if that's OK. Make a night of it.'

Ed watched him go, already back into work mode and sweeping the loose bits of gravel back into place as he walked.

His first staff member to leave. One down, four to go. The Blooming Marvellous empire was already beginning to shrink, and he wasn't at all sure how he felt about it.

Or about the fact that every other bloke in the world seemed to have a girlfriend, except him!

★ ★ ★

Jess wasn't totally sure why she had let Gary Roche back into her life.

Yes, she had loved him once, but that had changed in recent months and now she didn't know what she felt, except confused. Of course, the main thing he had going for him was that he was Poppy's dad and, as her own dad had been so eager to point out, Poppy needed a father. Whether he was ever going to be the sort of father Poppy deserved was another matter, but she had to at least let him try.

She had told herself to tread carefully, to take things one step at a time. She had to be sure of his feelings, and her own, before anything important was allowed to change. There would be no mad rush to let Gary move into the flat . . . or back into her bed.

That first evening, when he had all but chased poor Steve out of the room, he had only stayed for half an hour or so. Long enough to meet his daughter and make vague apologies for taking so long to have done so. Sitting together over mugs of tea and a packet of Gary's favourite garibaldi biscuits, it had almost felt like old times for a while, his jacket discarded on the edge of the armchair, his feet, with shoes still on, propped up on the pouffe, those slurping noises he made as he swallowed his tea. She had forgotten about those. He couldn't stay longer, he had said, as he was expected down at football practice, but he would come back again, soon.

After he'd gone, Jess had sat for a long time, Poppy asleep in her lap, and remembered.

They had been good together once, and had a lot of fun. Nights out, dancing, eating, drinking, going to the cinema and having a snog in the dark. It was only when the serious stuff had happened, like impending parenthood and the possibility of committing to a permanent life together, that Gary had backed away. He may be thirty-four but there was still a huge streak of immaturity running right through him, like the words through a stick of seaside rock.

For some odd reason, a vision of Ed flicked into her head. Ed who, at only twenty-five, was running his own business, taking life and the future seriously, and who seemed to really care about Poppy. Maybe about her too . . . or was that just her being fanciful?

She had gone to bed that night more confused than ever.

Did Gary really want to be a part of Poppy's life, a proper father, who wouldn't just drop out again when the novelty wore off? Or had he only come because his mother had shamed him into it? Whatever the truth, she had to give him a chance to prove himself, for their daughter's sake. That was why she had agreed to let him call in again, the following Sunday.

They had walked around the local park, Jess pushing the buggy, Gary's arm slung carelessly around her shoulders, and had stopped for a while to sit on a rusty metal bench by the pond. Jess had brought bread for the ducks, and turned Poppy's buggy to face the water so she could see the birds scrabbling about for it on the bank.

'So, this is what it's like, is it? Having a kid?' Gary had lolled back, stretched his long legs out onto the path and watched in amusement. 'Walking about aimlessly, pushing a baby who can't walk or talk, has no idea what you're doing or saying, wouldn't know the difference between a duck and an elephant, and will probably go to sleep on the way home?'

'There's quite a lot more to it than that, Gary. Keeping her fed and clean, and happy. You can change the next nappy if you like! And she may not communicate well yet, but she's watching and listening, learning all the time. How else will she make sense of the world if we don't take her out and show it to her?'

'Well, I still haven't made much sense of the world myself, so she's got no hope!'

'She has every hope! I want her to be bright and inquisitive and caring, and she won't learn any of that by staying indoors doing nothing. She needs stimulation.'

'Yeah, so do I,' he said, laughing, taking Jess's hand and laying it in his lap as he moved in for a kiss. 'I've missed you, Jess. I miss . . . well, what we had . . . let me stay tonight and I'll show you how much.'

Jess pulled her hand and her lips away.

'I don't think so, Gary. One step at a time, eh? I thought you'd come to see Poppy, not me.'

'You come as a package now though, don't you? Can't really have one without the other.'

'Lots of separated parents manage to share their children without getting back together.'

'Who said anything about getting

back together? I just thought it would be good to spend a bit of time together, that's all. See how it goes, where it takes us . . . you know, go to bed together, wake up together . . . '

'Gary, I am not going to bed with you. I am pleased you've decided to get involved with Poppy, but I'm not automatically part of the deal.'

'But I've changed, Jess.'

'Prove it.'

'And how exactly do I do that?'

'I don't know. Just be a good dad, I suppose. Get to know her, love her . . . '

'Can I get to know you and love you again?'

'We'll see. You've been gone for months, Gary, and I've got used to that. I can't say I've been happy about it, because I would have loved things to work out properly for us, but they didn't, did they? You weren't ready, you said. So, why should I believe you're ready now?'

He shrugged. 'I guess we'll have to find out, won't we? Now, where's this nappy you were talking about? You'll have to show me how to do it though — and lend me a clothes peg for my nose if it's a stinker!'

Jess laughed. She couldn't help it. In tiny flashes, the old lovable Gary was still there, but she would never forget how he'd walked out on her. Could he change? Now that he'd met Poppy, could he really want a future with her — with both of them?

Only time would tell.

★ ★ ★

The For Sale sign was up outside the chip shop.

'Wow, that was quick!' Ed said, pointing in the direction of the sign through the window as Leanne piled the usual enormous heap of chips onto a sheet of white paper, sprinkled them with salt and vinegar, and wrapped them up for him. 'Has your dad got somewhere else already?'

'Yep. A much bigger place, a few

streets away. It's been a café for years, so I don't think we'll have a problem with change of use or anything like that. The Cosy Kettle. It's quite an old-fashioned place at the moment, all checked tablecloths and china cups, and they have loads of plants hanging from the walls outside. The lady's retiring. You might know it. Or the plants anyway!'

'I do. Never been inside though. So, when's the move?'

'I think Dad wants to do it side-by-side. You know, keep this shop going for now while we do up the other, so we don't have a period of being closed altogether. Should take a few months, I guess. Just need to find a buyer for here . . .'

'How big is it? Have you got a yard or anything out the back? Any storage?'

Where had that come from? The words were out of his mouth before he'd even had time to think about them.

'Why? Are you interested? I didn't

have you down as a fish and chip man. Other than eating them, of course!' She laughed.

'Would it work as a nursery, do you think? I mean plants, not children, before you ask!' Ed's thoughts were already running away with him.

'Dunno. Depends on what you need. Do you wanna take a look while we're quiet? I can always put the Closed sign up for five minutes.'

'That'd be great. It won't get you in trouble with your dad, will I?'

'What, for five minutes? He won't even know. Come on, follow me. Leave your chips there in the glass cabinet to keep warm.'

She flicked the bolt across on the door and turned the sign over, lifted up the hinged counter and led him through to the back of the shop.

'Are you thinking of expanding then? Business must be good at that garden centre of yours.'

'Something like that.'

They walked into a large room,

immediately behind the shop, with a sink, wall to ceiling shelving loaded up with cans of oil and flour, and two enormous freezers, presumably housing the fish. Well, it wasn't going to be fresh, was it? They were miles from the sea. There were at least twenty sacks of potatoes piled next to what must be the chip-making machine.

Ed stood and gazed around. Yes, this part could be opened up, made into part of the actual shop. Lots of floor space, keep the shelving . . .

'Is there more?'

'Of course.'

Leanne opened a door at the back and they went into a small staff room. There was a desk in the corner, strewn with papers, two armchairs, an old TV, and an open door off to the side revealed a toilet and wash basin. The carpet was a bit threadbare, the walls were in need of decorating, and the choice of old magazines on the coffee table was not to his taste, but he could already imagine himself and Carol here, sorting it all out, her swishing about with her duster and him with a paintbrush.

It could work. It really could.

'This is great. How about outside? Upstairs?'

'There's a small flat upstairs. Comes with the lease, but we've never lived in it. Dad uses it as an office and for more storage. It's a waste, really, but he never wanted strangers living up there. Who'd want to, with the smell of chip fat all day long? I'm used to it. Never even notice it anymore, but others would.

'There was talk of me moving in up there one day but, to be honest with you, I prefer it at home, with Mum cooking the meals and doing my washing! I don't really fancy being on my own.'

Ed knew how that felt. He'd never had much of a hankering for stepping out and going it alone either. His mum liked having him at home, especially as it was just the two of them now, since his big sister Kate had moved out.

'Here, come out to the yard. It's a fair size. You could probably squeeze a greenhouse or two in, if that's what you're after. It's walled all round, pretty high, so not likely to get burgled. Then I'll take you upstairs. Now, there's a proposition for you!' She nudged him in the ribs and gave him an exaggerated wink. 'Only joking! There's no bed up there anyway!'

The tour was over in minutes, and Leanne had to deal with two irate customers who were banging on the window as soon as they walked back into the front of the shop, so Ed was able to leave without talking about it any further, but plans were roiling in his head all the way home.

Of course it would be a lot smaller than his current premises, and he'd have to scale down the range of stock. But the location was ideal, right in the middle of town, and with a public car park just around the corner for those buying and carrying heavier stuff. There would definitely be enough work to keep Carol on, and probably Trish as well, and young Andy might want to do a few hours at the weekends if trade was good.

First he had to talk to the estate agent and find out the price. What had Leanne said about change of use? He'd have to make enquiries at the council about that. He couldn't imagine anyone would be likely to object to replacing a smelly chip shop with all that litter that inevitably got dropped outside, with a nice place full of flowers. The council should say yes. They owed him that much, surely, after as good as throwing him and his business out on the street?

He really should go and look at other premises too, to make comparisons, before he leaped in feet first. He should, but he probably wouldn't. Heart over head, that was the way he worked. The way his grandad had always worked too. If you loved something enough, you'd find the way to get it.

That was when he remembered Jess.

He wanted to see her again, to talk to her, tell her what he was doing, everything that he was planning and imagining . . . could she ever be a part of it all?

He pulled out his phone.

The estate agent could wait. He needed to run all this past his mum, and his gran. Work out the finances, see if he'd need a loan, draw out his plans on paper. But that was all head. Heart came first.

His heart was telling him that, before he did anything else, he needed to speak to Jess.

12

Cornflower —
Otherwise known as bachelor's button,
it was worn by young men in love. If
the flower faded too quickly, his love
was not returned. Sow it next to pop-
pies for extra brightness.

Doreen and Margaret seemed to have
become very pally lately. They had
arrived unexpectedly, and very much
together, at Jess's flat, laden with carrier
bags from a shared shopping trip and,
as Doreen said, sinking into a chair,
'absolutely gasping for a cuppa.'

They had been lucky to find Jess at
home, as she'd only ten minutes earlier
got back from the library. She had
meant it when she'd told Gary she
intended to make sure Poppy went out
and about to as many places as
possible, and had every opportunity to

see and learn and experience new things. Now her daughter was the proud owner of a library membership card, and a lovely pack given to her by the librarian containing a couple of free picture books and some printed nursery rhymes. She'd borrowed another five books too, one of which had a finger puppet sheep attached, which would come in very handy when they sang *Baa-baa Black Sheep* at bedtime.

'So . . . ' Doreen blew on her tea, decided it was still too hot and put it down again. 'What's this we hear about you and Gary?'

Jess could see Margaret draw in a sharp breath as both women's eyes turned towards her.

'There is no me and Gary.'

'Well, that's not what he says. Is it, Margaret?'

'He has sort of implied . . . ' Margaret began, looking suddenly embarrassed and a bit out of her depth. 'He has hinted, shall we say, that the two of you are seeing each other, that you're a couple again.'

'It's the first I've heard of it, if we are! No, he's been round a few times, as I'm sure you know. He says he wanted to meet his daughter, and I'm hardly going to stop him doing that. But that's all.'

'And the money?' Doreen cut in. 'Does he know about that? Because that would seem, to me anyway, to be a very good reason why he may have had such a sudden change of heart.'

'I haven't told him about that, no.'

'Why not? Sorry, Margaret, but I do have to ask Jess this. Don't you trust him?'

Jess didn't answer. Did she trust him? How could she, when he'd left her once before? Admittedly, she'd decided not to say anything about the premium bond win, but she didn't really see him as some kind of gold-digger. She just hadn't felt it was any of his business any more.

'Oh, it's all right,' Margaret said, lowering her gaze. 'He may be my son, but I do know what he's like. I have a little confession to make. He does know about the money, because I told him. Well, I was excited when I heard. Excited for little Poppy and what a difference it could make to her future. And I just blurted it out. Well, it didn't seem to matter at the time. The two of you weren't together any more, and he didn't seem to have any intention of changing that. It's not as if he has any claim on the money, is it? It's Poppy's, and you'll be in control of it, so what was the harm? I thought he'd be pleased, that his daughter was well provided for, especially as he's not been exactly forthcoming with coughing up much cash for her himself. But now he's sniffing around again, I can't help but question his motives.'

'Sniffing around?' Jess felt a cold stab at her heart. 'Is that what you think he's doing? Just hanging about with me and taking an interest in the baby to see what he can get? Trying to worm his way back in to get his hands on her money?'

'I don't know, dear.' Margaret had gone a little red in the face. 'It could just be a coincidence and me being overly suspicious, but . . . '

'But tread carefully, Jessica,' her nan said gently, laying her old bony hand over one of Jess's on the arm of the chair. 'Margaret knows him better than I do, probably better than you do too, so I think you should listen to her. Be on your guard. I don't want to see you hurt again.'

'Oh, I won't let that happen, Nan. He's going to have to work pretty damn hard to win me round again, I can tell you. For now, it's just good to see him getting involved with Poppy. Do you know, he even changed a nappy the other day. Not awfully well, but we all have to learn, don't we? And he wants to take us out for a meal on Friday. Well, he wants to take me, I suppose, as our daughter isn't likely to eat more than a mushed-up rusk.'

'Would you like me to babysit Gigi?' Doreen was very quick off the mark. 'So the two of you can go out by yourselves? Like a proper date?'

'Her name is not Gigi,' Jess laughed. 'How many times do I have to tell you?'

'Oh, stuff and nonsense. I like to call her Gigi. It's our own special name, isn't it, sweetheart?'

She leaned over the basket where Poppy was still sound asleep, and proceeded to make little cooing noises in the hope that she might encourage her to wake up.

'Your nan's right. About going on a date, I mean. It's the only way you're ever going to find out what that boy of mine actually wants,' Margaret added. 'If he even knows the answer to that himself. And I'm sure you don't really want to take Poppy everywhere you go. It'll be your chance to dress up a bit maybe, put your glad rags on, and talk to him, properly, about things that don't involve nappies or milk, or money. Find out if there's still a spark . . .'

'Well, I suppose it might be nice to have a drink or two, and to wear something without sick on the shoulder. But I don't know about any spark, or even if I want there to be. Right now, I'd probably just settle for a bit of adult conversation.'

'That's decided then. Maybe Margaret might like to pop round and help me.'

'Oh, Doreen, I'd love that. We could get one of those children's DVDs and watch it together. *Bambi,* maybe. I always loved that one, even if I do cry every time.'

Jess was about to say that Poppy was still a bit young for watching DVDs, but of course she wasn't. New things to see and hear, new experiences, new people, were exactly what she had promised to give her.

After months of single parenthood, so many evenings spent in the flat with just the TV or a good book for company, she could do with some of that herself at the moment, so a night out might be just what the doctor ordered. As to it leading anywhere? Well, she was going to have to be cautious.

Her visitors left with a promise to be back nice and early on Friday evening, and Jess was washing up the cups, hoping for a few minutes to herself before Poppy woke up from her nap, when her mobile started to ring in the bottom of her bag. After quickly wiping the soapy suds from her hands, she had to rummage about for it under a mound of tissues and dummies and used bibs. Oh, how her bag needed a sort out!

When she eventually located the phone, she was surprised to see Ed's name flashing up on the screen. Although they had exchanged numbers a while back, he had never actually called her before.

'Ed?'

'Hello, Jess. I hope you don't mind me ringing. If it's not a convenient time . . .'

'Of course I don't mind. It's fine.'

In fact, it was more than fine. Jess was surprised at how pleased she was to hear his voice.

'How are you? It's ages since I've seen you.'

'It is. That's why I'm calling, really. To make sure everything's OK with you, and with Poppy. It's not like you to stay away so long. From Poppy's bench, I mean. It's felt a bit lonely sitting there with a coffee on my own.'

'Oh, Ed, I'm sorry! Were you worried? Everything's fine. Well, almost fine. It's just that Gary's back, you see.'

'Gary? Poppy's dad?'

'Yeah. He just turned up one day, saying he wanted to meet her, and he's been here a few times now. Joined us on our walks, when he's had the time. He's given me a lot to think about, I suppose.'

'Ah, I see . . . '

'What do you see?'

Jess quietly moved over to a kitchen

chair and sat down.

'I'm sorry, Jess. I don't want to get in the way, tread on anyone's toes. If the two of you are . . . '

'We're not back together, if that's what you think, Ed.'

'Right. Only, I was going to ask if you fancied meeting up? Coffee, a chat, a visit to the bench. Or the pub, if you prefer? But, if you and Gary . . . '

'There is no me and Gary. Well, I don't think there is. And I'd love to meet up. How's tomorrow? On the bench, at eleven?'

'That sounds perfect. There's something I need to tell you.'

Ah, yes. She remembered now. There had been something, a few weeks back, something that had been pushed aside by her own news, but he'd never had the chance to say what it was.

'Can't you tell me now?'

'No, I can't, so you'll just have to be patient, won't you?'

He was laughing down the phone. It was the last sound she heard as he hung up. He had a nice laugh, did Ed. She'd missed it. There wasn't a lot of laughter with Gary. Come to think of it, there never had been. She couldn't remember a time when she'd been able to just sit and feel so absolutely at ease as she had with Ed. It had never been that way with Gary. Ed was different, Ed cared, and he had the most beautiful deep brown eyes. In fact, he was a very good-looking man. She didn't know why she hadn't realised it before, but she really liked Ed Burton. Really liked him.

Suddenly, tomorrow couldn't come fast enough.

*　*　*

Ed was already there, sitting on the bench, when Jess arrived. He'd pulled a little wooden table over and there was a tray on top of it, with two coffees in china cups on saucers, a plate of sandwiches and two cream doughnuts laid out on pretty floral plates she was sure she had never seen in the small café area.

He stood up as she approached and kissed her gently on the cheek, immediately taking over the handles of the buggy and guiding it into position next to the bench.

'Hi, Jess,' he said. 'It's good to see you.'

'You too.' And she meant it. Wow! He was like a different person today. He had never kissed her quite like that before, so confidently, so naturally. And the jeans and plain black T-shirt he was wearing showed off his long, lean figure. No sign of his usual green overalls. And the food . . . It was laid out like something from a posh cafe. He had made a real effort here. All that was missing was the paper doilies!

'Here.' He handed her a coffee. 'Drink it while it's still hot. I know I should have waited until you got here, but I'd counted on you being on time, and of course you are!'

'Ever punctual, that's me. I've got years of teaching to thank for that. Can't ever be late for a class, not with thirty kids waiting.'

'And now there's just one.' He took hold of Poppy's tiny hand and gave it a stroke. 'Oh, she is so cute. And she's grown so much bigger since I last saw her.'

'Really? I don't notice it so much, seeing her every day.'

'She looks huge. Blooming! She'll be munching on the sandwiches soon.' He laughed, and little creases appeared at the sides of his mouth. 'So, how have you been? Keeping busy?'

'Always. No chance of taking it easy with this little one around. But drop the baby talk. I have enough of that all the time. I want to hear about you. You said you had something to tell me.'

'Yes. It's not good news, I'm afraid.' His smile faded. 'This bench . . . our bench . . . well, it won't be here for much longer.'

'What? Why?'

Jess put her drink back down and grabbed for his hand. It felt warm and quite unexpectedly soft. There was no soil under his nails today.

'I'm closing up, Jess. The whole place has to go. No choice in the matter, unfortunately. It's council land, and they want it back. They're building houses here.'

'Oh.' She couldn't think of anything to say.

'We've only got a few months left. So this will be our last Christmas here. I want to make it a good one. Some real fir trees, lots of lights and decorations, maybe even get a Santa in and give away packets of seeds or mini spades or something to the kids. Get them gardening young!

'Then, come the new year, I'll sell all the stock, wind things down, and start again. Somewhere much smaller, of course. I'd never find anywhere else like this around here, and I do want to stay in the area. Near to my mum, and my gran ... Grandad's grave. I want to hang on to the customers I've already got, if I can.'

'But this is such a lovely place. The plants, the gift section, the little café . . . '

'The outside toilet?'

'Don't mention that toilet. I never want to see that again as long as I live!'

'One thing neither of us will miss, then. Yes, it's sad. All Grandad's hard work up in smoke, but I've had time to think about it and I'm determined not to let it defeat me. Or him.'

'So, where will you go? Do you know yet?'

'I've got my eye on a place right in the centre of town. A shop. I still need to do my sums, make sure it will work, but I'm hopeful.'

'And the bench? Will there be room for it?'

'I don't think so. There's a small outside area, but I'll probably have that set aside for plants, pots, bags of compost, that sort of thing. I don't think I'll be selling furniture or pet supplies, or anything like that. That was fine while we had the room, but I fancy concentrating on the growing side of things from now on. Plants, flowers, seeds, maybe even holding a few gardening classes for kids. Getting back to my roots, if you'll excuse the pun. No café — it's not the sort of place where customers will want to just sit and admire the view, because there won't be one.'

'Oh, dear. So, what will you do with the bench?'

'Jess, the bench is yours, not mine. Well, it's Poppy's, really. I want you to take it.'

'But I told you, I don't have a garden.'

'But you might, if you move to Devon . . . '

'Ah, Devon . . . I haven't totally made up my mind about that yet. But I would like a garden of my own. It's something Poppy's going to need once she starts running about, riding a bike, pushing a doll's pram around. And now we have the money, I've been thinking it could be time to move. Use her win as a deposit, get a mortgage and buy a little house. I'm not sure where yet, but a proper family home — even if we're only a family of two.'

She tried to picture Gary as part of that family, but his face just wouldn't slot into her dream. Not any more.

'I need to think hard about Poppy's future. It's no good leaving all that money in the bank, earning a pittance in interest. I want to invest it for her, in property, not be renting for ever, or staying in a first floor flat. All those stairs, just to get to our front door!'

'So that's decided, then? We have a strategy, a master plan. Of sorts, anyway, even if we can't do much about it for a while. We're both going to be moving on, taking charge of our futures, starting over. It all sounds exciting, doesn't it? And so simple, when I say it like that.

'We might even still be able to meet

up on the bench from time to time, if you stay living around here — and I hope you do. Then I could come and help you plant things, to make your little patch of land into a real garden, while you make the coffees, for a change!'

'I like the sound of that.'

Jess could picture it already. A garden, the bench, Ed sitting there with his fork and spade propped up beside him, the usual muck under his fingernails. Somehow he fitted into the vision so much more easily than Gary ever could.

'So now we've put the world to rights, shall we eat these delicious-looking sandwiches?'

'Only if Poppy can join in. OK, maybe no bread for her just yet, but I've been dying to get her out of that buggy and give her a cuddle. Maybe walk her around and show her the flowers. I need some practice if I'm going to start teaching kids about plants. She could be my first customer.'

'Feel free. She's all yours! Give her her bottle too, if you like. I'm moving in on the ham and cheese, and I may be some time!'

*   *   *

'We wanted you to be the first to know . . . we've set a date!'

Mel was standing on the doorstep, jigging up and down with excitement, holding out a Save the Date card in one hand and a bottle of bubbly in the other. Behind her Steve just grinned like the cat that got the cream.

'Well, come in and tell me all about it.'

Jess took the card from Mel's hand and peered at it as her guests went in and sat down.

'February? That's only three months away.'

'Couldn't see much point in waiting. Steve's divorce has been finalised, and Valentine's Day is such a romantic time, isn't it? Not that we could get the

232

actual day — that gets booked up years in advance, apparently — but there'll be hearts and flowers in all the shops, lots of pink everywhere, maybe even snow if we're lucky.

'Three months is plenty of time to arrange the sort of wedding we want. Just a simple one, with close friends and family, and a nice meal. We don't want to spend every penny we have on just one day. It's more important that we use it for our future, start working out where we'll live.'

'You're trying to tell me you're moving away?'

'Well, it is important that Steve lives near to his children, Jess. As soon as his ex went back up north to be near her parents, it was always on the cards that he'd want to follow. I mean, can you imagine being miles away from Poppy? It's heartbreaking, and it's not as if we can't get jobs up there. We've been looking already.'

'I'm happy for you, Mel. Really, I am. I'll miss you, though.'

'Not as much as I'm going to miss you and Poppy. I'm getting used to babies now, since she's been in my life, and I have to say I'm warming to them rather a lot. Maybe we'll have one of our own one day soon.'

'Soon? Mel, you're not pregnant, are you? Is that why you're rushing things?'

'That's exactly what my dad said, and no, I'm not! If we're rushing it's just because we want to be together, that's all. No need to hang about, because there are no doubts. He's the one, Jess.'

She looked adoringly at Steve.

'You know how sometimes you just know? The fluttery tummy, the warm tingles, the not being able to think about anything else . . . '

Jess smiled. 'If you say so,' she said.

She took the bottle that Mel had still been clutching and went to the kitchen to find glasses.

Had she ever felt like that about Gary? About anyone? Had she ever felt so sure she was in love, so overcome with the sheer physical joy of it, that it had shone out of her the way it did now for Mel? She couldn't honestly say that she had.

'So, who will you be bringing?' Mel said as Jess put a cool glass of bubbly into her hand, her engagement ring still looking incredibly new and shiny as it glistened in the light.

'Bringing?'

'To the wedding, silly. You have to bring a plus-one. Can't have you being all Billy-No-Mates by yourself in the corner all evening. Although, as chief bridesmaid, you're bound to get a lot of attention. Action, even, if you feel so inclined. It's traditional, isn't it? To get off with the best man!'

'Who is . . . ?'

'Oh, you haven't met him,' Steve said, finally getting a word in. 'Bill, an old mate of mine. Probably not your type though, I have to say. Bill's a bit of a rough diamond. All straggly beard and baggy trousers . . . '

'And married,' Mel said with a pout.

235

'Oh, yes, that too,' Steve added with a grin.

'So, even more reason to bring someone with you. Poppy too, of course. I thought she could be a sort of honorary flower girl, even if she can't walk yet. We can make her one of those little head-dresses from artificial flowers and pop a tiny basket over her arm. Oh, I can't wait!'

'Well, you'll have to. Still, three months will go by really quickly, and there must be things I should be helping you with if I'm going to be chief bridesmaid — not that you've actually asked me yet. You've just assumed . . . '

Mel giggled and said, 'Jessica Markham, would you please do me the great honour of being my chief bridesmaid?'

'Er . . . I'll have to consult my busy diary.'

'Jess!'

'Oh, all right then. I'd love to!'

'So, who are you bringing then? Gary?'

'I don't know. Can I hold back on that question for a while? Gary's still . . . well, he's still on probation, shall we say.'

'Of course. How's it going with that, anyway? Has he asked if he can move in yet? More importantly, has he offered to pay you any maintenance? Because he really should, you know. Whether you've won the premium bonds, or the pools, or the lottery makes no difference, he should still be paying his share. You can make it official, get the CSA people on the case. After all, he is Poppy's dad, whether he likes it or not.'

'I think maybe he is starting to like it. Like her, I mean. He's actually very good with her. He brings her little things . . . a rattle, and a little white cardigan his mum must have knitted. It was a blue teddy last time, with a football scarf round its neck. Not entirely suitable for a five-month-old baby, but it's the thought that counts. I think he must have got it in the supporters' club shop. Trying to make her a fan already.

'But, you're right, it's time to make some sort of proper arrangement about money. Teddies won't help pay the bills or put shoes on her feet as she grows up, and I'm not going to use her winnings for any of that.

'I'll ask him on Friday, when we go out. Get a couple of pints down him to soften him up a bit before I hit him with it!'

'Well, make sure you do. And if he says no, or makes some excuse, just hit him!'

'It won't come to that,' Jess laughed. 'I can be quite persuasive when I need to be.'

'Low-cut top, you mean? And high heels. That should help you get your own way. Your Gary always was shallow like that.'

'He's not *my* Gary! But give him a chance, Mel. I'm hoping he's changed since Poppy's come into his life. Like you said, babies have a way of getting to you, melting your heart.'

'Ah, but he'd need a heart in the first place.'

'That's a bit below the belt, Mel.'

'Below the belt is exactly where his so-called heart is! It's the only bit of the body that matters most for men like Gary. So make sure you've got your chastity belt locked on tight, or you might find yourself with another little Poppy on the way before you know it. I bet you haven't done anything about contraception since she was born, have you?'

'There hasn't been any need.'

'Well, make sure you remember that on Friday.' Mel was getting so agitated that her drink was slopping dangerously close to the rim of her glass. 'The last thing you want to see if you find yourself pregnant again is the same man running away from you for a second time!'

'Drink your champers and shut up, Mel.' Steve reached over and put a restraining hand on Mel's arm. 'Jess is a grown woman who can make up her own mind. And, besides, it's really none of our business.'

'If you say so,' she pouted.

'Now, can we have a play with Poppy?' he said, in a complete change of tone. 'I don't know about Mel, but that's what I've really come for, to see my favourite girl.'

'I thought I was your favourite girl!'

'Girl? Mel, you may not always act like one, but you're a grown woman. Now, get that drink down you and start planning your veils and trains, and your table favours, and whatever else you women think no wedding should ever be without, while I have a little cuddle with Poppy.

'Is that *The Three Little Pigs* I see down there, Jess? Pass it over and I'll read it to her. Let her see what a real big bad wolf looks like, because I don't think it really looks like Gary, no matter how much Mel might want to think so.'

★　★　★

240

It was Ben's last day at work on Friday and, once everything at the garden centre was locked up for the night, Ed nipped home for a quick shower and change of clothes before the planned meet-up at the pub.

As he stood under the warm spray, letting the water cascade over his head, his mind flashed over to Jess.

She'd mentioned that she'd be seeing that Gary bloke tonight, going out to eat and talk. Just the two of them, without the baby. Something about that set-up unsettled him. A gnawing fear that Jess was about to make a huge mistake kept working its way into his thoughts.

The man had left her, for God's sake — and when she was pregnant with his child too! There should be no going back from a thing like that. No forgiveness, and certainly no reconciliation. Whatever was Jess thinking by even agreeing to go out with him? Unless it was to dump him, once and for all.

It was hard to imagine anyone not wanting to know their own child, not wanting to be involved at every step. If he ever had a child of his own, he'd want to go to every scan, every appointment, hold the mother's hand throughout the birth, be the first to hold it and help choose its name.

This Gary person had done none of those things, yet here he was back on the scene as if he'd never left. It wasn't right. He may never have met him but he knew his type, and he'd very happily knock his block off if he ever got his hands anywhere near him!

Seeing Jess again this week had only served to remind him how special she had become, and how much she meant to him. And little Poppy too. Good God, he had done more for that child than her so-called father ever had!

He'd even — almost — been at the birth.

How was he supposed to stand by now and let Jess make what could be such an appalling mistake in getting sucked back in by the man who'd betrayed her so badly?

If only he knew which restaurant they were going to, he'd barge in there and . . .

And do what exactly? Pull them apart, make a scene, punch the guy where it hurts? Or say something? Say what? That she belonged with him? That he loved her? Because he did. He knew that now.

'Jess Markham, I love you,' he said to his reflection in the misty mirror, not knowing if he would ever get the chance, or the courage, to say it for real, and wondering, if he did, just what her reply might be.

He dried himself quickly and threw his wet towel into the laundry basket. Throwing in the towel. Ha! How apt!

He couldn't do that, though, could he? Couldn't give up on her. Not until he knew what Jess wanted. And if that was Gary, and making a new life for herself and Poppy with him, creating that little family unit she so clearly craved, then he'd walk away, leave her alone, let her be happy.

It would hurt like hell, but more than anything in the world he wanted to see Jess happy.

With or without him.

13

Ivy —
A creeping plant that clings to build-
ings and trees, although it does not
penetrate the roots. It needs to be con-
trolled before it causes lasting damage.

Gary leaned across the table and held the wine bottle over Jess's empty glass. 'Another drink, Jess?'

'I've had three already. Are you trying to get me drunk?' She giggled.

'Of course I am. Go on, let your hair down. First night out without the baby, you should make the most of it. We both should.'

He ran his fingers up and down her bare arm while using the other hand to pour.

'There's still a lot left in there. You can't have had much yourself. Or is this a second bottle?'

'Who's counting? Just enjoy it. This wine always was one of your favourites, I remember.'

'Do you?'

'Jess, I remember lots of things about you. We were together for — what — a year or more?'

'OK, prove it. What's my favourite colour?'

'Er, that would be purple . . . no, blue, I think.'

'Lucky guess. And my favourite food?'

'Chocolate, obviously.'

'Ah, but what kind?'

'Every kind. I've never known anyone eat so much of the stuff.'

'I do not!'

'I licked little bits off your bare tummy that one time, when you were eating it in bed, remember?'

He moved his chair closer, so his face was inches from hers as he whispered in her ear.

'In fact, that turned out to be quite a night, didn't it?'

His hand had moved from her arm and was snaking around her shoulders, touching the side of her breast through the thin fabric of her dress.

'Now, that's giving me ideas. Let's order something chocolatey for dessert, shall we? Something a bit messy. For old times' sake.'

'Gary, no!' She pushed his hand away. 'I didn't come here for . . . well, that!'

'What did you come for? I thought this was a date, a chance to get close to each other again.'

'It was meant to be our chance to talk, Gary. About Poppy. About her future, and that means you starting to contribute. Financially, every month, like proper fathers do.'

'You have to put a dampener on things, don't you? Just when I was starting to enjoy myself. Look, I can't afford to pay much, Jess. You know that. I have the car loan to pay off, and it needs a new clutch, and there's my rent, and my season ticket, and — '

'So, your football matches are more important than your daughter?'

'I didn't say that. Look, you earn more than I do, we both know that. And you've got your parents to help you out. They're not short of a bob or two. And, besides . . . '

'Yes?'

Jess felt suddenly stone cold sober. He was going to mention the premium bond money, wasn't he?

'Besides,' he side-tracked, 'we don't live together, do we? You can't expect me to start helping to pay your bills as well as my own. You always managed before she came along. Rent, electric, water, and all that. What extras can a baby possibly add to the mix? A few nappies, a bottle of milk a day . . . '

'You have no idea, do you?' she snapped.

'Look, Jess, we both know you don't need the money. I know about the win, even though you didn't see fit to tell me yourself. You're just doing all this to prove some point. Trying to trap me, pin me down again. I don't want that. Never did, and never will. I'm her dad, I accept that, but she's richer than I am. All that money. Blimey, Jess, think what we could do with it.'

'We? It's Poppy's money, not ours. Is that what we're really here for tonight? So you can try to get your hands on the cash?'

'Like you already have, you mean? Mum said the cheque had your name on it.'

'Someone has to take charge of it. She can hardly make decisions herself, can she? Someone has to act in her best interests, make sure it's used wisely, and that does not mean buying you a fancy sports car or a fortnight in the Caribbean!'

'Well, all I can say, Jess, is that you don't need my money. You should probably be paying me, not the other way around.'

He gazed at her for a moment, took another swig of wine and changed the subject.

'Now, why don't we forget all this maintenance nonsense and have another drink, eh? Did I tell you how sexy you look in that dress? Even sexier out of it, I bet. Having a baby's definitely added a few curves that weren't there before . . . '

Jess sat in silence for a while. He was right, of course. He didn't earn as much as she did, and that big fat hundred thousand pounds was still sitting there untouched. He hadn't wanted to be a father, hadn't asked for any of this, but surely having met Poppy now things should be different. He should really want to be more involved, to help out as much as he could, even if, financially, it wasn't possible for that to be much. He could still give her his time, his attention, his love . . .

'Let's have the profiteroles, shall we?' Gary talked on, oblivious to her feelings. 'And a couple of brandies. You're very tense, Jess. Loosen up a bit, eh? Let's enjoy the rest of the evening, have a bit of fun like we used to. You seem to have forgotten how to do that.'

'I know how to have fun, Gary, but this isn't it.'

She laid her napkin on the table, picked up her bag and stood. This wasn't working. It wasn't a date, and it certainly wasn't fun. It was a revelation.

'I'll leave you to pay the bill. It's the least you can do. As for the child support, you'll be getting a letter about that as soon as I've been on to the CSA people. I should have organised things long before now but I was waiting for you to do the right thing of your own free will. I can see that's never going to happen, so let's make it official, shall we? You'll only be asked to pay what you can afford, but it has to be something, Gary, something to make you realise you have a responsibility now, even if you don't particularly seem to want a daughter.'

* * *

Jess walked home. It was a nice evening, already dark but not too cold, and she needed time to think.

Gary was never going to be the father Poppy deserved, never the long-term partner or husband that Jess had wanted him to be. He was just a waste of space, as her dad had said, a man who had disappeared from her life without a backward glance. Finally, she knew her dad was right.

She had to admit that she had quite liked the feel of Gary's fingers against her skin. It had been a while since she'd had that closeness with any man. Just for a few seconds, it had felt like old times, before her pregnancy had changed things and shown him up as the man he truly was.

Any thoughts of letting Gary back into her life were quashed now, once and for all. In fact, she couldn't imagine why she had ever entertained the idea at all. They had nothing in common. She had moved on and he very clearly hadn't.

Her priorities were different now, and Gary's probably never would be. Football, his car, nights out, sex . . . leopards don't change their spots.

There were a few people hanging about outside the chip shop as she hurried by, the smell of vinegar on the air, an overflowing litter bin spilling crumpled paper and tin cans onto the pavement.

'Hello.'

Jess jumped as a hand reached out and touched her on the shoulder. She spun round, one of her unfamiliar high heels turning over and making her wobble, but the hand steadied her.

'Ed! What are you doing here?'

'On my way home from a few drinks with the guys from work. Thought I'd take a bit of a detour and have another look at my future empire.'

'Empire?'

'The chip shop, the place I told you about.'

'For Blooming Marvellous?'

'Yep. Nice central location, lots of

shop floor space, a yard out the back . . . '

Jess stood still and looked back at the shop thoughtfully.

'It's hard to imagine it full of plants instead of fish, but, yes, I can see its advantages. The location is perfect. Quite a drop in size though.'

'It has to be, but it'll be all mine. Something I can do for myself, something I can feel proud of. But what are you doing here, and on your own too? Wasn't it the big dinner date tonight? Where is he, this ex of yours? Not in there treating you to chips, I hope!'

'No.' Jess wasn't sure she really wanted to have to explain. She felt a bit stupid, falling for Gary's nonsense, not immediately seeing him for what he really was. 'We finished early.'

'And he didn't offer to see you home? Where's your car?'

'I've been drinking. I should have got a taxi home, I suppose, but I fancied the walk. Nan's with Poppy, so there's no rush to get back home.'

'Then you've time for another drink. With me.'

Jess hesitated. Two men in the same evening? 'Out of the frying pan and into the fire' came to mind. She'd already had more than enough alcohol.

'Maybe a coffee?'

'Of course. Come on,' he said, hooking her arm through his. 'You can tell me all about it. I take it things didn't go the way you'd hoped?'

'You could say that.'

'It helps to talk, you know. And I'm a very good listener. My ear, as they say, is all yours.'

'Just the one?' Jess laughed. 'What's your name — Van Gogh?'

'Ha, ha. I'm no artist. He did a nice line in sunflowers though, so we do have something in common.'

Jess could feel her mood lighten as they strolled along, arm in arm.

The Cosy Kettle tea shop was closed for the night, and she didn't fancy another noisy pub, so they grabbed a window seat in McDonalds and drank their coffee gazing out at the high street.

Despite her protests that she had already eaten more than enough, Ed bought a couple of doughnuts as well.

She smiled at the contrast between the beautifully laden restaurant table, the candlelight, the glasses of deep red wine and promise of gooey profiteroles and cream that she had walked away from, and where she found herself now, elbows resting on a plain Formica table, licking sugar from her fingers, sipping from a cardboard cup.

Amazingly, she felt suddenly happier, less stressed, more in charge of her own life.

'So?' he said.

'So . . . '

'It's OK, you don't have to tell me. None of my business really, I suppose. We can talk about something else, anything you like. Politics, books, the weather . . . '

'How about if we don't talk at all? I

could really do with a bit of thinking space right now.'

'Suits me. Sitting in silence with a beautiful woman and a doughnut sounds like a little slice of heaven to me!'

Jess felt herself blush and quickly lowered her face to take another sip of her coffee.

Beautiful?

Well, she wasn't sure about that, but one thing was crystal clear. Ed was a lovely, kind, and caring man. She suddenly realised that she felt comfortable with him, warm and cosseted, at ease. Because Ed didn't pressure her, he had no hidden agenda, he made no demands on her.

Ed understood.

* * *

He stood on the pavement outside Jess's flat and looked up at the first floor window.

There was no way he could have let

her walk home alone at night, and the short, warm hug they'd just exchanged on the doorstep before she'd gone inside had made every one of the two miles he would now have to walk back worthwhile.

He could just picture her nan up there peeking at him through the curtains and muttering about her granddaughter going out with one man and coming back with another! And Gary's mum was in there too, apparently. An odd arrangement, but he'd better get off quickly before she came out. Keeping his distance from Gary and anyone associated with him made a lot of sense.

However, keeping his distance from Jess and Poppy was never going to happen.

Oh, she had looked gorgeous tonight. He'd never seen her dressed up like that for a night out. This Gary must be mad to have abandoned her the way he did. Some men just didn't appreciate what they had.

There were stars in the clear night sky as he walked back into town, one bigger than all the others. The North star? Pole star? He was no astronomer, but the sight of it threw his thoughts forward to Christmas. Wise men following the star, bringing their fancy gifts.

He was no man of wisdom, or of wealth. He was more of a shepherd himself. Linked to the land, nature, nurturing. Would — could — Jess ever want a man like that?

He shoved the thought aside, because he had no way of knowing the answer, and spent the rest of his walk planning what he was going to do to make Blooming Marvellous's last Christmas in its present home a memorable one.

His mum was still up when he got in. She was sitting with her feet up watching some old weepie film on TV.

'All right, son?' she said. 'Did you give young Ben a good send-off?'

'Yeah, it was OK, no tears. Carol and Trish only stopped for one drink, and Ben had his girlfriend there, and some of his mates. I left them to it in the end. Ran into a friend on the way back and stopped off for a coffee.'

'Who? Rich?'

'No, no. Not anyone you know, Mum. Not yet, anyway.'

'Now I'm intrigued. It wouldn't be a girl, would it?' she teased.

'Might be.'

'Well, about time, that's all I'm going to say.'

'Sure about that?'

'It's your life, Ed. You'll tell me when you're good and ready. Now, do you fancy a hot chocolate before bed?'

'OK, go on, budge up and make room. I'll watch the rest of the film with you. I'm in the mood for a bit of romance. Then I'll make the chocolate.'

14

Poinsettia —
A cheery plant, widely grown indoors
over Christmas. Take care when trans-
porting poinsettias home in winter,
as the cold outdoor temperatures
can cause damage.

December swept in, in a flurry of tinsel and pine cones and poinsettias. Blooming Marvellous, under its strings of twinkling coloured lights, looked as though a ton of glistening snow had been sprinkled all over it, which it more or less had, albeit the fake kind.

Ed sat in his small office and worked his way through the latest invoices and stock lists. Everything was on track for a final sales push before the inevitable winding-down and, instead of the sense of sadness he had expected to descend upon him, he was feeling excited, even exhilarated, at what was to come. Perhaps a little of the Christmas spirit was seeping in and working its magic.

Leanne's dad had agreed, in principle at least, to let Ed take over the chip shop premises in a few months' time when his own move had been completed, and the paperwork was already being prepared at the solicitor's.

The bank had been brilliant about the short term loan he would need to get him started, and things were in motion at the council to make sure there were no objections to the change of use. Now all he had to do over the coming months was sell everything off at the best possible price and organise the removal of all the things he would be taking with him, which hopefully would not be very much.

He planned to stay closed for at least a month, giving him time to re-fit and stock the new shop before opening its doors to customers.

Getting a tenant into the upstairs flat would help enormously with the bills, and the letting agents had assured him they would have no trouble finding someone quickly. All in all, things could not have been going better.

Except that Jess had taken Poppy off to Devon to spend an extended Christmas with her parents, and no doubt to lick her wounds and finally free herself from Gary's retreating shadow. She wouldn't be around to see him make a fool of himself when — having left it too late to book a professional — he planned to dress up as Father Christmas on Christmas Eve, with Carol as his elf. Still, that was probably a good thing. Carol might look cute in her emerald green outfit and big pointy ears, but his own red ensemble, bushy white beard and padded belly did not add up to a particularly sexy look!

He would miss them both though, and would have loved the chance to see little Poppy's eyes light up with wonder as she opened her very first Christmas presents.

What if Jess decided not to come back? What if spending so much time down there in Devon made her want to go and live there permanently? It wasn't an option he had any desire to contemplate.

Since her final split with Gary just a few weeks earlier, Jess had visited Blooming Marvellous often. Whatever the weather, they'd resumed their regular meetings on the bench, and their game of 'Getting to know each other better', which had moved on to all sorts of ridiculous questions and topics that had them in hysterics and meant he was now an expert on all things Jess, just as she was on him.

He knew what sort of takeaways she favoured, what her favourite book was, that she had a collection of socks with jungle animals on them, how many boys she'd kissed (he thought it would be a bit too cheeky to ask how many had gone further), and even what she wore in bed. That question had been more of a dare than anything else, especially when he'd described his bright red Superman pyjama bottoms, courtesy of his gran, and she'd insisted that no, she did not sleep naked but, just like Marilyn Monroe, always wore a dab of perfume!

It was quite surprising what their five-year age gap meant when it came to remembering their favourite childhood programmes — who on earth were The Rug Rats or Ace Ventura? And the music they'd danced to — she had been amazed that he didn't know all the words to *Barbie Girl*! And yet, somehow that just gave them more to talk about, as they each laughingly explained what was so great about a particular TV show or pop group and tried to justify their choices.

All the while, little Poppy sat on one of their laps, passed from one to the other, and babbled away to herself as if she knew exactly what they were talking about and couldn't wait to join in.

On the last day, before she'd set off for Devon, she had left Poppy with

Gary's mum for an hour, and they had gone across to the pub, settling into armchairs on each side of a blazing fire and sharing a plate of scampi and a mound of skinny chips, taking it in turns to dip them into a tiny bowl of ketchup.

'I thought you preferred mayonnaise,' she'd said, remembering one of their silly conversations.

'I do.'

'Then go and get some, and leave all the ketchup for me!'

Her eyes had shone in the flickering light from the fire and he'd had to fight the sudden urge to just lean over and sweep her up into his arms and kiss her, ketchup lips and all!

However, he hadn't, and now she had gone.

He stared at the invoices in front of him.

What was he doing, sitting here indoors, poring over paperwork? He should be out there, getting his hands dirty, doing what he did best. He was, first and foremost, a plants man. All those evenings and weekends he'd spent working alongside his grandad, sowing and planting and pruning, had been the best times of his young life. He was at his happiest when his hands were in the soil and, although December was hardly the growing season, there was always something he could be doing outside, especially since Ben had left. Tidying, sweeping, weeding, watering. That would be the beauty of the new, smaller place. Not so much admin, and a lot more time spent with his plants.

★　★　★

Jess and Poppy sat on a low wall and looked out to sea. The water was still and grey, a few birds hovering over it looking for food, tiny waves lapping at the shingly sand. They were both wrapped up warm against the chill wind, Poppy's furry hat pulled low over her forehead, her hands enveloped in chunky woollen mittens, at least two sizes too big, that Nan had knitted as an early present, even though she would be coming next week to join them for Christmas and could have waited until then to hand them over.

Taking a walk along the seafront had become a regular ritual for Jess now, just as their walks at home had been, but without the lure of their own bench and Ed's coffee (and company) to look forward to at the end.

The sea air was bracing, yet calming, and there was always something new to point out to Poppy, whether it was a dog snuffling among the pebbles, or a piece of gnarled driftwood, or a pretty shiny shell they could hold to their ears later on, back at the house, and try to hear the echoing sounds of the sea.

She had come here to finally get Gary out of her system, but already he had phoned her twice. The first time had been to ask what he could buy Poppy for Christmas and then to complain, as if he really cared, when he realised she would be away until after it had passed by. Jess doubted that any present would actually materialise.

The second call had been to let her know a letter had arrived with forms he was supposed to fill in, expecting him to tell all and sundry exactly what he earned and what he spent. His voice had grown louder and louder the more he ranted. She had hung up on him halfway through that one.

At least he was unlikely to turn up at the door while she was here. A combination of work and anger and distance would keep him away.

The village where her parents lived was so much more peaceful than her busy street at home. At night she could lie in bed and hear nothing at all except the distant rumble of the waves. No traffic, no people coming and going, no banging of doors on the landing. And yet, she still couldn't decide if this was good or bad. Country life was idyllic in its own way, and for her parents, at their stage of life, she could easily understand its attraction. But for a thirty-year-old — and more importantly, a six-month-old baby — was it able to provide enough variety, stimulation . . . life?

She would be going back to work straight after Easter. Her maternity leave would be nearing its close and it made sense to ease herself back in at the start of a new term. She would not have a class of her own to teach until September, and could make herself useful for those first few weeks, standing in for anyone who went off sick, helping out with planning and playground duties, and by July a long summer break would await.

She loved her job, and the school she had been so lucky to find. Going back would present problems over finding childcare and the inevitable wrench of leaving Poppy behind for most of the day, but still she looked forward to it. Giving that up to move down here and look for a new job had seemed a possibility before, with cheaper housing, free childcare on tap, all those green fields and open spaces, but now . . .

Now, with Poppy's long-term future to consider, her schooling, the friends she would make, Jess had begun to appreciate the huge range of facilities and activities London life would make available to her. She wanted more for her daughter than a quiet, uneventful country life. And now they had more money to put towards a new home than she had ever imagined possible, and that made her own familiar much-loved area of outer London suddenly affordable, doable.

Then there was Ed . . .

Jess was growing fonder of Ed. Was that the right way to describe her feelings — fond? They had certainly stretched friendship to its boundaries and stepped cautiously into the beginnings of something more. Watching him growing more and more at ease with Poppy had been wonderful. The way he talked to her, as a real little person, and took her off to see the flowers, cradling her tiny body the way he would a handful of delicate petals, it was as if he was helping yet another little flower to turn her head towards the sun and become the best she could be.

Jess could never imagine Gary doing anything like that. Teaching her to use a computer maybe, or how to drive, but the wonders of nature . . . never. When Gary had picked up Poppy's library card, he sniggered at the very thought that a baby who couldn't talk, let alone read, would have any need for books.

Jess remembered the words engraved on the plaque on Poppy's bench, words she had quickly learned by heart: *This bud of love, by summer's ripening breath, may prove a beauteous flower when next we meet.*

Poppy was the bud Ed had been thinking of when he'd had the plaque made, way back before he had known her. Even then he had thought of her as a tiny new flower that would grow and flourish with the seasons. Maybe that was the way Ed looked at the world and everyone in it, good or bad. Like seeds, buds, flowers, trees, weeds . . . the things he understood the most.

Yet there was more meaning in that quote, wasn't there? It was about love itself starting small, like a bud, and growing over time into something beautiful. Was any of that in Ed's mind, the way it was gradually working its way into hers?

When next we meet . . .

Jess shook herself out of her fanciful imaginings and walked home.

★   ★   ★

'Hello, love. Good walk?'

Her mum met her at the door as she got back to the house.

Jess lifted a sleepy Poppy from her buggy and slipped out of her boots.

'Lovely.'

'Tea's still hot if you fancy a cup.'

It was good to be here, being looked after and cosseted, even if it was only for a few weeks.

Jess sank into a big, squishy armchair as her dad fussed over Poppy and her mum brought her tea and a fat slice of home-made fruit cake.

'You've cut the Christmas cake already?' Jess said, taking a bite.

'No, this was my trial run, to make sure I got the recipe right-and I did,' her mum said, looking smug. 'The real thing's still in its tin, waiting to be iced. You might like to help me with that, Jess. You used to love doing it when you were a child.'

'You're not going to do the same with the turkey, are you, dear?' her dad chipped in. 'Magnificent though I'm sure it will be, I don't think I could face two enormous Christmas dinners, trial run or not!'

Jess ate every crumb, then laid her head back and closed her eyes.

What a luxury, to be waited on hand on foot, to be able to take a nap if she wanted one, and still have icing the Christmas cake to look forward to. She could get used to this!

Yet there were definite attractions in going back home too — and it was an image of Ed's face, mingled with roses and coffee cups and ridiculous Superman pyjamas, that drifted hazily (and crazily) through her mind as she nodded off to sleep.

★   ★   ★

By Christmas Eve, Ed was tired.

It had been a fantastic few weeks at Blooming Marvellous. Business was up, the building had buzzed with activity and, since word of their imminent closure had got around, many of his customers had made the effort to express their regret and offer support.

The new loyalty card scheme had taken off like a rocket, with hundreds already signed up and collecting stamps on their cards every time they shopped, ready to use as money-off coupons as soon as the new shop opened.

In the office, with the blind pulled down, Ed stepped into his big red heavily-padded Santa costume and pulled the elasticated beard over his ears. He went through to the staff toilet and peered at himself in the mirror, laughing at the transformation. Even his own mother wouldn't recognise him!

Out on the shop floor, Carol was already working her elf-like magic, singing along with the Christmas music and forming excited children and their weary parents into an orderly queue.

Ed wasn't quite sure how he was going to get from the office to the little grotto they had constructed inside a small snow-sprayed garden shed without being seen, but it seemed Sandra was one step ahead of him as she and Trish appeared, right on cue, carrying a large fence panel. Ed crouched behind it as they waited at the office door and then sidled along as they walked it across the floor until it was leaning up against the back wall of the grotto. From there it was a quick but extremely ungainly climb through the back window, well out of public view, and Ed was finally in place.

He had deliberately opted for a dark interior, lit only by an arch of flashing fairy lights that rose up and over his makeshift throne, just in case any little person should recognise him and spoil the magic. As he made himself comfortable, he could hear the hum of excited voices outside the door and Carol promising that Santa would be ready any moment now. And, with a sack of wrapped red and green plastic gardening tools to one side of him and a big box of wildflower seed packets on the other, he was.

All morning the children streamed through, some brave enough to come and sit on his lap while photos were taken, some simply hovering nervously in front of him until they could be persuaded to reach out and take the offered present. One or two of the younger ones disintegrated into floods of frightened tears as soon as they looked at him!

Unlike the big department store in town, he was not charging for tickets. But then, he wasn't handing out cheap boxed games or flimsy dolls either. Giving the gift of growing to the next generation didn't come with a price, he felt.

By lunchtime he was glad of a break as Carol flipped a makeshift glittery sign over to say *Closed for Lunch*.

This time, he took the costume off before quietly and unceremoniously exiting the grotto through the door, smiling to himself that he hadn't thought to get dressed inside it in the first place so he could have avoided using the window.

The small café area was doing a fantastic trade in turkey sandwiches, mince pies and hot chocolate, and it would have looked bad to jump the queue, so he made himself an instant coffee in the office, found a bag of crisps in his drawer and took them outside to Poppy's bench.

Sometimes customers decided to

take the weight off their feet and sit down on it, but today he was lucky. Everyone was in too much of a hurry to see Santa, snap up their last minute gifts and get off home, so the bench was empty.

He had always loved Christmas Eve, probably more than the day itself. Every year of his childhood it had been the same. A drive through the darkened streets to his gran and grandad's for tea, on to an early evening carol service at the local church, everyone wrapped up warm in woolly hats and scarves, and then he and Kate being allowed to take the first chocolates from the tree, and maybe a sneaky sip of mulled wine, before a game of Monopoly that was usually abandoned long before anyone reached millionaire status.

Then they'd go home to their own beds, often far too excited to sleep, the empty pillow cases draped at the end of the beds, just waiting for Santa to drop by and fill them. Funny to think that, in his own small way, he was now bringing that same sense of excitement and anticipation into the lives of the children waiting to see him in his little wooden grotto. And sad to think that, this year, there would be a Grandad-shaped hole in their family gathering that nothing would ever be able to fill.

The afternoon whizzed by, darkness falling quickly, so by the time he waved the staff away with a collection of thank you gifts, turned off all the lights and locked up, his was the last car left in the car park. The pavements were already glistening with the beginnings of frost under the yellow glow from the streetlamps as he pulled out into the street and joined a crawling line of traffic. So many people still out and about, making their way home or going to join family and friends, all no doubt looking forward to a few days of relaxation and celebration, himself among them.

He breathed a long sigh of relief. The worst was over now. By the time he re-opened in January, he could start concentrating on closure — and on new beginnings. In a strange sort of way he was looking forward to it.

He pulled up on the drive and climbed out, opening the rear door of the car to lift out a big box of particularly pretty left-over Christmas decorations he couldn't bear to leave behind and, balanced precariously on top, an ornate terracotta pot containing a lovely bright red poinsettia he had set aside for his mum.

He felt his foot start to slide almost as soon as he straightened up, but with so much balanced in his arms, and his keys looped over a finger, he had no free hand to try to save himself.

The pot fell first, the rim of the brittle terracotta shattering as it hit the hard frost-covered ground.

The decorations followed, a jumble of big green and silver baubles rolling like giant marbles beneath the car and under his feet as he tried desperately to grab for the last of them and to right himself before it was too late.

He felt his arms flailing, suddenly emptied of their burden. One knee smashed awkwardly against the open door of the car, his ankle turning awkwardly. Then he was flat out on the drive, pain shooting through him so instantly it was as if a knife had been thrust into his leg. Did he cry out? He must have done because, within seconds, his mum was at the door.

'Ed! Oh, my God, what have you done?'

★   ★   ★

It was the first year in living memory that they hadn't followed the traditional carols and Monopoly routine and, despite piped versions of *We Wish You a Merry Christmas* and *Silent Night* coming through the speakers on an irritating loop, and a game of Solitaire played on his phone to help pass the time, spending three hours in A&E was no substitute!

Ed had seen a doctor quite quickly,

and been dosed up with painkillers, but there was a wait for X-rays and, once it had been established that his leg was broken and would almost certainly need surgery, there had been yet another wait until they could find him a bed.

Christmas in hospital. That was not a prospect he was looking forward to.

'I'll be back as soon as I can tomorrow,' his mum had promised, fussing around before she left for the night and trying to tuck the blankets around him without touching the splint or anything that might hurt. 'Once I've peeled the potatoes and got the turkey in the oven. I'll gather up all your presents, and bring you a couple of mince pies. And your gran and Kate will want to come too, I'm sure. Oh, Ed!' He was sure he saw tears in her eyes. 'What a thing to happen at Christmas.'

'Mum, you stay at home and enjoy your dinner. They're not going to let you in if I'm in theatre, anyway, and if

I'm not, I'll still be lying here waiting, so there's nothing you can do.' He squeezed her arm. 'Look on the bright side, Mum — at least the garden centre is shut now until the New Year, so I don't have to worry about work for a while. There'll probably be something extra laid on for tomorrow. Nurses singing carols, maybe a special dinner . . . '

'Ugh! Hospital food! I doubt you'll feel much like eating it anyway, if you're having surgery. I'll see if they'll let me bring your dinner in on a plate, in the evening. Proper home-cooked food. And some of my Christmas pudding. They must have a microwave here somewhere.'

'I'll be OK, Mum. I'm a big boy now. I'm not going to starve. But, look, they have extra large pillow cases. Do you think, if I left mine at the end of the bed . . . ?'

She took a few seconds to catch on.

'Presents from Father Christmas, do you mean? Oh, you are a tease!'

He could hear her chuckling as she went, the imprint of her lipstick still fresh on his cheek.

Then it was quiet, just the bustle of nurses coming and going from their desk at the end of the ward, and a few coughs and grunts from neighbouring beds as his fellow patients settled down for the night.

He took a tentative look at what was visible of his leg, already covered in bruises and swollen like a half-inflated balloon. The painkillers had kicked in and he felt drowsy, yet wasn't sure if he would be able to sleep.

And surgery in the morning — on Christmas Day? He felt guilty for dragging some poor surgeon away from his family, but he guessed it was all part of the job. Sickness and accidents don't restrict themselves to sociable hours.

'Anything I can get you?' A young student nurse appeared at his bed. 'More pain relief? Tea?'

'No, I'm fine, but thank you,' he said, smiling as she retreated.

He reached for his phone, lying on top of the bedside cabinet, and scrolled through his contacts list until he came to Jess's name.

His thumb hovered for a moment over it. Should he? But a glance at his watch told him it was ten o'clock. She would be with her parents, perhaps helping her mum with the food preparations or watching TV with her dad, or stuffing little presents into a stocking for Poppy.

He didn't want to spoil things for her, didn't want to intrude. Christmas was for families, and the best thing he could do was to let her enjoy it.

15

London pride —
Otherwise known as Look Up And Kiss
Me. Symbolic of the resilience of ordi-
nary Londoners, and of the futility of
seeking to bomb them into submission.

Jess unpacked her case and piled most of its contents into the washing machine. She had enjoyed her time away from London, but there was only so much sitting back and being fussed over that she could put up with and, after the quietest and most sober New Year's Eve she had had for years, she was just glad now to be home and back to some sort of normal.

A new year had begun and a new start awaited. No more dithering over Gary, no more wondering about a permanent move to Devon. It was time to start guiding her own future, not letting others do it for her.

It had been a long, slow drive home on roads chock-a-block with other holiday returnees and, having called into a petrol station shop for bread and milk, and dropped Nan back at her own house, all Jess really wanted to do now was have a nice hot bath and an early night.

Tomorrow she would drive down to Blooming Marvellous and see if Ed was there.

She had been so tempted to call him over Christmas, but she had fought against it. She liked him — she really liked him — she realised that now. Absence makes the heart grow fonder, as they say, and her own heart was sending out the kind of unexpected but unmistakable messages she couldn't help but listen to. But would Ed want to hear them? They were at different stages of life, and she came with baggage, she knew that.

Not that she liked to think of Poppy as baggage, but to a young single man, even one as caring as Ed, there was still fun to be had and having a baby in tow could be a step too far.

She had no idea what she was going to say, only that the time had come to say it.

Their relationship, such as it was, had reached a point where it had to change. Whether it went forward or fell back into casual friendship, she had no way of knowing, but she needed to find out, and doing that over the phone wouldn't feel right. There were some things that could only be properly said face to face.

The thought of her own face close to Ed's — close enough to kiss — was one she could not get out of her head.

Poppy had slept for hours in the car, lulled by the movement and the thrum of the engine. Even Nan's constant chatter hadn't woken her. But now she was wide awake and hungry, and Jess's longed-for bath would have to wait.

She took a jar of baby food from the kitchen cupboard, tipped its contents into a bowl and put it into the microwave to warm. Turkey and vegetable risotto. She may have eaten enough turkey in all its guises in the last week or so to last her a lifetime, but Poppy wouldn't mind. It was all just spoonsful of mush to her, and Jess had to admit that it smelled nice.

Propping Poppy up in her bouncer chair and feeding her with one hand, she decided to give Mel a call. She had expected to feel envious when Mel had told her of her New Year plans, the party she and Steve were going to, of the new shimmery dress and heels she had bought. However, she'd been surprised by just how nice it had been to stay in with her family, share a bottle of wine and join in with an off-key *Auld Lang Syne* in front of the fireworks on TV.

Motherhood had changed her, settled her and made her appreciate what really mattered in life. And that included Ed.

'Mel? Hi!'

'Keep your voice down. My head is thumping . . . '

'You can't still have a hangover from last night, surely?' Jess said, laughing.

'I might have . . . '

'It was a good party then?'

'The best, or what I can remember of it anyway. Let's just say the drink flowed. A lot.'

'Serves you right. You should know when to stop at your age.'

'Yes, Mum! Since when did you get to be so righteous? I remember when you poured half a bottle of champagne into your shoe and drank it.'

'Yes, and it was an open-toed sandal, so most of it fell straight onto the carpet!'

'Just shows how drunk you were!'

'Enough of the embarrassing reminiscences. What are you doing later on in the week? I've missed you, and it's time we got together. I want to hear all about your wedding plans, and if there's anything you need me to do to help.'

'Have you got your plus-one sorted? And if you tell me it's Gary, I'll be round there to drag you to the psychiatrists and get your head examined!'

'Gary's gone — history. There will be no more Gary, I promise. Actually, I was thinking of asking Ed, if that's all right with you?'

'Ed? The garden centre guy?'

'Yes.'

'Since when have you two been an item? Not that I'm complaining. I like him.'

'We're not. Well, not yet . . . '

'But?'

'Well, I like him too, so I'm hoping we might be an item, soon.'

'Well, it's obvious he's interested in you. I could see that as clear as day when we were all in that pub garden. But you were still stubbornly clinging to the ridiculous notion that Gary might come good and turn into some kind of knight in shining armour overnight. Not to mention Father of the Year.'

'I was not!'

'Never mind. You've come to your

senses at last. So, how does Thursday suit you? Let's go out somewhere. Steve too. We can have some food and a couple of drinks, and I can talk you through all the latest nuptial notes! Right now I don't think I could face alcohol if you paid me, but I should have recovered enough by then. Bring Ed along, too.'

'OK. I'll try. Got to go now, Mel. Poppy's just spluttered a mouthful of goo all over the carpet.'

Jess put the phone down and cleaned up her daughter. The carpet could wait. But talking to Ed couldn't. She had never done it before in her life, but she was going to have to ask a man out on a date. Before Thursday.

She swallowed hard. What was so hard about that? This was Ed she was talking about here. Her good friend Ed who, thanks to their many conversations on the bench, probably knew more about her than her own mother did. There was nothing to feel nervous about.

Except that he might say no.

16

Viola —
Also known as heart's ease, heart's
delight, tickle-my-fancy, Jack-jump-up-
and-kiss-me, come-and-cuddle-me, or
three faces in a hood. It can always be
relied upon to flower in winter.

Blooming Marvellous looked very different. Although there were still a few days left until Twelfth Night, all the Christmas decorations had come down and there were big red *Closing Down Sale* signs all over the place, with red stickers attached to almost everything, announcing reduced prices.

Sandra looked up from her position at the till and waved distractedly, but there was a long queue of customers with bargains piled into their trolleys and offering their loyalty cards to be stamped, so Jess didn't stop to say hello.

It was good to see the place so busy but, at this rate, she thought, the entire stock would be gone in days. What would Ed do then, with several months left until the move?

Jess took a slow stroll around the indoor area, browsing the shelves, picking up a few bits she wouldn't mind buying herself and putting them down again, then went outside to take up her usual position on the bench.

Ed would find her soon enough.

His office window overlooked the outdoor plants area, so he always saw her eventually, even when he had not been expecting her.

It was a chilly day. Poppy was wrapped up in yet another of her nan's hand-knitted cardigans, this time with a fur-edged hood and matching mittens. Jess had opted for simple slim-fit jeans and a plain black jacket, her hands dipped into the pockets to keep them warm. She hadn't wanted to make too much obvious effort. If Mel was right and Ed did have any interest in her at all, it was the real Jess he had taken a liking to, not the made-up, dressed-up version she had always presented whenever she had spent time with Gary.

She hadn't been sure before just what she would say, but Mel's invitation had at least given her a starting point. A few drinks with her closest friend and her fiancé, a way of evening up the numbers, making a foursome, stopping her from being a gooseberry! And then, once they all knew each other better, it would be one easy step from there to suggesting he come to the wedding.

She took a hand from her pocket and nibbled at a fingernail. Where was he? She would chicken out and run back home if she didn't see him soon and blurt out her rehearsed speech before she lost her nerve.

'Hi, Jess.' Carol had spotted her and come out to have a chat, two cups of coffee in her hands. 'You're not here to see Ed, are you?'

'I was hoping to, yes.' She took one of the drinks Carol held out to her, grateful for its instant warmth against her fingers. 'And thanks for this. You must let me pay — '

'Nonsense. Call it a perk of the job, or in your case a perk of being friends with the boss.' She sat down beside Jess and laid a hand on her shoulder. 'You haven't heard then, love? About what happened to Ed?'

'No.' Jess felt an involuntary tremble of fear. 'Tell me. Is he all right?'

'He only managed to slip over and break his leg. Quite badly, actually, in two places. Oh, don't look so worried. He's OK now, but he had to spend Christmas in hospital. He had an op to put in a few screws or pins or whatever, and he's all plastered up and on the mend now, but it'll be a while until he's properly back on his feet.'

'Oh, no! So who's running things here?'

'His mum's taken over. She's quite enjoying it too, I think. Well, it's always been a family business, so she's pretty used to the way things are done. Not that Ed is a good patient, from what I hear. It's all she can do to keep him at home with his feet up. Come into the office, and I'll introduce you.'

'Oh, no. I'm sure she's busy, what with the sale and everything to manage.'

'Rubbish. She'd love to meet you. Any friend of Ed's . . . Still, it's up to you, love. I'd best drink up and be getting back to work anyway. See you again soon, I hope.'

She stood up, blew a silent kiss towards Poppy and headed off.

Jess finished her coffee and was about to go when a small middle-aged woman with grey hair and twinkling eyes came bustling towards her, her loose navy slacks flapping at the ankles.

'Ah-ha!' she said, plonking herself down on the other end of the bench. 'So, Carol tells me you're my Ed's mystery friend! I knew you'd turn up sooner or later.'

'Hello.' Jess smiled, a bit bemused by the woman's sudden and excitable arrival. 'I'm Jess. There's no mystery about me!'

'Hello, Jess. I've heard so little about you that I knew you must be someone special — if that makes any sense! Only, that's the way he is, you see . . . my Ed. Keeps things close to his chest. Well, until he decides it's time to reveal them. But I knew something was going on. He has that look about him lately. And this little one . . . ?'

'This is Poppy.'

'Ah, Poppy! Now it all makes sense.' She half turned and pointed at the brass plaque between them. 'You're the girl who went into labour here, aren't you? And Poppy is the result! I'm Denise, by the way — Ed's mum, as you've probably gathered. It's so good to meet you at last. He was so excited the day your little one was born, but I had no idea he was still seeing you. Oh, I knew there was someone, but I had no idea who.'

'I think you may have got the wrong idea, Denise. We're not seeing each other, as such. If there is someone, then it's not me.'

'Are you sure about that, dear? Because from where I'm sitting, I strongly suspect it is! Now, we can't have you both sitting out here in the cold, can we? You've heard about Ed's accident, I take it? He's pretty fed up, you know, out of action and stuck at home all by himself. Now, here's what I'm going to do. I'm going to get my coat and my car keys and drive you over to my house. It'll be such a lovely surprise for him to see you! There's plenty of tea, and I'm sure I still have some Christmas cake left — if you're not sick of it by now. I know I am!'

'Thank you, but I've got my own car here, Denise. And mine has Poppy's baby seat in it.'

'Of course. Silly me! In that case, you'd best go by yourself, dear. That's probably a better idea anyway. You two won't want me getting in the way. Now, let me just write down the address . . . do you have one of those satnav thingies? It's easy enough, if not.'

Jess tried to wriggle out of it. It felt wrong somehow, just turning up. What if he was asleep, or in pain? Or didn't want her invading his home territory, unannounced?

'How about if I ring him first? Let him know I'm thinking of calling in?'

'And spoil the surprise? Where's the romance in that?' Denise smiled broadly.

'I've told you, there is no romance. I don't know if he'll even want to see me.'

'Oh, he definitely will.'

It wasn't Denise who spoke this time.

Jess turned round and there he was. Ed. Standing behind them on the gravel, leaning on a pair of crutches.

'Edward! You're supposed to be taking it easy.'

His mum jumped up and gave him a playful pat before guiding him, mother hen-like, to the bench and helping him to sit down.

'Some people just can't keep away from work, no matter what,' she tutted at him good-naturedly, then started to back away. 'Or maybe it's not work you're having trouble staying away from? Anyway, I'll leave you two young people to talk, or whatever else you might want to do . . .'

Ed held the laughter back until she was out of earshot.

'I'm so sorry about my mother,' he said. 'If she's not fussing over me she's doing her best to match-make!'

'Mine's the same. My dad's even worse.'

Jess gazed at his leg, his jeans cut short at the knee, the exposed part of his right leg encased in plaster that was already covered in signatures and doodles, and several pictures of flowers she suspected he had drawn himself.

'Oh, dear, you have been through the wars, haven't you?'

'Yup. 'Fraid so,' he replied dolefully.

'Does it hurt?'

'Not now. It did at the time though. Worse than childbirth, I reckon.'

'As if! You men don't know what real pain is,' she teased. 'Oh, hang on. I know what to do. I'll bring a dog blanket and a bottle of water. That should do the trick!'

'Very funny! You're never going to let me forget that day, are you? What did I know about women in labour? I was doing my best.'

'I know, I'm sorry. I couldn't help it. And it's a day I'm not exactly likely to forget either.'

'Because it was the day you met me?'

'Well, I actually meant . . . '

'Poppy being born. Yes, that too, I suppose.'

Jess giggled. Oh, how she had missed this man, this easy banter between them.

'It's good to see you, Ed. If I'd been here, if I'd known what had happened, I would have come to the hospital, brought you something, like you did for me. Flowers, a balloon maybe . . . '

'Ha, ha. I've got enough of those here to last me a lifetime. Well, until they're all sold anyway. No, my needs are few. Just having you come to visit would have been enough.' He took hold of her cold hand and rubbed it between his warm fingers. 'More than enough.'

'Oh, Ed . . . '

'Oh, Jess . . . '

They both spoke at once, both stopped at once, both waited for the other to carry on, both laughed when that didn't happen.

'I really have missed you, Jess Markham. More than I ever thought possible. And I was wondering . . . '

He hesitated for only a few seconds, but it was long enough for Jess to know she wasn't going to have to pluck up the courage to ask a man to go out with her. She could see the look on his face, feel the tension running through his fingers. He wanted her just as much as she wanted him.

'Look, we've become friends, haven't

we? Great friends. But, as far as I'm concerned, it's not enough any more. Would you like to take things a step further?'

'A step?' She made a point of looking at his leg. 'Are you sure you're able to take any steps at all right now?'

'Oh, you know what I mean, Jess! I'm serious. Let me have my moment here . . . now, where was I? Ah, yes. I wondered if maybe you would be my . . . well, my girlfriend, I suppose is the word for it. If you would go out with me, stay in with me, do all the things people in love are supposed to do together.'

She could feel her heart start to pound. Love? Had he said love?

'But I've got Poppy.'

'So? I adore Poppy! You know I do. And I'd make a great . . . babysitter . . . ' He paused, then quickly added, 'I won't say dad, because she already has one of those. I could babysit for you when you go to your mate's wedding.'

'You dork! Nan will do that. Actually, I was kind of hoping you'd be coming with me to the wedding. Leg permitting, obviously.'

She leaned over the buggy, pretending to check on Poppy, peeping in at her beneath her furry hood, but really giving herself time to think and breathe and take it all in, time to think what to say next.

'As for the girlfriend thing . . . ' she went on, blustering a bit, but hoping beyond hope that he would give her the answers she needed to hear, 'I have to remind you that I'm older than you. Wouldn't you rather find someone your own age? Someone who's free to go out at night, who likes the same TV as you, the same music?'

'Where's the fun in that? Variety is the spice of life, Jess, and who else is ever going to teach me the words of *Barbie Girl?* Besides, as my mother is constantly telling me, I was born with an old head on young shoulders. I own a business, Jess. I don't go clubbing or whatever it is guys my age are meant to do. I'm responsible and respectable, and a bit old-fashioned — some might even say boring, and . . . ' His eyes danced with amusement. 'And there may be plenty more fish in the sea, but you'd have to look a long way to find a better catch than me.'

'Don't forget to add modest to the list, will you?' she laughed, squeezing up closer to him and putting a tentative hand on his bare knee. 'Aren't you cold?'

'Not any more.' He put his arm around her shoulders and drew her closer. 'Not if you're saying what I hope you're saying.' Jess nodded and smiled. 'Good, because I've got enough to deal with over the coming months without having to worry myself sick about you making the biggest mistake of your life — and mine — by running off with that ex of yours.'

'No chance! I've got a lot to think about, too. I have to decide where to live, for a start — oh, it won't be

Devon. I'm sure about that now. I want to stay here. With you. Or close to you, anyway. I thought maybe I could look into the houses they're going to build here.'

'Right here, you mean? On the Blooming Marvellous site?'

'Why not? It will solve the question of where to put this bench. We'll still be able to find it and meet up for our little chats if it can stay exactly where it is!'

'Well, maybe not *exactly* where it is. This spot could end up right in the middle of a road or in someone's new front room! But buying here's not a bad idea, actually.'

'I'll have to keep a look out for the publicity. They're bound to have plans available long before any of them are built. In the meantime, Nan says she'll keep the bench in her back garden. You never know, she might even invite you over for tea, if you promise to prune her roses in return.'

'Oh, Jess. Everything's going to work

out just fine now, isn't it? For both of us.'

'I hope so. But that leg of yours had better hurry up and mend. I need you up and dancing for Mel's wedding! We're going out with her and Steve on Thursday, by the way.'

'We are? And how exactly did you manage to get that arranged before I'd even asked you out?'

'Oh, call it telepathy. Like you communing with your flowers. Or just a lucky guess.'

'And what does this so-called telepathy tell you might happen next?'

He lifted his hand and very gently touched her chin, turning her face towards his.

A customer strolled by, running a trolley noisily over the gravel, but Ed took no notice. It was as if they were in a tiny bubble, untouched by anything going on outside it.

'Because, whatever it's saying, I have to tell you, I've been dying to do this for so long . . .'

Then he kissed her, and it was a kiss that sent shudders through Jess's whole body and told her that this was real. Finally real. It was the kiss of her dreams, and Ed — lovely, gorgeous, wonderful Ed — was the man of her dreams.

'Shall we get out of here? Go somewhere and talk properly?' he said, pulling away, although his face didn't move more than a few inches from hers. 'Maybe go over to The Gardener's Arms?'

'The only gardener's arms I need are right here,' she murmured.

She fell happily back into Ed's arms then, her face pressed against the warmth of his chest, where she could hear his heart beating, solidly and steadily, in perfect time with her own.

We do hope that you have enjoyed reading this large print book.

Did you know that all of our titles are available for purchase?

We publish a wide range of high quality large print books including:
Romances, Mysteries, Classics
General Fiction
Non Fiction and Westerns

Special interest titles available in large print are:
The Little Oxford Dictionary
Music Book, Song Book
Hymn Book, Service Book

Also available from us courtesy of Oxford University Press:
Young Readers' Dictionary
(large print edition)
Young Readers' Thesaurus
(large print edition)

For further information or a free brochure, please contact us at:
Ulverscroft Large Print Books Ltd.,
The Green, Bradgate Road, Anstey,
Leicester, LE7 7FU, England.
Tel: (00 44) **0116 236 4325**
Fax: (00 44) **0116 234 0205**

Other titles in the
Linford Romance Library:

SAVING ALICE

Gina Hollands

Naomi Graham is the best family lawyer in the country. But beneath her professional demeanour lies a broken heart. When the man who caused that heartache — billionaire ex-husband Toren Stirling — returns to her life after a ten-year absence, Naomi doesn't want to know. Their painful struggle to start a family tore their relationship apart, so when Toren reveals that he has a young daughter, Alice, it comes as a shocking blow. Not only that, but he's now fighting a custody battle — and needs Naomi's legal expertise to help him win.

FLIGHT TO LOVE

Penny Oates

It's 1975, and starry-eyed air hostess Anthea is about to embark on her first international flight. An incident on the way to the airport — involving her car, an icy road and an irksome gentleman — leaves Anthea slightly dishevelled, but little does she know what drama still awaits her, both in the skies and in exotic Thailand. Against her better judgement, she falls under the spell of aristocratic Captain Sebastian Orly — and incurs the wrath of super-efficient yet standoffish senior stewardess Zara Vine, who happens to have designs on him herself . . .

THE ARTISTS OF WOODBRIDGE

Jean M. Long

Isla Milne intends to stay with her relatives in Woodbridge only until she has put her life back in order. But then she meets a group of local artists, amongst them talented sculptor Jed Rowley. Soon she becomes integrated in village life and involved with the summer school at Rowley Grange, and things take on an interesting dimension as she builds new and discovers old connections in the area. Meanwhile, Isla finds herself becoming increasingly attracted to Jed — but he is already dating the glamourous and possessive Nicole . . .

T R A V E L E R ' S
MEXICO
C O M P A N I O N

The 2000–2001 Traveler's Companions
ARGENTINA • AUSTRALIA • BALI • CALIFORNIA • CANADA • CHILI • CHINA • COSTA RICA • CUBA •
EASTERN CANADA • ECUADOR • FLORIDA • HAWAII • HONG KONG • INDIA • INDONESIA • JAPAN •
KENYA • MALAYSIA & SINGAPORE • MEDITERRANEAN FRANCE • MEXICO • NEPAL • NEW ENGLAND •
NEW ZEALAND • PERU • PHILIPPINES • PORTUGAL • RUSSIA • SOUTHERN ENGLAND • SOUTH AFRICA •
SPAIN • THAILAND • TURKEY • VENEZUELA • VIETNAM, LAOS AND CAMBODIA • WESTERN CANADA

Traveler's MEXICO Companion
First Published 2000 in the United Kingdom by
Kümmerly+Frey AG,
Alpenstrasse 58, CH 3052 Zollikofen, Switzerland
in association with
World Leisure Marketing Ltd
Unit 11, Newmarket Court, Newmarket Drive,
Derby, DE24 8NW, England
Web Site: http://www.map-world.co.uk

ISBN: 1-84006-065-4

© 2000 Kümmerly+Frey AG, Switzerland

Created, edited and produced by
Allan Amsel Publishing
53, rue Beaudouin, 27700 Les Andelys, France.
E-mail: Allan.Amsel@wanadoo.fr
Editor in Chief: Allan Amsel
Editor: Fiona Nichols
Original design concept: Hon Bing-wah
Picture editor and designers: David Henry and Laura Purdom

Printed by Samhwa Printing Co. Ltd., Seoul, South Korea

TRAVELER'S
MEXICO
COMPANION

by Maribeth Mellin
Photographed by Nik Wheeler

Kümmerly+Frey

Contents

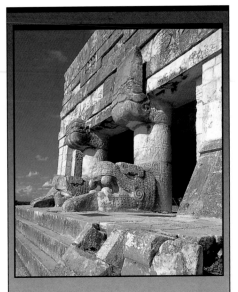

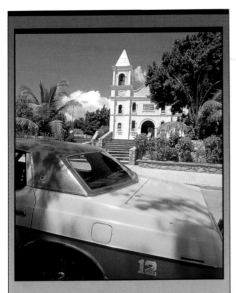

TOP SPOTS

Belt Out a Bolero

MUSIC IS ETCHED IN THE SOUL OF MEXICO.
Conch shells, clay pipes, and jaguar-skin drums accompanied the earliest rituals in the ceremonial centers of Teotihuacán, Chichén Itzá and Palenque. **Mariachis** have come to be identified as the national music makers, found throughout the country. Once you've heard a truly sensational 12-piece mariachi band perform, you'll never hear the music the same way again. Mexico's mariachis appear to have originated in Guadalajara during the period of French interventions. Their name is derived from the French word for marriage, and no bridal dinner is complete without at least one session of trumpets, bass, and a lot of brass wailing venerable old songs. Mexicans simply cannot resist their need to sing along, hands clutched to their chest. No troupe misses the chance to belt out *Paloma* and *Guadalajara*; as time goes by, you'll learn to request *Amor* and *Sabor a Mí*. Every town has its mariachi band, though the singers may

wear worn-out jeans and the instruments may need some tuning.

A natural derivative of the mariachi is the trio, including bass and guitar players crooning love ballads (called *boleros*). Agustín Lara, one of the most famous **bolero** composers, was born in Veracruz and spent much of the 1940s and 1950s entertaining Hollywood crowds and the elite in Acapulco. Every current singer worth attention includes a few Lara compositions in his or her repertoire — my favorites include *Noche de Ronda* and, aptly enough, *Veracruz*. Visit Veracruz and you'll learn about the *sones jarochos*, with small harps and guitars; their songs can be either lively and filled with double meaning, or languid and lilting. Veracruzanos take their dancing quite seriously, and perform quite formal *danzónes* in plazas and dance halls. The *danzón* came to Veracruz with Cubans who came for work, and who in turn had learned it from Andalucian and African transplants. It's considered gauche to smile or act like you're enjoying the rapid mincing steps and swaying hips required for proper form. Those who can't hold back their emotions dance salsa and cumbia at local clubs.

Marimba players haul their xylophone-type instruments to plazas and restaurants in many colonial cities, especially in Chiapas, Oaxaca and Veracruz. Restaurateurs throughout the country have come to appreciate marimbas as a pleasant background to dining, and you can hear excellent groups at the Bazaar Sábado in San Angel, Mama Mia's in San Miguel de Allende, and *palapa*-covered bars along all coasts. Each region of Mexico has its favorite songs. Ask for *Peregrina* in Yucatán, *La Bamba* in the north

Folkloric dancers OPPOSITE perform traditional courting rituals in the Mexican Hat dance. The Acapulco Sheraton presents a weekly fiesta ABOVE with Mexican food, music and games.

and *Guadalajara* in — you guessed it — Guadalajara.

Which brings us back to mariachis. As one might expect, Guadalajara's Plaza de los Mariachis is a wild and festive spot. The same can be said for Mexico City's Plaza Garibaldi. Both host competing mariachi bands who stroll from table to table proffering their songs — a tip of US$5 for two or three songs is the going rate. The revelry doesn't get serious until close to midnight and can last until dawn. Leave your purse in your room, keep your wits intact and join the fun.

Climb Toward Nature's Domain

EARLY ONE MORNING, WHILE THE CHACALACAS WERE CACKLING LIKE CROWS AND LIZARDS SLITHERED THROUGH THE HIGH GRASS, I hiked to a secret back trail to the Caracol in Chichén Itzá. Climbing the crumbling steps to the circular tower of this ancient Mayan observatory, I felt the glow of the rising sun warm my back and watched gray walls turn golden. I sat at a corner of the ruin's raised platform, notebook in hand. I glanced up and my eyes met those of a snake barely a meter (three feet) from my knee. I looked away, figuring there wasn't much I could do and the snake — which I later learned was one of the most poisonous in the region — backed away. I decided I had earned the right to explore the ruins in peace. Ever since, I've scouted for trails to the archaeological sites that make Mexico so mysterious. I've rested atop **Nohuch Mul**, the highest tower at Cobá and watched noisy wild parrots flock by. Huge, hairy tarantulas once accompanied me on a walk through Uxmal and I yearn to revisit Palenque now that the monkeys have returned.

The few wild creatures left in Mexico tend to gravitate toward the country's oldest cities, preserved in acres of barely tamed land. For this reason alone, it's best to visit the ruins in early morning or late day. I refuse to climb the **Pyramid of the Moon** in Teotihuacán when hundreds of humans are trekking down the Avenida de los Muertos in the blazing noon sun. I much prefer the still light of early morning or the lengthening shadows at dusk and always spend a night near whatever site I'm visiting. There are wonderful hotels by most of the ruins; my all-time favorite is the **Mayaland** at Chichén Itzá, perhaps because it was my first. I'm immensely fond of the **Villa Arqueológica** at Cobá. Buried in the

The pyramids of Teotihuacán outside Mexico City are among the most dramatic in the country.

jungle a 30-minute drive from the Caribbean Coast, this small hotel sits beside one of Cobá's seven lakes, where freshwater turtles feed on insects and bits of bread thrown by their fans. There are several Villas Arqueológicas located in the vicinity of Mexico's main ruins, including ones by Teotihuacán, Cacaxtla and Uxmal. Campers can still sleep beside the jungle-swathed structures at Palenque in southern Chiapas and can overnight fairly close to the seaside ruins of Tulum. It's more difficult finding lodging close to the ruins in Oaxaca.

Like all archaeology buffs, I have developed a favorite list of ancient structures and isolated lodgings. One of the best to come along is **Chicanná** in the Río Bec area of southwest Campeche. Sample a few during your wanderings; you're sure to come back for more.

Get Eye to Eye with a Mama Whale

IMAGINE CRUISING ALONG IN A KAYAK, SHIVERING IN THE DAMP SALT AIR, SCANNING THE SEA FOR SPOUTS. Suddenly, a sloping gray form slices the water wider and wider until a 20-ton whale appears on your starboard side. You lock onto the eye, much larger than your face and try to communicate affection. The whale, crusty with mollusks, looking as old as age itself, shelters a smaller form with her fin. As trust is ensured, the mother gradually allows her newborn to nudge the boat and perhaps accept a stroking human hand. The same thing happens again and again as you paddle slowly through lagoons that seem as big as the whole sea.

Every winter since before man can remember, great gray whales have swum miles from the Bering Strait to their birthing grounds in isolated Pacific lagoons. Whale watching has been a Baja tradition since long before whalers threatened the existence of these fast-moving leviathans, marine giants who supplied tons of oil for the world during the nineteenth century. The whales were all but killed out by the end of the century and it has taken much of this century to bring them back. Whale watchers now mob the lagoon from December through March, when the whales are giving birth.

Once the whales were proven to be near extinct, the Mexican government enacted laws protecting **Scammon's Lagoon** near Guerrero Negro, site of the largest whale slaughter in history. For a while, the whales had a fighting chance for survival. International environmental groups kept a close eye on the whales' progress

and tour companies became more responsible and protective of the lagoons and their residents. The sightseers spread out to **San Ignacio Lagoon** and **Magdalena Bay** along the remote southern Pacific side of the peninsula, where the whales increased in numbers annually. Then, in the middle of whale-watching season in 1998, the Mitsubishi Corporation won permission to mine salt at San Ignacio lagoon. The mines are expected to bring some 10,000 jobs to an area with almost no permanent population; the whales will surely have to move on.

Wherever they go, whale-watchers are bound to follow. Some will arrive via boat from La Paz, Los Cabos and San Diego, California. Others will drive from base camps in San Ignacio, Loreto and La Paz. All will be rewarded with an incomparable sight.

Hang Out in a Hammock

IN THE LAND OF SIESTAS ONE MIGHT EXPECT A GOOD SELECTION OF SLEEPING DEVICES. The best is the Yucatecan hammock, a supple cocoon woven from thousands of tiny strings. Nothing else will do when you're snoozing on a white sand beach, lulled by tropical winds rustling palm fronds overhead.

The Maya perfected the art of the hammock in the fourth century and have used them as beds ever since. The typical Maya house, called a *na*, always has hammocks hanging in the main room; and some of the smartest mansions in Mérida have hammock hooks in the bedrooms. A Yucatecan yard or terrace isn't complete without a few hammocks hanging about and savvy hoteliers always have a stash on hand. Guests in the finest suites in Cancún's Camino Real have hammocks on their balconies overlooking the sea. Nearly all hotels in Playa del Carmen have hammocks swaying under *palapas*, delightful palm-thatched structures, or suspended on porches and balconies. I once spent a week swinging to sleep in a rustic *palapa*-roofed house on the beach south of Tulum; it remains one of my most cherished memories.

Smart travelers pick up a Yucatecan hammock the minute they reach the peninsula and keep it and two long ropes stashed in their bags. Mérida has the best overall selection of hammocks to choose from, including multicolored silk ones that are like expensive works of art. Hammocks come in three sizes — single, double and matrimonial. I always go for the largest no matter how many bodies will be sleeping in

it. Cotton hammocks are the least expensive, but they tend to fade in the sun. Nylon ones are more durable. The more strings the better — loosely woven hammocks tend to pinch delicate skin. My favorite place to shop for hammocks is in **Tixcokob**, less than an hour's drive from Mérida. Nearly every home on the main street has a hammock loom in the front yard and families invite you into their homes to inspect their wares. Sellers from similar hammock-weaving centers display their collections in Mérida's markets and parks; you can pick up a few bartering techniques while watching them converse with customers.

Some things to remember when buying and using a hammock: Choose one that's larger and more finely woven than you think you'll need; pick up a skein of nylon or jute rope at a neighborhood market and keep it

with your hammock at all times; use a light sheet or beach towel to protect your backside when sleeping on the beach, since no see-ums and mosquitoes have no problem poking their stingers through hammock threads. Hang a new hammock up high when you first use it to allow the ropes and threads to stretch and support your body.

Nearly any beach is suitable for hammock hanging. I've used mine in the intense July heat in Baja, during rain showers in Akumal and (with the addition of a sleeping bag) in pine forests on mountain tops. On the Caribbean, Isla Mujeres, Playa del Carmen and Tulum all once had hammock campgrounds, though they're getting more difficult to find. Zicatela beach on the Pacific

Travelers lounge in hammocks on peaceful beaches beside Huatulco's chain of bays.

Coast near Puerto Angel still has some of the best hammock-hanging grounds.

Cruise the Lonely Peninsula

MY FAVORITE LONG-RANGE DRIVE IN MEXICO IS THE SURREAL TRIP DOWN THE BAJA CALIFORNIA PENINSULA, past mesas that could pass as UFO landing strips, sky-high cacti and spouting and breaching whales in the sea. Baja's topography is unlike any other in the world. Stretching nearly 1,600 km (1,000 miles) southward from the United States border, splitting the Pacific Ocean and the **Sea of Cortez** (Mar de Cortés) Baja dwindles from its widest point at the United States–Mexico border to a single peak of stone at its southern tip. Though largely composed of desert, the peninsula is far from barren. I dream of a month-long drive when I can stop as I please and wait for the best light of the day and brilliant stars at night. I yearn to camp by the cathedral-sized boulders at Cataviña and ride horses through the forest at San Pedro Martir. As a southern Californian, I've had dozens of opportunities to explore Baja. I'll never get enough.

Baja is a cult destination where hundreds of Californians spend their whole lives studying just a few of its unique phenomena. Much of the attention is focused on the waters framing the desert peninsula. Great **gray whales** cruise down the Pacific Coast each winter (see above) from the Bering Strait to reach Baja's isolated, windswept lagoons. Manta rays, dolphins, flying fish and guitar whales perform between the horizon and turquoise waters in the Sea of Cortez, one of the richest marine habitats on Earth.

Baja's landscape is as entrancing as its seascape. Even a drive of three days is enough to whet the appetite for life. The road itself is always a challenge with its potholes and *vados* (sudden dips in the road) and flat areas where rivers rush suddenly through sand during fierce rainstorms. The **Transpeninsular Highway** is a challenge; numerous crosses, shrines and bunches of plastic flowers at its side provide the evidence. I've driven the peninsula several times, most often in the searing heat of July when sport fishing is at its peak. It's a fabulous ride, once you get past the first 100 km (62 miles) or so of urban, border congestion.

South of Ensenada, just 128 km (80 miles) below the border, ramshackle neighborhoods are gradually replaced by vineyards crosshatching the foothills of the San Pedro Martir Mountains. Green valleys give way

to broad mesas, which gradually evolve into fields of giant boulders. Spectacular *cardón* cacti beg to be photographed, especially those so high as to tower over a child or full-grown man. At Guerrero Negro and the state line between Baja California and Baja California Sur, the highway begins to climb into the Sierra de la Giganta Mountains, peaking at the mission town of San Ignacio before descending toward **Santa Rosalía** and the Sea of Cortez.

Bahía de Concepción, south of the riverside town of Mulegé, gives drivers their first breathtaking view of the sea. Burnt-sienna peaks and points frame soft sand beaches and water so clear and still that kayaks and canoes glisten on its surface. In **Loreto**, *pangas* and yachts rock offside Islas Carmen and Danzante as anglers aim for dorado, tuna and the occasional marlin.

Drivers may find the next stretch of inland road boring; my speedometer hits 128 km (80 miles) per hour far too recklessly. But the Transpeninsular Highway eventually dips toward the sea again at **La Paz**, the capital and largest city in Baja Sur. Sensible (and weary) drivers plan for a night or two here, where they can sleep in relative luxury, shop in huge grocery and auto parts stores, eat some good pasta and meat dishes and partake of the sea's abundance. La Paz is the launching point for scuba diving trips to seamounts where hammerhead and whale sharks migrate in summer; the calm waters around nearby islands are perfect for snorkeling and kayaking. Anthropology and history buffs ride donkeys to hidden caves to study petroglyphs painted on rock walls in 700 BC. Whale watchers head across or around the peninsula to **San Ignacio Lagoon** and **Magdalena Bay**.

Nature gives way to astonishing commerce as you drive farther south to Baja's tip and Los Cabos. Sure to soon be Mexico's trendiest resort — and its most expensive — **Los Cabos** is truly the end of the road. Presenting the ultimate in vacation luxury, this man-made destination is filled with championship golf courses, world-class hotels, fine restaurants and exclusive boutiques. It feels as if one has driven 1,600 km (1,000 miles) only to arrive in a semi-Mexican version of Southern California. But man, what a ride!

For more on Baja, see BAJA CALIFORNIA, starting page 317.

Baja California is a narrow peninsula that stretches south from the border splitting the Pacific Ocean from the Sea of Cortez. Cacti dot the arid landscape and palm-frond *palapas* provide a little shade on Baja's broad beaches.

Ride the Rails

THE STENCH OF CIVILIZATION EVAPORATES INTO PINE-SCENTED AIR AS THE RICKETY COPPER CANYON TRAIN climbs 2,700 m (9,000 ft) from the Gulf of California into the Sierra Madre Mountains. These are foreboding peaks, sharp and distinct, sheltered deep gorges carved between sheer cliffs. The *Chihuahua al Pacifico* train line, constructed over the better part of a century, between 1872 and 1961, proves man's insistence that nature can be confronted, if not tamed. The American Albert Kinsey Owen first conceived of the train as the fastest means of transporting goods from the central United States to the gulf port of **Topolobampo** in Sinaloa, Mexico, where he ran what might now be called a New Age retreat for fellow socialists. Kinsey eventually abandoned his attempt to lay rail lines in unknown territory. American railroad contractor Edward Arthur Stillwell took up the project in 1900 before the Mexican government took over in 1940. Comparable with trains through the Canadian Rockies or the South American Andes, the rail line from **Chihuahua** to the coast runs 1,450 km (900 miles) through terrain inhospitable to all but the hardiest human inhabitants.

I first rode the Copper Canyon (Barranca del Cobre) train in the early 1980s, in the dead of winter, with hardly a thought of what I might be confronting. The dilapidated train cars offered little in the way of comfort and the windows were grimy. I spent much of the time hanging out by an open window or between the cars, feeling the rush of cold air against my cheeks and tremors of fear each time we approached a tunnel or bridge. My camera shutter clicked furiously much of the time as I tried to capture the sensation of traveling higher and higher into increasingly wild scenery. A friend and I spent two nights in **El Divisadero**, huddled together the first night in a single bed wearing every bit of clothing we had brought with us under flannel nightgowns. The heating oil, it seemed, had been used up. We spent the second night in our hotel's main lodge with a troop of hardy snowbirds (North America retirees who come south for the winter), listening to a tape of Eydie Gorme and Los Panchos singing *boleros* (love songs) as we mixed tequila and Squirt for barely passable margaritas until we faded into sleep before the wall-length fireplace.

The daylight was worth all of the shivering. We hiked into the snow-topped canyons behind Tarahumara Indians who somehow endured the chill in bare feet or thin sandals, dressed in little more than cotton shirts, flimsy dresses and pants. Their lives seemed so uncomfortable and their poverty nearly unbearable. But the Tarahumara thrived in these mountains long before gringos came bearing noisy machinery and ideas of slavery. Tarahumara men are known throughout the world as the fleetest of runners, covering endless miles of nearly invisible trails through the mountains and canyons to reach their nearest neighbors. Families live in hidden caves or rattletrap wooden houses and subsist on wild game and produce from humble gardens. Missionaries, loggers and marijuana farmers have all invaded Tarahumara turf; tourists, too, have invaded — witnesses to the fragile lifestyle of a people whose numbers total less than 50,000 in this modern age.

Over the past decade entrepreneurs have built more lodges and inns for travelers fascinated by this small slice of Mexico's beauty and history. Tour operators lead explorers into the canyons on mules, horses and on foot — one company offers hikes of a week or more into the four major canyons to wild rivers, hidden caves and Tarahumara settlements. The train hasn't improved all that much, though the tunnels and bridges have withstood natural forces — an amazing testimony to engineering. A few companies offer comfortable train rides in private rail cars at certain times of the year. But I still stick to the people's route, where Mennonites from towns outside Chihuahua board the train in their spanking clean overalls and black hats and huddle in solemn groups while tourists mingle with locals and pass the time with impromptu games of cards and dominoes. I alternate stops, spending nights in the Wild West town of **Creel** or in the mountainous isolation of **Batopilas** or **Cerocahui**. I am always pleased to return to the proud Tarahumara, whose continuing existence says much about personal choice and the strength of communities.

A Tarahumara Indian sells pine-needle baskets alongside the Copper Canyon train.

YOUR CHOICE

The Great Outdoors

Gray whales and sea turtles migrate to Mexico's shores to give birth. Monarch butterflies weigh down the trees of Michoacán as they seek refuge from the cold up north. Pink flamingos fly in rosy clouds to Celestún and Río Lagartos, resting in lagoons along the Gulf of Mexico.

Mother Nature's untamed creatures still find refuge in Mexico's protected terrain, though their numbers have dwindled appallingly. You hear about the jaguars and quetzals that inspired the Maya, the deer that once outran Tarahumara hunters in the Sierras, the toucans, parrots, monkeys and coatamundi so abundant in jungles and forests. Unfortunately, this aspect of Mexico has become rare and difficult to find.

But adventure travelers have also laid claim to vast sections of Mexico's terrain.

Mountaineers scale the snowy peaks of **Pico de Orizaba** in Veracruz and the steep cones of the volcano **Popocatépetl** (when it's not spewing ash over Puebla and Mexico City). On **Río Usumacinta** aficionados raft downstream through the rainforest canyons of Chiapas, past clusters of Lancandón Indians who persistently survive and resist civilization's invasions. Kayakers float with dolphins and pelicans around islands in the **Sea of Cortez**; divers head straight for **Cozumel** and Caribbean reefs.

Mexico is a large country (nearly four times the size of the state of Texas, for example). Its topography and wildlife are as varied as those of Australia or Costa Rica. Because of its size, exploring Mexico becomes an act of specialization. Amtave (Asociación Mexicana de Turismo de Aventura y Ecoturismo) makes it easier to grasp your options with its catalog of Mexican tour operators from throughout the country. The association has been operating since 1992 and brings more options in easy view annually. You can subscribe to their catalog by contacting **Amtave** ((5) 661-9121 FAX (5) 662-7354 E-MAIL ecomexico@compuserve.com.mx WEB SITE www.amtave.com.mx, Avenida Insurgentes Sur No. 1971-251, Colonia Guadalupe Inn, 01020 Mexico DF.

Several companies in the United States specialize in adventure travel throughout Mexico and offer tours to see whales, monarch butterflies, flamingos and other natural phenomena. For information contact any of the following:

OPPOSITE: Hardy hikers brave the desert heat in Sonora's Nacapule Canyon. ABOVE: Saguaro cacti tower over the rocks and sage in Sonora's Las Barajitas Canyon.

Mountain Travel Sobek TOLL-FREE (800) 227-2384 FAX (510) 525-7710 E-MAIL info@mtsobek .com WEB SITE www.mtsobek.com, 6420 Fairmount Avenue, El Cerrito, CA 94530.
Natural Habitat Adventures ((303) 449-3711 TOLL-FREE (800) 543-8917 FAX (303) 449-3712, 2945 Center Green Court, Boulder, CO 80301.
Overseas Adventure Travel TOLL-FREE (800) 221-0814, 625 Mount Auburn Street, Cambridge, MA 02138.
REI TOLL-FREE (800) 622-2236 FAX (253) 395-8160 E-MAIL travel@rei.com WEB SITE www.rei .com/travel, 6750 South 228th Street, Kent, WA 98032.
Above the Clouds TOLL-FREE (800) 233-4499 FAX (508) 797-4779 E-MAIL sconlon@world.std .com WEB SITE www.gorp.com/abvclds.htm, PO Box 398 Worcester, MA 01602-0398.
Backroads TOLL-FREE (800) 462-2848 FAX (510) 527-1444 E-MAIL goactive@backroads.com WEB SITE www.backroads.com, 801 Cedar Street, Berkeley, CA 94710-1800.
Remarkable Journeys ((713) 721-2517 TOLL-FREE (800) 856-1993 FAX (713) 728-8334, PO Box 31855, Houston TX 77231-1855.
Questers ((212) 251-0444 TOLL-FREE (800) 468-8668 FAX (212) 251-0890, 381 Park Avenue South, New York, NY 10016.

Two natural wonders attract a large number of travelers. The **Copper Canyon** (Barranca del Cobre), wider and deeper than the Grand Canyon in the United States, is a must-see. Several companies offer tours on the *Chihuahua al Pacifico* rail line (see RIDE THE RAILS, page 21) that runs through tunnels, over suspension bridges and up steep mountainsides to small settlements on the canyon's rim. Country lodges tempt travelers to linger and ride mules, horses and pickup trucks to remote Tarahumara villages in caves and beside waterfalls.

United States companies specializing in Copper Canyon tours include **American Wilderness Experience** ((303) 444-2622 TOLL-FREE (800) 444-0099 FAX (303) 444-3999 WEB SITE www.gorp.com/awe, 2820-A Wilderness Place, Boulder, CO 80301; **Columbus Travel** ((830) 885-2000 TOLL-FREE (800) 843-1060 FAX (830) 885-2010, 900 Ridge Creek Lane, Bulverde, TX 78163; and **DRC Rail Tours** TOLL-FREE (800) 659-7602 FAX (281) 872-7123, which offers South Orient Express train tours through the canyon in a private rail car.

Whale watching off the Baja California Peninsula is another experience Mexico fans cannot resist (see GET EYE TO EYE WITH A MAMA WHALE, page 16). Environmentally responsible tours from the United States are available through **Baja Expeditions** ((619) 581-3311 FAX (619) 581-6542 TOLL-FREE (800) 843-6967, 2625 Garnet Avenue, San Diego, CA 92109; **Baja Discovery** TOLL-FREE (800) 829-2252 E-MAIL bajadis@aol .com WEB SITE www .bajadiscovery.com, PO Box 152527, San Diego, CA 92195; and **Special**

Expeditions ℂ (212) 765-7740 TOLL-FREE (800) 397-3348 FAX (212) 265-3770, 720 Fifth Avenue, New York, NY 10019.

Sporting Spree

Every tourist destination in Mexico has its natural attributes and it would take a lifetime to explore them all. **Scuba diving** is an option along nearly all of Mexico's coastline. **Cozumel** and the chain of reefs stretching down Mexico's Caribbean Coast are magnets for divers who favor clear, warm water and an abundance of tropical fish. Caves and sinkholes called *cenotes*, in the limestone shelf of the Yucatán Peninsula, offer advanced divers an added rush; open-water fans prefer the **Revillagigedos Islands** off the tip of Baja California, where manta rays, sharks and huge tuna converge. Though I'm a diehard diver, I haven't yet tried the ultimate trip — a Jeep ride up some 4,270 m (14,005 ft) to a crater lake, at the **Navado de Toluca** volcano outside

Puebla, where the water temperature averages 15°C (59°F). If chilly craters are your bent, contact **Buceo Total** ℂ (5) 688-3736 FAX (5) 604-2869, Xicoténcatl No. 186, Col. del Carmen Coyoacán, Mexico DF 04100.

There are dive operations at nearly all coastal destinations, from Guaymas in the northern Gulf of California to Xcalak by the border with Belize. Scuba shops all over the world have contacts within Mexico and can arrange most types of dives. A few dive sites require further planning. Amtave (above) is your best overall source of information.

To reach the Revillagigedos Islands some 400 km (250 miles) off Los Cabos, Baja California, contact **Solmar V** TOLL-FREE (800) 344-3349 FAX (310) 454-1686. The Chinchorro Banks, 29 km (18 miles) off the southern Caribbean Coast, is littered with

OPPOSITE: The Mexican Pipeline off Playa Zicatela in Puerto Escondido lures surfers with its mighty waves. ABOVE: Playa Los Algodones, Bahía San Carlos, is the perfect spot for a horseback ride.

shallow reefs and shipwrecks; the easiest approach is from **Costa de Cocos**. For reservations contact the **Turquoise Reef Group** TOLL-FREE (800) 538-6802 FAX (303) 674-8735, PO Box 2664, Evergreen, CO 80439.

Wherever the divers are, you'll likely find excellent **sport fishing** as well. The only requirement to fish in Mexico is a fishing permit, easily available by contacting the **Government of Mexico Secretariat of Fisheries** ((619) 233-6956, 2550, 5th Avenue, Suite 101, San Diego, CA 92103-6622. Yachts and small skiffs called *pangas* ply the waters in veritable armadas off the Baja California Peninsula as well as the Pacific and Caribbean coasts. (Besides those, there are the commercial fishing operations that occasionally rape the most fertile fishing grounds.) Los Cabos, Mazatlán, Manzanillo, Zihuatanejo and Cozumel are all cult destinations for fans of big marlin, sailfish, dorado and tuna. The flats around the Boca Paila Peninsula in the state of Quintana Roo are legendary tarpon and bone fishing grounds.

Tour operators that book fishing trips in Los Cabos include: **Los Cabos Sport Fishing** TOLL-FREE (800) 521-2281; **Solmar Fleet** ((281) 346-1001 on the East Cape; and **Playa del Sol** TOLL-FREE (800) 368-4334. All the fishing fleets have representatives at the Cabo San Lucas Marina. For trips on the Sea of Cortez, contact **Sea of Cortez Sport Fishing** ((626) 333-9012. These United-States-based booking companies organize trips on the Yucatán: **First Class Ventures** TOLL-FREE (800) 816-8016; **Boca Paila Fishing Lodge** TOLL-FREE (800) 245-1950. For trips throughout Mexico, try **Tropical Fishing Adventures** ((516) 668-2019 and **Mexico Sportsman** TOLL-FREE (800) 633-3085. In all areas, try a visit to the marina to talk with fishing operators there.

Sea kayaking has become a major draw in Bahía de Concepción and all along the Baja Coast, as well as around the islands off of Puerto Vallarta or in Huatulco. **River kayaking** and **rafting** are excellent in southern Chiapas and in Veracruz, which probably has more adventure options than any other single state in Mexico. In Veracruz you can climb Pico de Orizaba, raft the Río Bobos and hike through the rainforest, sighting birds.

Companies specializing in a variety of Veracruz adventures include: **Río y Montaña Expediciones** ((5) 520-2041 FAX (5) 540-7870, Prado Norte No. 450-T, Col. Lomas de Chapultepec, 11000 Mexico DF; **Expediciones Tropicales** ((5) 543-7984 FAX (5) 523-9659, Magdalena No. 311-10, Col. Del Valle, 03100 Mexico DF; and **Veraventuras** ((29) 189579

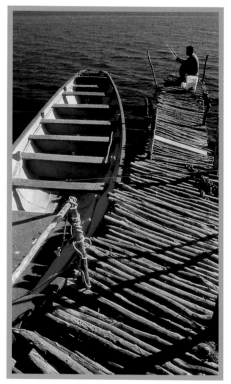

FAX (29) 189680, Santos Degollado No. 81-8, Col. Centro 91000 Xalapa, Veracruz.

Kayaking adventures in the Sea of Cortez are available through the companies listed above under whale watching.

Into a Desert Place by Graham Macintosh describes the ultimate Mexico trek, a month-long hike down and back the length of the peninsula. Macintosh did it the hard way: alone. **Hiking** and **trekking** tours provide support and comfort and are available with countless types of scenery. The Copper Canyon is inhabited by perhaps the best hikers and runners of all — the Tarahumara Indians. The volcanoes around Mexico City attract serious climbers. Several Mexican companies offer combinations of adventures in various parts of the country. Contact any of the following:

Turismo Ecológico Mexicano Quinto Sol ((5) 211-8130 FAX (5) 211-8208 E-MAIL kintosol @ienlaces.com.mx, Mexicali No. 36, Col. Condesa 06600 Mexico DF.

Intercontinental Adventures ((5) 255-4400 FAX (5) 255-4465, Homero No. 526-801, Col. Polanco, 11560 Mexico DF.

Expediciones Mexico Verde ((3) 641-5598 FAX (3) 641-0993, José Maria Vigil No. 2406, Col. Italia Providencia, 44610 Guadalajara, Jalisco.

Ecotours de Mexico ((303) 449-3711 TOLL-FREE (800) 543-8917.
Trek Mexico ((5) 525-6813 FAX (5) 525-5093, Havre No. 67-605, Col. Juárez, 06600 Mexico DF.

Bird watching is excellent throughout the Yucatán Peninsula. We suggest the following contacts: **Ecoturismo Yucatán** ((99) 252187 FAX (99) 259047, Calle 3 No. 235 entre 32-A y 34, Col. Pensiones, 97219 Mérida, Yucatán; **Amigos de Sian Ka'an** ((91) 849583, 873080 in Cancún, for bird watching tours in the Sian Ka'an preserve south of Tulum; **Field Guides** TOLL-FREE (800) 728-4953 FAX (512) 327-9231 E-MAIL fgileader@aol.com WEB SITE www .fieldguides .com, PO Box 160723, Austin, TX 78716-0723.

Golf has become a major attraction in **Los Cabos** at the tip of the Baja California Peninsula. Jack Nicklaus has designed a 27-hole desert course at the Hotel Palmila and an 18-hole course at the Cabo del Sol development. Robert Trent-Jones Junior has also been at work here, designing an 18-hole course at Cabo Real. These three courses have attracted worldwide attention and internationally televised competitions. Planners predict that by the year 2000 there will be 180 holes of golf in this desert between two seas. In **Cancún**, the Robert Trent-Jones Cancún Golf Club includes a small Maya ruin, while Caesar Park's 18-hole course abuts this modern resort's only archaeological site. Robert Von Hagge designed the 18-hole course at the marina in **Ixtapa**, and La Mantarraya Golf Links, beside Las Hadas in **Manzanillo**, was designed by Pete and Roy Dye. Every resort area now boasts at least one course, from the Club de Golf in **Huatulco** to **Acapulco's** two spectacular courses at the Acapulco Princess.

SPECTATOR SPORTS

Fiestas in many parts of Mexico call for a bullfight, one of Spain's many contributions to Mexican culture. World-class matadors swirl their capes at bullrings in Mexico City, Guadalajara, Tijuana, and nearly ever major town in the ranching country of northern Mexico. *Charreadas*, or Mexican rodeos, are held all over the country. The colorful costumes of the *charreada* have come to symbolize Mexican dress — tight

OPPOSITE: Makeshift piers offer fine perches for fishermen at the Lagunas de Chacahua in Puerto Escondido. BELOW: *Charreadas*, Mexican rodeos, are popular with Mexicans and tourists alike, and are less brutal than the Spanish-style bullfights that are sometimes staged in Mexico.

embroidered pants and wide-brimmed hats. They are usually held on a Sunday morning and involve demonstrations of roping, riding wild steers and unbroken horses, throwing steers by their tails and the *paso de la muerte*, where the *charro* (rider) leaps from the back of one galloping horse to another. These events are often followed by an *escaramuza charra*, where young women riding sidesaddle gallop around the ring accompanied by the music of mariachi bands.

The Open Road

Driving in Mexico can be a real pleasure. It is so easy to zoom in rented Volkswagens along empty stretches of straight road through the Yucatán and Baja California Peninsulas, to crawl up and down sinuous mountain passes in Veracruz, and to cringe with the crowds circling demonic *glorietas* (traffic circles) in Tijuana and other heart-pounding cities. Valuing my life, I have abandoned any ideas of driving in Mexico City. (I'm far from alone in this.) I've no need to tempt fate. But give me a rental car anywhere else in Mexico, and I'm content. The country's interior is best accessed on excursions and overnight trips from major cities and colonial centers (see SHORT BREAKS, page 44). In fact, I prefer traveling by bus in these congested, mountainous areas. But the coastlines are made for marathon drives. The most exciting drive in all of Mexico is the relatively arduous trek down the Baja California Peninsula (see CRUISE THE LONELY PENINSULA, page 18), but there are several others that lure me.

THE YUCATÁN PENINSULA
The Yucatán Peninsula has some of the best roads in the country — straight slashes of asphalt through scrubby jungle, much like the limestone *sacbes* used by the Maya to walk from one ceremonial center to another. The drive from Cancún to Tulum, on Highway 307, used to be one of my favorites, though it lost much of its charm when it was widened to four lanes and dubbed the "Riviera Maya." Entirely too many tour buses ply the road now, but I still find times, usually in early morning, when I can cruise unimpeded past bicycling, machete-toting workers from villages tucked away from the road. Highway 307's best attribute is its collection of crude signs: tires and coke bottles mounted on poles and other markers noting side roads to heaven. Though many of these turnoffs now

point to mega resorts, a few can still lead to superb discoveries. My favorites are the bumpy, sandy roads leading to Punta Bete Paamul, sections of Akumal and Casa Cenote. All offer access to uncrowded beaches, campgrounds with hammocks hanging over the sand, and clusters of sea grape and wild lilies. I've always treasured the road south of Tulum down the Boca Paila Peninsula, so I was horrified when I heard a few years ago that bandits had been robbing unwary wanderers by lying palm trunks across the road to impede escape. Always ask business owners and fellow travelers if they've heard such reports recently; if not, head out early for the tiny settlement of Punta Allen at the end of the road.

Potholes, ridges, sharp rocks and pockets of slippery sand all hinder progress and necessitate a few precautions. I always carry

at least 15 liters (three gallons) of fresh water, a good spare tire, a beach towel, a small first-aid kit and bug repellent. More cautious drivers would also suggest a tool kit, motor oil, and other accouterments. I rely on the inventiveness, good humor and curiosity of the dwellers along the road.

Past the Tulum ruins, hotels and campgrounds, you enter Sian Ka'an and 56 km (35 miles) of protected lagoons, beach and canals once used by the Maya to reach the sea. Punta Allen, located about three hours south of Tulum at the end of this tiny peninsula, is usually my first long stop. Once I've made it this far and checked the number of daylight hours left for the trip back, I pace myself accordingly. Lunch consists of fresh *ceviche* (marinated fresh fish) at one of the home-style restaurants run by a fisherman's family. I wander

through the sandy streets, take a photo or two of the town's few children playing on the beach, then head back north. With time to spare I stop at the wooden bridge over the Cuzan Maya's final canal to the sea and watch for herons and egrets. Nearly any road sign catches my attention; it's difficult to resist a dash into a few fishing lodges for the tarpon report. In need of a brief respite, I pull off at a secluded beach, take a dip in clear waters, and stretch out for a brief nap on the sand. Then it's back to the highway, where I've, perhaps, planned to spend the night at a small, beachfront inn.

The Xcalak Peninsula at the southern end of Highway 307 is equally alluring, and has

Mexico's highest volcano, Pico de Orizaba looms over field and highway in Puebla.

century monastery and surrounding buildings, and the plaza and side streets were repaved. Izamal is now one of the prettiest cities on the peninsula and is visited by tour groups from Mérida. Fortunately, the government built a tourism center on the outskirts of town; those with their own cars can skip the crowds and wander about in peace.

Mérida is a hub for several great drives to ancient cities and remote coastal communities. I love rolling through the Puuc Hills in the direction of Uxmal on Highway 180. When heading toward the coast, rocks turn to sand in the drive along Highway 281 toward Celestún. I've crisscrossed the peninsula's three states of Yucatán, Campeche and Quintana Roo dozens of times and always delight in finding a new route. Destinations sure to please include Oxkutzcab (the orange-growing capital of Yucatán); Santa Elena and the route on the ruins past Labná and Sayil; and the Hacienda Yaxcopoil. Ticul was always one of my favorites (it's got a great cemetery and market) until I caused a slight fender bender in the bus, bike, truck and car traffic that now clogs Ticul's confusing one-way streets.

one major advantage over Boca Paila. At the end of the road here, I stop for a night or two at Costa de Cocos. One of the few truly isolated beach resorts left on Yucatán's Caribbean Coast, Cocos rewards my body and soul with the sweet hospitality of owners Dave and Maria Randall, the comfort of a well-built *cabaña* on the sand and access to some of the best diving I've ever experienced.

Yucatán's interior is filled with rewarding drives as well. The old road from Cancún to Mérida, which runs roughly parallel to a new high-speed *autopista*, transports drivers from the twentieth century back to the first at the ruins of Chichén Itzá. En route, the road passes through villages of rough-hewn *nas*, the oval huts topped with palm fronds that rural Maya call home. There's usually a hammock swinging just inside the front door and gardens of crotea, spider lilies and corn in the front yards. Locals travel the road in *triciclos*, three-wheeled bicycles with baskets and seats for passengers. The bikes, and an abundance of *topes* (speed bumps), keep the traffic crawling at a sightseeing pace. Great stops between Cancún and Mérida other than Chichén Itzá include Valladolid (don't miss the plaster frog spurting in the central fountain), and Izamal, where Pope John Paul II met with thousands of indigenous peoples in 1993. As might be expected, the Ciudad Amarilla, or Yellow City, was mightily beautified for the pope's visit. A new coat of golden paint was applied to the seventeenth-

VERACRUZ

Highway 180 runs the length of Veracruz's gulf coast from Tampico to Tabasco, and is one of the least frequented byways on the tourist circuit. I usually approach the highway from the city of Veracruz, heading north to the ruins of El Tajín or south to Lake Catemaco. The northern route necessitates a stop at La Antigua and the mysterious crumbled hacienda where Cortés is said to have found refuge during his first voyage to the Americas. New Agers in particular are enchanted with the ruins of Cempoala and its Circle of the Equinox, where visitors say they feel strong cosmic energy during the winter solstice. Coffee fields and an occasional peek at Pico de Orizaba, Mexico's highest volcano, soothe the eyes as you drive north, stopping again at the Hacienda El Lencero, the country estate for early Spanish ranchers and revolutionary presidents. Here one must decide whether or not to veer over to Jalapa to visit one of the most wonderful archaeological museums in the country. You must stop if you're at all interested in understanding the riches along the Gulf of Mexico. Then you can move on over mighty

OPPOSITE: In rural towns, *loncherias* serve simple fixed meals, called *comidas corridas*. ABOVE: A modern suspension bridge at the Río Mescala links the highway between Acapulco and Mexico City.

rivers beside dense rainforest toward El Tajín. Plan on spending at least two nights before driving back and hitting any highlights you missed while heading north.

South of Veracruz city the highway becomes more intriguing, tempting travelers toward towns like Tlacotalpan that appear like living museums perched beside rivers. The two Tuxtlas are irresistible. Santiago Tuxtla, where *Romancing the Stone* was filmed, is marked by its 40-ton Olmec head which has been sitting here since at least 400 BC. San Andrés Tuxtla is known for its tobacco and cigars — I like the inexpensive vanilla cigarillos from Santa Clara. I've never had the

opportunity to stay at Lake Catemaco, but can easily understand why many city residents have country homes here. The third largest lake in Mexico, Catemaco is beloved for its natural beauty, clean air and *brujos* or witches, also called *curanderos* (healers). A colony of wild macaques imported from Thailand live on an island in the lake, while its shores hold private estates and a rainforest reserve. This is a wonderful area for drivers, as side roads lead away from the lake to hidden villages.

PACIFIC COAST

Each resort area on the coast has its byways to colonial and natural scenery. I like the quick drive from **Mazatlán** to **Copala** on Highway 15, past forests of palo verdes with white and yellow blossoms, and the longer cruise to Teacapán, a small peninsula where residents are trying to protect the abundance of birds and fish who flourish here. Outside **Puerto Vallarta**, Highway 200 leads south through the Sierra Madre del Sur Mountains, past raging rivers to gorgeous, expensive inns, where the rich and famous hide away. **Acapulco's** best side trip travels up Highway 95 through the same mountains to the silver-mining city of Taxco, where addicted shoppers should plan to spend the night. The small beach communities north of **Huatulco** offer a change from the modern resort climate, with scenes of fishing villages and lagoons filled with migrating birds.

Backpacking

Despite rampant tourism, which has driven up the cost of vacationing in Mexico, the country still has many budget destinations. For those with plenty of time, buses cover every corner of the country, obviating the need for more expensive plane tickets and rental cars. Though the resort areas and major cities cultivate high-end hotels and expensive entertainment, many Mexicans survive on a subsistence economy. Backpackers with strong boots, warm jackets and adequate food are still far better off than the villagers they meet in Oaxaca, Chiapas, Chihuahua and Michoacán.

When the peso was devalued in 1995, all of Mexico was a bargain for a short time. The mainstream areas quickly upped their prices, but travelers who stick with small towns can still keep daily food costs to about US$4 (about the basic day wage in Mexico). Hotels in the $4-for-two range have virtually disappeared, but you can get a good room for twice that amount. Toilet seats, shower curtains, decent screens and hot water are scarce in the cheapest places; ear plugs and eye shields are essential. Reservations are often difficult to arrange in remote areas, but can usually call ahead when you're in the area.

Mexico was a hippie paradise in the 1960s and 1970s, and communal campgrounds (with little more than pit toilets and hammocks

under palms) sprouted along the Caribbean Coast, especially on Isla Mujeres, and around Playa del Carmen and Tulum. Most of those hangouts are gone; some that remain charge a day fee to use their facilities. The Pacific Coast still has Playa Zicatela's strip of rundown *cabañas* on the sand, sandwiched between the mega-resorts of Huatulco and the moderately-priced small inns of Puerto Escondido. Many of the least-expensive places to travel are those frequented by Mexican tourists. I'm always delighted to see prices posted in pesos in old mansion-style hotels in Mérida, Oaxaca, Guadalajara and Veracruz, and in the older sections of Mazatlán, Puerto Vallarta, and Acapulco. The Central Valley of Mexico is filled with small colonial towns and rural villages where indigenous people live much as their ancestors did in past centuries. Courteous budget travelers find many reasons to extend their stays in these areas.

Mexico has a youth hostel system called CREA, with dormitory rooms and minimal amenities. They're often located a long walking distance from major sights, but are usually on bus routes. For a list of hostels contact the office in Mexico City at CREA, Agencia Nacional de Juvenil ((5) 252548,

OPPOSITE TOP: Sunset on a rocky promontory on one of Puerto Escondido's uncrowded beaches. BOTTOM: A sunbather wades at Playa Zicatela. ABOVE: Small skiffs called *pangas* float in the calm waters off Puerto Escondido's Playa Principal.

Glorieta Metro Insurgentes, Local CC-11, Col. Juaréz, CP. 06600 Mexico DF.

Food is cheap in Mexico, but restaurants can be quite expensive. Frequent Mexico travelers learn quickly about *tortillerias*, *panaderías*, taco stands and produce markets, and make a point of carrying extra bags for their purchases. Even if you strictly follow the peel, cook and purify laws of healthy eating (see TRAVELERS TIPS, page 363), you can fuel up quite nicely on beans, rice, fresh tortillas and endless varieties of salsas and condiments.

Living It Up

The magnitude of wealth among some Mexican families is truly astounding (and the source of many rumblings about impending revolutions). Though the high life has been curbed somewhat by peso devaluations and political scandals, there are still plenty of ways to engage in expensive pleasures.

EXCEPTIONAL HOTELS

Sixteenth-century convents, twentieth-century high-rises and timeless coastal resorts all cater to elite sensibilities and ample wealth. The Pacific Coast has long been dotted with stunning, private enclaves tucked between jungle and sea. The **Bel-Air Costa de Careyes**, south of Puerto Vallarta, set the architectural standard for the coast when it was originally designed by Italian architect Gianfranco Brignone. The **Camino Real Las Hadas** in Manzanillo took the Moorish dome and minaret to fairyland extremes when Bolivian tin magnate Anterior Patiño completed his dream palace in 1974. The **Westin Las Brisas** has long been Acapulco's landmark, revered for its pink and white villas with private pools and its matching Jeeps which come with accommodation.

A wave of boutique beach hotels rose along coastal cliffs in the 1980s and early 1990s; most have withstood hurricanes and fiscal fluctuations with aplomb. **La Casa Que Canta** in Zihuatanejo pioneered the new breed of luxury hotels, with its blend of traditional Mexican design, contemporary Mexican art, and world-class linens and furnishings. There's simply no reason to leave your terrace tucked amid vines and trees above the sea. Similarly seductive rooms are set right on the sand at **Villa del Sol** also in Zihuatanejo. **Maroma**, just south of Puerto Morelos and Cancún, has become the ultimate escape.

Las Ventanas al Paraíso changed the face of luxury in Los Cabos when it opened in 1996; nothing in the country compares with its idyllic setting, design, cuisine and comforts. The resort area at the tip of the long-forgotten Baja California Peninsula has become the most costly in the country. Venerable lodgings like the **Hotel Palmilla** have responded with drop-dead beautiful suites on scenic cliffs over the Sea of Cortez, backed by a championship golf course and million-dollar villas. The intimate **Casa del Mar** is soothingly small, sumptuous and classically Mexican, while the **Westin Regina** startles the senses with its soaring pink and yellow walls, then pampers the body with flowing pools and wonderful food.

The colonial-era cities dotting inland Mexico all have superb small inns. At the **Camino Real Oaxaca** guests sleep within stone walls which first rose in the sixteenth century to protect and house Catholic monks. The **Casa de Sierra Nevada** in San Miguel de Allende is housed in a stunning sixteenth-century mansion and is considered by many to be the ultimate colonial hotel in Mexico. **La Casa de la Marquesa** in Querétaro makes the most of eighteenth-century opulence and a fascination with all things European. Earth-toned brick and stucco *casitas* at **Villa Montaña** in Morelia have fireplaces to cut the mountain chill; guests dine on French and gourmet Mexican cuisine with a stunning view of treetops and city lights.

Chain hotel companies have not ignored Mexico's allure. **Camino Real**, a longtime favorite of knowledgeable travelers to Mexico, offers hospitable service, dramatic architecture and superb cuisine at its dozen or so properties throughout the country. **Fiesta Americana Mérida**, part of Mexico's largest hotel company, blends Mérida's colonial architecture with modern amenities. The same chain has three distinctive hotels in Cancún, all bearing the Mexican touch; another is going up in Los Cabos. **Quinta Real**, another Mexican company, has created three outstanding properties in Huatulco, Guadalajara and Monterrey, all reflecting the highest tastes among Mexico's elite. The **Ritz-Carlton** has made its mark in Cancún by adding a few coastal touches to its refined style; rumors have a second Ritz rising in Los Cabos. **Four Seasons** is going coastal in Punta Mita (opening in 1999) after achieving urban success in Mexico City, where high-end hotel competition is fierce. Had I money to burn, I would alternate staying at the capital city's **Marquís Reforma**, **Hotel Nikko**, **Presidente Inter-Continental**, and **Camino Real** hotels.

Palms shade the peaceful pool at the Fiesta Americana Hotel in Acapulco.

Mexico hasn't kept pace with other countries when it comes to small inns that combine adventure travel with luxury, but there are some exceptional countryside lodges. The Copper Canyon has inspired builders and explorers to create several outstanding hostelries, including the **Hotel Posada Barrancas Mirador** in El Divisadero, the **Copper Canyon Sierra Lodge** in Creel, and the **Copper Canyon Riverside Lodge** southeast of Creel in Batopilas. All have stunning settings, cozy rooms and immediate access to the canyon's natural attributes.

EXCEPTIONAL RESTAURANTS

Mexico City has the best overall dining scene in Mexico, followed by Cancún, Acapulco and Puerto Vallarta. All four destinations attract worldly, experienced chefs and have fine Asian, French, seafood and regional Mexican restaurants. International cafés line the pedestrian streets in Mexico City's Zona Rosa — there is always exquisite smoked salmon at **Konditori** and the freshest of sushi at **Daikoku**. **Cicero Centenario** and **Los Girasoles** are the capital's in restaurants of the decade. **Bar L'Opera** near the Bellas Artes has long been a favorite after-theater spot for handsome couples. **Fonda el Refugio** in the Zona Río has been my favorite regional Mexican restaurant in Mexico City for nearly 20 years.

Puerto Vallarta reminds me of Los Angeles with its hip dining scene. European chefs seem particularly fond of the city's communal ambiance, tropical setting and artistic residents. I've enjoyed fine meals at **Café des Artistes**, and **Chef Roger**, and wouldn't miss at least one seafood dinner in the jungles south of the city, probably at **Le Kliff**. **Coyuca 22** is said to be the most wonderful restaurant in **Acapulco**; unfortunately, it's closed from October through May. **Madeiras, Ristorante Casa Nova**, and **Spicey** please the residents of weekend homes in the Las Brisas hills and Acapulco Diamante. I thoroughly enjoy hanging out at the Sushi Bar at the **Boca Chica Hotel** in Playa Caleta and **Bambuco** at the Elcano.

I can't visit Mérida without at least one meal at **El Portico del Peregrino**; if I'm craving hummus, tabouleh, yogurt and lamb I visit **Alberto's Continental Patio**.

Boutique hotels throughout the country typically have excellent dining rooms; among the most exceptional are those at **La Casa Que Canta** in Zihuantanejo, **Casa de Sierra Nevada** in San Miguel de Allende, **Maroma**, on the Caribbean Coast south of Puerto Morelos and Cancún, **Las Mañanitas** in Cuernavaca and the **Quinta Real** hotels in Guadalajara and Huatulco.

Cookbook authors such as Diane Kennedy and Patricia Quintana tend to favor Mexico's regional cuisines in their publications, and a few exceptional chefs have made Mexico's *moles, pozoles,* chilis and spices their palettes. One of the most impressive Mexican menus I've ever seen is at **Maria Bonita** in Cancún, where the tequila list provides dozens of fine choices for sipping. Oaxaca, Puebla, Veracruz, Yucatán and Chiapas all have a plethora of neighborhood restaurants serving an abundance of regional dishes. See GALLOPING GOURMETS, page 48, for a description of some must-try meals.

Family Fun

Mexicans treasure, cherish and even revere small children, and are always delighted to welcome families to their country and into their homes. The main plazas in cities, towns and villages are like giant playgrounds; they often include basketball courts or lawns big enough for a soccer match, albeit with teams of two. Vendors hold cloud-sized bouquets of balloons, blow streams of bubbles toward their wide-eyed audiences, and encourage pleas to papa for enough pesos to buy a tempting toy. On Sunday afternoons, toddler girls in frilly dresses and boys in bow ties race after pigeons under the approving eyes of *las abuelas,* the grandmothers decked out in their church finery. The best plazas to join in the fun are in Veracruz, Cozumel, Oaxaca, Mérida, Plaza Tapatía in Guadalajara; and the Alameda in Mexico City.

Beach towns and resort areas always have some sort of family water park. There are parks with slides, river rides, wading ponds and all sorts of splashy stuff in Marina Vallarta, and Marina Ixtapa, Acapulco, and Cancún. **Xcaret**, south of Cancún, is the best all-around family park, with enough diversions to keep all ages happy for a very full day. Mazatlán and Veracruz city both have worthwhile aquariums, and Nuevo Vallarta and Isla Mujeres have well-run dolphin education centers. **Mexico City's zoo** in Chapultepec Park has undergone a much-needed renovation and its inhabitants, including two giant pandas, have more pleasurable living quarters. Chapultepec could be called the family center of the entire country, given its many options for kids.

Narrow cobblestone streets climb through colonial-era neighborhoods in Taxco.

Papalote, the Children's Museum completed in 1993, is one of the best in the world. Parque Agua Azul in Guadalajara and Mérida's El Centenario both have amusing kid's rides.

Some kids get a kick out of the **Museo Las Momias**, Guanajuato's collection of dressed-up skeletons. Others enjoy the silver mines in Zacatecas and La Valenciana in Guanajuato. They may grow tired of silver shopping in Taxco — reward their patience with a ride up the cable car to the Hotel Monte Taxco. Such simple pleasures are readily available in many places.

Cultural Kicks

Do you like museums, churches, galleries, architecture and fine art? Come to Mexico, for these are some of the country's greatest attractions. Mexico City's **Museo Nacional de Antropología** is one of the world's best archaeological museums; also noteworthy are those in Jalapa and those at the entrances to most archaeological sites. Entire Mexican cities are colonial-era National Heritage sites (or should be); among them are **Puebla**, **Morelia**, **San Miguel de Allende**, **Mérida**, **Oaxaca** and **San Cristóbal de las Casas**. Often built atop ceremonial centers constructed by Olmec, Aztec, Maya, Zapotec and Toltec laborers, these cities are nirvanas for art, architecture and history buffs.

Mexico's take on the fine arts has developed over many stages of its history. The **Pinacoteca Virreinal de San Diego** in Mexico City is housed in a colonial-era convent and houses a fine collection of Mexican art from the Virreinal, the Spanish colonial period of the late 1500s to the early 1800s. Mexican artists who showed promise were sent by the Church to study art in Europe; their paintings reflect the techniques and topics of that era, but always have a distinct Mexican touch in composition and content.

The mural movement after the 1910 revolution gave birth to Mexico's best-known artists, including Diego Rivera, Rufino Tamayo, José Clemente Orozco and David Alfero Siquieros, all of whose works can be found in several public buildings in the capital city. I never visit Mexico City without viewing at least a few of these masterpieces at the **Palacio Nacional de Bellas Artes**, the **Conjunto de San Ildefonso** and the **Palacio Nacional**.

Orozco's murals on the ceiling of the **Cabañas Hospicio** in Guadalajara are best seen while lying on one's back on a hard wooden slab in the former chapel. As befits the size of the man often called the giant frog, **Diego Rivera** was particularly prolific; he painted at least one mural in most of the capital's major buildings and left, upon his death, a **studio** open to the public in San Angel as well as his collection of pre-Columbian artifacts in a dramatic **Museo Anahuacali**.

Rivera's compatriots, including his wife Frida Kahlo, have also made an international impression. Kahlo has become a cult figure in her own right, much-admired for her tortured self portraits and distinctive lifestyle. The **Museo y Casa de Frida Kahlo** in Mexico City's Coyoacán neighborhood is like a religious shrine for Frida fanatics. Remedios Vara, a Spanish artist who lived in Mexico for many years, is also reaching cult status; her ethereal, surrealistic paintings can sometimes be viewed in Mexico City's **Museo Nacional de Arte** and the **Museo de Arte Moderno**.

The modern art movement is spread throughout the country; the best works are displayed in galleries in Mexico City, Guadalajara, Oaxaca and San Miguel de Allende. The **Museo José Luis Cuevas** in Mexico City is considered to be the best avant-garde museum in the country.

Several **cultural events** are held annually throughout the country. In May, both Puerto Vallarta and Cancún host jazz festivals. All of

OPPOSITE: The tile domes of Oaxaca's churches rise above colorful facades. ABOVE: Artifacts, such as this statue of a woman who died in childbirth, fill Mexico City's Museum of Anthropology.

Oaxaca state falls into a celebratory mode in July, when Oaxaca city hosts the annual **Guelaguetza**, a two-week folkdance and music show presenting the finest dancers in elaborate native costumes. San Miguel de Allende is the site of an international **Chamber Music Festival** in August; Guadalajara's mariachis strut their stuff during a two-week fiesta in September. The **Cervantes Festival** held in Guanajuato in October draws symphony orchestras, dance companies, jazz and rock groups and experimental theater companies from around the world.

Shop till You Drop

Should I ever win the lottery, I would undertake such a shopping spree as to vastly improve Mexico's economy. Granted, much of Mexico's folk art, fine art and furnishings are less refined than those of Portugal, Italy, or

France, but I have developed a deep affection for all things Mexican. In my backpacking days I kept my load and expenses down by purchasing necessities for the road — fine woven hammocks and *jipi* (similar to Panama) hats in Mérida, *huaraches* in Acapulco, herbal headache remedies and good luck charms in the markets of Mexico City. Then I started falling for the woolen rugs and black pottery from Oaxaca, the fanciful painted furnishings from Michoacán and Guadalajara, the silver from Taxco, tiles and dishes from Puebla, embroidered *huipiles* (blouses) from Chiapas and masks from Nayarit. Shopping has become an addiction, and my tastes have been refined to the point that I can hardly bear to tour the standard souvenir markets, appalled at their lack of creativity. In Mexico, one learns to shop at the source.

Tlaquepaque, outside Guadalajara, is one of Mexico's most famous shopping centers — its streets lined with art, jewelry and furniture galleries. I remember watching a troupe of interior designers from Texas blow through this picturesque village one day, with calculators, measuring tapes and cameras close at hand. Trucking companies eagerly await such orders and ship massive crates of dining tables, carved doors and cupboards to cities on both sides of the border. Those of us living in the southwest United States have a major advantage here, since we can pick up our purchases on the Mexican side of the border and avoid the expense of customs brokers and other bureaucracies. Many of Mexico's finest hotels are furnished with treasures from the region around Guadalajara — which, by the way, is also known for its fashionable women's shoes. **Michoacán** runs a close second for household items from lacquered tables to painted gourds.

When it comes to folk art, it's difficult to challenge the superiority of **Oaxaca's** artisans. Certain items from this artistically wealthy state seem to go in and out of fashion, though others endure and increase in value over decades and centuries. Nelson Rockefeller, one of the premier collectors of Mexican folk art in the 1930s, did much to focus attention on the black pottery of Doña Rosa Real de Nieto of San Bartolomé de Coyotepec, where one-meter (three-foot) high *ollas* (jugs) polished to

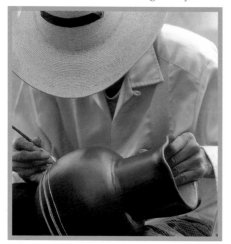

ABOVE: Detail from a bazaar in the San Angel district of Mexico City. LEFT: A potter paints a vase in Taxco. OPPOSITE: Ancient Mixtec and Zapotec designs are woven into woolen rugs at Teotitlán del Valle in Oaxaca. OVERLEAF: The eighteenth-century Iglesia de Santa Prisca stands out amid the multi-hued houses of Taxco at sunset.

an ebony-like gleam are fired without glazing in buried ovens. Rockefeller was also a fan of the Blanco sisters of Atzompa, who made fascinating clay *muñecas* (dolls).

Chiapas, on the Guatemala border, is so colorful and so filled with indigenous groups eking out a living that you're sure to find special treasures. I have a collection of woolen dolls carrying stick rifles, meant to resemble the Zapatista rebels who have brought so much attention to the plight of the poor in this most valuable state. I've seen these dolls, ever so briefly, sold by Indian women in the plazas of Mexico City, Oaxaca and Mérida. The police usually ban such sales quickly.

Folk art galleries are becoming more prevalent throughout the country as collectors grow to appreciate the skills of Mexico's artisans. You can get a good overview from an early-morning stroll through the **Mercado Sabado** (Saturday Market) in the Mexico City suburb of San Angel.

Some of the best folk art shops are in Puerto Vallarta, Puebla, Morelia, San Miguel de Allende and Cozumel. Cancún has been slow to break away from the tacky souvenir market and has a surprising dearth of authentic handicrafts on sale.

Short Breaks

Every major destination in Mexico offers a slew of convenient side trips, and the major airports are often mere drop-off points for explorers. **Cancún**, though far from the largest city in Mexico, has its second busiest airport. You can be sure that a good percentage of those airline passengers won't spend more than just a few nights at a luxury hotel on Cancún's white sand beach (though a fortnight at one of the luxury resorts is not a bad idea). There is more to Mexico than beaches! Those who have been there, done that head to the ruins of Chichén Itzá or Cobá, where small lodgings including the **Hotel Mayaland**, the **Hacienda Chichén** and the **Villa Arqueológica Cobá** offer sudden and total immersion into the world of the Maya. Cancún is also the entry point for the laid-back subtlety of **Isla Mujeres**, the underwater escapes of **Cozumel** and the chain of Caribbean hideaways down the highway to the ruins at Tulum.

The vast majority of Mexico's international visitors travel through **Mexico City** en route to their destinations. I often treat this overwhelming metropolis as a short getaway, squeezing in a few days' stay in the Historic District, the Zona Rosa or Polanco.

I'm particularly fond of the capital on holiday weekends. While everyone else is fleeing to the countryside or coast, I wander through Chapultepec Park, the Anthropology Museum, the Zócalo and San Angel in relative peace, and breathe air free of smog from commuter vehicles. The city is also the easiest embarkation point for quick breaks in Cuernavaca, Puebla and the Valle de Bravo, where country homes, ranches and spas pamper overworked psyches.

Festive Flings

Birth, death, marriage, revolution are all celebrated with equal fervor in Mexico. Rarely a day goes by when you don't hear fireworks or mariachis celebrating a significant event.

Most major holidays are tied into a religious, political or agricultural theme; few last only a day. Mexicans often turn holidays into a *puente*, or bridge, extending the celebrations for three or four days. Festivities typically include parades, dances, parties and an abundance of booming fireworks, which usually don't hit their peak until near dawn. Travelers staying near the site of major fiestas are advised to bring good ear plugs — sleep is not an option during Carnival in Mazatlán or Veracruz. Advance hotel reservations are a must for the big events.

The **Christmas season** is celebrated throughout December and on into January. Many Mexicans take two or three weeks off from work at this time, especially if they live away from their families. Offices run at half-tilt and hotels are packed. One could say the holiday season officially begins December 12, during the **Fiesta de Nuestra Señora de Guadalupe** (Feast of Our Lady of Guadalupe), the patron saint of Mexico. The Basílica de Guadalupe, outside Mexico City, is the religious center of the celebrations. Pilgrims begin their journeys to the Basilica from all corners of Mexico weeks in advance; they assemble on the streets of the capital near the Basilica, where many move in slow processions advancing on their knees until they reach the shrine. Smaller celebrations are held in Puerto Vallarta and other areas where Our Lady of Guadalupe is the patron saint.

On the 12 nights before Christmas, Mexicans celebrate **Las Posadas**, reenacting Mary and Joseph's search for a room.

OPPOSITE: The Virgin of Guadalupe, Mexico's patron saint, in souvenir form. RIGHT: Folkloric dancers in elaborate costumes perform at hotels and village plazas throughout the country.

YOUR CHOICE

Participants carry lit candles and sing carols as they travel from house to house, receiving gifts of food. **Posadas** are celebrated in every city and small town; some of the best are in Querétaro. On December 23, Oaxaca celebrates the **Night of the Radishes**, when elaborately decorated stands are set up in the main plaza for carvers to display their incredible radish creations. Querétaro has a big parade that same night. December 24 brings even bigger parades and celebrations throughout the country, with particularly dramatic fiestas in Oaxaca and Veracruz. Christmas Day is devoted to the family, and visitors are sometimes disappointed to find only their fellow travelers out on the street. **New Year's Eve** is also reserved for family celebrations, which continue on until January 6, the **Día de los Reyes** (Feast of the Kings).

The **Fiesta de San Antonio Abad** (Feast of St. Anthony of Abad), of special importance to ranchers and farmers, is celebrated on January 17. A variety of animals, from roosters to cows, are taken to the cathedral and other Mexico City churches to be blessed. In Veracruz, small towns celebrate the **Fiestas de la Candelería** in early February. **Día de la Constitución** on February 5 is a national holiday commemorating the signing of Mexico's Constitution; **Día de la Bandera**, on February 24, is Mexico's Flag Day.

Though Mexico's **Carnival** (*carnaval*) celebrations are no match for those in Río de Janeiro, Brazil, they are still massive parties with costumes, parades, dances and general revelry that lasts for a week or two. The best celebrations are in Mazatlán, Veracruz, Cozumel and Puebla. **Semana Santa** (Holy Week) competes with Christmas and the Fiesta of Guadalupe as the most important religious event of the year. The Tarahumara in the Copper Canyon come out of their cave dwellings to assemble in more populated villages where they participate in wild dances based on pre-Hispanic traditions. Major festivities are also held in San Cristóbal de las Casas, San Luís Potosí, Pátzcuaro and Taxco. Taxco Holy Week celebrations resembles those in Seville, Spain, with a touch of unique New World traditions that make the processions and performances more dramatic. The ceremonies begin on Palm Sunday, and each day the townspeople dramatize the episodes of the last days of Christ. Among the actors are black-hooded penitents, bearers of crosses and others with thorny vines wrapped around their heads. The crucifixion is reenacted on Good Friday and is followed by a silent midnight procession. The triumphal Easter

Sunday procession marks the Resurrection of Christ and the end of the festivities. **Good Friday** and **Holy Saturday** are national holidays.

The **Spring Equinox** is marked by an astonishing phenomenon at the ruins of Chichén Itzá in Yucatán. The ancient Maya considered the equinox to be the most significant event to determine their growing season and survival. They built the Temple of Kulkucán so that it aligns with the sun during the equinox, when the shadow of the plumed serpent slithers from the top of the building to the ground, where it joins the carved snake's head at the base. The spectacle brings hordes of visitors from throughout the world. **Día de Trabajo** (Labor Day) is celebrated on May 1 as a national holiday, when workers, many representing their unions, participate in huge parades, particularly in Mexico City (see also FESTIVALS AND SPECIAL EVENTS, page 112). The celebrations turn into fierce political protests in unstable times. **Cinco de Mayo** (May 5) is a national holiday celebrated with particular fervor in Puebla, where dances, fireworks and processions celebrate Mexico's defeat of the French. The **Fiesta de Corpus Christi** (Feast of Corpus Christi), 66 days after Easter, is celebrated throughout the country, but the best fiestas are in Papantla, Veracruz, where this region's famous *voladores* (flying pole dancers) perform by the ruins of El Tajín. In Mexico City, children dressed as Indians are blessed at the Catedral Metropolitana.

The **Fiesta de San Juan el Bautista** (Feast of St. John the Baptist) on June 24 is a national holiday, celebrated with parades and fiestas throughout the country, as is the **Fiesta del Virgen de la Carmen** (Feast of the Virgin of Carmen), July 16.

The biggest political holiday in Mexico is the **Día de la Independencia** (Independence Day), which officially begins at 11 PM on September 15. The Zócalo in Mexico City (see also FESTIVALS AND SPECIAL EVENTS, page 112) is decorated with larger-than-life-size portraits of Mexico's national heroes, made out of colored lights and suspended from buildings around the main square. As many as half a million people flood into the Zócalo, squashed shoulder-to-shoulder, to hear the president of Mexico cry out the traditional *grito*, or shout, that commemorates Padre Miguel Hidalgo's cry for independence in 1810. The crowd cries *Viva Mexico!* in unison response as fireworks,

Mexico's ubiquitous sombrero is intricately embroidered in the state of Jalisco.

horns, whistles and music explode in the air. It's a tremendously moving spectacle of national unity that continues on through the night and culminates, on September 16, with a parade of thousands from the Zócalo to the Independence Monument. Smaller celebrations are held throughout the country.

Días de los Muertos (Days of the Dead, November 1 and 2), known in the United States as **All Saints' Day** and **All Souls' Day**, are national holidays in Mexico. Deceased children are honored on November 1, adults on November 2. Altars to the dead are set up in homes and cemeteries; photographs of the departed are surrounded with flowers (especially marigolds), candles, and their favorite foods and beverages. The smell of copal incense fills the air, and candies and breads shaped like skulls and skeletons abound.

Aniversario de la Revolución (Anniversary of the Revolution), celebrated on November 20, is the anniversary of the Mexican revolution of 1910 and is honored with a national holiday (see also FESTIVALS AND SPECIAL EVENTS, page 112). Though Mexicans don't celebrate Thanksgiving, those living near the border sometimes join in the festivities, calling the United States holiday Día del Pavo (Turkey Day).

Galloping Gourmets

My kitchen cabinets and freezer are stocked with spices, condiments and staples from Mexican markets in Oaxaca, Mexico City or wherever I've been of late. Mexican cuisine has seeped into my daily regime. Consider the basics — corn, beans and rice — the universal diet of third-world countries. Whenever I need to shed a pound or two I switch to this diet, minus the lard that adds so much flavor to Mexican cooking. Vegetarians can enjoy Mexican cuisine too, but it takes some patience — and much insistence — as I have discovered over the years. Ask for a dish *sin carne* and you're assured it will lack beef. Instead, the chef might throw in some pork, ham, or chicken. *Sopa de mariscos* could well come with the head of the fish peering out from the soup, just to make sure you're well fed. During my first ventures into Mexico I lived on cheese in *quesadillas, queso fundido, tacos and enchiladas.* Since those days I've relaxed my dietary strictures and love nothing more than a plate full of *carnitas* (chunks of roasted pork) or *carne asada* (thin strips of marinated beef). But it's also become easier to stick to simple meals as more and more

kitchens have become accustomed to vegetarian requests, and an increasing number of resorts have at least one health-food restaurant. But travelers with strict dietary requirements are best off shopping in the public markets and preparing their own meals. On to the best of Mexican cuisine.

ANTOJITOS, BOTANES AND APPETIZERS

Whatever they're called regionally, small dishes accompanying large glasses of beer are as satisfying as most large meals. Bars and restaurants in all regions specialize in various types of *antojitos*. In Oaxaca you can order a Negro Modelo beer in the main plaza and receive a bowl of spiced peanuts or crispy deep-fried grasshoppers, called *chapulines*. In Yucatán, drinks are served with small plates of *cochinita pibil*, seasoned pork baked in banana leaves. You can get *queso fundido*, melted cheese similar to fondue, sometimes mixed with blackened chilis or greasy *chorizo* (sausage) served with homemade tortillas, in most cafés and bars. I once joined a group of locals at a dive bar called El Ultimo Tren in Manzanillo for an afternoon's merriment, complete with pitchers of sangria, bottles of beer, and an endless array of spicy shrimp, nuts, cheese, and *empenadas*, small turnovers filled with meat and beans. Two or three mariachi bands competed for attention as shoeshine boys, lottery-ticket and flower sellers, and vendors bearing various trinkets hustled out pesos from our pockets. Such bars are not the best places for women alone, but if you can find a group to join, they're great fun.

BREADS

The *tortilla* is the base of most Mexican cooking, so important that the government regulates their price during peso devaluations. Even the smallest village has its *molino de mixtamal* where housewives take their corn, which has been soaked in lime and water, to be ground into a paste called *masa*, ready to be patted or pressed into tortillas. Most towns also have *tortillerias*, where the *masa* is fed into machines that turn out tortillas by the kilo.

Tortillas are eaten as the accompaniment to a meal and are used for making *taco* (a fried tortilla filled with beans, meat, tomatoes, lettuce and cheese), *enchilada* (a tortilla folded over a meat or bean, and cheese filling, and covered with a sauce), and *quesadilla* (a tortilla folded over cheese). Tortillas accompany nearly every meal; in some places, they double as an implement for picking up food.

Nearly every town also has its *panadería*, turning out crunchy rolls with soft bread fillings called *bolillos*. Filled with beans, meat, cheese and lettuce, the *bolillos* are used for sandwiches called *tortas*. When cut in half, covered with cheese and beans, and broiled, they're called *molettes*. The *panaderías* also turn out long shelves of *pan dulce* (sweetened breads) and cookies usually made with lard or vegetable shortening rather than butter. Nearly every first timer who stands in a *panadería* holding a metal tray and tongs manages to pile the tray with goodies in no time at all. (Discipline is sometimes learned the hard way: these sweets have no preservatives and must consumed within a few hours of purchase!) When settling into a town for a week or two I usually research the *panaderías* early on, choose my favorite, and return every day for a small selection to serve with my morning coffee and afternoon tea.

Packaged breads are usually dreadful — the worst, and most popular, being carried under the label Bimbo. Many are the jokes

about Bimbo bread, which seems more suitable as food for fish or birds than for human sustenance. Some places now have whole-wheat and whole-grain breads, though they can be difficult to find.

CHEESE AND DAIRY PRODUCTS

Oaxaca and Chihuahua are the centers for cheese making in Mexico, and I'm addicted to the balls of fresh *quesillo* that tears off in long creamy strings. *Queso fresco*, freshly-made cheese, is crumbled much like feta cheese over tacos and *enchiladas*, as is *queso anejo*, aged cheese. *Requesón* is similar to ricotta or cottage cheese and is sometimes used in *enchiladas*. *Queso cotija* is a dry goat cheese sprinkled over beans and other dishes.

Pasteurized milk can be found in most markets and grocery stores. Most travelers are, and should be, wary of unpasteurized products. Look for packages that are well

Uniformed schoolchildren gather in Mexico City's plazas during lunch time.

onions and tomatoes. Grilled and steamed veggie platters are beginning to appear on some menus, and nearly every major town has at least one health-food restaurant where you can indulge yourself with fresh produce. Corn on the cob is a popular street food, either sprinkled with salt and chilis, or covered with mayonnaise. *Jicama*, a root crop that tastes something like a chalky apple, is served in salads, or alone sprinkled with lime.

Papayas as big as watermelons, melons as big as a small child, sweet juicy mangoes, oranges and grapefruits, succulent pineapples and firm, full-flavored bananas — Mexico grows them all in profusion. Fruit plates, sometimes served with granola and yogurt, are common on most menus, and street vendors all over the country sell sliced fruit covered with salt and powdered chilis. Fresh fruits are blended with milk or water into *licuados* — cool, refreshing drinks displayed in huge glass jugs at street stands and markets. I generally stay away from the market *licuados*, but drink them without worry at juice stands and restaurants.

sealed. Yogurt is very much in fashion these days and can be found in most grocery stores. Mexican butter is typically unsalted and creamy sweet.

VEGETABLES AND FRUITS

If you eat in restaurants exclusively you might begin to think that the only vegetables in Mexico are *chayote* and carrots. These two sweet root crops, which are served boiled or steamed with main courses, grow boring quite quickly. The *chayote*, a type of squash, is eaten whole like a baked potato in Chiapas but most often is diced into a vegetable mix. After this steady diet, it may come as a surprise when you stroll through a public market and find vegetables of every description — shiny deep red tomatoes (okay they're a fruit, but I prefer them in salads), all types of lettuces, green beans, eggplant and fresh peas (used in Yucatán liberally, even in egg dishes). The restaurants may be following the travelers' axiom — eat nothing that you can't peel or boil yourself. These days, most restaurants catering to tourists use purified water for cleansing vegetables; if you're not sure, just ask. Fortunately, the glorious avocado (*aguacate*) can be peeled and thus liberally eaten in tortas and *enchiladas* or big bowls of guacamole, made with mashed avocados, lime juice, tomatoes, onions and chilis. I always order salads in finer restaurants and hotels and am utterly gleeful when I find one filled with lettuces, sprouts, cucumbers,

RICE AND BEANS

Rare is the meal that is served without at least one of Mexico's staple foods, rice and beans, which are often the sole items on poor families' tables. Rice may be served plain or mixed with tomatoes, onions and chilis. Beans come in several varieties: *frijoles refritos* are refried pinto beans, first boiled then smashed and cooked in lard, and sometimes topped with crumbled cheese. *Frijoles charra*, or cowgirl beans, are served as a soup mixed with onions, tomatoes and chilis. *Frijoles negros*, or black beans, are becoming more common in coastal areas, served as a soup or side dish.

SEAFOOD

Given Mexico's many miles of coastline it should come as no surprise that fish (*pescado*) is found on menus throughout the country. I generally order seafood only in coastal areas, and even there I am mindful of heavy rains that may have washed sewage into nearby seas. I once spent a week in Campeche on the Gulf of Mexico without touching a bite of seafood. The rains were so bad that the streets were flooding, and I couldn't help picturing all that waste feeding the ocean creatures. Such restraint made me quite unhappy, since

ABOVE: Tempting arrays of Mexican-style fast-food lure diners to market counters. OPPOSITE: Tropical fruits are the hallmark of lavish buffets such as this one at Acapulco's Sheraton Hotel.

Campeche has some of the best regional seafood dishes in the country. I'm quite fond of Campeche's *arroz con mariscos*, rice mixed with shrimp, and the *cangrejo* or stone crab. In Yucatán, fresh fish is baked in banana leaves and seasoned with *achiote*, a ground red seed — the dish is called *pescado tik-n-xik*. In Acapulco, a similar dish made with ground chilis, vinegar and mayonnaise is called *pescado a la talla*. Veracruz's famous *huachinango veracruzano*, a red snapper covered with tomatoes, onions and green peppers, is served all over the country. *Pescado a la plancha* is simply grilled; *con mojo de ajo* is served with butter or oil and bits of fried garlic; *empenizado* is breaded and fried. Shrimp (*camarones*) are harvested all along the Pacific Coast and Baja; lobster is less abundant and is often imported. *Langosta a la Puerto Nuevo* has become a specialty of northern Baja, where crowds head to the tiny village of Puerto Nuevo for lobster, steamed and then fried in lard and served with rice, beans and homemade tortillas. *Tacos de pescado* (fish tacos) are another Baja specialty that's spreading through the land. They're made of deep-fried strips of fresh fish folded into a corn tortillas and served with an array of condiments including limes, cilantro (also called coriander), chilis and sour cream. *Ceviche* is an irresistible dish served all over the country — since it is made of raw fish that is "cooked" in lime juice, I usually limit myself to that prepared in fishing villages from the day's catch. My favorite *ceviche* is a simple mix of chopped or shredded fish, lime juice, tomatoes, onions and chilis. The Acapulco style (called *acapulqueño*) contains a ketchup-like cocktail sauce. And if I have the sad fate of suffering from a hangover I ask for spicy *sopa de mariscos*, supposedly guaranteed to *levante los muertos* (raise the dead).

MEAT

Beef cattle are raised in the northern states of Chihuahua and Sonora, and steaks imported from these two states are served throughout the country. As a rule, the beef is not as tender and flavorful as that found in the United States, and resort restaurants often advertise that they use imported beef. Mexicans use thinner cuts of meat than Americans and stretch this expensive treat far by pounding and marinating it as *carne asada*, a thin strip of beef served with grilled green onions and peppers, rice, beans, guacamole and tortillas. Pork (*puerco or cerdo*) is more common, served as *chuletas* (pork chops), or, in Yucatán, as *chochinita pibil*, with hunks of pork marinated in sour orange juice and achiote spice and

baked in banana leaves. *Chorizo* is a spicy pork sausage served with eggs. Chicken, called *pollo*, is roasted on large rotating spits in shops all over the country and is served as an inexpensive meal with beans and rice. Yucatán's *pollo pibil* is prepared like the pork dish mentioned above; and chicken is shredded and used in tacos, *enchiladas*, soups and stews.

SALSAS, CHILIS AND SAUCES

No Mexican meal is complete without at least one salsa. The simplest is a mix of chopped tomatoes, onions, chilis and cilantro, called *salsa cruda*, *salsa mexicana*, or *pico de gallo*. *Salsa verde* is made with *tomatillos*, a green tomato-like fruit; *salsa roja* includes roasted chilis and tomatoes and is usually quite spicy. Salsas are also made from cactus, papaya, mango and anything else the chef might think up; most families have a standard recipe.

Visit any Mexican market and you'll quickly learn that inventive chefs have dozens of chilis to chose from, including the fiery *habanero*, the robust *chipotle* and the humble, ever-present *jalapeño*. One of Mexico's most important dishes, served only on special occasions is the *chili en nogada*, a *poblano* chili stuffed with meat and fruits and covered with a white sauce and pomegranate seeds. *Chilis rellenos* are usually stuffed with cheese, lightly battered and fried; they are sometimes also stuffed with meat, fish, or shellfish.

Mexico's most famous sauce is *mole*, a complicated blend of spices with at least

20 ingredients. *Mole* comes in several colors — green, red, black, brown and yellow — and no two cooks prepare it exactly the same way. Some *moles*, such as those from Oaxaca, include bitter chocolate. Others incorporate ground pumpkin or sesame seeds, almonds, cloves, raisins, chilis (of course) and garlic. *Mole* is served over chicken, turkey and *enchiladas*. It is an acquired taste, and just when you think you've gotten a grip on its distinct flavor, you may be served something so different you won't believe it is *mole*.

SWEETS AND DESSERTS

The many tropical fruits of Mexico are often sweetened and dried, preserved in thick honey-like sauces, or blended into delicious ice creams. *Dulcerías* specialize in these sweet fruits, sugared candies and creamy nut bars. *Pastelerías* specialize in the frothy pastries so beloved by Mexicans; if you're in Mexico City stop by the two-story **Pastelería Ideal** for a peek at the gaudily ornate wedding and birthday cakes. Cakes are usually a bit crumbly and not too sweet; pies, called *pay*, are filled with fruit or nuts (*nueces*). *Cajeta*, a thick sauce made from caramelized goat milk, is absolutely wonderful in *crepas con cajeta*, a delicate crêpe dessert usually topped with chopped nuts.

BEVERAGES

Juices, *licuados and aguas* are a part of every meal. *Agua de Jamaica*, made with hibiscus flowers, is refreshing and its sugar content helps cut the burn from spicy food. *Horchata*, made with ground rice, is cool and filling. There are juice stands in nearly every town, where oranges, papayas, bananas and pineapples are peeled, chopped, blended and squeezed right before your eyes.

Mexican beers are among the best in the world and have entered the international, market with surprising strength. Negro Modelo, made in Yucatán, is the darkest and heaviest brew; Negro Montejo from the same region is equally satisfying. Bohemia, a lighter beer with a full flavor, can be found in most parts of the country, as can Dos Equis (look for their Noche Buena special Christmas beer), Corona and Pacifico. Tecate, made in the border town of the same name, is the working man's beer, served in distinctive red cans. Mexican's often add lime to their beer, squeezing a fresh slice into the bottle or can. The latest beer concoction is the *michelada*, served in an icy mug with an inch or so of lime juice in the bottom, salt around the rim and ice cubes. It makes a beer last much longer, especially on a hot day at the

beach. Some bartenders add Maggi sauce (somewhat similar to Worcestershire sauce) or spices to a *michelada*, and call the drink without sauce a *chelada*.

Tequila may well be considered the national drink, and is available in dozens of gradients of quality. Cheap tequila can certainly be harmful to your health, at least temporarily. If you feel a sharp pain in your temples after quaffing a few shot glasses of this stuff, stop drinking or switch to something more expensive. Also beware of slammers, poppers, and other party drinks, which usually consist of a splash of tequila topped with fizzing soda, shaken together and chugged. Suffice to say you'll be miserable if you indulge. Margaritas, the ubiquitous tequila drink served all over the world, are properly made with tequila, lime juice, triple sec, ice and salt. They can be blended into an icy slush or served on the rocks (*con las rocas*). Strawberry, mango, banana and other fruit-flavored margaritas are served in tourist restaurants; you can order one of these *sin* (without) tequila and still feel like you're joining in the fun. Not all firewater can be labeled tequila, which comes from just one region in the country. Mezcal, also distilled from agave, is made in Oaxaca and usually

LEFT: Tortillas are as essential to Mexico as wine is to France. ABOVE: Diners are treated to sublime regional cuisine in festive settings throughout the country.

has a worm in the bottom of the bottle. Pulque is yet another agave-based drink, harsh and unpleasant to most foreign palates. *Licores* (liqueurs) are produced throughout the country. Kahlua, made with coffee and vanilla beans is the most common. When in Yucatán, be sure to try Xtabentún, said to be a Mayan aphrodisiac. Damiana, made in southern Baja, supposedly has similar effects.

Mexican table wines, especially those produced in Baja California, Querétaro and Aguascalientes, are coming into their own, though it's difficult to make specific recommendations. I've enjoyed the reds from Santo Tomás, which has an excellent wine cellar in Ensenada.

South American wines are appearing more often on upscale wine lists, as are those from Spain and Italy. French and Californian wines can be prohibitively expensive. Imported alcoholic beverages are subject to enormous import duties and value-added taxes that price them well above their Mexican competition.

Special Interests

Students of art, archaeology, anthropology, language and cuisine look upon Mexico as a giant field lab where their interests can run wild. Nature buffs tend to cluster in Chiapas, Veracruz, Yucatán and Baja; those with other interests find like-minded souls in myriad locations in the country.

ARCHAEOLOGICAL, ANTHROPOLOGICAL AND HISTORICAL EXCURSIONS

Mexico offers amateurs and professionals a wealth of ruins, ancient civilizations and artifacts for study. Over 50 indigenous groups still follow the traditions of the Nahuatl, Huastec, Tarahumara, Mixtec, Maya and other cultures. Universities throughout the world offer archaeology tours, as do tour companies. For information contact the following: **Far Horizons** TOLL-FREE (800) 552-4575 FAX (505) 343-8076, PO Box 91900, Albuquerque, NM 87199-1900; **Remarkable Journeys** TOLL-FREE (800) 856-1993, PO Box 31855, Houston, TX 77231-1855; and **Smithsonian Study Tours** ((202) 357-4700 FAX (202) 633-9250, 1100 Jefferson Drive SW, Room 3045, MRC 702, Washington DC 20560.

Some tour companies are now using Veracruz as a launching point for a tour following the Ruta de Cortés (Route of Cortez) to Puebla, Teotihuacán and Mexico City. Contact **Tourimex** ((22) 322462 FAX (22) 322479 E-MAIL tourimex@mail.glga.com, in Puebla.

ART LESSONS

Oaxaca city, San Miguel de Allende, Puebla and Morelia all have a magical lure for artists of varying bents. Painters find inspiration in these landscapes; there are schools for advancing their talent at the **Instituto Rufino Tamayo** ((951) 64710 in Oaxaca and the **Instituto Allende** ((415) 20190 in San Miguel de Allende.

CULINARY LESSONS

Cooking lessons in the culinary centers of Oaxaca, Michoacán and Puebla are available through **Culinary Adventures, Inc.** ((206) 851-7676 FAX (206) 851-9532 in the United States.

LANGUAGE STUDY

It's easy to take Spanish lessons while touring Mexico, since schools offer everything from two-day immersion classes

to bilingual chat groups to month-long sessions centered around a particular interest. Most schools offer students the option of boarding with a local family or staying in a reasonably priced hotel. For information on other programs throughout the country contact: **Language Study Abroad** ((818) 242-5263 FAX (818) 548-3667 91207 E-MAIL cd002380@mindspring.com WEB SITE www.languagestudy.com, 1301 North Maryland Avenue, Glendale, CA; and **The National Registration Center for Study Abroad** ((414) 278-0631, PO Box 1393, Milwaukee, WI 53201, for a directory of schools throughout Mexico.

Nearly every vacation destination has at least one Spanish-language school. In **Mérida**, students can specialize in language, archaeology, medicine, law and other interests at the **Centro Idiomas del**

Sureste ((99) 261155 FAX (99) 269020, Calle 14 No. 106 at Calle 25. The University of Yucatán, also in Mérida, is affiliated with United States colleges and offers language programs for credit.

Oaxaca is another ideal learning center, and many travelers study Spanish, art and cooking here. Contact the **Centro de Idiomas** ((951) 65922 FAX (951) 91951 on Burgoa between Armenta and López.

In **San Cristóbal de las Casas**, the best place to study is at the **Instituto Jovel** FAX (967) 84069, Lores No. 21. **Guadalajara** has one of the largest communities of foreign retirees in the nation, and language centers abound. Check out **The American Institute**

The Zapotec and Mixtec temples of Monte Albán bear designs still used by weavers and potters in Oaxaca's villages.

for **Foreign Study** ((3) 616-4399 TOLL-FREE (800) 727-2437 extension 6083, Tomás V. Gómez No. 125, which can enroll students in their program at the University of Guadalajara. Nearly every vacation destination has at least one Spanish school. In **Mazatlán**, Dixie Davis teaches expatriates and snowbirds the words they need to live comfortably in Mexico. Contact her at the **Centro de Idiomas** ((69) 822053 FAX (69) 855606, Belisario Domínguez No. 1908.

SPAS

The Aztecs perfected the art of the steam bath at their *temazcal* sweat baths, oval-shaped structures where the steaming session was accompanied by chanting and drumming. Several of Mexico's modern spas incorporate *temazcals* in their facilities, but focus more on modern treatments such as seaweed wraps, aromatherapy and Swiss salt scrubs. The country is said to have more than 500 warm mineral springs, long used by locals seeking their soothing, curing properties. Now hoteliers from Baja to the Sierra Madre are tapping these waters in fancy, full-scale spas. The **Holiday Inn Vita Spa Agua Caliente** in Tijuana uses the same waters that attracted Hollywood types to the prohibition-era Agua Caliente resort in the 1920s. At **Rancho Río Caliente Spa**, in Zapopán near Guadalajara, soothing mineral waters fill soaking baths and pools; at **Hotel Hacienda Taboada**, near San Miguel de Allende, waters first discovered by the Otomi and Chichimeca Indians are still used to inspire tranquillity.

Rancho la Puerta near the United States border in Tecate is one of Mexico's most famous spas, attracting an international clientele to the harsh desert climate for weeks of exercise, spiritual regeneration and physical rejuvenation. Near the municipality of **Ixtapan de la Sal**, outside Mexico City, is a gorgeous spa facility beside a *balneario*, a public swimming pool, a large amusement park, and a variety of accommodations. The **Avandaro Golf & Spa Resort** in Valle de Bravo is surrounded by pine forests and set on a lake; the spa's name means 'dream place' and indeed inspires sweet sleep with its beauty treatments, fitness programs, and golf course. In Cuernavaca, **Hostería la Quinta** is both a romantic escape and a full-scale spa. Many of the finer resort hotels have incorporated full-scale spas in their facilities; among the best are **Las Ventanas al Paraíso** in Los Cabos, and the **Marriott Casa Magna** and **Meliá** in Cancún.

YOUR CHOICE

Taking a Tour

Several companies offer tours that give a good overview of the country's highlights. High-end tours include those with the following tour operators: **Abercrombie and Kent International** TOLL-FREE (800) 323-7308 FAX (630) 954-3324, 1520 Kensington Avenue, Suite 212, Oak Brook, IL 60523-2141; **American Express Vacations** TOLL-FREE (800) 241-1700, PO Box 1525, Fort Lauderdale, FL 33302; and **International Expeditions** TOLL-FREE (800) 633-4734 E-MAIL intlexp@aol.com WEBSITE www .ietravel.com/intexp, One Environs Park, Helena, AL 35080.

Those who appreciate lower prices and don't mind traveling en masse have several options with **Globus** and **Cosmos** TOLL-FREE (800) 221-0090 FAX (303) 347-5301 Federal Circle, Littleton, CO 80123-2980.

Other companies specializing in a variety of Mexico tours include: **Horizon Tours** TOLL-FREE (800) 395-0025 FAX (202) 393-1547, 1634 Eye Street NW, Suite 301, Washington DC 20006; **Sanborn Tours** TOLL-FREE (800) 531-5440 FAX (512) 303-4643, 1007 Main Street, Bastrop, TX 78602; and **Tauck Tours** TOLL-FREE (800) 468-2825 FAX (203) 221-6828, PO Box 5027 West Port, CT 06881.

Most airlines flying into Mexico offer vacation packages and tours that can save you considerable money. For package information contact one of the following numbers in the United States:

Aeroméxico TOLL-FREE (800) 245-8585
Air France TOLL-FREE (800) 237-2747
American Airlines TOLL-FREE (800) 321-2121
British Airways TOLL-FREE (800) 359-8722 or (800) 247-9297
Continental TOLL-FREE (800) 634-5555
Delta Vacations TOLL-FREE (800) 221-6666
Iberia TOLL-FREE (800) 772-4642
KLM TOLL-FREE (800) 800-1504
Lufthansa TOLL-FREE (800) 645-3880
Mexicana TOLL-FREE (800) 531-9321
United TOLL-FREE (800) 328-6877.

The flower-filled courtyard of the Camino Real Oaxaca.

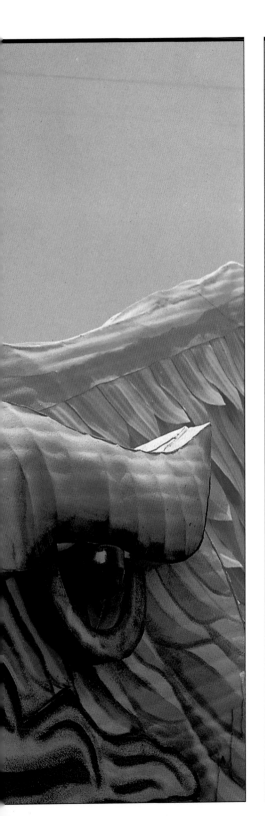

Welcome to Mexico

"MEXICO IS A STATE OF MIND," said Graham Greene. D.H. Lawrence described it as a smell. British journalist Alan Riding called it "ancient, complex and unpredictable." More simply, the American writer Edna Fergusson concludes that "Mexico is Mexico." With all of these one would have to agree. The people, the attitudes, the scenery, the languages, the history, the cultures, the architecture — everything in Mexico is uniquely Mexican. And, to have lived without knowing Mexico is to miss a profound and irreplaceable beauty and knowledge.

Mexico has enough natural and man-made attractions to please even the most jaded traveler. Its 1,972,544-sq-km (761,600-sq-mile) land mass is bordered by 10,145 km (6,290 miles) of shoreline, with innumerable stretches of fine sand beaches, and some of the world's longest and most beautiful coral reefs offshore.

The Pacific beaches are warmed by the Japan current; when the surf's up the waves rival those of South Africa and Hawaii. More sedate are the warm waters of the Gulf of California and the Gulf of Mexico. Best of all are the Mexican Caribbean's pristine white beaches, turquoise water, and multicolored coral reefs.

Mexico is a land of 10,000 ruined cities, towns, and pyramids, where ancient civilizations have left their mark deep in the countryside and culture. The country abounds with the remains of ancient towns of the Olmecs, Toltecs, Mayas and Aztecs whose civilizations were different from, but more advanced than, their European and African contemporaries. Few sites anywhere in the world rival the architectural glories of Teotihuacán, Palenque, or Chichén Itzá. The modern museums of Mexico City contain archaeological treasures and art that can be seen nowhere else on earth (though some of the most precious Mayan codices are housed in Dresden).

In the north, the stupendous Barranca del Cobre, the Copper Canyon, is not to be missed by anyone who has marveled at the more celebrated but smaller Grand Canyon in the United States. There are mountains everywhere in Mexico, except for in the northern deserts and on the Yucatán Peninsula, which is as flat as a tortilla. Every city in central Mexico has a volcano within view. Citlaltépetl (also called Pico de Orizaba), Popocatépetl and Iztaccíhuatl are, repectively, the third, fifth, and seventh tallest mountains in North America.

Mexico's mountains are surrounded by an amazing diversity of environments: tawny deserts, tropical jungle, arid plains, pine forests, broad cultivated fields, valleys, and canyons. Mineral springs, huge waterfalls, thermal waters, and spectacular caverns are etched in the mountainsides.

Despite centuries of production, Mexico continues to be a world leader in the production of silver, gold and copper. Its oil reserves are among the largest in the western hemisphere, and its silver mines continue to support colonial towns.

But Mexico's greatest asset is its people. Not at all like the caricature of a Mexican who sleeps all day under a large sombrero, they are productive and industrious. Like all southern people, they avoid working in the heat of the day. They work at their own even pace, often beginning at dawn and stopping well past dark. This is their "Mexicanismo," the identity created from a mixture of the Spanish culture with the more than 50 Indian tribes of the nation. Life, regardless of its difficulties, can at times be a fiesta, an explosion of fun and color. Or it can be dark and relentless.

There is no one place which reveals Mexico. So large is the country and so varied are its attractions that a lifetime could easily be devoted to its discovery. On a two-week vacation, set your sights on just one or two areas of the country. Even then you might feel rushed and find you would rather sit in a sidewalk café by a central plaza and watch the rest of the world go by. And there is no way to "do" Mexico, as some tour operators would have one believe. Nor can you get the vaguest sense of Mexico from sitting on the beach in a glossy resort. Land of 90 million people and 90 million viewpoints, Mexico has four thousand years of civilization behind it. Far more than a country, Mexico is a way of life.

OPPOSITE: Acapulco Bay is lined with highrise hotels and miles of sand, a playground for all ages. ABOVE: First communion and other religious holidays bring out the best in children's wardrobes.

The Country and Its People

THE GREAT PRE-HISPANIC CIVILIZATIONS

When Paleolithic nomads crossed the Bering Strait some 35,000 years ago, never could they have imagined the verdant meccas of Mexico that would eventually be built by their descendants. The early hunter-gatherer tribes moved south and east from the land bridge until they were scattered over the entire North American continent. When they reached warmer climates, they domesticated wild plants such as maize, chili peppers, pumpkins, and beans. They became rooted to the land and began to develop civilizations more sophisticated than contemporary European ones.

Artifacts discovered near Mexico City show that hunter-gatherers lived here at least 4,000 years ago. They used tools made of obsidian (a volcanically-formed glass used in place of metal) and had fire. A thousand years later they had established villages and become year-round farmers.

By 1500 BC, the first great civilization of Mexico, the Olmec people, had developed in what are now the states of Tabasco and Veracruz. They thrived for 1,000 years and are considered the ancestor of the empires that followed.

Jaguar carvings and sculpted human heads of enormous proportion typified Olmec art, much of which was associated with large ceremonial structures. The prevailing theories are that the Olmecs worshipped the jaguar as a deity and considered the human head the key to power. Their society is thought to have been dominated by priests and to have exerted commercial rather than military power. Ritual decapitation may have had religious significance; heads were probably considered the only appropriate sacrifices for the gods.

The Olmecs left not only their art, carved on gigantic basalt stone, but also the mystery of how they imported these stones not native to the area. Likewise no one understands the decline and disappearance of the Olmec around the year 500 BC.

The Olmec civilization was followed by a succession of various others. The next two most notable were the Teotihuacán in central Mexico, and the Maya in the Yucatán, Chiapas, Tabasco, Guatemala and Belize.

The Teotihuacán civilization was centered in a city of the same name built near Mexico City around 100 BC. It was at its peak from AD 150 to AD 600, when the city may have had as many as 250,000 inhabitants. From necessity an extensive system of irrigation to grow maize for the population was developed. Like the Olmec, the Teotihuacán was a commercial society ruled by its priests. They worshipped gods of the sun, moon, rain, and various animal forms, including the plumed serpent.

At this same time the great Maya cities and ceremonial centers of the Yucatán were thriving. Like the people of Teotihuacán, the Maya were farmers. Because of the peninsula's limestone crust, shallow soil, and lack of fresh water the Maya were more nomadic, practicing slash-and-burn agriculture. In some areas, they dealt with the problem by building raised beds and extensive water delivery systems. Maya art and architecture, more ornamental than those of other civilizations, is almost all that remains of their incredible accomplishments.

By AD 700 Teotihuacán was nearly deserted, and the Maya were battling the Toltecs, who dominated the region north of Mexico City. All of these

once-thriving civilizations sank from prominence; historians and archaeologists are not sure why. Several centuries of tribal warfare followed, and power shifted from tribe to tribe with little continuity. The greatest personage from this period appears to be Quetzalcoatl, the ruler of the Toltecs. The Toltecs were skilled metal workers, which may account for their military prowess. In any case Quetzalcoatl's power became legendary, and he was revered as a god by many non-Toltec tribes, including the Aztecs, the last of the great Indian civilizations. The Aztec tribe goes back to before the thirteenth century, but the true development of an empire did not occur until the middle of the

OPPOSITE: Palenque, located in Mexico's dwindling southern rainforest, is considered to be the most architecturally refined Mayan site. ABOVE: Each period of Mexican history is illustrated by a unique art style such as that shown in this Aztec god of fire.

fourteenth. In the year 1345, while wandering down from the north in search of a new homeland, the Aztecs, or Mexicas, saw an eagle with a serpent in his mouth perched on a cactus in the Valley of Mexico. This vision had been prophesied as the sign of the "promised land," and so here they built their capital city, Tenochtitlán, on a island in Lake Texcoco not far from Teotihuacán.

The Aztec civilization was based on both military might and commercial power, each enlarging the other. They revered Huitzilopochtli, the god of war who wielded a fire serpent, and Tláloc, the god of rain. They extracted tribute — metals, agricultural produce and other goods — and enslaved some humans for human sacrifices.

These early Mexican civilizations were, linguistically, scientifically and mathematically, more advanced than those of the Europeans who destroyed them. Their libraries were among the world's greatest, and their social and cultural organization highly effective. But, in the name of Christ and greed, the Spanish destroyed it all because the Mexicans worshipped pagan gods and held control over rich natural resources.

THE DOMAIN OF SPAIN

At the peak of the Aztec empire, Columbus reached the Americas, and the Spanish began their westward expansion which brought the adventurous, aggressive, and unprincipled young Hernán Cortés to seek his fortune in Cuba. Cortés is one of the more controversial figures in the history of the conquest of the Americas. While the treasures he found in Mexico are displayed proudly in Europe, esteem for him is so low in Mexico that there are no statues erected in his memory and few streets named in his honor.

Mexico's history might have been different had Cortés been less of a womanizer. At age 16, this young man of lower Spanish nobility gave up his studies at the University of Salamanca, one of Europe's finest seats of learning, to seek a more active life. In February 1502, he was to set sail for Haiti, but one last visit to his Spanish sweetheart was in order. Alas, he missed both boat and belle as he fell from a roof attempting to reach her window, and was still recuperating from his injuries when the ship left port. Two years later he set sail for Cuba.

Caught up in political jealousies in Cuba, the headstrong Cortés sailed for Mexico in February 1511 with, it is reputed, 11 ships, 550 soldiers, 109 seamen, 16 horses, 10 brass guns and four falconets, to claim Mexico's riches for King Charles and to tell the Indians about the Lord of the Christians. Although he destroyed the temples and idols of the indigenous peoples, he nonetheless played on their religious beliefs for his success. Horses, unknown in Mexico, were revered as gods and thus carried the conquistador unscathed through his first encounters on Mexican soil.

Cortés had little trouble convincing many of the coastal tribes to side with him against the Aztecs, to whom they paid tribute, particularly after he enlisted the aid of a shipwrecked Spaniard who had learned the native language, and of an Indian maiden, Malinche, who spoke several dialects. Malinche became Cortés' constant companion, and fathered his children. Like Cortés, Malinche is intensely hated still today by many Mexicans.

Along the route inland to Tenochtitlán, Cortés' entourage, which included warriors from the coastal tribes, committed one of the more bloody atrocities in the colonization of the New World — the Cholula massacre, in which 6,000 people were slaughtered in a single afternoon.

Days later, Cortés marched unchallenged into the Aztec capital. It is difficult to understand why the Aztec ruler, Montezuma, adopted a pacifist attitude in his dealings with Cortés. He could have easily brought a superior force against the small Spanish expedition and dealt with it swiftly and finally before the Spaniards allied themselves with other tribes. Perhaps he had decided the Spanish could be bought off with riches, but these only further tantalized the Spanish greed. As well, the legends of the Plumed Serpent Quetzalcoatl's return from the east may have impaired Montezuma's judgment.

Cortés entered Tenochtitlán more or less as visiting royalty. And, ignoring the old adage, "Never bite the hand that feeds you," he imprisoned Montezuma. A fifth of Montezuma's treasures, some 600,000 pesos of gold, along with 100,000 ducats of gold tribute from other tribes, was sent to Spain's King Charles, while Cortés stood guard over the remainder.

When Governor Velásquez of Cuba sent an expedition to recall Cortés, he left the capital city to confront them. The encounter between the two opposing Spanish camps was little more than a skirmish. Cortés managed to lure most of the 1,200 new men to his camp with promises of fabulous wealth and the commander returned empty-handed to Cuba.

With Cortés absent, the Aztecs prepared for the annual feast to honor their gods. The Spaniards attacked the Aztecs to prevent the ceremonies, killing over 4,000. The entire population of the city retaliated; the Spaniards retreated to the Aztec palace where they still held Montezuma prisoner. Fortuitously, Cortés returned in time to assist his forces. Fierce fighting continued for about a week, during which time Montezuma was killed. The Aztec monarch was sent to the roof of the

Taxco's Spanish heritage is evident in its narrow, cobbled streets.

The Country and Its People

palace to plead for peace. He was struck on the head by a stone hurled from the crowd and died three days later.

On the night of June 30, 1520, Cortés planned a secret retreat which resulted in a bloody ambush after a native woman sounded the alarm. The Mexicans call this *La Noche Triste*, in which thousands of Indians and over half of Cortés' soldiers lost their lives. With more than 400 men left, Cortés is rumored to have reasoned that God had spared the lives of as many soldiers as he had brought to Mexico; what further proof was necessary to show that it was the will of God that he return to Tenochtitlán?

He did return about a year later and succeeded in taking the city from Montezuma's successor, Cuauhtémoc, in a battle that lasted the better part of four months and ended with the utter destruction of the magnificent capital city.

Cuauhtémoc remained a captive for four years and is said to have nonetheless rallied forces to oppose the Spaniards. At least this was the version which Cortés used to justify the execution of Cuauhtémoc.

After the conquest of the Aztecs, Cortés was named governor general of a new colonial authority, and directed and participated in expeditions throughout southern Mexico, Honduras, Guatemala, and Belize, collecting riches at every opportunity.

Rumors of other cities like Tenochtitlán kept Spanish adventurers such as Ponce de León, Marcos de Niza, Cabeza de Vaca, and Francisco Vásquez de Coronado busy exploring and pillaging Mexico and the southern United States for several more decades. Meanwhile Spanish administrators set in place the colonial institutions which would serve as Mexico's government for the next 300 years.

The Council of the Indies, founded in 1522, was the supreme legislative and administrative power for Mexico and all other Spanish colonies, while the House of Trade controlled matters of commerce, navigation, and immigration. Both were answerable only to the monarch of Spain, whose representative in Mexico was the Viceroy. An *audencia* was established as high court and administrative body of the home government. Below this upper tier was a carefully divided and defined distribution of authority in cities, towns, villages, and Indian settlements all, of course, administered by Spaniards.

There also was the equally rigidly defined Church system which had to answer to the viceroy in all matters except those of dogma and doctrine. The nuns and priests, however, answered only to clerical courts for any misdeeds, be they corporal or spiritual.

In 1542 King Charles I put into effect the New Laws, which forbade *encomiendas* (trusteeships whereby a Spaniard could collect tribute from the Indians and enslave them in exchange for protection and instruction in the Catholic faith). The colonial government and the Church adopted their own loose and self-serving interpretations of these laws. In their opinion, Charles was taking humanitarianism too far.

Control of the land soon passed into the hands of a very few Spaniards born in Spain. Under them in the social strata were the *criollos* or creoles, Spaniards born in Mexico, who had prestige and land only if they remained true to crown and culture. Far below were the mestizos, persons of mixed Spanish and Indian blood. A mestizo might be a shopkeeper, ranch hand, soldier, mine foreman, or priest. At the very bottom remained the Indian, with little or no opportunity for education or freedom.

Mexico was directed by the two-edged Spanish sword. One edge was sharpened by economic greed for silver, gold, copper, and land, and the other by the Christian zeal for more souls for Christ. In the end the coffers of Spain and the Church were greatly enriched while the Mexican Indians, through no real choice of their own, became Catholic, Spanish-speaking, and impoverished serfs on their own land. During the 300 years of Spanish colonialism, Mexico had 61 viceroys who lavishly bestowed the bounties of the country on favored Spaniards. By the nineteenth century, two-thirds of all the silver in the world came from Mexico, where it was mined by Indian slave labor. The land was split about evenly between the Catholic Church and Spanish ownership. The population was approximately six million; three and a half million Indians, two and a half million criollos and mestizos, and 40,000 native-born Spaniards.

The colony was economically and intellectually dependent on Spain. Trade was forbidden with any nation except other Spanish colonies, and no goods which could be considered in direct competition with the mother country could be produced. Literature, which was almost entirely imported, was censored. Nonetheless the liberal ideas of Rousseau, Montesquieu, and Danton found their way into the colony, where at the beginning of the nineteenth century they gave rise to an independence movement among the criollos.

ENLIGHTENMENT AND INDEPENDENCE

Napoleon's invasion of Spain only fueled the fires of independence in Mexico. No one in the colony wanted to recognize Napoleon's brother, Joseph, as regent of Spain; thus ties between the two countries began to fray. When the Spanish monarchy

Morelia's cathedral is a stunning example of Mexico's seventeenth-century baroque architecture.

was restored two years later, loyalists were unable to regain complete control.

On September 16, 1810, Father Miguel Hidalgo y Costilla and several thousand Mexicans raised the battle cry of independence, the *Grito de Dolores*. The *grito* had been several years in the making in the state of Querétaro, where a "literary" society had been meeting to discuss the ideas of the French enlightenment. It was here that Hidalgo and Army Captains Ignacio Allende and Juan Aldama laid the plans for a *grito*, intended to begin in December 1810. But their plans were leaked to Querétaro's governor. When he issued orders for the arrest of all conspirators, his wife Josefa, who was sympathetic to the movement, warned Allende and Aldama, who made a frantic midnight ride to warn Hidalgo. Rather than see the movement shattered, Hidalgo called for immediate action. The *grito* began.

After taking control of the town of Dolores and imprisoning all Spanish sympathizers, Hidalgo and his makeshift army moved on to the rich mining town of Guanajuato, near the present-day San Miguel de Allende. For six months the revolution continued. Hidalgo's forces, which now numbered more than 80,000, took Guadalajara, Morelia, and Toluca. When the Spanish were finally able to organize a proper military effort, it took only 7,000 men to turn back the loosely formed ranks of the revolutionary forces before they reached Mexico City.

Before they could seek American aid, the three revolutionary leaders Allende, Aldama, and Hidalgo were captured. Allende and Aldama were executed on June 26, 1811 and Hidalgo a month and two days later because he had to be tried by the ecclesiastical court.

Although its leaders were dead, the independence movement was far from over. Others rose to take control. José Morelos y Pavon, a mestizo priest, led a movement for agrarian reform and national identity. He decreed that inhabitants of Mexico should no longer consider themselves mestizos, Indian, or anything other than Americans. He wrote the Constitution of Apatzingán, all copies of which the Viceroy ordered destroyed. On December 22, 1815, Morelos was shot by a firing squad.

Late in 1820, *criollo* Brigadier General Agustín de Iturbide marched out of Mexico City with troops to quell the revolution, but instead became the revolution himself. The Viceroy had sent Iturbide to subdue the rebel forces of Vicente Guerrero. However, instead of fighting, Iturbide and Guerrero joined forces and on February 24, 1821 jointly issued the Plan of Iguala. It was both a declaration of independence and a political plan for the new nation. Mexico would be a constitutional monarchy where Roman Catholicism would be the only recognized religion and where all

citizens had equal rights. With little opposition, Iturbide and Guerrero took Mexico City on September 27, 1821 and declared to the world that Mexico was free. Nine months later, Iturbide was declared emperor and, on May 22, 1822, was crowned Agustín I by the Bishop of Guadalajara.

The problems of the First Empire were immense. Departure of the colonial government had left no administrative structure on which to build. The treasury was empty. To pay the troops Iturbide printed money, which caused runaway inflation. Overwhelmed by it all, Iturbide took ultimate power, abolished the legislature, and imprisoned and executed many who disagreed.

Guerrero turned against his former ally and joined forces with a young ambitious *criollo* officer, Antonio López de Santa Anna, who was to play a major role in the shaping of Mexico as we know it today. With much of the army turning against him, Iturbide abdicated on February 19, 1823 and left Mexico for exile in Italy. When rumors reached him that Spain was going to attempt to reconquer the colony, Iturbide felt compelled to return, only to be imprisoned and shot as a traitor on July 19, 1824. History has nonetheless forgiven him his faults, and he lies buried in the Catedral in Mexico City and is honored as the "Author of Mexican Independence." Besieged with troubles on the continent, Spain left its former colony alone, except for one halfhearted invasion attempt in 1829.

With the fall of the First Empire, a military triumvirate was established to rule until a new constitution could be formed. On October 4, 1824, the Federal Constitution of the United Mexican States was adopted. Patterned on the United States Constitution, the Mexican proclamation split governmental powers into legislative, judicial, and executive branches. A 20% tax was imposed on all goods, and the country was divided into 13 states.

One of the members of the interim military triumvirate, Guadalupe Victoria, was elected president and another, Nicolás Bravo, became vice president. During the four years of Victoria's term little changed in Mexico, which then included all of present day Mexico and much of Texas, Arizona, New Mexico and California. Poverty remained, the treasury was empty, and power and land was still the property of a select few and the Church. It took most of the remainder of the century to build a workable government in Mexico.

The five ensuing decades saw a drastic seizure of Mexican land by the United States, as well as innumerable coups and executions, rigged elections, and foreign rule. Guerrero, like Iturbide, met a firing squad after serving a brief term as president. The only constant during this period was the conflict between conservatives and liberals. The former wanted a strong central government and were allied with the Catholic Church and most of the wealthy landowners. The latter favored a federal government like that of France and the United States. Power shifted back and forth numerous times. Throughout this period one memorable figure stands out, Antonio López de Santa Anna, who was in and out of the presidency eleven times, and in total held the position for 30 years.

THE MEXICAN-AMERICAN WAR

During the early years of independence, the government actively sought settlers for the remote areas of the territory, including the present southwest United States. With generous land grants available for the price of becoming a Mexican citizen and the nominal cost of $30 per league in an area where slavery was still legal, many Anglo-Americans moved in and were soon at odds with the Mexicans. This situation quickly set the stage for, as the settlers called it, the Texas War for Independence, or what has come to be known as the Mexican-American War.

The war brought Santa Anna from the Valley of Mexico; he won a lopsided victory at the Alamo, but was taken captive at San Jacinto. In exchange for his life and free passage on a United States warship to Mexico, Santa Anna signed a treaty with the Texans giving them independence.

As might be expected, the rest of the government refused to recognize the treaty; Santa Anna lost power and retired temporarily to his hacienda. Separatist movements sprang up in other parts of the country but were not long-lived.

Capitalizing on Mexican turmoil, the United States moved to claim New Mexico, Arizona, and California as part of the Texas territory that Santa Anna had ceded. In retaliation, the various factions in Mexico united in a decision to protect these borders. The United States forces soon dominated, but the tenacious Mexicans refused to negotiate a treaty. To solve the issue once and for all, American troops were sent to capture Mexico City.

The Americans landed at Veracruz where, during a short but bloody battle, they killed twice as many women and children as soldiers. They proceeded toward Mexico City. The last battle of the war was fought at Chapultepec Castle where 2,000 Mexicans and 700 Americans died before a further thousand Mexican cadets and soldiers at the castle's military college fought to the last man rather than surrender. This was September 13, 1847; on this day each year these *Niños Héroes* (Young Heroes) are honored.

A treaty was signed, and Mexico received $18 million for the stolen territories, less than half its annual budget. With its land mass cut nearly by half, Mexico spent several more years in political turmoil before Benito Juárez, a Zapotec Indian from a Oaxacan village, was elected president.

REFORM: BUT NO END TO STRIFE

The period of Mexican history from 1855 to 1861 is often termed the Reform Period, during which Juárez moved to redefine the role of the Catholic Church in Mexican politics. The Mexicans had successfully rid their country of the Spanish, but found the Church almost as stifling an influence. It owned approximately half of the land and had an income greater than the government. Yet it had refused to participate in lending funds for the Mexican-American War.

Under Juárez, a new constitution was instituted guaranteeing freedom of education (the Church ran all schools) and freedom of speech (the Church controlled most of the printing presses). Laws were enacted to make a clear separation between Church and state. One law required the Church to sell all its land not in cultivation or in use. Another required civil servants to take an oath of loyalty to the new constitution. The Church retaliated by threatening the excommunication of anyone purchasing its lands or taking the new oath. Its response was a bit tamer than the Spanish Inquisition, but nonetheless drastic when one remembers the hold the Church held on the minds of relatively uneducated and isolated Mexicans. Those who were educated had received their schooling from the Church, and a substantial portion of the population earned its living working for the Church.

The country was again split into conservative and liberal factions. For three years Mexico sank into a civil war, with the liberals, led by Benito Juárez, finally victorious in 1861. Church properties were nationalized, civil marriages and burials were allowed, and the government set standard fees for church services, such as baptisms and marriages.

THE FRENCH CONNECTION

While liberals and conservatives fought at home, arch-conservatives, led by Gutiérrez de Estrada, lobbied abroad for a European monarch to take control of the nation. Not wishing to find themselves in conflict with the United States, European nations adopted a hands-off policy until 1861, when the United States was occupied with its own Civil War. Using the pretext that they were collecting defaulted debts, France, Spain and England sent troops to Mexico in January 1862. It appears that Spain and England had clear intentions, but the French emperor Napoleon III had grander designs.

Some say he was unduly influenced by his Spanish-born wife, Eugénie, and her arch-conservative Mexican friends; others claim he was just greedy; and still another school of thought suggests he wanted to weaken the Austrian House of Hapsburgs by luring the young Archduke Ferdinand Maximilian Joseph away from Europe. In any event, the idealist Maximilian and his Belgian wife, Charlotte, were sent to Mexico with false assurances that Mexicans were in favor of having a monarch. They arrived in Veracruz on May 28, 1864, to find the French army in pursuit of the retreating Mexicans. On June 12, Maximilian became the Emperor of Mexico. Napoleon, Mexican arch-conservatives, and the Church were all unaware of Maximilian's surprisingly liberal views. He endorsed the Juárez Laws of Reform, the nationalization of church properties and the establishment of a civil registry. But he was ill-equipped as an administrator and unaware of Mexican politics. His reign was a disaster.

At the end of its Civil War, the United States began pouring arms into Mexico and Napoleon immediately recalled his troops to France, deserting Maximilian, who now faced armed opposition from Juárez. Charlotte sailed for Europe in the hope of convincing Napoleon to change his orders. When this failed, she appealed to the Vatican, but her pleas fell on deaf ears. In despair and desperation, her mind gave way and she lived out the 61 remaining years of her life in a convent in Belgium without regaining her sanity.

Proud, headstrong and without a Hapsburg title (he had renounced it to become Emperor of Mexico), Maximilian stayed in Mexico and was captured on May 15, 1867. He was executed on the Cerro de las Campanas (Hill of the Bells), near the city of Querétaro, on June 19. "Maximilian of Hapsburg only knew the geography of our country; [the monarchy was] the crime of Maximilian against Mexico," wrote Juárez, who assumed control of the country after the execution.

Striving to develop the nation's economy, Juárez fought to reduce the debt, create jobs and establish an infrastructure. Unfortunately he had little success. He could get no credit in the international markets and never succeeded in absorbing the thousands of uprooted soldiers back into society. By the time of his death in 1872, the country was again threatened by civil war.

"DÍAZ-POTISM"

Sebastián Lerdo de Tejada followed Juárez as president and continued Juárez's policies, much to the dismay of Tejada's former political ally, General Porfírio Díaz. Like Juárez, Díaz was from Oaxaca, but was a military man rather than an intellectual. With backing from the United States, Díaz took control of the presidency in 1877 and remained as dictator until 1911.

Cinco de Mayo Parade, Puebla.

Neither he nor his collaborators had much political experience; but following their motto "little politics, all administration," they put their country on such a sound basis that it enjoyed its first period of international respectability. They invited foreign investment on easy terms and built a new landed aristocracy. Díaz came to an agreement with the Church not to enforce the anticlerical laws; his strong army and rural police discouraged dissidence; and the Indians became poorer.

Díaz ruled as dictator for 34 years, and probably would have remained longer if he had not given in to the request for free elections, proposed by his Vice President, Francisco Madero, who wanted to run for president. Exhibiting a rare moment of insecurity, during the elections Díaz jailed Madero who, on his release, decided to launch an armed rebellion. Within six months the government of Díaz had collapsed and Madero assumed the presidency. Thus began ten years of civil war known as the Revolution, called "an explosion of reality" by Octavio Paz.

REVOLUTION

A rich idealist, Madero believed that all people have an inherent capacity for democratic life, and before consolidating power he granted freedom of the press and encouraged workers to form unions. When opposing factions realized that Madero had no organization to implement his policies, rebellions broke out. In the south, Emiliano Zapata organized an army of Indians and poor mestizos to protest their landless condition; in the north, the United States was anxious to maintain the economic privileges that it had obtained from Díaz. Madero was assassinated, some claim by an officer in the pay of the United States, and Victoriano Huerta became president. Huerta was a bloodthirsty drunkard; his government was repressive and ineffectual.

Soon after taking office in the United States, President Woodrow Wilson recalled the United States ambassador and instituted an arms embargo against Mexico, but revolutionary leaders were organized. In the south, Zapata and his men continued their raids on the haciendas of the rich, while in the north Venustiano Carranza, Alvaro Obregón, and Pancho Villa plotted to overthrow the Huerta government.

Huerta relinquished power in 1914 and was followed by Carranza who was a shrewd politician. In 1917, a new Constitution which included social rights that never existed before, the confiscation of foreign-owned and Church property, and no reelection of public officials, was drawn up and is still in effect today. By the end of Carranza's term, power had gotten the best of him; prohibited by his own Constitution to run for reelection, he conceived the idea of a puppet government.

The Country and Its People

He failed and in 1920 fled Mexico City with the coffers of the treasury; he was assassinated before he could leave the country.

The Revolution was costly; one out of every eight Mexicans was killed — between one and a half and two million people in all. Alvaro Obregón followed Carranza and brought Mexico into a period of stability. The Constitution of 1917 was put into practice. Labor leaders were incorporated into the state apparatus, and land reform was put into effect. Church properties were seized and priests and nuns who remained in the country had to go underground. Obregón selected Calles as his successor; Calles continued Obregón's policies, suggested that Obregón return to power, and modified the Constitution to allow it. Obregón was reelected in 1928, but was assassinated a few weeks later by a religious fanatic who has since been canonized by the Catholic Church. The country remained under the control of Calles through a series of puppet presidents.

MODERN MEXICO

In 1934, Calles chose Lázaro Cárdenas to succeed to the presidency; the astute Cárdenas quickly freed himself from Calles' domination. He sided with the popular movements pushing for agrarian reform and established an impressive number of public works projects. Much to American and British dismay, he expropriated all the foreign-owned oil fields. The retaliatory embargoes on Mexican oil were lifted five years later when the Allies needed fuel.

Cárdenas established a single official party, the PRI (Partido Revolucionario Institucional) that, until the late 1980s, remained the mechanism for selecting candidates for public office. Political power was institutionalized to such an extent that it thereafter hardly mattered who exercised it. Under the pretext of a call for nationalism brought on by World War II, social demands were silenced, agrarian reform and labor movements lost strength, and foreign capital flowed into the country and became increasingly powerful.

In 1946 Miguel Alemán Valdés was elected president. He consolidated the activities of the previous regime, and has been termed by historians the architect of modern Mexico. For the average Mexican, however, he did little. He felt that wealth has to be created before it can be redistributed, and he inaugurated a period of vast economic expansion. Foreign investments were indiscriminately sought and accepted; agrarian reform ground to a halt, and corruption was

ABOVE: Palms, an abundance of lounge chairs and an ocean view are essential at all coastal resorts.
BELOW: The Centro Cultural Tijuana hosts a fascinating array of cross-border art shows and performances.

rampant. Once again wealth was concentrated in the hands of a few, but now the "few" were the politicians and their cronies. Many a Mexican claims that the few numbered, then as now, no more than 150 families.

Alemán's successor, Adolfo Ruíz Cortines, gave women the vote and tried to eliminate graft and harness uncontrolled growth by devaluating the peso, but little changed. Alfonso López Mateos, the next president, distributed land to the peasants, expanded the social security system and built more schools. After Cuba's revolution, he refused to break ties with the new government; as a result, foreign companies and banks withdrew their capital from Mexico.

Through the middle of the twentieth century, Mexico's presidential and local elections were carried out peacefully with no breakdown in public order, and Mexico's economy grew at a rate of six percent, higher than in most Latin American countries. This political stability and rapid economic growth were cited as models for other developing countries, and Mexico was chosen as the site of the 1968 Olympic Games.

However, the wealth within the country was still very unevenly distributed. Ten percent of the population received almost half of the national income. On the eve of the Olympic Games, protests erupted and were suppressed by force ordered by then-president Díaz Ordáz. Three hundred people were killed, thousands arrested, and press coverage was censored.

Luis Echeverría Alvarez became Mexico's next president in 1970 and immediately freed these political prisoners and adopted what foreign investors and national capitalists considered leftist rhetoric. He began a program of land redistribution, encouraged tourism, brandished Mexico's economic independence from the United States and took up the causes of the Third World. This precipitated a large-scale flight of capital from the country and he had to borrow heavily from abroad to finance his public-works projects. Just before leaving office he devalued the Mexican peso, and successive presidents have not yet been able to recover its stability.

Although growing oil production in the late 1970s brought a small economic boom, the peso continued to have problems during the presidency of López Portillo. It was devalued twice in less than three years and fluctuated regularly, even though Portillo was quick to cut inflation. But he also ran afoul of foreign investors by supporting Cuba, Sandinista Nicaragua and other freedom movements in Latin America. Capital flight intensified and corruption spread. The complex of lavish homes that Portillo built for himself and his family on a hill in the outskirts of Mexico City was nicknamed the Colina del Perro (Dog's Hill).

In 1982, Miguel de la Madrid inherited a nightmare. Mexico had staggering national and foreign debts, annual inflation of over 100% and a peso that had been devalued almost 500% within a single year. A technocrat with a degree in public administration from Harvard, he approached the task with determination and confidence. He slashed government spending while raising the price of government-supplied services, began a trade liberalization policy, joined the GATT (General Agreement on Trade and Tariffs), renegotiated the foreign debt, instituted a Solidarity Pact to try to control inflation, and engineered an export-oriented economic strategy. Still, purchasing power declined over 50% during his administration and there was rampant unemployment.

In the wake of the earthquake that struck the country on September 19, 1985, the population began to organize massive rescue and relief efforts out of which came citizen's groups that offered a united voice to Mexico's people. As never before, people began to recognize and actively support the possibility of peaceful change through elections. Opposition political parties were formed.

To no one's surprise, Carlos Salinas de Gortari, the government's candidate, won the next presidential election in 1988, but by barely 50%. The opposition parties won an important number of seats in the House of Representatives as well as four seats in the Senate.

Salinas promised to reach out to some of Mexico's more impoverished people, and formed a "Pact of Economic Stability and Economic Growth." The main elements of the plan included a program of deregulation and the negotiation of a new foreign debt arrangement. He courted the national and international business communities, promising more opportunities to both and making tremendous efforts to promote Mexico internationally. His government nearly stabilized inflation by 1991, strengthened ties with international investors, and loosened regulations for foreign purchase of Mexican land and other assets. In 1993, the United States, Canada and Mexico signed the North American Free Trade Agreement (NAFTA). Salinas pledged Mexico would be a First-World country by the year 2000.

THE FATEFUL NINETIES

Carlos Salinas de Gortari was considered by many to be Mexico's savior, a brilliant economist and technocrat on par with other world leaders. But the end of his term saw the beginning of intense civil unrest in the country. On January 1, 1994, the Zapatista Army for National Liberation attacked the colonial city of San Cristóbal de las Casas in Chiapas. Leading villagers armed with no more than mock wooden rifles, Comandante Marcos, a mysterious character in a stocking cap and mask, exposed the miserable plight of the rural Indians in that southern state. His act inspired other rebel groups throughout the country and threatened the long-standing power of the PRI. Opposition parties began to gain strength in several states including Guerrero, Michoacán and Baja California, which elected the first opposition party governor in the country. In autumn 1994, Salinas' chosen successor for the presidency, Luis Donald Colosio, was assassinated during a political rally in Tijuana; further assassinations of PRI dignitaries, religious leaders, judges and politicians soon followed. Ernesto Zedillo Ponce de León, the subsequent PRI presidential candidate, won the election by a small majority. Shortly after he took office in 1995, the peso plunged to half its value and the country was thrust into financial chaos.

MEXICO TODAY

As the twenty-first century approaches, Mexico is withstanding an intense period of internal strife. Poverty, violent crime and political unrest are on the rise, and ex-President Salinas has become a national pariah. Living in self-imposed exile in Ireland, Salinas has become the butt of jokes, ridicule and scorn in the country that not so long ago treated him as a hero. The PRI, which held the country so firmly in its control since the 1930s, is suspect on all levels. Mexicans suffering under the effects of a deflated economy are no longer willing to let "dinosaur" politicians and wealthy families rape the country and its people for their own benefit. In 1997, Mexico's congressional elections resulted in an elected majority of opposition party members; by early 1998, conflicts between the PRI and other parties were nearing crisis proportions. Mexico's next presidential elections will be held in 1999 and observers predict the country will soon have its first non-PRI president in 70 years.

Mexico's economy is said to be improving, though the trickle-down effect to the lower classes has slowed to an occasional drip. Crime, on the other hand, is increasing to levels unheard of since the 1910 Revolution. Drug lords have taken control of vast areas along the border, where they terrorize the local population, corrupt public officials and kill those who stand in their way. Everyday crimes such as robbery, theft and assault have reached epidemic proportions in Mexico City, where just taking a taxi can be a life-threatening proposition (see SAFETY AND SECURITY, page 364). Those on the outside who love Mexico are shaken by current events and fear for the country's future. Those within are becoming ever more enraged with their social conditions. The next decade is bound to bring unprecedented changes to the country ex-President Salinas swore was on the path to prosperity and stability.

The Country and Its People

THE PEOPLE

More than 52 indigenous groups still live within Mexico, but the majority of the people now called Mexicans are descendants of Indian and European ancestors. Although there has been much intermingling of blood, there are still distinct regional differences and many Mexicans proudly retain their non-Spanish languages and traditions.

When traveling through the country the cultural differences are evident. The Maya are the predominant inhabitants in the Yucatán Peninsula, despite the influx of people from throughout the country who work in the tourism industry. In both

Oaxaca and Chiapas there are numerous Indian groups living in rural villages and visiting the cities to buy and sell their wares. The twentieth century has left barely visible marks in the mountains of the Northern Central Highlands and the far southern border with Guatemala; in both areas indigenous groups have survived extraordinary indignities and extreme poverty. Today, their existence is threatened by environmental and political concerns, but urban Mexicans have begun to realize the cultural worth of their ancestors.

Until the 1940s, Mexicans were primarily rural dwellers. A shift toward industrialization since World War II has rudely overturned this tradition. In 1944, 35% of the population lived in urban areas; by 1980 this figure had grown to more than 60%. Such in-migration to the cities has been coupled

A Lancandón Indian canoe across Lake Hana.

with a veritable population explosion during the second half of the twentieth century. Although family planning programs helped to diminish the annual growth rate from three to 2.4% between 1976 and 1982, the 1990 population was estimated to be 90 million, with nearly 20 million people living in the greater Mexico City area alone.

Most visitors to Mexico are struck by the crowded conditions in the cities and the enormous disparity between rich and poor. The wealthiest five percent of Mexicans live on a scale comparable to European royalty, sporting several homes, domestic staffs, bodyguards, swimming pools, numerous cars and horses. Together with the upper-middle class professionals, high-level corporate executives, business owners, and politicians (all of whom make up 10% of the population), they control over 70% of the country's wealth.

Middle and lower-middle class bureaucrats, office employees, teachers, shopkeepers and skilled technicians can usually afford decent housing (by Mexican standards), food, a car and possibly even private schools for their children. But they live well below their European or American counterparts. The peso devaluation of 1995 exacerbated this situation; those who had learned to put all their faith in credit cards and bank loans found their interest payments doubling and their loans revoked during the worst financial crisis since the 1970s. Though Mexico's economy was reported to be on an upswing in the late 1990s, little was certain and many Mexicans were living hand to mouth.

Some of the poor, particularly those in Mexico City and along the border with the United States, live in conditions so appalling that words could never prepare the visitor for the shock. The rural poor have a lifestyle little different from their ancestors except for the frequent presence of electricity and television in their adobe, stucco, cement block, or thatch houses. While nearly all houses, huts, shanties and shacks are equipped with television antennae, they often lack running water and bathrooms. It has been suggested that the television set with its ever-visible antenna and more modern satellite dish is a status symbol among the poor, just as the wringer washing machine on the front porch was for the American poor in the Appalachian Mountains 60 years ago. I have visited the rural homes of artisans whose work sells for thousands of dollars in foreign galleries; often the most obvious manifestations of their new-found wealth are additional television sets and giant refrigerators.

Many Mexicans with strong regional ties prefer their village lifestyle, with its abundance of extended family members, built-in support systems and relative simplicity.

The people of Mexico are hardly backward, however. Those with even minimal education are

typically bilingual and speak either an Indian dialect and Spanish, or Spanish and English. The federal government provides free schools, and the first six years of elementary school are mandatory. In villages, towns, and tiny settlements children assemble for school in matching impeccably clean uniforms, a sign of modest prosperity and abundant pride.

The people of Mexico, ever aware of their ancestry and history, fiercely defend their national character and independence. Ever suspicious of outside interference (and rightly so), they sustain a nearly xenophobic resistance to attempts by the United States, Japan and Korea to label Mexicans as the cheap labor force of the twenty-first century. Many Mexicans are reluctant to see national treasures such as oil, silver, seafood and human labor exploited or appropriated by foreign countries. "Solitude — the feeling and knowledge that one is alone, alienated from the world — is not an ex-

clusively Mexican characteristic," writes the late Octavio Paz. But it lives within all Mexicans, who appear to feel alone in the world, subjugated and scorned, conquered and subdued.

Yet Mexicans have long embraced all things foreign and new. European and Asian furnishings were considered necessities in the nineteenth-century; plastics, electronics and international trademarks are the rage of the late twentieth century. Most Mexicans take great pleasure in encountering foreigners and will try to initiate conversations with innocent questions. Children who notice your wristwatch may ask for the time; adults want to know where you've come from. Travelers who attempt to speak Spanish, however awkwardly, are usually rewarded with effusive praise for their linguistic skills and gentle nudges toward correct pronunciation and vocabulary. I shudder to think how many times I've slaughtered the Spanish language in animated conversations with

cab drivers or waiters, yet I've never been mocked (at least not openly). Mexicans working in the tourist industry are eager to learn phrases in English, Italian, German and French, and will trade language tips with all travelers interested in sharing their skills. When off the tourist circuits, travelers who speak Spanish may find themselves helping locals with English, French, German, or Italian phrases they might need for the next non-Spanish speaking guest.

Mexico's social history has been recorded by the country's many great muralists. Diego Rivera painted *La Gran Tenochtitlán,* which graces Mexico's City's Palacio Nacional.

Mexico City

IMMENSE, SWARMING, CHOKING, FRENETIC, dense, colorful, violent, miserable, unbreathable, dangerous, exciting — these words touch on the quite extraordinary nature and contradictions of the world's most populated city.

Your own response to Mexico City will depend on what you want from it and on how you feel about cities. There is no city in the world like this one. Frequent comparisons with Cairo, Calcutta, or Río de Janiero do not even come close. No one even knows how many people it holds: current estimates have more than 23 million living in the metropolitan center and millions more in the surrounding suburbs and slums. Some 3,000 Mexicans from the rest of the country flock to this city every day, all in search of work that probably does not exist, in search of shelter that will probably be less than they had at home, to live in unbelievable poverty and hopelessness in slums in this unimaginably polluted, occasionally beautiful, and always fascinating city.

To this incredible capital-bound migration must be added the city's birthrate of nearly one million children per year. In this still-Catholic country, birth control, particularly among the poor, is often the exception rather than the rule. Estimates indicate that Mexico City's population, already more than a quarter of the nation's, may exceed 35 million by the year 2000, despite the exodus of the city's middle classes to less teeming, more livable suburbs and provinces.

Mexico City is situated in a wide, 7,800-sq-km (3,000-sq-mile) rolling valley more than 2,200 m (7,200 ft) above sea level, surrounded by mountains. Two of North America's highest peaks, snow-capped Popocatépetl, 5,452 m (17,761 ft), and Iztaccíhuatl, 5,286 m (17,343 ft), tower over the valley's southeast rim, dividing it from the vast and growing city-suburb of Puebla. To the east rise the peaks of the Sierra Nevada, to the west those of the Sierra Las Cruces, and to the south is the Sierra Ajusco. The city is nearly entirely enclosed by mountains, responsible for its once-superb microclimate and now, unfortunately, for the world's worst air pollution. Thermal inversions, the valley's trapped air, and millions of cars on the street contribute to the appalling air quality.

It has been said that no one has experienced air pollution until they have seen and experienced Mexico City's. Often so thick as to reduce visibility to less than a kilometer (a half mile) on an otherwise clear day, this shifting, thick cloud of noxious, malodorous fumes is a result of vehicle exhaust, industrial and chemical pollution, countless burning open-air dumps casting their tons of hazardous residues into the breeze, the windstorms from the overlogged and overgrazed rural areas of the valley, and dust storms from the dry beds of Lake Texcoco to the east, carrying their tons of silt, dried sewage and trash back into the city. As a result of all this toxicity, the health effects of living in Mexico City are described as similar to that of smoking two packs of cigarettes a day. A program to cut the number of cars on the road has helped somewhat, but not enough.

The problems of transport in Mexico City are legion. The Metro, as the subway is called, is riotously jammed at peak hours and yet serves only a small fraction of city dwellers needing transport. Many workers are forced to leave home at 5:30 AM to reach work by 8 AM, only to endure a similar hegira at the end of the workday. Traffic jams are indescribable, particularly during the

rainy season, with its flooded underpasses, malfunctioning traffic lights and increased vehicle usage.

Although this sprawling megalopolis occupies only one-tenth of one percent of Mexico's land surface, it holds a quarter of its population and all of the national government and bureaucratic institutions. In the last decade's financial downturn, Mexico City's debt grew larger than that of many entire nations, and continues growing faster than tax and other revenues can rise to quench it. Sadly, there is little sign of a change in policy that will quickly improve the condition of the city and that of its residents.

Although some social scientists see in Mexico City the dreadful harbinger of the chaotic breakdown of the world's developing cities in the twenty-first century, there remain countless fascinations in this weird, enticing megalopolis and there are reasons enough, depending on your interests, to stop for a while.

With over two millennia of pre-Columbian remains and 450 years of architecture since the Spanish conquest, Mexico City is an immense treasure of ruins, remnants and differing styles. Over

OPPOSITE: A costumed dance of Sonora performed by the Ballet Folklórico. Mexico City ABOVE on a relatively smog-free day.

50 churches of the early Spanish period remain, as well as hundreds of public buildings, mansions and quiet courtyards barely changed in 400 years. There are 70 significant museums containing the world's best surviving treasures of Mexican archaeology as well as fine European art from the Renaissance to the twentieth century. The wide, tree-lined boulevards and the city's blend of Indian, European and twenty-first-century international cultures, the cafés and open air restaurants, fashions, hectic pace and warm climate (see CLIMATE, page 361) make the city truly different, even in its most positive aspects, from any other on earth.

And day or night, Mexico City is vibrant, alive. There are color, music and vitality in its commerce, flower markets and crowded parks. The streets are jammed with cars, buses and bicycle carts. There are peasants at street corners swallowing fire for small change to feed their families; beggars, sad-eyed skinny children and miserable old women; boys with rags cleaning windshields at intersections. Sidewalk vendors sell everything from candy and juice to balloons, cutlery, wicker furniture and lottery tickets.

Safely isolated from the squalor and misery of most of the city are the fancy districts of expensive restaurants with international names, the boutiques with Paris fashions, the glittery high-rise hotels, the discotheques and night clubs.

LONG AGO…

Once, long ago, Mexico City was undoubtedly one of the world's loveliest urban sites, a mosaic of pyramids, towers, temples, homes, canals and markets surrounded by a wide, sparkling lake.

"The other morning we arrived on the wide causeway of the city. We saw so many cities and towns set in the water, and other grand towns on dry ground, to which led the straight and level causeway, that we were stunned with admiration, seeing things of such enchantment, great towers and quays and buildings rising from the waters, and all of roughcast stone, such that some of the soldiers said it must be a dream. There was so much to ponder that one could not count it: to see things never seen, nor even dreamed of, as we have seen.

"We were lodged in palaces of such grandeur and fine workmanship, of finest stone, of cedar and other beautiful and fragrant wood, with grand patios and rooms and things beautiful to see, with embroidered cotton hangings. And each house was surrounded with gardens and orchards so lovely to pass through, where I could never tire of seeing the diversity of trees and fragrant bushes, each one with paths filled with roses and other flowers and many fruit trees and rose bushes, each with a freshwater pond. And another thing marvelous to see: One can enter into these orchards from the lake with huge canoes, by an opening that has been made, without getting out on land, and all of this whitewashed and gleaming, and decorated with many kinds of stones and fine paintings exceedingly well conceived, and filled with birds of many diversities and species."

This was the city of Tenochtitlán on November 8, 1519, the day when Hernán Cortés and his men first set foot in it. Named "place of the cactus fruit" (in Nahuatl) by the Aztecs, it may have been, even then, the world's largest city; with an estimated 300,000 to 500,000 inhabitants, it was three times the size of any in Europe in the Middle Ages. When the Spanish arrived, its beauty reminded them of Venice, although it was far cleaner and more orderly.

But there had been large and lovely cities here even long before the Aztecs came. The valley in the shadow of Popocatépetl was home to an earlier magnificent city, Teotihuacán. The valley's first residents lived here much earlier, but they have left few traces. At that time there appears to have been five shallow lakes filled by the rivers and streams draining the valley's surrounding mountains. The first residents may have lived on the shores of these lakes and, eventually, for greater protection, inhabited islands which they constructed in the lakes.

Between 1000 and 500 BC, an advanced civilization took over the valley, centered in Tlatilco. It expanded transportation routes and traded with the Olmecs on the Gulf Coast. It was superseded by another, even more advanced, settlement at Cuicuilco. Here, it is now known, the first stone pyramid in Mexico was built. These were followed by Teotihuacán, a city which, during its period of greatest power from 150 BC to 700 AD, had a population of 250,000, vast esplanades, temples, markets and causeways: probably the world's greatest city at that time.

Serving as a continental crossroads for commerce in obsidian, a volcanically-formed glass which was used in place of metal for arrowheads, knives, lances and other cutting implements, Teotihuacán traded as far north as New Mexico in the United States, as far south as Guatemala, and eastward with the Mayan civilization of the Yucatán. In its time it was the most advanced culture in the world in astronomy, mathematics and some technologies; its people probably spoke Nahuatl and worshipped the rain god Tláloc.

Some time after AD 700, Teotihuacán was destroyed and was followed by Tula, a Toltec city established by a Chichimeca tribe in AD 958. Like the Chichimeca Aztecs who were to follow them, the Toltecs expanded their civilization at first principally through war, but also devoted themselves to writing, medicine, mathematics, the sciences and the arts. Under their king Quetzalcoatl, whom they later deified, they banned human sacrifice; this angered the priests, and Quetzalcoatl was forced to flee to the Yucatán, where he died promising to return to Tula. In 1168 the city itself fell, 200 years after its founding.

But it was not until after 1200 that the group of Chichimecas who called themselves Mexica, later to become known as the Aztecs, even reached the valley that is now Mexico City. According to their own legends, they had originated from the Seven Caves, near a place they called Aztlán. Under the guidance of their priests and accompanied by their god, Huitzilopochtli, they appear to have wandered widely in central Mexico, perhaps moving slowly down from the north, halting at propitious places to grow crops then moving on as the soil gave out or their neighbors became aggressive. When they arrived at Lake Texcoco they were, by local standards, barbarians — an unruly, savage and untutored tribe.

At Lake Texcoco the Aztecs saw the sign long foreordained by Huitzilopochtli as indicating the place where they must finally settle: an eagle devouring a serpent while perched on a cactus growing out of a rock. It was the year 1345; the Aztecs settled on two deserted islands in the lake, began to forge alliances with local city-states, and sold their services as mercenaries to the more advanced cultures in the valley. They linked their two islands by means of *chinampas*, man-made structures of mud and dirt on a bed of reeds anchored to the lake's shallow bottom. By 1350 they had founded Tenochtitlán. In 1428, allied with the neighboring Texcocos and Tlacopans, they conquered the valley's largest city, Azcapotzalco, for which they had formerly served as mercenaries.

Basing their own warlike culture on the earlier Chichimeca Toltec civilization at Tula, the Aztecs adopted the Toltec god Quetzalcoatl, and copied the Toltecs' and other cities' methods of learning and architecture, soon advancing these far beyond their previous heights. With amazing speed they expanded their control over the trade routes of what is now Mexico and Central America, at the same time establishing military dominance over nearly all neighboring nations, and receiving enormous amounts of goods in tribute from civilizations as far away as Guatemala. Only the Tarascans (now known by their original name, the Purépecha) to the west and the Tlaxcalans to the east remained undefeated by the Aztecs; it was the Tlaxcalans who eventually became the Achilles heel which doomed the Aztec empire.

The great Aztec city of Tenochtitlán soon measured more than 13 sq km (five square miles) surrounded by a 16-km (10-mile) dike to keep the saline waters of Lake Texcoco from flooding the city's freshwater interior, with a well-planned network of canals faced with houses, gardens,

temples, markets and public squares. It received its freshwater from an aqueduct crossing saline Lake Texcoco from the mainland. In the city's center was the Sacred Precinct and huge pyramids dedicated to the gods of war and rain, Huitzilopochtli and Tláloc. Also within the Sacred Precinct were the homes of the king and nobles; the entire area was surrounded by a vast stone wall covered with carved snakes.

Like the warrior society of the Spartans in ancient Greece, the Aztecs lived by a very stringent code of behavior and relationships. Social position from the king downward was based on courage in war, a character trait difficult to feign. The king was responsible for the wealth and happiness of his subjects; each class had rigid rules regarding dress and deportment; to contravene them could bring death. Education was revered; religion was a serious matter and its ceremonies adhered to. The priests were at the top of the social pyramid but had the strictest laws governing their behavior: they were required to honor the gods in all their actions, to live in celibacy, never tell falsehoods and never scheme or seek for position above their individual station.

The Aztecs, like the Toltecs before them, also believed they were the Chosen People of the Sun and that only they, by constant human sacrifice, could keep the sun circling the earth and rising anew each morning. To provide the poor souls thus needed to mollify the sun, the Aztecs conducted incessant "Wars of the Flowers" on their neighbors; some estimates indicate that up to 20,000 lives were sacrificed solely to dedicate the Great Temple of Huitzilopochtli.

Barbarous as this may seem, it should be remembered that the Catholic culture, which conquered the Aztecs, sacrificed millions of innocent lives in a religious rite known as the Inquisition.

By the year 1502, when Montezuma II was named emperor and high priest of Huitzilopochtli, the Aztec city of Tenochtitlán with its vast temples, universities and other public buildings was the world's largest and probably most prosperous city. It was a seat of learning, science and the arts, the center of a culture that had militarily and commercially united most of what is now Mexico and Central America. It was time for new barbarians to enter on the scene.

THE THREAT FROM THE EAST

These new Catholic barbarians came from the east, the direction from which Toltec and Aztec legend had foretold that Quetzalcoatl would return. After having landed at Cozumel and followed the Gulf Coast to Veracruz, Hernán Cortés turned inland with his 550 men and 16 horses, accompanied by at least a thousand Tlaxcalan allies, his mistress-interpreter Malinche and the interpreter Geronimo

de Águilar. Fearing that Cortés might be the white, bearded god Quetzalcoatl, Montezuma sent a tribute of silver, gold, gems and embroidered cloth, in the hopes of satisfying him so that he would leave. These gifts only further convinced Cortés that the reports he had heard of Tenochtitlán's wealth were true: "Spaniards," he said, "are troubled with a disease of the heart for which gold is the only remedy."

The Spaniards were not long in attempting to remedy their "disease." After being lavishly feted for several weeks by the Aztecs, Cortés had Montezuma kidnapped and imprisoned in the Spanish quarters, along with several leading nobles. Perhaps still under the sway of the Quetzalcoatl myth, or desiring peace, Montezuma did not rebel, instead insisting he had joined Cortés of his own will and passed on to his people Cortés' orders that the kingdom's gold be gathered at Tenochtitlán.

But things came to a head when Cortés had a statue of the Virgin installed in the Great Temple to Huitzilopochtli. The nobles and priests began to warn the populace; Cortés then went to Veracruz to deal with a Spanish force sent to arrest him, leaving about half his original Spaniards in Tenochtitlán. These men slaughtered 200 unarmed nobles in the Sacred Precinct and 4,000 other Aztecs. When Cortés returned from Veracruz with 900 more Spaniards and more Tlaxcalans, he was immediately besieged. He ordered Montezuma to make the Aztecs retreat; Montezuma was then killed by a stone hurled from the crowd as he urged them not to go against Cortés, and Cortés, accompanied by his troops and allies, attempted to flee Tenochtitlán.

This was *La Noche Triste*, the "Sad Night" of June 30, 1520 when, overloaded with gold and silver, the Spaniards and Tlaxcalans retreated along the causeways in the rain and darkness. Four thousand Tlaxcalans and over half the Spaniards perished — either killed by the Aztecs, or, weighted down by their booty, drowned in the lake.

The furious Aztecs pursued the Spaniards and Tlaxcalans to the latter's territory. But in May 1521, Cortés returned to attack Tenochtitlán along the causeways and from 13 frigates which the Spaniards had built in Tlaxcala and carried overland. With a total of 900 Spaniards and 50,000 Tlaxcalans and other allies, Cortés was able to surround the city and cut it off. In two and a half months of bloody battles, he slowly wore the Aztecs down. On the verge of starvation, their numbers vastly diminished by smallpox and other European diseases, the few remaining Aztecs and their emperor Cuauhtémoc surrendered on August 13, 1521. "Broken spears and torn hair lie on the road," says a 1528 Nahuatl poem of the defeat, "Houses are roofless, their walls now stained with blood."

"THE NEW CITY OF MEXICO"

Cortés had "the city of enchantment" burned and razed, and the canals filled in with debris. "The new city of Mexico," he proclaimed, "shall be built upon the ashes of Tenochtitlán."

The battle was followed, in the words of one Padre Toribio de Benavente, by a series of seven plagues afflicting the Mexicans. The first six were diseases of European origin, the seventh was "the building of the huge city of Mexico, which in its first years took more people than in the building of the temple of Jerusalem in the time of Solomon."

These hundreds of thousands, perhaps millions, of people were immediately enslaved to construct Mexico City, using the stones of Aztec temples to build the first churches and official buildings. A mixture of Spanish Catholic architecture and Mexican Indian stonemasons and other workers soon created a new style, Spanish Colonial. Many fine sixteenth-century examples of this style can still be found in many parts of Mexico City, not a few directly atop Aztec edifices that preceded them and whose walls contributed to their construction.

Further hard times, however, awaited Mexico City. Already named the capital of New Spain, it expanded rapidly at first. In 1523 the Spanish king,

OPPOSITE: The seventeenth-century altars of Mexico City's Catedral Metropolitana are wonders of Mexican baroque art. ABOVE: A child in the Parade of Chimeras at Xochimilco.

Charles V, proclaimed it the Most Loyal, Noble and Imperial City, and gave it its municipal coat of arms. In 1535 the first major school was created, the Colegio de Santa Cruz. By 1540 the city's population had climbed to 100,000 Mexicans and over 2,000 Spaniards. The first hospital in the New World was founded and, in 1551, the first university.

But the Aztecs' superb urban engineering had been devastated by the Spaniards; the dikes which had held back Lake Texcoco's saline waters were gone and the lake frequently flooded the city. Sanitary conditions broke down; the aqueducts were damaged. In 1600, Mexico City's population was reduced to some 8,000 Mexicans and 7,000 Spaniards, many of the latter priests and monks. Overall, nearly 70% of all Mexicans had died of European diseases by 1600. Added to this came the countless tortures and slow executions of the Inquisition, initiated by the Catholic kings of Spain and Pope Sixtus IV in 1480, but which had its greatest impact on Mexico between 1574 and 1803.

In the ensuing century little that was grandiose occurred in Mexico City. Defeated, their families and tribes torn asunder by slavery and disease, the Mexicans descended into a psychology of permanent melancholy, broken only occasionally by intermittent attempts at freedom such as the uprising of 1692, which burned the viceregal palace, Cortés' former home. The 1810–1821 War of Independence caused significant damage in the city when pro-Spanish forces used it as a last redoubt. The city was again occupied by the United States Army in the Mexican-American War; major battles occurred at Chapultepec Castle and the former convent of Churubusco.

Mexico City was again occupied by foreign troops from 1863 to 1867, this time the French. During the French conquest of Mexico, the Emperor Maximilian built one of the city's finest architectural monuments, the Paseo de la Reforma, according to the style of the grand Parisian boulevards, to connect his residence at Chapultepec Castle with the downtown area. During the dictatorship of Porfírio Díaz (1877 to 1911), Lake Texcoco was drained, the Reforma was expanded to copy the Champs Elysées, and other French touches were added to parts of the city, including construction of the elegant Palacio de Bellas Artes and the installation of art nouveau gas streetlights.

The emptying of Lake Texcoco had the unfortunate effect, besides its impact on wildlife and aesthetics, of lowering the city's water table, and in no time many of the finer edifices began to tilt and sink. Although they have since been buttressed, a few maintain noticeable Pisa-like angles.

The long and savage Revolution from 1910 to 1920 resulted in the deaths of over two million

people in Mexico City alone. The Cuidadela (Citadel) was the headquarters for Emiliano Zapata and other revolutionaries battling the regime of Francisco Madero, and is now an outdoor market selling handicrafts and tourist trinkets. The Revolution had the further effect of forcing many peasants off their land; they came to Mexico City in search of an alternative, and the vast slums for which the city is now known began to grow.

The city was slowly rebuilt between the two World Wars, but the worldwide depression from 1929 to 40 had extensive secondary effects on the Mexican economy. By 1940 the city's population had reached one and a half million, but there were

few automobiles, and the air remained clear and the surrounding mountains were still sharply etched against the blue sky. World War II brought economic growth to the valley as foreign goods vanished and Mexico was forced to develop its own consumer industries; the city grew quickly as the focal point for national economic planning and development. By 1950 its population was three million and by 1960, five million.

Attracted by this economic growth and motivated by the government's poor agricultural policies in the countryside, peasants began to swarm into the city. Social conditions throughout Mexico were worsening; the endemic poverty which had been the life of the majority since the Spanish conquest grew more insupportable as the wealth of the elite classes soared; at the same time many intellectuals, labor leaders, educators and students were questioning the validity of

Mexico's authoritarian government and pressing for social change.

The 1968 Olympic Games provided the catalyst. Protesting the expenditure on the games at a time when many people were hungry and demanding changes in government, students, families and even office workers poured into the streets. After demonstrations of 150,000 and 300,000 people in late August, the government struck back. Fearing the unrest on the eve of the Olympics would taint the country's image, on October 2, 1968 the government ordered the Army to open fire on 10,000 people gathered in the Plaza de Tlatelolco. Some 200 to 300 people, including many children, were massacred; hundreds more

GENERAL INFORMATION

Mexico City is eager to accommodate travelers; information booths are located at the airport ((5) 762-6773, as well as main highway entry points. A wealth of printed material is available at the **Mexico City Tourist Information Office** ((5) 525-9380 and 533-4700 FAX (5) 525-9387 in the Zona Rosa at Amberes No. 54 at Londres; open daily 9 AM to 6 PM. **LOCATEL** ((5) 658-1111 is a 24-hour information hotline. To check flight arrivals and departures, call Benito Juárez Airport ((5) 762-4011. There is also a security line ((5) 571-3600 should you have any problems.

were arrested. Ten days later the Olympics began. Although the Olympics loom large in Mexican history books, it is difficult to find a mention of the Tlatelolco massacre.

The city continued to expand exponentially, reaching eight million inhabitants by 1970 and 15 million by 1980. Living conditions were worsened by the devastating earthquake of September 19, 1985, which killed 8,500 people, left 100,000 homeless and destroyed vast sections of the city.

Although it still functions, in many areas Mexico City's services are the exception rather than the rule; money needed for schools, water lines, electricity, roads and other urban infrastructure is siphoned off by corruption, poor planning, grandiose schemes and interest payments for the city's expanding debt. That the city survives and functions remains a miracle.

Mexico City

WHAT TO SEE AND DO

Mexico City is divided into 16 *delegaciónes*, or districts; each *delegación* is divided into several *colonias* or boroughs. There are 240 *colonias* in all. The street names of each *colonia* usually share a common theme. For example, in the Colonia Juárez, where the Zona Rosa is located, all of the streets are named after European cities: Londres, Atenas, Florencio, Hamburgo, Liverpool, Berlin, Sevila, and so on. Once you are in the part of the city you want to explore, walking is usually the best way to get around and definitely the best way to get the flavor of Mexico City.

OPPOSITE: A Diego Rivera mural decorates the Palacio Nacional. ABOVE: More modern murals, such as *Liberation* by Camerena, adorn the Palacio de Bellas Artes.

HISTORIC DOWNTOWN

The entire Historic Downtown area, some nine square kilometers (three and a half square miles), including 1,436 buildings from the sixteenth to nineteenth centuries, has been preserved as a National Historic Monument by the Mexican government, and is under constant restoration. The area is bounded by the Paseo de la Reforma and Calle Abraham Gonzáles on the west, by Calle Amfora on the east, by the Avenidas Arcos de Belén and José María Izazaga on the south, and by Bartolomé de las Casas in the north. So many extraordinary sights are included within this area that it is impossible to recount them all: There are the Palacio Nacional and its astounding Plaza de la Constitución, the Catedral, the Palacio de Bellas Artes, Parque de Alameda Central, and many fine mansions and homes of the early colonial period. This area is best explored on foot, beginning early before the crowds, smog and heat of midday close in.

The Zócalo

Constructed atop the ruins of Tenochtitlán's Great Temple, the Zócalo, or **Plaza de la Constitución** (Constitution Square), is one of the largest open squares in the world. In the past it has been used for bullfights, executions, public markets and mass meetings. Though the city has sprawled into regions far from the Zócalo, it remains the heart of this vast metropolis. Mexicans from throughout the country gather here to protest social injustices and to celebrate Independence Day on September 15 and 16. The daily raising and lowering of the flag is an impressive civic show; when I'm in the city I enjoy starting and ending the day here. Bordering the Zócalo in the south is the **Palacio del Ayuntamiento** (Old Town Hall), first built just after the conquest and extensively remodeled about 1700. It now contains offices of the Federal District of Mexico, as does the facing New Town Hall, built to match the older architecture in the 1930s. Across Avenida Pino Suárez is the **Corte Suprema de Justicia** (Supreme Court), built in 1953 in the colonial style. José Clemente Orozco's bitterly ironic mural "Injustice of Justice," covers the walls along the stairway.

The **Palacio Nacional** (National Palace) fills the entire east side of the Zócalo. The seat of the Mexican government, it was originally built of red stone by Cortés on the site of Montezuma II's New Palace. The original Bell of Independence, rung by Father Hidalgo in the village of Dolores on the night of September 15, 1810 to initiate the War of Independence, now hangs over the Palacio's main gate. In commemoration of the event, the President rings the bell every year on this date at 11 AM, and repeats the *grito*, the call to revolution.

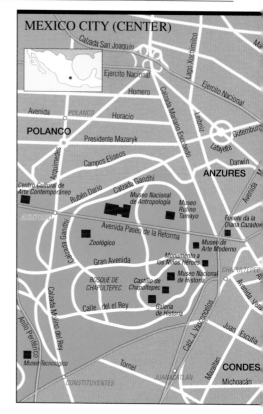

MEXICO CITY (CENTER)

The Palace was the seat of the Spanish Viceroys but was extensively damaged during the Indian uprising of 1692. Its façade stretches an impressive 200 m (650 ft) and it has 17 courtyards, only a few of which are open to visitors, including the lovely arcades of the Grand Courtyard.

In the Palacio's Grand Courtyard there is a central stairway with superb murals by Diego Rivera portraying the history of Mexico from pre-Columbian times to 1929, covering a total of 450 sq m (4,800 sq ft). The Palacio Nacional also holds a large library, the Biblioteca Miguel Lerdo de Tejada, and the state archives. An honor guard marches out from the Grand Courtyard before sundown every afternoon to lower the flag flying over the Zócalo.

The **Catedral Metropolitana** (Cathedral of Mexico City) fills the north end of the Zócalo. Sited on the ruins of the Aztec Sacred Precinct, in the area of the former temple of Xipe Totec and the Wall of Skulls, it was built of the latter's materials (stones from Montezuma's Great Temple can be seen in the Cathedral's walls). It is one of the largest and most ancient churches in the western hemisphere, 118 m (387 ft) long, 54 m (177 ft) wide, and 55 m (180 ft) high.

Construction of the first church on the site was started in 1525 by Father Toribio de Benavente

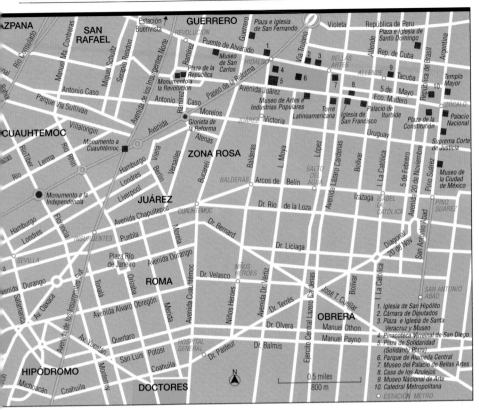

four years after the fall of Tenochtitlán. This first structure was intended by the Church and the Spanish government as provisional and was rebuilt beginning in 1563. The principal façade was completed in 1681; the cupola surmounting the Latin cross of the Catedral's floor plan was not completed until 1813. Its superb baroque façade has two nearly matching towers completed in 1793, a 5,600-kg (five-and-a-half-ton) bell and fancy stonework; the vast interior includes 15 altars, some fashioned out of magnificently ornamented marble, silver railings, gold-leaf icons and numerous, fine baroque paintings.

Most memorable within the Catedral is the extraordinary **Capilla de los Reyes** (Chapel of the Kings) and its altar, the Gothic-vaulted sacristy decorated with paintings by Cristóbal de Villapando and Juan Correa and the choir with its immense organ located in the middle of the Catedral. The overall feeling within this building is also memorable, akin to that of fine Spanish cathedrals but more somber in lighting and atmosphere.

To the right of the Catedral is the **Sagrario** (Sanctuary), completed in 1760 in churrigueresque style, and consecrated in 1768. Built in the form of a Greek cross, it is functionally separate from the cathedral, serving as a parish church, and has itself

a finely detailed baroque façade. Inside are a beautiful high altar and Capilla del Bautisterio (Chapel of the Baptistery). Poor cementation of the stonework and subsidence of the walls due to the draining of Lake Texcoco have affected the structure, which continues to sink into the dry lake bed.

Directly behind the Sagrario are the remains of the Aztecs' **Templo Mayor** or Great Temple of Tenochtitlán (small admission fee; open Tuesday through Sunday from 9 AM to 6 PM) dedicated to Huitzilopochtli and Tláloc, respectively, the gods of war and rain. Needless to say, this building was one of the most ravaged by the Spanish, and its remains were not uncovered until 1978. During excavations a huge stone disk was found that had reliefs depicting the moon goddess Coyolxauhqui who, in the history of the Aztecs, was Huitzilopochtli's sister. She had rebelled against him and had been defeated, beheaded and dismembered by him during the Aztecs' long diaspora from Aztlán.

The disk, which measures over three meters (10 ft) and weighs some 8,500 kg (8.5 tons) was installed in the **Museo de Templo Mayor** (Great Temple Museum) located behind the excavations (admission fee except on Sunday; open Tuesday through Sunday). The Museum is built following the concept of the Aztec temples themselves, with the northern galleries depicting the Temple of Tláloc and the southern galleries that of Huitzilopochtli. A large scale model of Tenochtitlán is situated on the museum's main floor, surrounded by maps and explanations of Aztec history. A separate area holds displays of the Spanish conquest, including Aztec accounts of the destruction of Tenochtitlán. English-speaking tours of the museum are available.

The site also contains remnants of at least 10 earlier pyramids over which the Great Pyramid of Tenochtitlán was built. There are major walls of two earlier temples and a sacrificial altar; buried beneath these walls archaeologists found skulls of sacrifice victims and thousands of tribute offerings sent from all parts of the Aztec empire to sanctify the construction of the Great Pyramid. The **Fuente Modelo de la Ciudad de Mexico** (Fountain Model of Ancient Mexico City) is an outdoor model of the city of Tenochtitlán; it sits in front of the Templo Mayor ruins.

Up the street from the ruins is the **Conjunto de San Ildefonso** (Saint Ildefonso Complex) ((5) 702-2843, Justo Sierra No. 16 and República de Argentina (admission fee; open Tuesday through Sunday). One of the finest museums in the city, it is housed in a former college founded in 1588 as a Jesuit school. During the 1920s, Education Minister José Vasconcelas enlisted several promising young artists to paint murals on the school's walls. Diego Rivera painted his first mural in the school's amphitheater, then continued on to cover the walls of the Ministry of Education building next door. The complex also contains murals by José Clemente Orozco, David Alfaro Siquieros and Fernando Leal, and presents traveling exhibitions of Mexican art and artifacts.

Also facing the Zócalo and to the west of the cathedral the **Monte de Piedad** is a state-run pawnshop and auction house, well worth a visit for flea market aficionados. The **Gran Hotel** on Calle 16 de Septiembre is an art nouveau building that was once Mexico's first department store. It has a stained glass domed ceiling, open ironwork elevators and a superb marble staircase.

Venturing a few blocks off the Zócalo in any direction, one can find a variety of historic buildings, monuments and churches. Just behind the Palacio Nacional is the **Antigua Casa de Moneda**, Calle Moneda No. 13, an eighteenth-century government mint that now houses the **Museo de las Culturas**, a small art museum with an international collection.

Opposite this is the baroque **Palacio del Arzobispado** (Archbishop's Palace) and three blocks farther east, on Calle Moneda, is the remarkable baroque, jewel-like **Iglesia de la Santísima** whose churrigueresque façade is said to be one of the city's finest. (The churrigueresque style was erroneously named after architect José de Churriguera and is used to describe a style that evolved in the early 1700s, characterized by an ornate and highly worked form of decoration applied to the façades and interiors of churches.) Constructed on the site of a former hermitage and then a convent, the church was designed principally by Lorenzo Rodríguez, also architect of the Sagrario, and was completed in 1677. Its foundation and walls have suffered severely from the extensive settling of the land in this area of the city. Trends in modern art scandalize or please visitors to the **Museo José Luis Cuevas** ((5) 542-8959, Calle Academia No. 13 (admission fee; open Monday, Tuesday, and Thursday through Sunday). Considered to be one of the country's best avant-garde artists, Cuevas has installed his private collection of more than 30 works by Picasso in the Sala Picasso, and holds rotating exhibitions in the gallery space.

Returning to the Palacio and going south from the Zócalo on Avenida Pino Suárez four blocks to the Avenida República del Salvador brings one to the impressive Casa de los Condes de Santiago de Calimaya, now the **Museo de la Ciudad de México** (Mexico City Museum) ((5) 542-0487 at Pino Suárez No. 30 (free admission; open Tuesday through Sunday from 9:30 AM to 5 PM). Here is a diverse display of the city's history from pre-Columbian to recent times, including models of the city in Aztec and contemporary periods.

PLAZA DE SANTO DOMINGO

Returning north and going three blocks behind the Catedral, one finds the **Iglesia de Santo Domingo** (Church of Santo Domingo) and the plaza of the same name, bounded by República de Brasil, República de Chili, República de Cuba and the República de Perú. One of the best-preserved colonial squares in Mexico, Plaza de Santo Domingo was also one of the first parts of Mexico City settled by the Spaniards after 1522. The first church of Santo Domingo was begun here in 1539 by the Dominicans and was the headquarters of an influential convent. It was later partially destroyed by floods from Lake Texcoco, of which the worst occurred in 1716. It was replaced by a new structure completed in 1736, which has a splendid façade, a tower decorated with tiles and six richly embellished chapels.

The **eighteenth-century building** at Calle República de Cuba No. 95 stands where the Tabascan woman, known as *la Malinche*, and who served as Cortés' mistress and translator, lived with her husband after the fall of Tenochtitlán. Many locals consider the site accursed because of Malinche's role in the fall of Tenochtitlán.

On the west side of the Plaza at the **Portal de los Evangelistas**, public scribes (*evangelistas*) are available to type letters and other documents for the illiterate. At nearby Calle República de Brasil and Calle República de Venezuela is the eighteenth-century **Palacio de la Inquisición**, a notorious prison and headquarters for the Catholic Inquisition in Mexico City, and now a Museum of Medicine.

Not far away, on Calle Justo Sierra between Calles República de Argentina and República de Brasil, is the **Convento de la Enseñanza Antiguo**, a baroque former-convent constructed by Francisco Guerrero y Torres in 1754. Inside is a fine small chapel known for its extraordinary *retablos* (retables or altars) in churrigueresque style, also a repository of various relics of significance including an ivory image of the Virgin of Pilar. The

on the corner of Calle Isabel la Católica and Calle de la República de Uruguay is the charming **Iglesia de la Profesa**, a church first constructed by the Jesuits in 1585 with donations received from the treasurer of the national mint (Casa de Moneda) and others. The flood of 1629 drastically damaged this structure; many of the interior's fine paintings perished in a later fire. La Profesa was the site of secret meetings between opponents of Mexican Independence that led to the decision to name Agustín de Iturbide as Commander of the southern Independence Army, after which he joined with the Independence forces under Vicente Guerrero and was instrumental in winning the battles for Mexico City.

convent has a lovely courtyard, rooms for the habitation and education of daughters of the aristocracy, and a tower with three bells.

Farther east, off Calle Loreto, is the Plaza Loreto and its superb neoclassical Iglesia de Nuestra Señora de Loreto with its towering cupola, elegant nave windows and fine late Virreinal paintings by Miguel Cabreras, begun in 1809 and completed in 1816. One block farther east is the Iglesia de Santa Teresa la Nueva. Finished in 1715, the church has an interesting façade of baroque portals and sculptural niches, and a tiled sacristy.

CALLE MADERO

Returning to the Zócalo and turning west, one soon encounters a further series of fascinating monuments and structures along Calle Madero, a largely pedestrian boulevard. Two blocks from the Zócalo

Following Calle Madero brings one to the **Palacio de Iturbide** ((5) 518-2187, Calle Madero No. 17 (free admission; open Monday through Friday from 9 AM to 5 PM), one of Mexico's most beautiful buildings. A magnificent baroque structure built to resemble the original owner's home in Palermo, Italy, the building now houses the administrative offices of the Banamex corporation. It was occupied in 1821 to 1822 by Mexican Independence leader Agustín de Iturbide, who had himself made emperor while living in this building. Rotating exhibitions from Banamex's large art collection can be seen in the main floor gallery, the only part of the building open to the public.

In the next block going west on Calle Madero is the fine **Iglesia de San Francisco** and its adjoining former cloisters, now a separate church.

Letter-writer and client, Easter Saturday.

The stone arch portal and façade are considered among the world's greatest achievements of the churrigueresque style. Once part of a much larger monastery initiated by Cortés in 1525, most of the remaining structure was actually dedicated in 1716. The earlier monastery, which had once been the administrative headquarters in Mexico for the Franciscans and thereafter a religious school for lay Aztec teachers, was destroyed in 1856 by order of President Ignacio Comonfort. The goods of the Franciscans were nationalized and, after 1860, the monks were excluded from the church, and parts of the adjoining cloister were sold off in lots.

As an exercise in outright eclecticism, the **Casa de los Azulejos** (House of Tiles) ((5) 525-3741, Calle Madero No. 4, on the other side of Calle Madero from the Iglesia de San Francisco, has few equals (open daily from 8 AM to 10 PM). Built in 1596 for the Counts of El Valle de Orizaba, it offers, with its façade covered in blue and white tiles, a stunning contrast to the somber magnificence of the church. The tiles, from Puebla, were added in the middle of the eighteenth century. The vast glassed-in Moorish courtyard, now a Sanborn's Restaurant, has cloister-like two-story columns leading to a carved and tiled balcony. The staircase has fine frescoes done by José Clemente Orozco in 1925.

A more recent Mexico City landmark is just east of the Iglesia de San Francisco on Calle Madero. The **Torre Latinoamericana** (Latin American Tower) on Calle Madero at Avenida Lázaro Cárdenas (small admission fee; open daily 10 AM to midnight) is 47 stories high. On a day with minimal smog, there are spectacular views of the city, valley and mountains from the tower's observation deck on the 44th floor. On a reasonably clear night it seems the city lights below extend to the ends of the earth. There are also a bar and restaurant one floor down (semiformal dress, including coat and tie for men, may be required).

Turning two blocks north off Calle Madero brings one to the superb Italianate art deco **Palacio Nacional de Bellas Artes** (National Palace of Fine Arts) ((5) 521-9225 (free admission; open Tuesday through Sunday from 10:30 AM to 6:30 PM). Built of white Carrara marble, and designed by the Italian architect Adamo Boari who also designed the Post Office diagonally opposite (see below), it is so heavy it has sunk over four meters (13 ft) into the subsiding soil. It was begun in 1900 by Porfírio Díaz but not completed until 1934, having been delayed by the Revolution. The **Teatro de Bellas Artes** (Opera and Concert Hall) ((5) 521-9225 within can house an audience of 3,400 spectators. Its stage has a 22-ton beaded stained glass curtain made by Tiffany of New York that portrays the great volcanic peaks of the Mexico Valley, Popocatépetl and Iztaccíhuatl. Considered the

cultural center of Mexico City, and thus of Mexico, the Palacio has frequent performances of opera, symphonies and ballet. It is the home of the famed **Ballet Folklórico de México** ((5) 521-3633, which performs here Wednesday at 9 PM, Sunday morning at 9 AM and Sunday evening at 8 PM.

Bellas Artes also contains one of the finest collection of murals in the city. On the second and third floors are remarkable works by Rufino Tamayo and murals by José Clemente Orozco, David Alfaro Siquieros and Diego Rivera. These four artists have created such a prodigious series of master works here that it is difficult to imagine an equally outstanding and sizable exhibition of twentieth-century murals anywhere else in the world. It is here that Rivera moved his celebrated mural of modern man, that had previously been commissioned by, and hung in, New York's Rockefeller Center only to be removed because of its leftist overtones. The palace was renovated in 1994 and a parking lot installed underground with fine gardens at ground level. The bookshop here is one of the best in the city for information on Mexico's artists and muralists; the café is a pleasant spot for coffee and dessert.

Across from the Belles Artes is the **Dirección General de Correos** (Post Office) ((5) 521-7760, Ejército Central at Calle Tacuba (open Monday through Saturday from 8 AM to midnight and Sunday from 8 AM to 4 PM). This building is also an Italianate masterpiece of sumptuous white marble, which was cleaned and restored in 1994. The interior is replete with marble, carved wood, bronze and wrought iron. Upstairs there is the Postal Museum with a variety of stamp displays and depictions of the postal history of Mexico.

Around the corner at Calle Tacuba No. 8 is the **Museo Nacional de Arte** (National Museum of Art) ((5) 512-7320 (small admission fee; open Tuesday through Sunday from 10 AM to 5 PM). Designed by Italian architect Silvio Contri, the museum houses an imposing collection of twentieth-century Mexican landscapes, including magnificent pastoral paintings of the Valley of Mexico by José María Velasco. These lovely oils are enough to make one weep over the damage done by "progress." Also on display are superb exhibits from all phases of Mexican artistic history, from pre-Columbian to the present.

In front of the National Museum of Art is the extraordinary sculpture **El Caballito** (The Little Horse), often termed the most beautiful equestrian statue in Mexico. Cast in bronze in 1802 by Manuel Tolsá, it portrays the Spanish king, Carlos IV, atop his steed. Two of the city's fanciest restaurants have opened by the statue; plan an

ABOVE: The art nouveau Palacio de Bellas Artes, commissioned by General Porfírio Díaz, was designed by the Italian architect Adamo Boari. BELOW: Remains of the Aztec Templo Mayor.

early lunch here, before young elite professionals head for their regular tables.

Across Tacuba is the **Palacio de Minería** (Palace of Mining), also designed by Tolsá. Its beautiful façade and vast staircase have been termed the finest examples of neoclassical architecture in Mexico. Once the College of Mining, it is now part of the National University's Engineering School. Just east and north of the National Museum of Art are the two chambers of the **Mexican Parliament**, the **Cámara de Senadores** (Senate) and the **Cámara de Diputados** (House of Deputies).

West along Tacuba (which changes name to Hidalgo) is the delightful **Parque Alameda**, the historic district's largest park (see below). Across Hidalgo is the eighteenth-century **Iglesia de Santa Veracruz**, standing on the site of an earlier church built in about 1550. It contains the grave of Manuel Tolsá. On the other side of a small square is the **Iglesia de San Juan de Dios**, built in 1727, with its seashell-topped façade.

Behind them is the fascinating **Museo Franz Mayer** ℂ (5) 518-2267, Hidalgo No. 45 (small admission fee; open Tuesday through Sunday from 10 AM to 5 PM). Mayer was a German immigrant who arrived in Mexico in 1905 to seek his fortune and, soon thereafter, found it. As his wealth grew he collected a wide variety of Mexican, German and Asiatic art from the Middle Ages to the nineteenth century. Mayer was particularly interested in applied art, ceramics, furniture, religious artwork in gold and silver, tortoise shell and ivory inlays, tapestries and textiles, glassware and timepieces, but was happy also to acquire fine oils and sculptures when they came his way. Prior to his death in 1975 he established a fund creating a permanent museum for this extraordinary collection. The museum, installed in the beautifully restored sixteenth-century hospital of San Juan de Dios, opened in 1986. English-speaking guides are available, but it is advisable to call ahead for guide reservations.

PARQUE DE ALAMEDA CENTRAL

A shady, lovely area of promenades, fountains, pools and ancient trees, **Alameda** is Mexico City's oldest park, developed in 1592 under the orders of the Spanish Viceroy Luis de Velasco. Originally it was surrounded by a wall to keep out the peasants and Indians. It was placed over the remnants of the Tenochtitlán *tianguis*, or marketplace, of which Cortés' soldier Bernal Díaz de Castillo said, "I wish I could tell all the things that are sold there, but there were so many and of such varying quality, and the great market with its surrounding arcades was so filled with people that we could not have seen or learned about it all if we had two days." Many of the soldiers, he said, who had seen the great markets of Europe had never seen one

so large and well-arranged, with its separate town-sized subsections each given over to trade in a single commodity, such as jaguar skins, gold, silver, gems, live animals, rope and clothing.

The park acquired a particular notoriety during the Catholic Inquisition, for it was here that many people were burned at the stake, in the **Plaza del Quemadero** (The Burning Square), on the park's western side. Standing in this area, it is almost possible to imagine the feelings of those poor innocents, the majority of whom did not even understand the religion against which they had supposedly sinned, as the flames rose around them and they looked for the last time on the new city the Spanish had built on the ruins of Tenochtitlán.

On the Alameda's western edge is the **Pinacoteca Virreinal de San Diego** (Viceregal Art Gallery) ℂ (5) 510-2793, Calle Dr. Mora No. 7. This former Convent Iglesia de San Diego (small admission fee; open Tuesday through Sunday) was begun in 1595 and completed in 1621. Originally there had been a *mercado* (market) in front of it, but in July 1596 this was transformed into the Quemadero for the Inquisition, and remained so until 1771. In the 1850s much of the fine churriguseresque furnishings of the church's interior were destroyed; in 1861 the church was closed by the government and the adjoining convent was sold off. Quite innocently, it now houses a fine collection of Mexican art from the Virreinal, Spanish colonial period of the late 1500s to the early 1800s. To those not yet aware of the magnificent diversity and quality of this epoch of Mexican painting, and also to those who love this unique resource, the Pinacoteca museum is a most valuable resource.

The Alameda was much improved over the centuries, particularly during the brief reign of the French-imposed Emperor Maximilian and in the presidency of Porfírio Díaz, both of whom added many fountains and French sculptures, and adapted the park's form to French patterns of landscape architecture.

At the east end of Alameda is the **Hemiciclo Juárez**, a 1910 monument to President Benito Juárez (1806–1872), where concerts are often held on Sunday and holiday mornings. The park is always lively, but is especially festive in December and January, when it is filled with Santa Clauses, the Three Kings, strolling minstrels, balloon and toy vendors, food stands and many families bringing their children to see them.

Across Avenida Benito Juárez, on the south side of the Alameda, is the **Museo de Artes e Industrias Populares** (Museum of Popular Arts and Crafts), which contains displays of folk art from all parts of the country, some of which are available for purchase at reasonable prices. One of the finest folk art stores in the city, the museum closed in 1995 for ongoing renovations which have lasted three years. It is scheduled to reopen in 1999. Those eager to purchase Mexican handicrafts will also find a variety of government-run shops along Avenida Juárez on the park's south side.

On the Alameda's western edge is the **Plaza de Solidaridad** (Solidarity Plaza) and the **Museo Mural Diego Rivera** ((5) 510-2329 on Balderas at Colón (admission fee except on Sunday; open Tuesday through Sunday from 10 AM to 6 PM, but closed at midday). The museum houses Diego Rivera's famous colorful and autobiographical mural, *Sueño de una Tarde de Domingo en la Alameda* (Dream of a Sunday Afternoon in the Alameda), which was salvaged from the old Del Prado Hotel

Tenochtitlán and the mainland. It was along this causeway, then called the Calzada Tlacopan, that Cortés' men and their Tlaxcalan allies attempted to flee with their plunder on *La Noche Triste*, bringing such great loss of life on that rainy night of June 30, 1520. Although most of the enormous amount of gold and other wealth they had stolen was lost in the lake, a few pieces have recently been discovered and are on display in the Museo de Templo Mayor.

The Alameda is now one of the most popular parks in the city, filled with office workers on lunch breaks, vendors selling balloons, cotton, candy and fried *churros* (similar to donuts), preachers and politicians lecturing the crowds, and magicians

after it was severely damaged by the 1985 earthquake. The mural portrays the park at the turn of the century and depicts a promenade with Rivera as a boy and then a young man with his family and friends. It satirizes many of the prominent cultural and political figures of Mexico's history from the conquest to the Revolution. This lovely mural became the center of a national controversy because of the words Rivera painted on a sheet of paper held by one of the historical figures, *Dios no existe* (God does not exist). He was later forced to recant and replace them with the insipid Conferencia de San Juan de Letrán. The mural is part of a park built to commemorate the thousands of people killed in the 1985 earthquake.

On the north side of Alameda is the east-west boulevard **Avenida Hidalgo**, a continuation of Tacuba, and originally the major causeway crossing Lake Texcoco between the Aztec city of Mexico City

and musicians performing for a few pesos. I thoroughly enjoy sitting here during daylight, watching the parade of city characters. The park is, however, less hospitable at night.

There are two other interesting churches a block or two northwest of Alameda Park. The first is the **Iglesia de San Hipóllito**, dedicated to the city's patron saint and built in the early 1600s in baroque style. The sculpture standing in front of the church commemorates the loss of Tenochtitlán to the Spanish; it portrays an Aztec warrior being carried off by an eagle. Two blocks farther is the second interesting church, the slightly less imposing Iglesia de San Fernando, in whose graveyard Benito Juárez and several other prominent Mexicans are buried. This church was begun in 1735

Mexican dancers spice the fare at Zona Rosa's Focolare Restaurant.

and suffered much damage after the secularization of Mexico, when its magnificent paintings and numerous architectural details were destroyed.

A few blocks farther west is another excellent museum, the **Museo de San Carlos ℂ** (5) 566-8522, Puente de Alvarado No. 50 and Avenida Ramos Arizpe (small admission fee; open Monday and Wednesday through Sunday). Housed in what was formerly the Palacio de Buenavista, designed in the early 1800s by Manuel Tolsá, the museum holds a formidable collection of European paintings and sculptures.

Although there are literally thousands of other interesting sites in the downtown area, the visitor might be well advised at this point to return to the

In Maximilian's time the Reforma was a showcase of fine colonial architecture, but like the Champs Elysées on which it was modeled, it has seen the replacement of esthetics by commercialism. Along it can be found, however, some of the most expensive and classiest restaurants and shops of the city.

The **Zona Rosa** (Pink Zone), an area on the south side of the Reforma between the traffic circles of El Angel and Cuauhtémoc, was (until a few years ago) considered the city's most elegant commercial area. It contains an imposing array of restaurants, boutiques, high-class hotels, offices, movie theaters, night clubs, handicraft shops, cafés and other places to spend money

Paseo de la Reforma and follow this wide boulevard westward, toward Chapultepec Park and Castle, and one of the world's very finest museums, the Museo Nacional de Antropología.

PASEO DE LA REFORMA

Once, before the advent of cars, the Paseo de la Reforma was the most beautiful boulevard in Mexico. The Reforma was built by the Emperor Maximilian to connect his home in the Castillo de Chapultepec with the Palacio Nacional. It is now the main crosstown (east-to-west) thoroughfare in the city, an eight-lane highway with a dividing strip and banked on either side by trees backed by parking lanes and tall buildings. From time to time it is broken by *glorietas* (traffic circles) which, like those in Paris or Rome, take some time to learn how to navigate with a semblance of safety.

quickly, but with the more recent gaudy and bawdy overtones of Times Square.

In a sense the Reforma, and the crossing north-south Avenida de los Insurgentes, is the lifeline of Mexico City, the place which mirrors the city's future just as the Zócalo mirrors its past. Even the Reforma's name, taken from the Laws of Reformation instituted under Benito Juárez in 1861 which led to the savaging of so much of the city's ecclesiastical architecture, suggests an optimism about improving the human condition which any long stay in Mexico City is likely to dampen.

Traveling southwest from the Alameda park area on the Reforma, there are a number of sites worth remarking as one approaches Mexico City's tour de force, **Bosque de Chapultepec** (Chapultepec Park) and its anthropological museum. The first *glorieta* thus reached is that of Cristobal Colón (Christopher Columbus) with its **Monument of**

Columbus sculpted by the French artist Charles Cordier and erected here in 1877.

A short walk north from Cristobal Colón brings one to the imposing **Plaza de la República** with its huge **Monumento a la Revolución**. In the monument are buried revolutionary leaders Plutarco Calles, Lázaro Cárdenas, Venustiano Carranza, Francisco Madero and Pancho Villa. Returning to the Reforma one next passes the *glorieta* of Cuauhtémoc with the statue of this last Aztec ruler who was forced to surrender to Cortés and was later murdered by him. Here the Avenida de los Insurgentes, so-named for the country's many revolutionaries, crosses the Reforma.

After one more *glorieta* one arrives at the columnar **Monumento a la Independencia**, popularly known as El Angel, because of the winged and gilded figure with a laurel wreath in its hand surmounting the monument. The monument was inaugurated in 1910 to celebrate the 100th anniversary of the beginning of the war fought for independence from Spain. The figures at the base of the column represent heroes of the independence movement.

The original angel was destroyed when it fell from the monument in the earthquake of 1957. The entire column, like most of the structures in Mexico City, is slowly sinking into the soft soil. The neighborhood between El Angel and Chapultepec Park competes for attention with the Zona Rosa, and contains two of the city's finest hotels and several modern office buildings.

BOSQUE DE CHAPULTEPEC

Its serene groves of ancient, gnarled trees, its lakes, streams, pathways, gardens, playgrounds and lovely vistas, its architecture and its world-leading anthropological museum, all make Bosque de Chapultepec (Chapultepec Park) a site no visitor should miss. At over four square kilometers (two and a half square miles), it is Mexico City's largest and also its most varied semi-natural area, an area with strong spiritual and geographic links to its Aztec past.

Aztec legends indicate that when the tribe came to the valley of Mexico after its long wanderings from Aztlán, it first settled in Chapultepec, which in the Nahuatl language of the Toltecs and Aztecs meant "hill of the grasshoppers." According to some of the oldest Aztec sources, in what are now known as the Florentine and Aubine Codices, the Aztecs had lived in the valley much earlier, perhaps at or before the time of the Toltecs and, having been set upon by their neighbors, had been forced to flee northward. After their diaspora in the desert, under the direction of their priests who interpreted what they believed was the will of Huitzilopochtli, the Aztecs returned to the valley and at first settled in the area of

Azcapotzalco, but the powerful Tepanecas soon drove them out.

They retreated to Chapultepec, which because of its hills and dense forests they felt was easier to defend and would be an excellent location for marauding among the more developed city-states of the valley. But the city-states, annoyed by these upstart and dangerous barbarians from the north, banded together and chased the Aztecs from Chapultepec in 1319, whence, again exiles, they wandered to the two islands in Lake Texcoco that became their last and greatest home.

Chapultepec retains many remnants of the Aztecs and of the valley's earlier inhabitants. In the height of their reign, after they had dominated

the entire valley, the Aztecs returned to Chapultepec to build summer homes for the nobility, carving on the rocky slopes large likenesses of their kings, some of which remain. The Aztecs also channeled water from the Chapultepec springs by aqueduct to the Sacred Precinct in Tenochtitlán. Visitors may still visit the area of one of these springs, the **Fuente de Netzahualcóyotl**, named for the king of the city-state of Texcoco who supposedly first developed Chapultepec as a park in the early 1400s.

Before one leaves the Reforma to enter Chapultepec Park there is, however, one more interesting site. In the small plaza between the Reforma and Avenida Melchor Ocampo is the **Fuente de Diana Cazadora**, a fountain with a statue of Diana the Huntress, perhaps hearkening back to the days when Chapultepec was the Versailles of Mexico City and a hunting preserve for the city's Chichimeca rulers. The **statue** at the park's entrance depicts Simón Bolívar.

Once you pass by the Bolívar Monument at the entrance to the Park, the first major building on your left is the **Museo de Arte Moderno** (Modern Art Museum) ((5) 211-8045 on Paseo de la Reforma at Calzada Gandhi (small admission fee;

OPPOSITE: The gates at Castillo de Chapultepec. ABOVE: Wedding car with fairy-like carriage.

open Tuesday through Sunday from 10 AM to 6 PM). Designed by Rafael Mijares and Pedro Ramírez Vázquez and completed in 1964, the museum has extensive collections of twentieth-century Mexican painting, sculpture, photography, lithography and the plastic arts, along with ongoing temporary international exhibitions of modern art.

Across the street is the excellent **Museo Rufino Tamayo** ((5) 286-6519 on Paseo de la Reforma at Calzada Gandhi (admission fee; open Tuesday through Sunday from 10 AM to 6 PM), which was built in 1981 to house the personal collection of one of Mexico's most famed modern painters. On exhibit are the works of Miró, Warhol, Picasso, Moore, and other of Tamayo's contemporaries.

and as such was the last Mexican stronghold to fall to United States troops in 1847. In 1863 it was taken over by the French-imposed Emperor Maximilian and his Belgian wife, the Princess Charlotte. It served thereafter as a summer residence for several Mexican presidents and was made a national history museum in 1940 by President Lázaro Cárdenas.

The **Museo de la Historia Nacional** (Museum of National History) is situated within the Castillo and has the same opening hours. It contains 19 rooms of exhibits of varying interest. The majority of the ground floor exhibits deal with Mexican history from the time of the conquest until the 1910-1921 Revolution, and include Spanish

The **Monumento a los Niños Héroes** (Monument to the Young Heroes) south of the Reforma entrance is a semicircular series of columns and fountains commemorating six military cadets who, rather than accept capture by American troops in the battle for Chapultepec Castle (Castillo de Chapultepec) during the 1847 United States invasion of Mexico, wrapped themselves in Mexican flags and jumped to their deaths.

The **Castillo de Chapultepec** ((5) 553-6246 (admission fee; open Tuesday through Sunday) overlooks the park on Chapultepec Hill. It was built by the Spanish Viceroy Conde de Gálvaz on the site of an Aztec summer palace, site of one of the last stands of the Aztecs against the Spanish. After the fall of Tenochtitlán the area was used as a Catholic hermitage and later for a gunpowder plant. Construction of the Castillo itself began in the 1780s; in 1841 it was made a military academy,

weapons and armor, military maps and other documents, historical materials of the wars of Independence and the Revolution, as well as a vast array of coins, furniture, horse-drawn coaches, clothing, books and other historical materials of the post-Columbian epoch.

Also on display are a number of reproduced codices of the Aztec and earlier periods, as well as other pre-Columbian relics. Visitors may tour the apartments inhabited by Maximilian and his wife, containing the furniture, *objet d'arts*, fabrics and other decorations the ill-fated couple brought with them from Europe. From Maximilian's balcony, the views of Mexico City are spectacular. Visiting this spot, one can easily imagine the deep commitment that this well-intentioned but doomed Hapsburg came to feel for the country which would finally reject and assassinate him.

MUSEO NACIONAL DE ANTROPOLOGÍA

The crowning glory of Chapultepec Park, and of Mexico City, and one of the very best, if not the best, anthropology museums in the world, is the **Museo Nacional de Antropología** (National Museum of Anthropology) ℂ (5) 553-1902 on Paseo de la Reforma at Calzada Gandhi (admission fee except on Sunday; open Tuesday through Sunday). Even those who generally avoid museums will find plenty to entertain and fascinate them in this magnificent place.

Designed by one of Mexico's finest contemporary architects, Pedro Ramírez Vázquez, the

In 1997, workers began a multi-year renovation of the museum, slated for completion after the year 2000. Some of the exhibits described below may be closed when you visit, but the museum is, nevertheless, open and not to be missed.

The first thing one sees on entering the building is a vivid mural by Rufino Tamayo of a feathered serpent fighting with a jaguar. It is easiest to begin at the Sala de Orientación (Orientation Room), which offers an audiovisual display of Mexican archaeology and history from the earliest human habitation to the arrival of the Spanish. Here also is a summary of what the museum has to offer. All information displays are in Spanish, but English-speaking guides are available at a very

museum is a splendid example of the country's often-great (and underestimated) modern architecture. Completed in 1964, it covers some 30,000 sq m (320,000 sq ft), with over five kilometers (three miles) of exhibition halls. The entire building is composed of two levels surrounding a spacious rectangular patio shaded by an immense flowing water sculpture on a pedestal, known as the "umbrella."

Rising in stern reproval in front of the museum building itself is the famous seven-and-a-half-meter (23-ft) pink stone statue originally thought to be Tláloc, the Aztec god of rain, but now considered by many experts to represent Tláloc's sister, the water goddess **Chalchiuhtlicue**. Weighing 167 tons, this unfinished monolith was found not far from San Miguel Coatlinchán, south of Texcoco, and brought by a special trailer to Chapultepec.

Mexico City

reasonable price. And if hunger, thirst or aching feet call, the museum has a very pleasant restaurant (follow the stairs off the fountain patio) in which to take a short break.

To the left of the Sala de Orientación there is a gift shop and bookstore where excellent guidebooks of the museum are available in several major languages; they are a must for heightening one's appreciation of the pleasures to follow.

On the first floor there are 12 main display rooms, each covering a major period of Mexican civilizations prior to the Conquest. It is here one begins to get a sense of the incomprehensible richness of Mexican history and archaeology, and the diversity of civilizations the country has produced.

OPPOSITE: The Olmec god of maize LEFT and carvings RIGHT from a Mayan temple. The Museo Nacional de Antropología ABOVE has artifacts from every period of Mexican history.

Turning right at the Sala de Orientación, one finds three rooms devoted to special exhibits and recent excavations. Next, following the right side of the main patio, there is a hall devoted to anthropology and archaeology, which illustrates many of the methods used for finding and identifying some of the displays to be seen later in the museum.

Next on the right is the Sala de Meso-America, displaying the many advances in weaponry, hunting, astronomy, writing and medicine which enabled the early civilizations of Mexico to advance. Following this is the Sala de Preistoria (Prehistory Room), depicting the arrival of humanity in the western hemisphere, the social structures and habitations of the first inhabitants in the Mexico City region.

Next on the right is the Sala del Periodo Preclásico (Pre-classical Hall), covering early civilizations of the central highlands, particularly the area of Tlatilco. Then, the Sala de Teotihuacán is not to be missed, for its amazing relics of this complex early civilization. This room is well worth visiting as a preview to a trip outside of Mexico City to Teotihuacán's nearby ruins. Thereafter one arrives at the Sala de Tula (Toltec Hall), with its excellent art, pottery, *stelae*, and sculptures from the nearby pre-Aztec city of Tula.

It is in the Sala Mexica (Aztec Hall) that one can get an intimation of the majestic power of the Aztecs. This enormous display at the far end of the museum houses many of the great stone carvings of Tenochtitlán, the fearful Aztec gods and smaller statues depicting their more quotidien occupations. The Aztec Hall also contains the Aztec Calendar Stone, three and a half meters (11.8 ft) in diameter, and weighing 24 tons, more accurate than European calendars of the same period. It was found during excavations undertaken by the Viceroy of Spain in 1790, and for many years thereafter was affixed to the wall of the Cathedral. Also exhibited are intricately detailed dioramas of the market in Tlatelolco and the heart of pre-Hispanic Tenochtitlán.

In the Sala de Oaxaca is displayed a sampling of the complex and fascinating earlier cultures of Monte Albán and Mitla, including tomb findings, masks, jewelry, and clay sculptures. Again, this is a worthwhile visit to make before exploring Monte Albán itself or the other sites in the Oaxaca region.

The Sala Olmec (Olmec Hall) has an astounding display of the breadth and depth of Mexican civilization. Here one finds a cross-section of one of the most fascinating cultures ever to inhabit the planet, and considered the source of later Mexican civilizations. Exhibitions include massive stone heads, superb jade sculptures, and other fine semi-precious stone carvings.

The Sala Maya (Mayan Hall) represents yet another unique and incomprehensibly rich culture: that of the Yucatán Peninsula. With its superb limestone *stelae* (large flat carved bas-reliefs), jewelry, death masks, fine ceramic sculpture, and reproductions of the famous Bonampak war murals, this room offers a remarkable vision of the Yucatán's cultural richness.

The less-known but lovely art of the Sala de las Culturas del Norte (Northern Highlands Hall), includes treasures from Casas Grandes south of Ciudad Juárez and the United States border. Adjacent to it is the Sala de las Culturas de Occidente (West Mexico Hall), an essential stop for anyone planning to visit the states of Nayarit, Jalisco and Colima, on the central Pacific Coast in the triangle between Guadalajara, Mazatlán and Manzanillo. Here are the famous clay dogs of Colima, and superb examples of the region's fine pottery and other ceramic sculpture.

The museum's second floor is devoted to ethnographic displays, including the crafts and contemporary art produced by Mexico's Indian tribes in modern times. Again following the edge of the patio on the right, one first reaches a display room on general ethnology, followed by halls given over to individual tribes or groupings. Among the tribes whose work is shown are the Tarahumaras and Yaquis of the northwestern desert, the Mayans, the Huichols, Nahuas and Coras. Exhibits include photos, clothing, holy objects, carvings and portrayals of contemporary life.

For historians and anthropologists the museum contains a wealth of material in the form of the National Anthropology Library, with its nearly 350,000 books.

Returning to Chapultepec Park one finds a plethora of other sights and activities. The large lake stretching between the Anthropology Museum and the Castillo is a pleasant spot for a rest. Boats are available for rent and are filled with families and couples seeking escape from the eagle eyes of their chaperones on weekends. Continuing along the Paseo de la Reforma, one passes the **Parque Zoológico** (Zoo) at Paseo de la Reforma between Calzada Gandhi and Calzada Chivatito (free admission; open Tuesday through Sunday). Animals were kept here as early as the sixteenth century, when exotic creatures from all over Meso-America lived amid the forests of Chapultepec. The zoo was in dreadful condition for years and was finally remodeled in 1994 by architect Ricardo Legoretta. Today, the zoo is one of the most popular attractions in the park and is filled with animal lovers on weekends. Four giant pandas attract big crowds and the aviary contains two golden eagles, the symbol of Mexico. The gardens are a delight, with waterfalls, clusters of sky-high bamboo and tropical pathways. **Los Pinos**, the residence of Mexico's presidents, is nearby.

At the western side of the park is the **Papalote Museo del Niño** (Papalote Children's Museum)

((5) 237-1781 on Anillo Periférico at Constituyentes (admission fee; open daily in two sessions, the first from 9 AM to 1 PM, the second from 2 PM to 6 PM). Papalote, which means butterfly in Nahuatl, opened in 1993 to immediate acclaim and enormous crowds. The museum contains over 300 exhibits on scientific and technological themes, along with mazes, tunnels, small rainforests, police cars and fire engines and plenty of activities to keep kids and adults delighted. Tickets are sold in advance for each session.

Nearby is the **Chapultepec Mágico**, an amusement park with children's rides and games, including a large roller coaster; the **Technological Museum** (admission fee; open Tuesday through Saturday from 10 AM to 5 PM) with hands-on exhibits; and the **Natural History Museum** (admission fee; open Tuesday through Saturday from 10 AM to 5 PM).

Located between the children's rides and the Technological Museum is an interesting mosaic fountain, designed by Diego Rivera, called the **Fuente del Mito del Agua** (Fountain of the Water Legend), representing his interpretation of the Aztec rain god Tláloc.

The Paseo de la Reforma exits Chapultepec Park and continues west through Lomas, one of Mexico's most exclusive and luxurious residential areas, and eventually runs into the highway to Toluca.

POLANCO

North of the museum and park is **Polanco**, a trendy and fast-growing residential area that is replacing the Zona Rosa as the place to eat, shop and drink. The **Centro Cultural Arte Contemporáneo** (Cultural Center of Contemporary Art) ((5) 282-0355 on Campos Eliseos at Elliott (admission fee; open Tuesday through Sunday), is the most innovative of its kind in Mexico, with modern art, sculpture and photography. The museum holds fascinating rotating exhibits on modern art, and has a gift shop worth hours of browsing time.

COYOACÁN

Coyoacán (the coyote place) was an important Indian settlement long before the arrival of the Spaniards, and is where Cortés and some of his officers chose to live after they had reduced Tenochtitlán to rubble. Coyoacán is still a residential community deeply entrenched in colonial atmosphere. Many of the cobblestone streets are bordered with trees, the colonial mansions concealed behind high stone walls.

Avenida Francisco Sosa, one of the most typical streets, leads to the **Jardín Centenario**, the public gardens, and Coyoacan's main plaza. Facing the gardens is the **Casa de Cortés**, the site

where Cuauhtémoc was imprisoned and tortured by the Spanish before he was killed. Coyoacán's Town Hall is constructed of stones taken from Cortés' home. Facing the square, the **Parroquia de San Juan Bautista**, one of the first churches to be built in Mexico, was begun in 1538 and completed in 1582. A gilded altar was added two centuries later.

The Jardín Centenario is particularly lively on Sundays, when there is usually some organized entertainment, and it is filled with vendors, mimes, groups of wandering musicians and fortune-telling birds. Streetside cafés facing the park are packed with studious, literary types on weekends; the neighborhood is much calmer on weekdays, and is a great place to imagine yourself living in this massive city.

The **Museo de las Culturas Populares** (Museum of Popular Culture) ((5) 554-8968, Hidalgo No. 289 (free admission; open Tuesday through Sunday) is a fascinating place to explore Mexico's popular culture, with exhibits of soap operas, the Day of the Dead rituals and *lucha libre*, the highly amusing form of masked wrestling.

Art lovers make pilgrimages to the blue **Museo y Casa de Frida Kahlo** ((5) 554-5999, Calle Londres No. 247 (admission fee; open Tuesday through Sunday), on the corner of Calle Allende. This fancifully decorated house is the birthplace of Frida Kahlo, one of Diego Rivera's three wives and a famous and prolific artist in her own right. Kahlo, who has developed a worldwide cult following, was an early Mexican feminist whose Bohemian lifestyle was not abated by crippling injury and disease. The house where she was born and lived all her life, and where Rivera lived after their marriage, displays many of her works, many eighteenth- and nineteenth-century Mexican paintings, a variety of Rivera's early works, and folk and other art collected by Kahlo and Rivera. Also displayed are many mementos of her marriage to Rivera, of her extraordinary personal life and the fascinating intellectual turbulence of the period, and of her own renown as a painter.

Five blocks from the Kahlo Museum is the **Museo Leon Trotsky** ((5) 658-8732, Calle Viena No. 45 on the corner of Calle Morelos (admission fee; open Tuesday through Sunday). Here Trotsky lived after fleeing Stalin in 1938 until he was killed by one of Stalin's agents on August 20, 1940. His grave is in the garden, beside his wife's. His study has been kept as it was the day he died.

SAN ANGEL

The San Angel area began to grow when it was chosen as the site for a Carmelite monastery in the seventeenth century. It is now one of the most charming sections of greater Mexico City, known for its colonial atmosphere and wealthy homes set in fine gardens. With its narrow cobblestone streets and visually fascinating mix of eighteenth and nineteenth-century buildings, parks and plazas, it is best explored on foot. On Saturdays its **bazaar** is a special attraction. The town's chapels, with their gilded altars and their domes inlaid with hand-painted ceramic tiles, are also of special interest.

The **Plaza San Jacinto**, a lovely square surrounded by colonial homes and restaurants, is where part of the famous **Bazaar Sábado** is held. This fine art and folk art bazaar fills a colonial building facing the plaza and spills out into adjoining parks and streets. On exhibit are some of the best works by artists and artisans from through-

tiled fountain and a collection of Colonial and European paintings from the eighteenth and nineteenth centuries.

It was on the Plaza San Jacinto that United States soldiers executed 50 Irish soldiers of the Mexican Army during this war. Considered heroes by the Mexican people, the Irish soldiers still receive a special tribute every September in the plaza. Prior to the war, when Texas was still part of Mexico, these Irish soldiers had lived in Texas but had belonged to the United States Army. When war broke out they chose to fight on the Mexican side because of long-standing allegiances between Mexico and Ireland, and are remembered as being among the Mexican Army's fiercest troops.

out Mexico. Stands and shops are filled with high quality woodcarvings, lacquered boxes and trays, textiles from Chiapas and Guatemala, silver from Taxco, *talavera* dishes and tiles, hand blown glassware and everything else imaginable. The Bazaar Sábado restaurant in the main building has tables set around a flower-filled central courtyard and fountain; the buffet served all day is quite good, and the restaurant a wonderful spot to listen to marimba musicians and watch shoppers show off their purchases. The bazaar is immensely popular with city residents and tourists; arrive early in the day or you'll be overwhelmed by the crowds.

Calm as it seems today, the Plaza San Jacinto has a martial history. The **Casa del Risco ☏** (5) 616-2711, Plaza San Jacinto No. 15, open Tuesday through Sunday, was the headquarters of the United States troops from North Carolina during the Mexican-American War. It has a wonderful

A scarce two blocks away is the lovely **Convento y Iglesia del Carmen**, Avenida Revolución No. 4, on the corner of Avenida de la Paz — two streets forming an interesting juxtaposition (admission fee; open Tuesday through Saturday from 10 AM to 5 PM). Constructed after 1617, it has tiled domes and fountains, a museum of colonial paintings, religious relics and period furnishings, and a basement room with the mummified corpses of nuns and priests.

The **Museo Alvar and Carmen T. de Carrillo Gil ☏** (5) 550-6289, Avenida Revolución No. 1608, a few blocks north of Avenida de la Paz (small admission fee; open Tuesday through Sunday from 10 AM to 5 PM) houses a private collection of works by twentieth-century Mexican painters, including murals by Rivera, Siquieros, and Orozco.

Farther east, returning toward Coyoacán, is the **Monumento al General Alvaro Obregón**, the revolutionary and president who was shot here in a restaurant in 1928.

The **Museo Estudio Diego Rivera** (Diego Rivera Studio Museum) **(** (5) 616-0996 on Calle Altavista (small admission fee; open Tuesday through Sunday from 10 AM to 6 PM) is a monument to the painter's life more than to his art. Designed by Juan O'Gorman and used as a museum since 1986, it offers exhibits on the main and first floor. The top floor, Rivera's studio, houses an amazing selection from his personal art collection and mementos of his life. Even more fascinating is the **Museo Anahuacali (** (5) 617-4310, a short cab ride away on Calle de Museo at Montezuma (admission fee; open Tuesday through Sunday).

ish Viceroy Antonio de Mendoza, and approved by King Philip II of Spain, making it the oldest college or university in the western hemisphere, nearly 100 years older than Harvard University in the United States.

The present campus, inaugurated in 1952, is located in Ciudad Universitaria (University City). Its 325 hectares (800 acres) contain the largest educational complex in Mexico, and one of the largest in the world, with nearly 100 buildings and over 300,000 students. It is undeniably one of the finest exercises in social architecture conceived in the world, with a variety of astounding murals and shapes conveying the extraordinary intellectual vitality of Mexico.

Rivera had this museum built to resemble a volcanic stone pyramid and filled it with his private collection of pre-Columbian sculptures and artifacts. The enormous second-story studio contains sketches of his famous murals.

To those eager for a bit of fresh air after a time in Mexico City, San Angel is the gateway to the nearby **Parque Nacional del Desierto de Los Leones** (Desert of the Lions National Park). Despite its name, it is a heavily conifer-forested mountain park of beautiful vistas and crisp air, a lovely alternative to the city's polluted atmosphere. It can, however, be crowded on weekends.

Of special interest are the murals which adorn the exteriors of several of the buildings. Juan O'Gorman designed a magnificent, brilliantly colored, 12-story nouveau-baroque mosaic mural on the library building, depicting the history of Mexico from early human occupation through the Spanish invasion to the present. As with many of Mexico's great murals, it is a hopeless task to try to convey the power and majesty of this work of art; it must be seen.

David Alfaro Siqueiros's mural on the Rectory building is a three-dimensional portrayal of the role of education, entitled, "People for the University and the University for the People." On the School of Medicine building is a mosaic by Francisco Huelguera depicting the various roots of the

CIUDAD UNIVERSITARIA

The Universidad Nacional Autónoma de México (National Autonomous University of Mexico) was created in 1551 on the initiative of the Span-

OPPOSITE: Shopping for gold in Mexico City.
ABOVE: A bustling market LEFT and colonial *posada* RIGHT in Mexico City's San Angel suburb.

Mexican people. Jose Chávez Morado created the two vast murals on the Science Building, which depict the role of energy and the harmony of all human life.

For those with a botanical bent, the university also houses one of the world's great **nurseries and greenhouses** (open Monday through Saturday 9 AM to 4 PM), with extensive examples of Mexico's fabulous tropical vegetation.

The enormous Estadio Olímpico, one of the world's largest, has excellent murals by Diego Rivera showing the role of sports in Mexico from earliest times to the present. And the university's modern Cultural Center, on the southern part of the university complex, is the location of the Sala de Nezahualcóyotl, a wraparound concert hall which seats 2,500 and is considered to be one of the most acoustically perfect performance halls in the world.

PIRÁMIDE DE CUICUILCO

South of Nezahualcóyotl, where Avenida Insurgentes crosses the Periférico, is the Pirámide de Cuicuilco (Pyramid of Cuicuilco), which in Nahuatl means "singing and dancing place" (free admission; open Tuesday through Sunday from 10 AM to 5 PM), a circular structure believed to be one of the oldest constructions in the Valley of Mexico, constructed probably about 500 BC. According to archaeological analysis, it was apparently abandoned by its population about 200 BC and then buried under lava a hundred years later when the Xitle volcano erupted. Time and earlier excavations have not treated it well: it is reduced from an estimated former height of 27 m (88 ft) to today's height of less than 18 m (59 ft). Yet it and the surrounding excavations are well worth a visit to gain a sense of early history in this part of the valley. There is also a simple museum on site (admission fee; open Tuesday through Sunday from 10 AM to 4 PM).

XOCHIMILCO

Moving east, at the Jardines del Sur exit off the Periférico, are the famous "floating gardens" at Xochimilco, a name which means "the flowering fields" in Nahuatl. This is one of the most colorful sites in all of Mexico. Threaded with a maze of canals, it is the only remnant of the many lakes that once existed in the Valley of Mexico. The "floating gardens" were originally *chinampas*, a type of raft woven from branches, covered with soil, and planted with vegetables and flowers. Over the years, the roots of the vegetation anchored the rafts to the bottom of the lake.

Flower-bedecked launches, called *trajineras*, can be rented, with boatman included, at the docks (follow signs to the Embarcadero), and

used to wander the canals. These launches usually carry up to 12 people, but smaller groups and even couples can be accommodated, particularly during the week when there is less demand. Mariachis and marimbas also cruise the canals offering serenades.

Although official prices for the *trajineras* are posted at the docks, they are often ignored, particularly for gullible tourists. Be sure to agree on the price in advance. Xochimilco is filled with Mexican families on weekends and the canals tend to become bottlenecks unless you get there early. During the week it's more peaceful but less jolly.

Xochimilco's Iglesia de San Bernardino, built at the end of sixteenth century, has a superb

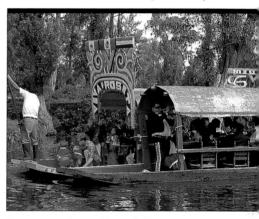

Renaissance altar and beautifully carved portals. The town also has an interesting Saturday market and a daily flower market. Also of interest in Xochimilco is the **Museo Dolores Olmedo Patiño** ((5) 525-1016, which houses the largest private collection of works by Mexican painter, Diego Rivera. It is located at Avenida Mexico No. 5843 and is open by appointment.

TLATELOLCO

Located in the northern section of Mexico City, Tlatelolco was a major city in itself and a rival to Tenochtitlán until the latter defeated it in a battle in 1473 and killed the Tlatelolcan king, Moquihuix, by throwing him off the top of a pyramid. Even after its conquest by the Aztecs of Tenochtitlán, it remained an important ceremonial center, and it was the site of what was probably the largest market in Mexico when the Spanish arrived. According to Spanish accounts, over 60,000 people visited the market every day. Vestiges of pyramids from that epoch, a wall of skulls, Aztec calendar carvings, a seventeenth-century colonial church and modern buildings form what is called the **Plaza de las Tres Culturas** (Plaza of the Three Cultures).

OPPOSITE: Xochimilco's Parade of Chimeras.
ABOVE: Go to Xochimilco early to beat the rush.

The church, the **Iglesia de Santiago de Tlatel-olco**, is a simple baroque structure built in 1609 on the site of an earlier Franciscan chapel. It contains a baptismal font supposedly used to baptize Juan Diego, to whom later appeared the Virgin of Guadalupe.

BASÍLICA DE NUESTRA SEÑORA DE GUADALUPE

The **Basílica de Nuestra Señora de Guadalupe** (Basilica of Our Lady of Guadalupe) is off the Calzada de Guadalupe, starting at the Glorieta de la Reforma. It is the most important religious center in Mexico and honors Mexico's patron saint, the Virgin of Guadalupe. According to the legend, the Virgin appeared here to a peasant, Juan Diego, and asked that a church be built on the spot.

The Bishop asked for proof of the Virgin's request and, on December 12, Juan Diego returned with roses she had told him to grow on a cactus hill. When he attempted to show the Bishop the flowers, they had disappeared and in their place was the Virgin's image, stamped on the inside of his cloak. Now the cloak is exhibited on the main altar of the modern-style basilica. The first basilica was constructed in 1536 and remodeled and enlarged over several centuries. The basilica now houses a fascinating collection of ex-votos, paintings, usually on tin, beseeching the Virgin to cure some ailment or rescue a repentant sinner. The modern sanctuary, which holds 10,000 worshipers, was designed by Pedro Ramírez Vázquez and built in 1976. Unfortunately, the building has none of the mystic warmth one would expect of such a monument. Instead, it is a startling pile of glass and steel.

Juan Diego's cloak, which is exhibited over the main altar, can be seen from any point in the building. For a closer look, get on the moving sidewalk under the altar. The grounds around the basilica are filled every day of the year with religious pilgrims from throughout the country. On December 12, the Feast of Our Lady of Guadalupe, all of Mexico comes to a halt with religious processions and fiestas honoring the country's patron saint. Pilgrims fill the streets around the basilica, many waiting their turn to move forward on their knees until they reach the church.

The nearby **Capilla del Pocito** (Chapel of the Little Well) is a perfect example of eighteenth-century baroque architecture. It is said that a spring burst forth on this spot from a rock where the Virgin stood. Coincidentally (or perhaps inevitably), it is the same spot where a shrine to Tonantzin, the earth mother god of the Aztecs, once existed.

Thousands of pilgrims and tourists flock each year to the Basilica de Nuestra Señora de Guadalupe. OVERLEAF: A display of crucifixes at Mexico City's Mercado Guadalupe.

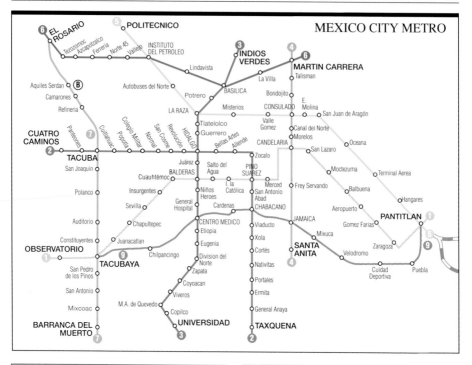

MEXICO CITY METRO

FESTIVALS AND SPECIAL EVENTS

Don't miss Mexico City's huge parades which mark the celebration of **Labor Day** (May 1), **Independence Day** (September 15 and 16) and the **Anniversary of the Revolution** (November 20). Father Hidalgo's cry for independence, the *Grito de Dolores*, is reenacted by the President in the Zócalo on the evening of September 15 and is best seen from the restaurant of the Hotel Majestic. Some people even rent a room facing the Zócalo at the Gran Hotel de la Ciudad de México to view the celebrations. The main square of Coyoacán is another lively place to join in the celebrations. See also FESTIVE FLINGS, page 45.

Colonia Ixtapalapa is noted for its reenactment of the Passion of Christ during Easter Week. On Holy Saturday papier-mâché figures representing Judas or the evils of the previous year (corruption, inflation, etc.) are exploded to the accompaniment of fire crackers on the esplanade of the Museum of Anthropology and in the Plaza Santo Domingo.

The **Noche de Muertos** (Night of the Dead) is especially colorful in the town of Mixquic near Xochimilco (night of November 1). The festival is marked by visits to cemeteries, with offerings of flowers and food, and candlelight vigils.

Pastorelas, reenactments of the birth of Christ, are held from December 13 to 23 at the museum in Tepotzotlán and in various museums in Mexico City. The price of admission includes dinner, *ponche* (a hot alcoholic drink), music and souvenir *piñatas*.

GETTING AROUND

Invariably, you'll find yourself walking for miles when visiting Mexico City, especially since pedestrians can often reach a destination faster than drivers stopped in the clogged streets. Driving here is not advisable, but if you must, get a copy of the *Guia Roji*, which lists all streets and has excellent maps. Mexico City's traffic is horrendous except during Christmas and Easter weeks when *chilangos* wealthy enough to own cars are out of town. Parking lots cost less than US$1 per hour. Don't be tempted to leave your car in a no-parking zone; it will be towed away, or at best the plates will be removed by a policeman, and you will have to undertake the expensive and time-consuming effort of recovering them.

TAXI

Taxis are abundant but come fraught with dangers that make some travelers unwilling to ever set foot in the city. Since 1996, robberies of taxi passengers have become a common occurrence. A passenger gets into a cab and within a few blocks is accosted by one or two men who jump into the cab. In some cases victims have been forced to remove money from bank machines with their ATM cards, usually at gunpoint. Some have been stripped of all their possessions, even their shoes and clothing. Travelers aren't the only victims; important government officials have fallen prey as well. Foreign companies and embassies have taken to hiring drivers for their employees. As a result, you must follow certain procedures when hiring a cab. Do not flag one down on the street. Instead, go to a *sitio* (cab stand) or hotel, and choose a cab with the driver's license clearly posted. Most hotels and the tourist information offices have a list of radio cab companies thought to be reliable. Though these cabs cost more than those on the street, you at least have some means of making a claim if trouble occurs. Once you've chosen a cab, make sure the meter is working; if it's not, agree on a fare with the driver before the cab starts moving. Keep your doors locked and don't carry more money than you'll need for the moment.

METRO

Mexico City's rapid transport system, the Metro, is only marginally safer than taxis. Pickpockets abound; keep your wits and possessions about you. Despite this, the Metro is the city's most efficient mode of transportation. Designed and partially outfitted by the French, it would be a pleasure if it were not so packed. Extra cars, for women and children only, are added during rush hours. Maps are posted at each station and in the cars, and are easy to read. There are several lines that intersect at certain stations. The train's direction is indicated by the name of the last stop on the line. Transfer stations are noted on the maps with the colors of the lines that stop at that particular station. Baggage or extremely bulky packages are not permitted on the Metro.

PUBLIC BUS

Public buses must contend with the city's abominable traffic and are often impossibly crowded. Stops are clearly marked with signs reading *parada*. The Paseo de la Reforma line is the most useful, running from Chapultepec Park to the Zócalo, and stopping within a few blocks of most attractions.

WHERE TO STAY

Mexico City is generally the most expensive place to stay in the country, especially during weekdays when the finer hotels are filled with business travelers. Room rates in some hotels drop by more than $100 per night on weekends and over holiday periods; always ask about such bargains. As in most major international cities, there are plenty of reasonable places to stay if one chooses carefully. As always, a final choice should be made on the basis of overall location, relative tranquillity, ambiance and proximity to what one wants to see and do. I find it easiest to stay in the Historic District, the Zona Rosa, or Polanco; all are within walking distance of major attractions.

An important factor in looking for a room in the smaller, less expensive places is traffic noise. Rooms facing busy boulevards tend to be noisy even late into the night. As a general rule, look at any room (including the bathroom) before you take it, and don't be reluctant to ask for a larger or quieter room if the one you see doesn't please you. Ear plugs are a must in most inexpensive hotels. And, always be careful of baggage while inspecting rooms.

VERY EXPENSIVE

Polanco, close to Chapultepec Park, is one of the inner-city's ritziest neighborhoods and home to

the city's most luxurious hotels. The most famous is the **Camino Real** ((5) 203-2121 TOLL-FREE (800) 722-6466 FAX (5) 250-6897, Mariano Escobedo No. 700. There are 720 rooms and suites, with every facility the jaded might dream of, including a telephone in the bathroom, minibar, four pools, tennis courts, gorgeous architecture, discos, six restaurants and a business center.

Also famous is the **Presidente Inter-Continental** ((5) 327-7700 TOLL-FREE (800) 327-0200 FAX (5) 327-7750, Campos Eliseos No. 218. The 870 large rooms and suites have the same amenities as above; those on the highest floors have lovely views of Chapultepec Park. Facilities include six restaurants and a business center.

I spent 24 soothing hours without ever leaving my room at the **Hotel Nikko** ((5) 280-1111

Hotels and restaurants offer havens from the clamor and crowds of the city.

TOLL-FREE (800) 645-5687 FAX (5) 280-9191, Campos Eliseos No. 204. I had been traveling for weeks through southern Mexico by bus — after one look at the room's enormous bed and marble bathtub I put out the *no moleste* (do not disturb) sign and settled in. The 770 rooms in this shining tower come in a variety of sizes and styles, including Japanese rooms with sleeping mats. There are three restaurants, two pools, tennis courts, and a health club. The structure has a tendency to shake a bit in a high wind.

Newer on the scene is the colonial-style **Four Seasons Hotel Mexico City** ((5) 230-1818 TOLL-FREE (800) 332-3442 FAX (5) 230-1808, Paseo del la Reforma No. 500 (between Burdeos and Leija), designed after the colonial buildings around the Zócalo and those on rue St. Honoré in Paris. The hotel's 230 rooms frame a central courtyard; some have terraces overlooking the gardens and all have more than ample space for work and relaxation. Facilities include a health club, four restaurants and bars. The service here is outstanding and the location, between Polanco and the Zona Rosa, is ideal for walkers.

The **Marquís Reforma** ((5) 211-3600 TOLL-FREE (800) 525-4800 FAX (5) 211-5561, Paseo Reforma No. 465 (at Río Elba), is across the street from the Four Seasons. Sparklingly modern inside and out, this hotel's 209 rooms and suites are decorated with art-deco furnishings while the lobby has a European ambiance.

A little farther away from the park but directly off the Reforma is the **María Isabel Sheraton** ((5) 207-3933 TOLL-FREE (800) 325-3535, Paseo de la Reforma No. 325, with superb views from the upper floors, 850 lovely rooms, three restaurants, health club, pool, and tennis court.

The **Galería Plaza** ((5) 211-0014 TOLL-FREE (800) 228-3000 FAX (5) 207-5867, Hamburgo No. 195, is located in the Zona Rosa close to good shopping and dining areas and has 435 classy rooms.

EXPENSIVE

The **Fiesta Americana Reforma** ((5) 705-1515 TOLL-FREE (800) 343-7821 FAX (5) 705-1313, on Paseo de la Reforma at Ramírez, is a favorite of Mexican business travelers familiar with this national chain. The hotel has 610 rooms, a fitness center, pool and sundeck, and good Mexican restaurants, along with a popular dance club.

The **Krystal Zona Rosa** ((5) 228-9928 TOLL-FREE (800) 231-9860 FAX (5) 211-3490, Liverpool No. 155, has 302 rooms, a very good Japanese restaurant and excellent service.

La Casona ((5) 286-3001 TOLL-FREE (800) 223-5652 FAX (5) 211-0871, Durango No. 280 at Cozumel, a restored mansion, is refreshingly small, with only 30 rooms. The guestrooms and public spaces are decorated with the European antiques

and the formal lamps, rugs and armoires so popular among the wealthy in the late nineteenth century. You can walk from here to the Zona Rosa in less than 10 minutes, and yet come back each evening to a quiet residential neighborhood.

The **Calinda Geneve** ((5) 211-0071 or 525-1500 TOLL-FREE (800) 221-2222, Londres No. 130, is one of my favorite Zona Rosa hotels. An older property with 318 continually renovated guestrooms, the Geneve has the feeling of a slightly worn grande dame, her surfaces always polished to a brilliant sheen. The belle époque Salón Jardín is a marvel with its abundance of plants under a stained glass ceiling.

Of great relief to travelers stuck at the airport, the **Marriott Aeropuerto** ((5) 230-0505 TOLL-FREE (800) 228-9290 FAX (5) 230-0134 is located right at the national terminal. Its coffeeshop is a popular layover spot for those in the know who are stuck for hours between flights. The rooms are extraordinarily expensive, yet unremarkable — the price of convenience.

MODERATE

When I'm more interested in sightseeing than business I always choose the **Hotel de Cortés** ((5) 518-2121 TOLL-FREE (800) 528-1234 FAX (5) 512-1863, Hidalgo No. 85 (at Paseo de la Reforma). Right across from the Alameda, the hotel is a national monument — an eighteenth-century hospice for Augustinian monks. The 29 rooms face a luxuriant courtyard filled with trees and dotted with umbrella-shaded tables. Though the rooms are far from fancy, they're quite comfortable.

Nearly as enchanting is the **Gran Hotel** ((5) 510-4040 FAX (5) 512-6772, 16 de Septiembre No. 82. This nineteenth-century department-store-turned-hotel has one of the most opulent lobbies imaginable, with a stained glass dome, crystal chandeliers and wrought-iron elevators. The 125 rooms can be noisy; some face walls and rooftops. Keep looking until you find one that suits you.

The **Hotel Majestic** ((5) 521-8600 TOLL-FREE (800) 528-1234 FAX (5) 512-6262, Madero No. 73, faces the Zócalo. I always plan at least one off-hours meal at its seventh floor Terraza restaurant, but only if I can get a table at the edge of the terrace looking out to the National Palace. There are certain drawbacks to the hotel's 85 rooms. The street noise can be considerable, especially during political demonstrations and parades. Though this is a good place from which to view the Independence Day celebrations, your window may be blocked by strands of colored lights. Still, you must stay here at least once to fully appreciate the Zócalo scene — just be sure to bring ear plugs.

An abundance of marble adorns hotels around Mexico City's Zócalo.

There are few moderate hotels in the Zona Rosa. One exception is the **Hotel Vasco de Quiroga (** (5) 566-1970, Londres No. 15, with 50 rooms in an older building. If you need a bed near the airport, the **Riazor (** (5) 726-9998 FAX (5) 654-3840, Viaduct Miguel Alemán No. 297, is your best choice.

Inexpensive

The best inexpensive hotels are located on side streets in the Historic District, in the midst of the downtown noise and action. The **Hotel Catedral (** (5) 512-8581 FAX (5) 512-4344, Calle Doneceles No. 95 between República de Argentina and República de Brasil, is a real find, with 116 well-maintained rooms. Your sleep will be accompanied by the tolling of the cathedral's bells. The **Hotel Gillow (** (5) 518-1440 FAX (5) 512-2078, Isabel la Católica No. 17, has 110 modern rooms, some with windows facing interior walls. A better choice is the **María Cristina (** (5) 566-9688 or 703-1787 FAX (5) 566-9194, Río Lerma No. 31, near the Zona Rosa. The building with its 156 rooms was built in the 1930s but has a colonial style and ambiance.

WHERE TO EAT

Like capital cities all over the world, Mexico City has something for every type of appetite. Sushi, pasta, steaks, *truite meunière* — all are available in Polanco, the Zona Rosa, or downtown. But the best dishes are prepared by chefs experimenting in nouvelle Mexican cuisine, giving old recipes new flavors and presentations. Fine dining is not exclusively the province of the rich; you can eat filling meals composed of appetizers and hearty Mexican soups at the best spots, or lower your standards just a tad and sample excellent regional Mexican cuisine. Every neighborhood has its casual cafés, as well, where the inexpensive *comida corrida* (meal of the day) served during lunch hours should suffice for hours. The residents of Mexico City dress up when they go out, and some of the most expensive restaurants have jacket-and-tie requirements.

VERY EXPENSIVE

Many of the Mexico City's finest restaurants are located in its super-deluxe hotels. **Fouquet's de Paris (** (5) 203-2121 in the Camino Real, Mariano Escobedo No. 700, is a branch of the Paris restaurant, whose world-famous chefs take over this kitchen for a culinary festival each autumn. **Maxim's de Paris (** (5) 327-7700 in the Presidente Inter-Continental, Campos Eliseos No. 218, has long been a magnet for the city's elite set, who dine on classic French dishes and a few regional specialties. A sixteenth-century colonial mansion is the setting for **Hacienda de los Morales (** (5) 281-4554, Vázquez de Mella No. 525, in Colonia

Los Morales near Polanco. Elegant and subdued, the restaurant has several dining rooms where diners feast on international cuisine.

The quality of the cuisine at the **San Angel Inn (** (5) 616-1527, Diego Rivera No. 50 in San Angel, has declined in recent years, but that hasn't detracted from its popularity or prices. This lovely colonial mansion was once the site of meetings between Emiliano Zapata and Pancho Villa. It is worth a visit, and a meal, solely for the beauty of its patio garden and lovely furnishings. A dress code is strictly enforced, even down to your shoes — sneakers and sandals are forbidden.

EXPENSIVE

Though the Historic District is hardly considered fashionable, two of the city's trendiest restaurants have been doing a roaring business since opening here in the early 1990s. **Cicero Centenario (** (5) 521-7866 at República de Cuba No. 79, is housed in a seventeenth-century mansion near the Portal de las Evangelistas. The owners have created a tribute to Mexican architecture, folk art and cuisine with the restaurant's handsome decor and outstanding menu of regional *moles* and other sauces, and a fine use of the more obscure chilis. The restaurant has done so well that there is now a second location **(** (5) 533-3800 in the Zona Rosa at Londres No. 195. **Los Girasoles (** (5) 510-0630, Plaza Tolsa No. 8 in front of the National Museum of Art, also features nouvelle Mexican cuisine in a colonial mansion with a pleasant outdoor patio. **Prendes (** (5) 512-7517, 16 de Septiembre No. 10, is the old-timers' favorite Mexican restaurant — it first opened in 1892. All of the legendary Mexican figures since then are supposed to have eaten here; murals on the back wall portray personages from Leon Trotsky to Walt Disney — all partying at Prendes.

MODERATE

El Taquito ((5) 526-7699 or 526-7885, Carmen No. 69, behind the cathedral, is another legendary spot long favored by matadors and movie stars. Live music is played during lunch time, when the crowd is festive and reluctant to return to work. **Café Tacuba (** (5) 518-4950, Tacuba No. 28, is absolutely packed for midday dining — don't worry about acting like a gringo — arrive around noon if you don't want to wait for a table. All the basics — *enchiladas, taquitos, carne asada*, tortilla soup — are served with brisk efficiency. Though full meals are overpriced at **Sanborn's Casa de los Azulejos (** (5) 512-2300, Madero No. 4, by the Alameda, you can sit in the café, lunch-counter area and feast cheaply on bowls of soup and *molettes*.

The Zona Rosa has an abundance of international cafés along its pedestrian walkways and nearby streets. Delicate sandwiches and pastries are the specialty at **Konditori (** (5) 525-6621, Génova No. 61. Homesick British get their fix of fish and chips at **Piccadilly Pub (** (5) 533-5306, Copenhague No. 23. **Mesón del Perro Andaluz (** (5) 533-5306, Copenhague No. 26, serves Spanish and Mexican *tapas*. Afternoon tea is a delight at the tiny café tables in **Duca d'Este (** (5) 525-6374, Hamburgo No. 164B. I'm particularly fond of the flaky apple strudel. **Focolare (** (5) 207-8850, Calle Hamburgo No. 87, serves Mexican specialties from all regions of the country and has a marvelous breakfast buffet. My favorite Mexican restaurant is **Fonda El Refugio (** (5) 525-8128, Calle Liverpool No. 166, also in the Zona Rosa. Situated in a remodeled townhouse with several dining rooms, the restaurant serves at least one dish from each region of the country and has an English-language menu for the uninitiated.

INEXPENSIVE

The **Hostería de Santo Domingo (** (5) 510-1434, Belisario Domínguez No. 72, claims to be the oldest restaurant in the city. It's one of the best places for home-style Mexican cooking at reasonable prices. Vegetarians are delighted to find **Yug (** (5) 533-3296, Varsovia No. 3, just off Paseo de la Reforma. What a joy to face huge plates of steamed veggies and brown rice, salads with sprouts, creamed spinach soup, and homemade yogurt with fresh fruit and granola. **Restaurant Danúbio (** (5) 512-0912, by the Alameda at Uruguay No. 3, is a classic Mexican coffeeshop, noisy and busy at all hours of the day and night. The restaurant offers a fixed price *comida corrida* at lunch, and decent entrées and sandwiches.

NIGHTLIFE

In Mexico City, most discos and dance clubs don't even open until 10 PM when a few early-comers claim tables before the crowds arrive around midnight.

Traditional mariachi music blares through the streets around **Plaza Garibaldi**. Here, fans (and tourists) sit at tables spread about the plaza and request their favorite songs from the itinerant groups of musicians. As the night wears on, the crowds grow. Use caution when wandering the streets in this area as pickpockets are common. **Guadalajara de Noche (** (5) 526-5521, next to the plaza, is a popular indoor cantina with live music that stays open till dawn.

Many of the finest hotels offer dinner shows; the best of the lot is at **La Bohemia**, in the Camino Real **(** (5) 203-2121 (see WHERE TO STAY, page 113) which presents popular Latin musicians, and dancing after dinner. Lobby bars at the better hotels are also good spots for live music. The **Presidente**

Inter-Continental ((5) 327-7700, and the **Camino Real**, are both popular venues. Hotel Nikko's discotheque, **Dinasty (** (5) 280-1111, is a well-patronized place while **Antillano's ((** (5) 592-0439, Francisco Pimental No. 78, near the Zona Rosa, is best for Latin dance music.

HOW TO GET THERE

Mexico City's Aeropuerto Internacional Benito Juárez **(** (5) 762-4011 (for general information is the country's main airport and receives flights from all over the world. International travelers often pass through this massive airport when traveling within Mexico. The airport has two connected

terminals, one each for international and national flights. There are several money exchange booths, tourist information offices, shops and restaurants in both terminals. Taxi booths outside each baggage claim area sell tickets for licensed cabs; always use these rather than the gypsy cabs whose drivers hustle customers in the terminals.

There are four major bus stations in the city offering first-class bus service to most parts of the country. Check with the tourist information office in the airport for the correct station for your destination.

The Terminal de Ferrocariles Nacionales de Mexico train station (also called the Buenavista Station) is located on Insurgentes Norte at Buenavista. Modern first-class trains depart from here for cities throughout the country.

Though there are car-rental booths for all major companies at the airport, I strongly discourage all travelers from renting a car in Mexico City. The traffic rivals that of Rome or Bangkok. If you are planning a driving tour of Mexico, try to pick up the car at an office on the outskirts of the city in the direction you'll be traveling.

Venerable restaurants in the Historic District are filled with office workers and tourists from dawn until dusk.

The Valley of Mexico

A VISITOR COULD SPEND MANY WEEKS exploring the valley surrounding Mexico City and never see all of the pre-Columbian ruins, colonial cities, monasteries, convents, villages and natural parks. Most of these sites can be seen on day trips from the city, but a more agreeable approach is to select one of the nearby cities or towns and visit Mexico City on one- or two-day trips from the countryside. For example, the colonial cities of Puebla and Cuernavaca are well within commuting distance of Mexico City by freeway or public transportation. Other advantages are lower-priced hotels and substantially less pollution.

The following are the major attractions, as well as the best of the lesser-known ones, in the area roughly 100 km (62 miles) around Mexico City. We begin in the north.

TEPOTZOTLÁN

To the north of Mexico City off the main highway (Highway 57D) and about a 45-minute drive from the Petroleum Monument on the Reforma, is Tepotzotlán, a small colonial city of 30,000 inhabitants.

WHAT TO SEE AND DO

Construction on the **Iglesia de San Francisco Javier** (open Tuesday through Sunday 11 AM to 6 PM) and a school for the Indians was begun by the Jesuit missionaries in 1670 but was not completed until the eighteenth century. The church is considered one of the most beautiful examples of churrigueresque art in Mexico. Entrance is through a stairway in the rear of the **Museo Nacional del Virrienato** (National Viceroys Museum), which is housed in the sixteenth-century monastery adjoining the church (open Tuesday through Sunday from 10 AM to 6 PM). Its walls and former cells are filled with outstanding treasures of Mexican religious art. The richly adorned novitiate's chapel is simply a foreshadow of what is to be seen in the adjoining church, with its richly decorated altars of gold and mirrors insets. In the basement is the old kitchen. Concerts and performances for children are held on weekends on the patio. Behind the museum is a lovely orange grove.

To the right of the main entrance to the church is the **Capilla del Virgen de Loreto**, a chapel which contains a brick house representing the home of the Virgin in Nazareth. Behind it is the octagonal **Camarín de la Virgen**, a robing room which is covered with richly colored angels and cherubs, all brown-skinned with Indian features. A mirror has been placed below the vaulted ceiling to enable visitors to appreciate the intricacy of the embellishments. From December 13 to December 23 *pastorelas*, passion plays that reenact the search for lodging for the birth of Christ, are performed in the patio of the museum. Tickets can be obtained beforehand through TicketMaster ((5) 325-9000 in Mexico City and ((587) 60243 in Tepotzotlán.

WHERE TO EAT

There are several restaurants at the market across the street from the colonial monuments, or you can grab a bite at the museum's coffeeshop.

HOW TO GET THERE

By car from Mexico City, take Highway 57D (the toll road to Querétaro). After approximately 38 km (22 miles) watch for the turn to Tepotzotlán. It is then about two and a half kilometers (one and a half miles) west of Highway 57.

TULA

At its height, from 950 to 1250 AD, Tula was famed for its advances in writing, medicine, astronomy and agriculture. Much of its knowledge may have been culled from earlier civilizations in the valley, particularly from the Toltecs, whose name means "enlightened being, sage," or "artist." The ruins of their civilization contain art of a quality and intelligence that confirms their name.

Although most of what made Tula one of the world's great cities was stripped away by the Aztecs when they conquered it in the 1300s, enough remains to get a sense of its power. The ancient city, located just outside modern Tula, is particularly worth a visit for its Pirámide de Quetzalcoatl (Pyramid of Quetzalcoatl) and the surrounding plaza.

WHAT TO SEE AND DO

The **Pirámide de Quetzalcoatl** (admission $4.50; open Tuesday through Sunday from 10 AM to 5 PM) stands on the north side of the main plaza, with a ball court on one side and a smaller pyramid on the other, surrounded by fields, walls, rolling wooded hills and mountains. The most stunning features of the pyramid are the colossal *atlantes*, four-and-a-half-meter (15-ft) stone columns of Toltec divinities clasping weapons in each hand and facing southward across the plaza. Each is composed of four stacked blocks of stones held together by tenons. Their towering headdresses are said to depict feathers and stars, the signs of divinity; their eyes and mouths may have been decorated with shells and semiprecious stones. From a distance their faces seem rigid and patterned, but on closer inspection they become

These impressive stone columns of heavily armored Toltec divinities once held up the roof of the temple of the Pirámide de Quetzalcóatl.

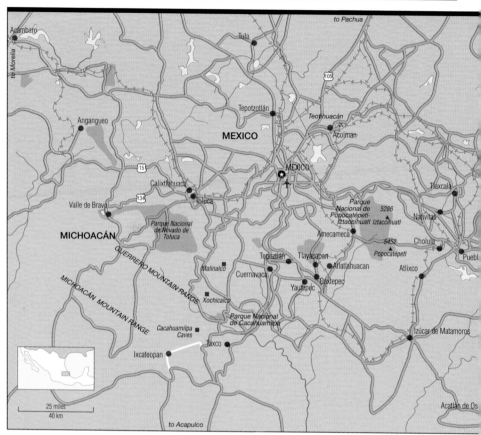

charged with emotion and are quite individualistic. Originally these *atlantes* held up the roof of a temple, now gone, which looked out on the roof of the lower colonnade, of which now only the columns (nearly 100) and a carved bench remain.

Carvings on the pyramid reflect this society's preoccupation with sacrifice, mortality, and human beings as prey to supernatural animals and forces. The pyramid's sloping stepped walls were originally covered by carved stone panels depicting jaguars, coyotes and eagles tearing apart human hearts; of these only the rear walls remain relatively intact. Behind the pyramid is the intricately sculpted **Coatepantli** (wall of serpents), a long frieze of painted stucco and geometric shapes in which a procession of rattlesnakes are swallowing human skeletons.

This vibrantly represented preoccupation with life and death is a hallmark of all pre-Conquest Mexican art, but particularly so among the Toltecs. Their greatest god, the divinity of Tula, was Quetzalcoatl, the feathered serpent made famous to the English-speaking world by D.H. Lawrence's novel of the same name. Quetzalcoatl's divinity was a fusion of opposites: darkness and light, earth and sky, life and death.

In the central area before the pyramid are two *chac mool*, reclining sculptures, each with a basin for human hearts. When one stands with one's back to the pyramid, the structure on the right is the so-called burnt palace, with more carvings, benches, fireplaces and columns.

Apart from the ruins, the **museum** holds an interesting selection of finds from Tula.

WHERE TO EAT

There are several restaurants located around the main plaza with reasonably-priced meals.

HOW TO GET THERE

Continuing north on Highway 57D from Tepotzotlán, drive a half hour to the right-hand turnoff to Tula. Take the second Tula exit.

TEOTIHUACÁN

No visit to the Mexico City area should exclude Teotihuacán, "the place where men become god." This vast and beautiful archaeological site rivals the Egyptian pyramids in its grandeur, ancient

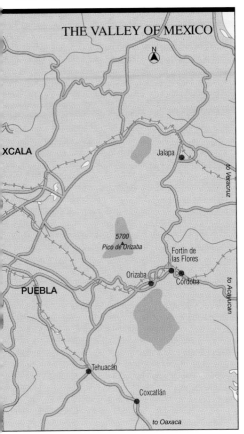

THE VALLEY OF MEXICO

N

XCALA

Jalapa

to Veracruz

5700
Pico de Orizaba

Fortin de
las Flores

Orizaba

Córdoba

to Acayucan

PUEBLA

Tehuacán

Coxcatlán

to Oaxaca

so-called "thin orange" pottery became a major trade item throughout much of Mexico, and the outskirts of the city extended with apartments, markets, temples, and other structures. At this point the city's architecture became most refined, based on a combination of vertical and sloping elements, the *talud-tablero*. The society became equally complex, composed of well-organized social, religious, and political groups, probably all under the rule of a governing class of priest-rulers who controlled trade, manufacturing and education, and wielded their knowledge of science, astronomy, and religion.

If the ancient cultures of Mexico illustrate one axiom better than any other it is: A great civilization bears within itself the seeds of its own destruction. Thus the most imposing city in the world fell apart after AD 650, was burned, and its population dispersed. But even long after its destruction, it apparently remained a major religious site for the Toltecs and later for the Aztecs.

WHAT TO SEE AND DO

Allow at least three hours to explore the vast site of Teotihuacán, and a full day if you are a devoted archaeology buff. The entrance is located at the **Unidad Cultural** (admission fee except on Sunday; open Tuesday through Sunday, 8 AM to 5 PM), a visitor center with an excellent small museum, restaurants, several book and souvenir shops, public restrooms and snack stands.

Directly opposite the museum is the enormous **Plaza of the Ciudadela** (Citadel), a sunken plaza with temples and pyramids that is one of the world's great architectural sites. It measures over 400 m (1,300 ft) square and could contain over 60,000 people during religious ceremonies. The plaza once held 12 major buildings on three sides, including homes for priests and other official residences. There may also have been palaces, as well as the graves of humans offered as sacrifice. Their bodies have been found, with their hands still bound, buried in the plaza to the north and south of the Pirámide de Quetzalcoatl.

By far the most prominent and ancient feature of the plaza is the **Pirámide de Quetzalcoatl**, originally covered by another and bigger pyramid. It was built in *talud-tablero* style, with both the short sloping elements (*taludes*) and the taller vertical *tableros* covered with sculptures and bas-relief. The *taludes* display incredible side views of a feathered serpent which seems to undulate along the wall; the *tableros* are studded with huge stone heads of the gods Tláloc and Quetzalcoatl — the former with his round-eyed, fanged robot-like features, the latter a dinosaur-sized creature with a grinning jaw of bared teeth and round staring eyes.

The main thoroughfare and axis of the city is the **Avenida de los Muertos** (Street of the Dead),

Rome in the complexity of its architecture, and Baalbek and Babylon in its power and expanse. Probably in no other great city on earth, ancient or modern, has urban planning reached such refinement, nor the standard of the architecture been so uniformly excellent.

BACKGROUND

Extending over a total of 40 sq km (15 sq miles), Teotihuacán was the largest and most important city in Meso-America between 150 BC and AD 700, probably reaching its zenith between AD 200 and 500, when archaeologists estimate its population was over 250,000, greater than that of Imperial Rome. Its beginnings as a small village date back to about 600 BC and are still obscure, but according to archaeologists it had become a city of 50,000 people by 200 BC, its economy largely based on trade in obsidian. Over the next 500 years the city continued to enlarge along the north-south axis of the Street of the Dead, supposedly named by the inhabitants because of the similarity of its large pyramids to *tumuli* grave mounds.

During the following 300 to 400 years the **Temple of Quetzalcoatl** was built, the city's

The Valley of Mexico

a 43-m (140-ft) wide boulevard running two and a half kilometers (just over one and a half miles) north to south from the Pirámide de la Luna past the Ciudadela. In its glory, the Avenida de los Muertos supposedly continued at least one and a half kilometers (one mile) past the Ciudadela, for a total length of at least four kilometers (two and a half miles).

Despite the grandeur of the site, one can barely imagine what Teotihuacán really looked like at its peak. It was originally densely composed of buildings, nearly all faced with stucco walls and murals painted in many different colors and decorated with a stunning variety of stone sculptures of animals, gods, and humans. Much of the site was tampered with by nineteenth-century archaeologists whose determination far exceeded their respect. The seven-meter (22-ft) thick exterior stone and stucco facing of the Pirámide del Sol (Pyramid of the Sun) was removed by overly ardent archaeologists in the 1910s.

Turning north on the Avenida de los Muertos, one next arrives at a long series of smaller sites, including the "1917 excavations" (so-called for the date of their archaeological dig), and across from them the Edificios Superpuestos (two-story buildings). These give a good sense of how construction in many pre-Columbian Mexican cities was accomplished: each older level was knocked down and used as fill for those built on top. Here the various levels have been excavated in order, so that the observor can literally descend into the past.

Continuing up the gentle rise of the Avenida de los Muertos, one approaches the Grupo Viking (Viking Group), named for the United States foundation which provided the funds for its excavation. Two large floors of mica, six centimeters (some two inches) thick and nearly nine square meters (97 sq ft) in area, are laid here, their ceremonial or other purpose now lost in time.

Next on the right one finds remnants of the Casas de los Sacerdotes, houses used by priests, then the enormous Pirámide del Sol (Pyramid of the Sun). The latter is oriented so that the sun shines directly over it at a certain time of the year; during the summer solstice the setting sun is directly opposite the western façade. Covering an area roughly the size of the great pyramid of Cheops in Egypt (although not as tall), this superb structure was intended to provide a focal point for the entire city and this portion of the valley. It is almost perfectly square, measuring 225 by 222 m (738 by 728 ft) at its base, and rising 63 m (207 ft) tall, and was completed about 100 AD. Archaeologists estimate the fill material used to build it at nearly four million tons, all carried to the site by humans.

Like many of the buildings at Teotihuacán, the Pirámide del Sol has been marred by unwise restoration attempts. Nevertheless, the climb up the central staircase to the top gives one a unique,

almost sublime, sense of the vast power and intellectual genius which created Teotihuacán. At the top, where originally a temple was situated, the fine expanse of the city is visible.

Not to be missed are the superb wall paintings of the apartment complex of Tepantitla ("thick-walled place" in Nahuatl), located behind the Pirámide del Sol. Families of artisans or priests may have lived here; the walls have excellent paintings of priests in ceremonial garb, a superb mural depicting Tláloc creating rain from the sea, and other paintings of swimmers, animals, priests, and a sacrifice victim.

Returning to the Avenida de los Muertos, its last section rises toward the Pirámide de la Luna. On the left is the Patio de los Cuatro Templitos (Patio of the Four Little Temples), followed by two other temple structures, that of the Animales Mitológicos (Mythological Animals) and then the Templo de la Agricultura. The former has copies of murals depicting animals, and the latter, plants. The original murals have been transferred to Mexico City's National Museum of Anthropology in Chapultepec Park. Original animal murals, including crouching jaguars with feathered head dresses blowing ceremonial conch trumpets, can be found in the Palacio de los Jaguares (Palace of the Jaguars). Next door is the Palacio del Quetzalpapálotl (Palace of the Quetzal Butterfly). Probably a dwelling area for priests, this beautiful structure was burned well before the fall of Teotihuacán, but has been thoughtfully restored. Built around a wide central patio of columns with bas-relief carved birds and butterflies, the palace also had a rear patio, called the Patio de los Tigres (Patio of the Tigers), where priests may also have lived.

Directly beneath the palace is the much older Subestructura de los Caracoles Emplumados (Substructure of the Feathered Snails), accessible by tunnel from the Palacio de los Jaguares. There remain superb carvings and murals showing birds, flowers, and feathered snail shells which may have been used for music or other ceremonies.

Here, at the upper end of the Avenida de los Muertos, is the mystically beautiful Pirámide de la Luna (Pyramid of the Moon). At a height of 46 m (151 ft), it is 17 m (56 ft) shorter than the Pyramid of the Sun, but was designed, given the rising slope of the Avenida, to be exactly the same elevation at the top. Set in a wide plaza of the same name, it is again nearly square (140 by 150 m or 460 by 492 ft). Originally it was surrounded by 12 temples and adorned on its peak by a thirteenth. From the top of the Pirámide de la Luna one looks all the way back down the Avenida de los Muertos, with the Pirámide del Sol in the distance on the left side, and the mountains far beyond. It takes but a little

The baroque Iglesia de Santa Maria de Tonantzintla has one of the most ornately decorated interiors in the world.

imagination to see it all as the vast city of which now only these massive ruins remain. Use care when climbing both the sun and moon pyramid, as they are very steep. The first time I visited Teotihuacán I reached the top of the Pirámide de la Luna just as a thunderstorm arrived over the mountains. Standing atop the pyramid with lightning flashing over the site was one of the most moving experiences of all my travels in Mexico; climbing back down the steep steps was one of the most unnerving.

NEARBY SITES

Also not to be missed are the excellent murals and frescoes at **Tetitla** and the **Palacios de Zacuala** and **Yahuala**. To reach this area, leave the main parking area, continue straight and turn right at the signs. A little farther on the same road is **Atetelco** with two patios richly decorated with frescoes of animals and priests.

WHERE TO STAY AND EAT

The only hotel we can recommend at Teotihuacán is the Club-Mediterranée-operated, **Hotel Villa Arqueológica** ((595) 60244 or 60909. There are 20 expensive rooms, a good dining room and a swimming pool.

There is a pleasant small restaurant on the third level of the Unidad Cultural called **Las Pirámides** ((595) 60187. The meals aren't cheap but the view is worthwhile. **La Gruta** ((595) 60127 or 60104, behind the Pirámide del Sol, is also a good bet.

HOW TO GET THERE

Teotihuacán is located 48 km (30 miles) northeast of Mexico City. If you are traveling there by car, take either Highway 85D, a toll road, or the free Highway 132D. The scenery is better from the free road, which is also the slower route. You can also take a bus from Mexico City. They leave every half hour from the Terminal Central de Autobuses del Norte. The trip will take approximately one hour.

TLAXCALA

Only an hour to the east of the capital city is Mexico's smallest state, Tlaxcala, with its fascinating combination of Mexican history and culture. The state's capital, also called **Tlaxcala**, was in pre-Hispanic times headquarters of the fierce Tlaxcalans with whom the Aztecs were constantly at war. Thus it would appear logical that, after testing the strength of the white Spanish invaders in 1519, they sided with Cortés and were instrumental in assuring eventual Spanish victory over the Aztecs. After the fall of Tenochtitlán, they

converted to Christianity and remained strong supporters of the Spanish.

In appreciation of its assistance to Cortés, Emperor Charles V granted special status to the city and it became the most prosperous settlement in New Spain. However, this glory was short-lived, as the population was destroyed by a three-year plague (1544 through 1546). The town never rebounded; today its population is less than 30,000.

What makes the area attractive to travelers is the relative tranquillity of its colonial town center, the shrine outside the town, and the nearby Cacaxtla archaeological site.

WHAT TO SEE AND DO

Tlaxcala's main square, **Plaza de la Constitución**, is surrounded by colonial government buildings that show a strong Moorish influence. The second floor balcony of the **Palacio de Gobierno** might easily have been spirited here from Granada's Alhambra. Northeast of the plaza is the **Ex-Convento de San Francisco**, founded in 1526. Its magnificence attests to the early importance of Tlaxcala; check out the church's geometric carved cedar ceiling. The side chapel (the oldest portion of the complex) is where the Tlaxcala chiefs were said to have been baptized.

On a hill, about one and a half kilometers (one mile) away, is the **Santuario de Nuestra Señora de Ocotlán**, erected on the site where the Virgin appeared in 1541 and promised an end to a drought and subsequent epidemic. It is not as overwhelming in stature or popularity as Mexico City's Basílica de Nuestra Señora de Guadalupe, but the church is more beautiful. Designed by Francisco Miguel and constructed in the eighteenth century, it represents perfection in the churrigueresque style. The interior has an exceptional octagonal shrine to the Virgin, which is decorated with an overwhelming profusion of baroque art and statuary on the walls and dome.

WHERE TO STAY

The best hotel in the area is the expensive **Hotel Posada de San Francisco Villas Arqueológica** ((256) 26402 FAX (256) 26818, Plaza de la Constitución in Tlaxcala, which is operated by Club Mediterranée. Opened in 1992, this beautiful hotel offers 68 comfortable rooms and suites in the turn-of-the-century Casa de las Piedras (House of Stones). The lobby leads to a courtyard with a large pool. There is also a good restaurant, meeting facilities and a tennis court.

CACAXTLA

Approximately 20 km (12 miles) southwest of Tlaxcala, near the village of Nativitas, is the

Cacaxtla archaeological site (admission fee except on Sunday; open Tuesday through Sunday from 10 AM to 5 PM), which dates from AD 700. The site's well-preserved frescoes, showing colorfully attired figures of various ethnic groups, were discovered in 1975, and have since been instrumental in helping historians understand the chaos that followed the collapse of Teotihuacán. The largest mural, 22 m (72 ft) in length, depicts a battle with surprising realism. Seventeen of the original 42 figures remain completely intact. Several other murals and buildings have been discovered since, and it appears that Cacaxtla was an important trading center for groups from throughout the country. The murals are protected by a steel roof, and photography is allowed only with an additional fee and a permit. Cacaxtla and Tlaxcala can been visited as a one-day excursion from Mexico City or a two-day excursion that could include Puebla. Accommodation is available at Tlaxcala and Puebla.

PUEBLA

Capital of the state of the same name, Puebla is an old colonial city with more than 60 churches set in a high valley. Less than two hours by freeway from Mexico City, it now counts a population of over 1.5 million people, but it has managed to retain some of its former colonial flavor.

GENERAL INFORMATION

Tourist information may be obtained at the **Tourist Information Office** ((22) 461285 or 462044 FAX (22) 323511, Avenue 5, Oriente No. 3, near the cathedral and the library. It is open Monday to Friday, 8 AM to 8:30 PM, Saturday from 9 AM to 8:30 PM and Sunday from 9 AM to 2 PM.

BACKGROUND

Puebla was founded in 1530 on a site chosen for its strategic location from which the colonists could keep a sharp eye on the surrounding villages, and on the shipping routes between Veracruz and Oaxaca. The city's old buildings reflect the origins of the colonists, most of whom came from the region around Talavera in Spain. They adorned their homes and churches with brightly-colored brick and hand-painted tiles. Puebla is one of the most photographed cities in the country, thanks to its exuberantly colorful buildings set against the intense blue sky and the brilliant snow-capped volcanoes backing the city. With good reason the city has received World Heritage designation from UNESCO (United Nations Educational, Scientific and Cultural Organization).

The Spanish who founded Puebla were not fortune-seekers looking for gold and silver. They came with their families to start a new life in New Spain; with them came a love of learning and strong religious beliefs. By 1537, Puebla had a university and by 1539, a bishop. The town soon developed into a prosperous agricultural and industrial center. By the end of the sixteenth century, its tiles were almost as important a cargo for Spain-bound galleons as silver and gold. Later, exports of wool and textiles added to the town's prosperity; in 1835 the nation's first mechanized textile plant began operating in Puebla.

Puebla's peaceful existence was disrupted in the nineteenth century when Antonio López de Santa Anna confronted the United States Expeditionary Corps commanded by General Winfield

Scott, who occupied Puebla briefly. On May 5, 1862, Puebla was again a battlefield; this time, General Ignacio Zaragoza was victorious over French troops led by General Laurence. **Cinco de Mayo**, one of Mexico's major holidays (and a street name seen in almost every city, town, and village), is celebrated in honor of this victory. In 1863, the town was again besieged by the French and was defeated. The French remained until they were driven out by General Porfírio Díaz on April 4, 1867.

Aside from its historic, architectural, and cultural contributions, Puebla is also renowned for its cuisine. *Mole*, a rich piquant sauce made from more than 20 ingredients including almonds, chocolate and red peppers, was created at Puebla's Santa Rosa Convent. The shops surrounding the

Puebla's cathedral shows close links with Spanish late gothic architecture.

convent specialize in ingredients for *mole*, which has become the sauce for special occasions. Another Puebla delicacy is *chilis en nogada*, chilis stuffed with ground meat, nuts and fruit, topped with a walnut cheese sauce and pomegranate seeds. This is only available during pomegranate season from mid-April to mid-October.

WHAT TO SEE AND DO

The magnificent **Plaza Principal**, also called the **Plaza de la Constitución**, is surrounded by colonial government buildings and the country's second largest **cathedral** (open daily from 10:30 AM to 12:30 PM and from 4 PM to 6 PM). Construction

volumes is a sixteenth-century polyglot bible in Chaldean, Hebrew, Greek and Latin. The collection also includes early maps of Mexico's central valley and works by its inhabitants.

Señor Bello, a tobacco magnate and art collector, donated his home and art collection to the city for the **Museo Bello (** (22) 419475, Avenida 3 Pte. No. 302 (admission fee except Tuesday; open Tuesday through Sunday from 10 AM to 4:30 PM). Bello's collection of European art, antique furnishings and Talavera tiles is truly impressive. Visitors must be accompanied by guides; tours are available in English and Spanish.

North of the plaza is the **Capilla del Rosario** (Rosary Chapel), Calle 5 de Mayo No. 405 (open

of this beautifully proportioned edifice began in 1575, but was not completed until 1649, when Juan de Palafox y Mendoza, archbishop of the city, donated much of his personal fortune to complete its main tower. The interior is a showplace of Mexican religious art, and includes a main altar by Manuel Tolsá and José Manzo, carved choir stalls by Pedro Muñoz, a mural on the dome of the Capilla Real by Cristóbal de Villalpando, and baroque paintings in the sacristy by eighteenth-century artists Pedro García Ferrer and Miguel Carbrera.

Just round the corner from the cathedral is the **Casa de la Cultura** (Cultural Center) at Avenida 5 Oriente No. 5, housed in the former archbishop's palace. Its library, **Biblioteca Palafox** (admission fee; open Tuesday through Sunday from 10 AM to 6 PM), was founded by Bishop Palafox and donated to the city. Among its 43,000

daily from 7 AM to 1 PM and from 3 PM to 8:30 PM), housed in the **Iglesia de Santo Domingo**. The chapel has been referred to as the eighth wonder of the world. Its extravagantly adorned Virgin of the Rosary, surrounded by polychrome statues and gold-laminated carvings, is somehow miraculously harmonious with the equally extravagantly decorated walls, ceilings, arches and doorways. This is perhaps the finest example of high Mexican baroque art in the country.

The **Museo Amparo (** (22) 464200, Calle 2 Sur No. 708 (admission fee but free on Monday; open Wednesday through Monday from 10 AM to 6 PM), one of the most renowned archaeological museums in Mexico, is housed in a colonial-era building and contains two floors of outstanding artifacts. There are seven rooms on the first floor and five on the second, each with its own archaeological focus. The Sala Arte Rupestre houses examples of cave paintings from around the world, offering a comparison between the petroglyphs in Baja California and those in France. The Sala Codice del Tiempo has an intriguing wall-sized timeline marking important world events from 2500 BC to AD 1500.

The Talavera-tiled kitchen of the **Convento de Santa Rosa**, on Avenida 12 Poniente at Calle 3 Norte, is famous as the site where Sister Andréa de la Asunción invented *mole* sauce. Today the Convent is the **Museo de Artes Populares** (Handicrafts Museum). Folk art from throughout Mexico and regional costumes are displayed here (admission fee; open Tuesday through Sunday from 10 AM to 4:30 PM); there is also a small shop. Up Calle 3

of *alfeñique*, an almond-sugar paste. The Parian Market, which dates from the eighteenth century, has dozens of stalls selling crafts items. Sunday is market day in Puebla and **Plazuela de los Sapos**, Avenida 7 Oriente and Calle 4 Sur, is transformed into Puebla's version of a flea market.

WHERE TO STAY

There are many hotels in Puebla; prices are quite reasonable when compared with Mexico City.

Expensive

The **Camino Real Puebla** ((22) 328983 TOLL-FREE (800) 7226466, Calle 7, Poniente No. 105,

Norte is the seventeenth-century **Convento de Santa Monica**, Avenida 18 Poniente No. 103 (small admission fee; open Tuesday through Sunday 10 AM to 4:30 PM), which operated clandestinely for 80 years after Benito Juárez's Reform Laws of 1857 made convents and monasteries illegal. Its secret tunnels, disguised doorways and hidden passages are master works of deception.

West of the plaza on Avenida 6 Norte, between Calle 2 Oriente and Calle 8 Oriente, are the **Teatro Principal**, **Casa de Alfeñique** and the **Parian Market**. The Teatro Principal is one of the oldest theaters in the Americas. Completed in 1759, it is still in use today. There are usually performances once a week. The Tourist Office has the schedule. Across the street is the **Museo Regional de Puebla** (small admission fee; open Tuesday through Sunday from 10 AM to 4:30 PM) in a building called the Casa del Alfeñique, because it looks as if it is made

occupies a restored sixteenth-century convent in the historic center of the city. The handsome hotel has 83 rooms and suites as well as three restaurants, and is an excellent choice for those who want to be within walking distance of all Puebla's major attractions. Popular with tour groups is the **El Meson del Angel** ((22) 243000 FAX (22) 487935, Hermanos Serdán No. 807, situated on four hectares (10 acres) of beautifully landscaped grounds, complete with two pools, a tennis court, modern health club, putting green and convention facilities. The hotel's 192 rooms have balconies, refrigerators and cable television; 10 suites come equipped with fireplaces.

The city of Puebla is an entrancing mixture of old and new. OPPOSITE: The city's old buildings, such as the flamboyant town hall, reflect the origins of Puebla's Spanish colonists. ABOVE: Sunday is market day in Puebla.

The Valley of Mexico

Moderate

For the traveler looking for value for money, the **Royalty** ((22) 424740 on the Plaza Principal, is a good choice, with 47 rooms in a four-story colonial style hotel with an outdoor café.

WHERE TO EAT

Everyone who visits Puebla should try *mole poblano*, the city's famous dish. Most places have it, but the best is **Fonda de Santa Clara** ((22) 422659, Avenida 3 Poniente No. 307. If someone in your party does not want Mexican food, **Bodegas del Molino** ((22) 490399, at Molina de San Jose del Puente, on the edge of town, offers good variety.

HOW TO GET THERE

Puebla is located 125 km (80 miles) east of Mexico City and is accessible by car from either Highway 190 or Highway 150D. I recommend the latter, since it is a new toll road and much faster than the old and winding Highway 190. Neither is advisable if you are staying in the center of Mexico City, since exiting the city by car could easily discourage you from going any farther. Far better is the first-class bus service from Mexico City's TAPO bus station; buses run every half-hour and the trip takes about two hours.

CHOLULA

Cholula was once as significant as Teotihuacán in size and ceremonial importance. When Cortés arrived on his march to Tenochtitlán, he found a Toltec city of some 400 temples and 100,000 inhabitants under Aztec dominance. Fearing an ambush, he ordered an assault on the city that turned into a massacre in which some 3,000 men, women and children died. The town was virtually destroyed by Cortés' Tlaxcalan allies. The destruction left Tepanapa, said to have been the largest pyramid in the world, in rubble.

WHAT TO SEE AND DO

Cholula is one of the prettiest towns in central Mexico, thanks to its abundance of church cupolas set against a backdrop of snow-capped volcanoes. Its most significant structure is the **Tepanapa Pyramid**, a five-minute walk from town on Avenida Morelos. The site and a small **museum** are open daily from 10 AM to 5 PM, and English-speaking guides are available to conduct individual tours (admission fee except on Sunday).

Dedicated to Quetzalcoatl, the pyramid has a 425-sq-m (1,395-sq-ft) base covering 17 hectares (42 acres). It originally rose to a height of 62 m (200 ft). When the Spanish returned to Cholula to colonize it after Montezuma's defeat, more of the city and pyramid were destroyed and a church, la **Virgen de los Remedios**, was built on and of the pyramid's rubble. In the course of excavations archaeologists have burrowed over six kilometers (four miles) of tunnels (open to the public) through the hill. They discovered that the pyramid is actually composed of four others superimposed over a small one dating from 900 to 200 BC. The museum at the entrance to the site has a scale model of the pyramid as it is believed to have looked.

A steep path leads up a hill from the tunnels to the Spanish church and a view of the town, which appears as a sea of spires and domes. It is said that Cholula has 365 churches, one for each day of the year. The most significant is that of **San Francisco Acatepec**, 6.5 km (four miles) south of town. The church is completly covered with tiles, and often decorated with flowers and paper banners for holidays and weddings. The town of Cholula certainly does not have the magnificent buildings that distinguish Puebla, but many find it preferable. It is the site of **University of the Americas**, which gives the town a youthful atmosphere.

HOW TO GET THERE

Twelve kilometers (seven and a half miles) west and a suburb of Puebla, Cholula can be reached by car or bus from Puebla via Highway 190.

THE VOLCANOES POPOCATÉPETL AND IZTACCÍHUATL

Nothing can replace the stunning sensation of leaving Mexico City or Puebla and rising into the cool, pine-scented heavens toward the snow-covered volcanoes of Popocatépetl and Iztaccíhuatl. Soaring above the clouds, above the imagination, they look down on the valley of Mexico with the kind condescension of giants from another world, dominating the Sierra Nevada mountain range and dividing the valley from Puebla to the east. After a stay in the polluted, clogged cities, or after the humid, hot lowlands and coast, a trip to the volcanoes clears the lungs and spirit, for they are the soul of Mexico.

In Nahuatl, Popocatépetl (usually called Popo) means "smoking mountain," and Iztaccíhuatl (Izta) "white lady." Like Mount Fuji in Japan and Kilimanjaro in Tanzania, they have come to be

valley, including Mexico City. Thus far, Amecameca's pleasant plaza and sixteenth-century Dominican convent and cloister have remained unharmed.

According to Nahuatl legends, the warrior Popocatépetl fell in love with the lovely princess Iztaccíhuatl. But her father would not accede to the marriage until Popocatépetl first conquered one of the tribe's most formidable enemies. When Popocatépetl returned victorious from the battle, he found that the princess, fearing him dead, had died of a broken heart. He carried her in his arms and placed her body on a hill, lit a torch — and remains there, still, watching over her body in silent grief. When seen from the valley, the extended

identified with Mexico, and can sometimes be spotted from planes flying into the capital city. Except for the Pico de Orizaba, they are the tallest peaks in Mexico, with altitudes of 5,456 m (17,900 ft) and 5,230 m (17,159 ft) respectively. Together with their foothill regions, they compose the **Parque Nacional de Iztaccíhuatl** (better known as Izta-Popo Park), the largest national park near Mexico City.

Situated at 2,500 m (7,500 ft) above sea level, the pretty town of **Amecameca** is nestled in the foothills of the towering volcanoes. The town's 37,000 residents have been evacuated several times since Popo started rumbling in 1994. Popo's last serious eruption was in 1802, but it has been increasing in activity in the past few years (perhaps in protest against the horrid air quality in the nearby metropolis). The volcano occasionally sends clouds of ash and smoke over much of the

peaks and ridges of Iztaccíhuatl bear a striking resemblance to the outline of a reclining woman's head, breast, belly and legs. The outline of Popocatépetl is more towering and severe, the classic profile of a young volcano.

On his march to Tenochtitlán from Veracruz, Cortés crossed between these two mountains, near what is now the road known as the Paso de Cortés, and sent his men up to the crater of Popocatépetl to get the sulfur they needed for making gunpowder. According to Bernal Díaz's *The Conquest of New Spain*, it was from here that Cortés and his men first saw the spectacular sight of Tenochtitlán. Today's climbers are less fortunate, since the Aztecs' former home is now obliterated from view by dense haze and smog.

OPPOSITE: The azuelo-tiled tower of Puebla's cathedral. ABOVE: The serene central courtyard of Santa Rosa Convent.

CLIMBING POPOCATÉPETL AND IZTACCÍHUATL

A climb to the summit of either Popocatépetl or Iztaccíhuatl is a strenuous undertaking and should be approached as an overnight trip. These volcanoes are similar in altitude to Mounts Blanc, Whitney, Rainier or Kenya; they are accessible to experienced climbers in good health who have the wisdom to turn back in the case of bad weather or exhaustion. The round trip up Popocatépetl takes at least two days, but it is better to allow for three days. You can camp at the top of both peaks; the view on a clear and starlit night is incompa-

get information on the climb. Guides for the ascent of Iztaccíhuatl or Popocatépetl can usually be found in La Joya or Tlamacas.

HOW TO GET THERE

From Mexico City, take the Puebla road (Highway 190), turning right onto Highway 115. A few miles past the village of Chalco is Amecameca. Continue from Amecameca 23 km (15 miles) toward Cholula and Puebla on the Paso de Cortés. Near the crest you can turn either south toward Tlamacas and the trailhead for the hike to the summit of Popo, or head north toward La Joya and the trailhead for the trail up Izta.

rable. If you haven't brought sleeping bags and camping gear, they can usually be rented in Tlamacas. Check for reports of volcanic activity and weather conditions at the Mexico City Tourist Office before beginning your climb.

WHERE TO STAY

There is a park shelter at the 4,000 m (13,300 ft) marker on Popocatépetl, accessible by a road from the main highway. Conditions are very basic — all you get for a few dollars is a cement-slab bunk; bring your own sleeping bag, water and food. The **Albergue Vicente Guerrero** in Tlamacas ((5) 553-5896 (a Mexico City number) is a beautiful mountain lodge with bunkrooms, showers and a restaurant. It's best to call the Mexico City number in advance to reserve a bed. The Albergue Guerrero is also the best place to

CUERNAVACA

Known as the city of eternal spring, Cuernavaca has long been the favorite retreat for Mexico's wealthy inhabitants. Before the Spanish conquest it was home to the Tlahuicas, a people conquered by the Aztecs scarcely a hundred years before the latter were overthrown by the Spanish. Some maintain that Montezuma I was born here of a liaison between the Aztec chief Huitzilíhuitl and the magician-daughter of the ruler of Cuernavaca, and that he built a summer residence at nearby Oactepec. Later Hernán Cortés built a palace and a hacienda, at which he introduced sugar cane to the area. Even Maximilian chose Cuernavaca to escape the trials and tribulations of his brief reign.

Connected by freeway to Mexico City, Cuernavaca is today an exclusive suburb of Mexico's privileged, whose magnificent homes and gardens are jealously hidden behind high walls. All the casual visitor sees are walls, burglar alarm systems, and the tips of palms and exotic flowers. Between Christmas and Easter, the local Ladies' Guild offers guided tours to some of the most impressive estates. The Sunday travel section of the *Mexico City News* usually carries the schedule and information on reservations. Fortunately, there are several gardens and museums where you can get a sense of the city's beauty.

GENERAL INFORMATION

The **State Tourist Office** ((731) 43860 is located at Avenida Morelos Sur No. 802. It is open Monday through Friday from 9 AM to 8 PM, Saturday and Sunday from 9 AM to 5 PM.

WHAT TO SEE AND DO

Though the country palaces of Aztec kings have long been destroyed, you can visit the **Casa de Cortés**, which now houses the **Museo de Cuauhnáhuac** ((73) 12-817, Leya No. 100 and Juárez on the Alameda (admission fee; open Tuesday through Sunday from 10 AM to 5 PM). As was often the custom of the conquistadors, Cortés had his home built over a pre-Hispanic structure, bits of which can still be seen. The building, which dates from the 1530s, served as a home for Cortés and his son, and then as the headquarters for subsequent governments. In its current incarnation as a museum, it contains exhibits on Mexico's history and displays of clothing, carriages and furnishings from the colonial era. Most important is the large mural by Diego Rivera depicting the history of Mexico from the time of the Spanish conquest through the Revolution. It was donated to the museum by former United States Ambassador to Mexico, Dwight Morrow, the father of writer Ann Morrow Lindbergh.

The museum faces the **Alameda**, a park connected to the larger **Jardín Juárez**, with its *kiosko* designed by Gustave Eiffel. The larger **Plaza de la Constitución** sits across the street from the garden. All three are pleasant places to sit on a park bench and watch vendors sell crafts from around the area. The fortified **Catedral de la Asunción** on Avenida Hidalgo at Morelos was built by Franciscan monks in the early part of the sixteenth century. It contains seventeenth-century frescoes that tell the story of 25 Franciscan missionaries who were crucified in 1597 near Nagasaki, Japan. It is likely that these missionaries had come from Spain and crossed Mexico, setting sail for the Orient from one of Mexico's Pacific ports.

Visitors often travel to Cuernavaca just to see the **Jardín Borda** (Borda Gardens), Avenida Morelos No. 103 (small admission fee; open Tuesday through Sunday from 10 AM to 3 PM).

The gardens are basically the private park of an enormous estate developed by Frenchman Joseph de la Borda, who made his fortune in mining in the eighteenth century. Complete with a pond where the owner and his wealthy friends boated beside rose gardens, the park is said to have evoked memories of Versailles in the homesick eyes of Emperor Maximilian and his bride Charlotte (known as Carlotta in Mexico). They used the Borda estate as a temporary home until their palace south of the city was completed. Visitors can imagine the scenes of royal parties held amid the lawns, fountains and flowers, which are depicted in paintings displayed in a gallery in the gatehouse.

In 1866, Maximilian established his country residence in the southern suburb of Acapantzingo. Part of this short-lived royal residence has been turned into the **Museo de la Herbolaría** (Herb Museum) ((73) 125956, Avenida Matamoros No. 200 (admission fee; open daily from 10 AM to 5 PM). The house has a small museum of traditional herbal medicine and the extensive gardens contain over 200 orchid plants along with patches of herbs. The small cottage on the estate was built for Maximilian's mistress, *La India Bonita* (the pretty Indian girl).

To the east of the train station is the pre-Columbian site of **Teopanzolco**, "the abandoned temple" in Nahuatl. These twin pyramids dedicated to the Aztec gods Tláloc and Huitzilopochtli are the only remaining relics of the Tlahuican city.

WHERE TO STAY

On most weekends the hotels of Cuernavaca are fully booked, so one is wise to visit during the week or make reservations well in advance for a weekend stay.

OPPOSITE: The town of Cholula crowns a high hill with the volcano Popocatépetl (Smoking Mountain) in the background. ABOVE: Hotel Hacienda Bella Vista in Cuernavaca.

Very Expensive

Long considered the best hotel in town, **Las Mañanitas** ((73) 141466 FAX (73) 183672, Ricardo Linares No. 107, is worth visiting even if you can't get a room. This Relais & Chateaux property has 23 rooms and suites, gorgeously furnished with antiques, ornate brass, gilded accessories and hand-painted tiles; some have balconies overlooking the lawns where peacocks stroll and strut. There are fireplaces in some rooms and a heated pool in the garden. The **Camino Real Sumiya** ((73) 209199 TOLL-FREE (800) 722-6466 FAX (73) 209155, about 15 minutes south of town at Interior del Fraccionamento Sumiya was built as a private home by Woolworth heiress Barbara Hutton in 1959. The 12-hectare (30-acre) estate was converted into a hotel in 1993, with rooms scattered about the property. Fascinated with all things Japanese, Hutton used materials and designers from Japan to create a serene hideaway with formal Japanese gardens and a kabuki theater. The 169 rooms and suites reflect the Asian theme with scrolled wood doors and minimalistic furnishings. There are tennis courts and a pool in the grounds, and the main house has been turned into an elegant lobby, lounge and restaurant.

Expensive

Those wanting a truly self-indulgent getaway head to **Hostería la Quinta** ((73) 183949 FAX (73) 183895 E-MAIL hquintas@intersur.com, a hotel and spa located at Avenida Pte. Gustavo Díaz Ordáz No. 9 at Col. Cantarranas. The 52 terrace suites are designed for ultimate comfort; six have indoor whirlpool baths. The hotel is set within a beautiful 7,000-sq-m (7,700-sq-yard) garden with a large variety of exotic trees and flowers. There are two heated swimming pools and a full-service spa offering massages, facials, exfoliating scrubs with Dead Sea salt and other beautification rituals. A comprehensive gymnasium helps keep the body toned, while the restaurant serves excellent Mexican and continental dishes.

Moderate

The conquistador is said to have slept at the **Hotel Hacienda de Cortés** ((73) 158844 FAX (73) 150032, Plaza Kennedy No. 90. This seventeenth-century hacienda was converted into a 22-suite hotel in the 1970s and was one of the first hacienda hotels in the country. The rooms are decorated with antique furnishings.

Inexpensive

The **Hotel Cadiz** ((73) 189204, Alvaro Obregón No. 329, has 17 simple, clean rooms with private baths and an inexpensive restaurant. Another good deal is the **Hotel Colonia** ((73) 886414, Agustín y León No. 104. This popular little hotel fills up fast so get there early.

WHERE TO EAT

The price of dining out in Cuernavaca reflects the fact that restaurants are catering to the affluent of Mexico City. However, the quality is similarly high. In fact, the **Las Mañanitas** ((73) 141466 restaurant is considered among the top 10 in the country. The specialty here is Mexican food with international touches, and several specials are offered daily. Reservations at this world-class dining room are highly recommended.

For a less expensive meal, try **La Cueva**, Galeana No. 2 at the corner of Rayon, or **Restaurant Los Arcos**, Plaza de Armas No. 4. Both offer reasonably-priced Mexican food and can be reached conveniently from the center of town.

HOW TO GET THERE

Cuernavaca is located 100 km (64 miles) south of Mexico City and 80 km (50 miles) north of Taxco. By car from Mexico City, take Highway 95D, the toll road on the far south of town that goes toward Cuernavaca. From the Periférico take the Insurgentes exit. At the signs for Cuernavaca/Tlalpan, choose either the toll road or the older free road on the right. I much prefer taking the bus, which departs frequently from the Central de Autobuses del Sur. There are direct express buses to Cuernavaca; non-express buses bound for Taxco, Acapulco or Zihuatanejo will also get you to Cuernavaca.

TEPOZTLÁN

Although the area is developing rapidly, one can still find Mexican towns that cling to their pre-Hispanic traditions. **Tepoztlán**, 25 km (15 miles) south of Mexico City, has capitalized on these traditions and is gaining popularity as a tourist spot. Attempts by developers to build a golf-oriented getaway for Mexico City's wealthy residents near Tepoztlán have been greeted with near-violent protests from the 13,000 residents. Far more welcome are visitors who consider the area to have nearly magical properties — New Agers have migrated here to practice yoga, meditation and natural healing, and to learn from the *curanderos* (healers) of the area. The town is noted for its September 8 celebration that honors the Virgin and Tepoztécatl, the town's patron god of intoxication and *pulque* (fermented juice of the maguey plant), and its Holy Week Fiesta del Brinco. In addition, the **Convento de Tepoztlán**, a former fortified monastery, is a national monument, while the Sunday market attracts many from Mexico City.

OPPOSITE: Tepoztlán's Sunday market is a kaleidoscope of color.

The best feature of Tepoztlán is the **Pirámide de Tepoztec**. It is a one-hour climb up a forested hill to the site. Here sits a three-story Tlahuican temple to Tepoztécatl. The ruins are not exceptional, but the carved columns of the third-story shrine and the view make the climb well worth the effort.

South of Tepoztlán are several other villages (with populations under 10,000), many of which have beautiful sixteenth-century convents and monasteries. The most interesting of these monasteries and convents are found at Yautepec, Oaxtepec, Tlayacapan, Atlatlahuacan, Yecapixtla and Ocuituco; there are few hostelries or restaurants in these villages.

Xochicalco, "place of the house of flowers" in Nahuatl. Considered to have been an important ceremonial center from AD 750 to 900, evidence of Teotihuacán, Zapotec and Mayan influences can still be seen at the site. Scholars believe that Xochicalco may have been a pre-Conquest university for the study of astronomy and the calendar; the Toltec god-king Quetzalcoatl may himself have studied here.

The central pyramid, **Pirámide de Quetzalcoatl**, is adorned with carved reliefs of plumed serpents (Quetzalcoatl) on all four sides, human figures with strong Mayan features seated cross-legged, and hieroglyphics bearing some traces of the original paint. On the western side of the

MORELOS

Cortés chose several areas for country estates; in Morelos, a one-hour drive southeast of Mexico City, he built the beautiful Hacienda Cocoyoc. It fell into ruins over the subsequent centuries, but in the 1970s a Mexico City developer came upon it and decided to create a spa. The result is **Hacienda Cocoyoc** ((735) 22000, built from the ruined hacienda sugar mill, stables and stone aqueduct. The 300 rooms and suites have a Spanish colonial theme; golf and fine dining are available. But it's the spa, with an abundance of beauty treatments that brings *chilangos* for rest and relaxation.

XOCHICALCO

Southwest of Cuernavaca are the little visited, but nonetheless archaeologically important, ruins of

pyramid is the entrance to a tunnel which leads to a domed, circular structure. This structure is thought to be an observatory where, at the time of the equinoxes, the sun casts its rays directly into the room. Also at the site are the **Templo Stelae**, a well-preserved ball court, and evidence of a sophisticated sewage system. It is well worth visiting also for its splendid setting amid rolling hills and the backdrop of the distant sierras of Morelos.

TAXCO

Taxco is the most famous of Mexico's preserved colonial towns. With quaint red-roofed, white houses and cobblestone streets winding down a rugged hillside in the Sierra Madre, it is one of the must-see cities on a colonial-oriented itinerary; those who love silver jewelry can't pass it by.

GENERAL INFORMATION

The **Tourist Office** ((762) 21525, Avenida de los Plateros No. 1, is open weekdays from 9 AM to 2 PM and from 4 PM to 7 PM. Taxco is located 1,800 m (6,000 ft) above sea level and the air is crisp and clear. Average temperatures are 22°C (72°F), with the months of April and May the warmest, and December and January the coolest.

BACKGROUND

When the Spanish conquerors arrived at "Tlachco," as it was then called, they discovered

to town to write a book. A friend convinced him to turn his artistic talents to designing silver objects. He found a few apprentices among the locals, brought in experts to teach them the trade and eventually turned his small workshop into a prosperous factory, from which came Taxco's reputation as the Silver Center of the world.

Today, there is probably nowhere else in the world that has as many silver shops per capita as Taxco. At least 200 shops are the backbone of the town's economy, supporting its 87,000 residents. The National Silver Fair, which takes place the last week in November and the first week in December, is an international event. Taxco remains a traditional Mexican city, as well, and its Semana Santa

rich deposits of silver and gold. However, real prosperity did not come until the eighteenth century when the Frenchman Joseph de la Borda (who Mexicanized his name to José) discovered a rich lode of silver. In gratitude for his good fortune, he built several of Taxco's most important structures including the magnificent **Iglesia de Santa Prisca y San Sebastián**, the church that stands on the central plaza. It is said that he promised to pave the road between Taxco and Mexico City with silver coins, if only the Pope would visit. But the Pope never came and, over the years, Taxco's importance as a mining center waned. Fortunately for Taxco, the Mexican Government had the foresight in 1928 to declare the town a National Colonial Monument, which means original façades must be preserved and new buildings have to conform to the old architectural style. In the early 1930s an American named William Spratling came

celebrations during Easter are among the most elaborate in the country.

WHAT TO SEE AND DO

José de la Borda's masterpiece, the pink stone **Iglesia de Santa Prisca y San Sebastián** on the Plaza Borda, is said to have cost more than US$8 million when it was built in the eighteenth century. This twin-towered church is unquestionably the center of interest for tourists visiting Taxco, as well as the focal point of the town. The carved façade and tiled dome are oft photographed while the gold-leafed saints and angels inside prove Borda's wealth. Several paintings

OPPOSITE: The plumed serpent of Xochicalco. ABOVE: Looking down on Taxco LEFT, and RIGHT ornate window and portico moldings adorn a downtown street.

by Miguel Carbrera, Mexico's most famous colonial-era artist, hang in the church and in the sacristy beyond the altar.

Behind the church is the **Museo Guillermo Spratling ((762) 21660 at Porfirio Delgado and El Arco (admission fee; open Tuesday through Sunday from 10 AM to 5 PM). Though one might expect to see Spratling's silver work, this small museum instead contains Spratling's personal collection of pre-Columbian artifacts and an exhibit on colonial mining. The **Museo Virreyenal de Taxco ((762) 25501, on Calle Juan Ruíz de Alarcón, (admission fee; open daily from 10 AM to 5 PM) is housed in the Moorish-styled **Casa Humboldt**. Once an inn for travelers between Mexico City and Acapulco, the house's German name comes from that of scientist-explorer Baron Alexander von Humboldt, who resided here briefly in 1803. The museum contains eighteenth-century paintings, costumes and historical artifacts along with a small display on von Humboldt's expeditions.

William Spratling's hacienda home and silver workshop are now open to the public as the **Spratling Ranch Workshop ((762) 26108, located nine kilometers (six miles) south of town on Highway 95. A visit here helps explain how Spratling managed to revive the town's silver industry. Though Spratling died in 1967, his designs are still created by craftsmen he trained and their workmanship is truly outstanding. Silver fans should also visit the workshop of **Los Castillo ((762) 20652, eight kilometers (five miles) south of town on Highway 95. Castillo was one of Spratling's students who went on to develop his own distinctive style. The items in the workshop are not for sale, but you can purchase Los Castillo silver pieces at the shop of the same name on Plaza Bernal in the city. Los Castillo shops are also located in upscale shopping centers and hotels in major resort areas.

Taxco is a wonderful city for those who love to walk; I can never resist following narrow cobble-stoned streets up and down hills, and around neighborhoods. It's difficult to get truly lost, since the spires of Santa Prisca are always in sight. These detours off the beaten track are a relief after visiting several silver shops in a row; after a while, all those potential purchases get overwhelming. Those not prone to acrophobia can get a marvelous view of the town from the cable car to Hotel Monte Taxco on a hill north of town.

WHERE TO STAY

There are plenty of hotels to choose from in Taxco; one caveat is worth keeping in mind, however. The city's steep hills are murder on transmissions, brakes and sensitive ears; after a few nights of listening to grinding gears the place loses its charm. Many of the finer hotels are located outside the city. If you choose to stay close to the plaza, bring the best ear plugs you can find.

Expensive

Guest cottages are set about a landscaped hilltop at the **Hacienda de Solar ((762) 20323 FAX (762) 20687 on Calle del Solar. The 22 rooms are individually decorated with fine Mexican folk art; the restaurant's view is better than its food.

Moderate

Tour groups and Taxco aficionados enjoy the colonial-style ambiance at the **Hotel Monte Taxco ((762) 21300 at Franc. Lomas de Taxco. A funicular runs up a steep hill to the hotel (there's a road

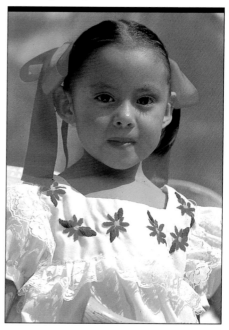

for those burdened with luggage), which has 160 rooms, a nine-hole golf course, pool and tennis courts. The 150-room **Posada Misión ((762) 20063 FAX (762) 22198, Cerro de la Misión No. 32, is worth visiting to view Juan O'Gorman's murals by the pool area. For families traveling with children, the **Hotel de la Borda ((762) 10015, 20225 at Cerro del Pedregal No. 2, is a good choice. This hotel offers a children's pool and playground, as well as cable television, tennis courts, room service and a restaurant.

Inexpensive

**Hotel Santa Prisca ((762) 20080, Cena Obscuras No. 1, has 38 rooms. The hotel is colonial style; breakfast is included in the room rate. **Posada de

OPPOSITE: The eighteenth-century Iglesia de Santa Prisca y San Sebastián has an elegantly carved façade. ABOVE: A charming Mexican child.

Las Castillo ((762) 21396, located on Calle Juan Ruíz de Alarcón, with 15 rooms is smaller than the Santa Prisca, but the rooms are clean and the service pleasant.

WHERE TO EAT

Restaurants in Taxco are generally good and reasonably priced, especially when compared with other towns around Mexico City. The classier hotels have expensive international menus, but Mexican restaurants with great food and reasonable prices are abundant. The home style *enchiladas*, soups and egg dishes are excellent (and moderately priced) at **Santa Fe** ((762) 21170, Hidalgo No. 2. **Cielito Lindo** ((762) 20603, Plaza Borda No. 14, offers pleasant decor and good food with plenty of ambiance. It's a busy place at lunch time when the waiters are hopping. The food ranges from Mexican dishes to soup and roast chicken. **Señor Costilla's** ((762) 23215, Plaza Borda No. 1, has a prime location overlooking the plaza and good, abundant meals served in typical Carlos Anderson style. Like others in this chain, the restaurant is decorated with tacky kitsch and patrons are meant to have fun. If you don't mind blatantly looking like a tourist, be sure to claim one of the few tiny balcony tables for an early dinner; almost anything you order, be it barbecued ribs, tortilla soup, or *carne asada*, will be hearty and filling. I had one of my favorite meals ever at one of these tables when I first started traveling alone in Mexico; the waiters and the plaza's denizens provided much camaraderie and entertainment.

HOW TO GET THERE

If you are driving from Mexico City, take Highway 95D on the south side of town. From the Periférico, take the Insurgentes exit to the sign reading "Cuernavaca/Tlalpan." You may take either the toll road or the free road. Continue south to the Amacuzac interchange and go straight on to Taxco. The drive will take about three and a half hours. If you prefer to do it by bus, then catch one at Central de Autobuses del Sur station.

AROUND TAXCO

CACAHUAMILPA CAVES

The **Cacahuamilpa Caves** (admission fee; open daily from 10 AM to 3 PM), 32 km (21 miles) northwest of Taxco in the **Parque Nacional de Cacahuamilpa**, are worth exploring if you are fascinated by tunnels and stalactites. I don't find them as impressive as the caves in the Yucatán Peninsula, but the 16 km (10 miles) of tunnels are good spots for a long, cool walk. A light-and-sound show detracts somewhat from the natural beauty. Far-

ther north are the equally impressive but less developed **Estrella Caves**, also worth a visit.

IXCATEOPAN

In the parish church in Ixcateopan, 40 km (25 miles) west of Taxco, is the altar under which Cuauhtémoc, the last Aztec ruler, was supposedly buried. Historians and archaeologists cannot agree, but many claim that after Cortés ordered Cuauhtémoc's death in Honduras in 1423, his body was brought back here for burial.

TOLUCA

Less than an hour southwest of Mexico City, at 2,680 m (8,793 ft), Toluca has a cooler climate and escapes much of the pollution of its metropolitan neighbor. As the capital of the state of Mexico, Toluca has grown into a large city of about 500,000 residents. It has long been a market center for groups living in outlying villages and has now become an industrial center as well. Toluca has always been known for its Friday market, which used to sprawl along the streets surrounding the central plaza. The market is still held on Friday, but was moved to the periphery of the city near the bus station on Paseo Tollocán in the 1970s. At first glance, it seems that plastic household items and blaring CDs have overtaken the market (formally called **Mercado Juárez**), but if you dig deep into its narrow byways you'll find some unusual handicrafts and memorable market scenes. The folk art selection is better a few blocks east at **CASART**, Paseo Tollocán No. 900, with its excellent assortment of crafts from around the state. Prices are reasonable, but fixed.

The old art nouveau iron structure that housed the former central market has been converted into the **Cosmovitral Botánico**, a botanical garden, at the corner of Juárez and Lerdo (admission fee; open Tuesday through Sunday from 9 AM to 4 PM). The gardens are framed by the building's 54 stained-glass panels, which cast shadows on tropical and desert plants. Toluca's historical center is worth a wander once you've finished with the market (Friday tours to the market and city are offered by several companies in Mexico City). There are several art and history museums within walking distance of the main plaza and the city's famed nineteenth-century *portales*, or arcades.

AROUND TOLUCA

CALIXTLAHUACA

North of Toluca is the pre-Columbian site of Calixtlahuaca (Nahuatl for "place of houses on the plain"), which is believed to have been the location of the only round temple in Mexico. The four-storied circular temple is thought to have been dedicated originally to the Huastec wind god Ehecatl and later rededicated to Quetzalcoatl by the Aztecs after they conquered the city in 1474. Among the more than 20 structures found at the site, the most interesting but macabre is the cross-shaped **Altar of the Skulls**. Some structures are still under excavation and are not yet open to the general public.

MALINALCO

Set in the forested hills southeast of Toluca and directly west of Cuernavaca is the village of **Matlalzincan**. Surrounded by steep cliffs, this village, with a population of less than 30,000, is laid out today much as it was at the time of the Spanish conquest.

When the Spaniards arrived here in 1521, they found the Matlalzinca people living under Aztec rule at the site of **Malinalco**. This small indigenous group built their ceremonial centers by carving into the rocky hillsides. As was their practice, the Spaniards destroyed much of the center and used its stones to build a nearby Augustinian monastery. Up 400 steps is the **Templo del Jaguar y Águila** (Temple of Jaguar and Eagle), the exterior of which is the head of the "earth monster" with jaws open, eyes and fangs clearly visible, and tongue spread out as a door mat. The inner sanctuary is probably where Aztec initiation rites were performed. On the floor is a small receptacle that archaeologists presume was used for the hearts of sacrificial victims. As the name of the temple would suggest, there are many sculptures and carvings of jaguars and eagles.

NEVADO DE TOLUCA

The **Parque Nacional de Nevado de Toluca** surrounds the snow-capped extinct volcano Nevado de Toluca or Xinantécatl ("the naked man" in Nahuatl), which rises 4,558 m (14,954 ft) and is located 44 km (27 miles) southwest of Toluca. Hiking trails circle the slopes and lead to the rim of the giant crater containing two lakes, known as the **Lagos del Sol y Luna** (Lake of the Sun and the Moon). This spectacular sight is not limited to hikers: A dirt road goes to the summit, from which one can usually see the volcanoes Popocatépetl and Iztaccíhuatl and the mountain ranges of Guerrero and Michoacán. The park caters to hikers, not tourists, so one is well-advised to bring food and drink. Guides proffer their services to drivers and hikers at the entrance to the park.

VALLE DE BRAVO

Another escape route for *chilangos* (as the wealthy residents of Mexico City are known) is the three-

hour drive west to the **Valle de Bravo** about 100 km (62 miles) beyond Toluca. Valle de Bravo is an old Mexican village with cobblestone streets and red-roofed white houses on the shores of a large artificial lake. The town is known for its pottery, textiles and embroidery, all of which are plentiful at the Sunday street market around the central square. The countryside around the lake has hiking trails along riverbanks to waterfalls, but most visitors come here for waterskiing, sailing and windsurfing.

Where to Stay

If you would like to pamper yourself for a weekend or longer, make a reservation at the very ex-

pensive **Avandaro Golf & Spa Resort (** (726) 60366 TOLL-FREE (800) 525-4800, Vega de Ríos/n, Fracción Avandaro. In addition to its golf course, the resort has a a wonderful spa where you can indulge in a relaxing massage or rejuvenating facial. There are 110 suites, all with fireplaces. The amusement park beside the spa is a popular weekend thrill for *chilangos*.

If you are looking for slightly more moderate accommodation, try the **Hotel Rancho las Margaritas (** (726) 20986 at Carretera Valle-Villa Victoria Km 10. This hotel offers a swimming pool, restaurant and lounge, a coffeeshop and conference facilities. There are also horses available for hire.

Dramatizing the last days of Christ, Taxco's Easter Week celebration is a blend of Catholic and pre-Columbian rituals.

Central
Mexico

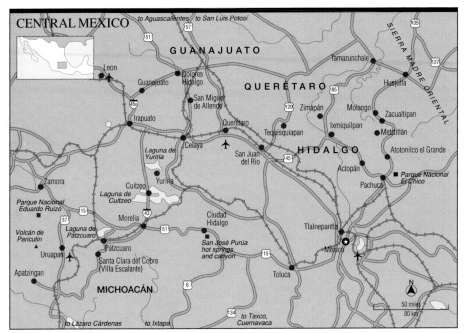

CENTRAL MEXICO

MORE THAN 250 YEARS after the conquistadors arrived, it was the heartland's wealthy, liberal *criollos* who first dared to speak out against Spanish rule. Many of the battles for independence were fought in the central Mexico states of Michoacán, Guanajuato, Querétaro and Hidalgo. Among the heartland's most famous leaders are Ignacio de Allende, José María Morelos, Melchor Ocampo, Padre Miguel Hidalgo y Costilla and Lázaro Cárdenas. Its history is one of the main reasons for visiting this area. But there is also a wealth of fine colonial architecture in the cities of Morelia, Guanajuato, San Miguel de Allende and Querétaro. Michoacán is filled with villages where artisans create some of the country's finest folk art. It also has wonderful forests and is home to an amazing natural phenomenon — the annual migration of monarch butterflies to the sanctuary at El Rosario.

INLAND MICHOACÁN

Of the many regions of Mexico admired for their natural beauty, Michoacán is among the most diverse. It is a panoply of soaring plateaus, towering volcanoes, sheer pine-forested slopes, crashing rivers and tropical valleys, vibrant towns and, on the Pacific Coast, thundering surf, coastal marshes and white beaches.

Cortés and his conquistadors wasted no time after the razing of Tenochtitlán in finding the Aztec ore mines of Central Mexico. The Spaniards quickly set about extracting their wealth of gold, silver and precious metals at rates previously unimaginable to the native residents. Here,

among the rolling hills of the larger region surrounding Mexico City, the Spanish colonialists built their cities and adorned them with lavish cathedrals, monasteries, convents, universities and private mansions.

In pre-Hispanic times Michoacán was home to the Purépecha — or Tarascans, as named by the Spaniards. They lived mainly by fishing, hunting and cultivating maize. Details of their religious life are obscure, as are their linguistic roots. Divided into two classes — warrior-priests and peasants — the society developed a high sophistication in feather-work, pottery, textiles and stonework. The warriors possessed exceptionally fine metal weapons. Indeed, they were one of the groups able to rebuff the fierce Aztecs, insatiable in their thirst for sacrificial victims.

Their skills as craftsmen were reinforced by the Spanish colonizers and are still today a trademark of the region. From Michoacán come some of the finest handicrafts in Mexico.

MORELIA

About 280 km (174 miles) or two and a half hours by car, west of Mexico City on Route 15, Morelia sits, surrounded by gentle hills, 1,951 m (6,401 ft) above sea level. It is the commercial and cultural capital of Michoacán; most of its buildings are of *cantera rosa* (a pink stone mined throughout the area) and date from the sixteenth and seventeenth

Although not far from Mexico City, central Mexico retains its rural flavor, particularly around Pátzcuaro.

centuries. Local ordinances require new construction to conform to the colonial style and, with some unfortunate exceptions, they do.

BACKGROUND

Before the arrival of the Spaniards, Morelia lay within the territory of the Purépecha, whose center was Lake Pátzcuaro. The first permanent European establishment here was a school aimed at converting the local populace, established by Juan de San Miguel in 1531; the town itself was founded in 1541. Originally known as Valladolid, it was renamed Morelia in 1828 in honor of José María Morelos, a native son and well-loved hero in the War of Independence.

Another man beloved and honored throughout the state is Don Vasco de Quiroga, the first bishop of Michoacán, who converted the Purépecha to Christianity and then fought to protect them from exploitation by their Spanish "saviors." Tata Vasco, as they called him (*tata* being a term of great respect which means "father") was a fervent follower of the philosophies of Thomas Moore and wanted to create a Utopia in Michoacán. He built hospitals and schools, and traveled from village to village teaching trades and crafts. Many consider his teachings to be responsible for the quality and variety of folk art still produced in the region.

GENERAL INFORMATION

The **Tourist Office ℂ** (43) 128081 or 120415 FAX (43) 129816, Calle Nigromante No. 79, is open weekdays from 8 AM to 8 PM and weekends from 9 AM to 4 PM.

WHAT TO SEE AND DO

Morelia's majestic central square, known as either the **Plaza de Armas** or **Plaza de los Mártires** (Martyrs' Square) is the very heart of the city. During the War of Independence several rebel priests, including Father Matamoros, a disciple of Morelos, were murdered in the square. Today the past seems all but forgotten as one strolls under geometrically cut Indian laurels and tulip trees with bright orange blossoms.

At the east end of the plaza is the **Catedral**, the third largest in Latin America and one of exquisite proportions. Its two 65-m (200-ft) baroque towers are perfectly balanced with its massive body. Work began on the cathedral in 1660; it wasn't completed until 1744. The interior, once richly adorned, is barren by Mexican standards—much of its precious metals were stripped to help fund the War of Independence. The silver pedestal, on which the Eucharist is displayed, and the baptismal font are wonderful reminders of how ornate

the interior must once have been. Any present lack of ornamentation is certainly compensated by the magnificent three-story organ, which was built by the House of Wagner of Germany in 1905 and has nearly 5,000 pipes. An international organ festival is held here each May during the State Fair (usually May 1 to 21). The Tourist Office has information on this and other organ concerts.

Across Avenida Madero is the **Palacio de Gobierno ℂ** (43) 127872, Avenida Madero No. 63 (free admission; open daily from 9 AM to 2 PM and from 6 PM to 10 PM), the former Tridentine Seminary, built in the eighteenth century. Morelos, Melchor Ocampo and the infamous Emperor Agustín de Iturbide all studied here. Murals by Alfredo Zalce, a native of the state, decorate the second floor and the stairwell.

At the southwest corner of the Zócalo is an eighteenth-century mansion in which Emperor Maximilian stayed. Today it houses the **Museo Michoacán ℂ** (43) 120407, Calle Allende No. 305, (small admission fee; open Tuesday through Saturday from 9 AM to 7 PM) whose exhibits are dedicated to Mexican history and art. A block south of the museum on Hidalgo is **Iglesia San Agustín**, a simple church surrounded by a tranquil park that was once a patio of its adjoining convent. On the east corner of the park is the **Casa Natal de Morelos ℂ** (43) 122793, Calle Corregidora No. 113, the house where Morelos was born on September 30, 1765. The colonial building is now an historical library and national monument (free admission; open Monday through Friday from 9:30 AM to 2 PM and from 4 PM to 8 PM; Saturday and Sunday from 9:30 AM to 2 PM).

Another block south and east is the **Casa Museo de Morelos ℂ** (43) 132651, Avenida Morelos Sur No. 323 (small admission fee; open daily from 9 AM to 7 PM), home to generations of the Morelos family until 1934. Now owned by the state, it is filled with memorabilia.

Northeast of the Plaza de Armas, on the **Plaza San Francisco**, is the **Casa de Artesanías de Michoacán ℂ** (43) 121248, Calle Vasco de Quiroga at Calle Humboldt (open daily from 9 AM to 8 PM). This combination museum and shop is a good place to learn about the region's handicrafts. Upstairs the crafts are organized by village, each one running its own tiny cooperative. Prices are reasonable, so hard bargaining is not necessary.

To the northwest of the cathedral on Avenida Madero Poniente at Nigromante is the former **Colegio de San Nicolás de Hidalgo**, the second oldest college in the Americas, founded by Don Vasco de Quiroga in 1540. Father Miguel Hidalgo was a student here and then later a professor. It still serves as a school and visitors are welcome (during school hours) to view the courtyard enclosed by two floors of arcades, and the mural of Purépecha life in pre-Hispanic days.

The **Palacio Clavijero**, across Nigromante, was built as a Jesuit seminary at the end of the sixteenth century. Named after Francisco Javier Clavijero, Mexico's most famous eighteenth-century scholar, the Palacio has been converted to offices and the public library. The tourist information office is also located here.

North along Nigromante at the intersection of Santiago Tapia is the **Jardín de las Rosas**, around which is clustered the beautiful **Iglesia Santa Rosa**, the internationally famous **Music Conservatory** and the **Museo del Estado** (State Museum). The Music Conservatory building was the former Convent de Las Rosas, the first Dominican convent in Morelia, and the oldest music school in the

century, when it was built as a Carmelite convent. Today it is the center of the city's cultural life and a gathering place for young people. It has some large, whimsical soldered metal statues in the courtyard, a small café and usually a list of upcoming cultural activities.

A 15-minute walk northeast of the city center is **Plaza Villalongín**, Avenida Madero Ote and Santos Degollado, which contains a fountain that has become the symbol of Morelia. Three bare-breasted Purépecha maidens hold aloft a huge tray filled with the riches which make Michoacán famous. Across the street from **Bosque Cuauhtémoc**, Morelia's largest park, begins the **aqueduct**, almost two kilometers (just over a mile) long,

Americas. It is now the home of the Children's Choir of Morelia, which has performed all over the world. Occasionally rehearsals are open to the public. The Museo del Estado ((43) 130629, Guillermo Prieto No. 176 (free admission; open Monday through Friday from 9 AM to 2 PM and from 4 PM to 8 PM), has ethnological exhibits on the people of Michoacán. One room is a reconstruction of Morelia's first drugstore, founded in 1868.

One block west, and heading back south along Gómez Farias, is Morelia's **Mercado de Dulces** (Sweets Market). Here are enough candy shops to satiate even the most insistent sweet tooth. (Just the sugary smell of the confections is enough to add calories!)

The **Casa de la Cultura** ((43) 131320, Morelos Norte No. 485 (open daily from 10 AM to 8 PM), is one of the oldest and most impressive structures in Morelia. Construction began in the sixteenth

with 253 arches. It was built during a drought in 1785 to bring water to the city. A couple of blocks beyond Bosque Cuauhtémoc is the **Contemporary Art Museum** ((43) 125404, Avenida Acueducto No. 18 (free admission; open Tuesday through Sunday from 10 AM to 2 PM and from 4 PM to 8 PM), which has both a permanent collection and interesting rotating exhibits.

WHERE TO STAY

Most hotels in Morelia are unheated. With winter temperatures averaging 15°C (59°F) — and not infrequently even lower — it is advisable to bring some warm clothing. April through June, when temperatures are about 20°C (68°F), are the region's warmest months.

Muraled cloisters of Morelia's Museo del Estado.

Very Expensive

The most luxurious lodging is at **Villa Montaña**
((43) 140231 or 140179 TOLL-FREE (800) 525-4800
FAX (43) 151423 on Calle Patazimba s/n. Overlooking the city, this deluxe 55-room hotel has a heated
pool and tennis court, and an excellent restaurant
with international and Mexican cuisine. Some of
the rooms have fireplaces; all have special touches
such as antiques and cozy sitting areas.

Moderate

Located on the southwest corner of the Plaza de
Armas is the recently remodeled, eighteenth-
century mansion that is now **Hotel Virrey de
Mendoza** ((43) 126719 FAX (43) 126719, Portal
Matamoros No. 16. The marble-floored lobby is
immaculate, practically oozing colonial opulence.
The exterior accommodations are noisy because
of traffic below, and interior ones are just slightly
better. Nonetheless, the 52 rooms are beautifully

decorated and have bathtub and cable television.
The elegant restaurant is open all day.

The colonial **Posada de la Soledad** ((43) 121888
FAX (43) 122111, Zaragoza No. 90, has 60 rooms,
some nicer (and pricier) than others. Compare
them for street noise, furnishings, cost, and ambiance before accepting. Some rooms have fireplaces
and bathtubs. In low season, you might be able to
negotiate a better room at near the standard price.

Hotel Mansion Acueducto ((43) 123301
FAX (43) 122020, near the aqueduct, Avenida Acueducto No. 25, provides a quieter atmosphere than
do downtown hotels, but it is frequently full. All
36 rooms are equipped with telephone and cable
television. There is a swimming pool.

Morelia has a very inexpensive **Youth Hostel**
((43) 133177, Calle Chiapas No. 180 at Oaxaca, with
76 beds, near the bus station. There is an 11 PM
curfew and you must share a double bunk-bed
room with other travelers, but the place is clean,

the owners friendly and the restaurant serves breakfast, lunch and dinner at reasonable prices.

WHERE TO EAT

Moderate

A thoroughly charming restaurant is **Fonda las Mercedes (** (43) 126113, Calle León Guzmán No. 47, where flocks of attentive waiters in formal black-and-white attire attend well-heeled Mexicans, enjoying both the food and the elegant yet comfortable atmosphere. Warm bread with herbed butter arrives shortly after you are seated. The varied menu highlights international food, with six varieties of crêpes and refreshingly different salads, such as the salad of gruyère cheese and fresh mushrooms in vinaigrette sauce.

Although the name means "the dinner guests," **Los Comensales (** (43) 129361, Zaragoza No. 148, is a good choice for breakfast, lunch, or

dinner. Just north of the Zócalo, it has location, atmosphere and tasty Mexican food — although service can be slow.

The huge buffets for breakfast, lunch and dinner make **Cenduria Lupita II (** (43) 244067, Avenida Camelinas No. 3100, Col. Jardines del Rincon, a good place to sample a variety of regional cooking. It's a short taxi ride from the town center, near the Gigante grocery and the movie theater.

Inexpensive

One of the best taco stops is **Los Pioneros (** (43) 134938, Aquiles Serdán No. 7, popular with locals for the enormous portions of delicious *alambre* (grilled meat, onions, peppers and cheese) in various presentations — but always served with fresh tortillas, homemade salsa and lots of napkins. Takeout is also available. For a light snack, try the small and aptly named **Café (** (43) 128601, Santiago Tapia No. 363, in the garden across from the Conservatorio de las Rosas. Symphonic music plays inside, drifting through to those reading books or newspapers at the white wrought-iron tables outside. The baguette sandwiches come with French fries or salad. The menu also offers meat or spinach pies, cakes, and coffee or tea; red and white wine is also available.

HOW TO GET THERE

Morelia's Aeropuerto Francisco J. Mugica is about a half-hour drive from the city center. The airport receives flights on regional carriers from Mexico City, Guadalajara and Tijuana. The main bus terminal is downtown at Ruíz and Goméz Farías, north of the cathedral. There is frequent bus service to Mexico City, Guadalajara, Pátzcuaro and Querétaro.

AROUND MORELIA

EL ROSARIO

A 10-hour day trip out to the **Monarch Butterfly Sanctuary** at El Rosario is worthwhile for nature buffs and can be arranged through tour operators in Morelia. The butterflies, which make a 4,800-km (3,000-mile) trek twice each year between Canada and the northern United States and the pine forests of Central Mexico, can be seen from November through March, but the best time is after mid-December. The butterflies travel this great distance to escape the harsh northern winters and to feed on the *oxamel* tree and reproduce. You'll see monarchs in the air, as well as blanketing the evergreen trees (making them appear brown); butterflies

Morelia's seventeenth-century baroque cathedral is the venue for an international organ festival held each May.

that have died form a gold and brown patterned mosaic on the forest floor.

Of the eight protected nesting sites in Michoacán, only the El Rosario site is open to the public. It's a bit of a hike up the steep slope to see the butterflies, so wear sturdy shoes and bring a walking stick. Also, dress in layers if possible, as the weather can get chilly as the elevation rises.

CUITZEO

About 24 km (15 miles) north of Morelia, on the banks of a shallow saltwater lake, lies the picturesque town of Cuitzeo. Its **convent**, built by Augustinian monks in the sixteenth century and

profusely decorated with carvings and painting by Indian artisans, is worth a visit. A four-kilometer (two-and-a-half mile) causeway connects the south shore to the town situated on a spit in the center of the lake. In the summer the lake is almost dry, hardly the place for a bathing vacation.

YURIRIA

An hour's drive farther north (55 km or 34 miles), in the state of Guanajuato about halfway between Morelia and Celaya, is the convent town Yuriria. Before the Conquest, Yuriria was a major Purépecha settlement; and now this town is a national historical monument because of its sixteenth-century Augustinian church and monastery. Purépecha converts to Christianity put their talents to work on this impressive structure, which is a

mixture of medieval and Gothic styles and a tribute to the native peoples' skill and artistry.

PARQUE NACIONAL SIERRRA MADRE OCCIDENTAL

About 70 km (44 miles) east of Morelia is the Parque Nacional Sierra Madre Occidental. The serpentine roads of the park's jagged terrain should be negotiated with care. Luckily, buses and trucks are not allowed on these roads; nonetheless they are crowded on weekends and holidays. The park has good hiking trails and camping sites, as well as fabulous views of steep forested slopes, narrow valleys and tree-lined, precipitous crests.

PÁTZCUARO

Set in the hills that rise from the shores of Lago de Pátzcuaro, the town of Pátzcuaro is situated about 57 km (36 miles) southwest of Morelia — an easy hour's dirve from Morelia and a four-and-a-half-hour drive from Mexico City. Despite its 65,000 inhabitants, it remains an Indian village, and the locals seem to live up to the meaning of its name: Place of Happiness.

One of the few tribes in Central Mexico able to resist Aztec domination, these noble people call themselves Purépecha. The Spaniards renamed them Tarascans, although today they prefer to be called by their true name. Tzintzuntzán, near Pátzcuaro, was the Purépecha capital and an important ceremonial center until the Spanish renegade leader Nuño de Guzmán arrived. His reign of terror and residency here lasted only long enough to destroy the site and send the surviving natives fleeing to the mountains. In 1537 Don Vasco de Quiroga, the first bishop of Michoacán, came to the area and began the slow process of regaining the Indians' confidence; the town was slowly repopulated. Tata Vasco installed his bishopric here and staunchly defended the rights of the indigenous people. After his death the bishopric was moved to Morelia.

Many towns just outside Pátzcuaro are famous for their Day of the Dead celebrations — ceremonies combining Catholicism with pre-Christian beliefs. On November 1, All Saints' Day, parents and family honor their children who have died, calling it "Dia de los Angelitos" (Day of the Little Angels), as children are believed to be without sin. Families build altars to their little angels, beginning on October 31, filling them with favorite foods and drinks of the deceased to draw them to the altar.

All Souls' Day celebrations begin the evening of November 1. Purépecha in their colorful clothes stream down from their villages to stage candlelight vigils at the graves of loved ones, bringing food and other offerings for the spirits who are expected to return on this night and the following day. On **Janitzio Island**, on Lake Pátzcuaro, a ceremonial duck hunt is held several days before the Day of the Dead. Ceremonies on Janitzio have been well publicized and, in recent years, throngs of tourists converge on the island. Although it creates a bit of a carnival atmosphere, island residents go about their business with impressive dispassion. Other communities with equally impressive ceremonies, and fewer tourists, are those of Yunuen and Jarácuaro Islands and Tzintzuntzán, as well as other villages. Many public events — including concerts, art exhibitions and traditional dance — take place in Pátzcuaro at this time. The tourist office usually distributes a comprehensive schedule of the area's events. Hotel reservations at this time must be made months, or even up to a year, in advance.

If you want to avoid the avalanche of tourists around the Day of the Dead, you can come any time of year to visit the many artisan towns and country hostelries in this culturally rich area of Mexico. In the communities around the lake, 60 different traditional dances are performed at different festivals throughout the year, although in Pátzcuaro you will see only the Dance of the Old Men. There are also over 300 traditional crafts created throughout the region. The enthusiastic staff at the tourist information office will happily make recommendations for day excursions or longer trips. The Semana Santa (Holy Week) is also celebrated here with much aplomb.

GENERAL INFORMATION

Blessed with a year-round temperate climate, Pátzcuaro has a thriving tourist industry and a helpful **Regional Delegation of Tourism Information Office** ((434) 21214, on the Plaza Vasco de Quiroga on Ibarra 2, Interior 4, open Monday through Saturday from 9 AM to 2 PM and from 4 PM to 7 PM, as well as Sunday from 9 AM to 2 PM.

WHAT TO SEE AND DO

Pátzcuaro has two squares: the larger, more formal, **Plaza Vasco de Quiroga** with its ancient trees, stone benches and circular fountain surrounding a **statue** of the town's benefactor (for which it is named), and the busy **Plaza Gertrudis Bocanegra** one long block north. Formerly Plaza San Agustín, the latter has been renamed for the town's local heroine and martyr of the War of Independence.

The **public market** on the west side of the Plaza Gertrudis Bocanegra is one of the best of its kind in Mexico. Many tourists make a day trip to Pátzcuaro just to shop here, but the town, its people and the lake are worth far more than a shopping spree. Although many of the stands in the market are permanent emplacements, craftspeople from the outlying villages often come only on certain mornings to sell their wares. The area is particularly recommended for its handwoven goods and woodcarvings.

At the north edge of the Plaza Bocanegra, in what was an Augustinian monastery, is the **Biblioteca de Gertrudis Bocanegra** (open Monday through Friday from 9 AM to 7 PM). Inside this public library you can see an enormous mural depicting the Conquest and the history of Michoacán from pre-Conquest times through to the Revolution. Muralist Juan O'Gorman (a contemporary of Diego Rivera) has included the Plaza's namesake in his pictorial history as well as Erendira, the niece of the last Purépecha ruler, who

is supposed to have been the first Indian woman to mount a horse. Also depicted is a famous battle in which the Purépecha defeated the Aztecs in 1478, killing 20,000 of them.

Further east is the **Basílica de Nuestra Señora de la Salud** (Basilica of Our Lady of Good Health) on Calle Lerin near Calle Cerrato, in which Bishop Vasco de Quiroga is buried. It is not so much the structure that makes this building interesting as the statue of the Virgen de Salud (Virgin of Health) made of a paste of ground corn stalks, orchid essence and other ingredients. On the eighth of every month special devotions are held in her honor.

South of the Basilica, the **Museo de Artes Populares** (Museum of Popular Arts) ((434) 21029, Calle Enseñanza at Calle Alcantarillas (admission fee; open Tuesday through Saturday from 9 AM to 7 PM and Sunday from 9 AM to 3 PM), contains an extensive collection of typical Michoacán crafts. The building was formerly the Colegio de San Nicolás, which was founded by Bishop de Quiroga in 1538 and was the first seminary in the Americas. The rooms surround a beautiful patio. At the back of the museum is a full-scale model of a typical Purépecha house.

OPPOSITE: Bustling downtown Pátzcuaro. ABOVE: The street-side vending stalls of Santa Clara del Cobre are filled with copper vessels.

Continuing south to a narrow street with stairs, one finds the local crafts cooperative in **La Casa de las Once Patios** (House of the Eleven Patios) on Calle Madrigal de los Altos No. 2 (open daily from 10 AM to 2 PM and 4 PM to 8 PM). This seventeenth-century Dominican convent now has only five patios, but is nonetheless a magnificent piece of architecture. Most of what is for sale in the boutiques is locally made and usually there are craftspeople at work in their studios or in the courtyards.

In between the museum and the crafts center is the crumbling sixteenth-century **Iglesia de La Compañía**, and the **Iglesia de El Sagrario** where the Virgen de Salud was kept until she was transferred earlier this century to the Basílica.

WHERE TO STAY

There are several hotels in town and, although none is deluxe, a few are full of colonial charm.

Moderate

The one large resort-type hotel is **Posada de Don Vasco** ((434) 23971 or 22490 FAX (434) 20262, Avenida de las Américas No. 450. The Posada has 100 rooms and is located between the town and the lake. This property has extensive grounds, with a heated pool, badminton and tennis courts and bowling; the pretty restaurant has a huge fireplace at one end. The older rooms could use the services of a good interior decorator, but all of the rooms have telephone and cable television.

Inexpensive

Hotel Posada de la Basílica ((434) 21108 or 21181, Calle Arciga No. 6, 103 rooms, is among the most charming in town. Seven of its rooms have fireplaces; it is best to take one of these as the others have no heat and nights can be chilly.

A three-story restored colonial property, the **Hotel Plaza Fiesta** ((434) 22515 or 22516 FAX (434) 22515, Plaza Bocanegra No. 24, has 92 rooms and is a mixture of old and new. Although the building itself is nicely restored, the furnishings are modern and rather plain; rooms have small cable television sets and telephones. The large interior courtyard is rather bare. There is a small restaurant and a parking lot. Somewhat down-at-heel but reliable and quiet is the **Meson del Gallo** ((434) 21474 FAX (434) 21511, on Calle Dr. Coss No. 20, with 25 rooms. Rooms have telephone, but no television.

For a unique experience, spend the night on Yunuen Island in Lake Pátzcuaro, at the **Cabañas Yunuen** — run by the regional tourist board. There are six comfortable cabins to accommodate two, four or 16 persons. The price of a night's lodging includes transportation to and from the island and one meal. Each cabin has a kitchen-

ette with small a refrigerator and limited cooking utensils. There's not much happening on this tiny island, whose families survive by fishing or commute to Pátzcuaro. Bring a good book, or better yet, pass the time chatting with the villagers and brush up on your Spanish. Reservations must be made through the tourist office ((434) 21214, on Plaza Quiroga, Calle Ibarra No. 2.

WHERE TO EAT

Lake Pátzcuaro is renowned for a tender white fish known simply as *pescado blanco*; however, in recent years pollution of the lake has made this a dubious delicacy. The *boquerones* and *charrales* (tiny minnow-like fish that are fried, salted and eaten for a snack like French fries) are at least fried in hot oil, possibly killing any bacteria. Adventurous eaters might hit the many vendors at the **Plaza Chica** (Plaza Gertrudis Bocanegra): they sell many hot meals, including grilled chicken with fresh tortillas and salsa, tortas and steamy hot *atole* (a rice drink).

On the whole, Pátzcuaro's sit-down restaurants lack variety. After a few bowls of *sopa tarasca* or *quesadillas* with guacamole, one's eyes begin to glaze over when the menu arrives. While this is to be expected in small towns, it is surprising since Pátzcuaro receives a large number of tourists each year. A few exceptions, however, are beginning to brighten the culinary scene in Pátzcuaro.

Moderate

El Primer Piso ((434) 20122, Plaza Vasco de Quiroga No. 29 (closed Tuesday) on the second floor overlooking the Plaza Grande, has some interesting eclectic international dishes, including salads with roquefort or goat cheese and a daily special. There are usually several tempting desserts to choose from, such as a lovely fruit tart or a white chocolate mousse. It is a cheerful place, decorated with rotating art exhibits by local artists. Soft jazz in the background, dimmed lights and candlelit tables make it one of Pátzcuaro's more romantic spots.

The restaurant at **Hotel Los Escudos** ((434) 20138, Portal Hidalgo No. 73, caters to tourists and offers American plates such as filet mignon with mushroom sauce, breaded steak, or a club sandwich, in the recently remodeled dining room. Mexican food is served as well. The Dance of the Viejitos can be seen here, over dinner or drinks, usually on Saturday evenings at 8 PM.

El Viejo Gaucho ((434) 30268, within the Hotel Iturbide, entrance at Iturbide No. 10, specializes in *churrasco argentino* (Argentine barbecue), served with potatoes and salad Wednesday through Sunday evenings. Dinner or drinks are served to the accompaniment of live music after 8 PM.

Inexpensive

The food at the restaurant in the **Hotel Posada de la Basílica** ((434) 21108 or 21181, is nothing new: tiny fried fish, *enchiladas* and *sopa tarasca*, although breakfast can be interesting. Service is slow at times; absorb yourself in the view of the town's red-tiled rooftops as you wait for your server.

The four-course fixed-price lunch at **El Sotano** ((434) 23148, Cuesta Vasco de Quiroga N° 12, is worth investigating. You may choose among three soups, two appetizers, two main dishes and top it off with either dessert or coffee — for under $4. The à la carte menu is more limited.

HOW TO GET THERE

Buses travel from Mexico City and Morelia to Pátzcuaro's downtown bus station daily.

AROUND PÁTZCUARO

THE ISLANDS OF LAKE PÁTZCUARO

One can hardly visit Pátzcuaro without a trip to the lake, four kilometers (two and a half miles) from town. The lake is sedgy around the edges and deep blue in the center. A boat ride on the lake with a stop at one of the islands, **Janitzio**, **Jarácuaro**, **Pacanda**, **Tecuén**, or **Yunuén** can be both relaxing and rewarding. The lake's villagers have maintained much of their old way of life and impart a rare serenity. Only in the past 15 years have the traditional butterfly nets (*uiripu*) of the lake's fishermen been replaced by more modern techniques, but there are usually a few men who will demonstrate their use in return for a small tip. The Day of the Dead, the powerful ceremonies which begin on the night of November 1, All Saints' Day, and end in the morning of November 2, All Souls' Day, is also celebrated on the islands, and small ferries make the trip back and forth from Pátzcuaro.

Janitzio

Regular ferries run to Janitzio, the closest and most populated of the islands, which unfortunately means that it is often overrun with tourists. Nonetheless, it is worth the visit, if only for the boat ride and the view from the top of the island. Ferries operate from 8 AM to 5 PM and the trip takes half an hour. Fares (inexpensive) are annually set by the Tourist Board.

VOLCÁN DE ESTRIBO GRANDE

Pátzcuaro has not only the lovely lake and surrounding verdant hills, but also a volcano with a matchless view over the ensemble. A cobblestone road to the top of the extinct Volcán de Estribo Grande (Stirrup Peak) begins at the Church of San Francisco, a few miles west of the town center.

Formerly accessible only on foot, automobiles can now make the trip, but walking the eight-kilometer (five-mile) round trip gives one a much better chance to absorb the beauty and uniqueness of one of Mexico's finest scenic offerings.

THE COPPER TOWN OF SANTA CLARA

Santa Clara del Cobre, sometimes referred to as Villa Escalante, (16 km or 10 miles south of Pátzcuaro) is the regional center for copper crafts. Here, Quiroga de Vasco brought a group of Spanish craftsmen to teach new techniques for working the copper extracted from the nearby Inguarán mines. The **Museo del Cobre** (no phone) on Calle Morelos at Piño Suárez (free admission; open daily from 10 AM to 3 PM and 5 PM to 7 PM) has exhibits that trace the development of copper crafts in Mexico, and displays pieces that have won prizes in the national copper fairs held here every year from August 10 to 17. Copperware is for sale here, as well as almost everywhere in this town.

Eleven kilometers (seven miles) to the west is the "place where it steams," the often mist-covered **Lago de Zirahuén**, one of the most beautiful lakes in the area. You can have a meal or spend the night at the lakefront El Chalet cabins ((434) 20368, Cerrito Colorado, Zirahuén. These cabins, affiliated with the Mansion de Iturbide hotel, in Pátzcuaro, are equipped with kitchenettes and fireplaces. There are also other worthwhile restaurants in this charming town of adobe houses, red-tiled roofs and tall pines and oaks. Special days of celebration here include Easter Week and the feast of the Holy Cross (May 3). Zirahuén is also known for its finely carved wood and its music and folk dancing.

ERONGARÍCUARO

Continuing around Lake Pátzcuaro to the northwest is the village of Erongarícuaro — "lookout tower in the lake" — in the Purépecha language, at 2,025 m (6,824 ft) above sea level. André Breton and other French Surrealists made this their home during World War II. It has grown little since then. Off the main roads, Erongarícuaro remains a fishing village of about 4,000 with a sixteenth-century Franciscan convent. The women historically produced fine handwoven cambric and embroidery to be sold at the Sunday market; however, this art is on the decline. One of the town's most lucrative industries is the unusual carved and painted furnishings that can be purchased at the workshop. Some of the chairs, tables, bureaus and other one-of-a-kind pieces produced here are completely decorated with fine art reproductions, whimsical scenes and much more. Pieces can be made to order; they are not cheap. As this is a working factory, lookie-loos are discouraged.

Among this county seat's most important festivals are those of Easter Week, Corpus Christi, the Holy Cross (May 3) and the large and small feasts of Our Lord of Mercy, held respectively January 6 and June 6.

TZINTZUNTZÁN

Above the northeast shores of Lake Pátzcuaro is the "place of the temple to the god hummingbird": Tzintzuntzán. Olive trees planted by Quiroga de Vasco still grow in the patio of the sixteenth-century convent and church, **Convento e Iglesia de San Francisco**. The age of the olives trees is significant, but more interesting is the fact that Tata Vasco, in planting these trees here, defied a Spanish edict that forbade the cultivation of olive trees in New Spain. In the church, the figure of Christ — like that of the Virgen de Salud in Pátzcuaro's Basílica — is made from a paste of beaten corn husks and orchid extract.

If one has time and patience, one of the taletellers who pass their time beneath the olive trees can be persuaded to share stories of the Purépecha and their buried wealth. Historians believe there is some truth to these legends. They also acknowledge the existence of the legendary Erendira, a courageous Purépecha princess, who, with a white feather in her hair, led the tribe against the Spaniards — a Purépecha Joan of Arc.

The town is noted for straw goods and, to a lesser extent, ceramics and weavings. These are sold at the large artisans' cooperative at the entrance to town. The Day of the Dead is also celebrated here, and during Easter Week there are reenactments of the Passion of Christ. The tourist office in Pátzcuaro can provide information on schedules of events and the town's limited accommodation.

YÁCATAS AND IHUATZIO

Atop the hill just south of the town of Tzintzuntzán is the Yácatas Archaeological Zone, the most important town and religious center of the Purépecha, dating from the Toltec period (eleventh century). It surrendered peacefully to the Spaniards in 1522, but was nonetheless heavily damaged by Nuño de Guzmán seven years later. Here, amid excavation begun in the late nineteenth century, are the remains of five pyramids built over a rectangular platform 400 m by 250 m (1,312 ft by 820 ft). Originally these pyramids had low-lying T-shaped bases with oval or circular superstructures which were tombs of the rulers and their families. These were topped by wood and straw temples dedicated to the fire god Curicaveri. The site has a completely different feel from those of the Maya and Aztec ruins. Maybe the arid mountain top and lack of vegetation make it so, but the people who

built it had a much different vision of the world than the more intellectual Maya or the power-hungry Aztecs. They were a simple people, tied more to their land and lakes.

Four kilometers (two and a half miles) away is another old Purépecha city, Ihuatzio, "place of the coyotes" which once had a population of about 5,000. The ruins are not yet excavated.

URUAPAN

The state of Uruapan, which roughly translates as "where the flowers bloom" in Purépecha, is set in a valley of lush tropical vegetation some 60 km (38 miles) from Pátzcuaro. The attraction here is

the **Parque Nacional Eduardo Ruizo** (open daily, dawn to dusk). The park, which is filled with moss-covered trees, lush vegetation and man-made waterfalls, protects the source of the Cupatitzio River. During the week it is practically deserted, but city dwellers from Morelia and Guadalajara come for the hiking and horseback riding each weekend. The **Hotel Mansion del Cupatitzio** ((452) 32070 or 32100 FAX (452) 46772, at the park boundary, has 57 inexpensive rooms and provides easy access to hiking trails. The hotel's restaurant features international dishes and is open daily. Ten kilometers (six miles) downstream are the imposing 45-m (150-ft) **Tzaráracua Falls**.

The city of Uruapan (population approximately 300,000) has some charm and can be toured in a few hours. The cathedral faces the main plaza, and the adjacent former nunnery and hospital now house the **Museo Huatapera** ((452) 22138 (free admission; open Tuesday through Sunday from 9:30 AM to 1 PM and 3:30 PM to 6 PM). It now contains a good display of local crafts. Uruapan is not really worth a special side trip unless you're interested in hiking in the park. The State Fair which begins on Palm Sunday each year, is definitely worth visiting.

The other hiking attraction is Michoacán's volcano, **Paricutín**, 35 km (22 miles) away. It is now considered to be extinct, but many local residents still remember when it last erupted on February 20, 1943. You can hike to the top of the volcano from the town of Angahuán, crossing an immense lava field. The village of San Juan Parangaricutirorícuaro was buried in the 1943 quake; only the

Guanajuato's silver mines, now largely worked out, were the richest in Mexico and its valleys produced wheat, grains and cattle for the country's growing cities.

Later, many battles of the War of Independence were fought here, leaving towns in ruin, farms destroyed and silver mines inoperable. Guanajuato has been rebuilt over the last century and a half but not at the pace of Mexico City and Guadalajara. The most popular tourist destinations in the state are the capital Guanajuato city, along with San Miguel de Allende, Atotonilco, Dolores Hidalgo and Yuriria.

High in the Sierra Madre, the city of Guanajuato sits nestled among arid mountains at 2,000 m

upper portions of the church poke through the thick layer of lava. The terrain leading to the summit is rough, but not treacherous. Guides with horses are more than willing to give those with weak ankles a ride.

GUANAJUATO

A region rich in minerals and fertile soil, Guanajuato state ("hilly place of the frogs") was the center of the Mexican economy and culture during the colonial period. Although Guanajuato's countryside is hilly and certainly lush enough to be the home of many a frog, its Purépecha, or Tarascan, name is said to come from the frog-shaped boulders above town. After taking over the area in the early sixteenth century, the Spanish found silver instead of the gold for which they were searching. They were not disappointed, however.

(6,700 ft). Although the city has spread out to the adjoining hills, the old colonial center has remained so well preserved that it was declared a UNESCO World Heritage Site in 1988. Since 1972, Guanajuato has sponsored the **Cervantes Festival**, a two-week event in October when the city becomes a stage for some of the best performing arts groups from around the world. The number of people attending has grown by leaps and bounds; expect large crowds and make hotel reservations more than six months in advance. The schedule for each year's festival can be obtained from Festival Internacional Cervantino ((473) 26487 or 25796 FAX (473) 26775 or in Mexico City's Ticket Master at ((5) 325-9000, Plaza de San Francisco No. 1.

Guanajuato's downtown is a maze of narrow streets OPPOSITE which wind up and down the slopes of the Sierra Madres ABOVE.

Central Mexico

BACKGROUND

The city has been saved from being overrun by the automobile by some clear thinking in the 1950s. The dry riverbed of the Guanajuato River was transformed into an underground avenue that winds its way underneath the city for about three kilometers (nearly two miles). Above this, and under the sun and stars, the arched bridges and overhanging balconies are reminiscent of much earlier times. The city center has remained a maze of narrow streets illuminated with old-fashioned lanterns, romantic fountains, tree-shaded parks, flower-decked homes and richly decorated churches. In some places, the streets are so steep that the foundation of one house seems to be perched precariously atop the roof of the one below.

Once a Purépecha and then an Aztec settlement, Guanajuato became a colonial boom town when silver was discovered in the mid-sixteenth century. After the Veta Madre de Plata (one of the richest lodes of silver in the world) was discovered, Guanajuato's population grew to about 80,000, the same as it is today. For centuries its mines produced a quarter of Mexico's silver, and some mines are still in operation. The local economy, however, is now based on government services, commerce, tourism and the university.

GENERAL INFORMATION

Visitors will find a mother lode of information at the **Tourist Office** ((473) 20086 or 21574, on Avenida Juárez at Calle Cinco de Mayo. It is open Monday through Friday from 8:30 AM to 7:30 PM and Saturday and Sunday from 10 AM to 2 PM. There is also a **State Tourism Office** ((473) 27622 FAX (473) 24251, Plaza de La Paz No. 14.

WHAT TO SEE AND DO

Guanajuato city is Mexico's version of San Francisco — minus the ocean. It extends along a narrow valley and up and down the slope of the surrounding hills. As no street is straight for longer than a block or two, getting one's bearings and following directions is a challenge. The best approach is to stop at the Tourist Office and pick up a map and then, as you wander around, try to memorize landmarks.

The dominant landmark of the city is an old grain elevator, now the regional museum, **Alhóndiga de Granaditas** ((473) 21112, on Calle 28 de Septiembre No. 6 (small admission fee; open Tuesday through Saturday from 10 AM to 2 PM and from 4 PM to 6 PM, Sunday from 10 AM to 3 PM). The Alhóndiga was the site of an important victory by Hidalgo's troops during the War of Independence.

After his execution, his head and those of Jiménez, Aldama and Allende were brought from Chihuahua and displayed on the four corners of the granary. The hooks remain as reminders. The museum has exhibits of local history, crafts and archaeology. Murals by Chavez Morado depicting the fight for independence decorate the stairwell.

To the east are the **Jardín Reforma** and the **Plaza de San Roque**, where Mexican concerts are presented year-round. The plaza is the venue for the Cervantes Festival's performances of *entremeses*, one-act plays written by the author of *Don Quixote*. Farther along Avenida Juárez is the Bancomer bank building with its lacy wrought-iron balconies and massive doors carved with seal of the Marquis de San Clemente. The Avenida winds past the majestic **Palacio Legislativo** (Legislative Palace), with its grey-green façade, to the Plaza de La Paz. South of the plaza are an assortment of *plazuelas*, little plazas, surrounded by narrow streets. Here one finds Guanajuato's illustrious **Callejón del Beso**, Kissing Lane, so-named because the street is so narrow that lovers on opposite balconies can share a kiss.

On the Plaza de La Paz is the **Mansión del Conde de Rul y Valenciana**, now housing the Superior Court of Justice. This neoclassic mansion was designed by Francisco Eduardo Tresguerras at the end of the eighteenth century for the Conde de Rul, a wealthy mine owner. The **Basílica de Nuestra Señora de Guanajuato**, across the Plaza, dates from 1671. The wooden image of Our Lady of Guanajuato is said to date from the seventh century and was a gift to the town from King Philip II of Spain.

The next plaza up Avenida Juárez, **Jardín de la Unión**, is as close as Guanajuato gets to having a central plaza. Wedged in the center of the city, the park and its wrought-iron benches, shaded by old laurels, attract students and intellectuals. The outdoor café of the Hotel Posada Santa Fe is a good vantage point from which to watch the comings and goings. The **Teatro Juárez** (open Tuesday through Sunday from 9:15 AM to 1:45 PM and from 5:15 PM to 7:45 PM) faces the park. It is a veritable explosion of art, with a Doric exterior, French foyer, Moorish interior and a few extra touches of art nouveau: a turn-of-the-century monument to the prosperity of the nineteenth century and the penchant of Don Porfirio Díaz for all things European.

The **Museo Iconográfico Cervantino** ((473) 26721, on Calle Miguel Doblado (small admission fee; open Tuesday through Saturday from 10 AM to 1 PM and from 4 PM to 6 PM, Sunday from 10 AM to 1 PM), exhibits a collection of works inspired by Don Quixote. The collection was a gift to the city by Eulalio Ferrer, a refugee of the Spanish Civil War. Among the collection are pieces by Dalí, Rafael and Pedro Coronel, a native of Zacatecas.

From de la Jardín Unión, one can climb the hill southwest to **El Pípila Monument**, about 500 m (550 yards) as the crow flies or one and a half kilometers (a mile) on foot, for a splendid view of the city. The monument, a rough-hewn statue of a half-naked miner, was erected to honor the young man who enabled Hidalgo's forces to capture the Spanish Royalists hiding in the Alhóndiga when he crawled into the building and set it on fire. His name, José M. Barojas, is remembered by few, as he is best known by his nickname, El Pípila. The slogan on his statue is often fondly recounted: *Aún hay otras alhóndigas para incendiar!* (There are still other granaries to burn!)

Back in the city, behind the Basílica is the **Universidad de Guanajuato**, founded in 1732. Its somewhat overpowering façade was built in 1955 to harmonize architecturally with its surroundings — you be the judge of how well the architect succeeded. Next door, the lovely original church in the city, **La Compañía de Jesús**, remains the dominant structure. Its elaborate churrigueresque pink stone façade belies its stark neoclassical interior, decorated simply with a collection of Miguel Cabrera paintings.

Heading back toward the Alhóndiga, Calle Pocitos runs past the **Museo del Pueblo de Guanajuato** (Guanajuato Museum) ((473) 22990, Calle Pocitos No. 7 (small admission fee; open Tuesday through Saturday from 10 AM to 2 PM and from 4 PM to 7 PM, Sunday from 10 AM to 2:30 PM). The museum is housed in the seventeenth-century home of the Marquis de San Juan de Rayas, and it contains a large collection of colonial religious art and murals by José Chávez Morado depicting the history of Guanajuato. The **Museo Casa Diego Rivera** (Museum and House of Diego Rivera) ((473) 21197, Calle Pocitos No. 47 (small admission fee; open Monday through Saturday from 10 AM to 6:30 PM and Sunday from 10 AM to 2:30 PM), is the place where Mexico's most famous muralist was born and lived part of his childhood. The museum is decorated with turn-of-the-century furnishings and displays a collection of Rivera's early works. Upper galleries are used for contemporary art exhibits.

Two kilometers (just over a mile) west of the Alhóndiga, following Avenida Juárez to Tepetapa, is the **Museo las Momias** (small admission fee; open daily from 9 AM to 6 PM), with its macabre display of mummies. The dry air and the composition of Guanajuato's soil mummifies bodies buried in the municipal cemetery. Until 1958, bodies were ritually removed from the cemetery after five years if the grave sites hadn't been paid for. Someone had the idea of putting these naturally preserved bodies on display. Now more than 50, some with hair and clothing intact, they present a rather bizarre sight, a reminder of life's brevity and a sure draw for necrophiles.

WHERE TO STAY

Guanajuato is very much like parts of old Spain, with its up-and-down, narrow cobblestone streets. Many hotels provide extra blankets but have no heating, and it can get chilly in this part of the country in fall and winter. Bring comfortable, warm indoor lounging clothes. Hotels are reasonably priced, for the most part, except during the Cervantes Festival, when rates may double. Newer motel-like establishments, can be found on the major roads leading into and out of Guanajuato; however, these deny the visitor the chance to experience the city's charm and intimacy close at hand.

Moderate

Among the most central accommodation, and certainly the oldest in Guanajuato, is the three-story **Hotel Posada Santa Fe** ((473) 20084 or 20207 FAX (473) 24653, Jardín de la Unión No. 12. Reincarnated from a hotel erected in 1862, the 47 comfortable rooms have satellite television and telephone. There is a hot tub on the roof, and on the first floor there is a bar and indoor dining room, with an outdoor café right on the Jardín de la Union, Guanajuato's most central square. A former hacienda, **Parador San Javier** ((473) 20626, 20650 or 20696 FAX (473) 23114, at Plaza San Javier, has some nice touches reminiscent of its former grandeur. The 15 rooms in the older wing have fireplaces, and the 100 newer ones in

One of several attractive and inexpensive small restaurants in Guanajuato.

the high-rise have parabolic television and clock radios. There is a large pool with a slide and a kid's pool set in the extensive grounds at the back of the hotel. Meeting rooms are available; the restaurant is open all day.

Inexpensive

Casa Kloster ((473) 20088, Alonso No. 32, is located just two blocks from the central Jardín de la Unión and managed by a friendly family. There are caged birds and plants in the central courtyard, and a snug sitting room on the second floor. The 18 rooms have worn but clean furnishings and bedspreads, but bathrooms (three of them) are shared. The managers sell soft drinks and bottled water from their living quarters–office. The **Hotel Socavón** ((473) 26666 FAX (473) 24885, Alhóndiga No. 41A, is also recommended. The mining-town decor is a bit oppressive, but the 37 rooms have television and telephone, and are relatively quiet.

WHERE TO EAT

Guanajuato is not renowned for its restaurants and has some of Mexico's least attentive waiters. Nonetheless it is pleasant to sit at some of the outdoor cafés, and meals in the small restaurants that cater to the city dwellers are reasonably good and inexpensive, even if the decor is utilitarian. The restaurants in the aforementioned hotels are a safe bet.

Moderate

Tasca de Los Santos ((473) 22320, is conveniently situated on the Plaza de La Paz, the main plaza, and has indoor and outdoor dining. The cuisine here is more Spanish than Mexican, offering *tapas* (Spanish appetizers) such as serrano ham, Pamplona sausage and Manchego cheese, in addition to full meals which include paella, the house specialty. **El Teatro** ((473) 25454, Sopeña No. 3, features international food, and stages small theatrical sketches or plays during the dinner hour on Friday and Saturday. **La Capilla Real de la Esperanza** ((472) 2141, Carretera Guanajuato a Dolores Hidalgo Km 5, is a bar, restaurant and gallery on the road to Dolores Hidalgo.

Inexpensive

El Truco 7 ((473) 38374, Calle Truco No. 7, is a snug restaurant where locals read the paper in the afternoon over a cup of coffee. The late lunch *comida corrida* is a great deal, and the sandwiches are good. There are three separate dining rooms in this restored colonial property, all tastefully cluttered with original art, photographs, and shelves with books and magazines. **Café Dada** ((473) 25094, Calle Truco No. 19, is a hip little restaurant on the same street, where service can be slow but the

coffee is great, from the house blend to the espresso and cappuccino. The American owner offers *comida corrida* between 1:30 PM and 5 PM for about $3. Crêpes are among the most popular menu items; there is also a selection of baked goods and full entrées. Crave some vegetarian food? Try the unassuming **Restaurant Yamuna** (no phone), behind the Juárez Theater, for its fixed price *comida corrida*, which attempts to replicate some popular Indian dishes.

HOW TO GET THERE

The Aeropuerto Bajío is about 30 minutes by taxi from downtown, and receives flights on major and regional carriers from Tijuana, Mexico City, Morelia and Guadalajara. The bus station is south of downtown and has frequent service to Mexico City and San Miguel de Allende.

AROUND GUANAJUATO CITY

MARFIL

Marfil, four kilometers (two and a half miles) west of Guanajuato on Route 110, is an old and charming mining town where several stately mansions have been restored. On the highway before Marfil, in a romantic, tree-shaded garden with bright multi-hued flowers and old laurels, is the **Museo Ex-Hacienda de San Gabriel Barrera** (small admission fee; open daily from 9 AM to 6 PM). This eighteenth-century mansion and its multiple manicured gardens have been restored and give an idea of the wealth some families possessed during the silver boom. The gilded private chapel contains a spectacular polychrome altar piece with scenes of the Passion of Christ.

LA VALENCIANA

The most profitable silver mine from the sixteenth to the early nineteenth century is located on Highway 30 going northwest from Guanajuato toward Dolores Hidalgo. The Valenciana silver mine, which was closed for some 40 years, is now open to the public. It was discovered in 1766 by Antonio Obregón y Alcocer. Obregón made the mine the most productive in the world, employing more than 3,300 workers in its shafts that descended to a depth of 500 m (1,650 ft). Its main shaft was often referred to as "the mouth of hell" by the Indians who slaved below.

Obregón became wealthy beyond belief, was granted the title Conde de Valenciana, and built a church to show his gratitude to God, provider of such inexpensive labor. The Count spared no expense in creating this ornate baroque masterpiece, known both as **La Iglesia de San Cayetano** and **El Templo de la Valenciana**. For some reason the tower on the right was never finished. Ornate gilded carvings adorn the altar and the richly carved pulpit was supposedly brought from China. Of the thousands of Indians who worked in misery to dig out his silver there is no trace.

SAN MIGUEL DE ALLENDE

Most of the churches, houses and public buildings in the city of San Miguel de Allende are colonial and, with its beautifully carved wooden doors set in stuccoed adobe walls in hues of colonial gold, indian red and myriad others, it is city of great beauty. Its cobblestone streets pitch down or climb past colonial buildings of native pink quarry stone (*cantera rosa*) and aging, moss-covered, red-tiled roofs. San Miguel sits at 1,870 m (5,900 ft) above sea level, and enjoys a mild and sunny climate with an average annual temperature of 18°C (64°F). As the town's many artists and artisans would no doubt agree, the town itself is a work of art; it was designated a UNESCO World Heritage Site in 1926. It is a place to spend a couple of days or even several weeks. It has attracted a considerable foreign community (mainly Americans and Canadians) and many expatriates have chosen this lovely place to spend the rest of their lives. In fact the town's population has doubled in the last few decades and is now over 100,000.

BACKGROUND

The town, originally known as San Miguel el Grande, was founded in 1542 by Franciscan friar Juan de San Miguel who was led to the site by his dogs seeking water. By the eighteenth century, wealthy mine-owners and hacienda owners from Guanajuato and Zacatecas had built their homes in the town, directing their operations from the thriving cultural, agricultural and commercial center. Without doubt the abundance of hot springs was one of the major attractions of the area. In the days before hot-water heaters, who wouldn't have chosen to live near a perpetual source of hot water?

After Mexico's War of Independence, the town's name was changed to San Miguel de Allende in honor of its local hero, Captain Ignacio Allende. Following the Mexican Revolution in the early twentieth century, the huge haciendas in the area were broken up, and their lands were divided among the peasants who had worked for the landowners. Some of the hacienda mansions were left to decay; others were restored as private homes or museums. One became the **Instituto de Allende**, a school of fine arts founded in 1951, attracting students of all ages and nationalities. It has played an important role in giving San Miguel its impetus as a tourist and cultural center.

GENERAL INFORMATION

The **Tourist Office (** /FAX (415) 21747 is on the Plaza Principal and is open Monday through Friday from 10 AM to 7 PM, Saturday and Sunday from 10 AM to 5 PM. The staff does an excellent job promoting the area. A house and garden tour is offered each Sunday — sponsored by the public library, which has a large English-language section and serves as an informal cultural association and meeting place for expatriates and visitors to San Miguel. Two-hour tours of the historic center can be arranged through the **Instituto de Viajes (** (415) 20078 FAX (415) 20121, in the Hotel Vista Hermosa, Calle Cuna de Allende No. 11 interior. Try to make reservations a day in advance.

There are several worthwhile music festivals held each year in San Miguel. The Nigromante Art School hosts an international chamber music festival yearly during the first two weeks in August. The annual international jazz festival is now in its fifth year and takes place near the end of November. And, during the last two weeks in December, musicians from throughout Mexico and beyond its borders converge on San Miguel to participate in the winter classical music festival.

San Miguel is also known as Mexico's fiesta town, celebrating all the national fiestas, their local holidays and a few United States holidays to boot. Never a month passes without parades, fireworks, and dances and bands in the central square. The most elaborate take place during Christmas and Holy Week, and on Independence Day (September 15) and the Feast of San Miguel (September 29).

WHAT TO SEE AND DO

There is no one monument or museum that makes San Miguel an attraction; it is a place to be taken as a whole. Throughout the city are colonial houses, almost as many churches, and shops selling high-quality textiles, hand-crafted furniture, jewelry, ceramics and tin and brass objects.

San Miguel's focal point is the **Parroquia**, the parish church, which stands on the south side of the central square, **Plaza Allende**. It is almost too ornate to be real and is often described as the "gingerbread Gothic" church. Some parts of the structure date from the sixteenth century, but it was rebuilt approximately 100 years later. At the end of the nineteenth century, the remodeling of the façade was given to the self-trained Indian architect Zeferino Gutiérrez who, some say, incorporated a bit of this and a bit of that from picture postcards of several different European buildings, particularly the cathedral in Cologne, Germany. Inside the decor is more traditionally Mexican;

one chapel contains the interesting Nuestro Señor de la Conquista, a Purépecha figure made from corn stalk paste.

Across the street from the Parroquia, **Casa de Ignacio Allende**, Calle Cuna de Allende No. 1 (free admission; open Tuesday through Sunday from 10 AM to 3:30 PM), is the home in which Allende was born and lived. It is now a regional museum with permanent and rotating exhibits.

Several blocks northeast of the plaza, near the eastern end of Calle Insurgentes, is the seventeenth-century church **Oratorio de San Felipe Neri**, with a delicate rose-colored stone façade. Next door, **Santa Casa de Loreto** is an eighteenth-century edifice with a baroque façade. Reproducing the House of the Virgin in Loreto, Italy, it was build by the wealthy Conde de Canal as a sepulcher for himself and his pious wife.

To the west of the plaza is the **Bellas Artes Cultural Center** (also called El Nigromante) ((415) 20289, Dr. Hernández Macías No. 75 (open Monday through Saturday from 9 AM to 8 PM and Sunday from 10 AM to 3 PM). Once the largest convent in Mexico, it is now a branch of the National Institute of Fine Arts, offering courses in dance and literature. Directly behind it is the **Iglesia de la Concepción**, which has one of the largest domes in Mexico, strongly resembling the dome of Les Invalides in Paris. Zeferino Gutiérrez is credited with its design.

Uphill and four blocks south on Calle Zacateros, which becomes Calzada Ancha de San Antonio, is the elegant eighteenth-century home of Tomás de la Canal. The building now houses an international school of fine arts, a cultural center and a garden at the **Instituto de Allende** ((415) 20190 FAX (415) 24538, Ancha de San Antonio No. 20 (closed Sunday).

Going east from the Allende Institute, one arrives at San Miguel's largest park, **Parque Benito Juárez**, on whose northern edge is the Lavandería. Women gather daily around the spring-fed tubs to do their wash. Certainly the back-bending task gets a little easier with a bit of gossip and friendly chat to ease the chore.

WHERE TO STAY

Although the town is a major tourist destination the hotels and restaurants remain reasonably priced and of high quality. Breakfast is sometimes included in the price of a room. Many properties are heated by fireplace or not at all.

Very Expensive

At the top of the charts — in price, charm and comfort — is the lovely **Casa de Sierra Nevada** ((415) 20415 or 27040 TOLL-FREE (800) 223-6510 FAX (415) 22337, Hospicio No. 35, which has been enlarged to fill adjoining colonial properties. In

the main building is the concierge and front desk as well as the bar and restaurant, which spills out into the flower-filled central patio. Some of the 37 rooms and suites are located across the street, and a large pool is in another building. The appointments and furnishings are impeccable: Beautiful tiles from nearby Dolores Hidalgo, lace curtains, antiques and a blazing fireplace will make you feel as if you're staying in the home of a fabulously wealthy friend rather at a hotel. Golf and tennis can be arranged at nearby clubs, and the hotel has its own 202-hectare (500-acre) equestrian center for the exclusive use of its guests. Children under 16 are not permitted, and the atmosphere is definitely sophisticated and refined.

Equally outstanding is **La Puertecita** ((415) 22250 or 25011 FAX (415) 25505, Santo Domingo No. 75. Located in the residential neighborhood of Ascadero, the hotel is housed in the former home of a San Miguel mayor who obviously wasn't lacking money. The home, with its brick-domed ceilings, tiled stairways, circular and arched windows, and open fireplaces contains 24 individually decorated rooms; most have patios and fireplaces, and some have whirlpool tubs. Facilities include two heated swimming pools, a fitness center and an elegant restaurant.

Hotel Hacienda ((456) 20888, 24 km (15 miles) from town, is a spa built upon mineral springs used by the Otomi and Chichimeca Indians. The 100 rooms are surrounded by lush gardens; all the usual spa treatments are available.

Moderate

Villa Jacaranda ((415) 21015 or 20811 FAX (415) 20883, Aldama No. 53, is run by American expatriates Don and Gloria Fenton, who know how to make guests feel at home. The 16 rooms have heaters and cable television. You can relax after a day of sightseeing in the hotel's hot tub, or watch an English-language film in their video room. There is also an award winning restaurant.

Also worth mentioning in this category is the **Mi Casa B&B** ((415) 22492, Canal No. 58, with two guests suites and the **Pensión Casa Carmen** (/FAX (415) 20844, Correo No. 31, with 11 rooms all with private bath.

Inexpensive

The unpretentious **Quinta Loreto** ((415) 20042 FAX (415) 23616, Calle Loreto No. 15, has a clientele of longtime fans who return year after year. They like the 38 clean rooms with comfortable yet unexciting furnishings and the quiet, tree-shaded grounds. The rooms have heaters, telephones and televisions; the restaurant has a reputation all its own and many people who live in San Miguel come here almost daily for the large *comida corrida*.

The central arcade of San Miguel de Allende contributes to the town's European flavor.

There is a parking lot, a dilapidated tennis court and a swimming pool that is only cleaned occasionally. Also recommended in this category are the **Hotel Vianey** ((415) 24559, Aparacio No. 18, with 11 rooms, some with kitchenettes; and the **Parador San Sebastián** ((415) 20707, Mesones No. 7, with 13 rooms.

WHERE TO EAT

Very Expensive

The restaurant at **Casa de Sierra Nevada** ((415) 20415 or 27040 (see WHERE TO STAY, above) has award-winning fare which they describe as "contemporary cuisine with a Mexican touch".

Reservations are required and the setting is decidedly formal, so dress up a bit if you don't want to feel out of place.

Moderate

As has the restaurant at Casa de Sierra Nevada, the dining room at **Villa Jacaranda** ((415) 21015 (see WHERE TO STAY, above) has received several awards for excellence. The space is airy yet intimate and a delicious champagne brunch is served on Sunday. Both international and Mexican dishes are served; among their specialties are crêpes with *huitlacoche* (black corn fungus), and *chili en nogada* — chili pepper stuffed with ground meat, nuts, raisins and topped with a delicious cream sauce.

ABOVE: San Miguel's gingerbread-Gothic Parroquia. OPPOSITE: Like many towns in Central Mexico, San Miguel has many fine examples of Colonial architecture.

Popular with both locals and tourists, **Mama Mia** ((415) 22063, Calle de Umarán No. 8, has become a San Miguel institution. The pastas and pizzas are reasonably good, but what makes this place special is the lively ambiance on the flower-and-vine-filled covered patio and the fact that music in one form or another — be it jazz, marimba, reggae or rock — is performed most evenings. **El Arlequin** ((415) 20856, within Hotel Mansión del Virrey, Calle Canal No. 19, is warmed by a fire on chilly afternoons and serves a reasonably priced *comida corrida* including soup, main course, dessert and coffee. On the à la carte menu, try the *sopa azteca* (chicken stock with tomato, fried tortillas, avocado and sour cream), an appetizer of mushrooms with garlic and spicy chili sauce, or the chicken in white wine. It is open daily and has a full bar.

Inexpensive

Delicious breads (including superfine white, French, multigrain and rye) are served to go or to enjoy on the spot along with delicious, strong coffee at **La Buena Vida** ((415) 22211, Calle Hernández Macías No. 72-5 (closed Sunday). This tiny bakery also makes great muffins, cookies, pastries and scones, as well as simple breakfasts such as fruit with granola and yogurt.

HOW TO GET THERE

There is no airport in San Miguel, but several bus lines offer frequent service from Mexico City, Guanajuato, Querétaro and Dolores Hidalgo. The bus station is just west of downtown.

AROUND SAN MIGUEL DE ALLENDE

DOLORES HIDALGO AND ATOTONILCO

From San Miguel it is an easy day trip to Dolores Hidalgo, where the *Grito de Dolores* launched the Mexican War of Independence on the night of September 15, 1810. The city has never been as prosperous as San Miguel, but it has a certain amount of colonial charm and a sleepy atmosphere. History buffs can visit the **Casa Hidalgo** ((418) 20171, Calle Morelos No. 1 (admission fee; closed Monday), Padre Hidalgo's former digs, to inspect memorabilia from the Mexican War of Independence. Possibly more interesting is shopping for the pottery and tiles for which Dolores Hidalgo is famous, and which can be admired throughout the Bajío region.

On route to Dolores Hidalgo, one passes Atotonilco, "place of the hot water" in Nahuatl. From the sanctuary of the convent, Father Miguel Hidalgo's army took the banner of the Virgin of Guadalupe and declared her the patron saint of

Mexico's fight for independence. Pilgrims still flock to the church, sometimes to see the enormous frescoes, sometimes for religious instruction.

QUERÉTARO

Located at the country's geographic center, the state of Querétaro was colonized by the Spanish not because of its abundance of silver, but for its fertile plateau that was to produce much of Mexico's grain. There are ruins of the settlements of pre-Columbian tribes that inhabited the area at Las Ranas, which is easily accessible, and at Toluguilla, accessed by a dirt road and a strenuous uphill walk.

Querétaro, capital city of the state of the same name, is a city of many churches and plazas, and of palatial homes with geranium-filled balconies. It was first inhabited by the Otomí Indians and taken over by the Aztecs. In 1531 the Spanish and Franciscan monks founded the city of Querétaro, which became the headquarters of Franciscan monks who established missions throughout the area.

Since the early nineteenth century, Querétaro has played an important role in Mexican history. It was here that the insurgents drafted the "Querétaro Conspiracy" while supposedly attending literary soirées organized by Josefa de Domínguez and her husband. When their plot for independence was uncovered in 1810, *La Corregidora* (Doña Josefa) alerted the conspirators of their impending arrest.

When United States forces invaded Mexico City in 1847, Querétaro became the temporary capital of the nation until the Treaty of Guadalupe Hidalgo was signed here to end the Mexican-American War. Emperor Maximilian fought his

ABOVE: A little boy and his piglets. OPPOSITE: Atotonilco's convent was an early focus for Mexico's bloody struggle for independence. OVERLEAF: One of Querétaro's many charming sixteenth-century churches and plazas.

last battle here against the army led by Benito Juárez in 1867 and was placed before a firing squad on the Cerro de las Campanas to the northeast of the city. In recent years, Querétaro has grown to a population of nearly one million. Many of the new residents came from Mexico City after the 1985 earthquake and the population boom has given rise to enormous urban sprawl. However, after traversing the industrial and suburban sector, one finds at the core a charming colonial city at an altitude of 1,853 m (6,079 ft) which has, with a mean temperature of 18°C (64°F), a slightly warmer climate than that of Mexico City.

GENERAL INFORMATION

The State Tourism Office ((42) 121412 or 120907 FAX 121094, is at the Plaza de la Independencia at Pasteur 4 Norte, open Monday through Friday from 9 AM to 9 PM, Saturday and Sunday from 9 AM to 8 PM, and it offers walking tours of the old city for a small fee. English-speaking guides may be arranged for a sufficient number of people.

WHAT TO SEE AND DO

Querétaro has so many historic monuments and colonial buildings that UNESCO has included the city on its World Heritage list, citing it as a place of universal value, worthy of preservation. The city's main plaza, **Jardín Obregón**, at Calles Madero and Juárez, is surrounded by stately eighteenth-century buildings, including the **Iglesia de San Francisco** on the east. Many of the surrounding streets are now designated as pedestrian walkways, which has revitalized the downtown area. In the evening the streets are as crowded as during the day.

Founded in the seventeenth century as a Franciscan monastery, the Iglesia de San Francisco houses the **Museo Regional de Querétaro (** (42) 122031, at Calle 5 de Mayo (open Tuesday through Sunday from 10 AM to 4 PM). In addition to an extensive collection of regional historical documents and memorabilia of the area, the museum has colonial paintings by Mexican and European artists.

Farther east on Avenida 5 de Mayo is the **Palacio del Gobierno del Estado**, which is also know as the Palacio de la Corregidora. At the beginning of the nineteenth century it was the home of Doña Josefa and was where the Independence movement was born.

Around the corner, on the **Plaza de Armas** (or Plaza de la Independencia) is the former home of the Marquis de Escale, now called **La Casa de Escala**, with its magnificent baroque façade. The statue in the center of the tree-shaded plaza is of the Marquis de la Villa del Villar del Águila, who

was responsible for building the aqueduct which still delivers water to the city.

West of the Jardín, the street changes from Avenida 5 de Mayo to Avenida Madero. One block down is a lovely eighteenth-century mansion, now the five-star hotel La Casa de la Marquesa, which was formerly the residence of the Marquesa de la Villa del Villar del Águila. More interested in aesthetics than was her more practical-minded husband (who engineered the aqueduct), the marquise had the inner courtyard decorated in intricate Spanish *mudejar* (Moorish) style. Note the stone pomegranates carved in the interior arches; these signify that the Moors — who occupied southern Spain for 700 years — were about to fall.

One block further west is the **Iglesia de Santa Clara** on a plaza of the same name, which contains the neoclassical Fountain of Neptune, by Eduardo Tresguerras. The rather severe exterior of the church belies the interior's ornate carvings, with delicate ironwork and gilded cherubs everywhere.

To the south on Calle Allende at Piño Suárez, the church and ex-convent of Saint Augustine now houses the **State Museum of Art (** (42) 122357, Calle Allende Sur No. 14 (small admission fee; open Tuesday through Sunday from 11 AM to 7 PM). The collection focuses on colonial-era art, although modern exhibitions are sometimes shown. Note the unusual caryatids, each standing on one leg, in the flamboyantly baroque central patio.

At the corner of Calle Corrigedora and Avenida 16 de Septiembre you'll see the **Jardín de la Corregidora**, with a **monument** to Doña Josefa and the **Arbol de la Amistad** (Friendship Tree), planted in 1977 with a mixture of soils from around the world to symbolize Querétaro's hospitality.

East of Jardín Obregón, on Calle Independencia and Calle Felipe Luna, is the **Plaza de la Santa Cruz**. The **cross** of the church here marks the spot where the Spanish offered the first mass in the area in 1531, after having exterminated the locals. The monastery, adjacent to the church, served as Maximilian's headquarters and later his prison. In the interior patio is a tree with cross-shaped thorns which, many believe, grew from the walking stick of one of the community's most beloved monks, Fray Antonio Margil de Jesus Ros.

A short distance further east is the beginning of Querétaro's **aqueduct**. Designed by Antonio Urrutia y Arana, the Marquis de la Villa del Villar del Águila, it has 74 arches, with a maximum height of 23 m (77 ft); its construction took 12 years (1726 to 1738). While it remains an impressive sight by daylight, it is even more so when seen illuminated at night.

WHERE TO STAY

Querétaro is blessed with many colonial-era mansions and some of these have been turned into sumptuous hotels. Because of their age and design, these, although picturesque, may be slightly noisy (open patios draw noise up and amplify it). Still, they are charming and absolutely unique. There are a few hotels geared toward business travelers on the city's outskirts, and some no-frills and inexpensive hotels near the city center.

Very Expensive
La Casa de la Marquesa ((42) 120092 FAX (42) 120098, Avenida Madero No. 41, is the most recent incarnation of the mansion built by El Marquis de la Villa del Villar del Águila — it is not known whether it was intended for his wife or another object of his affection. In any case, it is a lovely building and each of the 25 tastefully furnished, large rooms is decorated slightly differently, with luxurian area rugs, antiques and original art. They offer air-conditioning, central heating and voluminous bathtubs — unusual for the region, but typical of the five-star hotel it is. Only children aged 12 and older are permitted, and the restaurant — which has 30 types of tequila on hand — is quite elegant and intimate.

Expensive
Located on the Plaza de Armas, the 300-year-old **Mesón de Santa Rosa (** (42) 242623 or (42) 242781 or 242993 FAX (42) 125522 E-MAIL starosa @sparc.ciateq.conacyt.mx, Pasteur Sur No. 17, is another remodeled colonial edifice. Each of the 21 accommodations is actually a suite facing a quiet courtyard, with satellite television, video player and minibar. There is a heated pool at the back of the hotel, as well as an excellent restaurant.

Inexpensive
For accommodation that is easier on the pocket but nowhere near the same quality as those mentioned above, there are the modern **Hotel Señorial (** (42) 143700 FAX (42) 141945, Guerrero Norte No. 10-A, with 45 rooms, as well as the very plain, yet adequate and centrally-located, **Hotel Plaza (** (42) 121138 or 126562, Avenida Juárez Norte No. 23, with 29 rooms which can be noisy even at night.

WHERE TO EAT

Querétaro has a variety of reasonably-priced restaurants serving Mexican food. Upscale restaurants, such as those in the better hotels listed above, generally have a selection of Mexican and international cuisine on their menus.

Expensive

Want something different? Try **1810**((42) 143324, at the Plaza de Armas, which serves French food in addition to some Mexican favorites. There are some original dishes such cream of partridge soup with mushrooms, and "mestizo" soup, made with camembert cheese and cilantro. There is rabbit stew for the main course and cheesecake with blueberries for dessert. Some people go just for coffee and dessert and to soak up the charming ambiance; others go for a full meal.

Moderate

La Fonda del Refugio ((42) 120755, on Jardín Corregidora Nº 26, is located on this quiet plaza shaded by jacaranda and Indian laurel trees, under which Indian women sell handmade cloth dolls. Beef is the house specialty, and it's pleasant to eat outside in the evening as the twinkling lights come on and the strolling guitarists begin their rambling serenades around the plaza.

Inexpensive

La Flor de Querétaro (no phone), Avenida Juárez No. 5, is fun because it's so authentically middle-class Mexican. It's no frills and no nonsense; the food — most of which is served à la carte — is quite tasty. The menu consists mainly of *enchiladas*, chicken, *chili rellenos* and similar standards. Breakfast is also served, as are massive side dishes of sautéed vegetables.

HOW TO GET THERE

Buses from San Miguel arrive at the main station south of town.

AROUND QUERÉTARO CITY

The spas at **San Juan del Río** and **Tequisquiapan**, both within an hour's drive of Querétaro, have provided weekend getaways for Mexico City dwellers and made the towns into large tourist resorts. San Juan, the larger of the two (population 50,000) is a center of basket-weaving and furniture making; but more visible is the semi-precious gem industry. Tequisquiapan is a pretty little town known also for its wicker items and for its numerous hot springs, most of which have dried up in the last decade, leaving behind a rather shaky tourist infrastructure.

HIDALGO

Hidalgo is one of the most scenic and least-visited states in the heart of Mexico. **Tula** in the south was the most important Toltec city in the state (see THE VALLEY OF MEXICO, page 121); the entire area is rich in mineral reserves. **Pachuca**, the capital of the state, was, in the colonial era, the center for

mining activities but never evolved to the size of the other Silver Cities. It is a miniature Guanajuato with narrow, winding streets, a multitude of small squares and colonial buildings. There is an extensive collection of photographs chronicling the Revolution of 1910, which is housed in the former Convent of San Francisco. The convent's chapel has a gilded churrigueresque altar whose radiance so overpowers the room that it has been named the **Capilla de la Luz** (the Chapel of Light).

The area around Pachuca is also known for its vast fields filled with row upon row of maguey cacti, from which the fermented drink, *pulque*, is made. The worm of the maguey plant, crisply fried, is considered to be a great delicacy.

PARQUE NACIONAL EL CHICO, CONVENTS AND TOLANTONGO CANYON

One could spend an entire vacation exploring the nooks and crannies of Hidalgo. Thirty-five kilometers (21 miles) northeast of Pachuca is **Parque Nacional El Chico**, with thick pine forests, intriguing rock formations and two lakes.

An interesting 500-km (310-mile) circuit is one that leaves Pachuca going north on Highway 105 to the pottery-making town of **Huejutla**, then west to **Tamazunchale** and returning to Pachuca via Highway 85. There are small hotels and restaurants in most of the towns along the route. From Pachuca to Huejutla, there is both excellent scenery and sixteenth-century Augustinian convents at **Atotonilco el Grande, Metztitlán, Santa María Xoxoteco, Zacualtipan, Molango** and **Huejutla**. On the return, there are lushly vegetated mountains of the **Sierra Madre Oriental**, the old mining town of **Zimapán**, another Augustinian convent at **Ixmiquilpan**, the Tolantongo Canyon and its caves, and the Convent de San Nicolás Tolentino in **Actopán**.

The **Convent de San Nicolás** is a spectacular fortified structure, more like a medieval castle than a house of prayer and learning. It was built in the sixteenth century and is noted for the frescoes on the stairwell and its outdoor chapel.

Tolantongo Canyon, accessed by 28 km (17 miles) of hair-raising, steep and sinewy dirt road, is one of the most beautiful sites in Mexico and certainly one of the natural wonders of the world. At the foot of a crystalline waterfall is the entrance to a series of caves which contain natural thermal springs. The further one goes in the caves, the warmer the water, which eventually reaches the temperature of a steam bath.

The Wonders of the West

BETWEEN THE PACIFIC COAST and Mexico's central valley, Spanish settlements in the Sierra Madre Occidental grew steadily, isolated from the main thrust of colonization. With a temperate year-round climate, fertile land and rich mines, they attracted settlers who were committed to remaining in the New World.

Only in the second part of the twentieth century did the western states of **Jalisco, Aguascalientes, Zacatecas** and **San Luís Potosí** emerge as tourist destinations, possibly heralded by the many early foreign visitors who fell in love with the Mexican spirit and stayed.

GUADALAJARA

Capital of the state of Jalisco, Guadalajara is the second largest city in Mexico. Its European atmosphere and colonial architecture, the friendly Tapatíos (as the inhabitants of the city are called), the lively mariachi music, *charreadas* (Mexican rodeos), tequila and the *jarabe tapatío* or Mexican Hat Dance for which the city is known, have made Guadalajara famous among Mexicans as nearly a shrine to national culture. Although completely cosmopolitan, the city has a slower pace than Mexico City and at times it seems as if all the inhabitants are out strolling in one of the many parks. While lacking both the depth of history and the wealth of museums of the nation's capital, Guadalajara remains a most attractive city to visit.

BACKGROUND

In pre-Columbian times, the Sierra Madre and Atemajac Valley were inhabited by Indian tribes of whom little is known. Archaeologists believe that they traded with the people of Teotihuacán and were also in contact with tribes in Central and South America. An abundance of metal objects has been discovered which seems to indicate a knowledge of metallurgy, one of the trademarks of South American cultures of that time.

Another similarity has been found in burial practices — deep-shaft tombs in which several generations of the same family were interred. The West Mexican Indian tribes occupied the area from 2500 BC to 600 AD, and most of what is known about them derives from the few tombs which have survived desecration and pilfering. The ceramic figures that have been recovered depict the dress and daily activities of men, women, and children, as well as battle and religious scenes. The most famous of these pre-Columbian figures are the so-called Kissing Dogs of Colima.

After the destruction of Teotihuacán near Mexico City the task of exploring the western Sierra Madres was given to Nuño Beltrán de Guzmán, the greediest and most scurrilous of the conquistadors. He demanded a tribute from every Indian

tribe, and no matter how much gold or silver was given it was never enough. Torture and slaughter ensued until Guzmán eliminated whole tribes by these forms of barbarism. Those surviving tribes not able to overcome the superior weapons of the Spanish retreated into the mountains.

With the Indians of the area gone, the Spanish settled in the Atemajac Valley in the early 1500s. Soon thereafter many of the early explorers left the settlement for what they heard were richer gold fields in Peru. With the Spanish forces depleted, the Indians regrouped and attacked in 1528. This, called the Mixton War, lasted four years. It ended in defeat and annihilation for the local Indians, but only after the Spanish equipped

their Indian allies from other parts of Mexico with guns and horses.

With no Indians left in the area Guadalajara was able to develop into the most European of Mexico's cities. It became the capital of Nueva Galicia, as the whole of western Mexico was then known. The wealth gained from the tons of silver extracted from the surrounding mountains by Indian slaves brought from elsewhere is reflected in the region's architecture.

By the nineteenth century, Guadalajara was a thriving metropolis with a booming textile industry. Most residents were born and raised here, and felt little influence from Mexico City or from Spain. It was hardly surprising, then, that Father Hidalgo was welcomed here with open arms in 1810 after the *Grito de Dolores*. From the steps of

Two young women of Guadalajara.

Guadalajara's **Palacio de Gobierno** he declared the abolishment of slavery, but his forces later met defeat here in 1811.

Even though Maximilian thought the city important enough to station French troops in during his reign, Guadalajara was seen by most as a remote provincial capital until the arrival of the railroads. In the late 1800s, it was linked by rail with Mexico City, and with the cities to the north in the 1920s.

Since the 1985 earthquake in Mexico City, many Mexicans have relocated to Guadalajara, pushing the population near six million. Pollution, overcrowding and street crime are becoming problems, but are still not of the same magnitude as in the nation's capital.

GENERAL INFORMATION

At 1,552 m (3,780 ft) above sea level, Guadalajara has a near-perfect year-round climate of perpetual spring. From November through February the average temperature is 15°C (59°F), from March to October it is 21°C (70°F). There is a rainy season that lasts from June to September, but even then the rain is interspersed with frequent sun.

The **Jalisco State Tourist Office** ((3) 616-3332 or 614-0123 FAX 614-4365, Calle Morelos No. 102, open Monday through Friday from 9 AM to 8 PM and weekends from 9 AM to 1 PM, has the best selection of local information and maps. Information is also available from **Teletur** ((3) 658-0222, 658-0305 and 658-0177, at Plaza Tapatía, where they have a bilingual staff and lots of information.

WHAT TO SEE AND DO

Guadalajara's highlights are clustered in the heart of the old colonial city which was originally laid out around four plazas forming a Latin cross: Plaza de los Laureles, Plaza de Armas, Plaza de la Liberación and Plaza de la Rotunda. *Tapatíos* have guarded the architectural and historic value of this area, preserving the old and blending the new to complement it. When the historic city became overrun with vehicles in the late '70s, an underground freeway was built and a five-block section adjacent to the old plazas was turned into a pedestrian esplanade, **Plaza Tapatía**. The absence of vehicles in even this small part of old Guadalajara makes a walking tour much more pleasurable.

The logical start for a city tour is the **Catedral**, facing **Plaza de los Laureles**, on Avenida Alcalde between Avenida Hidalgo and Morelos (open daily from 8 AM to 7 PM). Its construction was begun on July 31, 1561 and it was completed in 1616. Much altered in later periods, the Catedral is an intriguing mixture of baroque, Renaissance, Gothic, Byzantine and neoclassic styles. In accordance with a decree by King Philip II, the

church was designed with three naves, one for Spanish officials, another for landowners (primarily mestizos), and a third for Indians. The twin towers, dedicated to St. Michael and St. James the Apostle, were built at the end of the seventeenth century, but were destroyed in an 1818 earthquake and rebuilt according to the more modern design of Gómez Ibarra.

The interior is a compendium of religious art. The statue and altar of Our Lady of the Rose, patroness of the city, are from the early sixteenth century, unique in that they were carved from a single piece of balsa wood. The ten silver and gilt altars were gifts from King Ferdinand VII in recognition of Guadalajara's contributions of silver and gold to Spain during the Napoleonic wars. The sculpted white marble altar came from Italy in the mid-nineteenth century, as did the remains of St. Innocent I, the fifth-century pope whose body had been found in the catacombs of Rome.

The best of the paintings is the seventeenth-century *Assumption of the Virgin* attributed to Spain's Bartolomé Esteban Murillo. It is the gentleness of the characters' expressions that gives support to the theory that this masterpiece, hanging over the sacristy door, is Murillo's.

South of the Catedral, across Avenida Morelos, is the **Plaza de Armas**, the Zócalo of Guadalajara. European visitors may find that the central kiosk reminds them of Paris, and rightly so. It was cast there at the turn of the century and is similar to those found in many Parisian parks.

On the eastern edge of the plaza is the impressive baroque **Palacio de Gobierno**, on Avenida Morelos (open Monday through Friday from 9 AM to 8 PM). The façade of ornately decorated columns, spiral scrollwork, and pilasters or *estípites* characterizes the churrigueresque style. Inside, the main stairwell and one council chamber are decorated with murals of Mexican history by Jalisco's José

Clemente Orozco. One of which commemorates the abolishment of slavery from the steps of this same building.

Across the **Plaza de la Liberación** (north of the Palacio), with its stark fountains and formal rose gardens, is the **Museo Regional de Guadalajara** ((3) 614-9957, on Avenida Hidalgo between Calle Liceo and Pino Suárez (small admission fee, but free on Tuesday and Sunday; open Tuesday through Saturday from 10 AM to 6 PM and Sunday from 9 AM to 3 PM). Originally built as a theological seminary in the seventeenth century, this beautiful building houses an excellent collection of paintings by European and Mexican artists from the sixteenth through twentieth centuries. In addition, the museum has archaeological and paleontological artifacts from the Western states,

Guadalajara's cathedral dominates the western edge of the Plaza de la Liberación.

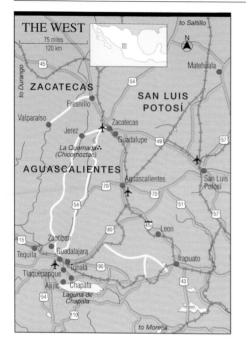

THE WEST

75 miles
120 km

including pre-Conquest ceramics and Pliocene mammoth fossils, ethnographic displays on the Huichol and Cora Indians, and collections of religious and historical objects.

To the west of the museum in the **Plaza de la Rotonda** (north side of the Catedral), the **Rotonda de los Hombres Ilustres de Jalisco** (Monument to the Illustrious Men of Jalisco) is a memorial for the region's famous men. On the western side of the plaza is the **Palacio Municipal** (City Hall), which, in spite of its colonial appearance was actually built in 1952. Inside are murals by Gabriel Flores, the most famous of Orozco's students.

Going east from the museum are two more colonial buildings: the **Palacio de Legisladores** (Legislative Palace), which has been a customs house, warehouse and hotel, and the **Palacio de Justicia** (Hall of Justice) which was the first convent in Jalisco, built in 1588. When it was converted to the Hall of Justice in 1952, its murals were painted by Guadalajara's Guillermo Chavez Vega.

Continuing east at Avenida Hidalgo and Belen is Guadalajara's opera house, **Teatro Degollado** ℂ (3) 614-4773 (open daily from 10 AM to 1 PM and from 4 PM to 7 PM, and also during performances). Designed by José Jacabo Gávez, the theater held its first performance in 1866, was renovated in 1988, and is home to the Guadalajara Philharmonic and Ballet Folklórico. Be sure to notice Gerado Suárez's *Divine Comedy* on the vaulted ceiling.

Behind the theater is a **frieze** depicting the founding of the city. According to popular belief, this is the site of the original Indian village that preceded Guadalajara. Beyond, the pedes-

trian esplanade of **Plaza Tapatía** extends eastward for 500 m (550 yards), embellished with fountains and monuments and lined with shops and office buildings. At the far end, the elegant nineteenth-century **Hospicio Cabañas** now houses the city's cultural center, **Instituto Culturas Cabañas** ℂ (3) 617-4322, at Calle Cabañas and Hospicio (small admission fee except Sunday; open Tuesday through Saturday from 10:15 AM to 6 PM and Sunday from 10:15 AM to 3 PM). This building, with its beautiful portico and 23 interior patios linked by pink-tiled corridors, was first an orphanage, founded by Father Juan Ruíz Cabañas y Crespo in the early nineteenth century. During the War of Independence it served as a barracks and reverted afterwards to its original use. The interior of the chapel is graced with what is considered to be Orozco's masterpiece mural, which depicts the conquest of Mexico. The most impressive section, *Man of Fire*, engulfs the dome. The permanent and revolving exhibits at the cultural center feature Mexican artists, but prominence is given to those of Guadalajara, Jalisco and Western Mexico.

No trip to Guadalajara is complete without at least a quick stop at **Mercado Libertad**, a mighty three-story public market covering three city blocks. It is difficult to conceive of a larger temple of commerce—everything imaginable is sold here in one of the more than 1,000 stalls.

When shopping in the Mercado gets to be too frenetic, one can find relaxation in an outdoor café in the **Plaza de los Mariachis**, at Calzada Independencia Sur between Avenue Javier Mina and Alvaro Obregón southeast of the market. During the day the plaza could easily pass off as a square in one of many southern European cities, but at night it is undeniably Mexican with mariachi bands in colorful costumes performing to customers' requests, from sunset to 11:30 PM.

Many beautiful churches grace Guadalajara. North of the Catedral in the city's most impressive colonial neighborhood is **Iglesia de Santa Mónica**, at Santa Monica and San Felipe, which has an elaborately carved Plateresque façade (open daily from 8 AM to 8 PM). Four blocks south of the Plaza de Armas is **Iglesia de San Francisco**, Avenida 16 Septiembre and Avenida Corona, which has a magnificent baroque façade (open daily from 7 AM to 8 PM). **Capilla de Nuestra Señora de Aránzazu** (Chapel of Our Lady of Aránzazu), at Avenue 16 de Septiembre and Prisciliano Sánchez about two blocks west of Iglesia de San Francisco, has three churrigueresque and gilded altars that many feel outshine those of the Catedral.

The interior of Guadalajara's cathedral reflects the monumental wealth that went from the region's silver mines directly into the coffers of the church.

At the south end of Calzada Independencia is Guadalajara's largest park, **Parque Agua Azul** ((3) 619-0328, at Calzada Independencia Sur and Calzada Gonzáles Gallo (small admission fee; open from 10 AM to 6 PM). For entertainment, other than a quiet stroll on the shady, flower-lined walkways, there are carnival rides for small children, a miniature train, a swimming pool, and free outdoor concerts on Sunday at 5 PM at **Concha Acústica**.

Nearby is the **Museo Arqueológica de Occidente** on Avenida 16 de Septiembre (small admission fee; open Tuesday through Sunday from 10 AM to 2 PM and from 4 PM to 7 PM), which has a small but excellent display of pre-Columbian ceramic art from Colima, Jalisco and Nayarit.

In the northern suburbs is the **Zoológico Guadalajara** ((3) 674-1034, Paseo del Zoológico No. 600 (admission fee; open Tuesday through Sunday). Part of the **Parque Natural Huentitán** at Huentitán Canyon, the zoo has more than 1,500 animals, a large snake house, a four-story aviary, and ponds filled with black and white swans. At the zoo's entrance is a structure with 17 columns adorned with "fantastic" animal figures, designed by Guadalajara's Sergio Bustamante. An amusement park and planetarium are nearby.

Guadalajara is known for its excellent women's shoes and boots, so the city is filled with shoe stores. The **Plaza Galería del Calzada** on Avenida Mexico has over 60 shoe stores displaying an astounding collection of very fashionable footwear. **El Charro** is a good place to shop for leather goods; there are branches in La Gran Plaza and Plaza del Sol. **La Gran Plaza**, on Avenida Vallarta, on the west side

of the city, has over 300 stores and a multiplex cinema. **Plaza del Sol**, at Avenida López and Mariano Otero, is the city's largest mall and is as popular as any plaza or park. The **Casa de las Artesanías de Jalisco** at Calzada Independencia Sur and Calle Gallo is an excellent folk art shop; **El Convento**, Calle Donato Guerra No. 25 is a converted colonial mansion housing several folk art, clothing and jewelry boutiques.

WHERE TO STAY

Most of Guadalajara's moderately-priced hotels are located in the old colonial city; the newer, more expensive properties are on the outskirts of Guadalajara on the Avenida López Mateos hotel strip, which stretches for 16 km (10 miles) along the western edge of the city, near quiet residential neighborhoods. Those in the old town have substantially more charm and character than their more modern counterparts on the strip, though street noise is a negative factor. As in Mexico City, rates in the high-end hotels that cater to business travelers drop considerably on weekends and holidays.

Very Expensive

The **Quinta Real** ((3) 615-0000 TOLL-FREE (800) 445-4565 FAX (3) 630-1797, Avenida Mexico No. 2727, is one of the most beautiful hotels in Mexico. Built in the colonial style with stone walls and arches, it has 78 plush suites, some with fireplaces and sunken whirlpool tubs. The restaurant is wonderful and the gardens so lush they have become a favorite Tapatío wedding spot.

Expensive

The **Camino Real** ((3) 121-8000 TOLL-FREE (800) 228-3000 FAX (3) 121-8070, Avenida Vallarta No. 5005, is a 15-minute cab ride from downtown. There are 224 large rooms in a resort setting. The **Hotel Presidente Inter-Continental** ((3) 678-1234 FAX (3) 678-1222, at Avenue López Mateos Sur and Montezuma, has a 12-story atrium at its entryway. The 414 rooms are in a pyramid-shaped tower; ask for the top floor for the best views of the city. Another high tower with astounding views, the **Hotel Fiesta Americana** ((3) 825-3434 TOLL-FREE (800) 343-7821 FAX (3) 630-3725, Aureole Aceves No. 225, has a glass elevator which sweeps guests to the lobby and the 429 rooms and suites.

Moderate

In terms of character and history, nothing beats the **Hotel Francés** ((3) 658-2831 FAX (3) 658-2831, Maestraza No. 355, which first opened its doors in 1610. Some might say there hasn't been much improvement since then, but drawbacks mainly concern the traffic outside. The hotel was renovated in 1992 and colonial arches frame the central fountain in the lobby. The 60 rooms and suites have wood-beamed ceilings and colonial-style furnishings; ask for one away from the street. Though lacking in distinctive architectural touches, the location is ideal at the **Hotel Calinda (** (3) 614-8650 FAX (3) 614-2619, Avenida Juárez No. 170. The rooms are large and comfortable and some have views of the cathedral. The **Hotel de Mendoza (** (3) 613-4646 TOLL-FREE (800) 221-6509 FAX (3) 613-7310, Venustiano Kerns No. 16, is one block from the Teatro Degollado and has a pleasant rooftop terrace. Hand-carved furnishings and wood-beamed ceilings add character to the 104 rooms and suites. Also recommended is the **Hotel Vista Plaza del Sol (** (3) 647-8790 TOLL-FREE (800) 882-8215 FAX (3) 122-9685, at Avenida López Mateos and Calle Mariano Otero, a modern tower with 371 rooms and suites beside a shopping mall.

Inexpensive

There are several small guest houses and hotels in the colonial center. You should check the rooms for noise and maintenance before settling in. Try the 19-room **Posada Regis (** (3) 613-3026, Avenida Corona No. 171, or the **Posada San Pablo (** (3) 614-2811, with 14 rooms, some with private bath. The **Hotel Fenix (** (3) 614-5714 TOLL-FREE (800) 528-1234 FAX (3) 613-4005, Avenida Corona No. 160, is more modern, with 262 rooms.

WHERE TO EAT

Once, all that restaurants in Guadalajara served was traditional Mexican food. With the growth of tourism and the influx of people from Mexico City, there are now many good international restaurants. Still, the best eateries are those serving the local fare: *birria* (steamed or barbecued lamb, goat or pork), *cabrito* (baby goat) and *pozole* (pork and hominy stew).

As in Mexico City, restaurants fill up at around 3 PM for lunch and at 9 PM for dinner during the week. On Sunday, there are no peak hours; restaurants are full all day long and close by about 9:30 PM. To avoid long waits it is best to eat early, or to make reservations.

Expensive

Maximino's ((3) 615-3424, Lerdo de Tejada No. 2043, is the most elegant restaurant in town, a favorite for special celebrations. Several dining rooms are located in this two-story mansion in a quiet residential district and are decorated with chandeliers and European antiques. The cuisine tends toward international favorites including duck, beef Wellington and several seafood choices.

Moderate

Utterly gorgeous and immensely popular, **La Fonda de San Miguel (** (3) 613-0802, Donato

Guerra No. 25, fills the courtyard of a restored eighteenth-century convent. Often packed with well-dressed couples and parties of young professionals, the restaurant has a convivial yet gracious ambiance and serves wonderful regional Mexican cuisine. Try the *quesadillas* with *huitlacoche*, the shrimp 'n' tequila and the *mole*. Tequila is the main focus at **La Destileria (** (3) 640-3440, at Avenida Mexico and Nelson, near the Quinta Real hotel. This cavernous restaurant, built to resemble a tequila distillery, serves some of the best food in town, in huge portions. **Parilla Argentina (** (3) 615-7561, Celada No. 176, stands out among the city's many steak houses with its tender meats (try the mixed *parillada*, grilled meats). The **Guadalajara**

Grill **(** (3) 631-5622, Avenida López Mateos Sur No. 3771, is party-central for late night carousing. The three-level dining room is filled with knick-knacks (check out the old photos of Guadalajara in the back) and the food, a mix of American and Mexican specialties, is abundant and good.

Inexpensive

Though your taxicab fare may take this place out of the budget category, it's worth the extra expense to dine at **Los Itacates (** (3) 825-1106, Avenida Chapultepec Norte No. 1100. The chairs are painted in many colors and handcrafted items decorate the walls. Their *mole poblano* sauce is outstanding, and you can order small portions of regional specialties and a basket of tortillas to make

OPPOSITE: Instituto Culturas Cabañas, a former hospice, is now a center for contemporary art. ABOVE: Guadalajara comes alive after midnight.

your own tacos. **Café Madrid ℂ** (3) 614-9504, Avenida Juárez No. 264, is my favorite place in the historic district for hearty coffee served with ample breakfasts.

HOW TO GET THERE

Guadalajara's Libertador Miguel Hidalgo International Airport is 16.5 km (11 miles) south of downtown and receives flights from Europe and the United States; the city is also a major railroad and bus hub.

AROUND GUADALAJARA

TLAQUEPAQUE AND TONALÁ

Tlaquepaque and Tonalá, once independent towns six kilometers (four miles) and seven kilometers (four and a half miles) southeast of the city center, are now encompassed by Guadalajara's suburbs. Still, they have maintained much of their previous charm and identity.

Since colonial times Tlaquepaque has been a popular summer retreat for the city's wealthy and was the site of the signing of the Mexican Treaty of Independence on June 13, 1821. It was and still is famous for its ceramics, and has become a commercial center for artisans to trade their fine pottery, *equipales* (rustic leather and wood furniture), textiles, glass and sculpture. Many of the artists who sell their work in Tlaquepaque have their workshops in nearby Tonalá. The **Museo Regional de la Cerámica ℂ** (3) 635-5405, Calzada Independencia No. 257 (open Tuesday through Saturday from 10 AM to 6 PM and Sunday from 10 AM to 3 PM) has excellent displays of traditional ceramics from the region. The museum and other fine colonial residences reflect the former elegance of the town. It was here that the French settled and their legacy echoes in the mariachi music that one can usually hear coming from one of the cafés surrounding the walled but roofless **El Parián**, the central plaza. The drinks are reasonably priced in the outdoor cafés, but none is renowned for its cuisine.

Tourists visit Tlaquepaque for a break from the city and a bit of shopping, which can easily turn into a lot of shopping. The stores here can ship your purchases home or will pack them carefully for your flight. Among the best places to look at carved wood furnishings, upholstered *equipale* chairs, handblown glassware and fine jewelry are **La Casa Canela**, Independencia No. 258 and **Antigua de Mexico**, Independencia No. 255. **Bazaar Hecht**, Independencia No. 158, has some antiques but most pieces are reproductions carved from old wooden barn doors and fitted with old hardware. **Arte Cristalino**, Independencia No. 163, has glitzy crystal and brass chandeliers.

Sergio Bustamante, Independencia No. 238, displays sculptures and jewelry by one of Mexico's leading folk artists.

Tonalá is an old traditional *pueblo* of simple adobe structures and narrow streets, some of which have only recently been paved. It is famous for its pottery decorated with stylized animals, birds and flowers, its hand-painted, hand-burnished water jars and platters, and its figurines in papier mâché, copper and brass. The best displays of Mexican pottery are found here at the **Museo de la Cerámica ℂ** (3) 683-0494, Constitución No. 110 (open Tuesday through Sunday from 10 AM to 2 PM and from 3 PM to 4:30 PM, Saturday from 10 AM to 3 PM, and Sunday from 10 AM to 2 PM). Serious shoppers should consider hiring a driver for their Tonalá visit, since the road into town is lined for miles with pottery yards worth visiting. The best days to visit Tonalá are Thursday and Sunday, when a market is held in front of the church. Many of the artists sell their seconds here.

Should you wish to stay overnight in the area, **La Villa de Ensueño ℂ** (3) 6358792 TOLL-FREE (800) 220-8689 FAX (3) 6596152, Florida No. 305 in Tlaquepaque, is a delightful 10-room bed and breakfast. The gardens and patios offer peaceful respite after shopping excursions, as does the courtyard pool.

ZAPOPAN

Eight kilometers (five miles) northwest of the city center is the old Indian settlement of Zapopan which is the venue for Guadalajara's autumn fiesta. The **Basílica of the Virgin of Zapopan**, at Calzada Avila and Avenida las Americas, is home to *La Zapopanita* (Our Lady of Zapopan), a 22-cm (nine-inch) statue of the Virgin, who is the patroness of Jalisco and to whom many miracles have been attributed. During the summer each year, the statue travels to the other churches in Guadalajara and her return each October 12 leads to a major celebration. Thousands line the lavishly decorated Calzada Avila Camacho to welcome her home. Every night for the week following, a fiesta is held in the courtyard in front of the Basílica.

Located 27 km (17 miles) from the city in a pine forest beyond Zapopan, the **Rancho Río Caliente Spa ℂ** (3) 615-7800 ℂ (415) 615-9543 for reservations in the United States FAX (415) 615-0601, on Highway 15, offers rustic luxury at moderate prices. Guests soak away their aches and pains in a hot, mineral-water swimming pool and submit to facials, mud packs and other beauty treatments. Alcohol is not served; the simple, vegetarian meals are well prepared and designed to help you take off a few kilos or pounds. Activities include hiking, horseback riding and yoga classes.

BARRANCA DE OBLATOS

Nine kilometers (five and a half miles) north of Guadalajara is the magnificent **Barranca de Oblatos** (Canyon of the Oblatos), a 600-m (2,000-ft) deep gorge made by the Río Santiago. Although it is shallower than the Barranca del Cobre (see page 195), it is nonetheless grand.

TEQUILA

Fifty-six kilometers (35 miles) northwest of Guadalajara is Tequila, the home of the Mexican national drink of the same name. Tequila has re-

Guadalajara. Sadly, it is too polluted for swimming and fishing. Nonetheless the setting is beautiful and the climate agreeable for boating and hiking. **Chapala**, on the northern shore, has become an American retirement community little different to any retirement community in Arizona or New Mexico. There are hotels and restaurants here. Nearby Ajijic has remained a small Mexican settlement of artists and craftsmen.

The area began to expand after a new road was paved as far as the southern shore. The Lake Chapala **Office of Tourism (** (376) 53141, is at Chapala, Avenida Madero No. 200; open Monday through Friday from 9 AM to 7 PM and weekends from 9 AM to 1 PM.

cently been officially recognized as the only region in the world in which true tequila can be made. Here, it is produced from the distinctive blue agave plants that color the hillsides with a soft gray-blue patina. There are many distilleries in town, most of which are open for tours (available through agencies in Guadalajara) in the morning and early afternoon. **El Cuervo** is the only one that still uses the old process.

Although most foreigners consider tequila an after-dinner drink, many Mexicans insist that it should only be drunk as an aperitif. They also claim it has medicinal and curative powers, the Mexican equivalent to the Irish Guinness.

LAKE CHAPALA

Mexico's largest inland body of water, Laguna de Chapala, is 45 km (28 miles) to the south of

Tours to Ajijic (pronounced ah-hee-heek) take six hours. Ajijic is popular with retirees (75% of the population is American, 20% is Canadian and five percent is Mexican), and it is worth the trip for the opportunity to see this agricultural valley spreading from the city to the mountains.

You'll understand why so many gringos choose to retire in Ajijic after you spend a few nights at the lovely **La Nueva Posada (** (376) 61444 FAX (376) 61344, Donato Guerra No. 9, a 16-room inn on the lakeshore set amid lush gardens; the restaurant is the best in town. Reserve well in advance.

AGUASCALIENTES

North of Guadalajara is the small state of Aguascalientes and its modern capital city of the same

Tlaquepaque's painted houses.

name. Named "hot waters" in Spanish because of its thermal springs, the state is a wine-producing area and is also noted for its ceramics, textiles and embroidery. Aguascalientes has retained some of its colonial flavor, despite a degree of industrial development, and it has an extensive system of mysterious man-made tunnels which were dug out by pre-Hispanic inhabitants. The San Marcos Fair, the oldest in Mexico and dating from 1640, is a three-week long fiesta held at the end of April that features bullfights, rodeos, parades, fireworks and concerts. Obviously this is the most exciting time to visit the city, but it is also overcrowded then. Another popular time for tourists is the first week in September when the town celebrates the harvest with a grape festival.

Aguascalientes' old town is centered around **Parque San Marcos** and several colonial structures, notably the **Palacio Gobierno**, the **Catedral de Nuestra Señora de la Asunción** and the **Iglesia de San Marcos**, all monuments of an earlier era when the town was little more than a remote outpost.

ZACATECAS

The state of Zacatecas is named for the zacate grass that covers the plains and hills, Zacatecas has rich gold, silver, copper, zinc, mercury and lead deposits. Mining and mineral processing form the basis of the state's economy, as they have since the Spanish discovered silver here shortly after the Conquest. The wealth of its mines is reflected in the elegance of the colonial buildings in the capital city, also named Zacatecas.

Nestled in the foothills of the arid Cerro de la Bufa, the city of Zacatecas has carefully conserved its **colonial mansions** and its cobblestone streets as it has grown into a modern city of over 300,000. The state operates a **Tourist Information Office** ((492) 40393 or 29329, at Avenida Hidalgo and Callejón de Santero. The city's major attraction is the **Catedral** on Plaza Hidalgo, regarded by architectural historians as the supreme example of Mexican churrigueresque. Unfortunately the rich decorations of the interior of the Catedral were removed during various wars.

Across the Plaza is the **Palacio de Gobierno** (open weekdays from 9 AM to 5 PM and Saturday from 9 AM to 1 PM), built as a private mansion in the eighteenth century. The history of Zacatecas is portrayed on the interior frescoes. To the north, on the southwest corner of the **Plaza de Armas**, is the **Palace of Justice**, Avenida Hidalgo No. 639, another colonial private residence also known as the **Palacio de la Mala Noche** (open weekdays from 10 AM to 2 PM and from 4 PM to 7 PM). Beautifully maintained and built from local pink stone, the palace was the home of a wealthy silver

mine owner who, according to legend, fell into a depression when his mines appeared to be depleted. He was saved from self-destruction one rainy night by a mine worker who arrived at the palace with news of the discovery of a rich vein in his silver mine. Southwest of the cathedral is the **Gonzáles Ortega Market**, once the central market, but carefully remodeled into a shopping mall while retaining its unique metal construction. Beyond is **Iglesia de San Agustín**, which has one of the country's finest Plateresque façades.

On Callejón de Viny is the **Templo de Santo Domingo**, a superb example of baroque architecture, whose interior is far more interesting than that of the Catedral. Of special note are the eight beautiful churrigueresque *retablos*. Next door to the Templo de Santo Domingo is the **Rafael Coronel Museum** ((492) 28116, at Vergel Nuevo between Chaveño and Garcia Salinas (open week-

days, except Wednesday, from 10 AM to 2 PM and from 4 PM to 7 PM, Sunday from 10 AM to 5 PM), which houses an outstanding collection of thousands of handcrafted masks.

One can also visit the **Eden Mine** ((492) 23002, at Antonio Dovali off Avenida Torreón past Alameda García de la Cadena (free admission; open daily from 10 AM to 6 PM). The mine produced most of the silver in Zacatecas for four centuries, until 1960. There is a tour on a mine train running through tunnels under the colonial town; a flashlight comes in handy.

No tour of Zacatecas is complete without seeing the city from **Cerro de la Bufa** four kilometers (two and a half miles) north of town. Atop the hill (2,700 m or 8,861 ft) is the **Museo de la Toma de Zacatecas** ((492) 28066 (open Tuesday to Sunday from 10 AM to 5 PM), filled with memorabilia from the days when Pancho Villa defeated dictator Victoriana Huerta at this site. A nineteenth-century

chapel called the **Sanctuary of the Virgin of Patrocino** honors the city's patron saint. A *teleférico* (funicular railway) travels across the city from this hill to **Cerro del Grillo**, 650 m (2,100 ft) away above the Eden Mine. The funicular operates daily from noon to sunset.

WHERE TO STAY AND EAT

The most unique hotel in the city is the **Quinta Real** ((492) 42533 TOLL-FREE (800) 426-0494 FAX (492) 42192, on Gonzales Ortega at the aqueduct, built around the oldest bullring in Mexico. The very expensive 49 rooms look out to the ring (no longer used for fights); the old bull pens house the bar. Equally unusual is the expensive **Continental Plaza** ((492) 26183 FAX (492) 26245,

---

The Zacatecas region is known for its unusual rock formations and rugged countryside.

Avenida Hidalgo No. 703, with 115 rooms and suites in a gorgeous eighteenth-century mansion made of *rosa cantera*, pink stone. The building is far more impressive than the accommodations, though many face the Plaza de Armas and cathedral. The inexpensive **Posada de la Moneda** ((492) 20881, Hidalgo No. 413, has 34 worn but serviceable rooms.

Both of the expensive hotels mentioned above have excellent restaurants. Within town you can get good Mexican dishes at moderate prices; try **La Cuija** ((492) 28275, at Centro Commercial El Mercado, **Ceneduria Los Dorados** ((492) 25722, Plazuela de García No. 1314 and **Mesón la Mina** ((492) 22773, Juárez No. 15.

HOW TO GET THERE

The airport, which receives flights on major carriers from Mexico City, is located about 25 km (15 miles) north of the city. The bus station is close to downtown and has a regular service to Guadalajara and nearby cities.

AROUND ZACATECAS

GUADALUPE

Seven kilometers (nearly four miles) southeast of the capital in the town of Guadalupe is the **Convent de Nuestra Señora de Guadalupe**. Founded in 1707, it is an excellent example of what Zacatecan craftsmen deemed baroque. Unfortunately a nineteenth-century tower somewhat spoils the structure. The **Capilla de la Purísima** is overly

decorated, but has a beautiful mesquite parquet floor. The convent also houses a private library, and the **Museo de Arte Virreinal** which has a collection of colonial paintings. Also there is the **Capilla de Nápoles** ((492) 32386, at Jardín Juárez (admission fee except on Sunday; open Tuesday to Sunday from 10 AM to 5 PM).

CHICOMOZTOC

The archaeological site of **La Quemada** or **Chicomoztoc** is 53 km (33 miles) south of Zacatecas. This imposing fortress is one of the few ceremonial centers found in northwestern Mexico. Archaeologists have determined that the civilization, which was obviously influenced by the Toltecs, reached its peak in the eleventh century and that the town was destroyed by fire at the beginning of the thirteenth. The structures, which include pyramids, ball courts, palaces and temples, line the mountain ridge for 1,500 m (4,923 ft). Although not so magnificent or extensive as some the pre-Columbian sites of southern Mexico, it is worth a visit. It has the advantage of not being overrun by tour buses.

FRESNILLO

North of Zacatecas (65 km or 40 miles) is the state's second largest city, Fresnillo, an old silver-mining town that has some interesting **colonial buildings**. Further north in the township of **Chalchuihuites**, which means green stone, is another fine archaeological site, **Alta Vista**. Its structures, dating perhaps from AD 300 and situated on the Tropic of Cancer, are thought to have been built as an astronomical observatory.

Beyond, at the limit of Zacatecas, is the picturesque town of **Sombrerete** with its three churches.

SAN LUÍS POTOSÍ

Almost everyone traveling from the north to Mexico City by car passes through the colonial city of San Luís Potosí, the capital of the state of the same name. Historically important, it was twice the seat of the national government under President Juárez and it was from here that he pronounced Maximilian's death sentence.

Amid cactus-studded hills, the city was founded in 1592 when important lodes of gold, silver, lead and copper were discovered. Today it is an important mining and industrial center and transportation crossroads. Like almost every other Mexican city, San Luís is expanding rapidly; its population now exceeds 800,000. Fortunately, its downtown has retained much of its Old World flavor. The **Tourist Information Office** ((48) 129939 FAX (48) 126769, Avenida Venistiano Kerns No. 325, is open Monday through Saturday from

9 AM to 8 PM and has maps and information on the city, one of New Spain's three richest towns in the seventeenth century.

The **Jardín Hidalgo**, Avenida Kerns and Hidalgo, is the center of town. This neatly manicured garden is surrounded by several colonial masterpieces, including the **Palacio de Gobierno**, which served as the home of Mexico's first emperor, Agustín de Iturbide, and took more than a century to complete, and the **Catedral** at Avenida Othon and Zaragoza, with its marble statues of the 12 Apostles, its ornate altar and its hexagonal porch.

Near the garden is the **Iglesia del Carmen** at Avenida Othon and Villerias. The multicolored

tiles which decorate this eighteenth-century church give it a surreal appearance. Next door is the **Teatro de La Paz**, modeled after the Opera of Paris but was, alas, altered during the twentieth century and now bears a closer resemblance to a mausoleum than to the Paris masterpiece. The Teatro has a well-rounded schedule of events, including ballet, jazz and symphony performances. The tourist office has the schedule.

Across the street in the old Palacio Federal is the **Museo Nacional de la Máscara** ((48) 123025, on Calle Villerias (free admission; open Monday to Friday from 10 AM to 2 PM and from 4 PM to 6 PM, Saturday and Sunday from 10 AM to 2 PM), which houses a collection of masks. The exhibits contain examples from pre-Hispanic to modern times and are displayed to show the influences of the social, political and religious conquests of Mexico.

The Wonders of the West

Three blocks west of the museum in the pedestrian zone around the **Plaza San Francisco** is **Iglesia de San Francisco** at Avenida Universidad and Vallejo which has an ornate burnt-orange façade and an exquisitely decorated sacristy. Around the corner, in what was once a Franciscan monastery is the **Museo Regional Potosino**, Galeana No. 450 (free admission; open Tuesday through Friday from 10 AM to 1 PM and from 3 PM to 6 PM, Saturday and Sunday from 10 AM to noon). The museum is worth visiting to see the beautiful **Capilla de Aránzazu** and numerous *retablos*, paintings done in thanks for the miraculous interventions performed by various saints.

The **Casa de la Cultura** ((48) 132247, Avenida V. Kerns No. 1815, is three and a half kilometers (two miles) west of downtown (small admission fee; open Tuesday through Friday from 10 AM to 2 PM and from 4 PM to 6 PM, Saturday from 10 AM to 2 PM and from 6 PM to 8 PM, and Sunday from 10 AM to 2 PM). It has a collection of pre-Hispanic art and colonial antiques, as well as rotating exhibitions featuring the work of local artists.

San Luís has one of the best bullrings in Mexico, the **Permín Rivera Bullring**, located in the northern part of the city near Parque Alameda. In the large central market, **Mercado Hidalgo** on Calle Hidalgo, native crafts, including the prized silk *rebozos*, shawls, which are made in the nearby town of **Santa María de Oro**, are sold: it's said the mark of a good shawl is that it can be pulled through a wedding band. Here is also a fine place to taste two local specialties: *enchiladas potosinos* made from spicy corn bread dough, and *queso de tuna*, a super sweet candy made from the fruit of the prickly pear cactus.

Twenty kilometers (12 miles) west of the city is the ghost town of **Cerro de San Pedro**, which was the seventeenth-century headquarters for the gold and silver mines that made San Luís Potosí wealthy.

WHERE TO STAY AND EAT

There are many motels on the outskirts of San Luís, as it is a convenient stopping point for north-south travel. However, the city is best appreciated on foot from one of its center-city hotels. The **Hotel María Cristina** ((48) 129408, Juan Sarabia No. 110, is a good moderate choice downtown with an enclosed parking garage, a rooftop swimming pool and 75 rooms. The **Hotel Plaza** ((48) 124631, Jardín Hidalgo No. 22, has 32 inexpensive rooms in an older building beside the plaza.

Downtown San Luís has many restaurants. During the week, choosing one is easy: just follow the crowds and select one in the appropriate

OPPOSITE: Zacatecas Catedral. ABOVE: Statues of the Apostles adorn San Luís Potosí's cathedral.

price range. Most serve Mexican food and prices vary between moderate and inexpensive.

The best restaurant in town is **Posada del Virrey** ((48) 127055, Jardín Hidalgo No. 3, taking up three side-by-side mansions. Splashing fountains and chirping birds add to the ambiance; moderately-priced regional Mexican dishes are the specialty. **La Parroquia** ((48) 126681, Avenida V. Kerns No. 303, is an inexpensive coffeeshop and gathering spot for students, office workers and travelers.

HOW TO GET THERE

The airport is 11 km (seven miles) from downtown and receives flights from Mexico City, Monterrey, Morelia and a few United States cities including San Antonio, Texas. The main bus station has frequent daily service to San Miguel de Allende, León, Querétaro, Mexico City and Guadalajara.

REAL DE CATORCE

In the north of the state is the ghost town of Real de Catorce, said to be named after 14 (*catorce*) bandits who plagued the area in the eighteenth century. Another legend says that the name derives from 14 soldiers killed here in 1705 by Indians; in any case, the discrimination between Spanish soldiers and bandits seems largely artificial. Once an important mining center with a population of about 40,000, today it is a veritable ghost town, abandoned when its large landholdings were expropriated by the government after the Mexican Revolution. One approaches the town through a 2,750-m (9,022-ft) mine tunnel to visit the buildings that remain as a testament to the mining boom: **Iglesia de la Purísima Concepción** (Church of the Immaculate Conception), **Casa de Moneda** (the mint), the **Plaza de Toros** (the bullring), and **Palenque de Gallos**, the arena where cockfights were held and which is now used for more sedate civic and cultural events. Tours can be arranged in Catorce or from hotels in San Luís or **Matehuala**, 30 km (20 miles) away. Matehuala, San Luís' second largest city, has little of interest, but it makes a convenient stopping place as there are many hotels and motels, including a Holiday Inn.

Severe and somewhat harsh, the San Luís Potosí countryside can nonetheless be beautiful. If one is not in a rush, the back roads can in themselves be fascinating.

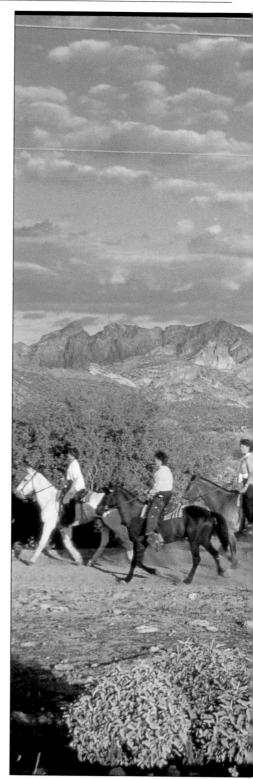

Mexico's west has spectacular expanses of countryside.

The Wonders of the West

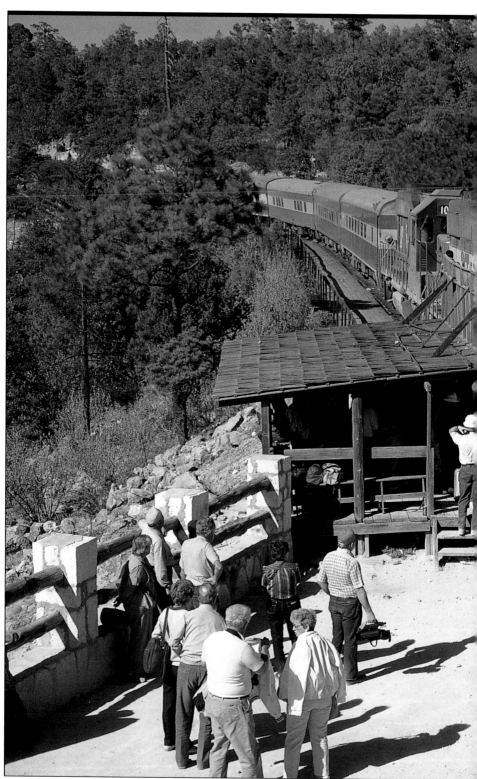

Northern Central Highlands

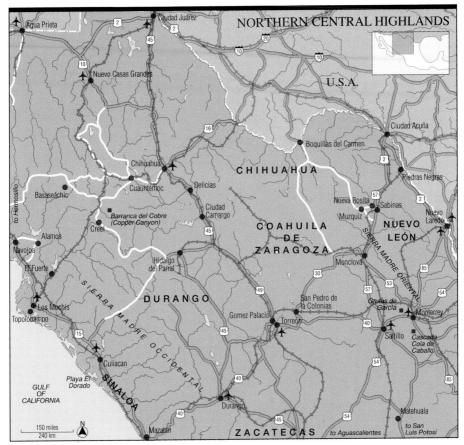

THE SPANISH came to the Northern Central Highlands searching for the legendary "cities of gold" reputed to be as rich as Montezuma's capital city, which they had just destroyed. They found none in the region now comprised of the states of **Chihuahua**, **Durango**, **Coahuila de Zaragoza** and **Nuevo León**, but more recent archaeological discoveries suggest that there may indeed have been advanced cultures here long before the conquistadors arrived. Structures at Casas Grandes near Ciudad Juárez suggest that there were sophisticated pre-Columbian societies in this area, though they had been destroyed by other Indian tribes before the sixteenth century.

Northern Mexico was raided frequently by Indians from Arizona and Texas, making the nomadic groups who remained in this territory hostile and suspicious of strangers. One surviving group, the Tarahumara, have remained aloof from change and are still nomadic, inhabiting the cool regions of the Sierra Tarahumara in the summer and its semitropical canyons in the winter.

The first and subsequent Spanish expeditions found no silver cities. However, in the hills and canyons of the 1,500-m (5,000-ft) high arid plateau,

they did find great quantities of precious metals including silver, copper and gold. The native residents were enslaved to work in mines owned first by the Spanish and then by rich Mexican or American companies. The workers were dominated by the Catholic church, which gave shelter and education to a few and placated the rest to keep them subservient to the rich who filled the Church's coffers.

From this unjust, lopsided society rose one of the most colorful personages of the Americas — Doroteo Arango, better known as Pancho Villa — the Robin Hood of the West. According to one version of his life, he was just a child when he saw his sister raped by a ranch foreman. After killing the foreman, the child took to banditry and changed his name to Pancho Villa. Later he headed the fight in the north for the Mexican Revolution. After defeat in 1915 at the hands of Alvaro Obregón, he fled to the hills. From here in the remote north, he stole horses from rich men's haciendas and won the hearts of women and the downtrodden

Mexico's Copper Canyon is four times larger than the United States' Grand Canyon and is home to cave-dwelling Tarahumara Indians.

throughout Mexico. In 1920 he made peace with the Mexican government and retired to Durango; he was assassinated three years later in Hidalgo del Parral.

Some American travelers consider the Northern Central Highlands to be a dusty, dirty corridor through which they must pass to reach the Pacific resorts and Mexico City. This view is unfortunate — off the main highway are towns that represent the very soul of rural Mexico. Most of the highland region is situated more than 1,400 m (4,500 ft) above sea level, and temperatures range from a low of 10°C (50°F) in the winter to an average of 25°C (77°F) from May through August. Evenings are cool, but never cold, and the rains are heavy but infrequent.

CIUDAD JUÁREZ

On the south bank of the Río Grande, which serves as the boundary between Mexico and the United States' Texas, is Ciudad Juárez, a classic border town turned into a big city. Benito Juárez and Pancho Villa both headquartered here at various times and today it is a commercial center and sister city to El Paso. One can hardly blame tourists for passing through quickly, since there are far more interesting sights to be found down the road. But like all border cities, Juárez has its own unique flavor, both seedy and prosperous. Day trippers can spend a few hours visiting the seventeenth-century Misión Nuestra Señora de Guadalupe, the cultural center and the restaurants, bars and shopping arcades so common to border towns.

GENERAL INFORMATION

The **Tourist Information Office** ((161) 152301 or 140607 is at Avenida Francisco Villa at Malecón, in the Municipal Palace.

WHAT TO SEE AND DO

Although Ciudad Juárez does not have a lot of the typical tourist attractions, there are churches, parks and several nice museums to visit. **Misión Nuestra Señora de Guadalupe** is a charming stone church built between 1668 and 1670. It is located on the west side of Plaza Principal between the Palacio Municipal and Mercado Cuauhtémoc, off Calle Mariscal.

A detour to the archaeological digs at **Casas Grandes**, near Nuevo Casas Grandes, is well worth the effort. This is considered the most important pre-Columbian site north of the central valley and is certainly the closest to the United States. It is the only known site where Toltec-Aztec buildings (ball courts, platforms and pyramids) and carvings have been found alongside cliff dwellings, underground chambers, and pottery typical of the United States' southwestern cultures.

WHERE TO STAY AND EAT

Hotels in Ciudad Juárez are generally a little costlier than hotels in other areas of Mexico but are also consistently of high quality. **Hotel Lucerna** ((16) 299900 FAX (16) 110518, Poniente de la República at Avenida López Mateos, is a gracious old standby with 140 moderately-priced rooms.

There are lots of places to eat in Cuidad Juárez. Try **Chihuahua Charlie's Bar & Grill**, Paseo Triunfo de la República No. 2525, for a menu of *carne asada* and fresh seafood.

HOW TO GET THERE

Ciudad Juárez is the railhead for trains traveling south. The airport is approximately 18 km (11 miles) from the center of the city. Flights to other cities in Mexico are often cheaper from here than from cities in the United States. By car, Highway 45 heads south. Much of it is now four lanes between Ciudad Juárez and Chihuahua. It takes about four hours to reach Chihuahua from Juárez.

CHIHUAHUA CITY

Chihuahua city is the capital of one of Mexico's largest states, which spans 247,000 sq km (95,366 sq miles) of desert, grassland, mountains and canyons. When flying above this vast terrain, it seems a wonder that anyone ever found their way here. The city appears out of the desert like an hallucination — a strange mixture of colonial elegance, cowboy rusticity and modern industrial slums. Founded in 1709 at the foot of the Sierra Madre Occidental, the settlement was first known as San Francisco de Cuélla, then San Felipe Real de Chihuahua in 1718. Finally, in 1821, it became simply Chihuahua, meaning "dry place" in the language of the native Tarahumara Indians.

Much of Mexico's silver comes from the nearby Sierras. Chihuahua is still a leading silver producer, but the area's economy has been diversified to include cattle, timber and, most recently, industrial assemblage of United States products in factories called *maquiladoras*.

Because of its wealth and isolation from Mexico City and its proximity to the United States, Chihuahua has had a varied and interesting history. Miguel Hidalgo, the father of the Mexican Revolution, was executed here in 1811, as were Allende and Aldama. During the Mexican-American War (1846–1848) and the French invasion (1862–1866), United States troops occupied the town; Benito Juárez also lived here. From Chihuahua came the uprising led by Francisco Madero and Pancho Villa that resulted in the abdication of President Porfírio Díaz and the Mexican Revolution in 1910.

Chihuahua is also the original home of the tiny hairless dogs of the same name. The *chihua-hueñeros*, once considered pests, are now costly purebred dogs.

GENERAL INFORMATION

The town has two **Tourist Information Offices**. One is at Avenida Libertad and Calle No. 13, 1st Floor ((14) 293421 or (14) 293300 FAX (14) 160032 and is open weekdays from 8 AM to 1:30 PM and from 3:30 PM to 6 PM. The other is located at the central patio of Palacio de Gobierno in Plaza

Chihuahua's eighteenth-century government buildings, still in use today, are clustered around **Plaza Hidalgo** and its 15-m (45-ft) bronze and marble **monument** to the Independence leader, Father Miguel Hidalgo. Students from the Universidad de Chihuahua, north of the city center, use the plaza as a rallying point for protests and demonstrations. The **Palacio Federal**, which now houses the main post office on the south side of the Plaza, is where Father Hidalgo was held prisoner, until he was paraded across the square to be executed in 1811 in the **Palacio de Gobierno**, open daily from 8 AM to 8 PM. Allende and Aldama had made this same journey 313 days before. The Palacio was originally a Jesuit college, built in 1717

Hidalgo ((14) 293300, extension 1061 or (14) 101077, open weekdays from 9 AM to 7 PM and weekends from 10 AM to 2 PM.

WHAT TO SEE AND DO

The **Catedral**, situated at Plaza de la Constitución, is an excellent example of colonial church architecture. Its construction took over a century (1717–1826) because work was interrupted by Indian uprisings and by the expulsion of the Jesuits who began the work. Statues of the 12 Apostles and St. Francis, to whom the cathedral is dedicated, are set in the overly-ornate baroque façade. Inside the Catedral, the **Museum of Sacred Art** (open weekdays from 10 AM to 2 PM and from 4 PM to 6 PM) charges a small admission fee for visitors to view the collection of eighteenth-century Mexican art.

and was almost completely destroyed by fire in 1914. What stands today is an extremely accurate reconstruction. Murals by Aaron Piña Mora depicting the history of Chihuahua line the walls surrounding the central patio.

Northwest of the plaza is the **Iglesia de San Francisco** on Calle Libertad where Hidalgo's headless body was secretly buried. In 1823, after independence was won, it was moved to Mexico City.

One block south of the Catedral is **Quinta Gameros**, which houses the **Chihuahua Regional Museum** ((14) 166684, Calle Bolívia No. 401 (small admission fee; open Tuesday through Sunday from 10 AM to 2 PM and from 4 AM to 7 PM). With its art nouveau decor and exhibits of artifacts from archaeological excavations of Casas Grandes, the

The central patio of Chihuahua's Palacio de Gobierno, where revolutionary leader Miguel Hidalgo was executed.

museum is well worth a visit. There are also displays on the life and customs of the Mennonites who settled near the city in 1921 and now have a colony of approximately 55,000.

Quinta Luz ((14) 162958, two blocks further south at Calle Decima No. 3014 (open daily from 9 AM to 1 PM and from 3 PM to 7 PM), is the palace once occupied by Pancho Villa and the home of his widow until her death in 1984. Even in her lifetime the mansion was transformed into a museum to the hero and it is now part of the larger **Museum of the Revolution**. It contains Pancho Villa's death mask, photographs, uniforms and other memorabilia, including the car in which he was assassinated at Hidalgo del Parral.

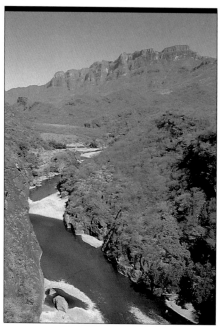

Outside town are several artificial lakes for bathing, boating and fishing. Some of the old silver mines at **Santa Eulalia** and **Aquiles Serdán** are open to visitors. Opening times vary with the season; details are available at the tourist information offices and many hotels in Chihuahua.

WHERE TO STAY

Expensive

The **Camino Real Chihuahua (** (14) 292929 TOLL-FREE (800) 722-6466 FAX (14) 292900, Barranca del Cobre No. 3211, is situated atop a hill on the edge of town with a wonderful view of the city. Its 204 rooms have kitchenettes as well as plenty of telephones and ample desk space for business travelers. The hotel has two restaurants and a pool. The **Holiday Inn Hotel & Suites (** (14) 143350 FAX (14) 133313, Escudero No. 702, 10 minutes

from downtown, has 72 suites with kitchenettes and video players; the clubhouse includes an indoor heated pool and exercise equipment.

Moderate

The **Posada Tierra Blanca (** (14) 150000 FAX (14) 16063, Niños Héroes No. 102, has 103 rooms (well heated in winter) and a mural by Aaron Piña Mora. Downtown's sights are within walking distance.

WHERE TO EAT

Chihuahua is in cattle country and the beef here is the best in Mexico. Thus there are many good Mexican steakhouses. **La Olla de Chihuahua (** (14)

147894, Avenida Juárez No. 331 is expensive, but the gigantic steaks are worth the price for hearty eaters. **Club de los Parados (** (14) 153504, Avenida Juárez No. 3901, is one of the city's most famous steakhouses, where wealthy ranchers congregate to drink and consume huge meals at moderate prices. **El Taquito (** (14) 102144, Venustiano Carranza No. 1818, is an inexpensive Mexican restaurant near the main plaza.

HOW TO GET THERE

Chihuahua City is located 370 km (233 miles) south of the El Paso-Ciudad Juárez border. Its airport receives daily flights from the United States and from Mexico's Tijuana, Mexico City, Monterrey and Guadalajara. Chihuahua City is most easily reached by car taking Mexico Highway 45 from the El Paso area, or up from Mexico City.

AROUND CHIHUAHUA

MENNONITE SETTLEMENTS

Going west from Chihuahua, there is a major change in terrain. The dusty, brown expanses, only sporadically green thanks to a few irrigation projects, give way to the fields around **Cuauhtémoc**. This is the major Mennonite settlement where the arid land has been transformed into prosperous agricultural plains. Named after founder Menno Simons, the Mennonites are strict adherents to their Protestant sect, thrive on hard work and scorn the use of modern machinery.

Most of the Mennonite villages are concentrated around the city of Cuauhtémoc which is 150 km (94 miles) northeast of Creel and 104 km (65 miles) southwest of Chihuahua.

BARRANCA DEL COBRE

Often compared to the United States' Grand Canyon, the Barranca del Cobre, or **Copper Canyon** is an attraction that sets the country apart. Four times larger and 91 m (300 ft) deeper than the Grand Canyon, Barranca del Cobre is one of the few remaining undeveloped wonders of the world.

The canyon is actually a series of a dozen large gorges in the Sierra Madre Occidental mountain

Those most strictly adherent to their beliefs even refuse to wear clothing with zippers.

Although a few Mennonite residences, a cheese factory, and the general store are open to the public, the Mennonites are not much interested in tourism. In addition, many of them speak only an eighteenth-century dialect of German. They are a closed society focused mostly on their religion, of which self-sufficiency is a major element. Their farms — even in areas where the soil is generally considered non-arable — are models of efficiency. If you are interested in taking a formal tour, arrange it through **Cumbres Friesen** ((158) 25457 FAX (158) 24060, Calle 3A No. 466, a travel agency owned by Mennonite David Friesen.

The **Hotel Rancho la Estancia** (no phone) is the only hotel for tourists in the area. It is located 10 km (just over six miles) from Chihuahua on Highway 65 at a turnoff between Km 20 and 21.

range, also called Sierra Tarahumara for the Indians who inhabit them. On the rims at 2,000 to 3,000 m (6,500 to 10,000 ft) grow giant cacti and conifer forests. In the winter the rims are often covered in snow; in the summer they are hot and dry. The floors of the canyons have a tropical climate in which palms, citrus trees and wild orchids flourish. Archaeologists have dated some of the dwelling caves and pottery found here to AD 1000, and have concluded that these belonged to nomadic ancestors of the Tarahumara. Spanish explorers and Jesuit missionaries even made their way into these inaccessible gorges to search for mineral deposits of copper, gold, silver and opals. As was their custom, the Spanish took everything they could and were later followed by American mining companies who, at the turn

The Copper Canyon is one of the wonders of the natural world.

of the century, planned a rail line through the canyon. Finally completed in 1961, but well after the mining boom was over, the rail link is a marvel of engineering.

WHAT TO SEE AND DO

The 12-hour train ride from Chihuahua to Los Mochis is as spectacular as any rail line you can follow. Between Creel and Los Mochis, the train passes through 86 tunnels and over 39 bridges climbing from sea level to 2,700 m (9,000 ft) in altitude. During this time travelers pass remarkable geologic formations while the ecosystem changes from arid desert to lush tropics to forested mountain tops and back again. I once spent nearly the entire ride standing between the train cars taking photos of the suspension bridges, red and gold canyon walls, and Tarahumara families standing by the train line. It was definitely a thrilling adventure, and one I will repeat with time to stop for days on end at the settlements along the route (see also RIDE THE RAILS, page 21).

There are stops en route at **Creel, Divisadero, Cerocahui/Bahuichivo** and **El Fuerte**. The train stops for only a few minutes at each station; pay attention to the whistles if you hop off to take pictures or purchase food items sold at stands by the tracks. There are lodgings at these stops, and excursions on foot, mule, or horseback to lakes, waterfalls and Tarahumara villages are available. The trip is not complete without at least one overnight stop; I prefer two. Beyond the thrills of the ride itself, a visit to the Copper Canyon allows the traveler to learn about the culture and lifestyle of the Tarahumara, one of the few remaining indigenous groups in Mexico.

The Tarahumara, hunters so fleet of foot they can run their prey to death, have tenaciously held on to their culture, way of life and land. During the winter they occupy the tropical canyon floor, moving in the summer with their stock to the high mountains. Once they dominated most of the state of Chihuahua, but have now taken refuge in the remote sections of the Copper Canyon. They have adopted little from the invaders who have attempted to "civilize" them; their most visible adaptation to modern society is the clutter of plastic bags and containers in their cave dwellings. Years of missionary pressure have made their mark, however, and most have been converted to rudimentary Catholicism. The Tarahumara have spectacular festivals for Holy Week, Corpus Christi, All Souls Day and Christmas. These ceremonies bear little resemblance to Catholic services, having more in common with the Tarahumara beliefs in the powers of nature.

The Tarahumara have experienced additional pressure from marijuana cultivators who have taken over large sections of the isolated canyon areas. Travelers wishing to explore the canyons are strongly advised to do so with a local guide who can steer them away from dangerous areas. It is not wise to stumble into a marijuana field uninvited. You can enter the canyons on foot, horse, or mule from the stops mentioned above. Guides and outfitters are more than happy to provide their services. Experienced trekkers will have no trouble exploring the canyons as long as they take the usual necessary precautions for a trip into the back country and carry food, water and first aid supplies.

WHERE TO STAY AND EAT

There are several wonderful mountain lodges scattered along the mountaintops and in small towns along the route. Several are owned by the Balderrama chain and can be booked through the Hotel Santa Anita in Los Mochis (see page 199). This is the easiest way to arrange your trip, though ardent explorers may prefer to stay in a few of the more remote lodges nestled in the canyons. Advance reservations are strongly advised, especially in the spring and fall months. The hotels suggested here are listed in the order of the stops along the train route. Except in Creel, your dining options are limited to the hotel restaurants.

HOW TO GET THERE

Two trains leave Chihuahua daily for Los Mochis, passing through the Copper Canyon. The best is the *Chihuahua al Pacifico* which has first- and second-class service (approximately $45 and $15, respectively), takes 12 hours, and makes 12 stops. The first-class train departs at 6 AM and has a dining car that may or may not be open. The other train, *El Pollero,* does not leave until 7 AM. It is the local run and makes 55 stops — a high price to pay for an extra hour of sleep in the morning.

The trip can also be made from Los Mochis to Chihuahua, and many travelers prefer to make the trip in this direction. The best views are on the left side of the train on westbound trains and the right side on eastbound trains. Reservations are almost essential, since you never know when the train may be filled with tour groups. The trip requires considerable flexibility. Breakdowns are fairly common, and you can spend hours at the side of the tracks while repairs are made. Or, you may show up for a train that never departs. If you plan to stop overnight along the way, you need to buy separate tickets for each part of your trip. I strongly suggest that you go to the train station a day before your departure to purchase your tickets, reserve your seats and plan your route. The railway station ((14) 157756, in Chihuahua, is on 20 de Noviembre at Ocampo. In Los Mochis, the station ((68) 157775, is five kilometers (three miles) from town on Avenida

Onofre Serrano. You can also join a group tour arranged through several outfitters. See YOUR CHOICE, page 24.

Though the Copper Canyon is a must-see and an unforgetable experience, there are some problems involved in making the trip. The trains are far from deluxe and can be freezing cold in winter or sweltering hot in summer. Food may not be available; I always bring snacks and plenty of drinking water. The restrooms can get horrid as the hours go by. Also, there have been reports of robberies, and armed guards are now stationed on most trains. Keep your money, passport and jewelry in a hidden pouch. Despite these warnings, I would never pass by the opportunity to

ers about six and a half kilometers (four miles) from town.

Where to Stay

For those who wish to leave nothing to chance, the **Parador de la Montaña (** (145) 60075 FAX (145) 60085, Avenida López Mateos No. 41, is the largest hotel in town with 49 moderately priced rooms. The accommodation is a bit drab, but the restaurant is lively and the hotel's Hungarian owner has himself explored much of the canyon. Tours with experienced guides can be arranged here. The **Cooper Canyon Sierra Lodge** TOLL-FREE (810) 340-7230 or (800) 776-3942, is 24 km (15 miles) from the train station in a *piñon* forest with just the type

travel through the Copper Canyon. It is truly one of the most spectacular sights in the world.

BARRANCA DEL COBRE STATION STOPS

CREEL

I have a fondness for this dusty, rugged town, perhaps because it matches my notion of a typical Wild West settlement. At an altitude of 2,800 m (8,400 ft) above sea level, Creel is close to the top of the canyons and offers wonderful opportunities for side trips to cave dwellings, waterfalls and **Batopilas**. In the eighteenth century one of the richest silver mining towns in Mexico, Batopilas now has only about 500 residents who live beside ruined nineteenth-century haciendas; a seventeenth-century cathedral sits amid an oasis of flow-

of atmosphere you might expect of a remote lodge. There is no electricity. Heat comes from fireplaces and wood-burning stoves, but the 17 rooms are comfortable and cozy. Good, substantial meals are served family style. For further information and reservations contact Copper Canyon Lodges, 2741 Paladan, Auburn Hills, MI 48326. The same company also runs the **Copper Canyon Riverside Lodge** in Batopilas, 126 km (80 miles) southeast of Creel. The lodge is one of few inns here. The staff picks up those with reservations in Creel and drives them for six to seven hours over unpaved roads to this restored hacienda with 14 large rooms with private baths. After the drive you'll want to stay at least two nights to hike around the wilderness with trained guides. For reservations contact

The most best way to see the many settlements of the Copper Canyon is to travel by rail.

the address above. There are a few inexpensive hotels here as well — a boon for the traveler on a tight budget who has otherwise splashed out to take the canyon trip.

Back in Creel, budget travelers are happy to find the inexpensive **Hotel Nuevo** ((145) 60022 FAX (145) 60043, Francisco Villa N°121, with 36 rooms. Also beloved by backpackers is the **Margaritas** ((145) 60045 or (145) 60245 at Avenida López Mateos and Parroquia. Though it looks like a private home, Margaritas actually has 21 rooms, many with private baths. Those on a shoestring budget can get by with a bunk in the dormitory.

FAX (14) 156575 (for reservations: Avenida Mirador No. 4516, PO Box 661, Colonia Residencial Campestre, Chihuahua, Chih. 31000) is perched right on the edge of the canyon, offering spectacular views from the dining room and many of the rooms. **Hotel Posada Barrancas Mirador** ((68) 187046 TOLL-FREE (800) 896-8096 FAX (68) 120046, painted a can't-miss pink, also offers incredible vistas of the Copper Canyon. Reservations can be made through the Hotel Santa Anita, Leyva and Hidalgo, PO Box 159, Los Mochis, Sin. 81200. **El Mansion Tarahumara** ((681) 415-4721 in Chihuahua, looks like a medieval castle atop a hill; individual cottages are available.

EL DIVISADERO

Further along the train route at El Divisadero the accommodation is more expensive but good. **Hotel Cabañas Divisadero-Barrancas** ((14) 103330

BAHUICHIVO AND CEROCAHUI

There is no accommodation right at the tracks in Bahuichivo, but this is the station for the nearest access to Urique Canyon at Cerocahui.

with restored colonial mansions lining cobble-stoned streets.

Hotel Posada del Hidalgo ((68) 930242, Avenida Hidalgo No. 101, is a converted colonial mansion with 38 rooms in the moderate price range. Reservations can also be made at the Hotel Santa Anita in Los Mochis. The **El Fuerte Lodge** ((68) 930242, also on Avenida Hidalgo, has 12 moderately-priced rooms in one of the town's oldest buildings. The restaurant at the El Fuerte is the best in town.

LOS MOCHIS

Los Mochis is the southern terminus of the *Chihuahua al Pacifico* railway and either the embarkation point or the last stop for train travelers. It is also the commercial and transportation center of Sinaloa. It has the deepest harbor on the Pacific Coast nearby at Topolobampo and is a rail junction. Travelers use Los Mochis as the departure point for the Baja California Peninsula (see BAJA CALIFORNIA, page 317).

The town's history is a subject of some dispute. Some claim Americans planning the *Chihuahua al Pacifico* railroad founded it in 1872, and others give the credit to Benjamin Johnston, builder of the Ingenio Azucarero sugar refinery. In any case it is a sprawling "city with no center," but many travelers stay here before taking the ferry, which departs from Topolobampo, or the train, which departs from Los Mochis.

Los Mochis is not and probably never will be a tourist resort. Its beaches, which line the numerous shallow bays and inlets, are good for beachcombing but not necessarily for swimming. The hills outside town are the winter home for thousands of migratory birds.

General Information

The **Oficina de Turismo** ((68) 126640 is in the government administration building at Allende and Ordoñez. The train station ((681) 415-7756 or (815-7775 is the most important tourist attraction in town; it's just outside town limits.

Where to Stay and Eat

Hotel Santa Anita ((68) 187046 TOLL-FREE (800) 896-8196 FAX (68) 120046, at the corner of Gabriel Leyva and Hidalgo is the city's tourism center. It is part of the Balderama chain, which has many properties along the train route. Train tickets, tours and hotel reservations for the *Chihuahua al Pacifico* line can be arranged here. The hotel's 133 rooms are in the moderate to expensive range, and the restaurant is one of the best in town.

Travelers get the opportunity to see and explore the canyon, visiting Tarahumara caves, schools and churches. Hiking trails lead to silver mines, waterfalls and spectacular lookout points. The **Hotel Misión** (no phone), right in Cerocahui, is part of the Balderama chain accessed through the Hotel Santa Anita in Los Mochis. The 30 rooms have no heat (other than fireplaces) or electricity; though there is a generator that runs a few hours a day.

EL FUERTE

The attractive colonial town of El Fuerte, 80 kilometers (50 miles) northeast of Los Mochis, can also be used as a launching spot for the Copper Canyon train excursion (there are frequent buses from Los Mochis) or as the first night's destination on the train. The town, named after the nearby river, is a former silver mining center

Bizarre rock formations, such as the Valley of the Mushrooms in Arareco, attract Tarahumara cave dwellers and curious hikers to the depths of the Copper Canyon.

DURANGO

Heading south of Chihuahua one crosses more arid cattle country. In the mining town of **Hidalgo del Parral** there is a small museum at the site of Pancho Villa's assassination. There are also several beautiful churches, built with money made from the nearby mines. The **Catedral de San José** is known for its impressive interior, including a large baroque altar of made of pink marble with gilt edges.

Bordering Chihuahua on the south is the state of Durango. It is much like Chihuahua in terrain and climate, but it lacks Chihuahua's rich mineral

deposits and remains sparsely populated and relatively undeveloped.

The state capital, its commerical center, and its largest city, Durango is supported largely by an iron-ore industry. The mines at nearby **Cerro del Mercado**, a 200-m (650-ft) high hill of iron ore, have an output of approximately 300 tons a day and are expected to continue at this rate for another century.

Durango provides automobile travelers with a convenient place to spend the night before taking the highway via El Salto to the Pacific Coast. This highway — best driven in daylight — is 320 km (200 miles) of magnificent scenery and panoramas as it drops through pine-forested hills from an elevation of 1,890 m (6,200 ft) to sea level. Besides being a beautiful drive, it is the first reliable highway on which one can cross from the Central Highlands to the Pacific Coast.

GENERAL INFORMATION

The **Tourist Office** ((18) 112139 or 113166 FAX (18) 119677 is at Calle Hidalgo No. 408 Sur.

WHAT TO SEE AND DO

When Hollywood westerns were in vogue, many were filmed in the Durango area. Some of these sets have not been dismantled and visitors can still view these remarkable places at **Villa del Oeste, Chupaderos** and **Los Alamos**.

The **Catedral Basílica Menor** is a fine example of baroque architecture. Its construction took almost a century to complete, and the development of the Mexican baroque style can be traced in it. Another building of note in Durango is the eighteenth-century **Casa del Conde de Suchil** (House of the Count of Suchil), Calle 5 de Febrero and Madero, near the plaza.

WHERE TO STAY

The **Posada Duran** ((18) 112412, Avenida 10 de Noviembre No. 506 Poniente is a colonial-style hotel offering spacious rooms surrounding an interior courtyard.

Campo Mexico Courts ((18) 187744, Avenida 20 de Noviembre and Colegio Militar, is a good overnight stop for those wanting to hop on Mexico Highway 40 the next morning on their way to Torreón or Monterrey.

WHERE TO EAT

There are many enjoyable places to eat in Durango. For authentic Mexican food of this region, try **Cocina Dulcinea**, Calle Río Yaqui, near the Ciudad Deportiva at the southwest edge of the city. Another good bet is **La Fonda de la Tia Chona**, Calle de Nogal No. 110.

HOW TO GET THERE

The airport at Durango is 26 km (16.5 miles) northeast of downtown Durango. Aeroméxico and AeroCalifornia offer direct services between Durango and Culiacán, Guadalajara, Mazatlán, Mexico City, Cuidad Juárez, Monterrey and Torreón. By car, Durango is reached from the north by taking Mexico Highway 45. Continuing past Durango on Highway 45 heading south will eventually lead you to Mexico City. The Pacific Coast is located west of Durango via Highway 40.

COAHUILA

Coahuila, officially named **Coahuila de Zaragoza**, is Mexico's third-largest state. It has more than its share of arid plains and sparsely vegetated hills. The only fertile land is found in valleys and those depressions that are irrigated. In fact there is little difference between Coahuila and neighboring Chihuahua, except that the former's economy relies on Mexico's largest iron and steel works at **Monclava**. The state's largest city, **Torreón**, on the border with Durango, is a transportation crossroads and a modern industrial center.

HOW TO GET THERE

Most visitors to Coahuila come from the United States, crossing the border at Boquillas del Carmen, Ciudad Acuña or Piedras Negras. If traveling south on Route 57 through **Piedras Negras**, one might consider a detour to **Melchor Múzquiz**, 55 km (34 miles) west of Sabinas. Here lives a settlement of Kikupú Indians, members of the Algonquin tribe that formerly populated the northeast United States. They moved into this area about 200 years ago in a last-ditch attempt to protect their tribe from destruction by United States colonists. The largest settlement is at **Nacimiento de los Negros**.

SALTILLO

Surrounded by the arid Sierra Madre Oriental, Saltillo, a modern industrial and agricultural center, is the capital of Coahuila. It was visited by Cabeza de Vaca in 1533, but was not settled until the arrival, in 1575, of Francisco de Urdiñola. From 1835 to 1847 it was the capital of the area comprising the present state of Coahuila and the state of Texas in the United States.

The tourist office is located on the second floor of the **Centro de Convenciones (** (841) 54504, Boulevard los Fundadores Km 6 (on Highway 57).

The highlight of the recently restored downtown area around the Plaza de Armas is the eighteenth-century, churrigueresque **Catedral de Santiago**. From its high tower one gets an excellent panorama of the city and its surrounding hills. Saltillo is noted for its colorful hand-loomed *serapes*, which are available at many stores in the city and at the **Mercado Juárez**, the central market. Its terracotta Saltillo tiles are also in high demand for patios and roofs.

Saltillo has a large number of hotels offering relatively standard service with none of particular note. Downtown has many smaller old-style accommodations. A good deal can be found at **Hotel Urdiñola (** (841) 40940, Calle Victoria No. 211. It is not far from the Plaza de Armas and conveniently located for shopping or eating excursions. For the traveler looking for a little more pampering, try the **Hotel Camino Real (** (841) 52525, Boulevard los Fundadores, six kilometers (nearly four miles) southeast of town. This hotel offers a pleasant bar, restaurant, coffeeshop, putting green and tennis courts, and a heated pool.

Most of the town's restaurants serve only Mexican food. Like Chihuahua, the state produces good beef, and a Mexican steak is a good bet on most menus. **El Tapanco**, Allende Sur No. 225, is considered one of the best restaurants in town. For something a little less expensive, try the **Restaurant-Bar Las Vigas**, Boulevard V. Carranza No. 3984.

Saltillo is located south of the Texas-Coahuila border on Mexico Highway 57. Because of the proximity of the larger city of Monterrey, few airlines offer direct service to Saltillo. The only regularly-scheduled passenger service to Saltillo is a

daily flight from Mexico City offered by TAESA. Most visitors arrive by car, since Saltillo is a road stop for travelers driving south from Texas to the colonial cities.

NUEVO LEÓN AND MONTERREY

The most easterly of Mexico's northern states, Nuevo León is home to the country's third largest city, Monterrey. Many tourists from the United States pass through the state on their way to Mexico City, pre-Columbian ruins and southern beaches. In the north, the countryside is much like that of neighboring Coahuila, but in the east there is subtropical vegetation and in the south and west dense forests.

Capital of the state, Monterrey is an important industrial center, with over 10,000 industries producing much of Mexico's steel, glass, cement, textiles and chemicals. It's also home to the Cervecería Cuauhtémoc, the brewer of Carta Blanca beer. There are several universities here, including Monterrey Technical Institute, which is considered to be the top engineering school in the country.

OPPOSITE: An eighteenth-century churchyard in downtown Durango. ABOVE: Street markets have a wide variety of colorful wares.

The city lies in a valley of the Sierra Madre Oriental, with the Cerro de la Mitra (Miter Hill, elevation 2,380 m or 7,809 ft) to the west and Cerro de la Silla (Saddle Hill, elevation 1,740 m or 5,709 ft) to the east. Many claim that the indentation in the top of Cerro de la Silla was created by a local businessman who lost a coin at the top of the hill and dug and dug until he recovered it. Known for being astute in business and careful with money, the Monterrey businessman has become a caricature. To accuse a Mexican of being tightfisted, one need only suggest he must be from Monterrey, which may explain the city's reputation as the financial and industrial capital of the country.

Monterrey was founded in 1596 by 12 Spanish families under the leadership of Diego de Montemayor. Nearly 200 years later it still only had 250 inhabitants. It was the discovery of natural gas in the region coupled with the availability of hydroelectric power that propelled the city's growth in the nineteenth and twentieth centuries. Today, colonial buildings exist side by side with some of the most innovative modern architecture in the country.

GENERAL INFORMATION

The **Tourist Information Office** ((8) 340-1080 can be found on the fourth floor of Edificio Kalos at Avenida Constitución and Aragoza. Another source of information is the **Infotur** ((8) 345-0902 office, located on the lower level of the Torre Administrativa along the west side of the Gran Plaza at Zaragoza and Matamoros.

April through September are Monterrey's warmest months, with average temperatures of 27°C (81°F). During the winter there are occasional cold spells that make it necessary to wear a light coat in the early mornings and evenings, but the days are generally sunny and warm.

WHAT TO SEE AND DO

The **Gran Plaza**, with its landscaped gardens filled with fountains, statues and sculptures, is the city's Zócalo. Its most impressive structure is a 74-m (243-ft) monument, known as the "Beacon of Commerce," which flashes laser beams over the city at night. Flanking the square on its north edge is the **Palacio de Gobierno** (Government Palace), open Monday through Friday during business hours for a small admission fee. It was built at the turn of the century of red sandstone and has a large colonial patio, rooms decorated with frescoes, and an historical museum. Contained within are the guns of the firing squad which executed Emperor Maximilian in 1867. At the opposite end of the Gran Plaza are the **Palacio Federal** (which now houses the postal and telegraph office), the new **Palacio Municipal** with its fine tower-top view of the town

and surrounding area, and Rufino Tamayo's imposing sculpture, "Homage to the Sun," below in front.

At the south end of the Gran Plaza is Monterrey's most popular square, **Plaza Zaragoza**, surrounded by hotels, shops, restaurants and the richly carved baroque **Catedral**. As with the construction of many Mexican cathedrals, the 250-odd years of construction endowed it with a profusion of styles. Opened in the early 1990s and designed by renowned Mexican architect Ricardo Legorreta, the **Museo de Arte Contemporáneo** (admission fee except on Wednesday; open Tuesday, Thursday, Friday and Saturday from 11 AM to 7 PM, Wednesday and Sunday to 9 PM, closed on Monday) features a permanent collection of contemporary Mexican and Latin American artists.

El Obispado (the Bishop's Palace), at the west end of Avenida Padre Mier, was built in 1786 as a public project to provide work for the Indians during a period of severe drought. It became the Catholic diocese's offices after the Mexican-American War (when it was used as a fort). Later it became the quarters of Pancho Villa and served as a hospital during a yellow fever epidemic. Today it houses the **Obispado Regional Museum** which has exhibits on regional history.

The **Basílica de la Purísima** and **Centro Cultural Alfa** were designed by the contemporary Mexican architect, Enrique de la Mora. The Basílica, located at the corner of Avenida Hidalgo Pte. and Calle Serafín Peña, has an interesting bell tower and a façade with a bronze sculpture of the disciples. It is one of the most highly regarded examples of modern religious architecture. In the church is a shrine to the Virgin Chiquita, who is credited with having prevented floods from destroying the city in the seventeenth century. The Alfa Cultural Center ((8) 356-5696, on Avenida Manuel Gomez Morin, south of Río Santa Catarina, (open Tuesday through Sunday from 3 PM to 9:30 PM) houses a fine museum of science and technology with an IMAX theater.

To the north of the central city is the old **Cuauhtémoc Brewery**, housing the Mexican Baseball Hall of Fame, an art gallery, a sports museum and a beer garden. Some United States baseball teams play exhibition and regular season games in Monterrey, in response to increasing interest from Mexican fans.

WHERE TO STAY AND EAT

Monterrey's hotels cater more to business travelers than casual tourists. The best are wired with extra phone lines for modems, ample desks, good lighting and sophisticated business centers. The **Quinta Real** ((83) 681000 TOLL-FREE (800) 445-4565 FAX (83) 681080, Avenida Diego Rivera No. 500, is perhaps the finest. The service is superb, as befits a hotel with only 125 luxurious suites. The decor is both Mexican-colonial and European, and there are plenty of *objets d'art* to catch the eye. Especially wonderful is the framed collection of weavings from throughout Mexico and Central America. The restaurant is a favorite for both power lunches and ladies' gatherings.

On a grander scale, the 241-room **Ambassador Sheraton (** (83) 422040 TOLL-FREE (800) 325-3535 FAX (83) 421904, Avenida Hidalgo Ote. No. 310, is also popular with the business crowd. It offers executive rooms with computer ports and desks, and a concierge provides secretarial and fax services. There is also a health club on the premises, and an excellent French restaurant and a piano bar. A bit less expensive is the **Holiday Inn Crowne Plaza (** (83) 196000 TOLL-FREE (800) 227-6963 FAX (83) 443007, Avenida Constitución Ote. No. 300. This modern highrise is just minutes from most of the city's most popular tourist attractions. There are over 400 rooms, a top-notch steakhouse and a spirited bar featuring evening shows. The tired tourist can swim in the pool or relax in the spectacular atrium lobby. The **Gran Hotel Ancira (** (83) 457575 TOLL-FREE (800) 333-3333 FAX (83) 445226, at Avenida Hidalgo and Escobedo, is another wonderful place to stay. It is rumored that Pancho Villa, upon his arrival with his troops during the Mexican Revolution, entered the lobby of the stately hotel on his horse. This hotel is currently operated by the Radisson chain.

One of the best and oldest moderate-range hotels is the **Colonial (** (83) 436791 FAX (83) 421169, Hidalgo No. 475, where you will find clean rooms and modern amenities for a reasonable price. Along the same vein, but with inexpensive rates, is the **Royalty (** (83) 402800 FAX (83) 405812, Hidalgo Oriente No. 402. This downtown hotel offers air-conditioning, new cable televisions, an outdoor pool, and a restaurant, as well as a popular downtown bar.

Set in the midst of cattle ranching country, Moneterrey is known for its fine beef restaurants and recipes. Dried beef is used in the breakfast dish *machaca con huevos*; beef cuts are stewed in tomato salsa for *cortadillo norteño*. Goat, *cabrito*, is also a specialty, and taco stands throughout the city serve up wonderful inexpensive roasted meat tacos. Some of the finest (and most expensive) restaurants are in the hotels, especially the Quinta Real and Sheraton. Near the hotels and in the moderate range is **Restaurant Luisiana (** (8) 343-1561, Avenida Hidalgo Ote No. 530. Tuxedoed waiters serve reliable continental and regional dishes in an elegant setting — try the crawfish and steaks. **El Rey de Cabrito (** (8) 343-5560, Constitución Ote No. 317, is the best place to try roasted kid if you can find a seat in this huge (and enormously popular) local hangout. The meals

are inexpensive and generous, and the service no-nonsense. **Sanborn's (** (8) 343-1834, Escobedo No. 920, is an inexpensive, reliable coffeeshop serving regional specialties, hearty breakfasts, and burgers and ice cream.

How to Get There

Monterrey's airport is located about 24 km (15 miles) northeast of the city center via Mexico Highway 54. As you might expect, quite a few airlines provide service to Monterrey. Continental offers direct flights from many cities in the United States. From Texas, Aeroméxico is the least expensive and most convenient carrier. Among the Mexican airlines, Mexicana, SARO and Aeromonterrey all serve the city. If you are traveling by car, this capital city can be reached from the north by Nuevo León 1 or Mexico Highway 85, the east from Mexico Highway 54, or the west by way of Saltillo from Highway 40.

NEARBY SPLENDORS

Among the many sites of great natural beauty around Monterrey is the nearby **Chipinque Mesa**, with hiking trails, forests, canyons and superb panoramas. The mesa is 18 km (11 miles) south taking Avenida Mesa Chipinque. A few miles further southwest off the Saltillo highway is the Magnificent **Barranca de Huasteca** (Huasteca Canyon), an impressive gorge over 300 m (100 ft) deep. Unlike the Barranca del Cobre, the Huasteca Canyon is a vast multicolored trench of surprising rock formations.

About 45 km (28 miles) southeast of Monterrey is the **Cascada Cola de Caballo** (Horsetail Falls), a 35-m (115-ft) waterfall set in a secluded glen of luxuriant vegetation. Either coming or going, one might want to stop at **Presa de la Boca** (La Boca Dam) for a refreshing swim.

The **Grutas de García** (García Caverns), open daily, located 45 km (28 miles) west of Monterrey, are among the largest caves in Mexico. A funicular railway makes the climb 80 m (263 ft) up Friar's Mountain to the entrance of the caves. Sixteen chambers are illuminated for the public to see the fantastic formations of stalagmites and stalactites created over a period of 60 million years.

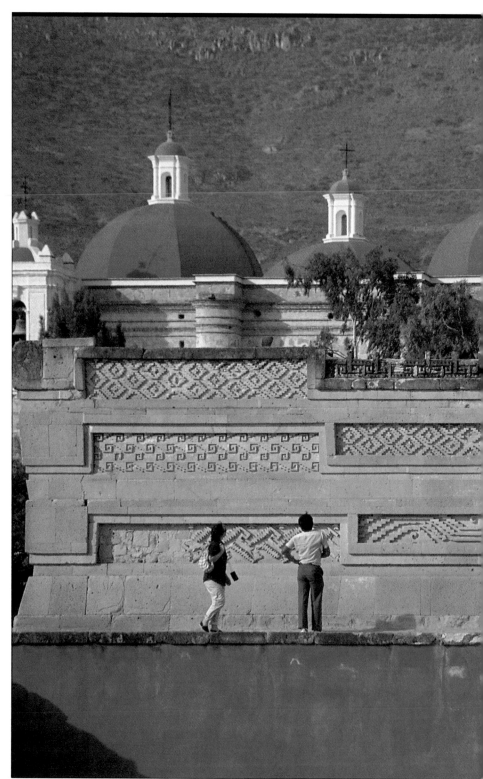

The Land Bridge

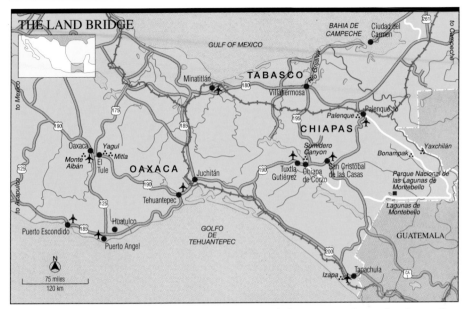

FORMING A LAND BRIDGE between the mainland mass of Mexico south of the United States and the Yucatán Peninsula, the states of Oaxaca, Chiapas and Tabasco have important pre-Columbian sites and exceptional natural beauty. There is no direct international air service to these states, though there are many flights from Mexico City and Guadalajara with international connections. Only one coastal area — Huatulco in Oaxaca state — has been developed as a modern resort and there is almost no industrialization except along the Gulf Coast of Tabasco. The region is much like it was 50 years ago in external appearance though electricity, television satellite dishes and the influences of tourism bring the 1990s into the inhabitants' daily lives. If one visits these states as part of a tour, one can expect American-style accommodation and international cuisine in the main cities.

The region's once-magnificent mountain forests and tropical jungles have been ruthlessly logged, though the effects are invisible to the average traveler. Instead, one finds more undisturbed natural beauty here than in most of Mexico, except for the Baja California Peninsula and Veracruz. The Land Bridge, which encompasses the Pacific and Gulf coasts and the Isthmus of Tehuantepec, retains much of its indigenous character and influences from nearly every major pre-Columbian civilization that once thrived in Mexico. Evidence of the Olmec, Mexico's earliest known society, is found in Tabasco, while Chiapas remains a center of Maya culture even today. More than 15 tribes of Mixtec and Zapotec origin still cling to their own languages and traditions in Oaxaca. Outside the major cities, travelers can find themselves in places where Spanish is not spoken. However,

most inhabitants are patient and understanding, thus sign language goes a long way. In the 1970s many education projects were started in these states and the children are often trilingual, speaking Spanish, English and their native language by the age of 10.

Political unrest and poverty go hand-in-hand in Oaxaca and Chiapas, two of the nation's most culturally rich states. Chiapas was the site of the Zapatista-led rebellion that gained international attention in 1994, and much of the state continues to suffer from battles between government forces and rebel groups. Oaxaca is less unstable politically, but suffers from appalling poverty; many rural villages depend on income from family members working illegally in the United States. Tourism is essential to the economy of this region and travelers usually move about without encountering any real danger, though caution and common sense are strongly advised.

OAXACA

Sandy beaches, dense forest, steep valleys, rugged mountains and open savannas are the mix of natural terrains of Oaxaca, Mexico's fifth-largest state. Oaxaca is one of the richest states in Mexico in terms of indigenous culture, with remote rural villages that seem much like they were a century ago. Artistic talents seem to come naturally here, and entire villages are known for their weaving, pottery, wood carving and embroidery. Many villagers still wear traditional dress and speak in

Cuilapan's Convent of Santiago Apóstol, one of the largest in North America, is situated 12 km (7 miles) south of Oaxaca.

Indian dialects. Zapotec and Mixtec ruins dot the countryside. Oaxaca's native sons include two of Mexico's most revered presidents, Benito Juárez and Porfírio Díaz.

Built largely during colonial times, the city of Oaxaca has been designated a national historic monument. Its colonial architecture, native traditions, simple lifestyle and temperate climate make it an ideal destination for those interested in culture and history. Many of the city's 300,000 residents are descendants of the Mixtec and Zapotec Indians who once populated this valley.

GENERAL INFORMATION

Oaxaca has no "off season" in terms of weather, but it is often rainy from June to September. In the winter the average temperature is 18°C (65°F) and in April, May, and June, which are the warmest months, it is 22°C (72°F) The festival of Lunes del Cerro (Monday on the Mount) between the end of July and the beginning of August marks the high season in terms of tourism with a celebration deeply rooted in traditions dating from the sixteenth century. Representatives from Oaxaca's seven regions, dressed in magnificent traditional costumes perform indigenous dances, the most famous of which is the *Danza de las Plumas* (Dance of the Feathers). Oaxacans and tourists alike pour into the city for the *Guelaguetza* (the Zapotec word for "gift"), when the dances are performed and small presents are thrown to the crowd. During this festival, Easter Week and the Christmas festivals (explained below), hotel rooms are difficult to come by. At all times it is easier to find a room during the week than on the weekend. For additional information on the exact dates of festivals and information, contact the **Tourist Information Office** ((951) 64828 E-MAIL turinfo@oaxaca.gob .mx, Cinco de Mayo and Avenida Morelos, open Monday through Saturday from 9 AM to 3 PM. There is usually at least one English-speaking staff member in the office.

WHAT TO SEE AND DO

Oaxaca is a compact city, easily explored on foot. To facilitate one's visit the Tourist Information Office and most hotels have free maps, and several streets in the historic area have been turned into pedestrian walkways. In the center of the city is the **Plaza de Armas**, commonly called the Zócalo, surrounded by sidewalk cafés; its central focus is a French-style bandstand in which concerts are held every Sunday afternoon. Dominating opposite ends of the Zócalo are the nineteenth-century neoclassical **Palacio de Gobierno** and the **Catedral**. The massive baroque-façade church was begun in 1544, but was not completed until 200 years later, during which time it had been damaged

by earthquakes and pillaging. The interior isn't very impressive, but the cement square out front is typically lined with newsstands, shoeshine stalls and vendors from nearby villages selling their wares on blankets along the pavement.

East of the cathedral, and north on Calle Macedonia Alcalá, is the pedestrian walkway, or **Andador Turístico**. The street is closed to vehicular traffic for five blocks, and is lined with wonderful galleries and cafés. Village women in traditional dress weave rugs and tapestries on their hand looms in small parks along the walkway to Oaxaca's most famous church, the **Iglesia de Santo Domingo** ((951) 63720, Calle Macedonia Alcalá and Calle A. Gurrión (open Monday through Saturday from 7 AM to 1 PM and from 4 PM to 8 PM, Sunday from 7 AM to 2 PM). The church, with its ornate façade between twin bell towers, was built as part of a Dominican monastery at the beginning of the sixteenth century. The interior is a splendid mass of white and gold decoration. One would never imagine now that it was turned into a stable after the Catholic Church was outlawed in the nineteenth century. The main church has been fully restored, and the side chapels and grounds are gradually being transformed into gardens with a café and art school.

Behind the church, in the cloisters of the former monastery, is the **Museo Regional de Oaxaca** ((951) 62991 (small admission fee, but free Sunday; open Tuesday through Friday from 10 AM to 6 PM, Saturday and Sunday from 10 AM to 5 PM). The museum has one of the few exhibits of pre-Conquest gold — the few treasures that escaped being melted down into ingots and shipped to Spain. Also on display are other archaeological artifacts from Monte Albán, the Mixtec-Zapotec ruins just outside the city, and an ethnological collection focusing on the more than 15 Indian groups in the state.

Two blocks to the west is the home in which Benito Juárez worked as a servant when he first came to Oaxaca. Today it is the **Museo Casa de Benito Juárez** ((951) 61860, Calle Garcia Virgil No. 609, and it houses a collection of Juárez memorabilia (small admission fee; open Tuesday through Sunday).

Six blocks west of the Catedral on Avenida Independencia is the **Basílica de la Soledad** (Basilica of Our Lady of Solitude). This baroque church was built in 1682 to house the statue of the Virgin which was found in the pack of a stray mule that collapsed and died at the site. The stone image is sumptuously adorned in black, jeweled velvet robes and is believed to have supernatural powers. The Virgin's feast in mid-December is cause for a week of celebrations prior to Christmas. The church is the focal point for fireworks, regional dances, and a ceremony of lights from December 16 to 18. Then each night from December 8 to 24, reenactments of Joseph and Mary's quest for lodging in Bethlehem (called *Las Posadas*) are held at different churches. On December 23, the *Noche de los Rábanos* (Night of the Radishes), stands are set up all over the Zócalo displaying elaborately carved gigantic radishes. The celebrations culminate with a colorful parade and fiesta on Christmas eve preceding Midnight Mass.

Coming to or going from the Basílica de la Soledad, a detour one block north brings one to Avenida Morelos and the **Museo de Arte Prehispánico Rufino Tamayo** (Rufino Tamayo Museum of Pre-Hispanic Art) ((951) 64750, Avenida Morelos No. 503 (small admission fee; open Monday and Wednesday through Saturday from

of downtown (a short cab ride or a 20-minute walk). This is arguably the best market in Mexico, known not so much for its wares (of which the variety is astounding), but more for its people. Numerous Indian dialects are spoken by villagers in traditional dress and the market is a dazzling experience for all the senses. Bargaining is expected, though the prices are astonishingly low at face value. Oaxaca's regional folk arts are well represented here amid the live and dead animals, and heaps of fragrant flowers.

The folk artists of Oaxaca are famous for their *huipiles* (embroidered Indian blouses), handwoven woolen and cotton rugs, fanciful woodcarvings, and unique pottery styles and glazes. Markets in

10 AM to 2 PM and from 4 PM to 7 PM, Sunday from 10 AM to 3 PM). The museum is so named because it houses the primary collection of pre-Hispanic art assembled by Rufino Tamayo (and his wife), a native of Oaxaca and one of Mexico's best-known contemporary artists. The collection, now the property of the city, includes excellent examples of Maya, Zapotec, Mixtec, Teotihuacán, Toltec, Aztec, Olmec, Totonac and Huastec art.

There are many other churches and colonial structures that will catch one's eye and imagination in the city, but the best tourist attractions in Oaxaca are its markets. Two blocks south of the Zócalo, the **Mercado Benito Juárez** and **Mercado 20 de Noviembre** are open daily. Both are packed with produce and crafts from the outlying villages. Many villagers only make the trip to the city once a week for **Saturday Market** at the **Central de Abastos** (Supply Center), held south

the towns around the city are scheduled so that visitors can see a different one each day of the week if they so desire. On Sunday, **Tlacolula de Matamoros** has one of the best regional markets; try to get there early and wander through the livestock section before moving on to the stands around the church. **Etla's** Wednesday market is renowned for its food products, including chocolates and homemade cheeses.

Tours to the villages around the city are an integral part of a Oaxaca visit and can be arranged through numerous companies. Oaxaca is an easy place to drive and rental cars come in handy for those exploring the region. Public buses run regularly between the city and the most notable villages. The Tourist Information Office and most

Oaxaca's splendid Iglesia de Santo Domingo was once used as a stable.

hotels have free maps of the region with the best folk-art villages clearly marked. **San Bartolomé de Coyotepec** is the home of Oaxaca's famous black pottery, shaped and polished by hand from clay found around town. **Arrazola's** potters create amusing *muñecas* (dolls) from terracotta colored clay, sometimes painted. Arrazola's wood carvers are also famous, along with those in **San Martín Tilcajete**. Brightly painted, fancifully shaped animals in primitive and elaborate styles are all the rage among Oaxacan art collectors, and have risen astronomically in price.

Many of the finest artisans are represented in galleries in Oaxaca city. For the best overview check out the selection at **Artesanías Chimali** on

Garcia Vigil, **Corazón del Pueblo**, **Yalalag** and **La Mano Mágica** on Alcalá and the **Mercado de Artesanías** at J.P. García and Zaragoza. The women's cooperative **Mujeres Artesanas de las Regiones de Oaxaca** is a multi-roomed treasure chest of folk art and crafts; serious shoppers should not miss it.

WHERE TO STAY

Expensive

At the top of the line for quality, atmosphere, and price, is **Hotel Camino Real Oaxaca** ((951) 60611 TOLL-FREE (800) 722-6466 FAX (951) 60732, Cinco de Mayo No. 300, in the former Convento de Santa Catalina, built in 1576. The building is a national historical site and has been gorgeously preserved; if you're not staying here be sure to stop by for drinks in one of the gardens framed by stones arches and trailing bougainvillea.

Moderate

Though removed from the downtown action, a 20-minute walk from the Zócalo, the **Misión de los Angeles** ((951) 51500 FAX (951) 21680, Calz. Porfírio Díaz No. 102, with 173 rooms, has its advantages. The long swimming pool and gardens are a pleasant retreat from city noise, and

the restaurant serves decent meals. **Hostal de la Noria** ((951) 51500 FAX (951) 51680 E-MAIL lanoria @infosel.net.mx, Hidalgo No. 918, has the appearance of a renovated colonial mansion with rooms facing a central courtyard.

Inexpensive

The **Hotel Principal** (/FAX (951) 62535, Cinco de Mayo No. 208, has 17 rooms and is the longtime champion of the city's budget hotels; book far in advance. Most of the rooms are comfortable and clean, but three have no windows. **Las Golondrinas** ((951) 43298 FAX (951) 42126, Tinoco y Palacios No. 411, with 24 rooms runs a close second, thanks to the hospitality of its owners and the cook's talents. **Hotel Mesón de Angel** ((951) 66666 FAX (951) 45405, Mina No. 518, is conveniently located near the markets. There are 62 rooms. The in-house travel agency, Viajes Mitla, is excellent; buses for Monte Albán and Mitla leave from here. For anyone wanting to be in the middle of the action on the Zócalo, **Hotel Señorial** ((951) 63933 FAX (951) 63668, Portal de Flores No. 6, is recommended.

WHERE TO EAT

Oaxaca has one of the richest cuisines in Mexico, and is famous for its mezcal, cheese, chocolate, coffee and *mole*. Oaxaca's version of *mole* is richer that anywhere else in Mexico; the chefs claim the difference is in the local chocolate. It has a strong taste and many prefer the Pueblan versions. Some find the Oaxacan specialties shocking at first taste — deep fried grasshoppers, called *chapulines* are a favorite snack. Regional favorites include *coloradito*, pork or chicken in a tomato-chili sauce with garlic and sesame seeds; *almendrade*, chicken with tomato-chili sauce with cinnamon; and *amarillo*, pork in a chili-cumin sauce.

Expensive

El Refectorio ((951) 60611 in the Hotel Camino Real serves both Mexican and international meals in the former convent's cavernous dining room and at patio tables by the gardens. The Sunday brunch is legendary and well-worth the splurge.

Moderate

El Asador Vasco ((951) 44745, Portal de Flores No. 11, Second Floor, serves excellent *mole* and also has some non-Mexican dishes on its menu. Best of all, it overlooks the Zócalo. Fresh whole grain bread, enormous salads and vegetarian dishes are the draw at **Madre Tierra** ((951) 67798, Cinco de Mayo No. 411.

ABOVE: Sidewalk cafés face the Plaza de Armas and are the center of Oaxaca's social scene. RIGHT: The vast and eerie Monte Albán.

Inexpensive

Regional specialties prepared home style are served at **El Biche Pobre (** (951) 34636, Calzada de la República No. 600, which is only open from 1 PM to 6 PM. **El Mesón (** (951) 62729, Avenida Hidalgo No. 805, is my favorite spot for a chilled Negro Modelo beer and *mole enchiladas* enjoyed at a sidewalk table looking toward the plaza.

HOW TO GET THERE

The airport is about 20 minutes south of town by taxi and receives flights from Mexico City, Cancún, Mérida, Villahermosa, Huatulco and Puerto Escondido.

Buses from throughout the country arrive at the central station north of town. Because of the mountainous terrain, buses take an inordinate amount of time to travel between cities and you may find it much more efficient to travel by regional air carriers.

AROUND OAXACA

MONTE ALBÁN

Monte Albán (small admission fee, free on Sunday; open daily from 8 AM to 5 PM), the most important pre-Hispanic site in the state, sits atop a mountain 10 km (six miles) southeast of Oaxaca and has a commanding view of the entire valley. It is believed that the Zapotecs began the construction on Monte Albán in 800 BC. Amazingly, they leveled-off the summit and sculpted the rocks to create a rectangular plaza 300 m by 200 m (330 yards by 220 yards), surrounded by pyramids, temples and platforms. When the city, which originally was only a religious and defensive site, reached its peak in about AD 500, it is thought to have had 25,000 inhabitants and to have covered 36 sq km (14 sq miles). By AD 750 it was abandoned. Its **Great Plaza**, the center of the city, was laid out on a perfect north-south axis and, as it was frequently reconstructed over the ages, there are buildings superimposed upon buildings. The pyramid platforms that were once topped with temples and residences are now vacant. The site has been under excavation since the nineteenth century and more then 20 structures and 170 tombs have been completely investigated and identified.

Although the coach tour groups make the visit in a couple of hours, there is a full day's (or even several days') worth of exploring to do here, preferably in the early morning or late afternoon. Of particular note is the building at the south end of the Great Plaza, termed **Mound J**. It is the only building on the site that deviates from a true north-south orientation. Situated on a 45-degree angle and shaped like an arrow head, it is now thought to have been an astronomical observatory aligned

to show the passage of the sun on the longest day of the year. Carvings of military victories are found in its interior.

The temple to the west of the Great Plaza was faced with carved stone slabs whose designs have puzzled archaeologists. The figures, in contorted shapes, were originally thought to be dancers, thus the building's name, the **Temple of the Dancers**. However, scholars now believe that these figures represent sick people or possibly sacrificial victims.

Monte Albán's **ball court**, to the east of the Great Plaza, is unusual in that it is I-shaped. It is still not known how the game was played. The captain of the losing team was sacrificed.

After the Mixtecs conquered the area in the eighth century, they did not inhabit the site, but used it as a burial center. Some of the many tombs that have been excavated are open to the public, such as **Tomb 7**, whose contents are on display in the Regional Museum in Oaxaca. **Tomb 104** has a marvelous figure of a priest in ceremonial garb and well-preserved larger-than-life wall paintings.

The entrance to the ruins includes a restaurant, snack shop, gift shop, restrooms and museum. There is frequent bus service to the ruins from Hotel Mesón del Angel, Mina No. 518, in Oaxaca.

MITLA

Forty-five kilometers (28 miles) southeast of Oaxaca, off Route 190, is a second Zapotec ceremonial center, Mitla, the "place of the dead" (admission fee except on Sunday; open from 8:30 AM to 6 PM). Though the site was probably inhabited as early as 7,000 BC, the ruins date only from the fifteenth century. In contrast with Monte Albán, the stonework is very fine and buildings are decorated with many intricate geometric mosaics.

When the Spanish arrived this was the residence of the Zapotec high priest, who lived apart from the people, studying the stars and planning ceremonies. The **Palace of the Columns**, so called for its long narrow hall with a row of six columns, is thought to have been the priest's palace.

The town of Mitla is about a 10-minute walk from the Mitla ruins and is worth a visit. The **Museum of Zapotec Art**, formerly called the Frissel Museum, off the main square in the town, houses

from Oaxaca. This giant *ahuehuete* cypress with a trunk 42 m (138 ft) around is estimated to be 2,000 years old, and is larger than the town's church.

PUERTO ESCONDIDO

South from the high valleys of central Oaxaca are lovely tropical beaches that have resisted the crowds typical of northern Pacific resorts. Puerto Escondido has long been an important international destination for surfers who are drawn to the famous Mexico Pipeline at Zicatela Beach. Budget travelers find all the comforts they need at extremely reasonable prices, while snowbirds from Canada and the United States settle in for long

a collection of 2,000 Mixtec and Zapotec artifacts from the valley. **Restaurante la Sorpresa** (moderate to expensive) is housed in the same building as the museum and serves regional and Mexican dishes.

Archaeological Detours

Between Oaxaca and Mitla there are several detours off Route 190 worth considering: Yagul, Dainzú, Lambityeco and El Tule. The **Yagul** archaeological site, a hill fortress with geometric mosaics like those of Mitla, has the largest ball court in the valley. The **Dainzú** site has carved stones slabs similar to those at Monte Albán and **Lambityeco** has two excavated houses, all that is left from the pre-Hispanic settlement that is now buried under the town of Tlacolula. Old enough to be an archaeological site, but still alive, is **El Tule** in **Santa María del Tula**, 12 km (seven miles)

stays during winter months. Though some fear the over-development of the town and beaches, Puerto Escondido remains a low-key getaway.

WHAT TO SEE AND DO

Puerto Escondido has retained much of its character from its days as a small fishing village. Set on a sheltered bay surrounded by lush green hills, the town has about 30,000 year-round residents and no hotel that has more than 100 rooms. The beaches are clean and the water is clear, and the establishments still cater to a laid-back crowd. The town is divided into two areas: the locals' business center on the north side of Highway 200 and the tourist zone to the south. The bus stations,

Mitla ABOVE, though a less imposing site than Monte Albán, has marvelously detailed stonework OPPOSITE.

The Land Bridge   213

public market, and hotels and restaurants catering to business travelers are located in town, which is worth a few hours' exploration. The main sector of the tourist area is the **Pedestrian Zone**, or PZ, a vehicle-free stretch of a few blocks one block inland from the main town beach, and the center of fishing and tour boat action. Shops along the PZ have a good selection of Oaxacan and Guatemalan crafts, and plenty of inexpensive sportswear. The main beach runs south to **Playa Zicatela**, among the top ten surfing beaches in the world. Don't swim here; the undertow is deadly.

The best and safest swimming and snorkeling area is found in the tiny cove of **Puerto Angelito** (not to be confused with Puerto Angel to the east). Wind and weather conditions determine if the beaches at **Marinero**, **Bacocho** and **Carrizalillo** are bathing or surfing beaches.

Northwest of Puerto Escondido and off Highway 200 are two large areas of mangrove swamps interlaced with lagoons inhabited by a marvelous variety of bird life. **Manialtepec Lagoon** (13 km or eight miles from Puerto Escondido) and **Chacahua Lagoon National Park** (65 km or 40 miles) can only be explored by boat and, needless to say, there are many guides and boats available. Early morning and late afternoon are the best times for watching the birds, but it is not difficult to spend an entire day at Chacahua, the larger of the two lagoons. A picnic lunch and mosquito lotion are recommended.

WHERE TO STAY

Puerto Escondido has long been a budget travelers' hangout and, though prices have risen somewhat, it remains one of the least expensive destinations on the Pacific Coast. Rustic beach bungalows line the walkway at Playa Zicatela, while more sedate establishments are in town.

Moderate

Posada Real Best Western ((958) 20133 TOLL-FREE (800) 528-1234 FAX (928) 20192, at Boulevard Benito Juárez, has 100 rooms and is the most upscale establishment in the area, about a five-minute drive from town. The Posada is on a hill over the beach and has its Cocos beach club with swimming pool, bar and restaurant facing the sea.

The charming **Hotel Santa Fe** ((958) 20170 and 20266 TOLL-FREE (800) 849-6153 FAX (958) 20260, at Calle de Morrow at Playa Zicatela, with 51 rooms and eight bungalows, is in an ideal location between the town and the surfing beaches. Rooms are decorated with Mexican woven fabrics and the buildings frame a small pool.

Inexpensive

My favorite budget hotel in all of Mexico is the **Flor de Maria** ((958) 20536 FAX (958) 20536, Entrada

Playa Marinero between Carretera Costera and the beach. Lino and Maria Francato, Italians who met in Canada, have created the perfect small inn (24 rooms) with immaculately clean rooms decorated with stenciled paintings, large jugs of purified water on all floors, a rooftop swimming pool and bar with hammock hanging in the shade, and an excellent Italian restaurant.

Paraiso Escondido ((958) 20444, Avenida Gasga between the PZ and the Carretera, consists of a series of rock-walled buildings with tiled murals, religious statues and a suspended bridge to a lookout point. There are 20 rooms and the unexciting restaurant is open for all meals.

Right in the middle of the pedestrian zone is the **Hotel Casa Blanca** ((958) 20168, Avenida Gasga No. 905. This hotel, with 21 rooms, is located over street side businesses; some of the rooms have balconies. Street noise is a consideration, but there is a small pool and restaurant and the town beach is a few steps away. On Playa Zicatela, **Hotel Arco Iris** ((958) 20432 FAX (958) 20432, at Calle del Morrow s/n (at Playa Zicatela), sprawls in three buildings amid lawns and gardens. The third-story restaurant and bar is a perfect spot to watch the sun go down.

WHERE TO EAT

There are an astonishing number of restaurants in Puerto Escondido, with seafood as the main selection, followed closely by pizza and pasta prepared by Italian emigres.

Moderate

Flor de Maria ((958) 20536, in the hotel mentioned above, is an amiable gathering spot where expatriates and tourists feast on Italian and American dishes. The daily specials are posted on a board outside the hotel — don't miss the spinach-filled pasta or the pork roast. The deserts are irresistible. The **Restaurant Santa Fe** ((958) 20170 or 20266, in the hotel mentioned above, is my favorite place in town for a breakfast of *huevos rancheros* (fried eggs, Mexican style) fresh orange juice and steaming *café de olla*. Sunset cocktails are popular here, as the restaurant overlooks the beach.

Inexpensive

Seafood reigns supreme at **La Posada del Tiburón** ((958) 20789, at Avenida Gasga s/n on Playa Principal. The stuffed fillet of fresh fish brims with crab, octopus and shrimp, and the seafood cocktails are generous enough to be your main course. Salads, pasta and pizza are the draws at **La Galería** (no phone), Avenida Gasga s/n between Avenida Soledad and Marina Nacional. The ambiance is subdued, with the owner's paintings hanging on the walls and soft jazz playing in the background. No visit is complete without a few meals at

Carmen's Patisserie, Entrada Playa Marinero between Carretera Costera and Playa Marinero. Just follow your nose toward the aroma of fresh baking bread and pastries to the simple bakery and restaurant with a few tables beside shelves of used paperbacks and magazines. Carmen's granola sprinkled over a bowl of fresh fruit and yogurt is great any time of day, as are the bulky sandwiches on whole wheat bread. There's a second location across from Playa Zicatela.

HOW TO GET THERE

Puerto Escondido's national airport receives daily flights from Oaxaca city and Mexico City. International airlines serve the Huatulco airport, 112 km (70 miles) south. Highway 175 from Oaxaca city to Puerto Angel is paved all the way; Highway 200 from Acapulco to Puerto Escondido continues south to Puerto Angel and Huatulco.

PUERTO ANGEL

About 83 km (51 miles) south of Puerto Escondido, Puerto Angel is one of the last little tropical paradises of Mexico. It is the home of a large Navy base but has no major resort development. Situated on a small well-protected bay, Puerto Angel has long beaches of fine sand that are generally good for swimming and body surfing. The most popular beach is **Playa Panteón**, a 15-minute walk from the base. The best beaches are at **Zipolote**, once beloved for its isolated beachside campgrounds where hippie holdovers spent weeks and months camping on the sand, sleeping in hammocks and sunbathing in the nude (illegal in Mexico). Zipolote, about seven kilometers (four miles) from town, remains popular with such travelers, but now is lined with bungalow hotels and a few campgrounds. The **Museum of the Sea Turtle** in **Mazunte** displays indoor aquariums sheltering the several species of sea turtles that migrate to these beaches to lay their eggs in the summer months. Outdoor tanks hold baby turtles, a joy to watch.

WHERE TO STAY AND EAT

La Posada Caóon de Vata ((958) 43048, Calle Cañon de Vata, with 10 rooms and six bungalows, is the most popular hotel in town with rooms hidden in a jungle of trees and vines. Hurricanes whipped this coast in 1997 and much of the foliage was destroyed, but the hotel is still a charming hideaway. **La Buena Vista** (/FAX (958) 43104, just south of the naval base atop a steep hill, is a simple spot with spectacular views. Guests must climb a precipitous stairway to reach the hotel. Both establishments have good restaurants.

Zipolote has several small establishments which you should inspect before booking. Many do not have hot water or screens to keep out the sand flies and mosquitoes.

HUATULCO

In 700 BC this area had a Zapotec settlement, during the colonial era it sheltered Spanish galleons and attracted pirates and after independence it became a lethargic but pleasant little fishing village. Now, FONATUR, the government's tourism development agency, calls Huatulco "paradise," in reference to its series of nine secluded and spectacular bays with 33 beaches covering a 36-km (22-mile) stretch of Oaxaca's Pacific Coast. You be the judge. As the Eagles once lamented, "Call somewhere paradise, kiss it good-bye."

Huatulco has struggled since 1974 to become a major resort, but faces some big drawbacks. Though there are many grand hotels and a golf course, there is little to do in this remote area other than snorkel, swim and sunbathe. Of course, if you're interested in relaxation, this may well be the perfect spot.

WHAT TO SEE AND DO

Huatulco has three major areas under development. **Bahía Tangolunda** is the site of most major hotels and the golf course. There are few restaurants outside the hotels and guests here tend to stay put, enjoying the beach and water activities. The main marina where tour boats depart for the undeveloped bays is at **Bahía Santa Cruz**, which has grown into a small town with moderately-priced hotels and restaurants. **Crucecita** is the main town, with shops, a small market, a main plaza and several good restaurants. Unfortunately, it's not possible to walk between these three areas, but public buses do run the route between 6 AM and 7 PM. Most guests make at least one trip to the towns away from their hotels.

The main side trip is a cruise of the undeveloped bays, with stops for snorkeling, swimming and lunch at a *palapa* restaurant on the sand.

East of Huatulco, Oaxaca becomes rural again and the coastline offers only intermittent stretches of sandy beach with little access. The towns of **Tehuantepec** and **Juchitán** are known for their communities run by women.

WHERE TO STAY

The majority of the hotels are in Tangolunda and many offer meal plans which encourage guests to remain within the resort compound. Smaller, less expensive places are located in Santa Cruz and Crucecita. If you like nightlife and a bit of action, Crucecita is your best bet.

The Land Bridge   215

Very Expensive

Architecturally stunning, the **Quinta Real (** (958) 10428 TOLL-FREE (800) 445-4565 FAX (958) 10429, Boulevard Benito Juárez, Tangolunda, with 27 suites, sits on a hill overlooking the bay. White-domed buildings house luxurious suites, some with private swimming pools, and there is a beach club on the bay. One of the first properties in Huatulco was the **Club Mediterranée Huatulco (** (958) 10033 TOLL-FREE (800) 258-2633 at Boulevard Benito Juárez, Tangolunda. Advance booking is mandatory. With 500 rooms, it sprawls over a 20-hectare (50-acre) spread at the edge of the bay and offers all the water sports imaginable, along with gourmet meals and a Teen Club.

Expensive

The **Sheraton Huatulco (** (958) 10055 TOLL-FREE (800) 325-3535 FAX (958) 10113, Boulevard Benito Juárez at the entrance to Tangolunda, has 348 rooms and is a full-service hotel offering water sports, a large pool area, several restaurants and shops. Meal plans are offered, and special packages can bring this hotel into the moderate price range.

Inexpensive

Hotel Posada Flamboyant ((958) 70113 FAX (958) 70121, Calle Gardenia at Calle Tamarindo, Cruce-cita, with 67 rooms, is one of the best choices by the plaza since it has a swimming pool; some rooms have kitchenettes. Less expensive by half is the **Hotel Las Palmas (** (958) 70060 FAX (958) 70057, Avenida Guamuchil No. 206 between Calles Carrizal and Bugambilias in Crucecita. The 10 rooms have ceilings fans and air-con-ditioning; 15 more rooms were be-ing added at the time of writing.

WHERE TO EAT

The all-inclusive plans at many of the hotels make it hard for independent restau-rants to survive. Those that do also cater to locals and offer good quality at reasonable prices.

Expensive

I recommend at least one sunset dinner at **Las Cupulas Restaurant (** (958) 10428, in the Hotel Quinta Real, Tangolunda. This elegant dining room (one of the few air-conditioned restaurants around) with chandeliers, crisp linens, and tables dressed with handcrafted dishes and glassware, overlooks the bay, which glows with pink light as the sun drops into the sea. The menu here is out-standing, offering fresh fish tartare, puff pastry with cheese and *nopal* cactus, excellent Oaxacan *mole* over chicken stuffed with fruit, and other treats you won't find anywhere else.

Moderate

One of the few restaurants outside the Tangolunda hotels is **Don Porfírio (** (958) 10001 at Boulevard Benito Juárez. Steak and lobster are the main draws; try the lobster flambéed with mezcal. The owners have a second dining room next door called **Noches Oaxaqueñas**, which is designed to look like a hacienda. The restaurant presents a folk-loric dance show on weekend nights. Oaxaca's regional dances and costumes are so famous that there is a special fiesta called the **Guelaguetza**,

celebrated outside Oaxaca city for two weeks each August. The show held at this restaurant is well worth seeing. Guests pay an admission fee to see the show and can order drinks, *botanes* (appetizers) and full meals from Don Porfírio's menu.

Inexpensive

Authentic regional Mexican cuisine is served in a colorful dining room at **El Sabor de Oaxaca** ((958) 70060, Avenida Guamuchil No. 106 in Crucecita. The Oaxacan sampler plate includes chunks of Oaxacan cheese, chorizo, *tamales*, seasoned pork and beef, and guacamole. Adventurous diners start with a dish of spicy *chapulines*, Oaxaca's legendary fried grasshoppers. Named after a famous Oaxacan medicine woman, **Restaurante Maria Sabina** ((958) 71039, Calle Flamboyant in Crucecita, is a casual sidewalk café with homestyle Mexican cooking.

Several seafood restaurants line the marina in Santa Cruz. The most famous of these is **Restaurant Avalos Doña Celia** ((958) 70128, at Bahía Santa Cruz. Try the shrimp or octopus sautéed with chilis and onions. Also by the marina is **Tipsy's** ((958) 70127, located at Paseo Mitla (behind the Port Captain's office). This is a beach club and restaurant

on the sand. Appetizers, *fajitas*, seafood salads and spicy crab are served on the beach, and guests can rent water sports equipment, join in volleyball games or swim in the clear water.

HOW TO GET THERE

A few national and international airlines serve Huatulco's international airport, though most involve a stopover or change of planes in Mexico City. The regional carriers Aerocaribe and Aeromorelos fly between Oaxaca and Huatulco.

CHIAPAS

East of Oaxaca is one of Mexico's most fascinating states: rich in culture, yet economically impoverished. Like the rest of the country, Chiapas has been much degraded in recent years by slash-and-burn agriculture and logging of the rainforest. Still, it remains a place of astounding beauty, with its steep green hills descending to the blue and white Pacific, its lowland rainforest and high country conifers, crashing rivers, fabulous Mayan ruins and towering plateaus — truly a land of myth and magic.

Turkeys ride to market in Chiapas.

Although the ruins of Palenque are the major attraction in the area, many travelers return time and again to the city of San Cristóbal de las Casas and the surrounding villages. Continuing conflict between the Zapatista rebels (officially known a the Ejercito Zapatista de Liberacion Nacional, the EZLN, or the Zapatista Army for National Liberation) and government forces has created a disconcerting military presence throughout the state, which affects Chiapanecos greatly but the average tourist very little. Be sure to carry your valid visa and current identification at all times.

The inhabitants of Chiapas are primarily of Mayan descent. The people maintain many of their traditions and the state has an interesting history. In January 1528, aided by a small troop of Spaniards and a large detachment of Tlaxcaltecs, Captain Diego de Mazariegos began the conquest of this area. After a series of battles, the fiercely independent tribes of Chiapas, with no arms or supplies, realized that they could no longer hold off the enemy, and 3,000 men, women and children threw themselves off the Peon de Tepetchia in the Sumidero Canyon, preferring death to slavery.

Once in control, the Spanish did everything possible to break the spirit of the *chiapanecos*. When Bishop Bartolomé de las Casas arrived in San Cristóbal, he was horrified by the cruelty shown the Indians and sent off a report to Spain. Twenty years later the king issued "The Ordinances Governing the Treatment of the Indians in the New World," which recognized the Indians as human beings, but in reality did little to change their plight.

Mexico's southernmost state, Chiapas has a total population of 3,200,000. Its low-lying coastal areas are hot and humid, while highland nights can get downright frigid. The state is an important agricultural area, with exportation of coffee, bananas and mangoes. It also produces 55 percent of the nation's hydroelectric power, generated by a total of four dams, and is third in petroleum production.

The Chiapas Coast has virtually no touristic development and little access to the water. Route 200, which descends the Pacific Coast beginning in the state of Nayarit, sees only a small number of tourists south of Huatulco until it terminates at Tapachula at the Mexico-Guatemala border. The area was destabilized by Guatemalan economic and political refugees and United States-built military staging camps during the decades-long Guatemalan civil war, and has never been exploited for tourism. Near Tapachula is one of the oldest pre-Columbian sites in Mexico, Izapa (in English, the "ditch in the plain") where more than 100 temple platforms dating from approximately 1000 BC have been found.

TUXTLA GUTIÉRREZ

The capital of Chiapas, **Tuxtla Gutiérrez**, is a modern commercial center of over 500,000 people. The town itself has little of touristic importance except the Miguel Alvarez del Torro Zoo and the Regional Museum of Chiapas. However, it does have the **State Office of Tourism** ((961) 34499 or ((961) 39396, Edificio Plaza de las Instituciones, Ground Floor, Boulevard Dr. Belisario Domínguez No. 950, which is open daily from 9 AM to 8 PM. It supplies brochures (some in Spanish only) and maps detailing destinations throughout the state.

Just west of the State Office of Tourism is the state-run **Casa de las Artesanías** (House of Handicrafts) ((961) 22275, Boulevard Dr. Belisario Domínguez Km 1083 (open Monday to Saturday from 9 AM to 9 PM), which sells crafts from the area and houses an interesting ethnological museum.

The **Museo Regional de Chiapas** (Regional Museum of Chiapas) ((961) 34479 or ((961) 20459 is at Calzada de los Hombres Ilustres s/n, Parque Madero (small admission fee; open Tuesday through Sunday from 9 AM to 4 PM). In **Parque Madero** is a modern structure designed by Pedro Ramírez Vásquez; it contains a history museum (handsomely redone in January 1997) and a small ethnological/anthropology museum as well as a cultural museum whose displays change several times a year.

The **Miguel Alvarez del Torro Zoo** (also known as the Tuxtla Zoomat) is southeast of town off Libramiento Sur (free admission; open Tuesday through Sunday from 8:30 AM to 5 PM). It is a remarkable ecological park. Only local fauna are exhibited in this tropical oasis filled with cedars, figs, mangoes and mahoganies, whose branches are weighted down by huge bromeliads and colorful orchids. A meandering path leads through the park, which houses more than 700 animals of some 175 species, including kinkajous, basilisk lizards, jaguars and howler monkeys. Many of the animal inhabitants are "volunteers," free-roaming creatures who were attracted to the place and decided to stay, often because of deforestation in surrounding areas.

Don't miss the twilight outdoor concerts at the new **Parque de las Marimbas**, Avenida Central and Ocho Poniente, Thursday through Sunday evenings at 7 PM. Old couples, young lovers, and mothers and daughters dance to a program of music that ranges from traditional to modern.

WHERE TO STAY

Tuxtla has several modern hotels. The luxurious and well-run Camino Real tops the list. Most hotels cater to business travelers, although tourists on their way to Sumidero Canyon or San Cristóbal de las Casas often overnight here. Several inexpensive hotels are clustered around the bus station; always check the room and gauge its noise and safety factors before settling in. It's always hard to guess when the city will be full, since much of the business revolves around sales and commerce, so try to at least make reservations by phone once you arrive in Mexico.

Expensive

The **Camino Real** ((961) 77777 FAX (961) 77799 E-MAIL tgz@caminoreal.com, Boulevard Dr. Belisario Domínguez No. 1195, was built from the ground up (and not converted from a historical building as others throughout Mexico have been) and is designed for comfort. Thick walls make all 210 rooms and suites quiet; purified water flows from the tap and all of the usual creature comforts expected at a five-star hotel are on hand. Terracotta and teal accents warm the comfortably furnished rooms; facilities include a business center, pool, gymnasium with sauna and steam, and tennis courts. The hotel's classy **Montebello** restaurant is especially recommended for the prime rib and the delicious stuffed *poblano* peppers with black corn fungus sauce (although it sounds dreadful, this black fungus is a delicacy). In **Azulejos Café** endless and scrumptious breakfast and lunch buffets are served in a bright, airy environment and different ethnic dinners are featured on each day of the week.

Moderate

The extensive grounds, large pool and buffet breakfast at the **Hotel Flamboyant** ((961) 50888 or 50999 FAX (961) 50087, Boulevard Dr. Belisario Domínguez Km 1081, attract tour groups and upper-class Mexican families. All of the 118 rooms — which are comfortable if a bit plain — are air-conditioned and have satellite television. It is located at the far west side of town, which is a bit of a drawback.

Inexpensive

The recent face lift given the 50-year-old **Hotel Bonampak** ((961) 32050 or 32101 FAX (961) 27737, Boulevard Dr. Belisario Domínguez No. 180, with 110 rooms, has certainly improved its appearance. Rooms on the first few floors have comfortable new mattresses and the walls gleam with new paint. The staff is professional and courteous, and the restaurant is popular with locals for its excellent regional cooking. There is a small pool on the back patio. Smack in the middle of downtown Tuxtla is the comfortable, clean, no-nonsense **Hotel Maria Eugenia** ((961) 33767 or 33769, Avenida Central Oriente No. 507. There are 75 rooms, all with pastel spreads and accents, color cable television, carpeting and air-conditioning. There is a pool on a pretty outdoor patio surrounded by lounge furniture; inside, the bar and the two restaurants blast overheated visitors with super cool air-conditioning. The hotel also has a travel agency and parking lot.

WHERE TO EAT

Tuxtla's dining scene is not particularly exciting; for an excellent meal, try the Hotel Camino Real (see above). Below are a few suggestions for good dining outside the major hotels.

Caudillo's Taco Restaurant (no phone) at Boulevard Dr. Belisario Domínguez No. 1982, is an informal, moderately-priced spot across from the Hotel Flamboyant, on the west side of town.

The specialty here is tacos, which you order by the piece. Although the menu is limited to tacos, *quesadillas* and *frijoles charros* (beans with sausage and pork bits), there are lots of drinks to choose from, including *horchata* (a fresh rice drink), beer, wine, sodas and coffee.

The following are good choices for inexpensive meals: **Restaurant Fronterizo** ((916) 22347, Avenida Central Poniente No. 1218, is recommended for its local cuisine. Meat dishes are accompanied by salad, refried beans and fried plantains or potatoes. Although this restaurant is open all day (daily except Sunday), it is most popular for breakfast and *comida* (late lunch). A longtime favorite with both locals and visitors is **Las Pichanchas** ((961) 25351, Avenida Central Oriente No. 837, which serves local cuisine to the tune of live marimba music and, at night, folkloric dances.

AROUND TUXTLA GUTIÉRREZ

SUMIDERO CANYON

Although it lacks the magnificence of the Grand Canyon, in Arizona, or the Copper Canyon, in

ABOVE: This region of Mexico is noted for its colorful handwoven cloth.

northern Mexico, Sumidero Canyon 18 km (11.2 miles) north of Tuxtla Gutiérrez is an impressive geological site. It is 1,300 m (4,265 ft) deep and 15 km (just over nine miles) long, and was formed 12 million years ago by the churning waters of the Río Grijalva. Its near-vertical sides and valley floor are covered with tropical vegetation which provide hiding places for raccoon and iguanas; butterflies and waterfowl are more easily spotted. There are lookout points at Ceiba, La Coyota and El Tepehuaje. Another excellent way to see the canyon is by boat. Two-hour boat trips cost approximately $7 and leave from the dock at Chiapa de Corzo, 17 km (11.5 miles) east of Tuxtla Gutiérrez, when there are sufficient passengers.

The tour continues to the massive hydroelectric dam at Chicoasen, which serves as a reminder that the river is no longer wild, and leads one to wonder what beautiful countryside must once have existed here.

CHIAPA DE CORZO

Located on the banks of the Grijalva River, **Chiapa de Corzo** is one of the oldest known pre-Columbian sites in Mexico (dating from 1400 BC), though few ancient structures remain. On the outskirts of town is a single-story **pyramid** that has been restored; the artifacts found here can be seen in the Museum in Tuxtla Gutiérrez.

Graham Greene disparaged Chiapa during his 1930s journey here because of the dust. The town's first settlers didn't stay long either, quickly decamping for San Cristóbal de las Casas because

of the many mosquitoes. Both may have judged this quiet town of 25,000 too harshly. Its Zócalo has the dubious distinction of being the only one in Mexico to have a central fountain (*la pila*) in the shape of the Spanish crown. The **Museo de la Laca** (open Tuesday through Saturday from 9 AM to 1 PM and from 4 PM to 6 PM, Sunday from 9 AM to 1 PM), located on the central plaza, has displays of lacquerware from throughout Mexico and from China. Finally, the sixteenth and seventeenth-century **Iglesia de Santo Domingo** (Church of Santo Domingo) has a bell made of silver, gold and copper that weighs 5,168 kg (2,350 lbs).

SAN CRISTÓBAL DE LAS CASAS

When Graham Greene came to San Cristóbal de las Casas in the 1930s, it was a trek of several days on horseback from Villahermosa, and there was only a dirt track, impassable in the rains, to Tuxtla or to the south. Today the roads are good and bus transportation quite convenient. This, the oldest Spanish settlement in Chiapas, was "discovered" by Americans and Europeans about 20 years ago and is now a well-worn stop along the so-called gringo trail. It is only 83 km (51.5 miles) east of Tuxtla Gutiérrez, but at an elevation more than six times higher (2,120 m or 6955 ft), with average daytime temperatures ranging from 13°C (55°F) in the winter to 16°C (61°F) in the summer.

The town had 14,000 inhabitants when Greene arrived and now has about 150,000. But despite its population growth, San Cristóbal still seems like a small town. The majority of the old town's houses still retain their red-tiled roofs, grilled windows and brightly painted stucco-over-adobe walls, which — along with narrow streets and arcades — give it a distinctly Spanish flavor. In addition, though founded as a Spanish town more than 450 years ago, San Cristóbal retains its Indian identity, and the religious ceremonies clearly demonstrate a blending of Catholicism and pre-Columbian religions. The uprising by the Zapatistas, the EZLN, on New Year's Day 1994 initiated a land reform movement that, after initial military battles, became a diplomatic campaign based largely on international awareness and support. Four years later, after the Mexican government reneged on promises made at the bargaining table, Zapatistas and government factions continue to spar. A massacre of villagers loyal to the Zapatistas in December 1997 has once again called the world's attention to the struggle.

GENERAL INFORMATION

The staff at the **State Tourist Information Office** ((967) 86570, Miguel Hidalgo No. 2, half block from the Zócalo (open Monday through Friday from 9 AM to 9 PM, Saturday from 9 AM to 8 PM, and Sunday from 9 AM to 2 PM), are helpful, speak English, and have an ample supply of information on San Cristóbal and surrounding areas.

WHAT TO SEE AND DO

The Mercado at Avenida General Utrilla at Calle Nicaragua is open daily and is one of the most famous of San Cristóbal's sites. It is most colorful on Saturday when the largest numbers of Chamula, Zinacantecan and Huastec Indians arrive from the surrounding villages to sell, among other things, medicinal herbs, live animals and flowers.

The Zinacantecan Indians are distinguished by their beautifully embroidered homespun wool *huipiles*, or loose-fitting blouses. The men's flat straw hats are decorated with ribbons whose colors indicate their village. If the ribbons are free flowing, the wearer is single; if they are tied, he is married. The dress of the Chamula is less elaborate. The women wear distinctive blue shawls over black wool skirts and white blouses. The men cover their *huipiles* with woolen tunics and the colors of their tunic sleeves identify their home town. The Huastecs dress the most elaborately. The women's *huipiles* are embroidered lengthwise with fine red lines over which bright diamond-shaped patterns are superimposed. The men's *huipiles* are embroidered only on the back shoulders, but also quite elaborately. They support knapsacks of their own design in which they carry their wares, in a manner similar to the Sherpas of Nepal.

As one would expect, the town's center is its **Zócalo**, faced on the north side by the **Catedral** (open daily from 10 AM to 1 PM and from 4 PM to 8 PM). On the west side is the **Palacio Municipal**, and on the other sides, shopping arcades and cafés. However, the most interesting building in town is the **Templo de Santa Domingo** (open Tuesday through Sunday from 9 AM to 2 PM), six blocks north of the cathedral. Its pink stone façade is similar to that of the church in Antigua, Guatemala, and its pulpit was sculpted from a single solid piece of oak. Adjacent to the church, in its former convent, is an Indian crafts cooperative and a regional history museum. On the eastern edge of town in a former seminary is the **Na Bolom Museum** (House of the Jaguar Museum) ((967) 81418 E-MAIL nabolom@sclc.ecosur.mx, Avenida Vincent Guerrero No. 33, a combination museum, library and hotel. The center was founded by Frans Blom, a Danish explorer and archaeologist, and Gertrude Blom, a Swiss socialist, who befriended the Lacandón Indians and opened their home to them. Mrs. Blom died in 1993; employees and volunteers continue the Bloms' mission for the cultural and ecological conservation of Chiapas. The residence-turned-museum features ethnological and archaeological artifacts from the area; the library

contains 5,000 volumes on Chiapas and the Mayan culture. The center has superb visiting scientist and artist-in-residence programs, and is a perfect venue for workshops, retreats, or other group events, as a staff member will coordinate excursions tailored for your group. The museum and library have variable hours and an English-language tour of the house ($2) is usually conducted at 4:30 PM, Tuesday through Sunday.

WHERE TO STAY

Very Expensive
A stay at the fabulous home of Percival and Nancy Wood, called **El Jacarandal** (Jacaranda Grove)

((967) 81065, Comitán No. 7, is unique, elegant and expensive. For $160 per person, double occupancy, you will get as many excursions and horseback rides as your hosts can arrange, as well as three eclectic, excellent meals a day. The magnificent libraries, gardens and sitting rooms of this restored nineteenth-century mansion are available to guests, and each of the four guestrooms has a bathtub.

Moderate
Resembling a tasteful art gallery more than a reasonably-priced hotel, the **Hotel Casa Mexicana** ((967) 80698, 80683 or 81348 FAX (967) 82627, Calle 28 de Agosto No. 1, with 50 rooms is clean,

OPPOSITE: Colonial San Cristóbal de las Casas. ABOVE: Eighteenth-century San Juan Chamula has the simplicity of an Andalusian church.

open and bright, with polished tile floors, comfortable beds and a welcome attention to detail. There is an equally attractive restaurant and a bar, with room service available. Massage, babysitting and free parking are other perks.

The 200-year old hotel **Posada Diego de Mazariegos** ((967) 81825 FAX (967) 80827, Calle Ma. Adelina Flores No. 2, is a San Cristóbal institution, although the old wing far outshines the new. Rooms in the original wing have fireplaces and open onto the glass-domed central patio where one can doze in comfortable chairs around the fountain. In both sections the interior decoration leaves a bit to be desired, but all 77 rooms have telephones and televisions and the hotel is agreeably close to the Zócalo and the action. The hotel has a bar, coffeeshop and restaurant as well as travel agency and car rental office. Also worth mentioning is the pretty **Hotel Flamboyant** ((967) 80045 or 80412 FAX (967) 80514, Español at Calle 1 de Marzo No. 15.

Without a doubt one's appreciation for the area can be enhanced by a stay at **Na Bolom** (/FAX (967) 81418 E-MAIL nabolom@sclc.ecosur.mx, Avenida Vincent Guerrero No. 33 (for more information see WHAT TO SEE AND DO, above), where staff and visitors eat together, family style. Unfortunately Na Bolom is small (14 rooms) and often full. It is recommended that one make reservations well in advance of arrival. Long term visitors to San Cristóbal gravitate to the **Posada Los Morales** ((967) 81472, Avenida Ignacio Allende No. 17, whose 13 small bungalows are scattered up a hillside: the more booked they are, the farther you'll have to climb. Approximately $16 a day gets you a dank two-room cottage with a fireplace and small kitchen with a very limited assortment of cooking implements. There is a bar and small restaurant open during most of the year.

Several small hotels are clustered within a few blocks of the main plaza; many are housed in colonial buildings and may be a bit drafty in winter. Promising choices are the **Hotel Don Quijote** (/FAX (967) 80346, Calle Colón No. 7, with 22 rooms; the **Hotel Fray Bartolomé de las Casas** ((967) 80932 FAX (967) 83510, Niños Héroes No. 2, with 26 rooms; and the **Hotel Real del Valle** ((967) 80680 FAX (967) 83955, Real de Guadalupe No. 14, with 36 rooms.

WHERE TO EAT

San Cristóbal's restaurants have improved noticeably in the past five years, although they still have a way to go. Nonetheless, there are lots of restaurants to choose from and you will no doubt find a few favorites. Restaurants are generally casual, unpretentious and unheated. Most budget and inexpensive restaurants do not accept credit cards; be sure to inquire before ordering.

Moderate

Delicious French and Italian specialties are served at the intimate **Restaurante el Teatro** ((967) 83149, Avenida 1 de Marzo No. 8; most dishes are served à la carte. The watercress salad, crêpes and pastas deserve consideration. In the evening, candles flicker on the white-clothed tables, adding to the ambiance. **Restaurant Bar Margarita** ((967) 80957, Calle Real de Guadalupe No. 34, is open daily and very popular with the tourist crowd after 9 PM, when the band, usually salsa, starts up. Go earlier for dinner to ensure a table on weekend or holiday evenings. **Emiliano's Mustache** ((967) 87246, Avenida Crescencio Rosas, near the post office, is recommended for its delicious tacos (served afternoon, although the restaurant opens at 8:30 AM) and lively ambiance. Also popular are the *queso fundido con rayas* (cheese fondue with slivers of jalapeno peppers) and *alambre* (Michoacán-style meat, grilled with onions, peppers

and melted cheese); there are, in addition, several vegetarian dishes, such as spinach quiche, veggie stir fry and *chili rellenos*. The band plays Latin music Thursday through Saturday after 10 PM. An expatriate hangout is the restaurant at the **Hotel Paraiso** ((967) 80085, Avenida 5 de Febrero No. 19; they go for the meat, as the Swiss owner's specialty is the thick steaks — which are otherwise difficult to find in Mexico.

Inexpensive

Both locals and budget travelers slide into the red Naugahyde booths at **El Tuluc** ((967) 82090, Avenida Insurgentes No. 5. The name means "turkey" in the Tzizoc language and it attracts visitors for the inexpensive fixed price lunch, which includes an aperitif, soup, rice, choice of three main dishes, dessert and coffee or tea, for less than $3. The sound track of elevator-music instrumentals (including the perennial favorite,

Raindrops Keep Falling on My Head) and an assortment of carved wooden toys and lamps for sale creates a slightly hokey atmosphere. Still, portions are huge, there is a full bar and it's open from 6:30 AM until 10 PM daily. The large à la carte menu focuses on national and international dishes — mainly sandwiches, soups and spaghetti dishes as well as meat and chicken. Locals frequent **El Payaso** (no phone), Calle Madero No. 35, for the large à la carte menu, vegetarian dishes and fixed price lunch. Don't come by on Wednesday; it's closed. **Café del Centro**, Calle Real de Guadalupe No. 15-B, is a budget restaurant with good deals at breakfast and the set price *comida*; other than that there's an abbreviated menu offering yogurt, tortas and *quesadillas*.

Palenque is at once the most architecturally refined and the most mysterious of Mexico's Mayan temple ruins.

The Land Bridge

HOW TO GET THERE

Most travelers get to San Cristóbal de las Casas by bus from Tuxtla Gutiérrez or Palenque. Both trips involve dizzying travel up curving mountainous roads. Buses arrive at the main bus station south of town. San Cristóbal does have a small airport, and there is occasional air service from Palenque.

AROUND SAN CRISTÓBAL DE LAS CASAS

SAN JUAN CHAMULA

When tourists came to San Cristóbal they also discovered San Juan Chamula, 11 km (seven miles) to the west, set in forested hills, with its lovely **church**. It has changed little since the eighteenth century and its religious festivals are a bewitching blend of ancient traditions and Catholic rituals. Realizing that these were an attraction, the city has attempted to control the influx of visitors who threaten to overrun the village. To attend Sunday mass conducted in Tzotzil, the native language, or visit the church, one must purchase a pass for a token fee at the local **Tourist Office** in the Palacio Municipal and promise to act respectfully. Photography and videotaping are not permitted in the church and the law is strictly enforced, with jail time and/or fines for scofflaws. The area's inhabitants likewise do not appreciate being photographed and will most often refuse requests.

LAGUNAS DE MONTEBELLO

Southeast of San Cristóbal de las Casas, on the Guatemala border, is the 7,000-hectare (2,900-acre) **Parque Nacional de las Lagunas de Montebello** (Montebello Lakes National Park) which has 63 lakes and lagoons, some quite spectacular and ranging in color from turquoise to emerald green to deep violet. The park has a magnificent variety of evergreen and other trees, with orchids in the branches and numerous birds. One highlight of the park is the **Arco de San Rafael**, a natural bridge of limestone under which the Río Comitán flows, dropping into the earth and disappearing. Unfortunately the area was somewhat destabilized during the Guatemala civil war and rumor has it that it isn't safe for camping. The closest accommodation is in Comitán at the **Museo Parador Santa María** ((963) 23346 or 25116, located 21.5 km (13.5 miles) from Chincultik en route to Lagunas de Montebello. The area can also be seen in a day trip from San Cristóbal.

Beyond the Lagunas de Montebello, a CIA-funded road follows the Guatemalan border east, turning northwest again to parallel the border and

the Río Usumacinta, past Bonampak toward Palenque. Once the most magnificent and hidden corner of Mexico, this area is being destroyed by slash-and-burn agriculture and illegal logging; and this once heavenly homeland of the Lacandón Indians, of the jaguar, quetzal and other rare wildlife, is disappearing rapidly. If you want to drive the Guatemalan border road, check with people at Las Lagunas or at Bonampak (depending which way you're traveling), to make sure the road is open and likely to be safe.

PALENQUE

Palenque is the most mysterious of Mexico's Maya sites, set in moist lowland jungle where moss creeps up the rubble of gray ruins. From afar, the temples resemble those of Tikal, in Guatemala, or even some in Nepal. The structures of Palenque are not as large or abundant as those at Chichén Itza or Uxmal, but the setting is far more beautiful. The town of Palenque, about eight kilometers (five miles) from the ruins, has long been a center for budget travelers, who escape into this dense jungle setting for days on end.

What to See and Do

What makes Palenque's ruins (admission fee except on Sunday; open daily from 8 AM to 5 PM) different are its roofs and tall, elegant open façades and roof combs that crest the façades. Archaeologists date the most important structures from the sixth through the ninth century, which coincides with the reign of Lord Pacal, whose long and impressive reign ended at the close of the seventh century. Earlier structures of inferior architectural style have been found west of the center. The **Temple of the Inscriptions**, on the right as one enters the complex, is one of the most magnificent temples containing undisturbed tombs in Mexico. The tomb, open daily from 9:30 AM to 4 PM, was the burial site of Lord Pacal; 80 steep steps down inside the base, with stalactites on the ceiling and walls caused by centuries of water dripping through the stone. In 1949 the 13-ton, elaborately carved, sarcophagus was found and inside was the Lord's skeleton, luxuriously adorned with a mask of jade, shell and obsidian. A reproduction is found in the Museum of Anthropology in Mexico City, but the sarcophagus lid remains here. A "psychoduct" (hollow stone tube) leads up into the temple to facilitate the passage of the soul. The tomb is eerie, damp and cool, but fascinating; particularly when one has time to examine the carvings of the slab and tomb walls in detail.

The trapezoidal **Palacio** dominates the site with a tower unlike any other Mayan architecture, which was probably used as an observatory. The palace has an intricate floor plan with multiple pillared galleries and inner courtyards.

Archaeologists think that it was mainly an administrative building, but the steam baths in the patio adjoining the tower suggest that it may have also been occupied by the ruler and priests. Much of the palace has been attributed to the grandson of Lord Pacal, and the family's history seems to be the theme of the hieroglyphics and stone carvings on the walls and staircases. Of particular interest is the **Oval Tablet**, which commemorates the coronation of Pacal. It is believed that the figure on the left is his mother, who ruled in his stead for three years before his ascendancy at the age of twelve and a half. To the north of the palace are five buildings of various periods and in varying states of disrepair, known as the **Grupo Norte** (North Group). The best preserved is the so-called **Templo del Conde** (Temple of the Count). The museum (open Tuesday through Sunday from 9 AM to 4 PM) to the east of this group has fragments of stucco work, *stelae*, grave artifacts and pottery. To the east of the palace and across the remains of the aqueduct and Río Otolun (just a stream now) are three temples with large roof combs. The **Templo de la Cruz** (Temple of the Cross) has a beautiful façade and the best view is from atop the **Templo del Sol** (Temple of the Sun).

The government built one of the country's better ruin entrances at Palenque in 1994, across the paved road in front of the ruins. My favorite path between the ruins and the museum, shops and restaurant ascends a hill beside the stream directly across from the museum. The official entryway is down the road a few steps, with a level path leading straight to the Temple of the Inscriptions.

The **town of Palenque** improves steadily with time. It can get quite congested when tourism is high and the streets around the bus stations are packed with travelers. Several small shops around the main plaza display high quality regional crafts and restaurants are becoming ever more diverse.

Where to Stay and Eat

I can't imagine visiting Palenque on a day trip from Villahermosa, since much of its mystical mood settles over the environs at first and last light. Plan to spend at least one night and preferably three or four. Properties on the road to the ruins have larger grounds and a tropical setting, and are interspersed with campgrounds. La Cañada, at the intersection between the roads to town and the ruins, is a neighborhood of several small lodges, many quite inexpensive and filled with character.

MODERATE

A tropical setting and three connecting, lagoon-style pools makes **Chan Kah (** (934) 50974, 50762 or 50945 FAX (934) 50820 or 40489, Carretera a las Ruinas Km 3, a tranquil place to get away from it all. The bungalows have wide terraces with comfortable porch furniture, large bathrooms, and large screened and glass windows from which to appreciate the lovely setting. There are televisions here, but only a few of the 70 units have telephones. There is also a bar, restaurant and meeting room.

A river flows through the extensive grounds of the **Calinda Nututún Palenque (** (934) 50100 or 50161 FAX (934) 50620, Carretera a las Ruinas Km 3.5. At a bend in the river a large natural swimming pool forms, a bit dangerous as the current moves swiftly through it. The well-respected restaurant overlooks the river and grounds. Television is available for a small daily fee; camping is permitted near the river.

INEXPENSIVE

The 47 rooms at the **Hotel Maya Tulipanes (** (934) 50201 or 50258 FAX (934) 51004, Calle Cañada No. 6, have both air-conditioning and fans, tile floors, reasonably firm beds and cable television with English-language channels. There is a basketball court where you can work up a sweat, but you're more likely to cannonball into the small pool to cool off. The staff is friendly and you can dine inside or outside by the pool. **Days Inn Tulija Palenque (** (934) 50166 or 50165 FAX (934) 50163, located at Carretera a las Ruinas Km 27.5, is clean and comfortable, with a friendly staff, pool and small restaurant. There are 72 rooms.

In addition to the hotel restaurants, there is **La Selva (** (934) 50363, Carretera Ruinas Km 5, which serves Chiapas cuisine and has a Sunday brunch.

How to Get There

Palenque is a four-and-a-half- to five-hour mountainous drive from San Cristóbal de las Casas — a trip that can be uncomfortable for those who suffer from motion sickness. Several bus lines cover the route; the fastest express buses have heavily curtained windows and video screens. Some of the low-end buses have windows you can open (the pine air as you rise into the mountains is a valuable part of the transition). After having met a family who survived a murderous bus crash on a similar road at night, I prefer taking this ride in daylight. Palenque is two hours from Villahermosa, and buses ply this road day and night. The small airport serves tour groups; regional airlines such as Aerocaribe fly between Palenque and Tuxtla Gutiérrez, San Cristóbal and some resort areas in Yucatán, but schedules are erratic.

The town of Palenque is about eight kilometers (five miles) east of the ruins; taxis run during daylight hours, but are less abundant at night.

YAXCHILÁN AND BONAMPAK

In the easternmost part of Chiapas, next to the. Guatemala border, are the Mayan ceremonial centers of **Yaxchilán** and **Bonampak**. Yaxchilán is situated on the banks of the Usumacinta River, along the former trade route between Palenque and Tikal. A trek here includes a short but colorful boat ride for 15 km (9.5 miles) along the river, arriving at this splendid monument to the Lancandón Maya, where one finds numerous archways exquisitely carved with figures of costumed gods, priests and women. There is also a sculpture of a god with his head separated from his body, which has religious significance for the Lancandón who still frequent the site.

Bonampak has the most extensive and best-preserved Mayan frescoes (although these are fading rapidly, despite "treatments" by concerned archaeologists). The richly colored murals represent scenes of rituals practiced before a war. Excellent reproductions of these murals and the temple in which they are found are in the Museum of Anthropology in Mexico City. For the less adventurous, this saves a long trip along a long road from Palenque, although the 13-km (eight-mile) dirt road between the ruins and Highway 198 has been recently graded and packed, making Bonampak more accessible. Flights in small private planes are also available via **Montes Azules** ((961) 32293 in Tuxtla Gutiérrez, and tour operators out of Palenque, Tuxtla and San Cristóbal can book air or land excursions to both ruins. There is no accommodation at these sites, although tour operators can arrange stays in small villages or the few jungle lodges that have recently begun to crop up.

TABASCO

When Graham Greene arrived in the state of Tabasco in the 1930s, there was prohibition (no intoxicating beverages except beer were allowed). The state was then controlled by Tomás Garrido Canabal, a puritanical anti-cleric who is said to have destroyed every church in the state, and unmercifully hunted its priests and nuns. This setting was Greene's inspiration for *The Power and the Glory*. The strong arm in control of the region today is no longer Canabal, but the all-pervasive oil industry. The state is flat, with numerous lakes and swamps and areas of overlogged rainforest. It has two of Mexico's few navigable rivers, Río Usumacinta and Río Grijalva, a number of pre-Columbian archaeological sites and one of Mexico's overlooked cities, Villahermosa.

VILLAHERMOSA

One could skip Villahermosa entirely if it were not for its proximity to Palenque. The majority of the city's visitors are conducting business, though many travelers eventually find their way here. The most interesting attraction for tourists is the **Parque**

La Venta at Paseo Tabasco (small admission fee; open Tuesday through Sunday from 9 AM to 5 PM). Also worth a visit is the **Centro de Investigaciones de las Culturas Olmeca y Maya** or **CICOM** (CICOM Museum of Anthropology), Carlos Pellicer No. 511 (small admission fee; open daily from 9 AM to 7:30 PM). Together these have the best displays of Olmec art in the world.

Parque La Venta is named for the most important Olmec site. The Olmec are considered to have been the precursors of the Maya and other better-known civilizations. Their most accessible impressive achievement are gigantic Olmec carvings of a thick-lipped, rotund face. As explorer-artist Miguel Covarrubias wrote in *Mexico South*, "The art of La Venta is unique. It is by no means primitive, nor is it a local style. It is rather the climax of a noble and sensual art, product of a direct but sophisticated spirit and an accomplished technique, and a sober dignified taste." Unfortunately almost all that remains of this mighty ancient civilization is the little that has been preserved in Villahermosa. In the park are more than 30 Olmec sculptures including altars, *stelae*, animal statues and giant heads, which have been transferred from La Venta archaeological site on an island of the Tonalá River, which has been completely taken over by oil wells. The most spectacular sights in the park are the heads, which weigh more than 20 tons and are up to three meters (10 ft) tall. The CICOM Museum contains the smaller and (relatively speaking) more delicate Olmec art, including bat gods and bird-headed humans as well as artifacts related to their jaguar cult, such as "were-jaguars" (half human, half jaguar), jaguar babies and jaguars swallowing human heads. The museum also has an extensive Mayan display as well as a cross-section of remains from archaeological sites across the country.

Where to Stay

With a population of almost 500,000, there are plenty of hotels in Villahermosa, but they primarily cater to business travelers and are therefore relatively expensive. Recommended are the **Hyatt Villahermosa** ((931) 134444 or 151234 FAX (931) 151234 or 155808, Avenida Juaréz No. 106, with 211 rooms; **Maya Tabasco Best Western** ((931) 144466 or 140360 FAX (931) 121097, Ruíz Cortines No. 907, with 156 rooms; and the **Hotel Miraflores** ((931) 20022 FAX (931) 120486, Reforma No. 304, with 64 rooms.

Agua Azul's famous waterfall is set in the last remnant of Mexico's vanishing rainforest.

The
Yucatán
Peninsula

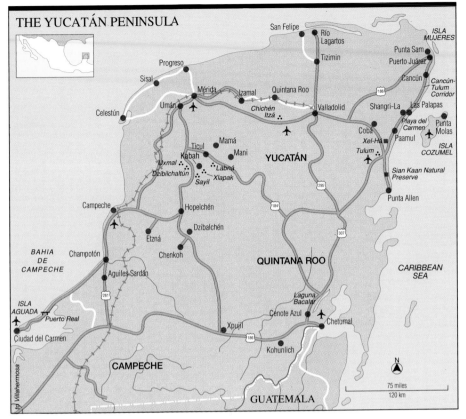

THE YUCATÁN PENINSULA

San Felipe
Río Lagartos
ISLA MUJERES
Punta Sam
Tizimin
Puerto Juárez
Progreso
Cancún
Cancún-Tulum Corridor
Sisal
Mérida
Izamal
Quintana Roo
186
Umán
Chichén Itzá
Valladolid
Shangri-La
Las Palapas
Celestún
Playa del Carmen
Punta Molas
Cobá
Xel-Há
Paamul
ISLA COZUMEL
Ticul
Mamá
Mani
YUCATÁN
Tulum
Kabah
Uxmal
Labná
Sian Kaan Natural Preserve
Dzibilchaltún
Sayil
Xlapak
295
Campeche
Hopelchén
Punta Allen
184
Dzibalchén
Etzná
307
BAHIA DE CAMPECHE
Champotón
Chenkoh
QUINTANA ROO
CARIBBEAN SEA
Aguiles-Sardán
261
Laguna Bacalar
ISLA AGUADA
Puerto Real
Cénote Azul
Chetumal
Xpujil
Ciudad del Carmen
186
Kohunlich
CAMPECHE
N
75 miles
120 km
to Villahermosa
GUATEMALA

THOUGH RELATIVELY REMOTE, the Yucatán Peninsula has become Mexico's most valued tourist destination. Its three states — Yucatán, Quintana Roo and Campeche — contain unparalleled beaches, fascinating ruins and distinct cultures that lure travelers from throughout Europe, the United States and Canada.

Warm, mysterious, sunny, redolent with tropical odors and the echoes of its Mayan past, the Yucatán is a place like no other and like no other part of Mexico. With impenetrable jungles and an impenetrable history lurking just below the surface, it seems nonetheless a very simple place. There are the beaches, among the world's best, pure white coral sand gently rising from the softly rolling surf of the aquamarine sea. Beyond the beaches are the reefs, vivid with fish and flowing vegetation in the aqueous, dreamlike light, a world entirely apart just feet beneath the surface.

And behind the beaches are the palms and coastal mangrove jungles, but stretching all the way to Chiapas and the mountains of Guatemala there is jungle, punctured intermittently by farms and ranches cut out of the brush, and by the Yucatán's few towns and cities.

The Yucatán is also about resorts, the jam-packed hotel zone of Cancún, or the fake Mayan villages along the coast with pseudo Mayan names where the dollar reigns, and the tourists come and go so frequently that no one seems to have a face, let alone a heart. But there is yet another aspect to this peninsula, that of historical cities such as Mérida, Chetumal or Valladolid, towns that are still Mexican, with an economy and lifestyle not yet maimed by the ceaseless coming and going of strangers, or by the endless purchase of meals, trinkets, hotel rooms and quick memories.

And there are the back-country Mayan villages, less impacted by the last 20 years of tourist boom, where life is still lived at a pace in harmony with history and earth. Places, as we've found by living there, that are slow to warm to strangers, but deeply giving when you stay a while.

And the Yucatán is also a region of ruins, concentrated here as nowhere else on earth, of stunning engineering design and of amazing culture. One by one being dispossessed of their cloaking jungle and serving now as attractions to the tourist trade, they have a mythic power and beauty that remains below the surface.

As it has been for more than 30 centuries, the Yucatán Peninsula is first and foremost the home

Women wait for a Yucatán village store to open.

of the Mayas, once the world's most advanced culture, now reduced to laboring in the tinseled tourist meccas of a northern race.

Hidden under the tropical vegetation, which quickly engulfs any abandoned site, are hundreds of pre-Hispanic towns and cities. The largest, such as Chichén Itzá and Uxmal, were first discovered by the Spanish; excavation of these ruins began in the nineteenth century and continues today. Others remained hidden until the last decade, when tourism brought development which reawakened the interest in Mayan history and architecture. Many remain obscured; no one is certain how many, but there are no doubt plenty, as the population of the area in the post-Classic era (AD 900 to 1200) is estimated to have been greater than it is today.

BACKGROUND

When the Spanish arrived in the early sixteenth century, the Maya opposed them with open hostility. The Maya had a highly sophisticated society that revered intellectual achievement, particularly in history, mathematics, astronomy and religion. They were the first human culture to invent and use the mathematical zero; they wrote with an advanced hieroglyphic script and created the most advanced and accurate calendar ever used. Their books, containing the wisdom of centuries, were burned by the priest Diego de Landa in 1562, two decades after the Spanish finally succeeded in founding a permanent settlement at Mérida in 1542. "We found many books," de Landa later wrote, "and as they contained nothing but superstitions and lies of the Devil we burned them all, which grieved the Mayas enormously, and gave them great pain."

There was neither gold nor silver in the Yucatán and thus the area stayed on the fringes of the colonial empire. Only rarely did viceroys pay it any attention. The Yucatán did not participate in the War of Independence or the Mexican-American War, but had its own brutal war over whether or not Yucatán should be part of Mexico. This struggle, called the Caste War, pitted *ladinos*, residents of European stock, against Mayas, and Mayas against Mayas. Finally federal troops were sent to the region in 1852, and Yucatán, Campeche and Quintana Roo became territories of Mexico. More than half of the population had been killed during the five-year war and the region's economic base had been destroyed. Sugar cane, the original cash crop of the area, was replaced by *henequén* or sisal, grown to produce hemp cords and ropes. The Maya were forced to work on the plantations, but had no right to own their own land. A select few settlers of Spanish origin controlled the land, power and lives of the people. When the Reform War came, the Maya welcomed

the resulting land reform laws and freedom from the Catholic religion to which only a small proportion of the population clung. However, in practice little changed for the Maya.

After World War II, man-made fibers reduced the value of sisal, and the economy of the peninsula took another dive until tourism began developing in the 1970s. As with previous booms in the Yucatán, however, tourism has principally benefited outsiders and disrupted traditional lifestyles.

Throughout the turmoil of the last four centuries, many Maya remained aloof, living in their small villages and towns in the impenetrable jungle. Life in some of these small villages changed little until roads, electricity and telephone lines connected them with the outside world. Life was and still is largely communal. In most remote areas, barter remains more common than currency exchange. A slaughtered pig is food for the community, its owner repaid in goods or labor.

Of the peninsula's three states — Yucatán, Campeche and Quintana Roo — Yucatán is the most developed. Large areas of Campeche and Quintana Roo can be crossed only on dirt tracks and foot trails. In the 1970s, the oil boom brought industrial development to Campeche's Gulf Coast and FONATUR, the tourism development agency, began to subject the northern coast of Quintana Roo to tourist development. The Maya were poorly prepared for all this development; as a result, there has been an influx of workers from other areas of Mexico and the larger Yucatán towns have lost their Mayan flavor.

CAMPECHE

There are few tourist destinations in the state of Campeche; one of its few claims to notoriety is as the homeland of Malinche, Cortés' Indian translator, advisor and mistress.

In the south, on the Bahía de Campeche, is Ciudad del Carmen on Isla del Carmen, once the favorite hangout of pirates who raided the prosperous Spanish Gulf ports. The 32-km (20-mile) long island has become one of the most profitable oil regions in the country, and the island's main city, Carmen, is the second largest in the state. The majority of the population of 100,000 residents is involved in the oil business; yet beaches just 16 km (10 miles) from the city are among the best along the Gulf of Mexico. A ferry at Zacatál brings visitors coming from the east (Villahermosa) to the island, and a bridge connects the island to slender Isla Aguada for travelers continuing towards the town of Campeche.

Champotón, midway up Campeche's coast, is thought to have been an important trading center and port in pre-Hispanic times. Today it is primarily a fishing port of about 50,000. There has been some attempt to create a beach resort along this stretch of coast, but the Caribbean is stiff competition. One of the few areas that has succeeded is the moderately priced, **Siho Playa** ((981) 62989, near **Sihochac** some 25 km (15 miles) away. It has 80 rooms and is a restored hacienda with pools, tennis courts and fishing facilities.

CAMPECHE CITY

When Hernández de Córdoba landed in Campeche in 1517, he found the Mayan settlement Ah-kin-pech, meaning, delightfully, "place of the snake and the tick." During colonial times, it was the only port on the Yucatán Peninsula and was constantly harassed by pirates, one of whom

GENERAL INFORMATION

The tourist information office in Campeche changes names and locales with unsettling frequency. The latest incarnation is the **Tourist Office** ((981) 52592 or 66829, on Avenida Ruíz Cortines across from the Palacio de Gobierno. It is open daily (closed during midday). The staff is unfailingly helpful, especially if you can speak Spanish.

WHAT TO SEE AND DO

A *malecón*, a waterfront sidewalk, runs along Avenida Ruíz Cortines on the west side of down-

was supposed to have been so brazen as to steal the doors and windows from private homes. For protection, the Spanish enclosed the city with La Muralla, a massive two-and-a half-kilometer (one-and-a-half-mile) long, two-and-a-half-meter (eight-foot) thick, eight-meter (25-ft) high wall with eight defensive installations. The remaining sections of the formidable walls and redouts give the city a distinctive military atmosphere, as if it were still encamped against invasion. Only a small portion of the travelers reveling in the beaches and ruins of Yucatán and Quintana Roo make it to Campeche City, which enhances its attributes for escapists. Those who linger enjoy some of the finest seafood in the country, a wealth of inexpensive hotels, a pleasant central square and side streets pocketed with parks, museums, handsome mansions and waterfront views.

town, providing a perfect setting for sunset strolls. Two blocks inland at Calle 57 and Calle 8 is the **Plaza de Independencia**, the central plaza for the old part of the city. The ornate **Catedral** faces the plaza, as do several pleasant cafés. East of the plaza on Calle 10, the early twentieth-century **Mansión Carvajal** houses offices for several social service agencies. Wander inside for a sampling of the handsome city-home mansions built by *henequén* plantation owners.

Only a few sections of the massive stone wall surrounding the city are open for touring. **Baluarte de la Soledad** (Fort Soledad) faces the plaza and houses a valuable selection of Maya stone writing tablets and other artifacts in the **Museo de los Estelae**, Calle 8 at Calle 57 (small admission fee;

Only vestiges of the late-seventeenth-century fortifications that surrounded Campeche still remain today.

open Tuesday to Sunday from 10 AM to 4 PM). Built in 1771 as an addition to the walled enclosure, **Fuerte San Miguel**, three kilometers (two miles) south of town (small admission fee; open Tuesday through Saturday from 8 AM to 8 PM and Sunday from 8 AM to 1 PM), houses the impressive **Museo Cultura Maya**, dedicated to the story of Campeche's Maya communities. **Baluarte Santiago** (Fort St. James) frames a well-tended botanical garden on Calle 8 at Calle 49 (free admission; open Tuesday through Sunday from 9 AM to 1 PM), while the views from atop the ramparts at **Fuerte San José** at the north side of the city on Avenida Morazán (small admission fee; open Tuesday through Sunday from 8 AM to 8 PM) are not to be missed.

WHERE TO STAY

Campeche has not been slated for tourism development, but there has been some spillover from the Mérida and Cancún explosion. Hotels are less expensive, service is good, and the beaches are nice for walking and viewing, though not necessarily for swimming.

The most dependable upscale establishment in town is the moderately-sized (and expensive) **Ramada Inn Campeche** ((981) 62233 TOLL-FREE (800) 228-9898 FAX (981) 11618, Avenida Ruíz Cortines No. 51, on the waterfront, with 149 rooms. Handsome tiled floors, patios with fountains and good views of downtown from some rooms, add character to the nineteenth-century mansion housing the inexpensive **Hotel Colonial** ((981) 62222 or 62630, Calle 14 No. 122, with 30 rooms.

In the old town there are several moderate and inexpensive hotels. Quality may vary from season to season, so ask to inspect your room. Campeche also has a **CREA Youth Hostel** ((981) 61802, Avenida Agustín Helger, near the university.

WHERE TO EAT

As a fishing port, Campeche has fine fresh seafood, particularly *camarones* (shrimp), *cangrejo moro* (stone crab) and *cazón*, a small shark used in stews and soups. There are many excellent seafood restaurants, from tiny storefront establishments in residential neighborhoods to several longtime local favorites. Among the best is moderately-priced **La Pigua** (13365, Avenida Miguel Alemán No. 197, with its glassed-in garden and a restful ambiance that tempts diners to linger over seafood cocktails, soups and entrées. **Miramar** (62883, Calle 8 No. 293, offers a good range of local fish preparations in a colonial dining room setting.

HOW TO GET THERE

There are few flights into Campeche city although there is usually one daily from Mexico City. The

bus service from Mérida is excellent, and the station is on Highway 261 (the road to Mérida).

EDZNÁ

Sixty kilometers (37 miles) southeast of Campeche is Edzná (small admission fee; open daily from 8 AM to 5 PM), a Mayan city occupied from 300 BC to AD 900, and covering six square kilometers (two and a half square miles). Edzná was built in a valley whose floor was below sea level, and the Maya developed an intricate hydraulic system that drained the land for urban development and farming and created reservoirs for irrigation. Part of this 23-km (14-mile) **canal**

system is intact. It is also believed that the first predictions of solar eclipses were made at the observatory here.

The site is not on the tourist circuit; in fact there is no public transportation directly to it. If touring without a car, the best way to get there is on an inexpensive tour from Campeche city. Thus travelers can examine its marvelous **Edificio de los Cinco Pisos** (Five-story Building), lesser temples, main plaza, ball court, and numerous *stelae* in relative solitude.

THE INTERIOR

Scattered throughout the interior of Campeche state are numerous Mayan sites in varying states of excavation. Using Campeche city as a base these can be visited on long day trips. At Edzná or Campeche there are often knowledgeable guides who will provide a tour. Equipped with a good map, sturdy vehicle, and determination, the adventurous traveler can reach most locations alone. However, remember that since human visitors are not in abundance, reptilian ones are. Beware of scorpions and snakes. Never put a hand into crevices and always wear shoes, not sandals or bare feet. As elsewhere on the peninsula, mosquito lotion is essential.

South of **Hopelchén**, which has a sixteenth-century fortified church, there are the ruins of **Dzehkabtún**, **El Tabasqueño**, **Dzibalchén**, **Hochob** near **Chenkoh**, and **Dzibilnocac** near **Iturbide**. In the north of the state near **Hecelchakán** are **Kacha**, **Xcalumkín** and many others that are only slightly uncovered.

THE STATE OF YUCATÁN

The state of Yucatán had the first Spanish settlements and has since been the most developed of the three states on the peninsula. Until the middle of this century, when the railroad and a highway were completed, it was far easier for Yucatecans to travel to Cuba or the United States than to Mexico City. Prior to 1951, anyone wishing to visit Mexico City had to travel by boat to Veracruz and then continue the journey by land. It was just as convenient to take a boat to New Orleans, Miami, or Havana. Even today, many Yucatecans feel somewhat independent and even alienated from the rest of Mexico.

MÉRIDA

Yucatán state's capital and largest city, Mérida, was the first Spanish settlement on the peninsula, founded by Francisco de Montejo in 1542 on the site of a Mayan city known as T'Ho. As was the Spanish custom, Montejo tore down the city's temples to build his new settlement, meeting with no small amount of resistance in the process. In the end the Spanish succeeded; T'Ho ceased to exist and Mérida became an important colonial center.

After the Caste Wars and with the hemp industry boom, Mérida grew rapidly. It became known as the "Paris of the West" because city fathers remodeled their Paseo Montejo after the Champs Elysées, along which the wealthy built palatial homes decorated with Carrara marble and filled with elegant European furnishings. Horse-drawn carriages, *calesas*, provided taxi service; today the same carriages are used for tours of the city. Mérida's golden era came to an end with the development of synthetic fibers, and the city's fortunes now rest on a mix of agriculture, industry, government and tourism.

The city retains much of its colonial ambiance and its people have guarded some of their Mayan

heritage. It is not uncommon to hear Mayan dialects spoken on the streets and many schools hold at least some of their classes in the native tongue. To our minds, Mérida is close to the perfect Mexican city, its only drawbacks being it does not have a beach and has become clogged with noisy traffic. Luckily, beaches are less than an hour away and Mérida is a good staging place for ruins, beaches and the countryside.

GENERAL INFORMATION

The main **Tourist Information Office** ((99) 248386 or 286547 in the Teatro Péon Contreras, on Calles 60 and 57, is open daily from 8 AM to 8 PM.

WHAT TO SEE AND DO

Mérida's **Plaza Principal** and major colonial structures were built upon the ruins of T'Ho. **Maya carvings** are still evident on some buildings, and the plaza remains Mérida's social center much as it was when the Spanish destroyed the Maya city. The plaza is particularly pleasant on Sunday, when the surrounding streets are closed to traffic and sightseers ride around in *calesas*. On the eastern side is the late sixteenth-century baroque Catedral, built from the stones of the Mayan temples. The **Capilla del Cristo de las Ampollas** (Christ of the Blisters) to the left of the main altar contains a statue that, according to local legend, was carved from a tree that burned all night, but was found intact

A hotel entrance OPPOSITE and an inviting streetside restaurant ABOVE convey the pleasant ambiance of Mérida.

the next morning. Beside the cathedral is the **Museo de Arte Contemporaneo (MAKAY)**, a colonial-era seminary converted into an impressive modern art museum. It is open daily except Tuesday, from 9 AM to 5 PM.

On the southern end of the plaza is the **Casa de Montejo** (Montejo's House), built by the conquering Montejo family in the 1500s. The house's carved façade shows two conquistadors standing on Maya heads. This image seems similar in intent to those of Mayan rulers standing on or over the heads of captured enemies, and is a cameo illustration of how the Spanish attempted to subjugate Mexico's peoples by turning their own practices and sacred places against them. As such, it is no wonder that there was no love lost between the Spanish and the Maya. The house was remodeled by architect Agustín Legoretta in the 1970s for Banamex bank, and can be visited during banking hours (Monday through Friday from 9 AM to 1:30 PM).

The **Palacio Municipal**, on the west side of the square, was originally a jail but was converted to municipal offices in 1929. The street in front of the municipal hall is often closed to traffic and used as a stage for music and dance performances. The newer, nineteenth-century, **Palacio de Gobierno** (open daily from 9 AM to 9 PM) dominates the north end. The murals lining the stairwells and the painting in the Hall of History were done by Yucatán artist Fernando Castro Pacheco.

A block north is **Parque Hidalgo** where marimbas play in front of outdoor cafés. This is the best place in downtown to linger over a coffee or beer and bargain with hammock sellers draped in their wares. Farther north on Calle 60 is the neoclassic **Teatro Péon Contreras**, housing the tourist information office and a stage where concerts, plays and folkloric dance shows are held.

Beginning at Calles 47 and 54 is Mérida's Champs Élysées, **Paseo Montejo**, a broad tree-lined avenue. At the corner of Calle 43 is the Palacio Cantón, formerly the official residence of the governors of the Yucatán. It now houses the **Regional Museum of Anthropology and History** (small admission fee, but free on Sunday; open Tuesday through Saturday from 9 AM to 6 PM and Sunday from 9 AM to 2 PM) that has exhibits on Mayan history and lifestyles as well as a comprehensive display on the archaeological sites of the Yucatán.

Several blocks east of the plaza is the **Museo de Artes Populares** (National Handicrafts Museum) on Calle 50 between Calles 57 and 59 (free admission; open Tuesday through Saturday from 8 AM to 8 PM). It has an extensive collection of Yucatán crafts and a representative display of handicrafts from elsewhere in the country. The shop on the ground floor has reasonably-priced embroidered blouses, ceramics and other fine handcrafted items.

North on Calle 50 at Calles 61 and 62 are Moorish-style arches, **Arco del Puente** (Bridge Arch) and **Arco de Dragones** (Dragon Arch), which are the vestiges of 13 gates that were built at the end of the seventeenth century to enclose and protect the city.

Between the plaza and Paseo Montejo, Calle 60 is Mérida's main shopping street with several folk art shops and galleries. South of the plaza, at Calle 60 and Calle 65 is **Mercado García Rejón**, a large crafts market. The **Mercado Municipal**, Calle 65 between Calles 56 and 58 (open daily), is the largest market in Yucatán; the surrounding streets are packed with shops specializing in hammocks, cotton shorts called *guayaberas*, Panama-style hats called *jipis* and other regional crafts.

On the southeast edge of the old city at Calles 77 and 65 is the small church, **Ermita de Santa Isabel**, which is also known as the Church of the Safe Journey. Travelers to Campeche used to stop here to pray for a safe trip. The old cemetery has been converted into a **garden** with a waterfall and Mayan artifacts. On Friday nights at 9 PM concerts are held in its open-air theater.

WHERE TO STAY

Mérida has an excellent selection of moderate and inexpensive hotels, many housed in colonial-era buildings. In recent years several luxury hotels have opened in the Paseo Montejo area; though truly elegant, these hotels often have rates at least one-third less than similar properties in Cancún.

Expensive

As befits the neighborhood, the 350-room **Fiesta Americana Mérida** ((99) 421111 TOLL-FREE (800) 343-7821 FAX (99) 421112, Paseo de Montejo No. 451 at Paseo Colón, is designed in the style of the nearby mansions constructed during the early twentieth century. The street-level entrance houses a shopping center and popular Sanborn's restaurant. Escalators lead to the elegant lobby replete with marble floors, chandeliers, atrium and fountains. The rooms are equally handsome and have satellite television, in-room safes, direct-dial phones and fax ports and small balconies. This is by far the best hotel in Mérida.

Located directly across the street from the Fiesta Americana is the **Hyatt Regency Mérida** ((99) 420202 or 421234 TOLL-FREE (800) 233-1234 FAX (99) 257002, Calle 60 No. 344, at Paseo Colón. Though similarly lavish, this property suffers from one disconcerting drawback — none of the windows in the guestrooms can be opened.

Moderate

More centrally located is the venerable **Casa del Balam** ((99) 228844 TOLL-FREE (800) 624-8451 and (800) 555-8842 FAX (99) 245011, Calle 60 No. 488

(between Calles 57 and 55), with 54 rooms and located only two blocks from the main plaza. Filled with antiques, elaborately tiled floors, fountains and gardens, this is a fine choice in the center of the action.

Nearby, overlooking Parque Hidalgo, the **Gran Hotel** ((99) 247730 FAX (99) 247622, Calle 60 No. 496 (between Calles 61 and 59) is said to have been Mérida's first hotel. As befits its age, the pistachio-green building is loaded with character, from the balconies overlooking the plaza to the rocking chairs set beside curving tiled stairways. The **Hotel Caribe** ((99) 249022 TOLL-FREE (800) 555-8842 FAX (99) 248733, Calle 59 No. 500, also overlooking the park, is similarly enchanting and benefits from quieter rooms located away from street traffic. Both have decent outdoor café-restaurants.

Inexpensive

The 23-room **Hotel Posada Toledo** ((99) 231690 FAX (99) 232256, Calle 58 No. 487 at Calle 57, is one of the most charming hotels in town, with rooms around a central courtyard. Ask to see the astonishing master suite, composed of two faithfully-restored high-ceilinged rooms with chandeliers and antique furnishings; at half the price of standard rooms in the expensive hotels, it's worth considering for a special occasion. The hotel's only drawback is its lack of a swimming pool. The owners of the **Hotel Mucuy** ((99) 285193 FAX (99) 237801, Calle 57 No. 481 (between Calles 56 and 58), have created a budget travelers' haven with rock-bottom room rates, a communal refrigerator, clothesline and garden, and inexpensive tours to nearby attractions (for hotel guests only). Book far in advance here. **Hotel Dolores Alba** ((99) 285650 FAX (99) 285650 and FAX (99) 283163, Calle 63 No. 464, offering 40 rooms, was my first favorite budget hotel in Mexico and remains a great choice if you don't mind the occasional mosquito bite. The Sánchez family has managed the hotel for decades, along with one near Chichén Itzá. The **Hotel Colón** ((99) 234355 FAX (99) 244919, Calle 62 No. 483, with 63 units, is amusing and bizarre, with Romanesque steam baths (reputed to be popular assignation hideouts) at the back of the first floor near the lawn and pool. The baths are open for a fee to non-guests. The rooms are dark and cozy, and guarded by two massive plaster dogs at the foot of the red-carpeted stairway.

WHERE TO EAT

Eating out in Mérida is a treat. In addition to a good variety of fresh seafood and traditional Yucatán specialties of *cochinita* and *pollo pibil* (pork or chicken marinated in achiote sauce), there is good Middle Eastern cuisine thanks to the city's many Lebanese immigrants.

Expensive

Alberto's Continental Patio ((99) 285367, Calle 64 No. 482, has an excellent menu of *tabbouleh*, *hummous*, stuffed cabbage and other Lebanese specialties, along with very good Yucatecan cuisine. The Salum family has operated this charming restaurant for decades, nourishing both their diners and the gardens of overgrown vines and trees that surround the candlelit tables. Reservations are essential on holidays and during busy weeks (Christmas, Easter, school breaks). Also recommended for its atmosphere and chef is **La Casona** ((99) 238348, Calle 60 No. 434, which specializes in Italian cuisine. **La Bella Epoca** ((99) 281429, Calle 60 (between Calles 59 and 57), is

memorable if you can get one of the tables for two in individual balconies overlooking Calle 60. The menu covers the full gamut of Middle Eastern, Italian, Yucatecan and Continental cuisines, with varying success. I never visit Mérida without having lunch or dinner in the vine-covered courtyard at **El Portico del Peregrino** ((99) 286163, Calle 57 No. 501 (between Calles 60 and 62). The meal I order is always the same — *berenjenas al horno* (baked eggplant, chicken and cheese) and at least one Negro Modelo beer.

Moderate

Students of Yucatecan cuisine appreciate the color photos and English-language descriptions in the English and Spanish menus at **Los Almendros** ((99) 285459, Calle 50-A No. 493 (between

Locals relax in an atmospheric Mérida coffeehouse.

Calles 59 and 57). The food preparation and portions are undependable, however.

Inexpensive
Businessmen hover over Middle Eastern and Yucatecan fare during their lengthy coffee breaks at **Café Alameda (** (99) 283635, Calle 58 No. 474 (between Calles 57 and 55 across the street from the Hotel Posada Toledo). Students prefer **Caféteria Pop (** (99) 286163, Calle 57 No. 501 (between Calles 60 and 62) despite its Formica-style ambiance. The coffee, breakfasts, and pastries are good and cheap, but the waiters will rush you along if you claim a table for too long. **Café Express (** (99) 281691, Calle 60 No. 509, is crowded with people day and night who come for a quick meal with a view of Parque Hidalgo. For drinks accompanied by *botanes* (similar to Spanish *tapas*) stop by **La Prosperidad (** (99) 211898, Calle 56 at Calle 33, where the snacks are free if you drink enough.

HOW TO GET THERE

The international airport south of the city receives flights from Mexico City, Cancún, Cozumel, Oaxaca, Villahermosa and Miami (Florida). Buses arrive from all major destinations on the peninsula at the main bus station, on Calle 69.

AROUND MÉRIDA

CELESTÚN AND SISAL

Gulf Coast beaches are within an easy hour's drive from Mérida. Eighty-six kilometers (53 miles) southwest is the Mayan fishing village of Celestún, with a 5,913-hectare (14,611-acre) wildlife refuge lagoon. Thousands of pink flamingos settle in the lagoon year-round, along with frigates, pelicans and egrets. North from Celestún, the road (if one can call it that) runs along the coast past 40 km (25 miles) of sandy beaches to the old sisal port, Sisal. This area is definitely off the beaten path. There are a few hotels at Celestún, but there are several great seafood cafés serving fresh shrimp, *ceviche* and snapper. During the winter season, many people come here to camp along this coast.

PROGRESO

Forty-five minutes north of Mérida by road, Progreso has been Yucatán's major port and Gulf Coast resort since Spanish times. The town is small and far from cosmopolitan, but has some architecturally interesting mansions along the waterfront and a strong local identity. The beaches away from the port have coarse brown sand and murky water, and are far less attractive than those on the Caribbean Coast. The area attracts weekend crowds from Mérida rather than tourists.

During the week Progreso is uncongested and quiet, except during July and August when Mexicans take their vacations. For anyone wanting to get away from it all, Progreso has just enough services to makes one's stay comfortable, and not enough to make it an attractive destination for the multitudes.

In town there are several inexpensive hotels, including **Hotel San Miguel (** (993) 51357, Calle 78, between Calles 29 and 31, with 20 rooms and **Hotel Progreso (** (933) 52478 FAX (933) 52019, Calle 29 No. 142. Bungalows on the beach are rented by the week or month as are many private homes. The Tourist Information Office in Mérida usually has a list of agents who manage rentals.

There have been several attempts to create major resorts along the beach northeast of Progreso, none them wildly successful. You don't need to stay in the area to explore it, however. The drive north from Mérida to Progreso and then east to the turnoff for Highway 281 south toward Izamal and Chichén Itzá can be completed in a day, even at a leisurely sightseeing pace.

DZIBILCHALTÚN

When the Mayan ruins of Dzibilchaltún were rediscovered in the 1940s, 17 km (11 miles) from Mérida, there was a flurry of excitement which quickly waned because no dramatic architecture was uncovered. Only during more recent examinations has it been determined that this may have been one of the largest Mayan settlements in Mexico. It was occupied from at least 600 BC until the arrival of the Spanish, who demolished much of the site to build haciendas and the Progreso–Mérida highway. Some 8,000 buildings have been identified, but little of the 65-sq-km (25-sq-mile) site has been excavated (admission fee, but free on Sunday; open daily from 8 AM to 5 PM). The major structure is the **Temple of the Seven Dolls**, which is believed to be the only Mayan temple with windows. It was named for the seven figurines which were found in the temple and which are now on display in the **museum** at the entrance.

The archaeological site is in the midst of an ecological park and preserve with *cenotes*, low-lying deciduous forest, cacti and palms. Hiking trails lead through the area.

Daily second-class buses travel to Dzibilchaltún from Mérida. You can also get part way to the ruins on the first-class Progreso-bound bus, but you will have to hike four kilometers (two and a half miles) from the highway to the ruins. If driving, take Highway 273 north from Mérida.

IZAMAL

Nowhere is the clash between the pre-Columbian and Spanish cultures more evident than at

Izamal, 75 km (45 miles) east of Mérida. Mayan structures form the base of the town's many colonial buildings. The sixteenth-century **Convent of San Antonio de Padua** is approached up the steps of a Mayan pyramid and occupies the location of a former temple. Prior to the Spanish Conquest Izamal was a Mayan pilgrimage center dedicated to Itzámna, the creator of the universe, the most powerful Mayan deity. Realizing its importance, Diego de Landa, the infamous priest responsible for the burning of the Mayan scrolls, selected the site as his bishopric, determined to make it the most important Catholic place of worship. The grandeur of his plans is evidenced by the atrium of the monastery, which was second

to town, and several companies offer Izamal day tours from Mérida.

The town, with about 25,000 inhabitants, has a few Mexican hotels and restaurants. The best place to stop for a meal or snack is the restaurant **Kinich Kakmó** at the foot of the ruins. Izamal is a marvelous off-the-beaten-path stop, particularly when religious festivals are held in the convent's atrium (April 3, May 3 to 5, August 15, October 18 to 28, and November 29).

THE PUUC HILLS

South of Mérida near the border with Campeche is the area called the Puuc Hills. The word "hill"

in size only to St. Peter's Square in Rome. Most of its 75 arches are still intact. The Mayan temples and pyramids were systematically incorporated into or taken apart for the new. Only **Kinich Kakmó**, dedicated to the sun god, escaped the colonial construction frenzy. The crumbled temple sits atop a slight hill; on a really clear day you can see across the scrubby jungle to Chichén Itzá.

Izamal garnered worldwide attention in 1993, when Pope John Paul II met with the indigenous peoples of Mexico and Central America in the town's main plaza. Already known as the Ciudad Amarilla (Yellow City) for the uniform gold tone of its buildings, Izamal went through a major beautification project before the pope's visit. It remains the most beautiful town in Yucatán and is gaining more tourism facilities. The state created a *Parador Turistica* (tourism center) with a museum, restrooms, a restaurant and shops at the entrance

is used very loosely, for the terrain is still relatively flat compared with almost anywhere else in Mexico. In this area are thousands of Mayan ruins, of which many of the major ones were originally "rediscovered" by John L. Stephens, a British adventurer and writer, and a companion, artist Frederick Catherwood, who explored the Yucatán Peninsula on horseback between the years 1839 and 1841.

UXMAL

Founded between AD 600 and AD 900, Uxmal is thought to have been a major center of learning, inhabited by priests and experts in astronomy, architecture and engineering. It appears that the

Viewing the unusual elliptical Pirámide del Adivino (Magicians' Pyramid) at Uxmal, one beholds the magic of classic Mayan design.

city was never invaded by groups other than Maya armíes and therefore is considered to be more genuinely Mayan than Chichén Itzá. The buildings are elaborately decorated with geometric designs similar to those at Mitla, Oaxaca, but the art has been taken a step further. The geometric friezes are overlaid with stylized caricatures that are somewhat like the gargoyle figures of Gothic architecture. Archaeologists believe these are representations of the rain god, Chac, who was of great importance to the region, as it was subjected to a long dry season each year. Apparently, the Maya had developed an intricate system of cisterns and reservoirs for collecting and storing rain, their only source of water. By the time of Stephens' arrival, the system had fallen into disrepair and the nineteenth-century Maya, under Spanish dominance, had lost their former knowledge of engineering and hydraulics.

The site, 80 km (50 miles) from Mérida (admission fee, but free on Sunday; open daily 8 AM to 5 PM), is dominated by the **Pirámide del Adivino** (Pyramid of the Soothsayer or Magician), which has five temples of different styles at various levels. Climbing the 118 steep steps to the top is worth the effort. The structure is alternately referred to as the Pyramid of the Dwarf or Wizard, because legend claimed it was built by the son of a witch, born from an egg.

Next to this pyramid to the west is a structure that has come to be know as the **Cuadrángulo de las Monjas** (Quadrangle of the Nuns), because the Spanish conquerors thought that its rooms were inhabited by Mayan clergy. Archaeologists, however, believe that the immense complex with intricately carved bas reliefs covering its walls was also used by Uxmal's scholars.

Facing the Nunnery to the south is the town's **ball court**, and beyond it the Casa de las Tortugas (House of the Turtles), the Governor's Palace, the Great Pyramid and the Palomar (the Dovecote).

The **Casa de las Tortugas** was dedicated to turtles which, according to Mayan belief, grieved for people during times of drought, and whose tears brought the rain. The cornice is decorated with turtles, each having a different pattern on its shell.

Often termed the most architecturally perfect structure in Mexico, Uxmal's **Palacio del Gobernador** is 100 m (328 ft) long, 12 m (39 ft) wide and nine meters (30 ft) high. On its terrace sits an unusual sculpture of two jaguars joined at the breast, with the head of one pointing north and the other south.

The **Great Pyramid** has been partially reconstructed and the Dovecote (so named because the lattice of its roof-comb resembles a pigeon house) is only the façade of what is thought to have been a structure similar to the Nunnery, but older.

Also at the site are other structures that have not been excavated or reconstructed, including the **Pirámide de la Vieja** (Pyramid of the Old Woman), the **Temple de los Falos** (Temple of the Phalli), named after its sculpted phalluses that serve as rain spouts, a *stelae* platform with 15 eroded **carved stones**, and the **Grupo del Cementerio** (Cemetery Group) decorated with skulls and crossbones, but probably not used as cemetery.

There is a **museum** and **cultural center** at the entrance and nightly there are two sound and light shows, one in Spanish at 7 PM and the other in English at 9 PM. The Tourist Information Office and hotels in Mérida have information and tickets for the show and tours to the site. However it

is more relaxing to make the trip at one's leisure by car or public transportation (bus).

Where to Stay

Most of the hotels at the site are expensive. The **Villa Arqueológica (** (99) 247053 TOLL-FREE (800) 555-8842, managed by Club Mediterranée, has 44 fairly expensive small rooms. It has a shaded courtyard pool and patio, and an expensive restaurant serving regional and continental cuisine nearing French standards.

Right across from the entrance to the ruins is the **Lodge at Uxmal (** (99) 289894 TOLL-FREE (800) 235-4079 FAX (99) 234744 (reservations in Mérida at **(** (99) 250621 FAX (99) 250087) E-MAIL mayaland @diario1.sureste.com, which opened in 1997. Built to blend with the surroundings, the lodge is an architectural gem with hardwood doors carved with Maya designs, long porches with rocking chairs looking out to the pools and lawns, ceiling fans and air-conditioning in the large rooms, and a *palapa*-roofed restaurant serving regional meals.

On the main roadway leading to the ruins is the 80-room **Hacienda Uxmal (** (99) 280840

OPPOSITE: The east building of Uxmal's quadrangle, with the Pirámide del Adivino towering behind it. ABOVE: Poolside at the Villa Arqueológica resort in Uxmal.

TOLL-FREE (800) 235-4079 FAX 234744 (reservations in Mérida at ((99) 250621 FAX (99) 250087) E-MAIL mayaland@diario1.sureste.com, located on Highway 261, approximately 100 m north of the ruins. For many repeat visitors Hacienda Uxmal is the *only* place to stay. They know the waiters, bellmen and housekeepers who have worked here for decades, amid hacienda-style buildings with intricately patterned tiled floors, heavy carved hardwood furnishings, slatted wooden shutters and jungle-high landscaping.

Rancho Uxmal ((997) 20277, Calle 26 No. 156, Ticul on Highway 261 about three kilometers (two miles) north of the ruins, with 20 rooms, has the only decent budget accommodation nearby. The

rooms have fans and there is a swimming pool, though it's often out of order. The ruins are a 45-minute walk away; buses from Mérida will stop here if you flag them down. The restaurant is one of the best in the area.

Where to Eat
The best dining options are the hotels mentioned above and the restaurant at the ruins' cultural center. If you eat at the Lodge at Uxmal you're allowed to use the pool area, well worth the extra cost of the meal as the ruins at midday are usually hot.

AROUND UXMAL

Kabah
About 20 km (12 miles) south of Uxmal is Kabah (admission fee, but free on Sunday; open daily

from 8 AM to 5 PM), interesting for the **Palacio de los Mascarones** (Palace of the Masks), and **Codz-Pop**, a palace whose Maya name supposedly means "rolled up mat," referring to the shape of the steps formed by the elephantine nose of the rain god Chac. Both structures have façades decorated with more masks of the god than anyone would like to count.

Other structures at the site, which is only partially excavated, are the stark **Teocalli** (Palace), the **Gran Teocalli** (Great Temple), the **Casa de la Bruja** (House of the Witch), and a superb **arch** with almost Moorish overtones, which stood over the entrance to the city and the beginning of the *sacbe* ("white road") leading to Uxmal (there is a similar arch at Uxmal, but the path to it has been overgrown).

Sayil, Xlapak and Labná
A short distance south of Kabah, accessible by paved roads, are the Maya sites of Sayil, Xlapak and Labná. **Sayil** (admission fee, but free on Sunday; open daily from 8 AM to 5 PM) has a large palace with some 50 chambers, and is noteworthy because its stone has an orange hue due to the iron oxides in the soil. **Xlapak** (admission fee, but free on Sunday; open daily from 8 AM to 5 PM) has a partially excavated palace with an unadorned ground floor, mask-decorated frieze, and similarly decorated towers at the corners and above the main entrance.

Labná (admission fee, but free on Sunday; open daily from 8 AM to 5 PM) has the best-preserved and most intricately decorated Maya archway in Yucatán, and **El Mirador**, a temple with a four-and-a-half-meter (15-ft) high roof-comb.

Located 29 km (18 miles) northeast of Labná, are the **Grutas de Loltún** (admission fee; open daily) where visitors are required to take a guided tour, offered throughout the day. Check at Uxmal for the schedule, as it changes with the seasons. These grottos are a subterranean wonderland. Amidst the stalactites and stalagmites are Mayan paintings and constructions. It is believed that the Mayas hid here during the Caste War, but the caverns were also in use long before this.

CHICHÉN ITZÁ

"At four o'clock we left Pisté," writes John L. Stephens on March 11, 1841, "and very soon we saw rising high above the plain the Castillo of Chichén. In half-an-hour we were among the ruins of this ancient city, with all the great buildings in full view, casting prodigious shadows over the plain and presenting a spectacle which, even after all that we had seen, once more excited in us emotions of wonder."

Stephens was describing his first view of the magnificent city of Chichén Itzá after having traveled over most of the peninsula and seen, in his words, "The remains of forty-four ancient cities." Much more visible today than in Stephens' time, Chichén Itzá (admission fee, but free on Sunday; open daily from 8 AM to 5 PM), 120 km (75 miles) east of Mérida, is probably the most famous of the Mayan ruins, and is also the most thoroughly excavated and restored. Consequently, it is also the most visited.

The site itself is enormous — nearly 10 sq km (four square miles) — although only a small part of the total city has been excavated. Some archaeologists estimate the total site is over 100 sq km (38 sq km) in size. Because of the extent of the ruins, the crowds, and the often crushing heat of the

Chichén Itzá was the major Mayan religious center from about AD 500 to AD 900, after which it seems to have been taken over, or heavily influenced by, northern tribes who may have been allied with the Toltecs from Tula. Recent theories suggest that rather than having been influenced by Tula, Chichén Itzá influenced it. In any case, the newer occupants of the site enlarged it and established their own structures.

Chichén Itzá is so extensive and complex that it deserves a guidebook all its own; indeed, they are available at gift shops at the site. Some visitors begin by studying a detailed map of the area and deciding on their itinerary in advance. Others prefer to wander around the site, taking it all in,

Yucatán jungle, it is best to visit this marvelous site early in the morning on two consecutive days. Thus you will visit one half of the ruins one morning — taking the afternoon off to swim in the hotel pool, relax and perhaps read more about the site — then return to visit the other half of the ruins the following morning.

At Chichén, one comes away with a keen sense of the awesome capabilities of the Mayan culture. To have constructed such a city out of enormous and beautifully carved stones, millions of them, yet without the wheel or pack animals, to have fed it and brought water to it, to have connected it to the other cities and centers of Mexico by superlative paved roads at a time when their European counterparts were largely dependent on dirt tracks, manifests a high degree of accomplishment.

Founded about AD 400 by Mayan tribes that had moved north from what is now Guatemala,

and then — only after they've gotten a taste for the ambiance — buying a guidebook and reading about what they've just seen… and then going out to explore the ruins once again.

Just past the cultural center, museum, and tourist services building by the parking lot, one may choose between entering the older area to the south or the newer area to the north. The northern side includes a vast open area faced on its south side by the **Pirámide de Kulkucán**. One of the wonders of the ancient Mayan world, the Pyramid was completed about AD 830. It is perfectly proportioned, with nine levels indicating the nine heavens, a total of 365 steps corresponding to the days of the year, and a 45-degree

OPPOSITE: The Mayan ruins at Sayil.
ABOVE: Chichén Itzá is the finest of the Mayan archeological sites. OVERLEAF: The imposing figure of Chac mool, the Mayan divine messenger.

staircase on each side, corresponding to the four cardinal directions.

It was built in configuration with exact astronomical measurements and topped with the square **Templo de Kulkucán** (the sun god). There is also an interior ascent of the pyramid, with views into earlier pyramids covered over by this one. From the Templo one has a marvelous view of the entire area, with its flat low jungle extending to the horizons.

As one stands atop the pyramid, the great **Templo de los Guerreros** (Temple of the Warriors) is to the east. One of the most beautiful sights in Mexico, this temple is surrounded by the **Mil Columnas**, the "thousand" tall white columns, and

virgins and the ill and infirm) may have been thrown. Over 80 m (260 ft) deep, the well has been explored by divers who have found over a hundred human skeletons and thousands of art, and other, objects.

There are numerous other fascinating sites on the north side, including a sweat bath, skull platform, the **Casa de las Águilas** (House of the Eagles), a market, other temples, colonnades and smaller structures. Even by itself, the north area is one of the major archaeological treasures of the world. But more, and equally fascinating, wonders await us to the south.

Upon entering the south area we are faced with the **Tumba del Gran Sacerdote** (Tomb of the Great

according to archaeologists is a larger version of the Toltec Templo de Tlahuizcalpantecuhtli at Tula.

Looking west from the Mil Columnas is the **Templo de los Tigres** (Temple of the Tigers), with a carved stone jaguar altar and numerous friezes of jaguars; inside are wall paintings of a battle between Toltecs and Mayas. Behind the Templo de los Tigres is the imposing and famous **Juego de Pelota** (Pelota Court), where contestants apparently had to knock a hard rubber ball through the round stone ring without using their hands, but only their legs and elbows. The ball was not supposed to touch the ground, for it symbolized the path of the sun through the sky. Reliefs along the walls show losing teams being taken to be sacrificed.

Beyond the north area a *sacbe* leads northward to the **Cenote de los Sacrificios** (Sacrificial Pool) where some of the losing ball players (as well as

Priest), also known as **El Osario** (the Ossuary). This older pyramid was probably, as its name suggests, the tomb of a major priest or priests. Several skeletons and many artifacts have been found in its graves, and the tomb and other sites in this area have been undergoing reconstruction during the 1990s.

Farther south is the astounding **Observatorio**, also called **El Caracol** due to its snail-like shape. Erected on a large flat pediment, it has an interior spiral staircase and slit windows that let direct sunlight in for a few seconds once or twice a year, allowing minute astronomical observations and calendar measurements.

To the south end of the presently excavated site is the series of buildings called, incorrectly, by the Spaniards, **Las Monjas** (the Nunnery), with richly carved friezes and intricate layered stone walls. Another nearby and beautiful structure was again incorrectly termed by the Spanish, **La Iglesia** (the Church), a tall rectangular building with superb friezes and cornice moldings.

Also fascinating are the **Azak Dib** (House of the Dark, or Obscure, Writing), the **Templo del Venado** (Temple of the Deer), the **Casa Colorado** (Red House) and another sacrificial pool, the **Cenote de Xtoloc**.

WHERE TO STAY AND EAT

A captivating option when staying at Chichén is the moderately-priced **Hotel Hacienda Chichén** ((99) 248844 TOLL-FREE (800) 624-8451 FAX (99) 245011, near the entrance to the ruins, offering

attraction, and the large dining room, with interesting stained glass windows, serves decent meals. Tour groups use the hotel's latest addition, a settlement of 24 villas just off the main highway with its own pool and dining room. Advance reservations are a must. Also near the site is the **Villa Archeológica** ((985) 203-3833 TOLL-FREE (800) 555-8842 off Highway 180 with 32 rooms, a lovely French-run hotel with pool, also often full in winter.

A mile away in **Pisté** is a good selection of hotels in all price categories, including the **Pirámide Inn** ((985) 62462, 44 rooms, an inexpensive place with pool and campground. South on the highway past the ruins is the **Dolores Alba** reservation in Mérida ((99) 285650 FAX (99) 283163, with 20 rooms — an

20 cottage rooms in an early 1900s hacienda with beautiful gardens, ruins and pool, built where explorer Edward Thompson made camp. The hotel is open year-round and advance reservations are strongly advised. The restaurant is open to non-guests.

Another enchanting lodge at the south entrance to the ruins is the **Hotel Mayaland** ((985) 10077 TOLL-FREE (800) 235-4079 FAX (985) 10129. For reservations in Mérida ((99) 250621 or 250622 FAX 250087 E-MAIL mayaland@diario1.sureste .com, located off Highway 180 at the southern road to the ruins. The hotel is set amid 40 hectares (100 acres) of jungle with blossoming red ginger and fuschia bougainvillea. The guestrooms are located in a main hacienda-style building and in several villas modeled after traditional Maya homes, with thatch roofs and front porches overlooking the garden. The pool is a welcome

The Yucatán Peninsula

inexpensive hotel and a great choice for budget travelers. Hammocks hang under palms by the small pool and meals are served for guests only in the small dining room. The owners will help you flag down buses en route to Pisté for rides to the ruins.

If all lodging is full in the area, plenty of rooms are also available in Valladolid, 44 km (27 miles) to the east (see VALLADOLID, below).

All of the hotels listed above have restaurants where the food is reliably good.

ELSEWHERE IN THE YUCATÁN

The state of Yucatán is the only state of the three on the peninsula that has any back roads to speak of where one can find anything other than jungle.

Chichén Itzá's stone carvings are unparalleled.

Surprisingly, it's possible to spend several days here exploring Mayan villages with remnants of colonial architecture. A few recommended destinations are **Umán**, **Ticul**, **Mamá**, and **Mani** in the south, and **Tizimin**, **Río Lagartos** and **San Felipe** in the north. Some of these destinations have restaurants but few have hotels.

VALLADOLID

Valladolid, in the center of the state, is Yucatán state's second largest city and is becoming a popular side trip from Chichén Itzá. It is a major transportation crossroads, commercial center and — for most tourists staying in Cancún and traveling

for lunch in the air-conditioned dining room and open-air courtyard.

Across the street from the Mesón del Marqués is **Casa de los Arcos** (inexpensive to moderate) which serves excellent local specialties.

QUINTANA ROO

In 1974 Quintana Roo became the thirtieth state of Mexico. At about the same time FONATUR decided to create Mexico's largest resort city on a tiny sandbar called Cancún. With statehood and tourism came paved roads, airports, electricity, telephone, televisions, congestion, and an influx of immigrants from other parts of Mexico to work

to Chichén Itzá — it is the closest they will come to the real Mexico. The market and the town's ambiance are definitely Mayan, and if one is not going to have the opportunity of visiting other colonial towns, Valladolid's sixteenth-century **Convento de San Bernardino de Siena** is well worth visiting. It is one of the town's few colonial buildings to have survived the Caste War.

The accommodation here is reasonably priced and without a lot of frills. The best accommodation in town is **Hotel Mesón del Marqués (** (985) 62073, Calle 39 No. 203. It has 38 inexpensive rooms and hosted former United States President Jimmy Carter in 1989. **Hotel María de la Luz (** (985) 62071, Calle 42 on the Zócalo, is also recommended.

Both the hotels mentioned above have good restaurants; my favorite is at the **Mesón del Marqués**, where local business people congregate

in the booming tourist industry. The state of Quintana Roo — which has remained independent and aloof from both the Spanish and Mexican central governments — appears to be riding high on a wave of success without considering the ultimate consequences of massive construction in a fragile ecosystem.

Such change was probably inevitable. Quintana Roo not only has an ideal climate with an average temperature of 28°C (82°F), but also is bounded on the east by one of the world's most beautiful bodies of water, the Caribbean Sea, and endless stretches of white sand beaches. The only factors that had disfavored development were a lack of infrastructure and the mosquitoes.

Quintana Roo has many drawbacks, but luckily many of the less-exposed villages have thus far escaped mega-development, and the Caribbean remains crystal clear and turquoise. The sea is the reason to visit Quintana Roo and water lovers will find it a paradise.

The Caribbean is a snorkeler's and diver's wonderland. Coral reefs can be reached from the shore, making the underwater world accessible to anyone who can swim. In fact, snorkeling is in many ways more rewarding than scuba diving, as one's time in the water need not be limited by air supply. We have spent hours floating around lagoons and over reefs watching the multicolored fish dart in and out of their coral cities, munch on plants and play continuous games of tag. Because the water is relatively warm and one can easily loose track of time, it is advisable to wear a T-shirt while snorkeling, for the sun's burning effect is

glossier version of Acapulco. It has no old town, and there are far more appealing beaches nearby. It's possible to spend a week in Cancún and never see an inch of the real Mexico, since the resort is dominated by the Hotel Zone — a development that runs the length of a 15-km (nine-mile) coral sand bar linked to the mainland by low-lying bridges at both ends. The Hotel Zone is mega-resort after mega-resort, each trying to out-glitter the next. As Cancún was primarily developed for Americans, many Mexican and European visitors have remarked that they feel out of place beside its overwhelming commercial culture, and because they don't speak English or have dollars to spend.

magnified by the thin layer of water covering one's back. It should go without saying that everyone should snorkel with a buddy and be aware of his or her location at all times.

Along the coast inside the reef sharks are rarely a problem, but they do exist. One should be particularly alert after a storm or when the waves are high. This is the time when a shark can be inadvertently carried inside the barrier reef that protects the beaches.

CANCÚN

Cancún is magnificent, with an ideal climate, perfectly clear turquoise water of the Caribbean Ocean, white sand beaches, and puffy white clouds in the azure sky.

Still, Cancún is not to everyone's taste. Some feel that Cancún is little more than a younger,

Some people use Cancún merely as a gateway to the many other more appealing destinations in Quintana Roo. If you choose a flight that arrives early in the day, you need not stay in Cancún (where hotel prices are inflated). Instead, you can pick up a rental car or bus and escape to Isla Mujeres or to one of the many less-developed beaches and resorts to the south.

GENERAL INFORMATION

Since most travelers arrive at the international airport, Cancún business owners have arranged to have their monthly English-language guide, *Cancún Tips*, handed to everyone clearing customs.

OPPOSITE: A colorful street corner in Santa Elena. ABOVE: A swimming pool blends almost imperceptibly with the ocean at a Cancún hotel.

The Yucatán Peninsula

The **Oficina de Turismo** (Tourism Office) ((98) 846531, is located on Avenida Cobá at Avenida Nader, downtown, and is open Monday through Friday from 9 AM to 5 PM.

WHAT TO SEE AND DO

Cancún is divided into two main areas: the Hotel Zone and downtown. Inexpensive buses run between the two and are the easiest way to get around. The downtown area lacks the charm of a traditional Mexican city. The main plaza is a drab slab of concrete with a few shady trees and benches, and the church is a modern structure lacking any grace. The main tourist-oriented businesses are on Avenida Tulum, where the artisans' market **Ki Huic** draws shoppers with its inexpensive manufactured blankets, sandals and T-shirts. Several good restaurants are located in this area, as are the least expensive hotels.

The Hotel Zone, running between the sea and several lagoons, is the center of the action. **Golf** is available at the 18-hole **Club de Golf Cancún** ((98) 830871 designed by Robert Trent-Jones Jr. and the 18-hole **Caesar Park Cancún Golf Club** ((98) 818000 at the hotel of the same name. **Tennis** is available at many of the hotels.

But it's the water that attracts the most attention. Several **water sports** centers offer wave runners, parasailing, kayaks, snorkeling and more. Check out the options at **Aqua Tours** ((98) 830400 on Paseo Kulkucán Km. 6.5; **Aqua World** ((98) 852288 Paseo Kukulcán Km 15.2; and Paseo Kukulcán Km 10.5. Think twice about scuba diving tours; the reefs near Cancún have been loved to death and are a great disappointment to divers. The chain of protected reefs off Cozumel is far better.

Theme cruises are also available, including ones that combine a beach lunch on Isla Mujeres with shopping in that island's small town. There are submarine and glass-bottom boat excursions, sunset "booze cruises" with dancing and unlimited cheap tequila and beer, and classier dinner cruises. Several depart from Playa Linda pier and nearly all are advertised in *Cancún Tips*. Talk with other travelers before choosing a cruise, as they vary greatly depending on the boat and crew.

Shopping is an enormously popular activity in the Hotel Zone and there are at least a half-dozen air-conditioned malls to choose from. All offer the same selection of brand-name clothing, sporting gear, accessories and jewelry as you would find in a big mall in the States, along with fast-food franchises. There are precious few folk art shops in the malls; the best selection is at Plaza Caracol. A large artisans' market is located near the Cancún Convention Center; prices here are a tad higher than at the Ki Huic market downtown.

Tours to nearby attractions are abundant. Several companies offer full-day trips to Chichén Itzá,

though these trips are usually disappointing for archaeology buffs. The tour buses typically arrive at the ruins as late as noontime, when the sun is at its hottest and the pyramids are packed with sightseers. Still, if your time is limited, this may be the only way to see Yucatán's most spectacular archaeological site. The ruins of Tulum are much closer to Cancún, and tours there usually include a stop for snorkeling and lunch. Xcaret, a water park-museum-zoo development 56 kilometers (35 miles) south of Cancún on the coast, has become a wildly popular day-trip destination. Buses for the park depart from the **Xcaret Terminal** ((98) 833143, at Paseo Kukulcán, Km 9.5.

WHERE TO STAY

Most of the hotels in Cancún's Hotel Zone are in the very expensive category (over $150 per room per night). So how do the thousands of visitors

afford to stay? The answer is package tours with airfare and accommodation booked together. In some cases a package tour can cost less than the price of a round-trip ticket from an American city.

With a long list of four- and five-star hotels, all offering similar services, it is almost impossible to choose. In fact, it is difficult to tell some of them apart. As the undertow on the eastern beaches is quite strong, a hotel on the north shore or at Punta Cancún is a better choice if one wants to swim and snorkel. The moderate and inexpensive hotels are located in downtown; some have shuttles to the beaches in the Hotel Zone.

Very Expensive

In the Hotel Zone the **Westin Regina (** (98) 850086 TOLL-FREE (800) 228-3000 FAX (98) 850296, Paseo Kukulcán between Punta Nizúc and Punta Cancún, is architecturally stunning with its soaring terracotta and pink walls and open niches painted

blue to frame vistas of sky and sea. The 385 rooms have both air-conditioning and fans; the sea breezes are usually enough to keep you cool.

Nearby, the impressive glass pyramid of the **Caesar Park Cancún Beach & Golf Resort (** (98) 818000 TOLL-FREE (800) 228-3000 FAX (98) 818080, Paseo Kukulcán Km 17.5, rises on a slight hill and sloping lawns. With 530 rooms it's one of the area's largest hotels, and benefits from its 18-hole golf course on the lagoon.

The **Club Méditerranée (** (98) 852409 TOLL-FREE (800) CLUB-MED FAX (98) 852290, Paseo Kukulcán, between Punta Nizúc and Highway 307, is one of the oldest hotels in Cancún. Its attractive all-inclusive programs and proximity to the overused coral reefs make it popular. The 300 rooms are sorely in need of remodeling.

More Miami than Mexico, Cancún winds its way along the Caribbean Sea.

The Yucatán Peninsula

251

A personal favorite because of its Mexican style and ambiance, the **Fiesta Americana Condesa** ((98) 851000 TOLL-FREE (800) 343-7821 FAX (98) 818000, Paseo Kukulcán Km 16.5, is topped by a peaked *palapa* roof. The 502 rooms are clustered around the pool, and the property resembles a Mexican hacienda. The **Meliá Cancún** ((98) 851160 TOLL-FREE (800) 336-3542 FAX (98) 851263, Paseo Kukulcán, Km 16, is the spot for spa lovers; try a moonlit massage in one of the outdoor tents. The 492 rooms are large and comfortable.

The **Marriott Casa Magna** ((98) 852000 TOLL-FREE (800) 223-6388 FAX (98) 851731, Paseo Kukulcán at Retorno Chacá, is also known for its spa and spacious 450 rooms and 38 suites. Like a grand European hotel on the beach, the **Ritz-Carlton** ((98) 850808 TOLL-FREE (800) 241-3333 FAX (98) 851015, Retorno del Rey 36 at Paseo Kukulcán, has such unusual touches as silk wallpaper, oil paintings of castles and hunting scenes, and elegant dining rooms.

One of the first and best hotels is the **Camino Real** ((98) 830100 TOLL-FREE (800) 722-6466 FAX (98) 831730, Paseo Kukulcán at Punta Cancún, which sits at the tip of a point and has both a freshwater pool and a saltwater lagoon filled with fish. Most of the 296 rooms overlook the sea; some have hammocks on the balconies.

Another older favorite is the **Presidente Inter-Continental** ((98) 830200 TOLL-FREE (800) 327-0200 FAX (98) 832602, Paseo Kukulcán Km 7.5, between Punta Cancún and downtown, sandwiched between private condos with a long stretch of uncrowded beach. The 298 rooms are colorfully decorated with woven drapes and spreads; best rooms are on the concierge floors.

Expensive

Misión Miramar Park ((98) 831755 TOLL-FREE (800) 555-8842 FAX (98) 831136, Paseo Kukulcán Km 9, between Punta Nizúc and Punta Cancún, is one of the few reasonably-priced hotels in the zone; its 189 rooms are popular with Mexican families.

Moderate

El Pueblito ((98) 850797 FAX (98) 850731 Paseo Kukulcán Km 17.5, between Punta Nizúc and Punta Cancún, is a real find in the zone. Its 239 rooms are located in several buildings arranged around various pools running down a slight hill toward the beach. The **Hotel Calinda Roma America** ((98) 847500 TOLL-FREE (800) 555-8842 FAX (98) 841953, Avenida Tulum at Avenida Brisa, downtown, is one of the better city hotels, with 177 rooms, a restaurant and pool.

Inexpensive

In the Hotel Zone, the best deal is the 700-bed **CREA Youth Hostel** ((98) 831377 on Paseo Kukulcán Km 3.

In town, the hotels are less expensive, but their drawback is that one must take a bus or taxi to get to the beach. Recommended are: **Plaza Caribe** ((98) 841377 TOLL-FREE (800) 555-8842 FAX (98) 846352, Avenida Tulum No. 36 at Avenida Uxmal, with 140 rooms; the 48-room **Hotel Antillano** ((98) 841532 FAX (98) 841878, Claveles No. 101 off Avenida Tulum; and **Hotel Plaza Carillo's** ((98) 841227 FAX (98) 842371, a 43-room inn near the plaza at Claveles No. 5.

WHERE TO EAT

All of the hotels in the hotel zone have at least one, if not three, restaurants from which to choose. Most are in the expensive category and some are among the best in Cancún. In the past, the emphasis was on American and Continental cuisine, and one was hard put to find a good Mexican restaurant in the whole city. Today, Cancún's chefs are more innovative and daring, and there are some excellent dining rooms serving regional Mexican cuisine. The Hotel Zone is filled with franchised takeout places for burgers and pizza, and several trendy theme restaurants such as the **Hard Rock Café**, **Planet Hollywood** and the **Rainforest Café**. Reservations are advised at the more expensive restaurants. None require a jacket and tie.

Very Expensive

The most popular restaurant among well-off locals during my last visit was the Hotel Camino Real's **Maria Bonita** ((98) 830100 extension 8060. Numerous dining rooms painted soft yellows, pinks and blues provide a sense of intimacy, and the menu is an absolute delight for those who crave authentic Mexican cuisine. There's also an excellent list of fine tequilas. This is one place that should not be missed. **El Mexicano** ((98) 832220, in the Hotel Zone in La Mansión Costa Blanca shopping center, presents folkloric shows with dinners of very good Mexican dishes. The **Club Grill** ((98) 850808 in the Ritz-Carlton is one of the most refined and elegant dining rooms in the Hotel Zone, serving steak, lobster, duck and seafood.

Expensive

Once a downtown landmark, **La Dolce Vita** ((98) 80161, on Paseo Kukulcán Km 14.6, is considered by many to be the best Italian restaurant around and offers a serene dining experience. **La Habichuela** ((98) 843158, Avenida Margaritas No. 25, downtown, is hands-down the most romantic spot, with its candlelit gardens, Maya sculptures and statues, and impeccable service. Try the *cocobichuela*, a coconut shell filled with curried lobster and shrimp. **Casa Rolandi** ((98) 831817, within Plaza Caracol in the Hotel Zone, is another Italian favorite with a fine antipasto bar.

Moderate

Many Cancún regulars swear the freshest seafood can be found at **El Pescador** ((98) 841227, Avenida Tulipanes No. 28 downtown. Lines form outside this casual restaurant with diners eager for huge platters of grilled fish and lobster served in a casual setting. There is another **El Pescador** ((98) 852200 at Plaza Kukulcán, Paseo Kukulcán Km 13 (between Punta Cancún and Punta Nizúc). Authentic Yucatecan dishes such as *pollo pibil* (marinated and baked chicken) and *poc chuc* (a marinated pork chop) can be sampled at **Los Almendros** ((98) 871332, Avenida Bonampak at Avenida Sayil, downtown. The English-language menu with pictures is a big help for the uninitiated. **Pericos** ((98) 843152, on Avenida Yaxchilán 71, downtown, is a wild and wacky place with waiters dressed as bandits, wall-sized murals of Mexico's most famous rebels and movie stars, and good Mexican food tamed a bit for tourist tastes.

A similar theme prevails at the half-dozen or so restaurants from the Carlos Anderson chain. These theme restaurants are famed throughout the country for their bountiful portions of *fajitas*, barbecued chicken and ribs, and Mexican combo plates served amid blaring rock 'n' roll. The most famous in Cancún is **Carlos 'n' Charlie's** ((98) 830846, Paseo Kukulcán Km 5.5, but you can also try **El Shrimp Bucket** ((98) 832710, next door to Carlos 'n' Charlie's; **Señor Frog's** ((98) 831092 at Paseo Kukulcán Km 9.5; and **Carlos O'Brian's** ((98) 841659, Avenida Tulum No. 107 downtown.

Inexpensive

When overindulgence has dulled your senses, go for the salads, fruit and vegetable juices, and healthy sandwiches at **100% Natural** ((98) 843617, Avenida Sunyaxchén No. 62-64, downtown, and **100% Natural** ((98) 831180, a second venue at Paseo Kukulcán at Plaza Terramar. **El Tacalote** ((98) 873045 at Avenida Cobá, downtown, is the best place for cheap tacos and *enchiladas*.

HOW TO GET THERE

Cancún's international airport is one of the busiest in the country, with daily flights from Europe, the United States, Mexico and South America. Passenger vans called *colectivos* transfer travelers to their hotels, and every major car rental company has a desk in the airport. If driving from Mérida you have two options: Highway 180 which passes through dozens of small towns the Autopista toll road which cuts driving time from six hours to four.

ISLA MUJERES

North of Cancún and half an hour offshore, Isla Mujeres is more relaxing and less pretentious than

Cancún. The island, only eight kilometers (five miles) long, has white sand beaches, lagoons with crystal-clear water, coral reefs with an abundance of multicolored fish and ample tourist facilities.

When the Spanish arrived in 1517, they gave the island its name because they found many female images carved in stone (none remain). It is believed to have been a pilgrimage center of some importance. Later, pirates and smugglers sought refuge here and the Allies used it as a base during World War II.

Twenty years ago tourism arrived with little fanfare and frills. Unfortunately Hurricane Gilbert destroyed most of the structures and vegetation on the island in 1988. Residents were quick

to rebuild, and the fresh coat of paint on the beaten Caribbean-style wood buildings helped improve the town's appearance. The island is far more appealing than Cancún for escapists and has a loyal following.

GENERAL INFORMATION

The **Office of Tourism** ((987) 70316 is located on the second floor of the Plaza Isla Mujeres on Avenida Hidalgo and is open Monday through Friday from 8 AM to 5 PM. The *Islander* tourist information pamphlet has a good map of the island and most of the information you'll need during your stay.

Vines spill and drape the balconies in the splendid atrium lobby of the Meliá Cancún, where stressed-out vacationers come for ultimate relaxation.

WHAT TO SEE AND DO

One of the charms of the island is that most attractions are within walking distance. The town, ferry terminal and major hotels are at the northern end of the island, and the only major road (which runs north to south) can easily be walked in two hours. Bicycles, mopeds and golf carts are available for rent by the hour or day, and taxis are inexpensive.

Playa Cocos, also called Playa Norte, on the north side of the island, is the main beach, lined with small rustic cafés, and vendors renting beach chairs, umbrellas and water toys. The beach marks the north end of town, which runs several blocks south to the Navy base. Once you've settled into your hotel you'll soon fall into the island pace, wandering to town for breakfast, and then back to the beach for swimming and sunbathing while the Cancún tour boats dislodge their passengers for frantic shopping sprees. Later, in the evening, you'll come back to town for shopping, dining and mingling with the residents and other travelers, who all seem to know each other. Shopping for folk art is far better here than in Cancún; don't miss the batiks of Maya gods at **Casa del Arte Mexica**, the embroidered blouses and black pottery at **Artesanías El Nopal**, and the masks, Guatemalan bags and Oaxacan carvings at **La Loma**.

South of town the island's main road, Avenida Rueda Medina, runs clear to the southern tip, passing by idyllic beaches and low-lying jungle. A turnoff to the west leads to Fraccionamiento Laguna, a small road past condo complexes and Laguna Makax to the **Puerto Isla Mujeres** marina and resort. The main road continues on to the ruins of the **Hacienda Mundaca**, a nineteenth-century hacienda supposedly built by a pirate named Mundaca for an island girl who nonetheless refused his advances and fled the island with another man.

Nearby, **Parque Garrafón Nacional** (admission fee; open daily from 8 AM to 5 PM) is a national park and marine life refuge filled with hundreds of varieties of colorful tropical fish. The best time for viewing the fish is in the early morning before the tours arrive from Cancún. North of Garrafón is **Dolphin Discovery** ((987) 70596, an educational center where a few lucky visitors are allowed to swim with the dolphins. You must make reservations in advance to visit the center.

The island's southern tip is topped with a lighthouse beside a small cluster of Maya ruins, thought to have been built as an observatory. The lighthouse keeper sells cold drinks and woven hammocks. The road continues along the wild west side of the island, where waves crash against sharp limestone cliffs; swimming is extremely dangerous.

Isla Contoy, 30 kilometers (19 miles) north of Isla Mujeres, is a bird refuge and breeding ground for some 70 species of birds including pelicans, flamingos, cranes, ducks and frigate birds. Boat trips can be organized from the **Isla Mujeres Fishermen's Cooperative** ((987) 70274, on Avenida Rueda Medina by the ferry pier, with local guides. The island has been closed to visitors since 1993 and you are allowed to view the birds only from the water.

For diving enthusiasts the big attraction is the **Cave of the Sleeping Sharks**, five kilometers (three miles) east and 21 m (70 ft) down. Here, in the caves made famous by "shark lady" Dr. Eugenie Clark, one can approach sharks when they "sleep." The sharks are attracted to the spot because of the low salinity of the water, and remain in a sedated state because of the high oxygen content of the water which slows down their metabolisms. Though many visitors are excited by the idea of the shark dive, it can be a major disappointment. Often there are no sharks there, or they are so deep that divers put themselves into danger trying to get to them. There are far better dive sites off the island, including the coral reefs at **Los Manchones** at the southern tip. The **Bahía Dive Shop** ((987) 70340, Avenida Rueda Medina No. 166, and **Buzos de Mexico** ((987) 70131, on Avenida Rueda Medina by the ferry pier, both offer several types of dive excursions and rental gear.

WHERE TO STAY

Isla's hotels are no longer the great bargain they once were, but there are still plenty of small places to choose from. Nearly every place on the island can be booked through **Four Seasons Travel** TOLL-FREE (800) 552-4550.

Expensive

Directly on North Beach is **Na Balam** ((987) 70279 TOLL-FREE (800) 223-6510 FAX (987) 70446, Calle Zacil-Ha No. 118. The 31 air-conditioned rooms are beautifully decorated with art and fabrics from Guatemala, and the restaurant is excellent.

Moderate

When it comes to friendliness, character, and great food and beverages, it's difficult to better **Posada del Mar** ((987) 70444 FAX (987) 70266, Avenida Rueda Medina No. 15A. The 40 rooms are well cared for, the pool is a delight and the clientele all seem to have been here before. **Hotel Cabañas Maria del Mar** ((987) 70179 FAX (987) 70273, Avenida Carlos Lazo No. 1, has a bit of everything within its 57 rooms, from inexpensive basic rooms

---

Isla Mujeres offers a peaceful escape from the glitter and crowds of Cancún.

to air-conditioned tower rooms with tiled floors and balconies. The hotel has a pool, restaurant and complimentary continental breakfast.

WHERE TO EAT

The above hotels all have excellent restaurants frequented by travelers and islanders alike. In addition, the courtyard dining room at **Rolandi's** ((987) 70430, Avenida Hidalgo No. 110, is often crowded with locals feasting on pizzas and pasta. **Mirtita's** ((987) 70232 on Avenida Rueda Medina near the ferry pier, is a coffeeshop with basic, inexpensive breakfast and lunch.

HOW TO GET THERE

The traditional passenger ferries to Isla Mujeres depart from Puerto Juárez, five kilometers (three miles) north of Cancún, where automobiles can be left in a parking lot. Service usually runs regularly from 6:30 AM to 8 PM, unless the water is rough. There is an automobile-passenger ferry from Punta Sam, but no one needs a car on the island. The Punta Sam ferry operates five times a day. The schedules change frequently and without notice. A faster, though slightly more expensive, Shuttle Isla Mujeres departs from Playa Linda Pier in Cancún's Hotel Zone several times daily. The price evens out if you have to pay for a taxi to get to Puerto Juárez. Ferries arrive at the pier in the heart of Isla Mujeres village; you can easily walk to most of the hotels from here.

COZUMEL

Mexico's largest inhabited island (48 km by 18 km or 30 miles by 11 miles), Cozumel is only 18 km (11 miles) off the mainland shore and faces the second-longest chain of coral reefs in the world. Though the island's population is about 55,000, only three percent of its land mass is developed. Dense jungle and mangrove lagoons cover most of the inland territory, a limestone shelf that supports a surprising amount of flora and fauna.

As early as AD 300, Cozumel was a Maya pilgrimage site dedicated to Ixchel, the goddess of the moon and fertility. Women arrived in bark canoes from throughout the Maya territories to honor the goddess.

Cortés landed on Cozumel in 1519, but the English buccaneer Henry Morgan became the first European inhabitant when he took up residency in the seventeenth century. Until World War II, when American military diving teams trained here, the island was home to only a few Maya fishermen. After the War, Cozumel's pristine environment attracted adventurous travelers, divers, fishermen, Jacques Cousteau and

eventually tourism on a relatively large scale. Cozumel is considered to be one of the top five dive destinations in the world, with dozens of idyllic dive spots submerged in crystalline water that rarely drops below 27°C (80°F).

Unfortunately, Cozumel has become an extremely popular port of call for **cruise ships** in the Caribbean. At least 650 ships come to call annually, disgorging thousands of passengers on the streets of the island's small town of San Miguel. The combination of large ships and fragile reefs concerns environmental groups worldwide, who staged major protests when plans for several new cruise piers were disclosed. The developers won out, however, and within the next

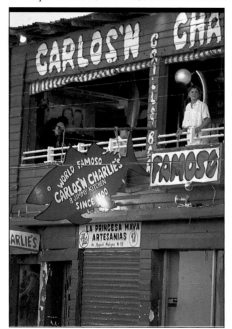

few years the island will likely have three giant piers stretching toward the reefs. Guests staying in hotels along the north and south shores can spot the ships from afar — stay out of town when they're around.

Cozumel's tourist facilities are more sophisticated than those on Isla Mujeres but still much less so than those at Cancún. Cozumel has a comfortable "lived in" feeling and soothing island pace that satisfies travelers seeking relaxation and just enough diversions to keep them happy for weeks on end. I once spent two weeks here without ever setting foot on the mainland; diving or fishing every few days, walking into town for meals and supplies, visiting with longtime islanders and

ABOVE: Diners ogle the waterfront from second-story bars across from Cozumel's *malecón*.
OPPOSITE: Nautical props line the entrance to the Museo de la Isla de Cozumel.

The Yucatán Peninsula

reading lightweight novels in a hammock beside the sea. It's a vacation I long to repeat.

GENERAL INFORMATION

The **Tourist Information Office** ((987) 20972 is located on the second floor of the Plaza del Sol on Avenida 5 facing the main plaza. There are also information booths at the ferry pier and in the airport.

WHAT TO SEE AND DO

The island's only village is **San Miguel**, where most of the shops and restaurants are located, as well as many small hotels. Unlike other Mexican Caribbean towns, San Miguel retains a traditional Mexican feeling. Locals gather under the feathery flamboyant trees surrounding Plaza Juárez, where bands often play in the white wrought iron *kiosko*, and stroll along the *malecón*, the waterfront sidewalk, running on the sea side of Avenida Rafael Melgar, the main street circling the island. Most of the shops and restaurants closest to the waterfront cater to tourists, but are above-average in quality and design. The **Museo de la Isla de Cozumel** ((987) 21434, on Avenida Rafael Melgar between Calles 4N and 6N (admission fee; open daily), is a must-see for first timers. Housed in the nineteenth-century La Playa Hotel, the museum has two floors of displays including a room of fascinating photographs, a relief map highlighting the island's natural topography, display cases filled with coral samples, and an outdoor exhibit featuring a traditional Maya house, called a *na*.

The island's 70 km (43.4 miles) of paved road can easily be explored with a rental car, moped or taxi. Traveling south from town Avenida Melgar becomes Carretera Sur, passing by several hotels, some dedicated to divers (the reefs begin south of town and diving sites are most easily accessed from here). **Parque Nacional Chankanaab** (admission fee; open daily from 8 AM to 5 PM; no phone), about 10 minutes from town, is a botanical garden and underwater reserve filled with colorful fish. In fact, the diving and snorkeling here is as good as at some of the reefs, since the fish have been protected for over a decade. It's easy to spend a full day here, wandering along pathways lined with more than 350 species of flowers, vines and trees before heading for the water. Showers, lockers and gear rental are available, and there is a very good restaurant, La Laguna, serving *ceviche*, grilled fish and sandwiches.

At Km 17.5 on the Carretera Sur, a dirt road leads east to **El Cedral**, the first Maya temple found by the Spanish invaders in 1518. The ruin is far from impressive, but the area is the center of Cozumel's small agricultural community and hosts a fiesta in early May. Another sandy road

leads west past isolated beaches (good for shelling) and a mangrove lagoon to **Punta Celarain**, where lighthouse keepers Primo and Maria Garcia live in an idyllic setting beside limestone boulders; look for the iguanas sunning themselves while facing the beach. For a small fee Primo will allow you to climb to the top of the lighthouse for a spectacular view of the island. Rumors have it that this area is slated for tourism development, *desafortunatamente* (unfortunately). At this point the road curves east along the island's southern tip to the largely isolated windward side and passes by gorgeous scenes of rough aquamarine waves crashing against gray cliffs. Several beach clubs dot the roadway and offer safe swimming in protected coves, rental beach gear, and simple cafés. Swimming in unprotected areas is not advised, as the waves and undertow are strong.

A ramshackle building on Playa Chen Río marks the site of Cozumel's **sea turtle** protection program, a largely volunteer effort aimed at protecting the endangered turtles who lay their nests on this beach in the summer months. Turtle meat and eggs have long been considered a delicacy among islanders, and it is now illegal to disturb the turtles or their nests. Guards patrol the beach in the summer months, when the Cozumel Museum sometimes offers midnight tours to the nesting sites. Few natural experiences are as moving as watching a 45-kilo (100-lb) turtle labor onto the beach and spend hours digging her nest in the sand, then laboring to discharge dozens of eggs before carefully covering and hiding the nest. The turtles shed tears during this laborious task; biologists tell me they're not actually crying, but I can't help welling up with tears myself while watching this scene under a moonlit sky.

The road does not go to the far north end of the island, but instead turns inland past Punta Morena to the ruins of **San Gervasio** (admission fee, but free on Sunday; no phone), 10 km (six miles) off the main road. Though not as impressive as the larger sites on the mainland, San Gervasio has been restored and offers an informative introduction to the Maya rituals that took place at this ceremonial center from AD 300 to 1500. Archaeologists estimate that there some 380 ruined buildings in the area, though less than a dozen have been restored. Most fascinating is **Las Manitas** (the small hands) where small handprints mark the wall. The **Estructura Los Nichos** (building of the niches) may have been a temple to the goddess Ixchel. A small **museum**, snack shop and souvenir stands mark the entrance to the ruins.

The main road becomes Carretera Norte as it turns along the waterfront north of town and

TOP: Translucent waters wash over coral outcroppings off Cozumel. BOTTOM: Once a budget travelers' haven, Playa del Carmen is now a cruise ship stopover and a major resort destination.

passes by another lineup of hotels. The beaches on this side of the island are less attractive than those to the south, but the hotels are generally less expensive and are good for families.

Scuba diving is irresistible here. Even nervous swimmers who can't imagine submerging themselves for any length of time are soon wooed by the unbridled enthusiasm of dedicated divers. A 25-km (16-mile) long chain of reefs is accessible from the island; over 230 species of fish float along the currents past brilliant purple sea sponges, waving coral fans, huge humps of brain coral and undersea caves. I call this drive-by diving, since you simply allow your body to ride the currents past mesmerizing scenes. With more than 30 dive shops to choose from, divers have unlimited opportunities. Several shops offer resort courses for non-divers that allow them to visit sites less than four-and-a-half meters (15 feet) deep. The island has two decompression chambers, and the Cozumel Association of Dive Operators oversees the operations of its member shops. Some of the established dive operations are: **Aqua Safari (** (987) 20101, FAX (987) 20661 on Avenida Rafael Melgar, between Calles 5S and 3S; **Caribbean Divers (** (987) 21080 FAX (987) 21426, Avenida Rafael Melgar at Calle 5S; **Dive House (** (987) 21953 at the Hotel Fiesta Americana The Reef on Carretera Sur; and **Dive Paradise (** (987) 21007 FAX (987) 21061, Avenida Rafael Melgar No. 601.

WHERE TO STAY

Cozumel has an excellent selection of one-of-a-kind hotels in all price ranges. Many offer dive packages, which can cut your costs considerably. Though dive boats will pick up passengers at hotels north and south of town, those planning frequent dives are best off staying toward the south, closer to the reefs. Advance reservations are strongly advised at all hotels.

Very Expensive

If I wanted to hang out for days on end in luxurious paradise, I would choose to stay at the **Presidente Inter-Continental (** (987) 20322 TOLL-FREE (800) 327-0200 FAX (987) 21360, Carretera Sur between Chankanaab and San Miguel. The best of the 253 rooms have terraces beside the sand and small *palapas* on what feels like private parts of the beach. The water here is excellent for snorkeling, thanks to the restaurant over the sea, where diners can't seem to resist dropping bits of bread into the water to feed the fish. The all-inclusive **Diamond Resort (** (987) 23443 TOLL-FREE (800) 858-2258 FAX (987) 24508, Carretera Sur Km 16.5, at Playa San Francisco, is an attractive complex of two-story, *palapa*-roofed buildings housing 300 rooms in a private complex near the best diving reefs. At the far north end of the island, the all-inclusive **Paradisus (** (987) 20411 TOLL-FREE (800) 336-3542 FAX (987) 21599, Carretera Norte Km 5.8, has 149 rooms in several buildings framing two pools and the beach.

Expensive

Divers are delighted with the facilities at the **Fiesta Americana The Reef (** (987) 22622 TOLL-FREE (800) 343-7821 FAX (987) 22666, Carretera Sur between Chankanaab and San Miguel. Though the 172 rooms are across the street from the beach, a walkway over the road leads to a great beach club and pier where boats depart for the nearby reefs. Accommodation includes several bungalows designed for divers with outside sinks and lockers for their gear. **Sol Cabañas del Caribe (** (987) 20017 or 20161 TOLL-FREE (800) 336-3542 FAX (987) 21599, Carretera Norte Km 6, Playa San Juan, is an ideal location for families. Some of the 48 rooms are located in small bungalows with double beds and fold-out couches, kitchenettes and front porches overlooking wading pools and the beach. There is an excellent windsurfing school on the premises. The **Scuba Club Dive Resort (** (987) 20663 TOLL-FREE (800) 847-5708, at Carretera Sur Km 1.5, used to be called the Galápagos Inn and is a longtime island favorite. The dive shop and restaurant are both excellent, and the 60 casual rooms face the sea, a small pool and a cluster of hammocks.

Moderate

Though the beach is across the street, the short walk is worth the low room rates at the **Fiesta Inn Cozumel (** (987) 22811 TOLL-FREE (800) 343-7821 FAX (987) 22154, Carretera Sur Km 1.7. Most of the 180 rooms face the gardens and pool. The **Playa Azul Hotel (** (987) 20199 FAX (987) 20110, Carretera Norte Km 4, has 31 rooms in older buildings by a good beach and pool.

Inexpensive

The least expensive hotels are located in **San Miguel**. The best place for divers is the **Hotel Safari Inn (** (987) 20101, with 12 rooms atop the Aqua Safari dive shop on Avenida Melgar at Calle 5S. The **Hotel Maya Cozumel (** (987) 20111, Calle 5 Sur No. 4, is close to the waterfront and has 30 rooms decorated with Maya designs. The **Hotel Mary-Carmen (** (987) 20581, Avenida 5 No. 4, is a simple 30-room inn above restaurants and shops.

WHERE TO EAT

Cozumel is blessedly free of the chain restaurants that litter Cancún's landscape. Most of the dining spots here are run by local families and expatriates in love with the island — all of whom favor character over trendiness. Most restaurants are

Cozumel's windward beaches offer long stretches of sand interspersed with rocky coves.

casual, requiring nothing more than shorts, shirts and shoes, and the majority accept credit cards.

Expensive
El Caribeño ((987) 20322, the seaside restaurant at the Hotel Presidente Inter-Continental is my favorite spot for the abundant breakfast buffet or a leisurely lunch of seafood salads and homemade breads. Lobster is the specialty at **La Cabaña del Pescador** (no phone), Carretera Norte. Diners choose their victim from a pile of lobsters on the front counter, then devour it at simple wooden tables. The same owners have a seafood restaurant next door called **El Guacamayo**. Locals have long sworn by **Pepe's Grill** ((987) 20213 on Avenida Rafael Melgar, for candlelit prime-rib and steak feasts. **Pancho's Backyard** ((987) 20170 on Avenida Rafael Melgar has a pretty courtyard setting and a menu featuring regional Mexican cuisine. Perched over the sea at the Sol Cabañas del Caribe, **Restaurante Gaviotas** ((987) 20161 is particularly magical at night, when floodlights illuminate the tropical fish in a feeding frenzy as diners drop bits of bread in the water.

Moderate
Romance and friendship seem to blossom under the trees and flowering vines at **Pizza Rolandi** ((987) 22040, Avenida Rafael Melgar No. 23. The wonderful pizzas are baked in a wood-burning oven, and there's a good selection of salads. Don't miss the coconut ice cream for dessert. **La Mission** ((987) 21641, Benito Juárez No. 23, is beloved by hardy eaters for its bountiful seafood platters and Mexican dishes. The owners have a second restaurant, **La Langosta Loca** ((987) 23518, on Avenida Salas between Calles 5 and 10. **Prima Trattoria** ((987) 24242, Avenida Rosado Salas No. 109, serves excellent homemade pasta on a rooftop terrace. **Joe's** ((987) 23275, Avenidas 10S No. 229, is as much a dance club as restaurant, where reggae and salsa bands keep the crowd dancing. Yucatecan dishes are available at **La Choza** ((987) 20958, Calle Rosado Salas No. 198.

Inexpensive
Many islanders return daily for breakfast at **Cocos Cozumel** ((987) 20241, Avenida 5S No. 180, feasting on eggs scrambled with cheese and chilis or huge homemade muffins. I typically alternate between Cocos and **Jeanie's Waffle House** ((987) 20545, Avenida Rafael Melgar No. 40, where the eggs are served with crisp waffles all day long. This is one of my favorite spots to fuel up after a dive.

HOW TO GET THERE

Several international and regional airlines have daily flights to Cozumel's international airport.

AeroCozumel and AeroCaribe ((987) 23456 in Cozumel, have several flights daily from Cancún. Ferries to Cozumel depart from Playa del Carmen on the mainland coast several times daily; the trip takes 30 to 40 minutes. Car ferries depart from Puerto Morelos south of Cancún; the schedule is erratic and you should get in line for the ferry several hours before it departs.

THE RIVIERA MAYA

In 1998, a new coalition of businesses and the government decided to change the name of the so-called Cancún–Tulum Corridor, Quintana Roo's Highway 307, running south from Cancún to the Belize border, to Riviera Maya. The road runs parallel to the coast, several kilometers inland, and almost every turnoff leads through the jungle to a magnificent beach, many of which are being developed. The day appears near when the entire Quintana Roo Coast will be endless concrete like Spain's once-lovely coast (indeed, Spanish developers are among the major investors ruining the Mexican coastline). A decade of serious development has carved the 160 km (100 miles) of coastline closest to Cancún into plantations for dozens of resorts. Some of the long-standing, most natural, hideaways have remained, but for the most part the Corridor is home to massive all-inclusive resorts hidden between the sea, lagoons and palm-peaked jungle. Playa del Carmen, the largest town between Cancún and Tulum, has become a mainstream destination in its own right, much to the horror of budget travelers who once held claim to its long strand of white sand beach. The Tulum ruins, long a magical center of Maya sea lore, have become gentrified with the addition of a massive *parador* (tourism center). Travelers who have long considered the Corridor an undiscovered paradise are appalled by the transformation. Fortunately, there are still plenty of special places to explore.

HOW TO GET THERE

Although there is good bus service up and down the corridor, a car is very useful if you want to get away from tour groups and the masses. Scores of sandy roads, some marked merely by a tire hanging on a pole, lead off Highway 307 to hidden beaches and coves. Public buses depart from the complicated terminal area in downtown Cancún; first-class express buses travel nonstop between Cancún, Puerto Morelos, Playa del Carmen and Tulum. Others buses make frequent stops at towns, villages and unmarked roads. Taxicabs ply the highway almost continuously and can be flagged down for trips down side roads.

PUERTO MORELOS

Though it's only 36 km (22.5 miles) south of Cancún, Puerto Morelos remains a small town of some 3,000 residents. It serves as the port for truck and car ferries to Cozumel and a bedroom community for Cancún's work force. Retirees have discovered the joy of small-town life on the north shores of town, and clusters of new homes (many with satellite dishes) have risen along paved and sandy streets. The center of town is a cement plaza-basketball court sandwiched between the town pier and a row of markets, shops and other businesses. Though it's not the most convenient base for day trips along the Corridor, Puerto Morelos has the singular distinction of retaining a sense of community.

WHAT TO SEE AND DO

Within town the major activities are diving, fishing, swimming, lounging and strolling around. On the highway just south of the Puerto Morelos turnoff is the **Jardín Botánico Dr. Alfredo Barrera Marin** (Dr. Alfredo Barrera Marin Botanical Garden), Highway 307 Km 38 (admission fee). This jungle of trees, shrubs and vines offers walking trails past labeled specimens; visitors are allowed to wander the trails or take a guided tour from Monday through Saturday. Horseback riding is available through **Rancho Loma Bonita (** (98) 875423 or 875465 in Cancún, on Highway 307 Km 42. The horses are well tended and the rides through jungle trails and along the beach are best in early morning or evening.

WHERE TO STAY AND EAT

My favorite place for a long-term stay is the **Caribbean Reef Club (** (987) 10191 FAX (987) 10190 TOLL-FREE (800) 322-6286 FAX (98) 832244, in Cancún. For reservations write to: Apdo 1526, Cancún, Quintana Roo 77500, Mexico. It is located south of the ferry dock and has 21 moderately-priced rooms. Apartment-style suites with kitchens and balconies face a flower-framed swimming pool, white beach and endless sea splashing over small reefs. The restaurant is the best in town, thanks to the talents of a Caribbean chef and the comforts of an airy dining room and seaside deck. Dive and fishing trips are easily arranged.

   Rancho Libertad ((987) 10181 and (719) 685-1254 TOLL-FREE (888) 305-5225, has 13 moderately-priced rooms and is located south of the town center past the ferry pier. It is similar to the Reef Club in its hideaway ambiance, but the emphasis is more nature-oriented. The beds are swinging mattresses hanging beside ceiling fans in airy

rooms with private bathrooms and purified water dispensers. The hotel is sometimes booked by yoga, meditation and other special-interest groups, who gather on the soft sand under a giant *palapa*. Dive and snorkel trips are available.

   Budget travelers have long extolled the cheap comforts at the 19-room **Posada Amor (** (987) 10033 FAX (987) 10178, just one block from the beach and town plaza, on Calle Javier Rojo Gómez. The basic rooms have cement slab beds with thin mattresses; some have private baths. The restaurant serves inexpensive, decent Mexican and American food with few frills and is a gathering spot for tourists and local families.

   The 36-room **Maroma (** (987) 44729 FAX (98) 842115 in Cancún, 24 km south of Puerto Morelos off Highway 307, is so exclusive you must have advance reservations to even enter the property or dine at the superb restaurant. The architecture, setting, comfort level and cuisine have all garnered rave reviews in stylish magazines.

Punta Bete

One of the few longtime hideaways is **La Posada del Capitán Lafitte** (no phone) reservations in the United States **(** (303) 674-9615 TOLL-FREE (800) 538-6802 FAX (303) 674-8735 or write: Turquoise Reef Resorts, PO Box 2664, Evergreen, CO 80439. It is located two kilometers (just over a mile) off Highway 307. It has 43 moderately-priced rooms and has survived numerous hurricanes and more than a decade of tourism fluctuations. The simple stucco rooms are booked solid over holidays, and many of the guests return annually for their dose of coastal camaraderie. The pool, restaurant, dive shop and long stretches of natural beach all encourage guests to abandon outside excursions. The Turquoise Reef Group, which manages Lafitte, once had the most magical campground on the coast, called Kailuum. The "camptel" had a cluster of rooms with *palapas* topping waterproof tents housing beds, tables and lamps, with hammocks hanging outside. It was destroyed by Hurricane Roxanne in 1995, but rumors of its reappearance elsewhere on the coast abound.

Shangri-La and Las Palapas

Shangri-la Caribe (no phone) on Highway 307 Km 56 is another good choice. For reservations in the United States: Turquoise Reef Resorts **(** (303) 674-9615 TOLL-FREE (800) 538-6802 FAX (303) 674-8735, PO Box 2664, Evergreen, CO 80439. The hotel is made up of two-story stucco buildings with thatch roofs; hammocks hang outside each of the 70 rooms. The restaurant serves three meals a day, and the pool is as popular as the perfect beach. Similar in architecture and ambiance is **Las Palapas (** (987) 30584 TOLL-FREE (800) 467-5292 FAX (987) 30458, Highway 307 Km 58, with 55 bungalows. Both offer water sports, fishing and other activities.

PLAYA DEL CARMEN

What a difference a decade makes! Seasoned fans of the Mexican Caribbean remember **Playa del Carmen** as a laid-back town with a wide range of services — gas, auto parts stores, groceries, banks and the ferry to Cozumel — and row upon row of inexpensive accommodations on the most beautiful beach north of Tulum. Imagine their surprise when they found a mini-city of 40,000 residents, a golf course, a massive mega-resort development right next door, and startlingly expensive hotel rooms. Playa del Carmen, just 60 km (37 miles) south of Cancún on Highway 307,

WHAT TO SEE AND DO

The **beach** here is among the best on the Yucatán Peninsula and far superior to Cancún's. Protected by Cozumel island, the shore is good for swimming, body surfing, sunbathing and snorkeling. Diving and sport fishing are both excellent here, and can be booked through most hotels. Tours and public buses to the ruins at Tulum and Chichén Itzá are readily available. The shopping is far superior to that in Cancún, with trendy boutiques featuring quality folk art, handcrafted jewelry, Guatemalan and Balinese clothing, and unusual twists on typical souvenirs. At the **Plaza Rincón**

is now the business and tourism center for the booming Riviera Maya, and its infrastructure can't keep up. Though new sewage lines and streets have been constructed in the past few years, traffic through town is horribly congested. Even the pedestrian walkway past Playa del Carmen's most popular restaurants and shops gets clogged with foot traffic. Cruise ships disgorge hundreds of lookie-loos onto Playa's main pier almost daily, which hasn't discouraged the hundreds more individual travelers who are content to lounge on her shores. Though there are dozens of hotels in town (and more constantly under construction), Playa is often booked solid, especially during holidays and in August when European and Mexican tourists arrive in hordes.

Coastal cities on the Caribbean and Pacific coasts have become havens for cruise ships and and their seething cargoes.

del Sol on Avenida 5N at Calle 8, check out the amber jewelry and wooden masks displayed at **Xop**, and the handmade paper and CD selection at **El Vuelo de los Niños Pájaros**. **Temptations** on Avenida 5N between Calles 6 and 8 has outlasted other boutiques featuring imported tropical sarongs and dresses. **La Calaca**, also on Avenida 5N, has the best overall collection of Mexican folk art.

WHERE TO STAY

The selection of one-of-a-kind hotels in Playa is truly astonishing. The best places for moderate to very expensive rooms are right on the beach, though several gems are tucked along side streets. Noise can be a problem in rooms close to the pedestrian walkway on Avenida 5N. Advance reservations are advised year-round.

Very Expensive

The all-inclusive **Diamond Resort** ((987) 30339 TOLL-FREE (800) 642-1600 FAX (987) 30348 is located deep within the Playacar development and is designed to encourage guests to remain on the grounds. The 300 rooms are quite comfortable and spacious for an all-inclusive tariff, and have television, ceiling fan and air-conditioning. Meals and many activities are included.

Expensive

The peaceful Mediterranean-style setting of the **Hotel Mosquito Blue** ((987) 31245 FAX (987) 31337 E-MAIL mosquito@www.pya.com.mx, on Avenida 5 between Calles 12 and 14, is unusual for Playa. The 24 rooms and suites have French doors, king-sized beds, air-conditioning and satellite television; the pool is framed by lawns, and a second-story lounge has videos on wide-screen television.

The first big hotel in Playa was the **Continental Plaza Playacar** ((987) 30100 TOLL-FREE (800) 882-6684 FAX (987) 30105 on Calle 10 at the entrance to Playacar. Similar to a Cancún establishment, the hotel has 188 rooms, several restaurants and bars, a huge pool and a watersports center. Large groups are often booked here.

Moderate

The majority of Playa's small hotels are in the moderate price range and, though longtimers are appalled at the increased rates, you can still get much more for your peso here than in Cancún. I'm particularly fond of the 31 white-on-white rooms and balcony hammocks at the **Albatros Royale** ((987) 30001 TOLL-FREE (800) 538-6802 FAX (987) 30002, on Calle 8 facing the beach. Similar in style and handled by the same reservation numbers is the **Pelicano Inn** at the end of Calle 6 on the beach.

Chichén Baal Kah ((987) 31252 FAX (987) 30050, for reservations contact Turquoise Reef Resorts ((303) 674-9615 TOLL-FREE (800) 538-6802 FAX (303) 674-8735, PO Box 2664, Evergreen, CO 80439, on Calle 16 at Avenida 4, is an adults-only complex with seven units all with bedrooms, kitchenettes and living rooms, and a pool. If I were to gather a group of friends for a vacation I'd reserve all five rooms at the **Hotel Baal Nah Kah** ((987) 30110 FAX (987) 30050, on Calle 12 between Avenida 5 and Avenida 1. This former home has a gigantic communal kitchen and living room, and plenty of restaurants nearby. One of the oldest gathering spots in Playa, the **Blue Parrot Inn** ((987) 30083 TOLL-FREE (800) 634-3547 FAX (987) 30049 (or contact ((904) 775-6660 FAX (904) 775-1869, 635 West Wisconsin Avenue, Orange City, FL 32763) is on Calle 12 at Avenida 5. It offers 45 rooms of varying sizes clustered along the beach and gardens. **Condotel el Tucan** ((987) 30417 TOLL-FREE (800) 467-5292 FAX (987) 30668, on Avenida 5 between

Calles 14 and 16, is a newer favorite with 67 units with kitchenettes and large balconies. Though a few blocks from the beach, this hotel has a large pool, peaceful gardens and a good restaurant.

Inexpensive

The **Hotel Alejari** ((987) 30374 FAX (987) 30005, on Calle 6 a half-block from the beach, has managed to keep its rates low while offering 29 rooms, some with air-conditioning and kitchenettes, in a lovely garden setting. Rock bottom prices and a friendly proprietor bring guests back time and again to **Posada Rosa Mirador** (no phone), on Calle 12. The nine basic rooms all have bathrooms; some have ocean views. **Mom's Hotel** ((987) 30315, on Avenida 30, is six blocks from the beach but has a small pool, a good restaurant and 12 basic rooms.

WHERE TO EAT

As Carmen is a tourist beach town, there are plenty of good restaurants at reasonable prices, most offering a fair variety of seafood and local dishes, as well as some international fare. The majority are in a string along Avenida 5N paralleling the beach, with a few good spots on the sand and up inland streets.

Moderate

Raising the standards for Playa restaurants, **Da Gabi** ((987) 30048, on Calle 12, is an excellent, serene Italian restaurant serving gourmet pizzas, fettucini with mussels, steaks, and imported wines. Playa's original Italian eatery, still a local favorite, is **Máscaras** ((987) 62624, on Avenida Juárez by the town plaza and pier. The outdoor tables are especially nice and a good spot for munching on fried calamari with a glass of Chianti. **La Parrilla** ((987) 30687 in the Plaza Rincón del Sol on Avenida 5, is the most popular spot for Mexican dishes, grilled meats and margaritas overlooking the pedestrian walkway. **Ronny's** ((987) 30996 in the Pelicano Inn at the beach, is the best spot for thick, juicy burgers and steaks.

Inexpensive

Healthy sandwiches, salads and decadent desserts are the draw at **Sabor** on Avenida 5. **El Chino** on Calle 4 between Avenidas 10 and 15 is my favorite place to escape the tourist crowds and dine on typical home cooking with local families.

FURTHER ALONG HIGHWAY 307

XCARET

I must admit to having felt utter horror when my favorite hidden cove complete with Maya ruins was turned into a tourist attraction in the mid-

1990s. The developer, who aimed to create "nature's secret park," used bulldozers, earth movers and hundreds of laborers to shape the jungle, limestone shelf, lagoons and cove into a gorgeously landscaped amusement park called **Xcaret** ((98) 830654 at Km 72 on Highway 307 (admission fee; open daily). The cove we used to snorkel in all alone has been enlarged and framed with a man-made beach, and tropical fish have begun to return close to shore. The *cenote* (underground well or sinkhole) and its adjoining caves were blasted into an underground river ride, where swimmers float in the cool water through dark underground tunnels. An aviary shelters tropical birds (this is the only place you're still guaranteed to spot parrots or macaws on the Yucatán Peninsula), and several small Maya ruins on the property have been restored. Maya culture is reenacted in a mesmerizing show called "Xcaret Nights," and several restaurants serve decent seafood and Mexican dishes. Day trippers from Cancún and Cozumel tend to rave about their time here; if you spring the big bucks for admission, plan to spend the whole day and half the night.

PUERTO AVENTURAS

A mega-resort with several hotels, condo complexes, a large marina and a nine-hole golf course, **Puerto Aventuras** ((987) 35110 FAX (987) 35182, off Highway 307 at Km 98, is worth visiting for a few hours. It is home to the **Museo Pablo Bush Romero** (no phone), devoted to the history of scuba diving in the area. **Mike Madden's CEDAM Dive Center** ((987) 22233 FAX (987) 41339 is one of the most renowned dive operations and is one of the best operators taking experienced divers to the *cenotes* and underground caverns buried in the jungle.

The restaurant **Papaya Republic** ((987) 35170 is set away from the resort complex on its own sheltered cove. I stop by for a meal or drink every time I'm in the area, and am always pleased that the peaceful setting with tables under a *palapa* and palms and innovative cuisine have withstood the intrusions of nearby development.

AKUMAL

An older cluster of hotels that have multiplied around a small beach village, Akumal has one of the coast's largest bays and was the site of early reef diving expeditions for shipwrecks. The largest resort in the area is **Hotel Club Akumal Caribe** ((987) 59012 FAX (987) 59019 (or contact Akutrame ((915) 584-3552 TOLL-FREE (800) 351-1622 FAX (915) 581-6709, PO Box 13326, El Paso, TX 79913) with villas, beach bungalows and a small hotel. All services — restaurants, water sports, diving and gift shops — are available in a low-key setting.

PAAMUL

The next sheltered bay with a good beach along the corridor is Paamul, 85 km (53 miles) south of Cancún. The lagoons are like salt water aquariums and the dirt access road and lack of public transport to the site have held development and tour groups at bay. **Cabañas Paamul** ((987) 62691 FAX (987) 43240, Highway 307 at Km 85, is the largest business, with seven bungalows on the sand, a campground and RV park, a great restaurant and full dive shop.

XEL-HÁ

Xel-Há, an important cult center in pre-Columbian times, is now known for its huge coral- and fish-filled lagoon. Snorkeling and swimming are permitted in this protected underwater preserve (admission fee; open daily from 8 AM to 5 PM). One need not get wet to enjoy the fish here, as they can be seen from the surface through the clear water. To appreciate the site fully, in or out of the water, visit early in the morning before others have time to stir up the sediment. The developers of Xcaret have taken over management of the park, and have plans for expanded facilities and diversions.

There are restaurants, shops and snorkeling equipment rental facilities at the park, and a hotel nearby.

TULUM

In his logs, Juan de Grijalva, a Spanish explorer who sailed from Cuba to the Yucatán Peninsula in 1518, mentions a town "as large as Seville," with a tower taller than he had ever seen. The site was probably Tulum, 220 km (135 miles) south of Cancún on Route 307, and the tower must have been El Castillo, the principal building on the site (admission fee, but free on Sunday; open daily from 9 AM to 5 PM).

Tulum, then called Zamá, is thought to have been an important trading center that flourished between 1200 and 1400. However, earlier dates have been found on *stelae*. It was the arrival of traders from all part of Mexico that accounts for the mixture of architectural styles found at the site. Here the Mayan vault is combined with flat roofs, and the small sanctuary and stucco sculptures with pillared porticoes faced with stucco in the Toltec style.

The town was probably fortified, as it is surrounded on three sides by a four-meter (13-ft) high wall that originally had a walkway on top. The fourth side is protected by the sea. The dominant structure, **El Castillo**, has a frieze whose three niches are occupied by stucco figures, the central one, the Descending God, appears in several places at the site. The castle was most likely a temple to Kukulcán, the feathered serpent deity brought to the Mayas by the Toltecs.

The Temple of the Frescoes, a two-story building fronted by four columns, contains some relatively well-preserved frescoes of Mayan deities.

The beach below the site is good for swimming (when the surf is not too high), and it is frequently deserted in spite of the numerous tour buses that arrive daily. The entrance to the ruins was moved a few yards away from the site and is now housed in a formal tourism center with all services.

Where to Stay

The beach south of Tulum ruins is dotted with small campgrounds and bungalow hotels, and has become one of the last places on the coast where you can hang out on the beach, sleep and eat relatively inexpensively. The best of the lot is **Cabañas Ana y José (** (987) 12004 FAX (987) 12004 or in Cancún **(** (98) 806022 and (98) 806021 E-MAIL anayjose@cancun.rce.com.mx, located about seven kilometers (3.5 miles) south of the Tulum ruins, with 16 rooms in two-story buildings, most facing the beach. The owners have two other properties in the area which can be booked through the same numbers listed above.

SIAN KA'AN BIOSPHERE PRESERVE

South from Tulum a partially paved road continues along the coast past more white sand beaches and a few primitive *cabañas* frequented by budget travelers, continuing on to the Boca Paila Peninsula and the Sian Ka'an Biosphere Preserve. The preserve encompasses the largest swath of beach, jungle and lagoons free of development along the coast. The Maya built a system of canals through the dense growth hundreds of years ago; travelers can arrange to ride boats through the canals past several small Maya temples; birdwatchers are particularly enthralled with the trip. For tours contact **Amigos de Sian Ka'an (** (98) 84983 FAX (98) 873080 in Cancún. The road ends at Punta Allen, at the mouth of Bahía de la Ascensión. There are a few fishing lodges specializing in bone and tarpon fishing in the saltwater flats; try the **Boca Paila Fishing Lodge** (no phone), Boca Paila Road, about 27 kilometers (17 miles) south of Tulum. For reservations contact **Frontiers International Travel** TOLL-FREE (800) 245-1950 FAX (412) 935-5388, PO Box 859, Wexford, PA 15090-0959.

COBÁ

Five lakes buried in the jungle surely attracted the Maya to create what may have been the largest city state on the peninsula during the post-Classic period. Archaeologists estimate some

50,000 people lived in this area somewhere between AD 400 and 1100 and that they built some 6,000 structures, most of which are now buried by the jungle.

The site was Cobá (admission fee, but free on Sunday; open daily from 9 AM to 5 PM), 39 km (24 miles) inland from Tulum. A causeway or *sacbe* (a paved, limestone road that was up to 10 m or 33 ft wide) extended from here almost to Chichén Itzá, and to Yazuna some 100 km (62 miles) away. What's more, there were 16 such roads crossing the Yucatán from Cobá. In their haste to eliminate all traces of the Maya culture and religion, the Spanish destroyed the Monjas, one of the most sacred buildings in the area, but Cobá is still a delight to visit. It has a wealth of *stelae*, two pyramids from which one looks far out over the jungle canopy, and very few tour buses. Unlike Chichén Itzá and Tulum, the buildings have not been reclaimed from the forest and visitors often have the opportunity to wander the trails past wild pigs and iguanas with nary another human in sight.

There are four main groupings of structures here: the Cobá Group, located near the entrance; Las Pinturas, named because of the pigment still visible on some of the friezes; the Macanxoc Group, located next to the lake of the same name; and the Chumuc Nul Group, the main structure of which is the "stucco pyramid" which still retains some of its original color. Towering above the treetops is the Nohuch Mul Pyramid, which with its 120 steps is the tallest in the Yucatán.

One needs walking shoes, mosquito repellent, refreshments and a vivid imagination to enjoy Cobá fully. English- and Spanish-speaking guides are usually available to explain the many different *stelae*, some of the best preserved in Mexico.

Less than a kilometer (around half a mile) west of the ruins and a short distance from the parking lot is the **Villa Arqueológica Cobá** (no phone). For reservations contact **(** (5) 2033086 in Mexico City or TOLL-FREE (800) CLUB-MED. It offers 40 small but comfortable rooms, an excellent restaurant and a pool. Closer to the town center and bus stop is **El Bocadito** (no phone). Theis restaurant serves well-prepared and copious Mexican food; from its tables one can watch the comings and goings of the town's inhabitants, who seem little affected by the tourists.

LAGUNA BACALAR

South of Tulum, Highway 307 travels past small villages and the town of Felipe Carrillo Puerto before reaching one of the peninsula's most spectacular natural sights, **Laguna Bacalar**, "the lagoon of seven colors," 36 km (22 miles) north of Chetumal and the border with Belize. The second largest lake in Mexico, Bacalar is 50 km (30 mile) long. Its color varies from navy blue to electric turquoise due to the mixing of fresh and saltwater. The lake is a popular vacation spot for residents of the peninsula, and their vacation homes line its shores. Laguna Bacalar is a good base for exploring the ruins and beaches in the area, and it is far calmer than Chetumal.

The best accommodation is at **Rancho Encantado** ((983) 80427 TOLL-FREE (800) 505-6292 FAX (983) 80427. For reservations in the United States ((505) 776-5878, FAX (505) 776-2102 PO Box 1256, Taos, NM 87571. It's located at Highway 307 Km 340, just north of the town of Bacalar, and has 12 *casitas* spread over emerald green lawns facing the lake. The restaurant here is very good,

and this is the best place to set up nature and archaeological tours in the area.

XCALAK PENINSULA

If you're looking for the Caribbean Coast of old, turn off Highway 307 at the side road to Majahual and the wild, largely undeveloped Xcalak Peninsula. But hurry! The government started paving this road in 1998, which should cut down the driving time, but it will inevitably increase tourism considerably. The fishing village of Xcalak sits at the end of the thin 64-km (40-mile) long peninsula. The biggest attraction here is the accessibility of the famed **Chinchorro Banks**, 29 km (18 miles) east of Xcalak. Divers are attracted to the 40-km (24-mile) long partially submerged reef for the dozens of shipwrecks that litter the sea nearby; pirate galleons are said to have crashed

here frequently leaving treasures at the bottom of the sea. The reef has been declared a national underwater park and it is illegal to take anything from the wrecks. A few small, rustic hotels line the southern tip of the peninsula and offer trips to the reef, but their boats are often unreliable. Far better is the operation at **Costa de Cocos**, 56 km (35 miles) south of Majahual. For reservations contact **Turquoise Reef Group** ((303) 674-9615 TOLL-FREE (800) 538-6802 FAX (303) 674-8735 PO Box 2664, Evergreen, CO 80439. Maria and Dave Randall, who have been in Xcalak for nearly a decade, have created an idyllic hideaway with 12 bungalows built of hardwoods imported from Belize. Meals are served under a large *palapa* on the sand, and swimming, snorkeling and diving are all excellent just offshore. The Randalls have helped develop wind-generated power for the resort and town, which still lacks telephones, reliable electricity and other modern comforts. It's the ideal destination for those who prefer isolation and the pleasures of wandering an empty beach or reading in a hammock under the palms with hardly a distraction.

CHETUMAL AND ONWARD

Chetumal, Quintana Roo's capital, is one of the country's most remote cities. Until the 1960s there were no well-paved roads to the city, which has a population of more than 50,000. The city cannot be termed a tourist destination, but it is unique. Cut off from the rest of the country, it developed without heavy Spanish and religious influences. Some claim it was a haven for outlaws and smugglers who insisted that individual privacy and property were to be respected at all cost. We are not certain whether this is true or not, but we can attest to the fact that theft is (or was until recently) almost unheard of.

On our first visit to Chetumal 15 years ago we carefully locked the car, only to notice that the windows of all the local vehicles were wide open and packages lay within easy reach on the seats. A local explained there was never a problem. A seasoned traveler who has spent many months in the area also told us the story of two Americans who left their backpacks unattended for three hours at the bus station with a camera sitting atop one. All was still there when they returned.

We would never recommend that one be this inattentive — even in Chetumal — but the stories do reflect the relaxed, friendly and calm atmosphere of the city.

Chetumal is not on the ocean and, without a car, the only thing to do here is shop and wander the waterfront *malecón*.

The population is primarily Maya, but each day hundreds of Belizians come from south of the border to shop for food, clothing and luxury items which are far more expensive or unavailable at home. Thus, it is not only the city's architecture — a mixture of modern concrete and clapboard — that makes it so different, but also the street life and language. It as almost as common to hear Creole, English, or Mayan as it is Spanish.

Belize (the former British Honduras) is just across the border and even more relaxed than Chetumal. Getting there is not a easy undertaking. It is generally impossible to enter Belize with a Mexican rental car. With a personal vehicle, extra insurance and patience at the border are essential. By bus it will take a good two hours to pass the two border control stations. A passport and visa (which can be obtained at the Belizian border) are required. On reentry one may have to reapply for the Mexican tourist visa.

This is not to discourage travel to Belize, but to make travelers aware that they cannot just hop down to Belize for a couple of hours. Time has little meaning in Belize and a couple of hours can easily turn into a full day. One would be well advised to plan Belize as a separate destination of several days or a week (we once spent three months there and it wasn't enough). It is as different from Mexico as France is from England.

It is also possible to continue through Belize to Guatemala. But beyond visiting the Mayan wonderland at Tikal, we do not recommend it. The deadly human rights record of Guatemala's United States-backed military dictatorship includes the murder of a fair number of tourists as well as 100,000 of their own citizens.

WHERE TO STAY AND EAT

Chetumal's most luxurious hotel is the **Hotel Continental Caribe (** (983) 21100, Avenida de los Héroes No. 171. It has 64 rooms and is moderately priced. **Hotel Los Cocos (** (983) 20544 FAX (983) 20920, Héroes No. 138, at Calle Chapultepec, has 60 rooms and is older and a bit musty, but serviceable.

Many small restaurants are scattered throughout the shopping areas. **Sergio's (** (983) 22355, Avenida Obregón No. 182, priced between moderate and inexpensive, has steaks, pizza and spaghetti, and is a favorite of those who travel from more isolated areas and long for a change in diet. **Emiliano's (** (983) 70267, Avenida San Salvador No. 557, is a large seafood restaurant serving outstanding seafood cocktails and platters of grilled lobster, shrimp and fish.

AROUND CHETUMAL

Outside Chetumal, it is easy to find things to do, but you will need a car.

Just before Laguna Bacalar, off Highway 307, is **Cenote Azul**, estimated to be 90 m (300 ft) deep.

Swimming here, or in any of the other Mayan *cenotes* is a memorable experience. Fourteen kilometers (nine miles) west of town is **Laguna Milagro**, smaller than Bacalar but charming just the same, particularly during the week when it is nearly deserted.

Maya ruins, some partially excavated and some still buried in jungle, dot the area between Chetumal and Campeche. Seventy kilometers (45 miles) east of Chetumal are the ruins of **Kohunlich** with their unmistakable masks of the sun god. Farther along Highway 186 are **Xpujil**, **Becán**, **Río Bec** and **Chicanná** in the Calakmul Biosphere Reserve. It has been difficult to visit this area because of its lack of facilities. But in 1995 a

new lodge opened near Chicanná. The **Chicanná Ecovillage Resort (** (981) 62233 in Campeche, is a delight, with 100 rooms spread through the jungle in one- and two-story buildings.

A weathered façade OPPOSITE and a sweet face ABOVE of the Yucatán.

Gulf
Coast

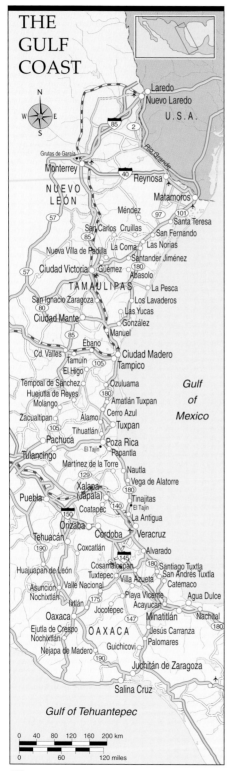

THE GULF COAST

THE GULF COAST HAS BEEN, for better or worse, Mexico's lifeline with the Old World. After various landings in the Yucatán, the Spaniards determined that the Gulf Coast was to be their entry point into the rich lands of Mexico. Veracruz became Cortés' first permanent settlement in New Spain, and the port from which Mexico's countless riches flowed to the Old World. Ironically, it was also the last city in which the Spanish flag flew before Mexican independence. British, United States and French troops have also tried to enter and control Mexico through the Gulf Coast.

Today the Gulf Coast remains a major shipping center for oil and agricultural and manufactured goods. It is not a major tourist destination but it does have palm-lined beaches, lush vegetated hillsides and some of the oldest pre-Columbian ruins in Mexico. Although the northern state of Tamaulipas, with its border towns and oil refineries, is less interesting than the south, this is the gateway to Mexico and thus the starting point for road trips from the United States.

THE BORDER TOWNS

Nuevo Laredo, Reynosa and Matamoros, in the state of Tamaulipas, are typical border towns. Trinket stands and money changing stalls line the roads at the southern ends of the bridges that cross the Río Grande or, as the Mexicans call the river, Río Bravo.

NUEVO LAREDO

Nuevo Laredo, the northernmost and smallest (population 300,000), had its heyday during United States prohibition, and today its major attraction is shopping for Mexican souvenirs by those who make a day excursion across the United States border. Although the street vendors along Avenida Guerrero, stretching south from the international border, specialize in rather tacky trinkets, good quality handicrafts can also be found, especially if you wander a bit east or west of the beaten track.

The **Tourist Information Office** ((87) 120104 is located at Guerrero near Puente Internacional; open daily from 8:30 AM to 8 PM.

Where to Stay

The inexpensive **Hotel Restaurant Reforma** ((87) 126250 FAX (87) 126714, Avenida Guerrero No. 822, with 38 rooms, is near the town center and popular with locals for the large fixed-price midday meal. It has a parking lot, which is a plus; rooms have televisions and telephones. The quiet and unpretentious **Hotel Posada Mina** ((87) 131473, Calle Mina No. 35, offering five rooms, is a tiny hotel with a small coffee shop. Rooms are small but have both air-conditioning and heat in addition to televisions.

Where to Eat

In addition to the Hotel Restaurant Reforma, mentioned above, is **The Winery** ((87) 120895, Matamoros No. 308 at Victoria. A large selection of Mexican wines is offered, along with the region's famous *carne tampiqueña*, which is a thin, marinated steak grilled with onions and peppers and served with rice, beans and tortillas.

REYNOSA

Reynosa, only a little larger than Nuevo Laredo, is an oil and gas town. It lies just across the border from McAllen, Texas, and is therefore a departure point for those traveling south to Monterrey or central Mexico, including Mexico City. While the downtown area has been improved by urban renewal projects, industrial installations dominate the area and there is no reason to stop long here. If you must have some souvenirs, Hidalgo Street is a pedestrian walkway radiating from the central square; here you will find many souvenir shops and itinerant vendors.

General Information

The **Tourist Office** ((89) 221189 is located at the international border crossing bridge and is open Monday through Friday from 8 AM to 8 PM.

Where to Stay

The newish **Hotel Hacienda** ((89) 246010 FAX (89) 235962, Boulevard Hidalgo No. 2013, has 34 moderately-priced units and is located just outside of town on the highway to Monterrey. It has lots of nice features, such as parking lot, car rental counter, restaurant/bar and direct-dial telephones. Rooms are clean, with cable television and pleasant furnishings. The **Hotel Nuevo León** ((89) 221310, Porfirio Díaz No. 580, is a converted ranch house with large yet not spotless rooms with private bath.

Where to Eat

In addition to the restaurant at the Hotel Hacienda, you can dine at the **Hotel San Carlos** ((89) 221280 Hidalgo No. 970, near the center of town, or **La Mojada** (no phone) Avenida Miguel Alemán s/n, which is a simple eatery specializing in roast goat. The **Café Paris** ((89) 225535, Hidalgo No. 815, is popular with both locals and visitors, especially at the fixed-price midday meal.

MATAMOROS

The largest of the three Mexican border towns, Matamoros (population 450,000) has the cleanest image; it competes with its Texan counterpart, Brownsville, for shoppers. Its main street, Avenida Alvaro Obregón, has had a facelift and is now home to some of the city's better restaurants and shops.

Still, a border town is a border town, and the more interesting sites are further south.

South of Matamoros, Highway 180 is sometimes in need of repairs and often floods during the June-through-November hurricane season. The road lies inland, bypassing the coastline, which has intermittent stretches of undeveloped beaches and numerous coastal lagoons. At La Comma the road splits, with Route 101 heading inland to the state's capital, Ciudad Victoria, and Highway 180 continuing south to Tampico.

General Information

Information is available at the **Tourist Office** ((88) 139045, Avenida Hidalgo No. 50, between Calles 5 and 6. It is open Monday through Friday from 9 AM to 1 PM and from 3 PM to 7 PM.

Where to Stay and Eat

Recommended for their moderately-priced accommodation as well as their restaurants, and representing some of the most respectable nightlife in town, are **Garcia's** ((88) 123929 or 131833, Calle Alvaro Obregón s/n, and **Gran Hotel Residencial** ((88) 139440, Calle Alvaro Obregón at Amapolas. The latter has a pretty garden with a pool and playground.

TAMPICO, MEXICO'S OIL CAPITAL

Tamaulipas' largest city, Tampico (population 600,000), is a mass of refineries, container docks oil tanks, and other port facilities sprawling from its very small old town. Located at the mouth of Río Pánuco (now polluted from the massive oil tankers stationed there), the city is nonetheless surrounded by lagoons and some decent beaches. The weather can be hot (36°C or 97°F) and humid, especially April through September, when hurricane season begins, usually lasting through the months of September and October. Gusty winds called *nortes* cool things off between November and March; while a blessing on hot days, they also send dust and sand blowing through the air.

The prehistory of the area, like that of the rest of Tamaulipas, is only now beginning to come to light. It appears that Tampico was settled about 1,000 BC by Huastecs, a tribe skilled in pottery-making. Nomadic, these tribes left little permanent mark on the landscape. The best archaeology finds are at **El Tamuín** 104 km (65 miles) west on Highway 110. The most famous Huastec sculpture, the statue of a youth with the symbols of the wind god, was taken from El Tamuín and is now in the National Museum of Anthropology in Mexico City. A copy can be seen in the **Museo Huasteca** located on Primero de Mayo (free admission; open Monday through Friday from 10 AM to 5 PM and Saturday from 10 AM to 3 PM) in Tampico's satellite town, **Ciudad Madero**. The museum has collections of artifacts that date from 1100 BC to AD 1500 and an extensive display of ancient arrowheads.

By the fifteenth century, the Huastecs were under Aztec rule; the city of Tampico was founded in 1534 on Aztec ruins. In the early years, it suffered frequent attacks by Apache Indians from Texas and pirates from the Caribbean. In the early seventeenth century Tampico was completely destroyed by pirates, not to be rebuilt until some 150 years later. Still later in its development, it was taken over by American and British oil men, becoming a typically tough petro-town. Somehow out of it all, the downtown around the Zócalo, **Plaza de Armas** with its **Catedral** and graceful **Palacio Municipal**, has maintained some of its colonial flavor. With oil pollution now under control, the nearby beaches are undeveloped and relatively clean, offering long stretches of pale sand and beautiful views from the cliffs above **Playa Escollera**, near the southeast end of the city. Some hotels along the beach rent towels and use of showers, as well as umbrella-shaded tables and chairs, from which you can order drinks and food.

WHERE TO STAY

Accommodation is utilitarian, catering to business travelers more than to tourists seeking luxurious beachside accommodation.

Moderate

Hotel Camino Real ((12) 138811 FAX (12) 139226, Avenida Hidalgo No. 2000, while not part of the Camino Real chain that stretches throughout Mexico, is one of the best hotels to be found in Tampico. Its 100 comfortable rooms are set in nicely landscaped gardens and have amenities such as direct-dial telephone and satellite television. There is a pool, restaurant and travel agency. The **Howard Johnson Tampico (** (12) 127676 TOLL-FREE (800) 654-2000 FAX (12) 120653, Calle Madera No. 210, is the reincarnation of the Colonial Hotel, which was thoroughly redecorated when it changed ownership. Amenities such as a restaurant/bar, travel agency and free parking make it very attractive for the low price. It is located just a few blocks southeast of the town's main plaza. There are 138 rooms. If the latter is full, the **Hotel Plaza (** (12) 141678, Calle Madero Oriente No. 204, with 40 rooms is just down the street.

WHERE TO EAT

Although Tampico is not known for its restaurants, there are several that serve decent seafood and Mexican specialties, including its namesake steak — *carne asada tampiqueña* — a delicious thin cut of beef marinated in oil, herbs and vinegar, grilled over an open flame, and often served with rice,

beans, guacamole and tortillas. Try the restaurants listed below in addition to the somewhat pricier ones at the hotels recommended above.

Inexpensive

Refresquería Elite ((12) 120364, Díaz Mirón Oriente No. 211, is a favorite among locals, who come in for a coffee and a chat or a refreshing dish of ice cream. Otherwise, the food is good, standard regional fare. **Restaurant Emi (** (12) 125139, Calle Olmos No. 207, offers huge portions of tasty seafood and meats at reasonable prices, and is open from dawn to well beyond dusk.

VERACRUZ

The state of Veracruz, with the rugged Sierra Madre Oriental and Gulf beaches, has long been an important center of culture and commerce. It was the homeland of the Olmec civilization (1200 BC

to 400 BC), which was more advanced than its contemporaries in Europe and the Middle East. Little is known about the Olmecs themselves, who founded the earliest advanced culture in Meso-America, and what is known about the culture comes from sites in Veracruz, Tabasco and Oaxaca.

After the Olmecs came the Huastecs and Totonacs, who were eventually conquered by the Aztecs. Then in the sixteenth century came the Spaniards. In 1519 Cortés landed near the present-day city of Veracruz and the Spanish Conquest began. Its ports were the most important during the colonial period, and the untold wealth that passed through them made them prime targets for daring Caribbean pirates. Today Veracruz has a mixed agricultural and industrial economy, and is one of Mexico's richest states. Veracruz has several important archaeological sites, including El Tajín. The latest discovery is El Pital, buried under forest vegetation just 98 km (60 miles) northwest

of Veracruz city. El Pital is believed to have been one of the largest seaports and a key trade center at least 1,500 years ago. The site is not yet open to the public, but archaeologists are working on it. Information can be obtained by writing E-MAIL mayaland @diario1.sureste.com.

EL TAJÍN

Located about 15 minutes from Papantla by car, 250 km (155 miles) south of Tampico and 260 km (160 miles) north of Veracruz, El Tajín ("lightning" in the Totonac language) is one of the most important archaeological sites in Mexico. It was so well hidden by jungle growth that no outsider knew of its existence until the end of the eighteenth century, and archaeologists are still excavating its extensive remains.

Old Veracruz was once Mexico's major link to Spain, and retains the flavor of its Colonial past.

Although originally ascribed to the Totonacs, structures within this 41-sq-km (16-square-mile) site also show the influence of Olmec, Huastec, Otomí and Maya civilizations. The city was a contemporary of Teotihuacán and flourished between AD 300 and 1100. Archaeologists have determined that it was both a ceremonial and administrative center whose influence was felt throughout Meso-America. The **Pyramid of the Niches**, 25 m (82 ft) high and 35 m (115 ft) square at the base, is unique in Mexico. The seven-level building is of the *talud-tablero* style common to many other pre-Columbian structures, but it has 365 niches, each dedicated to a day of the year. Impressive as it is today, it must have been even more so at its completion in the seventh century, when each niche was lined with stucco and painted with brilliant colors. South of the pyramid is the **South Ball Court**, which has six panels depicting the religious significance of ball games. To the north, in the newer area known as **Tajín Chico** (Little Tajín) is the **Building of the Columns** with its six pillars, which was probably one of the last buildings constructed at the site; it once supported a second story. Take advantage of the view from the top of this structure. Some of the buildings you'll see still show traces of the blue and red paint that once covered many structures. Admission to the site includes a visit to the small but worthwhile **museum**; both are open daily from 9 AM to 6 PM. There is also a restaurant and several small gift shops. The famed *voladores* of Papantla (see below) perform their historic flying act in front of the visitor's center at no set time (most often on weekends and for tour groups). If you hear the telltale flute and drum music while visiting the site, be sure to head for the visitor's center to see this historic ritual.

PAPANTLA

The closest town to El Tajín is Papantla (population 65,000), the vanilla capital of the world. However, it is neither the vanilla nor the ruins that are the town's claim to fame. It is famous for its *voladores*, fliers, who perform the pre-Hispanic **Flying Pole Dance** weekends at around noon and for the Feast of Corpus Christi. The chief dancer stands on a platform atop a 25-m (80-ft) pole and the four other dancers hang upside-down on ropes wrapped around their bodies and attached to the platform. As the chief dancer plays the flute, the others swing down from the platform, which rotates, spinning downward until the ropes are unwound and they have descended to earth.

GENERAL INFORMATION

The Papantla **Tourist Office** ((784) 20177, at the Palacio Municipal in the main plaza, is open

Monday through Friday from 9 AM to 3 PM and Saturday from 9 AM to 1 PM.

WHERE TO STAY

There are hotels and restaurants in Papantla, Tuxpán (population 130,000) and Poza Rica (population 170,000). Papantla, however, is the nicest of the three towns and has some pleasant accommodation.

Moderate

The **Hotel Premier** ((784) 20080 FAX (784) 21062, Calle Enríquez No. 103, is a reliable favorite because of its 20 large, clean, well-appointed rooms (some with small balconies overlooking the plaza below) and its central location. Other perks include satellite television and air-conditioning. There is no restaurant, but there are plenty of those in the streets surrounding the main plaza.

Inexpensive

Up the hill from the cathedral is the trim and tidy 59-room **Hotel El Tajín** ((784) 20644 or 21623 FAX (784) 20121 or 21062, Calle Núñez y Domínguez No. 104. All of the small yet clean rooms have either black-and-white or color televisions; some rooms have ceiling fans, others have air-conditioning. Horseback trips to the ruins at El Tajín can be arranged with advance notice.

WHERE TO EAT

Adventurous travelers head for the marketplace to find a good deal and an excellent local *tamal* (rectangle of steamed corn meal wrapped in banana leaves, with a sweet or savory filling) or other regional specialties. If you're not quite ready to indulge in market food, try the reasonably priced dishes from throughout Mexico which are served at the **Restaurant El Tajín** ((784) 20644 Calle Nuñez y Domínguez No. 104, in the hotel of the same name. Many go for the filling *comida corrida*, but the restaurant is open all day long.

Sorrento Restaurant (no phone), Enríquez No. 104, on the northeast corner of the main plaza, is a good choice for a seafood meal. It's not a fancy place and it's popular with locals. **Restaurant Plaza Pardo** ((784) 20059, Enríquez No. 105, is also on the plaza and is popular mainly for its tacos, fruit drinks, milk shakes and ice cream.

JALAPA

Jalapa or Xalapa (the Indian spelling meaning "sandy river"), capital of the state of Veracruz with 400,000 inhabitants, was one of the first inland Spanish cities. At 1,400 m (4,593 ft) above sea level, its moderate climate is a welcome break from the coastal heat and humidity. Modern development has depleted most of its colonial charm, and only on the infrequent mist-free day can one appreciate the magnificent view of the surrounding mountains: the 4,282-m (14,049-ft) **Cofre de Perote** (Nauhcampatépetl or "square mountain") to the northwest; and Mexico's highest mountain, the 5,700-m (18,700-ft) **Pico de Orizaba** (Citlaltépetl or "mountain of the star") to the south. The multilevel main square, **Parque Juárez**, has the requisite flowers, trees and benches, but it is unfortunately surrounded by several busy thoroughfares.

GENERAL INFORMATION

The Jalapa **Tourist Office** ((28) 128500 extension 126 or 127, is located at Boulevard Cristóbal Colón No. 5, Jardines de las Animas, Parque Juárez (open Monday through Friday from 9 AM to 9 PM). The staff is helpful, and will dispense city maps and general information.

WHAT TO SEE AND DO

What makes a visit to Jalapa worthwhile is the **Museo de Antropología de Jalapa** (Anthropology Museum) ((28) 154952, Avenida Jalapa s/n at Avenida Acueducto (admission fee; open Tuesday through Sunday from 10 AM to 5 PM) which is located two kilometers (just over a mile) from the center of town. It has the best collection of Olmec artifacts in the country. Set in perfectly manicured gardens, the building, designed by the New York firm of Edward Durrell Stone, is in itself a monument to museum design. It is built on descending levels, filled with light and interior gardens, and houses more than 29,000 archaeological pieces— which are displayed in rotating exhibitions. There are several overpowering, perfectly preserved Olmec heads, weighing about 20 tons each, and an exceptional collection of "laughing faces." Very haunting is the Priest of Las Limas, a scar-faced priest holding the body of a dead child. English-language guided tours are available Tuesday through Sunday from 11 AM to 4 PM; if possible call ahead to confirm and schedule one.

Another worthwhile museum is the **Hacienda Lencero** (no phone), Carretera Jalapa–Veracruz, 14 km (nine miles) southeast of Jalapa (small admission fee; open Tuesday through Sunday from 10 AM to 5 PM). This museum is named for the Spanish soldier who was presented with the sprawling 1,620-hectare (4,000-acre) ranch for his services to the Spanish crown. Later it was purchased by the ex-president of the republic López de Santa Anna. Most recently the state of Veracruz purchased the hacienda buildings and six-and-a-half hectares (16 acres) of land around it to create a museum of colonial country living. Mexican, European and Asian antiques fill the main house

and the former servants' quarters, now a restaurant. Spanish-speaking tour guides will show you around for no charge.

WHERE TO STAY

Moderate
Fiesta Inn ((28) 127920 TOLL-FREE (800) 343-7821 FAX (28) 127946, is located on Carretera Jalapa-Veracruz at Boulevard Cristóbal Colón, on the highway to Veracruz near the Anthropology Museum. With 120 rooms, this hotel is modern and comfortable, although not near the city center. The large rooms have conveniences such as air-conditioning, satellite televisions and bathtubs. There is a pleasant pool in a pretty garden setting and a good restaurant.

The former villa of a coffee baron, the **Posada Coatepec** ((28) 160544 FAX (28) 160040, Hidalgo No. 9, Coatepec, is located about 20 minutes outside of Jalapa in the town of **Coatepec**. Each of the 24 suites is tastefully decorated with handicrafts and handloomed rugs, and each has satellite television and air-conditioning; some are heated. Here you can arrange tours (river rafting, bird watching, ecotourism, or coffee plantations visits), or simply relax by the pool or in the charming bar.

Inexpensive
Hotel Maria Victoria ((28) 180501 FAX (28) 180501, Avenida Zaragoza No. 6, between Calle Valle and Avenida Revolución, is a good choice for those who want to be in the city center. Located just a block from the main plaza, it has good views of the streets below, clean rooms and a decent restaurant. The pool is another selling point. There are 114 rooms. The **Hotel Xalapa** ((28) 182222, Calle Victoria and Bustamante, with 200 units, although inexpensive, have bathtubs, mini bars and air-conditioning. There is also a covered parking garage and a disco. The large rooms are reasonably quiet. Coffee is the theme at the **Posada del Caféto** ((28) 170023, Canovas No. 12, and guests are invited to drink their fair share. The 23 rooms are decorated in bright colors, creamy white walls are painted with Mexican motifs, and ceramic tiles add another dash of color. This hotel was originally a townhouse, and rooms vary in size and layout. It's located about six blocks southeast of the Parque Juárez.

WHERE TO EAT

Besides the restaurants in the better hotels, there are several choice eateries on the pedestrian-only Callejón del Diamante, several blocks east of the Parque Juárez.

One of the best of those found on Callejón del Diamante is **La Sopa** ((28) 178069, Antonio M. de Rivera No. 3-A (a road also known as Callejón del

Diamante), which serves up a delicious yet inexpensive *comida corrida* including soup, main course, dessert and coffee or tea. Lighter fare is served in the evening, including such traditional favorites as tacos or *tamales*. Live music accompanies the meal Wednesday through Saturday after 1 AM. **La Casona del Beaterio (** (28) 182119, Zaragoza No. 20, serves good food in an unpretentious atmosphere near Parque Juárez. Choose from the appetizer menu or order a full chicken or beef dish served with the traditional accompaniments of rice, beans, fried plantains and salsa. Try to have at least one meal at the historic **Café La Parroquia (** (28) 174436, Zaragoza No. 18, just two blocks east of Parque Juárez. The plain tables accommodate groups of flirty teenagers, and retired gentlemen reminiscing their earlier escapades. There is a range of no-frills lunch and dinner items; breakfast centers around coffee, of course, served with sweet breads or more substantial fare.

FORTÍN DE LAS FLORES

Many of the flowers found in markets throughout Mexico come from Fortín de las Flores west of Coatepec. With fruit orchards and fields of gardenias, roses, and orchids (which bloom in May), this is a gorgeous spot, especially on a clear day when the snow-capped peak of Orizaba is in view. The **Hotel Fortín de las Flores (** (27) 130055, Avenida No. 2, was once a retreat for Maximilian and Carlotta, and is now a pretty hotel set amid gardens. There are 86 moderately-priced rooms.

VERACRUZ, CITY OF THE TRUE CROSS

Veracruz is near the spot where the gentle god Quetzalcoatl sailed away, deserting Mexico, and it is where Spanish rule began and ended. Hernán Cortés landed near here on Good Friday, 1519, the day of the Holy Cross, and began the conquest of Mexico. It was also here that the treaty recognizing Mexico's independence was signed in 1821.

During the colonial period, Veracruz became the most important port connecting the Old World and the New, and rich shipments of gold and silver tempted the likes of John Hawkins and Francis Drake. Legend says that there are about 200 galleons sunk off the coast of Veracruz, and these attract many treasure hunters to the port. Such was the harassment of the pirates that the Spanish built a wall and nine bastions to protect the city.

Its defenses were not always effective; Veracruz was briefly occupied by the French in 1838 and by the United States forces of General Winfield Scott in 1847, during the Mexican-American War. In 1862 a joint French, English and Spanish force took the city, demanding repayment of Mexican debts. The Spanish and the English withdrew, but the French

forces remained, marching inland to pave the way for Maximilian. United States troops again invaded Veracruz in 1914, with orders from President Woodrow Wilson to depose the dictator Victoriano Huerta, who had seized the presidency after assassinating President Madero.

Veracruz (population one million) is still Mexico's principal Gulf seaport. Some of the old colonial buildings and the Castillo de San Juan de Ulúa remain from the city's stormy past. The atmosphere of the city is sometimes frantic, sometimes calm; very much like music played by the city's strolling musicians on their harps and marimbas — at times romantic and languid and at times vibrant and gay.

GENERAL INFORMATION

May through September are the hottest and rainiest months in Veracruz, with an average temperature of 27°C (81°F). Hurricanes from the Caribbean are most likely between September and early November. Gusty winds blow down from the north between November and March; these *nortes* sometimes freshen the oppressive humidity, sometimes blow dirt in your eyes. From December to mid-April, Veracruz is a popular vacation spot for Mexicans. The season reaches its peak during Carnival (one of the best in Mexico), which occurs the week before Lent. Carnival is heartily celebrated with the burning of bad spirits and the burial of Juan Carnival.

The **Tourist Office (** (29) 321999 is located at Palacio Municipal in Veracruz, on the Zócalo, and is open Monday through Saturday from 9 AM to 9 PM and Sunday from 10 AM to 1 PM. It has a helpful, well-informed staff who can assist in arranging accommodation—something that is nearly impossible to find during Christmas vacation and Carnival.

WHAT TO SEE AND DO

Despite being short on sights, in the guidebook sense, Veracruz is a lovely place to stroll around or to sit on the *malecón* watching the boats in the harbor. Although no one ever seems to be in a particular hurry, the pace is at times frantic — one of many Jarocho contradictions!

Five blocks south of the *malecón* is the **Baluarte de Santiago** (Bastion of Saint James) **(** (29) 311059, at Calle Canal and 16 de Septiembre (admission fee, but free Sunday; open Tuesday through Sunday from 10 AM to 4:30 PM). Built in 1526, its medieval-styled tower and 12 cannons are all that remain of the wall that once surrounded the city. It now houses a museum exhibiting a small collection of weapons and pre-Columbian jewelry.

The **Plaza de Armas**, bordered by Calles Zamora and M. Lera, and Avenidas Independencia and Zaragoza, is Veracruz's Zócalo and the center of the city's evening social life. Residents and visitors alike spend hours strolling the plaza and relaxing in the cafés under the porticoes that surround this, the oldest Spanish plaza in North America. On some evenings couples dance the *danzón*, a type of waltz imported from Cuba. Other nights the marimbas, mariachis, or other musical ensembles take over the bandstand in the center of the Zócalo. The seventeenth-century **Palacio Municipal** flanks one end, and the eighteenth-century **Catedral de Nuestra Señora de la Asunción** the other.

The major tourist attraction in Veracruz is the **Castillo de San Juan de Ulúa (** (29) 385151, reached by a causeway from Veracruz city center (admission fee; open Tuesday through Sunday from 9 AM to 5 PM), which dates back to the sixteenth century. Although the Spanish constructed this fort on an islet to protect the harbor from marauding pirates, it was later used as a prison: one of the most wretched in New Spain (not an easy distinction to obtain). Visitors can see the cells which fill halfway with water at high tide. Today a causeway links the island to the city, but visitors can also rent boats for the journey. Once at the islet, you can hire an English-speaking guide, or tromp around on your own.

The newish **Aquarium** (Acuario) **(** (29) 374422 or 327984, at Plaza Acuario Veracruz, Boulevard Camacho at Playón de Hornos (admission fee; open Monday through Thursday from 10 AM to 7 PM and Friday through Sunday from 10 AM to 7:30 PM), is fun for kids and attracts tons of locals on the weekends. A huge tank reportedly holds 3,000 species of sea life, and there are films about sharks and other menaces of the deep to disturb your dreams at night.

Housed in a nineteenth-century mansion, the **Museo de la Ciudad** (City Museum) **(** (29) 318410, Zaragoza No. 397 near Morales (small admission fee; open Monday from 9 AM to 4 PM and Tuesday through Saturday from 9 AM to 8 PM), is an ethnological museum devoted to the history of the Jarochos. There are exhibits depicting carnival and other spiritual customs and interesting showings of current indigenous art. The scale model of the city should help first-time visitors understand the city's layout. South and west of the City Museum is the big market, the **Mercado Hidalgo**, Avenida Madero and Calle Hernán Cortés. Pop in to see the fantastic assortment of fruits and vegetables available in this rich agricultural land; or to buy coffee beans plucked and roasted on some of Veracruz's many plantations.

If you tire of the city, there are several beaches to visit. Don't expect white sand and turquoise water, however; the sand here is for the most part hard and packed like dirt, and the water close to town is murky at best, polluted at worst, from

the heavy maritime traffic. Nonetheless, locals flock on weekends to the palm-shaded beach **Villa del Mar**, which is about two kilometers (just over a mile) south of downtown. Here there are changing rooms and showers. The beaches get progressively nicer as you head south, past **Playas Curazau** (six kilometers or 3.6 miles south of Villa del Mar) and then two more kilometers (1.2 miles) to **Mocambo**, which is usually the least crowded. You can use the pool at the Hotel Mocambo for about $3, or sit under the umbrellas on the wide beach. Those interested in shipwreck diving should proceed another 11 kilometers (seven miles) or so south of Mocambo to the village of Antón Lizardo. Here you can rent snorkel or scuba

gear for an excursion to offshore reefs and wrecks. **Tridente (** (29) 340844, Pino Suárez at Avenida de la Playa, rents this equipment and arranges boat tours. If possible, call a day or two in advance to make a reservation. Back in downtown Veracruz, boats to the islands, including Isla de Sacrifícios and Isla de Pájaros (respectively, the Island of Sacrifices and Birds) depart from the dock next to the Instituto Oceanográfico, on Avila Camacho, and from the beach next to Plaza Acuario Veracruz.

Some tour companies are now using Veracruz as a launching point for a tour following the Ruta de Cortés (Route of Cortez) from Veracruz to Puebla, Tetihuacán and Mexico City. For information contact **Tourimex (** (22) 322462 FAX (22) 322479 E-MAIL tourimex@mail.glga.com.

Mexicans revel in music and dance.

WHERE TO STAY

There are three hotel districts in the Veracruz area: the **Zócalo, Mocambo Beach** — nine kilometers (five and a half miles) south of town — and **Villa del Mar** in between. All three have their advantages. Staying on the Zócalo places one in the center of the evening social scene, but away from the water and beach during the day. Be aware that accommodation near the Zócalo tends to be extremely noisy, especially during fiestas. The hotels on Boulevard Avila Camacho give one access to the Villa del Mar Beach and are much closer to the city than those at Mocambo. The latter is, in addition to being farthest from town, the most tranquil.

Expensive

"Cutting-edge" is the way to describe the new **Fiesta Americana (** (29) 898989 TOLL-FREE (800) 343-7821 FAX (29) 898904 at Boulevard Avila Camacho at Bacalao, which opened in 1996. Amenities include direct-dial telephone, voice mail, satellite television, in-room safe and bathtub; no-smoking and accommodation suitable for handicapped guests are also available. Business people will appreciate the business services lounge and its bilingual staff. There seems to be more than one of everything here: including three bars, two restaurants, three hot tubs and two pools. You can dine informally next to one of the pools at the Café la Fiesta, which serves a large breakfast buffet as well as enticing lunch and dinner entrées. Once the star of the Gulf Coast, **Hotel Mocambo (** (29) 220333 or 220205 FAX (29) 220212 Boulevard Ruíz Cortines No. 4000 at Carretera Boticaria-Mocambo, reminds one of a fading yet still-loved pageant winner. Its 123 rooms have been remodeled to vie with its newer competition; rooms at this 50-year-old hotel now have direct-dial telephones and cable television, but the overall effect is still of faded glory. The main draw is the relative isolation and quiet of the broad, palm-lined beach and the large pool set in brilliantly landscaped gardens. There is a restaurant, bar, coffee shop and gym.

Moderate

Located right on the Zócalo is the **Quality Inn Calinda (** (29) 312233 or 311124 TOLL-FREE (800) 228-5151 FAX (29) 315134, Avenida Independencia at Calle M. Lerdo, where there are 165 units. The public areas and room decorations are both tasteful and soothing, and the open-air restaurant on the second floor is a fabulous place from which to watch the action in the plaza below. You can cool off in the bathtub-sized pool. The **Hotel Emporio (** (29) 320022 FAX (29) 312261, Paseo del Malecón No. 210 at Avenida Xicoténcatl, with 240 rooms is located on the *malecón* downtown and has an impressive view of the harbor from its upper stories. Although geared toward business travelers (there are meeting rooms and a business center), a recent renovation makes it equally tempting for tourists. All of the pleasant rooms have bathtubs, air-conditioning and satellite televisions. On the grounds are three pools, including one with children's play equipment. Additionally, there are a gymnasium, sauna, restaurant and bar.

Inexpensive

The **Hotel Baluarte (** (29) 326042 FAX (29) 325486, Calle Canal No. 265, is well-situated for those who want to be close to the main plaza without the nighttime noise. Across the street diagonally from the Baluarte de Santiago, this modern five-story hotel with 123 rooms has views of the Gulf from the west side. There is a reasonably good restaurant on the premises and off-street parking.

Clean and comfortable describes the intimate (32 rooms) **Hotel Hawaii (** (29) 380000 or 310427 FAX (29) 325524, Insurgentes Veracruzanos No. 458. Both staff and management are warm and friendly, and will dispense city maps and recommendations upon request. The hotel, which is located right on the *malecón*, also has a coffee shop (with room service available) and free parking.

WHERE TO EAT

Veracruz specializes in seafood and the recipes in the city are in general more sophisticated than those found elsewhere in the state. Restaurants tend to serve white rice and black beans more than the seasoned rice and pinto beans found inland. An abundance of locally grown fruits are the basis for fabulous fruit drinks and desserts, and lunch really isn't finished until you sip a cup of the state's delicious Java coffee.

Expensive

Next door to the Agustín Lara Museum, **La Mansión (** (29) 371338, Boulevard Ruíz Cortines, Boulevard Avila Camacho, borrows a bit of the elegance of Maestro Lara in his heyday — the 1930s and 1940s. Those seeking stylish ambiance and a thick cut of steak will be happy here. There is an extensive list of domestic and imported wines.

Moderate

Although the original restaurant is outside of town in Boca del Río, the new **Pardiños (** (29) 317571 or 314881, Landero y Coss No. 146, Paseo del Malecón is equally good and certainly more central. The setting — in a bright, restored colonial mansion — is very charming and looks out across a busy street to the beach. In addition to standard Jarocho seafood favorites such as *huachinango a la veracruzana* (red snapper with a sauce of sautéed onions, tomatoes and green peppers), there are some succulent house specialties. It's fun also to visit the original **Pardiños** restaurant ((29) 314881, Calle Zamora Nº 40, in Boca del Río about 13 km (eight miles) south of downtown, which opened in 1950 and is still going strong. Imagine tiring of fresh seafood! If this should happen, try the Spanish restaurant **La Paella** ((29) 320322, Zamora Nº 138, right on the Zócalo. Although three meals a day are served, the most popular is the four-course *comida corrida* (fixed price lunch special) which highlights Spanish cuisine, including the restaurant's namesake, *paella valenciana*.

La Bamba ((29) 323555, on Boulevard Avila Camacho at Zapata, is popular with local families on weekend lunch. They enjoy the ocean view;

Mexico City. If you are traveling by car from Mexico City, take Highway 150; you will arrive in about six hours. If you are coming from the north, take Highway 180 and you should reach your destination in approximately eight hours. Both Mexicana and Aeroméxico airlines offer service to Veracruz. The local carrier, Aerocaribe, has flights from Cancún to Veracruz.

AROUND VERACRUZ

LA ANTIGUA AND CEMPOALA

La Antigua, a picturesque village about 23 km (14 miles) north of Veracruz, is the site of

indeed, this restaurant sits on stilts at the water's edge. Seafood is the specialty and you'll likely be serenaded by roving bands of mariachis.

Inexpensive

Gran Café de la Parroquia ((29) 322584, Gómez Farias No. 34 at Paseo del Malecón, is not just a café — it's an institution. Locals and savvy visitors delight in the ritual for the perfect *café con leche* (one waiter brings thick, dark coffee, a second brings the hot milk). While coffee and sweets are popular, there are, in addition, a variety of more filling items on the menu. The restaurant is open all day, every day.

HOW TO GET THERE

The city of Veracruz is located 502 km (320 miles) south of Tampico, 345 km (211 miles) west of

Gulf Coast

the oldest church on the North American mainland. The blue and white church remains in remarkably good condition today. According to historians, it was here that Cortés held Mass and the first Indian was baptized. This was the site of Cortés' first encampment and storehouse and where he scuttled his ships to squelch any ideas among his soldiers of a premature return to Cuba.

Cempoala (or Zempoala), about 40 km (25 miles) north of Veracruz, was the Totonac capital at the time of the Spanish landing and the site where Cortés met with the Totonac king Chicomacatl on May 15, 1519, 23 days after his landing. After a convincing show of might and firepower, Cortés succeeded in gaining Totonac allegiance in battling the Aztecs.

No visit to Veracruz is complete without a *cafe con leche* at the Gran Café de la Parroquia.

The **Ruins of Cempoala** (admission fee; open daily from 10 AM to 5 PM) in Cempoala are worth a visit. (There are public restrooms here, but no phone.) While the ruins are not as fully excavated as those at El Tajín, they are interesting, and there is a small museum on site. Spanish-speaking guides are available and *voladores de Papantla* usually give performances on weekends around noon. Among the structures that have been excavated is the main pyramid, or **Templo Mayor**, in which Cortés is said to have installed a Christian cross soon after his arrival, and the **Temple of the Little Faces** (Templo de las Caritas), where small faces once peered out from a multitude of niches. Uncharacteristic of Mexican ruins, many of the edifices here are from the fourteenth and fifteenth centuries, although the city flourished in the Classic period, between AD 300 and 900. It was still in use at the time of the Spanish invasion. The site is thought to have been of cosmic importance to the Totonac, and believers still converge on a ring of short pillars at the winter solstice (December 21) for special ceremonies.

LAGUNA DE CATEMACO

Inland and 166 km (102 miles) southeast of Veracruz, **Laguna de Catemaco**, Mexico's third largest lake, is surrounded by volcanic hills in which are hidden picturesque, traditional villages with colonial architecture. The lake and shore are one of the most beautiful and least developed in Mexico, and many of the area's sites are hidden away off dirt roads, sometimes inaccessible by vehicles. In the winter, birding enthusiasts come here to spot the approximately 550 species of migratory and native birds in residence. The lake itself is popular with fishermen, swimmers and skin divers. The 10-km (6.5-mile) long and eight-kilometer (five-mile) wide lake has several islands; on one of these, **Isla de Agaltepec**, is a colony of Thai monkeys which over the ages has learned to fish and swim. *(Carne de chango*, monkey meat, is often on the menus of the town's restaurants, although some say it is really pork.) At the north end of the lake, the Río Catemaco enters the lake, cascading over large rocks and forming several small waterfalls. In the region surrounding the lake are the communities of Santiago Tuxtla, San Andrés Tuxtla and Catemaco, among others.

To the uninformed, the small lakeside city of **Catemaco** (population 50,000) would appear to be nothing more than a sleepy Mexican settlement with a popular Sunday market, a quiet place to which stressed-out city dwellers flee on long weekends. This region, however, is more than a pretty landscape; it is the home of the *curanderos* (healers) and *brujos* (witches) — both male and female — who, it is said, have the power to heal and intervene in our day-to-day existence. For just how many centuries they have practiced here no one is certain, but many believe their powers date from the time of the Olmecs, who certainly inhabited the area. In addition to using their powers to understand the present and see into the future, these seers also prepare remedies for almost every ailment or problem. These arts are taken seriously by both the Mexicans and foreigners who visit the lake.

Boat tours of the lake are available through the **Cooperative de Lanchas** (boat cooperative) ((294) 30662 or 30081, Boulevard de Malecón s/n, across from the Siete Brujas restaurant. You may wish to ask that the tour include a stop at the **Proyecto Ecológico Educacional Nanciyaga** ((294) 30199 or 30666, a rainforest preserve and holistic retreat center. Visitors may stay overnight in rustic huts or come for the day to have a mineral bath, mud facial or massage. Other services available are spiritual cleansing, drum classes and a temazcal-style sweat lodge. The park can also be accessed by Carretera Catemaco Coyame, on the east side of the lake.

Less than 100 km (62 miles) farther along the Gulf Coast, one encounters the worst of Mexican industrialization. From Minatitlán to Ciudad del Carmen in the Yucatán, the coast has little to offer the tourist.

WHERE TO STAY AND EAT

One does not have to worry about finding rooms here except during Christmas and Easter vacations or July 15 and 16, when pilgrims arrive at the Church of the Virgin of Carmen to pray for miracles.

Inexpensive

With its economy based on sorcery, fishing and tourism, the town has more than 20 hotels, none of which, happily, are first-class resorts. The largest hotel on the lake, **Playa Azul** ((294) 30001, Carretera a Sontecomapan Km 2, off Highway 180, with 80 rooms, is two kilometers (just over a mile) outside town in the forest. Birders appreciate the huge windows. There is a pool, restaurant and bike rental. Closer to town, on the south shore of the lake is the smaller, more modern **La Finca** ((294) 30322, off Highway 180, offering 20 air-conditioned units in lakeshore cabins. Open for lunch and dinner is the **Restaurante Siete Brujas** ((294) 30157, Boulevard del Malecón, with a great view of the lake. Seafood is the specialty here and musicians play traditional tunes as diners chow down on stuffed crab or crayfish. The second-story, open-air dining room is especially pleasant.

Travelers of a metaphysical bent consider the ruins of Cempoala to be a sacred area during the winter solstice.

Pacific Coast

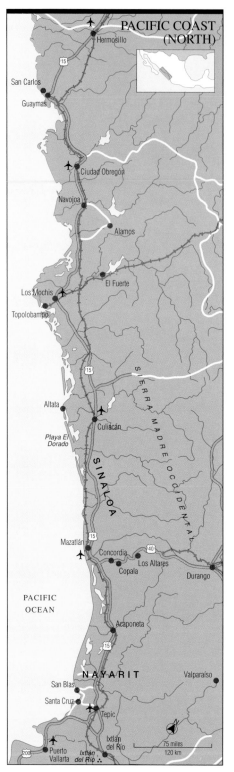

PACIFIC COAST
(NORTH)

ALTHOUGH EACH REGION of Mexico is unique, few areas are as diverse as the Pacific Coast. Lined with hundreds of miles of excellent beaches, and backed by hills and mountains ranging from desert crags in the north to precipitous rainforest in the south, the Pacific Coast offers much to see, with many parts still relatively undeveloped.

The northern Pacific Coast is sheltered from the ocean by the Baja California Peninsula and the Sea of Cortez, and bordered to the east by the Sonoran Desert. Thus, the climate is warm in winter and blazing hot in the summer. North of **Guaymas**, Sonora, there is little development and the few beaches are hardly worth the effort to get here. The major highway in this area runs north to south, inland through cowboy country much like Chihuahua but near sea level, from Nogales, Arizona, to Guaymas. The state of Sinaloa is little more that a coastal strip of bare semitropical terrain. Five rivers from the Sierra Madre Occidental cut the state to form swampy tidal flats at their mouths. In between are stretches of sandy beach and mangrove swamps.

Mazatlán, in the far south of Sinaloa, is due east of the tip of Baja and has long expanses of sandy beaches. Unprotected by the peninsula, the land south of Mazatlán has a more appealing year-round climate. Mexico's famous Pacific Coast resorts dot the coastline and are pocketed in protected bays from here to the Guatemalan border. Winters can be cool, but the ocean breezes keep the temperature pleasant all summer long.

Sections of the Pacific Coast were settled in the early sixteenth century by the Spanish, who were soon driven out by the Indians. A century later, the ever-persistent Jesuits succeeded in bringing enough Indians under control that commerce, mainly by sea, could be carried out. During the height of colonial dominance, Spanish galleons from the Far East made stops along the coast. Their goods were off-loaded, carted across the mainland to Veracruz and from there shipped to Spain. Few remnants of these colonial ports remain.

One can still arrive in several Pacific Coast ports by boat (cruise ship), but most tourists drop in by jet to Acapulco, Mazatlán, Puerto Vallarta, or Manzanillo. However, by car, bus, or train, the journey takes on the flavor of the real Mexico.

NORTHERN SONORA

To reach the Gulf Coast from the United States, one enters Mexico at Mexicali (see BAJA CALIFORNIA, page 326) or at one of three towns on the border with the state of Arizona: Sonoyta (Lukeville), Nogales (Nogales) or Agua Prieta (Douglas). In all four cases the trip south crosses desert terrain with intermittent irrigation projects until one reaches the Sonora capital, Hermosillo, at the confluence of Río Sonora and Río Zanjón.

HERMOSILLO

Surrounded by fertile land, Hermosillo, which literally means "little beauty," was actually named for José María González Hermosillo, a hero of the War of Independence. Originally settled in 1742, it has few structures remaining from the colonial era. Those that remain are in the central square and the **Plaza de los Tres Pueblos**, the site of the original settlement, and are sadly overshadowed by modern construction. Hermosillo is also home of the **Universidad de Sonora**, which operates the **Museo de la Universidad de Sonora**, on Boulevards Luís Encinas and Rosales, (free admission; open Monday through Saturday). On the south side of town is the **Centro Ecológico**, a huge park with over 300 species of plants and animals explaining the interdependence of the wide variety of flora and fauna in the mountain, desert, valley and tropical ecosystems of the state.

WHERE TO STAY AND EAT

As a government center and university city, Hermosillo has several good hotels and restaurants. The **Fiesta Americana (** (62) 596060 FAX (62) 596062, Boulevard Kino No. 369, is the best hotel in town, with 222 rooms in the expensive category. The **Holiday Inn Hermosillo (** (62) 144570 FAX (62) 146473, Boulevard Kino at Ramón Corral, is one of Hermosillo's oldest business hotels, with 144 expensive rooms. The **Hotel Gandara (** (62) 144414 FAX (62) 149926, Boulevard Kino No. 1000, is a moderately-priced older hotel with 154 rooms. Dining is good in all the hotels.

BAHÍA KINO

Bahía Kino (Kino Bay), 110 km (68 miles) southwest of Hermosillo, is the first of the North Pacific Coast beaches that is easily accessible, a lovely long stretch of clean sand against the blue sea. It is a fishing village where a few (mostly American) expatriates have built vacation homes, or arrive annually in self-contained campers. It is located near the Seri Indian camp. The major attractions here are tranquillity, fishing and the **Isla del Tiburón** (Shark Island), which is Mexico's largest island, 60 km (38 miles) long by 30 km (19 miles) wide. The island has been set aside as a wildlife sanctuary and game preserve and is, among other things, a turtle breeding ground. Special permits are required to visit the island; these can be obtained by the boatmen guides who are licensed to ferry visitors.

The Seri Indians make their living fishing and selling ironwood carvings, usually simple stylized animals. They are not fond of being photographed and may demand money if they realize

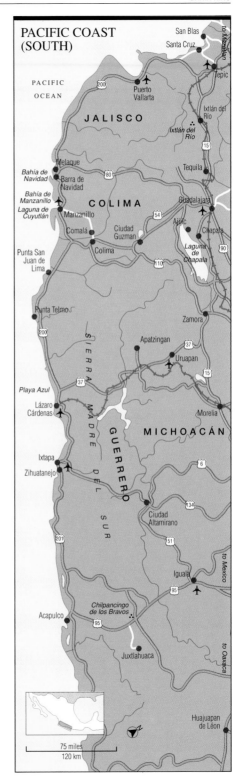

their image has been captured. To avoid an embarrassing scene here, or anywhere in Mexico, ask before you take a photograph and be prepared to pay for invading the subject's spirit. Better yet, avoid photographing any Indian.

WHERE TO STAY AND EAT

Most visitors to Bahía Kino are campers or vacation home owners; nevertheless, there are several hotels. The **Posadas Santa Gemma** ((62) 20026, Boulevard Mar de Cortés, in the expensive price range, has furnished bungalows with kitchens. The moderately-priced **Posada del Mar** ((62) 20155, Boulevard Mar de Cortés at Creta, offers 42 rooms and facilities such as a pool and restaurant. The most popular restaurant in town is **El Pargo Rojo** ((62) 20205, Boulevard Mar de Cortés No. 1426, specializing in fresh fish and local cuts of beef.

GUAYMAS

Guaymas is one of the best-kept secrets in Northern Mexico. Desert and mountains descend gradually to the Sea of Cortez, where sea lions, manta rays and tropical fish abound in calm waters. The beaches are superb and there is enough development to provide every need without totally destroying the character of the area itself. Even the Pemex refinery does not intrude too far into the beauty. Though there is talk of large-scale development, little progress has been made other than the installation of a marina and one golf course.

North of town in the bays of **Bacochibampo** and **San Carlos** (where *Catch 22* was filmed) are excellent bathing beaches, separated by rocky outcroppings around which there is great snorkeling. Nearby **San Nicolás**, **Santa Catalina** and **San Pedro Islands** are havens for sea lions and birds. Fishermen come from around the world to fish the bays and the Gulf of California.

In the hills around Guaymas are many **old haciendas** (most still occupied), the **Selva Encantada** (enchanted forest) of giant cacti in which parrots nest, and narrow gorges in which Indian paintings can be found.

BACKGROUND

The first Spaniards to explore the area arrived in 1535 and named the area Guaima for the Guaimas Indians who lived here along with the Seri and Yaquis. There was no settlement here, however, until the energetic Father Francisco Eusebio Kino founded Mission San José de Guaymas in 1702. Late in the eighteenth century, Guaymas became the shipping port for the precious metals extracted inland. Its commercial importance was underlined during the United States' occupation of the city in

the Mexican-American War and the French occupation in 1865. In 1854, the French count, Gaston Raousset de Boulbon, tried to establish a personal empire here, but he was arrested and shot.

GENERAL INFORMATION

Many tourists arrive by car and bus, and a few via the twice-weekly ferry from Santa Rosalía in Baja California. Those headed to the large hotels arrive at the airport, which has service to most Mexican cities, Los Angeles and Tucson, Arizona. The Guaymas **Tourist Information Office** ((622) 25667 is at Avenida Serdán No. 441 between Calles 12 and 13; it does not have fixed hours.

WHERE TO STAY AND EAT

Three large properties claim most of the area's hotel guests; all have good restaurants and

sometimes offer packages including airfare, accommodation and meals.

Very Expensive

I must admit to a feeling of apprehension when I checked in for an entire week's stay at the **Club Mediterranée Sonora Bay** ((622) 60166 TOLL-FREE (800) 258-2633 FAX (622) 60070, on Playa de los Algodones. I couldn't envision staying put for so long. Imagine my surprise when a week later I had never left the grounds except for repeated scuba diving excursions. The setting is magical, with 17 hectares (42 acres) of cacti, desert and lawns framed by the Sierra Madre and the sea. Though the 375 rooms have little charm, the compound seems to glow in the sun with the kind of light only the desert can provide. Horseback riding and lessons are available, as are tennis, sailing, windsurfing and diving. The buffet meals are outstanding: piles of tropical fruits, endless loaves

of chocolate and rye bread, plates filled with sushi, *ceviche*, and cheeses, and entrées that changed every day. Though hardly as glamorous as the clubs in Moorea or Martinique, this is one of my favorite Mexican escapes.

The **San Carlos Plaza Resort** ((622) 60794 TOLL-FREE (800) 654-2000 FAX (622) 60777, Mar Bermejo No. 4 on San Carlos Bay, is the most luxurious property in the area with 173 generously proportioned rooms and suites, a great swimming pool with a waterslide, and tennis courts, horseback riding and several restaurants.

Expensive

Overlooking the San Carlos Marina, the **Plaza Las Glorias** ((622) 61021 TOLL-FREE (800) 342-2644 FAX (662) 61035, at Plaza Commercial San Carlos,

Cruise ships still bypass the seaside town of Zihuatanejo, one of the Pacific Coast's most laid-back destinations.

Pacific Coast

has 105 rooms and suites, many with kitchenettes. The hotel also has a timeshare property where returning guests happily settle in for a week or more.

Moderate

The **Fiesta San Carlos (** (622) 60229 FAX (622) 63733, on San Carlos Bay, was one of the first hotels in the area. Some of its 33 rooms have kitchenettes and there is a restaurant by the pool.

ALAMOS

South of the modern cities of Ciudad Obregón and Navojoa and 53 km (33 miles) inland, is Alamos, an eighteenth-century silver city that is now a National Historic Monument. At its peak in the 1780s, it had at least 30,000 inhabitants; today there are less than 10,000. Indian attacks, drought, famines and the closure of the silver mines in 1910 left Alamos a ghost town, which luckily was never destroyed. After World War II, American artists and retirees began restoring many of the old homes around the **Plaza de las Armas**. They supported the Indian crafts and built a regional museum, **Museo Costumbrista de Sonora (** (642) 80053, Calle Guadalupe Victoria No. 1 on the Plaza de las Armas (free admission; open Wednesday to Sunday, closed at midday). The museum contains artifacts from the silver mining era, and a collection of clothing and furnishings from the miners' haciendas. The church, **La Immaculada Concepción**, built on the site of the original seventeenth-century Jesuit mission, dominates the central square, Plaza de las Armas. Alamos is one of the most beautiful settlements in the country and the residents take great pride in keeping the colonial-style houses in handsome repair.

WHERE TO STAY

The towns major hotels are all housed in restored eighteenth- and nineteenth-century buildings. The **Casa de los Tesoros (** (642) 80010 FAX (642) 80400, Avenida Obregón No. 10, has 14 expensive rooms, a pool and a restaurant in a restored convent. The home of a Spanish mine owner has been converted into the **Casa Encantada (** (642) 80482 FAX (642) 80221, Calle Juárez No. 20, just off the plaza. The nine expensive rooms have fireplaces and carved hardwood furnishings.

MAZATLÁN

Unlike many of Mexico's seaside resorts, Mazatlán has a life of its own outside of tourism. It is Mexico's largest commercial port on the Pacific and has the country's largest shrimp fleet. It also offers a full range of tourist facilities, set on a 57 km (35 mile) stretch of flat sandy beach.

Although it is an old port city from which Spanish galleons loaded with gold and silver set sail for the Orient, Mazatlán's oldest architectural landmarks are from the 1800s, when German farmers settled the area and enlarged the port for exporting produce and importing agricultural implements.

Today, this town of over 400,000 residents relies on its port — and the 1.5 million tourists who visit each year — for the bulk of its income.

GENERAL INFORMATION

The **Oficina de Turismo (** (69) 165160 FAX (69) 165166 is on Avenida Camaron Sábalo at Calle Tiburon. The English-language *Pacific Pearl* newspaper is available at most hotels and is filled with current information.

Temperatures range from 20°C (68°F) from December to April and 26°C (79°F) from May to July. July to October is the rainy season, when there can be hard rains. After the onslaught of Mexican tourists in August, hotel rates drop by about 20%.

WHAT TO SEE AND DO

Though most of Mazatlán's visitors stay in the *Zona Dorada* (Golden Zone), with its lineup of beachfront hotels, the city's most interesting attractions lie to the south in downtown. Since the 1980s, Mazatlán's civic boosters have dedicated considerable attention and money to *Mazatlán Viejo* (Old Mazatlán), and the neighborhoods of the center city. Architectural gems include the neoclassical **Teatro Angela Peralta (** (69) 82447, Calle Carnaval at Libertad, which first opened for a scheduled performance by its namesake diva in 1869. Peralta died from the bubonic plague before her appearance — perhaps an omen for the theater's progression from grand opera house to political hall during the 1910 Revolution, and then to a boxing ring and movie house. The rosy pink theater with its baroque interior was targeted as the centerpiece of Old Mazatlán in 1986, and reopened with a performance of Carmen. Travelers can (and should) tour the theater during week days. Performances are occasionally scheduled here.

The theater faces the **Plazuela Machado**, a pleasant green square with a Moorish style *kiosko* in its center. Buildings on the streets near the plaza have been restored and turned into galleries, shops, cafés and museums. The nearby **Museo de Arqueológia (** (69) 853502, on Sexto Osuna off Olas Altas (open Tuesday through Sunday, closed at midday), contains a good collection of historic photographs. Avenida Carranza climbs from Old Mazatlán to the top of **Cerro de la Vigía** (Lookout Hill), past the nineteenth-century mansion that houses the **University of Mazatlán** and the 1828

Customs House. The hill has been used as a sentry point for pirates, shipping concerns, and the military and drug enforcement agencies, and commands an impressive view of the Pacific Ocean, the city's port and downtown. Across the canal from this point is another steep hill called **Cerro de Creston**, which is topped with **El Faro**, said to be the world's second-tallest lighthouse. Constructed in the 1930s, its light can be seen 64 km (36 nautical miles) away. A trail leads from the end of Avenida Camarena up the hill (154 m or 505 ft above sea level); the climb takes about a half hour. Bring water, snacks and plenty of film.

The palm-lined 10-km (six-mile) *malecón,* or seaside walkway, begins north of the two hills at **Playa Olas Altas** (High Wave Beach). From **El Mirador,** a clifftop that drops six meters (20 ft) or so into the sea, one can watch divers plunge into the shallow water below. At the south end of the *malecón,* waves pound the beach — when the waves are up the surfers are in. The sea grows more calm as Olas Altas gives way to Paseo Claussén edging the center of downtown.

To the east is downtown's **Mercado Romero Rubio** (between Calles Juárez and Serdán). The enclosed cast-iron market was constructed in the 1890s and renovated for its centennial. It's a great place to bargain for souvenirs and buy snacks. The yellow-tiled spires of the nineteenth-century **Catedral de Mazatlán** can be used as a guidepost as you stroll around downtown. It is the heart of the city, facing the **Plaza Revolución** and its wrought iron *kiosko.* Visitors to the cathedral are requested to dress appropriately — no shorts or tank tops. In the city center, travelers would feel out of place in beach attire; this is where people work and shop.

Spreading north of the *malecón* is the longest of the downtown beaches, Playa Norte. It is popular with local residents and visitors staying in the part of town developed for tourism before 1970.

Midway down Playa Norte, a block inland from the beach, is the **Acuario Mazatlán** (Aquarium) ((69) 817815, Avenida de los Deportes No. 11 (admission fee; open Tuesday through Sunday from 10 AM to 6 PM). California sea lions perform in an educational show, and several large tanks contain more than 300 species of freshwater and saltwater fish.

At the north end of the waterfront walkway, is **Punta Camerón** (topped with the Moorish-style Valentino's disco) and the main tourist strip — the Zona Dorada. You can follow Mazatlán's stages of tourism by following Avenida Camarón Sábalo north to Punta del Sábalo and the **Marina Mazatlán,** the designated mega resort of the 1990s. The zone's older, family-style hotels are at its southern end, along with the souvenir-filled **Mazatlán Arts and Crafts Center** ((69) 135243, Avenida Loaiza, which is open daily.

Two kilometers (just over a mile) east of the Arts and Craft Center is the bullring, **Plaza de Toros Monumental** ((69) 841722, Boulevard Rafael Buelna, where bullfights are staged every Sunday from Christmas to Easter. October through January, baseball fans can see Mazatlán's triple-A team, Los Venados (Pacific League), at **Teodora Mariscal Stadium**, Avenida de los Deportes. Schedules for bullfights and baseball games are available at the Oficina de Turismo and hotels.

Playa Sábalo and **Playa las Gaviotas** in the Zona Dorada are Mazatlán's best swimming beaches, as they are protected from the heavy surf by Isla de los Pajaros (Bird Island), Isla de los Venados (Deer Island) and Isla de los Chivos (Goat Island). Excursions to these islands, where the beaches are less crowded, can be arranged through hotels or with any of the boat operators who will be eager to offer their services.

The best snorkeling and diving is off Isla de los Venados, but the avid snorkeler will be disappointed. The water is often too turbulent to see much. Mazatlán is best for surfing, windsurfing, body surfing, sunbathing and fishing. The fishing here ranks as some of the best in the world. Blue and black marlin run from March through December and striped marlin from November through April; dorado, shark, tuna and sailfish run year round. Prices for a fishing trip range from $80 per person on a party boat to $300 to charter an entire boat. It is best to shop around and negotiate. Having someone with you who speaks Spanish usually helps. For travelers on a tight schedule who want to plan a fishing trip in advance, contact the **Star Fleet** ((69) 22665 (or ((210) 377-0451 in the United States) FAX (69) 825155, which is located on Boulevard Joel Montes Camarena amid the fishing operators. The **Aries Fleet** TOLL-FREE (800) 633-3085 at the El Cid Marina in the Zona Dorada, schedules trips from the hotel zone.

The 18-hole golf course designed by Robert Trent-Jones at the El Cid resort ((69) 133333 is open to hotel guests only.

WHERE TO STAY

Room rates are lower in Mazatlán than in the newer Mexican resorts, and it is an immensely popular destination for retirees, students and travelers content with a lack of flash. Reservations are essential for Christmas and Easter vacations, spring break, national holidays and during Carnival (the week before Ash Wednesday). One of the best celebrations in Mexico, Mazatlán's Carnival began in 1898 and has grown into a major spectacle. Activities — selection of a queen, music, bullfights and fireworks — are scheduled every day for a week. A smaller religious fiesta is held on December 8; the Feast of the Immaculate Conception.

Very Expensive

Hacienda Las Moras ((69) 165044 FAX (69) 165045, located in the countryside about 20 minutes from the city (reservations can be made by writing to 9217 Siempre Viva Road, Suite 15-203, San Diego, CA 92173) is one of the most gorgeous guest ranches in the country, filled with folk art, fine paintings, hand-carved furnishings and a sense of country life. Individual *cabañas* have tiled kitchens, front porches, and sitting and sleeping areas — the latter artistically decorated with Mexican and Guatemalan fabrics and furnishings. These *cabañas* dot the rolling lawns, facing a stable of prize horses while flocks of guinea hens, peacocks and chickens roam the grounds. The dining room, living rooms and lounge areas are in the main house; meals are served inside, on the front terrace, or in the courtyard facing the swimming pool. Horseback rides — to the ranch's wedding chapel, up steep hills and along well-traveled paths to nearby small towns — and other exercise keep guests' appetites whetted for breads baked in a wood-burning oven, served with excellent Mexican cuisine.

Expensive

Situated at the far northern end of the Zona Dorada on Punta Sábalo is Mazatlán's most exclusive accommodation, the **Camino Real (** (69) 132111 TOLL-FREE (800) 722-6466 FAX (69) 140311, Camarón Sábalo. The soothing ambiance is a refreshing change from the more frantic activity farther south, and the 169 rooms are tastefully decorated. The hotel sits beside a small cove where swimming is safe and private, and the restaurants are very good.

Mazatlán's largest hotel is the 1,300-room **El Cid Resort (** (69) 133333 TOLL-FREE (800) 525-1925 FAX (69) 141311, Avenida Camarón Sábalo. In addition to rooms and suites in three highrise towers by the beach, the resort has 210 suites in the **Marina El Cid Yacht Club** by the 18-hole golf course, and several apartments and villas for rent. With 15 restaurants and bars, eight pools, a shopping arcade, disco, golf course, 17 tennis courts, and a beach club with water sports rentals and tour services, it is designed to keep visitors entertained on its grounds. Far more subdued and elegant is the **Pueblo Bonito Hotel (** (69) 143700 TOLL-FREE (800) 442-5300 FAX (69) 143723, Camarón Sábalo. Though many of the 247 rooms and suites are booked by timeshare residents, there are usually some accommodations set aside for hotel guests. Most have kitchenettes and balconies overlooking the lavish pool area (complete with wandering peacocks and squawking macaws) and the sea. Also recommended in this price range is the 118-room **Doubletree Club Resort (** (69) 130200 TOLL-FREE (800) 222-TREE FAX (69) 166261, Camarón Sábalo at Calle Atún.

Moderate

Unlike most Mexican seaside resorts where beach hotels are in the luxury and expensive range, many of Mazatlán's good hotels are in the moderate category. **Playa Mazatlán (** (69) 134444 TOLL-FREE (800) 762-5816 FAX (69) 140366 Rodolfo T. Loaiza No. 202 at Playa las Gaviotas, is enduringly popular with guests returning annually to stake out one of the 420 rooms. The restaurants are very good — there are even takeout stands by the lobby — and the hotel puts on a popular weekly Mexican Fiesta with buffet dinner, a show and fireworks. The **Hotel Costa de Oro (** (69) 135444 TOLL-FREE (800) 342-2431 FAX (69) 144209 Camarón Sábalo, south of the El Cid Resort, has 293 rooms in two sections, one across the street from the main hotel and the beach. The **Fiesta Inn (** (69) 890100 TOLL-FREE (800) 343-7821 FAX (69) 890130, Avenida Camarón Sábalo No. 1927, between El Cid Resort and the Camino Real, is a comfortable option with 117 rooms overlooking the beach, a long swimming pool, a workout room and reasonably-priced buffets, as well as à la carte meals, in the restaurant.

Inexpensive

Most inexpensive hotels are found outside the Zona Dorada closer to town or across the street from the beach. Some of the best are downtown in the Olas Altas area. My favorite is **La Siesta (** (69) 134655, Olas Altas No. 11, across from the pounding waves. Try for a room at the front with a balcony; though you'll have some street noise the surf usually overpowers other distractions. The **Hotel Belmar (** (69) 811111 FAX (69) 813428, Olas Altas No. 166 just down the street from La Siesta, would be a charmer if someone would take the time to renovate its tiled stairways and 150 run-down rooms. All have air-conditioning and cable television, a real plus in this price range. Try to avoid booking a room overlooking the back parking lot. Good choices on Playa Norte include the **Hotel Suites Don Pelayo (** (69) 831888 FAX (69) 840799, Avenida del Mar No. 1111, with 96 rooms and 72 suites with kitchenettes; and the **Olas Altas Inn (** (69) 813192 FAX (69) 853720, Avenida del Mar No. 719.

WHERE TO EAT

Mazatlán's restaurants serve up some of the best seafood in the country, prepared with local flair. The *parrillada de mariscos* is typically a spectacular heap of fish filets, crab, shrimp and oysters served on a hibachi grill. The *sopa de mariscos* is a similar blend of flavors in a bowl. Most of the restaurants are casual and moderate in price.

Expensive

Sr. Pepper ((69) 140120, on Camarón Sábalo across from the Camino Real, has long been the place for a special night out amid candlelight, crisp linen and courtly service. Sonoran steaks, lobster and shrimp are all excellently prepared.

Moderate

Twenty years ago the best seafood restaurant in Mazatlán was hidden on a narrow street three blocks from the beach. It is still one of the best places to mingle with locals over ample meals, though the competition has increased mightily. At **Mamuca's** ((69) 13490, Simón Bolívar No. 73, the specialty is shrimp prepared in any variety of ways: boiled in beer is one of the best. Another popular seafood restaurant is **El Paraíso Tres Islas** ((69) 142812, Rodolfo T. Loaiza No. 404 at Playa las Gaviotas. **La Costa Marinera** ((69) 141928, Privada Camarón at Camarón Sábalo, sits right on the beach. The dining room is filled with sea-shells and fishing nets, and it's hard to resist the *parrillada* here. For a change from fish, try down-town's most famous restaurant, **Doney** ((69) 812651, Mariano Escobedo No. 610, housed in a nineteenth-century mansion. Regional Mexican dishes are the specialty here; save room for pie. **Señor Frog's** ((69) 821925, on Avenida del Mar at Playa Norte, is a Mazatlán institution, so famous it has a separate shop for T-shirts and gear carry-ing its logos. The rock 'n' roll is deafening, the decor a wild jumble, and the platters of barbecued chicken, ribs or Mexican specialties are bountiful. A young crowd fills the place late at night for dancing and mingling. Irresistible pastries, great breakfasts, sandwiches and Mexican dishes draw crowds to **Pastelería Panamá** ((69) 851853, across from the Catedral on Benito Juárez. There's a sec-ond, fancier location in the Zona Dorada on Cam-arón Sábalo at Avenida Las Garzas ((69) 132941. Be prepared to submit to the bakery display; choose a few items for afternoon tea in your room. **Copa de Leche** ((69) 825753, Olas Altas No. 33 Sur, is my favorite restaurant near Mazatlán Viejo. Its sidewalk tables look out to sea, and are popular with office workers on midday break.

Inexpensive

Juices, salads and sandwiches on wholegrain bread are a welcome change of pace at **Pura Vida** ((69) 165815, on Calle Laguna one block in from Camarón Sábalo in the Zona Dorada. **Karnes en Su Jugo** ((69) 821322 at Avenida Del Mar, down-town, specializes in a savory beef stew served with homemade tortillas. **Baby Tacos** (no phone) on Calle Garzas between Camarón Sábalo and Rodolfo T. Loaiza, is a step above the typical street side taco stand and serves great cheap munchies.

HOW TO GET THERE

Most visitors arrive at Aeropuerto Internacional Raphael Buelna, which receives flights from

throughout the United States, Canada and Mexico. There is bus and rail service to Mazatlán, and it is the end of the spectacular drive down the mountains from Durango (see NORTH CENTRAL HIGHLANDS, page 200).

AROUND MAZATLÁN

CONCORDIA AND COPALA

Travelers arriving from Durango on Route 15 will have passed through Copala and Concordia. Each is worth a stop or an excursion from Mazatlán. Concordia, 48 km (31 miles) from Mazatlán is famous for fine carved furniture, baskets and

pottery. Twenty-four kilometers (15.6 miles) fur-ther is Copala, a sixteenth-century mining town. Its colonial buildings and cobblestone streets precariously perched on the side of the lushly vegetated mountain. Of particular interest are the Iglesia de San José and the main plaza. **Daniel's** (no phone) at the entrance to town, is the most popular restaurant, serving Mexican meals and its famous coconut cream pie. The small hotel here is the perfect place to escape outside distractions; once the tour buses are gone Copala is a delightful place to hang out, strolling the streets past immaculate whitewashed homes and watching small-town life at the plaza. Further east on Route 15, one continues to climb through steep, forested mountains with magnificent

Mazatlán's beaches are lined with lowrise and highrise resort hotels.

panoramas until Los Altares, across the border of Durango.

SAN BLAS

South of Mazatlán, in the state of Nayarit, is the quiet coast town of San Blas. Immortalized by H.W. Longfellow in the poem *The Bells of San Blas* this sleepy fishing village, once a colonial seaport, has long been popular with budget travelers. There is not much here other than a central square, **El Templo de San Blas**, the ruins of the customs house and Spanish fort founded in 1768, and more mosquitoes than inhabitants and tourists combined. (Mosquito repellent is a must.) Visitors

50308, on Calle Paredes Sur. The 47 moderately-priced rooms and suites are immaculate and have good screens to keep the bugs away, along with fans and air-conditioning. Guests gather by the two pools and in the restaurant, the best in town. The **Hotel Los Bucaneros** ((321) 50101, Avenida Juárez No. 75, has 33 inexpensive rooms, all with private bath.

Between San Blas and Santa Cruz is what the locals call Crescent Beach, where on average days the body surfing is excellent and the board surfing good. When the surf is up, some aficionados claim they can ride the waves from one end of the beach to the other, nearly five kilometers (three miles) away.

either love the town or hate it. Those who love it return time and time again.

On some days the waves are good for body and board surfing, and the beaches are relatively deserted most of the time. To the north of San Blas, the beaches are bordered by mangrove swamps which many describe as jungle. (This is a bit of an exaggeration if one compares them with those of the Yucatán.) They are, however, undisturbed stands of mangroves intertwined with numerous inlets that are home to innumerable species of birds. Canoes and/or guides can be engaged to explore the area.

WHERE TO STAY AND EAT

There are a few small hotels in San Blas, most catering to budget travelers. The nicest of the lot is the **Las Brisas Resort** ((321) 50480 FAX (321)

From here to the southern boundary of Nayarit and Puerto Vallarta are 150 km (90 miles) of relatively undeveloped beaches.

TEPIC

Tepic, capital of the state of Nayarit and home of several sugar refineries (it often smells of burnt sugar), is a crossroads for bus, rail and automobile travelers. The **Museo Regional de Antropología e Historia** (Regional Museum of Anthropology and History), Avenida México No. 91 (closed Mondays), has displays of archaeological finds from around the state, as well as ethnology exhibits on the Cora and Huichol Indians who inhabit the high country. The best time to visit Tepic is on weekends when the Indians come to town to sell their jewelry, woven goods, and "God's eyes" (crosses decorated with colorful yarns).

IXTLÁN DEL RÍO

In the southeast corner of Nayarit is one of the few pre-Columbian archaeological cities in western Mexico: Ixtlán del Río. Archaeologists believe the site was occupied as early as the sixth century AD, but the excavated portion, showing Toltec influence, is from the post-Classic period around AD 1000. No pyramids or castles have yet been excavated here, but if one is traveling only the west coast of Mexico and will not be able to see other pre-Columbian sites, Ixtlán is probably worth visiting.

COSTA AZUL AND NUEVO VALLARTA

The Nayarit Coast just north of Puerto Vallarta is feeling the effects of its neighbor's success. The Río Ameca separates Nayarit from the state of Jalisco; Puerto Vallarta is that state's major coastal resort. Since the mid 1990s the north side of the river has been experiencing resort development, especially in the man-made area of Nuevo Vallarta. Created primarily for charter groups staying at all-inclusive hotels, Nuevo Vallarta has a golf course, marina and several timeshare complexes. Development has spread north to **Punta Mita**, where locals used to escape to a pretty, sandy point jutting into the sea. Punta Mita is now becoming an upscale resort area, where a Four Seasons hotel will open in 1999, along with an 18-hole golf course designed by Jack Nicklaus. Of more interest to adventure travelers is **Costa Azul** TOLL-FREE (800) 365-7613 FAX (714) 498-6300 in the United States, north of Punta Mita on Playa San Francisco in **San Pancho**, Nayarit. This remote resort, just a 30-minute drive north of the Puerto Vallarta airport, covers two hectares (five acres) of isolated beach backed by jungle, and has 28 rooms in hotel buildings and villas on the beach; all have private bath, and the villas have kitchens, dining rooms and separate bedrooms. Adventure is the key here; guests can surf, kayak, fish, swim in the ocean or pool, go horseback riding in the jungle, and snorkeling around the **Marietas Islands**. The room rates are moderate, and reasonably-priced packages include activities, drinks and meals.

PUERTO VALLARTA

Until the 1960s, Puerto Vallarta was a remote fishing village, its red-roofed houses and cobblestone streets covering a small portion of the hillsides surrounding Bahía de Banderas (Bay of Flags). It was known only to a handful of travelers — the rich who arrived in their yachts or private planes, and the hardy explorers who made the 25-hour drive over the dirt road from Tepic.

Then film director John Huston chose it as the location for *Night of the Iguana*, starring Richard Burton, and the developers arrived, bringing their building materials by boat from Acapulco. Posada Vallarta, the first luxury resort, was completed before the highway from Tepic was blasted through the mountains in 1968.

GENERAL INFORMATION

The city operates a well-staffed, efficient **Office of Tourism** ((322) 12242 FAX 12243, Palacio Municipal, Avenida Juárez, which is open Monday through Friday from 9 AM to 9 PM and Saturday from 9 AM to 1 PM; two English-language monthly

publications, *Welcome* and *Vallarta Today,* list what to do and see in the area.

Year-round temperatures range from 24°C to 32°C (75°F to 90°F) with the coolest periods in December and January. The off-season months (June to October) are rainy. The air can be hot and very humid, and there are usually light showers during the day and heavy rains at night.

WHAT TO SEE AND DO

The town of Puerto Vallarta is completely given over to tourism. Buildings in the old town at the mouth of Río Cuale have mostly been converted to shops and restaurants. The **Palacio Municipal**, which houses the tourist office on the **Plaza de**

Puerto Vallarta — with its modern hotels OPPOSITE and downtown shopping ABOVE — was one of Mexico's first mega-resorts.

Armas main square has a mural by local artist Mañuel Lepe. One block east, the **Iglesia de Nuestra Señora de Guadalupe** has an unusual crown-shaped tower. Some claim it is a replica of the crown of Empress Charlotte, wife of Maximilian.

In the mouth of the river is **Isla Río Cuale** with tropical gardens, several galleries and cafés, and the small **Museo Arqueológico**, which exhibits pre-Columbian artifacts and Indian crafts.

The resort area lies north of town along Playa Norte, or **Playa de Oro**, to the **Marina Vallarta** development, where the newest luxury hotels are clustered around the beach, golf course and marina. The cruise ship pier is here, next to the dock for the numerous tour boats that ply the bay. Avenida las Palmas, which runs inland from Playa Norte, is filled with hotels, restaurants and shops, but despite a beautification project it is far better suited to vehicles and pedestrians.

The best people-watching beach in the area is south of downtown and the Río Cuale. Much to the city fathers' dismay, its original name, **Playa de los Muertos** (Beach of the Dead), has persisted rather than the more upbeat Playa del Sol (Sun Beach). Playa de los Muertos was the site of a battle between pirates and Indians. Many of Vallarta's least-expensive hotels are clustered in this neighborhood beside some of its best restaurants.

Farther south is the beach **Conchas Chinas** with numerous rocky pools. These are lovely natural aquariums where one can spend hours watching the tiny tidal creatures go about their daily routines. About 11 km (seven miles) south of town, where the jungle meets the water of the horseshoe-shaped bay, is **Playa Mismaloya**, the setting for *Night of the Iguana*. Until recently, Mismaloya was a small fishing village, but the residents have been moved away from the beach, where a gigantic hotel now stands.

Offshore are the giant boulders of **Los Arcos** (The Arches), an underwater preserve where snorkelers and divers can watch the fish undisturbed by human predators.

The more remote beaches at the fishing villages of **Yelapa** and **Animas** are accessible only by boat. There are restaurants at both, thus they make good destinations for day excursions. Boat schedules are available at the Office of Tourism and most hotels. Yelapa, the more developed of the two, but still without electricity and telephones, has a small hotel. A 15-minute hike up from the beach brings one to a lovely waterfall in the jungle.

For entertainment in Puerto Vallarta there are the beaches and the bay (waterskiing, parasailing, windsurfing, snorkeling, diving and swimming). The sport fishing is also good, with sailfish, red snapper, sea bass and tuna throughout the year. Fishing will cost approximately $70 per person on a party boat and over $300 for chartering an entire boat. Most hotels can recommend fishing guides or you can strike your own bargain at the marina.

Many of the hotels have **tennis** courts. The 18-hole **Marina Vallarta Club de Golf ℂ** (322) 10545, on Paseo de la Marina Norte, is open to the public.

Horseback riding along the beach and on jungle trails has become a popular activity; for reservations contact **Cuatro Milpas ℂ** (322) 47211 or **El Ojo de Agua ℂ** (322) 48240. **Kayaking** has also come unto its own as one of the best ways of appreciating the bay; for information contact **Open Air Expeditions ℂ** (322) 23310. Scuba diving when the water is calm is especially good at Islas Marietas; contact **Chico's Dive Shop ℂ** (322) 21895 or **Vallarta Adventure ℂ** (322) 10657. **Theme cruises** are an excellent way to view Vallarta from the bay, and are especially lovely at sunset. Most include unlimited beer and other drinks, and dinner on the beach. Contact **Vallarta Adventure ℂ** (322) 10657 or **Princesa Cruises ℂ** (322) 44777.

Puerto Vallarta is an excellent shopping town, filled with fine art, folk art, and clothing galleries and boutiques. Inexpensive souvenirs and friendly bartering are available at the **Mercado Municipal** on Rodríguez by the Río Cuale. Artists from throughout the country, as well as the many who live in Vallarta, display their work at fine galleries including **Galería Uno**, **Galería Pacifico** and **Galería Sergio Querubines**, **Alfareria Querubines and Rosas Blancas Bustamante**. Intricate and expensive beaded masks, animal figurines, and belts made by the Huichol Indians can be seen at **Arte Mágico Huichol**. Fine folk art from throughout the country is available at **Querubines**, **Alfareria Querubines** and **Rosas Blancas**. Serious shoppers return again and again to the downtown area, scoping out the scene before picking up treasures.

Vallarta's dining scene is excellent as well, with visitors and locals feasting on a late gourmet meal before heading for the hotel discos.

WHERE TO STAY

There is no shortage of hotel rooms in Vallarta, especially since the Marina Vallarta development opened with a half-dozen exclusive properties. The Marina area is best for those intent on golfing, sunbathing and relaxing amid luxurious surroundings, since downtown is a long cab ride away. The majority of the hotels are located along **Playa Norte**, where public buses to town pass by frequently. Smaller inexpensive hotels are located in the Los Muertos area. As with all resorts, it's best to have advance reservations during national and international holidays.

Restaurants come and go in Vallarta's tourist zones.

Very Expensive

One of the oldest and best hotels in the area is the **Camino Real (** (322) 15000 TOLL-FREE (800) 722-6466 FAX (322) 16000, hidden next to a peaceful cove south of town on Carretera a Barra de Navidad. The 250 rooms and suites in the original hotel tower all face the beach and are decorated with white walls, and vibrant yellow, pink and blue fabrics. Newer mini suites are located in the Royal Beach Club tower, connected to the main building by lovely landscaped pathways. *Palapas* line the curving beach and the restaurants are excellent. In the Marina Vallarta area choices include the sleek, modernistic **Westin Regina Vallarta (** (322) 11100 TOLL-FREE (800) 228-3000 FAX (322) 11141, Paseo de

la Marina Sur No. 205, with 280 rooms; the 433-room **Marriott Casa Magna (** (322) 10004 TOLL-FREE (800) 233-6388 FAX (322) 10760, Paseo de la Marina No. 5; and the smaller, more exclusive **Bel-Air Hotel (** (322) 10800 TOLL-FREE (800) 457-7676 FAX (322) 10801, Pelicanos No. 311, with 75 villas and suites on the golf course.

Expensive

My favorite Playa Norte hotel is the Mexican-style **Fiesta Americana Puerto Vallarta (** (322) 42010 TOLL-FREE (800) 343-7821 FAX (322) 42108, on Carretera al Aeropuerto. A sky-high *palapa* covers the massive lobby (the Christmas tree and decorations in this space are gorgeous), while the 291 rooms and suites are located in terracotta colored buildings framing the pool. The **Krystal**

Christina's disco, Puerto Valarta.

Vallarta ((322) 40202 TOLL-FREE (800) 231-9860 FAX (322) 40150, on Carretera al Aeropuerto, is another longtime favorite with 450 villas, suites, and rooms spread out along the sprawling gardens and lawns. Also recommended in this area is the conveniently located **Sheraton Buganvilias (** (322) 30404 TOLL-FREE (800) 325-3535 FAX (322) 20500, Avenida de las Palmas No. 999. You can walk to downtown from here. Away from the larger hotels, two and a half kilometers (one and a half miles) south of town is the "offbeat" **Quinta Maria Cortés (** (322) 21317, Playa Conchas Chinas, with six individually decorated suites. It is a short walk from the beach and each eclectically decorated unit has a terrace and kitchenette. Reservations must be made months in advance.

Moderate

At the north edge of the *malecón* and downtown is the 210-room **Hotel Buenaventura (** (322) 32737 TOLL-FREE (800) 878-4484 FAX (322) 23546, Avenida México No. 1301. Though the property resembles a low-end chain hotel, it benefits from its location and sea view. More charming is the smaller 65-room **Molino de Agua (** (322) 21907, Vallarta No. 130 with bungalows set in a lush garden on the banks of Río Cuale. South of town the **Hotel Playa Conchas Chinas (** (322) 20156 on Carretera a Barra de Navidad Km 2.5, has a loyal following with its 39 rooms set on a cliff over a rocky beach.

Inexpensive

Advance reservations are a must at the 13-room **Los Cuatro Vientos (** (322) 20161 FAX (322) 22831, Matamoros No. 520, set on a hill above town. Though it's a climb to get back from the beach and town, the airy rooms, small pool and gracious service are worth the exercise. The **Posada Río Cuale (** (322) 20450 FAX (322) 20914, next to Isla Cuale on Calle Vallarta at Serdán No. 242, has 21 rooms in a quiet setting. Just off Playa de los Muertos, **Posada de Roger (** (322) 20836 FAX (322) 30482, Basilio Badillo No. 237, is the best buy for budget travelers who don't mind a walk to the beach. Its 50 rooms are popular with an international set, many of whom have met each other elsewhere in their Mexican travels.

WHERE TO EAT

Puerto Vallarta can easily claim to have some of the most innovative restaurants in Mexico. The resort has attracted chefs from Italy, France, Switzerland and the United States, all of whom work hard to make a name for themselves. Budget diners aren't left out, as there are many small, casual places with great seafood and Mexican dishes. Many of the hotels can claim fine restaurants as well, but I prefer eating in downtown as often as possible.

Expensive

Simultaneously trendy and elegant, the **Café des Artistes(** (322) 23228, Guadalupe Sánchez No. 740, is the favorite among the see-and-be-seen local crowd, who gather by the piano bar late at night. Diners feast on prawn and pumpkin soup, roast duck in ginger sauce, smoked salmon in puff pastry and highlights from the ever-changing menu. The Sunday brunch in the garden is superb. **Chef Roger (** (322) 25900, Rodríguez No. 267, is less pretentious but equally pleasing to the palate, thanks to the Swiss chef Roger Dreier. Also highly recommended for its riverside ambiance and food is **Le Bistro (** (322) 20283 at the west end of Isla Cuale near the bridge at Insurgentes.

Moderate

My favorite place for seafood on the beach is **La Palapa (** (322) 25225 at the foot of Calle Pulpito on Playa de los Muertos. At first glance, it seems not unlike every other *palapa*-covered restaurant on the sand. But the soft sound of guitar *boleros* and the flickering candlelight are signs that this place is different. The fish dishes are prepared with tasty sauces made from *guajillo* chilis or *achiote* spices, and more mainstream dishes such as chicken *fajitas* keep all diners happy. **El Dorado (** (322) 21511, also at the foot of Calle Pulpito on the beach, is a more casual seafood spot where expatriates tend to assemble for sunset cocktails. **Archie's Wok (** (322) 20411, Francisca Rodríguez No. 130, in the Los Muertos neighborhood features Pacific-rim cuisine with Thai and Philippino preparations. **Las Palomas (** (322) 23675, on Díaz Ordáz, is the best spot for people-watching across from the *malecón*; breakfasts are particularly good here. Also on the *malecón* is **La Dolce Vita (** (322) 23852, Díaz Ordáz No. 67, serving good pizzas and pastas.

Jungle-style restaurants sit off the highway south of town, and offer both food and the chance to cool off in rushing rivers. **Chico's Paradise (** (322) 80747, off Carretera a Barra de Navidad Km 20, is one of the favorites, serving fish and Mexican meals under *palapas* beside a river splashing over giant boulders. **El Eden** (no phone), off Carretera a Barra de Navidad inland from Mismaloya, was the set for Arnold Schwartzenegger's *The Predator*. **Le Kliff**, off Carretera a Barra de Navidad south of Mismaloya, is a bit more upscale and an ideal spot for a sunset dinner overlooking the bay.

Inexpensive

There are many good inexpensive restaurants downtown. For down-home Mexican cooking, I prefer **Ceneduria Doña Raquel (** (322) 10618, Vicario No. 131, for its *pozole*, a traditional stew of hominy and pork or chicken. **Papaya 3 (** (322) 20303, Abasolo No. 169, is a health-food restaurant filled with plants and a great spot to feast on salads. Fruit and vegetable juices and sandwiches are available for takeout at **Tutifruiti (** (322) 21068, Morelos No. 552. And for breakfast you can't beat the staggering menu of flavored pancakes and eggs at **Memo's La Casa de Pancakes (** (322) 26272, Basilio Badillo No. 289.

HOW TO GET THERE

The Gustavo Díaz Ordáz International Airport receives flights from Mexico, the United States and Canada. Regular bus services connect Puerto Vallarta with other coastal towns and the capital.

SOUTH OF PUERTO VALLARTA

Between Puerto Vallarta and the boundary of the small state of Colima, are 200 km (120 miles) of relatively undeveloped and inaccessible beaches. Where there are paved roads, they generally lead to exclusive resort complexes beloved by wealthy recluses and honeymooners. The most famous is **Bel-Air Costa de Careyes (** (335) 10000 TOLL-FREE (800) 457-7676 FAX (335) 10100, 154 km (96 miles) south of Puerto Vallarta and 96 km (60 miles) north of Manzanillo off Highway 200, originally designed by Italian architect Gianfranco Brignone. A mix of Mediterranean and Mexican design was used to create a village of stunning private homes and villas tucked in the jungle overlooking the sea. A 60-room hotel has the least expensive rooms. Amenities include a full-service spa, a wide beach, horses for sunset rides, yachts for fishing expeditions and excellent restaurants. **Las Alamandas (** (335) 70259 FAX (335) 70161, set within a 607-hectare (1,500-acre) private reserve off Highway 200, 32 km (20 miles) north of Costa de Careyes, is so exclusive it has room for only 22 guests in gorgeous villas and *casitas* set amid fruit orchards, jungle and lagoons above the beach. Advance reservations are absolutely necessary, since the hotel is sometimes closed for high-powered gatherings. Activities include horseback riding, boat rides, hiking, exercise in the fitness center and, of course, lounging by the pool. The restaurant specializes in healthful cuisine.

BARRA DE NAVIDAD AND MELAQUE

The most developed areas between Puerto Vallarta and Manzanillo are the towns of Barra de Navidad, from which Miguel López de Legazpi set sail in 1564 to explore the Philippines, and San Patricio Melaque, both of which have tourist facilities and are popular with vacationing Mexicans.

The waves provide good surfing for the experienced, but unfortunately the undertow is so strong as to make the beaches not safe for swimming. However, for tranquillity this is a desirable destination. Coming from Acapulco, Puerto Vallarta, or one of Mexico's other glitzy resorts, the area may appear a bit tacky. It is not catering to the upscale market. Hotels provide the essentials and leave the traveler to find his own amusement.

The most resort-like of the establishments is the **Hotel Barra de Navidad** ((335) 55122 FAX (335) 55303, Legazpi No. 250. Its 60 rooms are inexpensively priced and most have large balconies overlooking the beach; guests rave about the restaurant. Also inexpensive and comfortable is the **Hotel Delfin** ((335) 55068 FAX (335) 55384, Morelos No. 23. South of the towns a massive resort development has risen at **Isla Navidad**, a peninsula between the Pacific and the Laguna Navidad. Thus far, the development includes a 27-hole golf course and the **Grand Bay Resort** on Isla Navidad ((335) 55050 TOLL-FREE (888) 80GRAND FAX (335) 56071 in the United States. The 158 rooms and 33 suites are in the very expensive category, and the resort is designed with all the amenities to keep guests from wandering away.

COLIMA, LAND OF THE KISSING DOGS

The high mountains and flat coastal plains of Colima have been inhabited since the second century AD, but no large archaeological sites have been found. When the Spanish arrived here in 1522, months after having destroyed Tenochtitlán, they victimized the locals with single-minded consistency and moved on. The area was later settled by Francisco Cortés de San Buenaventura, a nephew of Hernán Cortés. Still later, Sir Francis Drake supposedly visited the port of Manzanillo and, for a brief time at the end of the colonial era, Father Miguel Hidalgo was a parish priest in the capital city, Colima.

COLIMA, THE CITY

The state capital, Colima, lies at the foot of two large volcanoes, Nevado de Colima and Volcán de Fuego. The snow-capped Nevado, also called Zapotépetl ("mountain of sapodilla trees") is extinct and is the sixth-highest peak in Mexico (4,380 m or 14,376 ft). Volcán de Fuego (3,900 m or 12,796 ft) still emits plumes of smoke from its crater, which is 2,000 m (6,500 ft) in diameter. Both mountains can be climbed, and dirt roads go to an elevation of 3,560 m (11,680 ft) on Nevado and 3,130 m (10,270 ft) on Volcán de Fuego.

The city itself is a peaceful agricultural and government center. Several colonial era buildings remain, including the **Palacio de Gobierno**. Its **Museo de las Culturas Occidentales** ((331) 23155, Calzada Galván and Ejército Nacional (open Monday through Saturday from 10 AM to 1:30 PM) displays artifacts from Colima's past, including several *ixcunclis*, kissing terracotta dogs, for which

the area is famous, and which were held sacred by the pre-Conquest civilizations.

Outside the city is Lago de Carrizalillos, a lake with excellent boating and hiking opportunities, and the town of Comalá, which has a factory school and outlet store (closed Sunday) for furniture, ironwork and paintings.

MANZANILLO

Legend has it that trade existed between Manzanillo and the Orient long before Hernán Cortés set his sights on the area as Spain's gateway to the west. Cortés never got his way, and it was Acapulco to the east that became the major port for the Spanish galleons bringing goods from Cathay. Nonetheless, Manzanillo became a shipbuilding port that harbored not a few of the Spanish galleons trading with the Philippines. For unknown reasons, Manzanillo was more

susceptible to pirate raids than the other Pacific ports, and some local residents claim that there are pirate fortunes buried in the sand.

In spite of its idyllic setting — beautiful twin bays lined with white and black sand beaches — Manzanillo was passed over early in the twentieth century by the government tourism development planners. Again Acapulco came out the victor (or loser, depending on your point of view). Manzanillo seemed destined to remain little more than a commercial entry for goods to be transported by rail inland, though it is home to one of Mexico's most famous resorts — Camino Real Las Hadas — and is a popular vacation spot for Mexican families.

GENERAL INFORMATION

Today, Manzanillo remains somewhat on the fringes of the tourist circuit. Many fly into its

international airport (serviced by Aeroméxico, Mexicana and AeroCalifornia) to proceed north past Barra de Navidad to the remote self-contained resorts along the coast. However, the **Manzanillo Oficina de Turismo ((333) 32277, 32264 FAX (333) 31426, Costero Madrid No. 4960, is promoting the area. Their hours are erratic.

WHAT TO SEE AND DO

Tourist services are adequate and the town is worth an afternoon stroll, perhaps through the main plaza, called the **Jardín de Obregón**. The **harbor** is still a thriving commercial port, as are its shipyards. This gives the area a life and flavor of its own, something that is sorely lacking in the planned resort areas.

For a change a pace from the beach, Pacific Coast tributaries can be explored in small boats.

Pacific Coast

North of town on the twin bays of Manzanillo and Santiago, separated by the Península de Santiago, are 14 white or black sand beaches off which the snorkeling and scuba diving are good. For divers, there are remains of old galleons sunken off **Playa Miramar** and **Playa de Oro**. The surrounding countryside is flat coconut and banana plantations; the nearby **Laguna de San Pedrito** shelters flocks of flamingos and white herons.

It is hard to choose between the beaches, since all are good; Playa Miramar at the north end of Bahía de Santiago (the northern bay) is protected just enough by the Península de Juluapan to make it excellent for windsurfing. Across the spit to the north between two rocky outcroppings is **Playa**

WHERE TO STAY

Manzanillo has several all-inclusive resorts catering to families, a few chain hotels and several small mom-and-pop operations; reservations are usually not necessary except during national holidays.

Very Expensive

The most famous hotel in the area, featured in the Bo Derrick movie *10*, is the Moorish-style **Camino Real Las Hadas (** (333) 40000 TOLL-FREE (800) 722-6466 FAX (333) 41950, Rincón de las Hadas. A complete renovation in 1996 restored the 220-room hotel to its original grandeur and it is truly a

Audiencia, where Indians were supposed to have met with Cortés. **Playa Azul** runs most of the length of the Bahía de Manzanillo and has good swimming toward the south and high surf in the north. At Playa Cuyutlán, 45 km (30 miles) south of town, the sand is black and the waves have been known to reach heights of nine meters (30 ft). Often the waves here are green — the *olas verdes*, colored by phosphorescent marine organisms that glow in the dark.

If the sun, sand and sea are not enough activity or amusement, there are tennis courts at many of the hotels and the 18-hole **La Mantarraya (** (333) 30246 golf course at Las Hadas.

Manzanillo claims it is the sailfish capital of the world and holds an international sailfish tournament every November. Sailfish season runs from October to May, when red snapper, sea bass, and tuna are also abundant.

magnificent place. White-domed villas line several pathways planted with scarlet and white bougainvillea; all paths lead to the swimming pool and beach, both offering white fabric *cabañas* to shade guests from the sun. Tour boats depart from the hotel's marina, and the three restaurants offer expensive continental fare.

Expensive

Though far from luxurious, **Club Maeva (** (333) 36878 TOLL-FREE (800) 882-8215 FAX (333) 30395, on Costera Madrid at Playa Miramar, is one of the most popular places in the area. Families fill the 514 rooms, kids frolic in wading pools and playgrounds, parents play tennis on 17 courts, and a bridge leads over the highway to a beach. Similar in style, the 300-room **Vista Club Playa de Oro (** (333) 36133 TOLL-FREE (800) 882-8215 FAX (333) 32840, is on Costera Madrid at Playa Miramar.

Moderate
La Posada ((333) 31899 FAX (333) 31899, on Playa Azul in the Las Brisas district, is much like the old Mediterranean hotels where guests in the 24 rooms were residents for the season, sharing tables and becoming like family. It also has an unusual but practical tipping policy. Guests are asked to put 10% of their total bill in a tip box rather than leaving individual tips. This has led to a comfortably relaxed relationship between the clients and staff. The **Hotel Fiesta Mexicana (** (333) 31100 FAX (333) 32180, on Costera Madrid Km 8.5, between Las Hadas and downtown, is one of the best bargains on the beach, with its 200 rooms in a festive Mexican setting.

Inexpensive
For traditional hospitality, the **Hotel Colonial (** (333) 21080, Calle Bocanegra No. 28, downtown, is a real charmer. Somewhat rundown, the rooms have heavy wood furnishings and faltering ceiling fans. The dining room is a popular lunch spot for downtown workers.

WHERE TO EAT

The proliferation of all-inclusive and exclusive hotels keeps many diners away from independent restaurants, but there are a few places worth checking out.

Moderate
Willy's ((333) 31794, on Carretera Las Brisas near Highway 200, has long been considered the best French and seafood restaurant around, serving bouillabaisse, onion soup, grilled lobster and homemade pastries. **Carlos 'n' Charlie's (** (333) 31150 at Costera Madrid Km 6, is a lively spot serving barbecued ribs, *fajitas* and steaks.

Inexpensive
Nonresidents are welcome at **La Posada (** (333) 31899 (see above) for meals; the breakfasts — pancakes, French toast, eggs and bacon — are great. **Hamburguesas Juanito's (** (333) 32019, at Costera Madrid Km 14, is a popular hangout for American-style breakfasts, burgers and French fries. Downtown, the best spot for a plaza view is **Roca del Mar (** (333) 20302, 21 de Marzo No. 204.

MICHOACÁN — BEACHES WITHOUT TOURISTS

The beaches of Michoacán have remained undeveloped, primarily because they are not easily accessible. The best, Playa Azul, is a six-hour drive from Manzanillo, eight hours from Morelia and two hours from Ixtapa-Zihuatanejo. This is the most remote stretch of Mexico's coast and its most primitive. The high mountains of southern Michoacán descend steeply to beaches that are often rocky and there are no protected bays. Crashing waves are often too rough for body surfing and the undertow can be too strong for safe swimming.

There are beaches which have minimal facilities at the fishing villages of Punta San Juan de Lima, Punta San Telmo, Maruata, Caleta de Campos Chutla and Las Peñas. At the eastern boundary of the state, **Playa Azul** is the only developed resort of any size, and it does not cater to foreign visitors. This not to say foreigners are not welcome for they certainly are. It means that hotels, restaurants and entertainment are Mexican. During the week, the long beach is relatively deserted, but weekends bring families from Uruapan and the nearby port city of Lázaro Cárdenas with their accompanying happy noise.

IXTAPA–ZIHUATANEJO

The state of Guerrero has two of Mexico's most frequented tourist attractions — Taxco (see page 136) and Acapulco (see page 306). Tourism is 70% of the state's economy and visitors to its beach resorts are the biggest spenders. Thus, state and national funds have been used to renovate the country's best-known seaside resort, Acapulco, and to develop new facilities at the ever more popular resort area of Ixtapa–Zihuatanejo.

The resorts of Ixtapa and Zihuatanejo, or Ixta–Zihua, as they are often collectively called, is a

OPPOSITE: An Ixta–Zihua resort complex has been grafted on to Zihuatanejo, a hitherto calm, slow-paced fishing village. ABOVE: Guerrero artisans create picturesque souvenirs.

vacation destination that combines a modern, highrise resort complex with a working town. Picturesque Zihuatanejo was a calm, slow-paced fishing village that once vied with Acapulco and Manzanillo for trade with the Orient. Until 1978 its streets were unpaved; its laid-back atmosphere and fine protected beaches have made it a favorite vacation choice of savvy travelers for years. The old town now has paved streets, hotels, restaurants and tourist shops, and a population of more than 50,000 full-time residents. A few hundred of the original fishing families still claim some of the most valuable real estate but most of the residents come from Mexico City, Acapulco and Guadalajara to work in the tourism business. There is also a fair-sized population of winter residents from Canada and the United States.

Ixtapa, about six kilometers (four miles) northwest of Zihuatanejo, consisted primarily of coconut palm plantations until 1976, when the government began building stylish hotels along its protected bay. It has everything — hotels, golf, restaurants, shopping centers, discos — except a touch of Mexico. Luckily Zihuatanejo is nearby.

GENERAL INFORMATION

As in the other Pacific Coast resorts, the high season is from December through April, and year-round temperatures average approximately 26°C (80°F). Off-season prices are often one-third of high-season rates, but there may be light showers during the day and hurricanes in autumn.

The **Oficina de Turismo** (Tourism Office) ((755) 31270 FAX (755) 30819, is in Ixtapa at Plaza Ixpamar, Suite 18, and is open Mondays through Fridays. The office sometimes has copies of *What to Do, Where to Go*, a small pamphlet with hotel and restaurant listings.

WHAT TO SEE AND DO

Zihuatanejo is one on my favorite Pacific Coast destinations. It's small enough that one can get to know the major hangouts and streets easily, yet full of distractions. The first place most visitors learn to explore is the waterfront *malecón*, also known as **Paseo del Pescador**, running parallel to downtown from the fishing pier to the rocky trails along the south end of Zihuatanejo Bay leading to Playa Madera. Seafood cafés, artisans' stands and a few hotels line the *malecón*, which has an always busy basketball court in its center. The small **Museo Arqueológico de la Costa Grande** (Archaeology Museum) ((755) 32552, on Paseo del Pescador (open Tuesday through Sunday), fills a river-rock building with artifacts from Guerrero's sparse archaeological sites. Streets lead inland from the *malecón* past interesting shops and restaurants to the **Mercado Central**, on Benito Juárez at An-

tonio Nava, where locals stock up on produce, fish, giant coconuts and papayas. Stands in the area sell well-made *huaraches* and sandals. The **Mercado de Artesanías Turístico** on 5 de Mayo between Juan N. Alvarez and Catalina González, has 255 permanent stands along the narrow lagoon at the west side of the bay.

Playa Principal, the main beach, begins at the pier on the west end of the *malecón*; locals and travelers gather here to view the daily catch and take boat trips to **Playa las Gatas**, a remote beach on the far east side of the bay. **Playa Madera**, east of downtown and the *malecón*, is one of the better swimming beaches, though access is limited to rocky trails from town or the clifftop neighborhood above the beach. The best all-round beach is **Playa la Ropa**, backed by hotels. Beyond Playa La Ropa and a jagged cliff is **Playa las Gatas**. According to the local legend the rocks were put there by the Purépecha king Tangáoan II to create a swimming hole where his princess daughter could swim undisturbed.

With its highrise hotels lining the beaches of **Bahía de Palmar** (Palmar Bay) north to **Marina Ixtapa**, Ixtapa is different from Acapulco or Cancún in its location, the color and temperature of the water and its lack of franchise restaurants. Its best feature is **Isla Ixtapa**, a wildlife preserve. The swimming, snorkeling and diving off the island are better than from the mainland. All the hotels can provide guides, boats and equipment.

Golfers have two courses to choose from in Ixtapa; both are open to hotel guests and have such interesting hazards as crocodiles peering from ponds. You can partake in awesome **scuba diving** here in the summer, when manta rays, sharks and whales mingle with humans; contact the **Zihuatanejo Scuba Center** ((755) 42147 FAX (755) 44468 at Cuauhtémoc No. 3 in downtown Zihua.

Between Zihuatanejo and Acapulco there are many beaches which offer more secluded bathing. With the influx of tourism even these are beginning to be developed, but the rugged traveler can still find bungalows and restaurants down many of the dirt roads leading to the beaches.

WHERE TO STAY

There are exceptional hotels in Ixta-Zihua in all price categories, along with dependable chain properties. They book up quickly around holidays and in August.

Very Expensive

Among the most gorgeous hotels in all of Mexico is **La Casa Que Canta** ((755) 47030 TOLL-FREE (888) 523-5050 FAX (755) 47040 or reservations FAX (755) 47900 E-MAIL lcqcanta@internet.com.mx, on Camino Escénico a la Playa la Ropa. The 24 suites, some with private pools, echo the hillside's natural setting with their artistically carved wood furnishings, textured cotton upholstery and wood shutters which open onto terracotta-colored terraces. The buildings, which have an adobe-like finish blended with straw, nestle subtly against the jungle background. The suites are each named for a Mexican song and are the kind of rooms you simply don't want to leave. You may be tempted to descend the hill to the pool and hot tub by the sea, or wander to the elegant dining area by the *palapa*-roofed lounge. Room service is an option as well, as is breakfast in bed.

Villa Del Sol ((755) 42239 TOLL-FREE (888) 389-2645 FAX (755) 42758 on Playa de la Ropa in Zihuatanejo, is so exclusive that children under 14 are not allowed during the winter high season. The hotel is a member of Relais & Chateaux and the Small Luxury Hotels of the World, and offers beach front luxury to guests in its 45 suites. Children are readily welcome at the **Club Mediterranée Ixtapa (** (755) 43340 TOLL-FREE (800) 258-2633, on Playa Quieta north of Ixtapa's main beach, one of the better family clubs in the chain. Circus workshops (including trapeze lessons), scuba diving, kayaking, tennis, volleyball, archery and other activities keep guests busy; above average buffet meals with addictive homemade breads provide ample calories. Like other members of this Mexican chain, the **Krystal Ixtapa (** (755) 30333 TOLL-FREE (800) 231-9860 FAX (755) 30216, Boulevard Ixtapa at Playa del Palmar, has ample grounds to separate its 254 rooms.

Expensive

Set against a cove and a secluded beach at the eastern curve of Ixtapa Bay, the **Westin Las Brisas Resort Ixtapa (** (755) 32121 TOLL-FREE (800) 228-3000 FAX (755) 30751, at Playa Vista Hermosa off Paseo de Ixtapa, offers 428 stunning rooms with balconies hung with hammocks, excellent restaurants and a luxurious feeling of seclusion. The **Villa del Lago (** (755) 31482 FAX (755) 31422 and United States FAX (619) 575-1766, Retorno de las Alondras No. 244, next to the Ixtapa Country Club, is a private mansion turned guest house with six sumptuous suites, a peaceful terrace and pool, and an excellent chef. **Puerto Mío (** (755) 42748 TOLL-FREE (** (888) 389-2645 FAX (755) 42048, above Zihuatanejo on Cerro del Almacén, has 31 rooms in pastel *casitas* stacked up a steep hillside overlooking the west side of Zihua bay. The hotel sits above a cove and marina where guests dock their yachts and from which fishing and diving boats depart. The swimming pool seems to flow into the horizon and the restaurant commands a great bay view. The **Sheraton Ixtapa Resort (** (755) 31858 TOLL-FREE (800) 325-3535 FAX (755) 32438, on Boulevard Ixtapa, has the ultimate user-friendly swimming pool with plenty of space for wading, swimming and lounging around the swim-up bar.

The 331 rooms are tastefully decorated and have all the expected amenities.

Moderate

Amid more luxurious properties, the **Hotel Dorado Pacifico (** (755) 32025 TOLL-FREE (800) 448-8355 FAX (755) 30126, on Boulevard Ixtapa, offers 285 motel-like rooms, a huge pool, the best coffee shop in the hotel zone and friendly service. The **Best Western Posada Real (** (755) 31685 TOLL-FREE (800) 528-1234 FAX (755) 31805, on Boulevard Ixtapa, is another good choice for its 110 standard rooms, a kid-friendly pool and beach, and serviceable restaurants.

In Zihuatanejo, the **Hotel Paraíso Real (** (755) 42147 FAX (755) 42147, on Playa la Ropa (or write to Zihuatanejo Scuba Center, Calle Cuauhtémoc No. 3, Zihuatanejo 40880, Guerrero), is designed as an environmentally-responsible property bordering a mangrove forest at the edge of the beach. The 20 rooms in lush gardens do not have phone or television, a blessing for escapists. As crocodiles inhabit the lagoon by the property, only children 12 and older can stay here. There's a restaurant and bar, and kayak and windsurfer rentals.

Inexpensive

My first Zihua hotel has remained one of my favorites for its location, rates and second-story terrace overlooking the *malecón* and Playa Principal. The **Hotel Avila (** (755) 42010 FAX (755) 43299, Juan N. Alvarez No. 8, near the east end of the *malecón*, is far from fancy, but its 27 rooms are comfortable and air-conditioned, so you can shut the windows against the city noise. **Bungalows Pacificos (** (755) 42112 FAX (755) 42112 on Cerro de la Madera, is a great find on Playa Madera. Its six units have porches, kitchenettes and plenty of space, and the owner speaks several languages and is immensely knowledgeable about the area. Set in a garden on the slopes over the beach, the **Hotel Irma (** (755) 42025 FAX (755) 43738 at Playa Madera, Zihuatanejo, is one of Zihua's original hotels. It retains a low-key ambiance and many of the 80 modest rooms look out to the sea.

WHERE TO EAT

The restaurants in the Westin Las Brisas, Sheraton and Krystal hotels in Ixtapa are all quite good, as are those in Zihua's Puerto Mío, Casa Que Canta and Villa Del Sol hotels. Though Ixtapa's guests tend to have deeper pockets, many of the area's most innovative chefs have set up shop in Zihua, perhaps because of its friendly ambiance and proximity to markets and fishermen. Since taxi rides between the two towns can add up quickly, try to combine sightseeing with a good meal when venturing from your hotel.

Expensive

The view, tropical gardens and terraced outdoor dining rooms make **Villa de la Selva ℂ** (755) 30362, Paseo de la Roca, off Paseo de Ixtapa, the most romantic dinner restaurant in the area. Arrive early for sunset cocktails before dining on lobster and steak. Homemade pastas, tempting pastries and a serious wine list make **Beccofino ℂ** (755) 31770, near the lighthouse in Marina Ixtapa, the best Northern Italian restaurant in the area.

Moderate

In Zihuatanejo, **Kau-Kan ℂ** (755) 48446, on Playa Madera by the Hotel Brisas del Mar, is considered by many to be the most innovative restaurant in

the area, serving the catch of the day with *guajillo* chilis and manta ray in a black butter sauce. **Paul's** ℂ (755) 42188, on 5 de Mayo between Nicolás Bravo and Ejido, has as many followers who rave about the sashimi and shrimp in dill sauce. High quality regional Mexican cuisine served on *talavera* pottery in a peaceful dining room are the attractions at **El Patio ℂ** (755) 43019, 5 de Mayo No. 3 at Pedro Ascencio.

   La Sirena Gorda ℂ (755) 42687, on Paseo del Pescador near the pier, is the most famous of Zihua's *malecón* restaurants. Try the fish tacos offered with several types of fillings, including smoked marlin. Just a few doors down is **Casa Elvira ℂ** (755) 42061, at Paseo del Pescador near the basketball court. Though some say the food has gone downhill, I always like stopping here for chips, salsa and a chilled beer while watching the action. In Ixtapa, I'm particularly fond of the family feeling at **Mamma Norma Pizzeria ℂ** (755) 30274, in the La Puerta Mall, and the juice stand in the same mall. The **Golden Cookie Shop ℂ** (755) 30310, on the second floor of Los Patios Mall, is a German bakery and café serving huge sausage and cheese sandwiches, strudel and bratwurst. **Nueva Zelanda ℂ** (755) 42340, also at Los Patios in Ixtapa, and on Cuauhtémoc at Ejido in Zihua, is a great spot for *licuados*, salads and sandwiches. **JJ's**

306   *Pacific Coast*

Lobster and Shrimp ℂ (755) 32494, on Boulevard Ixtapa across from the Posada Real Hotel, offers fancy lobster meals in one dining room and cheap snacks next door.

Inexpensive

Lunch at **Tamales y Atoles Any ℂ** (755) 47373, a few blocks from Zihua's waterfront on Ejido at Vicente Guerrero, is an education in Mexican cooking. *Atole*, a hot drink made of ground corn meal or rice, comes in fruit flavors, and there are sweet and spicy *tamales* and *quesadillas* stuffed with cheese and squash blossoms for the sampling. You can get by cheaply by ordering conservatively and coming back often. **Rossy ℂ** (755) 42700, at the east end of Playa La Ropa, is a popular spot for snacks and drinks on the sand.

HOW TO GET THERE

Flights from the United States, Canada, and other points in Mexico arrive at the international airport near Zihuatanejo. Aeroméxico and Mexicana provide national and international service, and Continental and Northwest connect from several United States cities.

ACAPULCO

No matter how hard civic boosters and developers try, Acapulco seems unable to regain its title as the most dazzling and sophisticated coastal resort in Mexico. After its Hollywood boom in the 1950s and the surge in tourism in the 1970s, Acapulco slid downhill into disrepair. A massive redevelopment effort in the 1990s has brought new sewage systems and a concerted effort to clean up the waters in Acapulco's gorgeous bay. New resort areas have risen on the east side of the bay, in Punta Diamante, and many of the '70s-style hotels have been upgraded. Just when it seemed Acapulco was making a significant return, Hurricane Pauline hit in 1997. International attention was suddenly focused not on the resort but on the miserable living conditions of Acapulco's working-class residents. Torrential rains, high winds, mud slides and floods displaced thousands of people from their homes and caused many deaths. While the resort hotels quickly recovered from the hurricane's furious onslaught, entire inland neighborhoods went without purified water or sufficient housing for weeks and even months. Acapulco's image was tarnished.

   As Mexico's oldest glamour resort, Acapulco remains dear to Mexicans living in the capital and other major cities. Wealthy and middle-class

Acapulco — ABOVE: A flower vendor. OPPOSITE and OVERLEAF: With dazzling beaches, discos, hotels and villas, this is a coastal escape for Mexican and international vacationers.

families from Mexico City and Guadalajara built homes and condos long ago in the hills above the bay, where families escape from the city smog for quick fixes of sunshine, fresh air and partying. In August, Acapulco becomes almost purely Mexican as families settle in for weeks at the beach. International tourists find it a great escape, where they can drink and dance all night and spend the daylight ensconced in plush hotel rooms or dozing by the pool or sea.

BACKGROUND

In the sixteenth century, Acapulco was New Spain's largest Pacific port. Exotic goods arriving on galleons from the Orient were packed on mules and carried overland to Veracruz for shipment to Spain. The vessels were then laden with silver and spices for a return voyage. This thriving trade attracted pirates, among them Sir Frances Drake, who laid in wait to attack ships as they left the harbor.

After Mexico's War of Independence, trade with Spain and the Orient came to a sudden halt, and so did Acapulco. The few inhabitants who refused to leave their tropical paradise turned to fishing and agriculture for their livelihood. Then in 1927 a highway was cut through the mountains from Mexico City and tourism brought the city back to life. However it wasn't until 1955, when a new and faster highway was built, that Acapulco became a major tourist destination. At the same time, Mexican and American singers, dancers and movie stars were making Acapulco their coastal retreat. Titled Europeans followed, and for two decades the paparazzi kept the world informed about the dazzling villas and hedonistic lifestyles of the rich and famous. Tourism boomed in the 1960s and 1970s, and crashed in the 1980s as Cancún stepped onto center stage. Now Acapulco struggles to gain prominence once again by the turn of the century.

GENERAL INFORMATION

The **Oficina de Turismo** (Tourism Office) ((74) 848554 FAX (74) 848134 is located in the Oceanic 2000 Building, at Costera M. Alemán 311. It's open Monday through Friday from 9 AM to 5 PM. There is also an information booth in front of the Convention Center. The **Acapulco Convention and Visitors Bureau** ((74) 840599 FAX (74) 848134, Privada de Roca Sola No. 19 at Fracción Club Deportivo, is inconveniently located up a hill behind the convention center, and is open Monday through Friday.

WHAT TO SEE AND DO

In spite of its population (nearly two million), Acapulco is basically a one-street town. Costera

Miguel Alemán follows the curve of the bay, becoming Carretera Escénica on the east and Avenida López Mateos on the west.

Most of the major hotels and beaches are along Costera Miguel Alemán, from Playa Icacos on the eastern end and Playa Condesa, Playa Hornos, and Playa Hornitos on the west. The center of Old Acapulco and the downtown is the **Plaza Alvarez**, also called the Zócalo. Though not as charming as others in Mexico, the plaza is a gathering spot where newspaper vendors and shoeshine boys set up shop under shade trees and locals and travelers take a break at outdoor cafés. The plaza is backed by the **Catedral Nuestra Señora de la Soledad**, constructed in 1930.

Fishing and tour boats line up at the pier across from the plaza, where a seaside *malecón* leads east to the **Fuerte de San Diego** ((74) 823828, on Costera M. Alemán at Morelos (small admission fee; open Tuesday through Sunday). The star-shaped fort was built in 1616 by the Spanish to protect their galleons from pirate attack. Rebuilt after an earthquake nearly leveled it in 1776, it now houses a museum dedicated to the history of the area from pre-Conquest times through its heyday as a center of trade with the Orient, and up to today. Buried back in downtown is the **Mercado Municipal** on Constituyentes at Hurtado de Mendoza. This public market is one of the few places where outsiders can sample the local lifestyle; good tourist buys include leather sandals and *huaraches*.

The old hotels are at the western end of Costera M. Alemán where it becomes Avenida López Mateos. This is my favorite part of Acapulco's coastline, where locals gather for Sunday picnics on **Playa Caleta**. I enjoy staying in the Caleta area and wandering down to the beach for a drink at a snack stand on the sand, or following the *malecón* past the yacht club and marinas to the Zócalo. The bright purple **Mágico Mundo Marino** aquarium ((74) 831215 sits at the edge of the Playa Caleta off Gran Via Topical (admission fee; open Monday and Wednesday through Sunday). The building and outdoor attractions are packed with local families on Sundays and holidays. The aquarium displays indoor and outdoor tanks with tropical fish, alligators, and seals; an outdoor pool and waterslide keep the kids happy. Boats depart from here to **Isla la Roqueta**, where the beaches are less crowded, and hiking trails lead up steep hills through the now (thankfully) defunct Acapulco Zoo.

From Playa Caleta, Avenida López Mateos climbs the rocky cliffs to **La Quebrada**, where young men risk their lives diving 40 m (130 ft) from the cliffs into a small cove. These divers demonstrate their skills daily at 1 PM and in the evening.

Between downtown and the tourist zone is **Papagayo Park**, a 21-hectare (52-acre) greenbelt on Costera M. Alemán between Insurgentes and Aviles. The children's amusement park, with rides and life-size reproductions of space shuttles and Spanish galleons is the main attraction, though joggers and strollers enjoy the park's shaded paths. From here east, hotels, shopping centers, restaurants, artisans' markets and a general ambiance of jarring clutter fill the Costera. The **Acapulco Convention Center** sits near the east side of the bay; folkloric dance performances are sometimes held here. Centro Internacional Convivencia Infantil (Children's International Center) ((74) 848033, is a bit farther west on Costera M. Alemán at Cristóbal Colón (admission fee; open daily from 10 AM to 6 PM). The park is a delight for children, who can spend the entire day in the pools, playing on the waterslides and cruising in floats along the river ride.

In the eastern part of the bay, the Costera becomes the Carretera Escénica, the scenic road leading up to the Las Brisas hills and Acapulco's newest developments. The road climbs and curves atop the cliffs as it passes high-end hotels, discos, restaurants and private homes en route to **Puerto Marqués**, where pirates once wait for Spanish galleons.

Farther down the road is **Playa Revolcadero**, a long expanse of sand subject to rough open surf. Although there is a public section of this beach (at the eastern end), the beach is primarily the turf of the exclusive resort hotels, Princess and Pierre Marqués.

When one has had enough of the surf and sand, Acapulco has enough **shopping** to keep browsers busy. Most hotels have boutiques and there

are several air-conditioned malls on Costera M. Alemán. Shopkeepers have everything from Mexican handicrafts to designer clothes. Prices are usually high. Vendors are no longer allowed to sell their wares on the Costera's beaches and have been assigned stands in several permanent artisans' markets.

Most hotels also have **water sports** equipment rentals on the beach, offering everything from beach umbrellas to banana boats. Parasailing boats ply the water offshore.

Most major hotels have **tennis** courts, and **golf** is available at the nine-hole **Club de Golf Acapulco** ((74) 840781 on Costera M. Alemán at Lomas del Mar near the convention center, and at two

championship 18-hole courses at the Pierre Marqués and Princess hotels; call ((74) 691000 for information about either course.

As in Mexico's other Pacific Coast resorts, **sport fishing** is good in Acapulco. Sailfish, marlin, shark and dorado are the usual catches; check with boat captains at the dock across from downtown's Zócalo for information or arrange fishing excursions through your hotel. **Theme cruises** of the bay abound; again, your hotel tour desk is the best source of information.

Pie de la Cuesta 13 km (eight miles) west of the city, is a long, narrow strip of beach that separates the Pacific from Laguna Coyuca. The surf and undertow here make swimming difficult, but the sunsets are superb and many travelers book a

Sunset view OPPOSITE and waitress ABOVE at Las Brisas, reputedly Mexico's most expensive hotel.

side trip just to sit at a bar on the sand and sip tropical cocktails while watching the sun settle into the waves.

WHERE TO STAY

Acapulco has many hotels, and you should have no trouble finding a good room in your price range. Most of the major chain hotels are located along Costera M. Alemán in the midst of the action, and guests never need to even take a cab unless headed for a special night of dining and dancing in the Las Brisas hills. As a rule the least expensive places are near downtown and Playa Caleta at the west side of the bay, while the most expensive resorts are on the east side. Reservations are helpful during national and international holidays. Ask about hotel and air packages, which are abundant here.

Very Expensive

Acapulco's most famous hotel is the pink-and-white **Westin Las Brisas** ((74) 841580 TOLL-FREE (800) 228-3000 FAX (74) 842269, Carretera Escénica No. 5255. The 300 rooms are located in rows of small *casitas* stacked up the steep hillsides overlooking the bay. All rooms have private plunge pools, and coffee and sweet rolls are slipped through a small door onto a shelf inside the room each morning. Las Brisas pink and white jeeps are available with room rental, though many guests leave the property only to take the shuttle across the main road to the hotel's luxurious beach club. Equally glamorous, though far larger, is the pyramid-shaped **Acapulco Princess Hotel** ((74) 691000 TOLL-FREE (800) 223-1818 FAX (74) 691016 on Carretera Escénica at Playa Revolcadero. With 1,019 rooms, the Princess is one of the largest hotels in Mexico, and offers multiple pools and restaurants, a high-end shopping arcade, several excellent restaurants and two golf courses. The **Pierre Marqués** ((74) 691000 TOLL-FREE (800) 223-1818 FAX (74) 691016, on Carretera Escénica at Playa Revolcadero, on the same grounds as the Princess, is more intimate, with 344 luxurious rooms. The **Camino Real Diamante** ((74) 661010 TOLL-FREE (800) 722-6466 FAX (74) 661111, on Baja Catita off Carretera Escénica, is the centerpiece of the new Punta Diamante development of luxury villas and residences. Its interiors of jade-green marble and glistening chandeliers, pools terraced down a hill to the beach, a fitness center, and wonderful cuisine in the restaurants mark this Camino Real as an escapist's delight of the highest quality. It offers 156 deluxe rooms with grand baths for well-heeled vacationers.

Expensive

I would always be content to stay at the **Hotel Elcano** ((74) 841950 FAX (74) 842230, Costera M. Alemán No. 75, a 1950s-style hotel completely redesigned for the 1990s. A serene blue and white color scheme prevails from the tiled floors to the linen in the 340 rooms. White ceiling fans stir the air in the rooms and public spaces (though air-conditioning is available). The pool appears to flow into the horizon between towering palms. If you're not staying here be sure to stop in for a view of the enchanting murals of Acapulco's more glamorous era painted by artist Cristina Rubalcava, a Mexican expatriate living in Paris. You must dine here at least once.

Of the dozens of hotels on the strip the **Acapulco Plaza** ((74) 859050 TOLL-FREE (800) 343-7821 FAX (74) 855285, Costera M. Alemán No. 123, has always been a charmer thanks to its tropical-style

lobby with waterfalls, ferns and squawking parrots and macaws. The 506 rooms are renovated on a regular basis, and the large pool flows in several directions to provide plenty of swimming and lounging space. The **Fiesta Americana Condesa** ((74) 842828 TOLL-FREE (800) 343-7821 FAX (74) 841828, Costera M. Alemán No. 1220, is another perennial favorite with one of the best beaches on the Costera and 500 comfortable rooms. A complete overhaul in the mid-1990s restored the comforts of the 690-room **Hyatt Regency Acapulco** ((74) 691234 TOLL-FREE (800) 233-1234 FAX (74) 843087, Costera M. Alemán No. 1. The property benefits from being the last hotel on the east side of the bay; thus the beach feels more private than most.

OPPOSITE: Banana boats, jet skis and all forms of water toys entertain tourists on Acapulco's beaches. ABOVE: Beach vendor with local confection.

Moderate

The best escape from Acapulco's crowds is at the **Boca Chica Hotel** ((74) 836601 TOLL-FREE (800) 346-3942 FAX (74) 839513, Playa Caletilla No. 7. I love this place for its small rocky cove, its 45 simple and comfortable rooms, the perfect lap pool, the seaside restaurant and the wonderful staff. Guests feel like family here, trading paperback books and travel tips as they sunbathe and watch snorkelers in the cove. A sense of Old Acapulco seems to permeate the place, and one quickly loses interest in leaving the hotel to join the bustling crowds. A similar feeling prevails at the **Hotel Los Flamingos** ((74) 820690 FAX (74) 839806, on López Mateos near Avenida Coyuca. Another hotel long past its heyday, the Flamingo's 46 rooms have been recently renovated. The former Villas La Marina hotel in Old Acapulco was renovated in 1996 and reopened as the **Holiday Inn Hotel and Suites** ((74) 823620 TOLL-FREE (800) 465-4329 FAX (74) 828480, Costera M. Alemán No. 222. The 90 rooms and suites are in rock and brick buildings set amid gardens and draping bougainvillea. A pedestrian bridge leads over the road to the beach. The cliff divers of La Quebrada are the big attraction at the **El Mirador Plaza Las Glorias** ((74) 831155 TOLL-FREE (800) 342-2644 FAX (74) 824564, La Quebrada No. 74. Another gem from the 1950s, the El Mirador sits high atop a cliff and has 81 rooms, many with kitchenettes. Tour groups fill the restaurant when the cliff divers appear for their nightly performance. Closer to the Costera action is the 90-room **Howard Johnson Maralisa Hotel and Beach Club** ((74) 856677 TOLL-FREE (800) 446-4656 FAX (74) 859228 on Alemania off Costera M. Alemán.

Inexpensive

Tucked away on a side street close to the Zócalo, the **Hotel Misión** ((74) 823643 FAX (74) 822076, Felipe Valle No. 12, is a charmer with 27 rooms set around a courtyard. Other inexpensive hotels are clustered around the plaza; be sure to check the rooms before settling here.

WHERE TO EAT

Every palate can be satisfied by Acapulco's endless array of restaurants. There are dozens of franchise fast-food outlets for the feckless, and fine Italian, Mexican and Japanese restaurants for cosmopolitan tastes. The majority of the larger hotels have at least one first-rate dining establishment among their restaurant options, and a few of these are truly exceptional. Most of the high-end restaurants are in the Las Brisas Hill, so you'll have to add cab fare to your tab. In Acapulco it is fashionable to dine around 10 PM, before the discos open. During high season, reservations are recommended at the finer establishments.

Very Expensive

The most beautiful restaurant in town is aptly set in an Old Acapulco neighborhood by Playa Caleta. **Coyuca 22** ((74) 823468, on Calle Coyuca No. 22, looks like a partially restored Greek ruin with its Doric columns and statues around a small pool. Diners sample the *prix fixe* dinners or menu items at terrace tables overlooking the west end of the bay. Consistently mentioned as one of the best places in town is **Madeiras** ((74) 844378, on Carretera Escénica. Roast quail, duck, filet mignon and frog's legs are served in a series of elegant dining rooms overlooking the lights of the city. **Ristorante Casa Nova** ((74) 846815, Carretera Escénica No. 5256 is the best choice for elegant Italian cuisine. **Spicey** ((74) 81138, in the same neighborhood on Carretera Escénica at Fraccionamento Las Brisas, has a far more daring menu combining Pacific-rim and European ingredients. Spring rolls are filled with smoked salmon, fresh fish is glazed with honey and the *chilis rellenos* are covered with mango sauce. This is a see-and-be-seen spot for the pre-disco crowd.

Expensive

The shopping center setting doesn't detract from the romance at **El Olvido** ((74) 810214, in the Plaza Marabella on Costera M. Alemán. Large windows face the bay, visible from most tables in the multilevel dining room. The international cuisine features salmon, quail and fresh fish in fruit sauces. Sushi fans swear by the fresh ingredients and artful presentations at **Suntory** ((74) 848088, on Costera M. Alemán No. 36. Teppanyaki dishes with meat, seafood and vegetables are cooked at the table on a sizzling hot plate and tempura, sukiyaki and sashimi are all available. **Su Casa** ((74) 844350, overlooking the hotel and bay from atop a steep hill at Avenida Anhuac No. 110, fulfills the promises of its name by making diners feel as though they're eating on the terrace of a private home. Mexican dishes include grilled meats marinated in tropical juices. Shrimp, steaks and barbecued chicken are also available.

Moderate

I never visit Acapulco without lingering over breakfast at **Bambuco** ((74) 841950, a serene seaside café at the Elcano Hotel on Costera M. Alemán. Though power brokers prefer this spot for business breakfasts, there's no sense of urgency at the tables set amid palms by the shoreline. I crave the eggs and smoked salmon, the artful fruit plates and the courtly service, which prevail through meals served all day. **Señor Frog's** ((74) 848020 on Carretera Escénica, Lote No. 28, in the La Vista Center, is far from serene. Despite the loud music and cluttered decor, local leaders gather here on Thursday afternoons for the traditional *pozole* feast, based on a hominy stew with pork and dozens of condiments. The other menu items are tasty and served in bountiful portions. There's a second location, also lively, at Costera M. Alemán No. 999 ((74) 841285.

Paraíso/Paradise ((74) 845988 on the beach on Costera M. Alemán is the best of the many outdoor restaurants competing for attention at the center of the Costera. Seafood and steaks are served by merry waiters amid blaring music — you are expected to have fun here. **Pipo's Mariscos** ((74) 838801 on Costera M. Alemán near the convention center is a local hangout beloved for its giant lunches of seafood cocktails and grilled fish. There's a second location in Old Acapulco at Calle Almirante Breton No. 3, off Costera M. Alemán near the Zócalo.

Inexpensive

Fruit and vegetable juices, salads and healthy sandwiches are the draw at **100% Natural** ((74) 853982 on Costera M. Alemán near the Acapulco Plaza Hotel. **Zorritos** ((74) 853735 on Costera M. Alemán serves tacos, *huevos rancheros* and *enchiladas* to hungry dancers after the discos close; it's open during the day as well.

NIGHTLIFE

Acapulco's main attraction may well be its discos, where fashionable patrons start lining up at about 10 PM. The music and dancing don't really get intense until after midnight, when laser lights and fireworks over the bay announce that the fun has begun. The dress code is strict in most clubs — no shorts, sandals or sneakers — and it's obvious that patrons have spent much of the evening attending to their attire. The most glamorous discos, with steep cover charges and drink prices, are **Extravaganza**, **Fantasy** and **Palladium**, all on Carretera Escénica above the bay. **Baby O**, **News** and **Andromeda** on Costera M. Alemán attract a younger, trendy crowd.

HOW TO GET THERE

Acapulco's Aeropuerto Internacional Juan N. Alvarez receives national and international flights daily, and is located at the eastern edge of the resort, a half-hour drive from the center of the city. The drive from Mexico City, either by car or by express bus, takes three and a half hours on an expensive toll road (*autopista*), or six hours on the older highway.

CHILPANCINGO DE LOS BRAVOS

Chilpancingo de los Bravos, a city of 100,000 and capital of the state of Guerrero, is not a tourist destination in itself, but being only 133 km (82 miles) from Acapulco, it makes a good day

trip and a change of scenery, or a staging point for exploring the mountains. Of particular interest are the **Juxtlahuaca Caves**, 60 km (37 miles) southeast, beyond Colotlipa. These caves full of stalactites were discovered in the 1930s and were discovered to contain 3,000-year-old wall paintings. The paintings, which are found more than a kilometer (nearly a mile) from the entrance, represent typical Olmec motifs — figures of rulers and plumed serpents in black, red, yellow and green.

Going east from Acapulco to Puerto Escondido (see THE LAND BRIDGE, page 213), there is little tourist development. The road is no longer on the beach. It travels through several small towns, whose

inhabitants are descendants of runaway African slaves, and through areas of tropical vegetation with numerous rivers, lagoons and unusual rock formations.

Surf and sun draw millions of tourists — young and old — to Mexico's coastal resorts each year.

Baja California

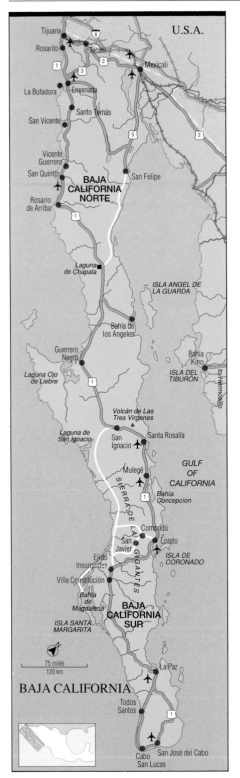

BAJA CALIFORNIA

WITH THE EXCEPTION OF THE VALLEY AROUND MEXICALI in the north, and its southern tip, the peninsula of Baja California is a mountainous desert bordered by sandy beaches and rocky shoreline. It is bounded on the north by the United States, and separated from the mainland of Mexico by the Mar de Cortés (Sea of Cortez) and the Gulf of California. Mountain ranges run north and south along the 1250-km (775-mile) long peninsula, a narrow finger of land which has an average width of 90 km (55 miles).

BACKGROUND

Baja California has been inhabited since approximately 7500 BC, when cave dwellers left petroglyphs looking much like those found in southern France. Little is known about these earliest inhabitants; the first written information about the area comes from Hernán Cortés. In 1535, while searching for the legendary kingdom of the Amazons ruled by the black queen, Calafia, Cortés landed a party at Baja's southern tip, near the present-day city of La Paz. Although the Spanish did not find the fierce women warriors here, they did give the land the queen's name — California.

Hearing rumors of an abundance of pearls in the bays along the peninsula, Cortés organized, but did not participate in, several later expeditions which, understandably, met with open hostility from the Indians. It was not until the late seventeenth century that any permanent European settlement began here. In 1697, three Jesuit missionaries arrived to begin proselytizing and converting native tribes. When more priests followed in 1720, they brought the additional spiritual benefit of smallpox, which decimated the native populations.

The missionaries persevered, believing it better to die as a Christian than live as an Indian. By 1750, there were few Indians left and their populations have never recovered. Today the Indian population of Baja is less then 1,500. In spite of their expiring clientele, the missionaries continued to work up and down the length of Baja, planting vineyards and olive and date groves. When the Jesuits were expelled from Mexico in 1767, these missions were prosperous enough to be coveted and taken over by the Franciscans, and then by the Dominicans in 1772.

The missions spread from Loreto northward into Alta (or higher California), where they grew and prospered. The lower (baja) peninsula remained part of Mexico after California became a US state in 1804. The peninsula was appropriated briefly by the United States during the Mexican-American War. After the Mexican War of Independence it was incorporated into the Republic as a territory and later, in 1931, divided along the 28th parallel into Baja California Norte and Baja

California Sur. Baja California became a state in 1952, and Baja California Sur in 1974. With more than 3,000 km (1,860 miles) of coastline, Baja has become a popular getaway for Californians. Although the climate on the Pacific Coast is cool in the winter, the Gulf of California is warm from November to April. When the weather becomes almost unbearably hot on the Gulf (May to October), the Pacific Coast is warm and dry. South near La Paz, the climate is pleasant year-round.

GENERAL INFORMATION

Baja Information ((619) 298-4105 TOLL-FREE (800) 522-1516 from California, Nevada, Arizona

have extra water, food and gasoline, and allow at least two days to drive from the United States–Mexico border between San Diego and Tijuana to Baja's tip. I've driven the peninsula several times, most often in the searing heat of July when sport fishing is at its peak. It's a fabulous ride past vineyards, mesas, boulders, cacti, desert and ocean views (see CRUISE THE LONELY PENINSULA, page 18). At Guerrero Negro and the state line between Baja California and Baja California Sur, the highway begins to climb into the the mission town of San Ignacio before descending toward Santa Rosalía and the Sea of Cortez.

Baja California's cities and towns have grown considerably since 1973 to accommodate the ever-

TOLL-FREE (800) 225-2786 from North America FAX (619) 294-7366 E-MAIL impamexicoinfo @worldnet.att.net, arranges hotel reservations throughout the peninsula; for printed information write: 7860 Mission Center Court No. 202, San Diego, CA 92108.

Baja California Tours ((619) 454-7166 FAX (619) 454-2703, 7734 Herschel Avenue, Suite O, La Jolla, CA 92037, offer informative trips to Baja's ranches, missions and wineries.

HOW TO GET THERE

Until 1973 most of Baja California was accessible only in four-wheel-drive vehicles. Now the sealed Carretera Transpeninsular (Transpeninsular Highway or Highway 1) goes the length from Tijuana in the north to Cabo San Lucas in the south. Anyone making the trip should always

growing influx of visitors, who make tourism the mainstay of the peninsula's economy.

There are airports in Tijuana, Mexicali, La Paz, Loreto and Los Cabos. First- and second-class buses regularly run the route from Tijuana to Los Cabos.

TIJUANA

Tijuana is Mexico's fourth-largest city, with an official population of one-and-a-half million and an actual population probably much larger. Dingy, crowded and poor at first sight, Tijuana is one of Mexico's fastest growing cities, and one of its most prosperous. To the casual visitor, Tijuana seems uniquely foreign yet familiar, since the city thrives

Tijuana's grand Jai Alai Palace ABOVE and bullring OVERLEAF attract fans from both sides of the border.

Baja California

on the thousands of tourist who hop, like Mexican jumping beans, across the border from the United States.

BACKGROUND

Tijuana may well be "the most visited city in the world," as its city fathers claim. The San Diego–Tijuana border crossing is said to be the world's busiest, used daily by commuters crossing to and from work on both sides of the border, by families visiting relatives and by tourists who typically cross the border both ways in a day. The city's name is said to be a derivation of the Indian word, *tiwan*, meaning 'nearby water.' But popular lore has

the name coming from *Tia Juana*, or Aunt Jane, the name of a ranch near the border. Either way, Americans insist on calling the city Tia-wana instead of its proper name, Ti-hwana.

Tijuana has been a popular getaway for Californians ever since the United States prohibition in the 1920s, when the border offered easy access to liquor for "dry" Americans. Even after the repeal of prohibition, Tijuana retained its reputation as a desirable destination providing types of fun frowned upon by many across the border — raucous nightlife, drugs, cheap liquor, bullfights and gambling on horses, greyhounds and jai alai. All such vices are still available (live horse racing has ended, but you can still bet on races transmitted via satellite from the United States). But Tijuana has many other attractions. Its Cultural Center introduces thousands of visitors to the history, archaeology and civilizations of mainland Mexico.

Its restaurants and markets offer a wonderful entree to the cuisines of Mexico, and its shops display the best of the folk art the mainland has to offer. Most travelers come only for a day; Southern Californians find themselves returning again and again for a quick taste of Mexico.

GENERAL INFORMATION

The **Tourist Information Office** ((66) 831405, just inside the border crossing, is open daily from 9 AM to 7 PM; the staff go out of their way to attract visitors and dispense information. There is another **Tourist Information Office** ((66) 840537 Paseo de los Héroes No. 9365, in front of the Centro Cultural in the Zona Río, open Monday through Friday from 9 AM to 5 PM.

WHAT TO SEE AND DO

Tijuana's civic boosters are constantly dealing with their city's negative image and finding new ways to attract tourists. Though most visitors just spend the day, there are several good hotels catering to business travelers and those moving on through Baja and Mexico. Most of Tijuana lies to the south of the usually dry riverbed of the Tia Juana River. The shopping, bartering and beseeching begin the moment you cross the border and walk along Calle 2 toward downtown. A large complex of pottery yards and souvenir stands lies between Ocampo and Nigrete; if you're walking, this is a good place to begin examining possible purchases and prices. Refrain from buying that terracotta pig, Ninja turtle, *piñata*, or beaded velvet sombrero that seems so irresistible. You may find something better later on; if not, you can pick it up on your way back through the border instead of hauling it around all day.

The city's main tourist zone, **Avenida Revolución**, once held a tawdry assortment of bars and brothels. It now caters to tourists seeking a good time and shoppers determined to find bargains. Stores, restaurants and bars seem to undergo constant renovation in an attempt to appear more hip, trendy and attractive to jaded visitors seeking something new. Burros painted like zebras still pose at street corners so tourists can don velvet sombreros and be photographed in the standard Tijuana cliché. But an element of class has managed to creep into the Avenida Revolución scene, and there are several fine stores and restaurants to compete with the tacky souvenir stands and rowdy bars.

The most significant building on the strip is the Moorish-styled **El Palacio Frontón** ((66) 384308 TOLL-FREE (800) PIK-BAJA, Jai Alai Palace at Avenida Revolución and Calle 8. Jai alai games begin at 8 PM every night except Thursday. The games are fast-moving and interesting, and the betting adds to the merriment. The palace serves as the loading and unloading zone for tour buses, and is a good place to reconnoiter with your friends after splitting up for shopping and partying. The **Bazar de Mexico** ((66) 865280, Avenida Revolución at Calle 7 and the **Mexicoach Terminal** ((66) 851470, Avenida Revolución between Calles 6 and 7, both offer a more soothing shopping experience than in the older arcades and have refreshments for sale. One of the newer attractions near Revolución is the **L.A. Cetto Winery** ((66) 851644, on Cañon Johnson at Avenida Constitución. Tours of the winery (a branch of one of Mexico's most famous wineries) are available along with wine tastings and sales.

most famous archaeological sites, colonial buildings, churches and parks. Designed to resemble a colorful colonial plaza, **Pueblo Amigo**, on Paseo Tijuana between Puente Mexico and Avenida Independencia, is a nightlife and dining center within walking distance of the border; though businesses change names rapidly here, there's always a good party restaurant and a nightclub.

Avenida Revolución becomes Boulevard Agua Caliente southeast of downtown; some of the city's wealthiest neighborhoods are located above the boulevard in the **Lomas de Chapultepec** (Chapultepec Hills). The smaller of the city's two bullrings, **El Toreo de Tijuana** is on Boulevard Agua Caliente. Bullfights are held here on Sunday afternoons from

The more dignified shopping centers, hotels, restaurants and nightclubs are located a few blocks east in the **Zona Río**, a 10-minute walk on Calle 8A across Avenida General Rodolfo Taboada. The globe-shaped Omnimax theater and boxy museum at the **Centro Cultural Tijuana** ((66) 841125, on Paseo de los Héroes at Avenida Independencia (free admission; open daily from 9 AM to 8:30 PM), have become Tijuana's most precious landmarks. Designed by architect Pedro Ramírez Vásquez, the Centro houses an excellent permanent exhibit of Mexican history and has rotating shows of contemporary Mexican artists. The center's bookstore has an extensive collection of books on Mexico in both English and Spanish. **Mexitlán** ((66) 384165, Avenida Ocampo between Calles 2 and 3 (admission fee; open Wednesday through Sunday from 9 AM to 5 PM), is a fascinating outdoor museum with miniature replicas of Mexico's

May to September. But the top matadors usually take on *el toro* at the bullring by the sea, **Plaza de Toros Monumental** ((66) 842126 or 878519 in Las Playas de Tijuana south of town. The Tourist Information Offices have the prices and schedules. Admission varies according the fame of the matador. Also held on Sunday afternoons are *charreadas*, Mexican rodeos, organized by amateur cowboy associations ((66) 842126. Golf is available at the **Tijuana Country Club** ((66) 817855 on Boulevard Agua Caliente east of downtown.

Beyond El Toreo de Tijuana is the racetrack, **Hippódromo de Agua Caliente** ((66) 862002 on Boulevard Agua Caliente at Salinas, or ((619) 260-0060 in San Diego, California. Horses no longer race at the track, but there are live — somewhat —

Colorful and varied, Tijuana's streets offer something for everyone at any time of day or night.

greyhound races on the weekends. The racetrack is now connected via satellite to racetracks in California, giving gamblers the chance to loose money in two countries at once.

Shopping is the number-one tourist activity in Tijuana. Visitors who have never been to mainland Mexico are fascinated by the abundance of silver jewelry, leather boots and jackets, wool *serapes*, cotton blankets, velvet sombreros, cartoon-character *piñatas* and every imaginable type of tacky souvenir. The shopping experience hits its height in the block-deep arcades along Avenida Revolución, where buskers can't resist pleading, pushing, and jostling for your attention. All the classic border scenes are here to greet you. Wide-

eyed boys and girls entreat passers by to purchase Chiclets, woven bracelets and Styrofoam balls covered with bits of mirror. *Marias* — as the locals call the Indian-looking women from Chiapas and Oaxaca who wrap themselves and their babies in blankets — beg on the street with heart-wrenching displays of poverty.

The most rewarding shopping experience is the instant Mexican immersion course one receives at the **Mercado Hidalgo** on Avenida Independencia at Avenida Sanchez Taboada, about six blocks east of Avenida Revolución. All household necessities from beans to rice to plastic mops can be found in the market stalls, interspersed with religious medallions, herbal potions and piles of produce. The setting is far classier at **Tolan (** (66) 883637 on Avenida Revolución between Calles 7 and 8. Folk-art collectors never miss a stop here to survey the latest collection of antique carved wood doors, stained glass panels, pottery, religious statues, and crafts from throughout the country. **Sanborn's (** (66) 841462, on Avenida Revolución at Calle 8, is part of a national chain of restaurants and shops displaying high-quality folk art, books and jewelry.

The beaches south of the city, **Las Playas de Tijuana**, are popular among locals. So far they have no major hotels and only a few small restaurants.

WHERE TO STAY

Tijuana's hostelries once consisted of cheap flop houses and few tourist hotels. The advent of the *maquiladora* (assembly plant) industry in the 1980s brought business travelers from mainland Mexico, Asia, Europe and the United States, and Tijuana's hotel scene changed immensely. Today there are several upscale hotels catering to a mixed clientele of business travelers and tourists. You can usually get more for your money on the Tijuana side of the border; those planning on sampling the city's night scene can rest comfortably close to the action. Inexpensive hotels are abundant and usually unpleasant (unless you enjoy constant noise and shabby conditions). Always check out a few rooms before choosing, and keep close watch on your possessions.

Expensive

You know a Mexican city has hit the big time when prestigious national chains invest in hotels there. The **Camino Real (** (66) 334000 TOLL-FREE (800) 722-6466 FAX (66) 334001, on Paseo de los Héroes, is a clear sign of Tijuana's prosperity. The modern-style hotel sits at a prominent intersection in the Zona Río and offers 235 rooms and 15 suites with all the amenities upscale travelers expect.

Back in the 1980s, when Tijuana began to boom, local entrepreneurs built twin mirrored towers on Boulevard Agua Caliente as a symbol of prosperity. One tower houses a hotel that has gone through several changes in management. It's now called the **Gran Hotel (** (66) 817000 TOLL-FREE (800) 472-6385 FAX (66) 817016, Boulevard Agua Caliente No. 4558. The atrium lobby is one of the most popular see-and-be-seen spots in the city, and the restaurant and bar are always buzzing with activity. The 422 rooms vary in maintenance and amenities; those on the highest floors command astounding views of Tijuana's sprawling tentacles.

Moderate

A favorite with those desiring traditional Mexican architecture and style, the **Lucerna (** (66) 647000 TOLL-FREE (800) 582-3762 FAX (66) 342400, Paseo de los Héroes and Avenida Rodríguez, is one of the Zona Río's anchors. Gardens about the pools are well established, and the 147 rooms and 28 suites are dark and comfortable, with colonial-style furnishings. The **Holiday Inn Vita Spa Agua Caliente (** (66) 346901 TOLL-FREE (800) 225-2786 FAX (66) 346912, Paseo de los Héroes No. 18818 in the Zona Río, has become one of my favorite Tijuana hotels, thanks to its wonderful spa. The hotel sits beside the underground spring that fed the pools at the prohibition-era Agua Caliente resort; the steaming mineral waters are now piped to the hotel's giant outdoor hot tub and private baths in the spa.

Mud and oil wraps, massages, facials, and other treatments fill out the spa menu. The hotel's 122 rooms and five suites are less luxurious than one might expect, but are nonetheless pleasant.

Inexpensive

I'm most comfortable suggesting **La Villa de Zaragoza** ((66) 851832 FAX (66) 851837, Avenida Madero No. 1120 for budget travelers. It's located right off Avenida Revolución, a major plus for those traveling by foot. The 66 rooms are serviceable and well maintained. This place books up quickly.

WHERE TO EAT

As with hotels, Tijuana's restaurant options have become more expansive, offering everything from gourmet dining rooms to bustling homestyle cafés. Most upscale and tourist-oriented restaurants are meticulous about health considerations, cleaning their produce with purified water.

Expensive

Cien Años ((66) 343039, on Avenida José María in the Zona Río, is the hit of the 1990s, offering an elegant ambiance and excellent nouvelle Mexican cuisine. Many of the favorite regional dishes from throughout Mexico are prepared and presented beautifully in a tasteful setting.

Moderate

The traditional favorite for regional Mexican dishes is **La Fonda de Roberto** ((66) 861601, in La Siesta Motel on the old Ensenada Highway, also called Calle 16 de Septiembre, near Boulevard Agua Caliente. **La Taberna Española** ((66) 847562, at Plaza Fiesta and Paseo de los Héroes, is the best of many ethnic eateries in this plaza, which fills up with hip young students on weekend nights. **Tia Juana Tilly's** ((66) 856024, on Avenida Revolución at Calle 7, has three locations on Revolución; this is the largest, and it has an outdoor café out front, great for people watching while munching on nachos. **Señor Frog's** ((66) 824964, in the Pueblo Amigo Center, Paseo Tijuana, is rowdy, raucous and fun, and serves good barbecued ribs and Mexican combo plates.

Inexpensive

My favorite spot for a taste of real Mexico is **La Especial** ((66) 856654, Avenida Revolución No. 718. The huge, busy restaurant is located at the foot of a stairway leading down from street level; *enchiladas, carne asada* and tacos are prepared homestyle, with a bit of spice. Baby goat is the draw at **Birrieria Guanajuato** (no phone), Avenida Abraham González No. 102, while roasted pork pulls in the crowds at **Carnitas Uruapan** ((66) 856181, Boulevard Díaz Ordáz No. 550. Both are informal places where you order the main course

Baja California

by the kilo along with beans, rice, salsa and tortillas, and prepare your feast at long wooden tables.

NIGHTLIFE

Border dwellers are heavily into Tijuana's nightlife scene, which offers everything from sleazy bars (clustered on the side streets off Avenida Revolución) to swank dance clubs. **The Hard Rock Café** ((66) 850206 on Avenida Revolución No. 520 between Calles 1 and 2, is the standby for cautious travelers; while **Rodeo la Media Noche** ((66) 824967, on Avenida Paseo Tijuana at Pueblo Amigo in the Zona Río, is a wild place where indoor rodeos are presented at midnight (hence the name). The

club also has several dance floors. **Como Que No** ((66) 842791, Avenida Sanchez Taboada No. 95 and **Dime Que Si** ((66) 842791, next door, are popular with fashionable young professionals from both sides of the border. **Baby Rock** ((66) 342404, on Calle Diego Rivera No. 1482, in the Zona Río, is the best place for the disco scene.

HOW TO GET THERE

Tijuana's Aeropuerto Alberado Rodríguez international airport is located eight kilometers (five miles) from the United States border, but no United States or European airlines fly to or from Tijuana. Aeroméxico, Mexicana, AeroCalifornia, Taesa, and a few regional airlines fly throughout Mexico and

OPPOSITE: Tilly's has good Mexican food at reasonable prices, but trinkets ABOVE are more expensive here than in other parts of Mexico.

Latin America (and Cuba). Travelers touring Southern California sometimes choose to move on to Mexico through Tijuana, where airfares are cheaper than those from San Diego or Los Angeles.

TECATE

Though most travelers head south along the Pacific Coast to the beach towns of Baja, some go 32 km (20 miles) east to the border town of Tecate. Famous for its brewery of the same name, Tecate is often an easier place to cross the border than Tijuana, unless you get caught in one the its summer fiestas or bicycle races, or arrive late — the border gates are closed from 10 PM until 6 AM. Work available at the *maquiladoras* rising outside town has increased the population to 100,000, but the main plaza, church and side streets still have the ambiance of a traditional small town where the pace is unhurried and the people friendly. There's not much to do here except sit in the plaza for a while and wander the side streets; several pottery yards outside town draw Californians shopping for flower pots and paving tiles. The biggest tourist draw is **Rancho la Puerta** ((665) 41155 TOLL-FREE (800) 443-7565 (from California you can also call ((619) 744-4222) FAX (665) 41108, on Highway 2 about five kilometers (two and a half miles) west of Tecate. This super-deluxe, very expensive spa is a haven for celebrities and stressed-out executives from both sides of the border. **Tourist Information** ((665) 41095 about Tecate is available on Callejón Libertad.

MEXICALI

Though Tijuana is far more populous and popular, Mexicali is the capital of the state of Baja California. Located 136 km (85 miles) east of Tijuana, Mexicali is a government and agricultural center with few tourist attractions. There is a **Tourist Information Office** ((65) 561072, at Calle Calafia and Independencia. There is also the **Convention and Tourism Bureau** ((65) 522376, Calle López Mateos and Calle Compresora. Mexicali is the border crossing used for travelers going south on Highway 5 to the beaches of **San Felipe**, and for those taking the *Ferrocarril Sonora Baja California* train south to **Hermosillo** and the interior of Mexico. The train station, **Estación de Ferrocarril** ((65) 572386, is at the south end of Calle Ulises Irigoyen.

In Mexicali, there is good accommodation in the expensive price range at **Crowne Plaza** ((65) 573600 TOLL-FREE (800) 227-6963 FAX (65) 570555, located on Boulevard López Mateos and Avenida de los Héroes. **La Lucerna** ((65) 661000 TOLL-FREE (800) 582-3762 FAX (65) 664706, Avenida Benito Juárez No. 2151, has 203 moderately-priced rooms and suites.

SAN FELIPE

San Felipe, 196 km (122 miles) south of Mexicali, has long been popular with serious deep-sea fishermen and escapists seeking an inexpensive destination on the beach. San Felipe is the first major town on the Gulf of California and though the waters here are not as clear as those farther south, they do provide an abundance of shrimp and seafood. Long the province of campers and those driving recreational vehicles (RVs or campervans), San Felipe now has several good hotels. The **Tourist Office** ((657) 71155, on Avenida Mar de Cortés, is open weekdays from 8 AM to 3 PM and is an excellent source of information.

WHAT TO SEE AND DO

Beaches are the town's biggest attraction; a *malecón* runs along downtown's main beach and is lined with simple cafés, bars and taco stands. A shrine to Our Lady of Guadalupe sits atop a hill overlooking a beach; local fishermen have traditionally visited the shrine before heading out to sea. **Fishing** for corvina, sierra and other game fish is available through **Alex Sportfishing** ((657) 71052, **San Felipe Sportfishing** ((657) 71055 and **Del Mar Cortés Charters** ((657) 71303. All fishing companies have representatives on the waterfront *malecón* in town. Spring break is San Felipe's busiest time, when college students from the United States and Mexico fill the town with unbridled revelry.

WHERE TO STAY AND EAT

Though many San Felipe regulars arrive in RVs and campervans, there are several good hotels. In the expensive range, the **San Felipe Marina Resort** ((657) 71568 TOLL-FREE (800) 225-2786 (if calling from California, Arizona, or Nevada TOLL-FREE (800) 298-4105) FAX (657) 71455, at Km 4.5 on Carretera San Felipe–Aeropuerto, is the fanciest place in town. The indoor heated pool is a major plus on windy winter days and there is a fitness center as well. Many of the 60 rooms have kitchenettes and balconies overlooking the sea. In the moderate range, **Las Misiones** ((657) 71280 TOLL-FREE (800) 336-5454 FAX (657) 71283, Avenida Misión de Loreto No. 130 is popular with tour groups, thanks to its well-maintained 185 rooms and 32 suites, its large pool and clean beach. **El Cortés** ((657) 71056 FAX (657) 71055, on Avenida Mar de Cortés, is an old favorite with beach bungalows and hotel rooms by the beach, an excellent restaurant and popular bar. The hotel is within easy walking distance of town.

Shrimp and seafood are the main staples in San Felipe's casual, inexpensive restaurants, including **George's** ((657) 71057 on Avenida Mar de Cortés and **Ruben's** ((657) 71091, RV Park north of town. **El Toro** ((657) 71032 on Highway 5 also north of town, is a great spot for bountiful breakfasts. **Tony's Tacos** (no phone) on the *malecón* at Avenida Chetumal, serves great fish and shrimp tacos.

ROSARITO BEACH

Heading south from Tijuana along the Pacific Coast, the first major town is Rosarito Beach. An enormously popular weekend getaway for Southern Californians, Rosarito has rapidly expanded from a small fishing village to a town of some 110,000 full-time residents. Tasteful and garish hotels, bars and restaurants line Boulevard Benito Juárez through the main part of town; bumper-to-bumper traffic is not uncommon. In 1996, Twentieth Century Fox chose Rosarito for the filming of *Titanic* and built a huge movie production studio south of town. The resulting attention added to the area's crowds and fame, and attracted hundreds of part-time residents with plenty of discretionary cash. Other films are expected to be made here, keeping Rosarito's fortunes rising.

GENERAL INFORMATION

The **Tourist Information Office** ((661) 20396 or 23078 is on Boulevard Benito Juárez on the second floor of the Quinta Plaza shopping center.

WHAT TO SEE AND DO

Rosarito's main attraction is its long, wide **beach** stretching the length of town. Vendors stroll the beach selling straw hats, fake silver jewelry, T-shirts and toys; others push carts holding cold drinks, cotton candy and snacks. Tourists play impromptu volleyball and football games, local families set out huge picnic spreads, and the beach is always festive. Swimming is safe here but only when the water is clear; if it's been raining recently chances are the water is polluted and you should stay on the sand. The beach runs parallel to Boulevard Benito Juárez, though the water isn't visible from the main street. Instead, what you see is a shoulder-to-shoulder collage of shopping plazas, bars and hotels. Hard to miss is the rollercoaster façade of **Festival Plaza**, a hotel and restaurant complex that has become the town's party center. The **Rosarito Beach Hotel** (see below) one block south was the town's first attraction, built during the prohibition era. The hotel, with its abundance of handcrafted tile, carved wood beams, murals and ballroom, is a must-see, though it's hardly as glamorous as photos of the 1920s indicate. **Misión el Descanso**, the original settlement from which Rosarito grew, is 19 km (12 miles)

south on the Old Ensenada Highway just past Cantamar (turn left under the toll road). A dirt road leads one kilometer (two-thirds of a mile) to the ruins of the mission, built in the late 1700s by the Dominicans.

The proliferation of vacation home developments along the coast has made Rosarito a profitable center for interior design shops, and most travelers spend at least a few hours browsing the strip. At the north entrance to town the road is lined with furniture and pottery stands; several good shops are located in the Quinta del Mar Plaza, the first major complex after you enter town. I never fail to stop at **Interios del Río Casa del Arte y La Madera** ((661) 21300, Quinta del Mar Plaza, for its selection of brightly-painted chairs and tables and unusual handicrafts from mainland Mexico. **Taxco Curios** ((661) 21877, Quinta del Mar Plaza, has a good selection of glassware. In the Rosarito Beach Hotel shopping center **Casa Torres** ((661) 21008 sells imported perfumes and cosmetics, **Margarita's** (no phone) has a good selection of handicrafts shops. Pottery yards line the street south of town leading to **Casa la Carreta** ((661) 20502, at Km 29 on the Old Ensenada Highway, and you'll also find the best woodcraftsmen in the area.

Golf is available north of Rosarito at **Real del Mar Golf Club** ((661) 31340, on the Ensenada toll road. **Horseback riding** on the beach is a favorite activity, and horses can be hired at the north and south ends of Boulevard Benito Juárez and on the beach south of Rosarito Beach Hotel. **Surfing** is not exceptional in Rosarito proper, but the waves are good at Popotla, Km 33; at Calafía, Km 33.5; at Costa Baja, Km 36; and at Km 38 on the Old Ensenada Highway.

WHERE TO STAY

Developers are racing to keep up with the demand for rooms in Rosarito; the result is an unattractive melange of architectural styles and construction sites. Rooms are scarce on summer and holiday weekends and should be reserved in advance. Several hotels are represented by **Baja Information** (see page 319).

Moderate

The **Rosarito Beach Hotel** ((661) 20144 TOLL-FREE (800) 343-8582 FAX (661) 21125 (or write: PO Box 430145, San Diego, CA 92143) Boulevard Benito Juárez, at the south end of town, would be the most desirable accommodation in Rosarito Beach if the rooms were better maintained. Unfortunately, the 275 rooms and suites vary widely in repair and comfort level; those in the unsightly tower beside the main hotel are in the best shape. The hotel has a pleasant health spa and a good restaurant.

Festival Plaza ((661) 20842 TOLL-FREE (800) 453-8606 FAX (661) 20124, Boulevard Benito Juárez No. 11, offers several types of rooms, from ocean-facing *casitas* to motel-type boxes; you're sure to find one to meet your comfort needs and price range among the 108 rooms, five penthouse suites, seven *casitas* and 13 villas. Noise is a concern here as the main courtyard area includes a working roller coaster and a concert stage.

Los Pelicanos Hotel ((661) 20445 FAX (661) 21757, Calle Cedros No. 115 at Calle Ebano (or write to PO Box 433871, San Ysidro, CA 92143), is a favorite of those seeking serenity close to the beach. The 39 rooms are well maintained; some have balconies facing the beach. There is no swimming pool, but the second-story restaurant and bar are perfect for sunset watching over drinks.

Inexpensive

Though it's located right on the main thoroughfare, **Brisas del Mar** ((661) 22547 TOLL-FREE (888) 871-3605 FAX (661) 22547 (or write to PO Box 18903, Coronado, CA 92178-9003), Boulevard Benito Juárez No. 22, seems quiet and secluded once you're within the complex. The 69 rooms and two junior suites are in good repair. Also recommended in this price category are the **Motel Colonial** ((661) 21575 on Calle Primero de Mayo with 13 rooms and **Motel Don Luís** ((661) 21166, on Boulevard Benito Juárez, with 31 rooms, some of which have kitchen facilities.

WHERE TO EAT

Gourmet restaurants are not Rosarito's style. Instead, the town is filled with places where drinking is as important as dining. Tacos and seafood are the main fare, along with plenty of tequila and beer.

Moderate

If steaks, lobster and conversation are your preferences, try **El Nido** ((661) 21430, Boulevard Benito Juárez No. 67. **La Leña** ((661) 20826, in the La Quinta Plaza, is a bit removed from the action and serves tasty and unusual beef dishes and Mexican food. **El Patio** ((661) 22950, on Boulevard Benito Juárez in the Festival Plaza, is the most reserved of this complex's restaurants and serves authentic regional cuisine including *mole* and chicken with *poblano* sauce. **La Taberna Española** ((661) 21982, on Boulevard Benito Juárez across from the Festival Plaza, is a branch of the popular Tijuana *tapas* bar.

Inexpensive

La Flor de Michoacán ((661) 21858, Boulevard Juárez No. 291, is the place to try *carnitas*, succulent chunks of roast pork with guacamole and homemade tortillas.

How to Get There

Rosarito Beach is 29 km (18 miles) south of Tijuana and is most easily accessed by the toll highway out of Tijuana. The Rosarito exit leads to Boulevard Benito Juárez and the Old Ensenada Highway, which travels south of town past hotels and residential areas. There is frequent bus service from Tijuana.

PUERTO NUEVO

Once a simple collection of fishermen's homes, Puerto Nuevo has become a major attraction. Why? Because it is said to have the best lobster restaurants on the coast: grilled or deep fried and served with lime wedges, melted butter, tortillas, beans and rice. The original bunch of small restaurants has expanded to at least three dozen set on a dusty clifftop. There's not enough lobster in local waters to meet the demand; consquently, much of what's served is imported. Prices and selection are the same at all the restaurants; few have phones or take reservations. I've always been fond of the family that runs **Ponderosa**, one of the older, smaller restaurants. **Ortegas** may well be the most popular, and has four restaurants here and two in Rosarito. Puerto Nuevo is 12 km (7.5 miles) south of Rosarito; you can tell you're getting close when you see an abundance of pottery yards along the roadsides.

WHERE TO STAY

There are several popular hotels in this area, some within easy walking distance of the lobster restaurants. Most book up quickly on summer and holiday weekends.

Moderate

The prettiest option is **Las Rocas** (/FAX (661) 22140 at Km 37 on the Old Ensenada Highway. The best of the 74 rooms and suites have microwaves and fireplaces. **Hotel New Port Baja** ((661) 41166 FAX (661) 41174, at Km 45 on the Old Ensenada Highway, has 147 rooms framing a large swimming pool. Excellent musicians play in the lobby bar. **La Fonda** (no phone) at Km 59 on the Old Ensenada Highway, is as popular for its restaurant as it is for the 26 rustic rooms perched in various levels on a cliff over the sea.

ENSENADA

Although very much a tourist town, **Ensenada**, 108 km (67 miles) south of the United States border

---

Ensenada attracts Southern Californians for its nightlife and dining.

on the Bahía de Todos Santos, is also an important seaport and Baja's largest commercial fishing port. In 1542, the Portuguese captain Juan Rodríguez Cabrillo was the first to chart this protected bay; the Spanish explorer, Sebastián Vizcaíno, gave it its name Ensenada-Bahía de Todos Santos. Missionaries and ranchers arrived in the late eighteenth century, discovered gold and Ensenada became boomed. The mines were soon depleted and Ensenada became a sedate agricultural and fishing community. It had two decades of glory as the capital of Baja California Norte from 1888 to 1910, and another during burst of fame during Prohibition when Americans came in search of liquid gold. Its popularity waned when Prohibition ended, but it has remained a weekend party town for Southern Californians.

GENERAL INFORMATION

The **Tourist Information Office** ((61) 782411 or 788588, is located on Boulevard Costero No. 1477, and is open weekdays from 9 AM to 1 PM and from 2 PM to 5 PM.

WHAT TO SEE AND DO

The toll highway from Tijuana ends at Ensenada's northern entrance at Boulevard Costero. The first attraction visitors come across, and one of the most popular, is the **Fish Market**, at the northernmost point of Boulevard Costero and Plaza de Marina. The market itself is a giant warehouse filled with stands displaying fresh shrimp, tuna, marlin, yellowtail and whatever happens to be in season, all spread out on heaping mounds of ice. Outside the market dozens of **taco stands** proffer their identical treat — the classic Baja fish taco. Strips of flaky white rock cod or other fresh fish are dipped in batter and deep fried, then wrapped in a corn tortilla. Condiments — including shredded cabbage, cilantro, onions, radishes, mayonnaise and several salsas — sit in small bowls on the counter; diners stuff their tacos and settle on stools at the taco stands to devour this concoction. The massive **Plaza Marina** now blocks the view of the market from the street, and is one of many partially inhabited structures marring Ensenada's scenery. South of the market is the **Plaza Cívica** at Boulevard Costero and Avenida Riveroll, where large busts of several Mexican leaders dominate a small park. The **Centro Artesenal de Ensenada** on Boulevard Costero was constructed to attract cruise ship passengers disembarking at the nearby pier. However, the few ships that still come to town anchor in the bay and passengers are tendered to the boat docks north of town. The Centro still has a few good shops. Most notable is the excellent **Galería de Pérez Meillón** ((61) 740399, displaying museum

quality pottery from Casas Grande. Ensenada's most cherished landmark is the Prohibition-era gambling palace called the **Riviera del Pacifico** ((61) 764310, at Boulevard Costero and Avenida Riviera (admission fee; open daily from 9 AM to 5 PM). The hacienda-style white building once housed a hotel, ballrooms, gambling halls and restaurants; it's now a civic center housing a small museum on Ensenada's history. Take time to wander through the ballrooms and gorgeous gardens.

Ensenada's main tourist area is one block inland along **Avenida López Mateos**. Shopping plazas, restaurants and hotels line this busy street, and you can easily spend a few hours browsing through folk-art shops and department stores,

taking time to stop for a cold drink or a meal. Among the best shops for good quality Mexican folk art and jewelry are **Artes Don Quijote**, **Artesanías Castillo** and **Girasoles**. The vineyards and wineries in the valleys around Ensenada produce some of Mexico's best wine. You can tour the in-town winery of **Las Bodegas de Santo Tomás** ((61) 783333, Avenida Miramar No. 666 (call ahead for tour hours). Across Miramar from the winery is **La Esquina de Bodegas**. This winery and others in the surrounding valleys are also open for tours. Most hotels and the Tourist Information Office have details on exact opening hours. **Lady of Guadalupe**, on Avenida Floresta at Avenida Juárez is Ensenada's largest cathedral.

Ensenada's beaches are not particularly attractive; the best are south of town at **Estero Beach**. The ocean puts on a grand show at **La Bufadora**, 31 km (20 miles) southwest of Ensenada. Waves explode in a blast of thunder and spraying water at this large blowhole in the coastal cliffs. Legends tell that the spray comes from a whale trapped in the rocks. La Bufadora was spiffed up in the mid-1990s and has become a bona fide attraction with craft stands, seafood restaurants and parking fees.

One of Ensenada's most important attractions is **sport fishing**. From May to October, fishermen come for yellowtail. Also abundant are barracuda, tuna, marlin, mackerel and bonita. Fishing trips can be arranged at the **Ensenada Sport Fishing Pier** at Boulevard Costera and Avenida Macheros. You should count on paying approximately $50 per person per day on a group boat. **Whale-watching** boats depart from the Ensenada Sport Fishing

Highway 1 north of town opened in the mid-1990s, offering a new level of accommodation for the city. The 600-slip marina attracts boaters from southern California, and many of the hotel's 140 rooms and suites have a view of the water. Facilities include a large pool and whirlpool, tennis courts, a gym, and decent restaurants. Similarly modern, **Las Rosas (** (61) 744320 FAX (61)744595, on Highway 1 north of Ensenada is the prettiest hotel on the coast. Its atrium lobby glows against the night sky, and the pool seems to float into the horizon. Some of the 32 suites have fireplaces and whirlpool bathtubs. The restaurant under the atrium has a beautiful view of the sea and serves good international cuisine.

Pier from December through April, when gray whales are migrating from the Bering Strait to southern Baja's lagoon. **Golf** is available at the **Baja Country Club (** (61) 730303, on Highway 1 south of Ensenada at Maneadero. **Kayaking** off Punta Banda is available through **Southwest Kayaks (** (619) 222-3616 in San Diego.

WHERE TO STAY

Regulars have their favorite hangouts and many of Ensenada's best hotels fill up quickly, even when you might not expect them to. Advance reservations are a good idea at most of the places listed below.

Expensive

The **Hotel Coral & Marina (** (61) 750000 TOLL-FREE (800) 862-9020 FAX (61) 750005 on Mexico

Moderate

Favored by the relaxed beach crowd, **Estero Beach Resort (** (61) 766235 FAX (61) 766925 (or write to 482 San Ysidro Boulevard, Suite 1186, San Ysidro, CA 92173), on Highway 1 between Ensenada and Maneadero, is the best hotel on the water in the area. Families pack the 110 rooms during the summer months; the most desirable suites (in the very expensive range) are the two-story ones right at the sand. The least expensive rooms face parking lots. The hotel's large complex includes several shops, an RV park, a pool, a large children's playground and a good restaurant with indoor and outdoor seating. In town, the **San Nicolas (** (61) 761901 TOLL-FREE (800) 578-7878,

OPPOSITE: Hussong's, a landmark Ensenada bar, has long inspired romance and revelry. ABOVE: Delicious fish tacos are sold at stands along Ensenada's waterfront.

located on Avenida López Mateos and Guadalupe, is an older hotel with plenty of character. The plain-looking two-story building houses 148 guestrooms and frames a long courtyard pool and gardens. The pool extends inside — a plus in the winter months — and the rooms are refurbished regularly. The restaurant serves good Mexican food.

Inexpensive
Though it faces the water near downtown, the **Corona Hotel** ((61) 760901 FAX (61) 764023 (or write to 482 San Ysidro Boulevard, Suite 303, San Ysidro, CA 92173), on Boulevard Costero No. 1442, doesn't have a beach. The 90 rooms are not always well maintained. If you're passing through town on route south, try the **Joker Hotel** ((61) 767201 FAX (61) 767201, on Highway 1 at Km 12.5 between Ensenada and Maneadero. The design is rather bizarre, emphasizing clown faces and such, but the parking lot is guarded and the 40 rooms are satisfactory.

WHERE TO EAT

Seafood is Ensenada's forte, from the humble fish taco to succulent fresh lobster and shrimp. The abundance of wineries in the area also encourages restaurateurs to experiment with Mexican and international cuisine with the result that there are a few exceptional restaurants. Most are casual, and nothing beats the simple taste of grilled fresh fish served at one of the city's landmark restaurants.

Expensive
El Rey Sol ((61) 781733, Avenida López Mateos No. 1000, has been owned and operated by the same family for decades. The owners operate their own vegetable farm, are well acquainted with local wines, and buy their fish and game from the best purveyors. French, Mexican and American recipes highlight the fresh ingredients; all the breads and pastries are baked in house. Though newer (it opened in the early 1990s), **La Embotelladora Vieja** ((61) 740807, Avenida Miramar No. 666, has acquired a cross-border reputation as an excellent restaurant in the quarters of the Santo Tomás winery. Teetotalers have a bit of a problem here, since the beef, poultry and fish dishes are typically prepared with wine sauces, but the chefs do all they can to accommodate individual tastes. The dark, wine cellar setting is perfect for intimate dinners amid candlelight and chandeliers.

Moderate
I've always been fond of **Casamar** ((61) 740417, Boulevard Lázaro Cárdenas No. 987, for standard seafood dinners made from the freshest fish. Order

your fillet of dorado, tuna or shark prepared *mojo de ajo*, with oil and garlic. Not fond of fish? Try **Bronco's Steak House** ((61) 761901, Avenida López Mateos No. 1525. The western cowboy decor, complete with branding irons, saddles and wagon wheel lamps, sets the mood for meals of *carne asada* (marinated beef strips) and robust steaks with charred green onions and chilis.

Inexpensive
Mariscos de Bahía de Ensenada ((61) 781015, Avenida Riveroll No. 109, Formica-table-top-type spot good for sampling seafood among locals. **El Charro** ((61) 783881, Avenida López Mateos No. 475, is the best place in the tourist zone for rotisserie chicken served with excellent tortillas, beans and rice.

NIGHTLIFE

Ensenada's nightlife scene can be rowdy during spring break and holiday weekends, when people of all ages escape nearby cities on both sides of the border.
    Hussong's Cantina ((61) 740145, on Avenida Ruíz at López Mateos, is the most legendary bar in all of Baja; few can resist strolling past the guard at the door to view the huge, semi-dark room packed with revelers, mariachi bands, lottery-ticket sellers and photographers. **Papas and Beer**, across the street from Hussong's, has a second-story terrace where beer drinkers can yell down to their friends on the street. Nearly any excuse is sufficient for staging a *fiesta*. Yacht, car and bicycle races attract crowds from Southern California, and all national Mexican holidays are celebrated with fervor.

HOW TO GET THERE

Ensenada does not have a commercial airport; transportation is available from the Tijuana airport to the Tijuana bus station, where you can catch a bus to Ensenada.

SOUTH OF ENSENADA

Below Ensenada, the traveler faces the wilderness of the Baja desert. Although the Trans-peninsular Highway is paved to Baja's southern tip, drivers should still have plenty of fuel and water, and be prepared to spend the night in humble lodgings. Gas stations are better equipped than ever, but sometimes the gas shipment is late, and if you let your fuel tank run low you may end up sitting in a long line waiting for

Young people stroll the streets of Baja California's cities, windowshopping and checking out their peers.

the gas trucks to arrive at the station. Always keep your tank at least half full.

South of Ensenada one passes through the vineyards of **Santo Tomás** and the last signs of major towns for many kilometers. Services are available in **San Vicente** and **Colonet**. The next town of any size, **San Quintín**, is said to be the windiest spot in Baja. It has beautiful white sand beaches, good fishing and clam digging.

The **Old Mill** TOLL-FREE (800) 479-7962, south of San Quintín on the dirt road leading to the bay, is the best hotel in the area. A magnet for anglers when tuna, yellowtail and dorado are abundant in the Bahía San Quintín, the hotel has 25 rooms and two suites, a marina and boat ramp, an RV park and an excellent restaurant. **La Pinta San Quintín** ((61) 762601 TOLL-FREE (800) 472-2427 is another good choice south of town.

After the town of **El Rosario**, the highway runs inland through rugged desert terrain. Huge boulders and mesas rise from the desert near **Cataviña**. The terrain remains harsh yet magnificent as the road travels past stark peaks and undulating raw ridges, dry *arroyos* and canyons, salt flats and cactus and a sprinkling of wildflowers.

BAHÍA DE LOS ANGELES

About 50 km (30 miles) south of **Laguna de Chapala** (a dry lake bed), a rough paved road turns east from the Transpeninsular Highway to **Bahía de los Angeles** (Bay of the Angels), 70 km (45 miles) away on the Gulf of California. Even before the road was paved in 1978, the bay had its own private airstrip and hotel, catering principally to fishermen, and a campground frequented by four-wheel-drive adventurers. Although the settlement has grown more touristy, it has little to recommend it but the bay itself, which is magnificent beyond description.

Protected by the **Isla Angel de la Guarda** (Island of the Guardian Angel), the bay has superb swimming, snorkeling and diving. Dolphins often play alongside swimmers; as you sleep on the soft sandy beach under the stars, you can hear the dolphins coming up for air while they cavort and feed along the shore. The rocky crags and ridges behind the beach turn a stunning purple-red at dawn as the sun rises white and molten from the bay. These mountains are excellent for hiking, but they are steep and dangerous, and have a sizable population of rattlesnakes. The best and only recommended way to visit Bahía de los Angeles is as a camper with a tent or sturdy RV.

GUERRERO NEGRO

The Transpeninsular Highway continues south to the town of **Guerrero Negro** (Black Warrior), named after a whaling vessel which ran aground

in 1858. The town is the commercial center for the salt mines at the edge of the **Desierto de Vizcaíno** (Vizcaíno Desert) which produces over 30% of the world's salt. A metal sculpture representing an eagle (look at it sideways and you'll get the picture) marks the 28th parallel and the state line between Baja California and Baja California Sur. Military checkpoints are often set up here to search vehicles for illegal drugs and firearms. A windy, dusty place, Guerrero Negro would have little attraction for tourists were it not for the gray whales that migrate to nearby lagoons (see below).

WHERE TO STAY AND EAT

There are very few places to stay in town, and it is unlikely any more will be developed. **La Pinta** ((115) 71301 TOLL-FREE (800) 542-3283 or (800) 522-1516 FAX (115) 71306, on the highway just north of town, is a good place to stop for the night, though the 26 rooms are overpriced and unremarkable. Within town, your best choice for dining and lodging is **Malarrimo** ((115) 70250 FAX (115) 70100, on Boulevard Zapata. The small hotel has 10 rooms and a trailer park; the restaurant is a favorite of Baja regulars. If you just want to stop for a meal, your best choice is **La Espinita** (no phone) on Highway 1 at the 28th parallel next to La Pinta.

HOME OF THE GRAY WHALES

Just across the 28th parallel into Baja California Sur, on the Pacific side of Baja, is the **Laguna Ojo de Liebre** (Hare's Eye Lagoon), also known as Scammon's Lagoon, for Charles Melville Scammon of Maine, the first whaler to discover the area in the 1800s. For ten years after finding this area, his and other whaling boats returned to these gray-whale breeding grounds until the population was practically exterminated. It took almost a century for the whales to return, and in 1940 whalers were prohibited from entering the lagoon.

Now protected as the **Parque Natural de Ballena Gris** (Gray Whale Natural Park), the lagoon is still the breeding ground for the world's few remaining gray whales. From December to April, these giant marine mammals take up residency, give birth to their young (which weigh approximately 500 kg or half a ton), nurse them, then turn back north to Alaska and the waters of the Bering Sea. Access to the park is severely restricted. No boats are allowed, and observers must watch from the shore. To see the whales, binoculars are essential. **Eco-Tours Malarrimo** ((115) 70250, on Boulevard Zapata at the Malarrimo restaurant, will arrange whale-watching excursions with English-speaking guides. Advance reservations are recommended.

Much of the whale-watching activity has moved south to **Laguna de San Ignacio** and **Bahía** de Magdalena, two remote areas where the whales have found protection. Mag Bay, as aficionados call the latter, has become one of the best places to see the whales in a relatively natural setting. Tour companies operate from campgrounds, some surprisingly comfortable despite the chill air and winds during whale season. Unlike Scammon's Lagoon, this is not a protected reserve. This means that it is up to visitors to act responsibly. It is important to remember that human intrusion can upset the whales' breeding, and one might be well advised to observe the whales from the sand dunes on the bay. A night spent on the beach where only the breathing of whales and lapping of waves can be heard is one of the great benefits of traveling off the beaten path and away from tourist haunts. Tours to these areas are available in San Ignacio, Loreto and La Paz, three points which have the easiest road access to this isolated stretch of the Pacific Coast. See THE GREAT OUTDOORS, page 24, for further information.

SAN IGNACIO

The Transpeninsular Highway (Highway 1) turns inland to cross the peninsula just south of Guerrero Negro. The road climbs into the mountains to the town of San Ignacio, which appears like an oasis in the desert. Its sixteenth-century mission church is one of the best preserved on Baja. The town is quiet, non-touristy, and friendly. The surrounding countryside is interesting to explore, on foot (wear hiking boots or sturdy shoes) or on muleback. Ancient **cave paintings** have been found nearby, and it is easy to arrange for a guide. Thirty kilometers (19 miles) to the east is the still-active volcano **Las Tres Virgenes** (The Three Virgins), 2,180 m (7,153 ft) high.

There is another **La Pinta** TOLL-FREE (800) 336-5454, or if calling from California, Nevada or Arizona TOLL-FREE (800) 522-1516, two kilometers (just over a mile) west of Highway 1 on an unnamed road into town, with 28 overpriced (moderate) rooms.

SANTA ROSALÍA

From San Ignacio the highway continues east to the Sea of Cortez. The view of the sea as you descend the mountains is spectacular. The town of Santa Rosalía, the only French settlement in Baja, was founded in 1885 as headquarters for the nearby Rothschild copper mines. The French not only built the town according to their architectural tastes, but also brought a prefabricated iron-framed church, **Iglesia Santa Barbara**, specially designed by Alexandre Gustave Eiffel, creator of the Eiffel Tower in Paris. The beaches are fairly good here (but much better farther south). A ferry departs from Guaymas on the mainland to Santa Rosalía.

three times weekly. Inland are the **Caves of San Borjitas** which contain the oldest cave paintings discovered in Baja. It takes a four-wheel-drive trip or hike (with guide) to reach these rock paintings of hunting scenes in which the human figures, some of which are life-sized, are colored half in red and half in black.

WHERE TO STAY AND EAT

The charming **Hotel Frances (** (115) 20327, on Calle Jean Michel Cousteau, is my favorite place to stay. This old wooden structure sits on a hill above town and has 20 moderately-priced rooms. The **El Morro Hotel (** (115) 20414, on Highway 1 at Km 1.5, just south of town, overlooks the water and has 30 moderately-priced rooms and a good restaurant. Baja regulars like to stop at **El Boleo Bakery (** (115) 20310, at Obregón and Calle 4 in town, for their fresh baked *bolillos*, soft rolls that make wonderful sandwiches.

MULEGÉ

Following the Transpeninsular Highway south along the coast, one reaches the lush green (by Baja standards) village of **Mulegé**, on the banks of the only year-round river (more like a stream) in Baja. Here on the shore of Bahía de Concepción, the largest protected bay in Baja, the Jesuits built the **Santa Rosalía de Mulegé** mission in 1705. The undistinguished church sits on a slight rise in town. Mulegé attracts anglers and kayakers drawn to the peaceful waters of the bay; it has a good collection of small hotels, restaurants and shops, and is a nice place to explore for an hour or so. The bay south of town is lined with many good beaches and several campgrounds.

Baja Tropicales ((115) 30409, PO Box 60, Mulegé, BCS 23900, offers kayaking tours and equipment rentals.

WHERE TO STAY

There are several small, inexpensive hotels in the Mulegé area, including **Hotel Hacienda (** (115) 30021, Madero No. 3, with 20 inexpensive rooms; the tour desk here is excellent, and you can arrange mule and hiking trips to cave paintings in the hills. **Hotel Las Casitas (** (115) 30019, Madero No. 50, has eight inexpensive rooms and a nice restaurant. The biggest establishment is the **Serenidad (** (115) 30530 FAX (115) 30311, three kilometers (nearly two miles) south of town. The 27 moderately-priced rooms are set in several buildings around the landscaped property, and the large swimming pool is a delight on summer afternoons. The restaurant is very good and hosts a weekly Saturday night pig roast. The camping is excellent around the bay.

LORETO

My favorite small town in Baja, Loreto, has all the charms of a traditional Mexican settlement with a tree-framed central plaza, a *malecón* along the waterfront, and a lovely mission church dominating the scenery. In the 1970s, the federal government included Loreto on its short list of areas to be developed for mass tourism; fortunately, their plans backfired. Rows of empty streets complete with a montage of power poles sit barren and neglected in the government's proposed development in Nópolo, about eight kilometers (five miles) south of Loreto. An 18-hole golf course and championship tennis center languish virtually ignored. The one large hotel in Nópolo has gone through several management changes and rarely holds a full house of guests. Meanwhile, Loreto continues to attract travelers seeking gorgeous water for fishing, diving, kayaking and snorkeling, and a quiet place to relax.

GENERAL INFORMATION

Despite having been to Loreto at least a dozen times, I've never found a working tourist information office. Most travelers rely on the hotels and sport fishing operations for information on tours and sports equipment rentals.

Alfredo's Sport Fishing ((113) 50165 FAX (113) 50590, on López Mateos near the boat ramp, serves as a one-stop information center and can set up fishing tours and winter whale-watching tours. **Arturo's Fishing Fleet** ((113) 50022 TOLL-FREE (800) 777-2664 on Juárez is another good source of information.

WHAT TO SEE AND DO

Once the capital of California (both Baja and the United States state), Loreto was the site of the first California mission, **La Misión de Nuestra Señora de Loreto**. Built in 1752, the church was almost completely destroyed in a 1829 hurricane, but has been restored. (The town was also destroyed, but rather than rebuild it, politicians decided to move the capital of California to La Paz.) Next to the church is **El Museo de los Misiones**, which contains artifacts from the early missions that extended from Loreto to Sonoma, California (just north of San Francisco) and other displays of life in nineteenth-century Baja.

Loreto's beaches are pleasant for sunbathing, but swimming is best around the many uninhabited islands offshore. **Isla Coronado** is the closest,

Dramatic vistas abound along the coastline from Tijuana to Ensenada.

while **Isla Carmen** is the largest, surrounded by small coves and rocky points where lobster, moray eels, parrot fish and sergeant majors feed in clear waters. Bottlenose dolphins, manta rays, finback whales and an occasional marlin splash in the fertile Sea of Cortez; few sights are as lovely as that from a boat ride at dawn, with the Sierra de la Giganta mountains glowing in the rising sun, and flying fish and porpoise glistening on the sea. Such natural wealth makes Loreto a popular destination for **sport fishing**, attracting a parade of trucks towing boats down Highway 1 from the border. Anglers arriving by air carry fishing poles and coolers aboard the plane; if lucky, they head home with fresh dorado and tuna filets. Those who wish to promote Loreto as a golf and resort destination constantly battle Loreto's enduring reputation as a sport fishing haven. Successful hotels provide their guests easy access to ice, freezers and reputable fishing fleets, and offer more upscale amenities after they've covered the anglers' basic necessities. Be sure to get a Mexican fishing license, as you can face a fine without one.

Loreto's islands and bays are perfect **scuba diving** territory; divers can arrange trips and rentals through **Baja Outpost (** (113) 51134 TOLL-FREE (800) 789-5625 FAX (113) 51134, Boulevard Mateos, by the marina. This company, which opened in 1998, also offers **kayaking** rentals and trips and has a few guestrooms. Kayaks are also available at **Villas de Loreto (** (113) 50418 (see below) and **Calafia Sea Kayaking (** (113) 50418 also on Boulevard Mateos by the marina.

Tennis is offered at the **Loreto Tennis Center (** (113) 50700 in Nopoló, a handsome complex with lawns, statues of archaeological sites, and nine, floodlit courts.

Golfers are served at the 18-hole **Loreto Campo de Golf (** (113) 50788 in Nopoló.

Hikers enjoy exploring the back-country terrain in the foothills of the **Sierra de la Giganta** (La Giganta Mountains) backing Loreto and the sea. Unfortunately, the weather is often either brutally hot or cold and windy, and hikers may face survival challenges when weather conditions shift abruptly. Anyone wishing to hike in the Sierra should have plenty of water, check with locals first, and watch out for rattlesnakes, scorpions, and the like. The views from the crest are incomparable. Those with wheels, or the cash to hire a driver, should travel 32 km (20 miles) southwest of Loreto on a paved and dirt road to the mountain settlement of **San Javier**. The mission church here is one of the finest in Baja, with a unique baroque façade and gilded altar. The church sits amid orange trees in the center of this settlement of some 300 residents, who are usually pleased to have visitors. Also recommended is the village of **Comondú**, 80 km (50 miles) northwest of Loreto

on the road to Las Parras. There is a superb 16-km (10-mile) canyon with a wealth of near-tropical vegetation amid the desert, but no food or lodging. Those with four-wheel-drive vehicles and plenty of time on their hands have an abundance of options — dirt roads on either side of Highway 1 lead to canyons, orchards, tremendous rock formations and all sorts of scratchy chaparral. Always carry plenty of water, fuel, a first-aid kit, and tools.

WHERE TO STAY

Loreto has several small hotels in town and along the highway. The only big hotel was constructed by the government in the late 1970s; it's a wonderful place when properly maintained. Known by locals as "the Old Presidente," the hotel has gone through several management changes in the past decade. The latest incarnation is an adults-only, all-inclusive resort catering to charter groups from Canada, called **Eden (** (113) 30700 FAX (113) 30377, on Boulevard Misión in Nópolo. Even in its current incarnation, it has undergone several transformations since 1996. One expects the doors to close any day.

I prefer staying in town, where the hotels have character and moderate rates. One of the best accommodations in Loreto are the **Villas de Loreto (**/FAX (113) 50586, on Antonio Mijares, at the beach. Located in a sea front neighborhood on the south end of town, the hotel has a good beach, a swimming pool, and a peaceful, friendly setting. The 10 rooms are spread out in several one-story buildings, many with front porches. Kayaking groups often book here, and equipment is available for rent. There's no restaurant, and the hotel is billed as a no-smoking property. Smokers tend to congregate in the parking lot and small RV park behind the buildings.

The **Oasis (** (113) 50112 FAX (113) 50795, on Calle de la Playa at Zaragoza, is a friendly hostelry with 35 rooms in several bungalows spread out near the edge of the sea. The **Hotel Misión (** (113) 50048 FAX (113) 50648, López Mateos No. 1, is closer to the marina but poorly maintained. The air-conditioning is suspect in many of the 36 rooms; the pool and second-story bar are popular on simmering afternoons. There is also a **Hotel La Pinta (** (113) 50025 TOLL-FREE (800) 336-5454, on Calle Davis, on the beach north of town. The property includes 49 rooms, a pool and a restaurant, but the architecture and character is rather bland. For economy rooms, try **Motel Salvatierra (** (113) 50021, on Calle Salvatierra. It's close to the bus station and can be noisy, but the 30 rooms are relatively clean and inexpensive.

Framed by the Pacific Ocean and the Sea of Cortés, the Baja Peninsula boasts miles of isolated beaches.

WHERE TO EAT

Loreto's cooks are accustomed to preparing their customers' catch of the day, rather unimaginatively as a rule. The best restaurant in town for a feast of margaritas and beef is the dark, friendly **El Nido** ((113) 50284, Calle Salvatierra No. 154. I always have at least one moderately-priced bountiful meal here. **Café Olé** ((113) 50496, on Madero, is an institution with a loyal following who stop in for breakfast, tacos, burgers, ice cream and fresh *limonada* (lemonade). Gringos congregate for great breakfasts, pizza, pasta, burgers and fish at **Anthony's Pizza** ((113) 50733, Calle Madero

No. 29. **McLulu's** (no phone), on Salvatierra, is a classic taco stand where hungry fishermen buy fish, chicken and beef tacos by the dozens.

HOW TO GET THERE

Loreto's international airport near Nópolo receives one flight daily from Los Angeles on Aero-California; the flight continues on to La Paz, where you can make connections to the mainland. Buses travel the route north and south through Baja daily.

SOUTH OF LORETO

Highway 1 cuts inland again south of **Puerto Escondido**, another potential resort development south of Loreto. The area's largest marina is located here, along with Tripui, a campground popular with those pulling boats with trucks and RVs.

Several international companies have considered building a hotel along the marina over the decades; none has come to completion. Divers and anglers are attracted to this area since it's close to **Isla Danzante** and **Isla de Montserrat**.

The ride gets a little boring along the next stretch up the mountains to **Ciudad Constitución**, where a paved road cuts west 55 km (35 miles) to the Pacific Coast and Magdalena Bay, a favorite whale-watching spot. South of Constitución the highway travels through the arid, sparsely populated southern reaches of the Sierra de la Giganta, whose varied tones of brown and gray are blanched to flat monotonous sandy color by the intense midday sun. At sunrise and sunset subtle variations in the sandy soil and rocks is strikingly beautiful against the pale blue and pink sky.

LA PAZ

The largest city in Baja Sur, with a population of over 150,000, La Paz is the state capital and main port on the Sea of Cortez. Most travelers spend a day or two here, recuperating from the drive, stocking up on supplies and enjoying the scenery. The city faces one of Baja's largest bays an fertile feeding grounds for large pelagic fish. A central plaza, large department stores and a cluster of businesses give La Paz a real city feeling; dump the car at your hotel and walk around. From March through September, runs of marlin, sailfish, yellowtail and tuna attract sport fishermen from around the world. Fishing tournaments are held several times during this season. The Baja 1000 car race passes through in late November.

BACKGROUND

The Spanish first landed in La Paz in 1535. Home of the Pericúe, Cochimi and Guaicura Indians, the region was unsuccessful as a mission site because of drought, famine and the hostility of the Indians, who were brought under control only after most of the indigenous population had died from diseases introduced by the Europeans. In 1853, William Walker, an American bent on establishing a country where slavery was legal, took over the city but was driven out by the Mexicans. But conquerors of all types kept returning because of the rumors of black pearls to be found in the bay of La Paz. The pearls were almost completely wiped out by disease and overfishing in the late nineteenth and early twentieth centuries. La Paz became the capital of the Californias in 1829 and the capital of the state of Baja Sur in 1974. La Paz is now a commercial and sport fishing port, a tourist destination and the largest city in Baja California Sur. Anyone living in the state ends up coming here frequently to shop and take care of business.

GENERAL INFORMATION

The **Tourist Information Offices** on Mariano Abasolo ((112) 40100 FAX (112) 40722, and on the *malecón* ((112) 25939 by Calle 16 de Septiembre, provides free maps of the city, and lists of hotels and services.

WHAT TO SEE AND DO

It takes a while to catch on to the charms of La Paz. At first it seems incongruous, and those who've been wandering through the more isolated parts of Baja are perturbed by the traffic and city

of Peace), a nineteenth-century church built next to the original 1720 mission. The **Museo Antropológico de Baja California Sur** (Anthropology Museum of Baja California Sur) ((112) 20162, Avenida Ignacio and Cinco de Mayo (free admission; open daily from 8 AM to 6 PM), has extensive displays of Baja cave paintings and Indian life, as well as copies of Cortés' writings. If the museum whets your appetite for Baja history, the **Biblioteca de las Californias** (Library of the Californias) ((112) 20162, Madero at Cinco de Mayo (open by appointment), is the repository for Baja historical documents. Most are in Spanish, but there are researchers in La Paz who can help you find and translate documents.

confusion. The best part of town is the *malecón*, which runs along the waterfront a few blocks from the heart of downtown. Fishing boats sway in the light currents at the center of the bay, across the street from longstanding hotels and restaurants. **Plaza Malecón** is a cement square at the foot of Calle 16 de Septiembre. I'm particularly fond of wandering in this area in the evening, when children run along the beach and play at brilliantly painted swing sets and slides. Teenagers sit hand-in-hand on benches watching the sunset, often closely supervised by parents and grandparents lingering nearby. On weekend nights youths cruise **Paseo Alvaro Obregón**, the street alongside the *malecón*, in their lowrider cars with radios blaring.

Calle 16 de Septiembre leads from the *malecón* inland to the main plaza and the **Catedral de Nuestra Señora de La Paz** (Cathedral of Our Lady

Paseo Obregón travels southeast from downtown and becomes Highway 11, leading along a point that stretches northward into the sea, cupping the **Bahía de La Paz**. Freighters and ferries dock at the pier in **Pichilingue**, where several seafood stands sell fresh fish and oyster lunches. The beaches at **Balandra**, **Coyote** and **Tecolete** are popular sunbathing and swimming hangouts; camping is usually allowed at these beaches, though you must be careful to keep your valuables locked up and bring all the freshwater you'll need.

Sport fishing is a big draw here; boats and gear can be chartered through the **Dorado Velez Fleet** operated by Jack Velez in the Los Arcos. La Paz is also well-known for its **scuba diving**, in

OPPOSITE: San José del Cabo on Baja's southern tip. ABOVE: A cocktail after a hot day in Los Cabos.

particular around **Isla Espíritu Santo** and the seamount offshore where hammerhead sharks, manta rays and nurse sharks sometimes congregate. Diving tours can be arranged through **Baja Diving (** (112) 21826, on Paseo Obregón, while the La Concha Beach Resort (see below) can also arrange dive trips. **Baja Quest (** (112) 35051 in the Hotel La Perla arranges whale-watching tours.

WHERE TO STAY

La Paz has an abundance of small, older hotels and a few modern properties. Advance reservations are advised for holiday weekends and during fishing tournaments.

Expensive

The best full-service property in the area is **La Concha Beach Resort (** (112) 16344 TOLL-FREE (800) 999-2252 FAX (112) 16218 at Km 5 Carretera a Pichilingue. The 107 unexceptional rooms are housed in several buildings facing a good swimming beach outside downtown. La Concha's beach club is the most complete watersports center in the area, offering scuba diving, snorkeling, fishing and kayaking tours. The restaurant is perfectly adequate. Newer rooms in the condominium building beside the older part of the hotel have kitchenettes, living room areas, and a separate swimming pool; some are used as timeshares or are privately owned.

Moderate

The traditional favorite across from the *malecón* is the colonial-style **Los Arcos (** (112) 22744 TOLL-FREE (800) 347-2252 FAX (112) 54313, on Paseo Obregón between Rosales and Allende. Some of the 180 rooms face the water; street noise can affect your sleep. Others are located behind the courtyard swimming pool. **Los Cabañas de Los Arcos** beside the hotel (same contact numbers), has 30 bungalows in a tropical setting; guests have use of the main hotel's pool. I'm fond of the hotel's coffee shop, which opens early, is blissfully air-conditioned, and offers snacks and full meals at all hours of the day. The tour and sport fishing operations within the hotel are among the town's best. **Hotel La Perla (** (112) 20777 FAX (112) 55363, on Paseo Obregón, is another *malecón* favorite with 101 rooms (some facing the waterfront) a pool, tour operators, and a pleasant open-air café facing the water.

Inexpensive

The **Hotel Mediterranée (**/FAX (112) 51195, Calle Allende No. 36, is one of the prettiest small hotels in La Paz. The blue and white decor, pale wood furnishings, and airy feeling of the five rooms create a pleasant setting just a few blocks from the *malecón*. Quirky and plagued by insects, the

Pension California ((112) 22896, Avenida Degollado No. 209, has 25 humble rooms and space for guests to mingle. The owners have a second hotel nearby.

WHERE TO EAT

Though seafood reigns supreme on all menus in La Paz, you can also get good pasta, meat dishes and poultry. Restaurants are casual.

Moderate

La Paz-Lapa ((112) 59290, on Paseo Obregón at Calle 16 de Septiembre, is a fun place to fuel up on barbecued ribs and chicken, and huge platters of tacos, *quesadillas* and steaks, while listening to blaring rock 'n' roll. **La Pazta (** (112) 51195, Allende No. 36, is a bit more refined, with a restrained black and white decor. The cooks prepare excellent homemade pastas with local herbs, vegetables,

and seafood. **El Bismark** ((112) 24854, on Santos Degollado and Avenida Altamirano, is the best place for huge seafood cocktails and grilled fish.

Inexpensive

Traffic is sometimes blocked by the crowds of lunchtime diners enjoying fish and pork tacos at **Tacos Hermanos González** (no phone) at Mutualismo and Esquerro. This simple taco stand is considered the best of all the downtown taco spots. For a healthy breakfast of yogurt, fruit and cereal, **El Quinto Sol Restaurante Vegetariano** ((112) 21692, Belisario Domínguez No. 12, opens at 8 AM. It also serves vegetarian lunches and dinners, and operates a well-stocked natural food store.

HOW TO GET THERE

La Paz's international airport receives flights from the United States and mainland Mexico on

Aeroméxico, AeroCalifornia and Mexicana. Vehicle and pedestrian ferries from Mazatlán dock at the port at Pichilingue east of downtown. There is express first-class bus service from La Paz to Tijuana and Los Cabos. La Paz also has several car rental companies at the airport.

LOS CABOS

Two decades ago it was hard to believe the southern tip of Baja would succeed as a major destination. But the government pulled off a winner here, combining the two small towns of **San José del Cabo** and **Cabo San Lucas**, 33 km (20 miles) apart, into one destination called Los Cabos. Long popular with anglers and boaters, the area has grown from a rustic escape with a few exceptional hotels into Mexico's most expensive, deluxe destination.

Marina Cabo San Lucas.

Baja California

Much of the upscale development has occurred in the Corridor between the two towns, where several championship golf courses have been carved into the landscape.

The transformation of Los Cabos started slowly back in 1974, when the government slated it for development. Until then, the tip of the peninsula was the province of hardy travelers arriving by car or wealthy travelers arriving by private planes and yachts. The completion of Highway 1 to Cabo San Lucas, at land's end, brought a trickle of adventuresome travelers; the addition of an international airport added more options for travelers curious about this narrow tip of land where the desert meets the sea.

In terms of topography, Los Cabos is uniquely beautiful. The Sierra de la Giganta bisects the land, gradually diminishing in height to a dramatic rock formation called **El Arco** at the end of the peninsula, where the Pacific Ocean and the Sea of Cortez swirl together in crashing waves. The two towns, which once consisted of a few small neighborhoods on sandy streets, have grown into a jumble of back street neighborhoods and tourist centers filled with restaurants, bars, and shops. I find the growth to be disappointing, yet inevitable, and still return annually for a dose of searing dry desert air, spectacular fishing, and the sense of escape — still possible if you know where to go.

GENERAL INFORMATION

The **Tourist Information Center** ((114) 22960 extension 148 in San José del Cabo, is on Zaragoza

between Hidalgo and Mijares, and Tourist Information Center ((114) 34180 FAX (114) 32211, on Madero between Hidalgo and Guerrero, in Cabo San Lucas.

WHAT TO SEE AND DO

Coming from the north on Highway 1 and the airport, your first stop is **San José del Cabo**, the municipal headquarters for the region. Despite bumper-to-bumper traffic on Boulevard Mijares, the main road through town, San Jose has retained a sense of tranquillity. Its central plaza with a traditional iron gazebo, fronts the **Iglesia de San José**, a modest church with yellow spires peaking above the town. Most tourist-oriented businesses are located on Mijares and the bisecting streets; there are several excellent interior design shops catering to the wealthy home owners buying into ever-growing vacation-home complexes. The master-planned hotel zone sits at the south end of Mijares, facing the Sea of Cortez. The **beaches** are gorgeous here, but the tides and surf are powerful, and swimming is not advised. The **Estero de San José** at the end of the hotel zone has been set aside as a protected zone with over 200 species of birds which migrate to the Río San José. The **Los Cabos Cultural Center** ((114) 21540, on Paseo San José (admission fee; open Tuesday through Sunday), has a small collection of photographs, fossils, and replicas of Indian cave paintings.

From San José the highway climbs a slight ridge toward the Corridor, where trucks and bulldozers are as common as cars. The changes here are incredible. What once was a barren yet beautiful landscape of seaside cliffs and fields of cacti has been transformed into huge swaths of fairways and greens framed by massive hotels. Million-dollar vacation homes sit hidden behind guarded gates. Some of the classiest hotels in Mexico have risen along the Corridor, attracting a clientele willing to pay $300 and up per night for luxurious pampering. Tucked between these palaces are a few of Los Cabos' first hotels, which have managed to keep up with the competition while retaining their individual character. Many visitors to Los Cabos spend a day wandering through the Corridor's hotels, stopping for drinks beside the tropical, landscaped gardens and pools. Two of the area's best snorkeling spots are also in this area. Dirt roads lead to **Bahía Santa Maria** and **Bahía Chileno**, where vendors rent snorkeling gear during the high season. Both are wonderful spots where you can get a sense of the region's natural beauty.

The Corridor gives way to **Cabo San Lucas**, or simply Cabo as it's usually called. Once a small fishing settlement with a few canneries and booming commercial fishing business, Cabo has become a rowdy party town with a garish assortment of bars and shopping plazas. **Boulevard Marina** is the main street along the waterfront, though you're hard put to spot the sea between the massive buildings that now block the town from cooling breezes. The **Marina Cabo San Lucas** is at the end of Mijares. Most fishing boats bring their catches in here, and the walkway along the marina is lined with vendors offering fishing, snorkeling, and glass-bottom boat trips. An open-air **Artisans' Market** facing the marina caters mainly to the cruise ship crowd, who arrive on tenders from enormous ships anchored in the Sea of Cortez beyond El Arco.

A few blocks inland on Avenida Hidalgo is the main plaza with an ornate white *kiosko* and shade trees. Unlike most Mexican plazas, this one doesn't attract local families; most live several blocks inland in the congested residential area of the town. The **Parroquía de San Lucas** on Calle San Lucas at Zapata, was established in 1730; the simple church is undergoing a long-term renovation funded by local parishioners.

Sport fishing endures as one of the area's biggest attractions. Most of the fishing boats leave from the Cabo San Lucas Marina, where anglers gather to watch each day's catch come in from noon to dusk. There are many excellent sport fishing operations and all have representatives at the marina; for information contact **Gordo Banks Sportfishing** ((114) 21147 or TOLL-FREE (800) 408-1199; **La Playita Sportfishing** ((114) 21195; the **Twin Dolphin** fishing fleet ((114) 30256; and **Minerva's Baja Tackle and Sportfishing** ((114) 32766. The largest fishing fleet belongs to **Solmar** ((114) 33535 TOLL-FREE (800) 344-3349. It has over 21 boats including the *Solmar V* which heads out on week-long dive trips to the Socorro Islands 645 km (400 miles) off shore.

You needn't be a fisher to have an excuse to get out on the water. Boat captains at the marina offer sightseeing tours, sunset cruises, and snorkeling trips. Check the condition of the boat and the availability of lifejackets before signing on. One of the most popular trips is to El Arco and **Playa de Amor**, a small beach tucked under the rocks. I find this beach to be overrated; the water tends to be rough here and you may have to swim from the boat to the beach. Be sure to bring plenty of drinking water and sunscreen lotion, and try to find a spot away from the pelicans and sea gulls who have covered the rocks with chalky white guano. Theme and sunset **boat tours** of the ocean and bay are available through **Operador Pez Gato** ((114) 33797.

Scuba divers are fascinated by the sandfalls at land's end, where underwater streams of sand flow over the rocks. The coral reefs north of Los Cabos at **Cabo Pulmo** are also popular, though they're a couple of hours away by boat. For information contact **Amigos Del Mar** ((114) 30505

TOLL-FREE (800) 344-3349, one of the oldest and most reputable scuba companies in Los Cabos. **Kayaking** in the sea's calm coves gives patient paddlers the opportunity to study the cliffs and perhaps spot a dolphin or whale. Kayaks can be rented at **Los Lobos del Mar** ((114) 22983 and **Cabo Acuadeportes** ((114) 30117. **Baja Expeditions** TOLL-FREE (800) 843-6967, 2625 Garnet Avenue, San Diego, CA 92109, is one of the premier dive operators for Baja, and can arrange anything from hiking and biking trips to kayaking and diving trips off of the peninsula. **Tio Sports** ((114) 32986, has water-sports equipment rentals and tours. **Tour Cabos** ((114) 20982 offers a full range of activities, including trips to La Paz.

Though Los Cabos began as a fishing destination, **golf** has become a major attraction and there are as many golf clubs as fishing poles on the inbound airplanes these days. The **Los Cabos Campo de Golf** ((114) 24166 FAX (114) 24166, on Boulevard Finisterra off of Boulevard Mijares, is the area's original golf course. Designed by Mario Schjetnan and built by FONATUR, it has nine holes and is par 35 and 3,000 yards. It also has six floodlit tennis courts and is open to nonmembers. The **Palmilla Golf Club** ((114) 45250 or (800) 386-2465, located across the highway from the Palmilla Hotel on Highway 1, is a gorgeous course with vistas of the Sea of Cortez. It was designed by Jack Nicklaus and has 27 holes, 72 par and 10,000 yards. **Cabo Real Golf Course** ((114) 40040, designed by Robert

Colorful Los Cabos: beach hats for sale OPPOSITE and cocktails ABOVE.

Trent-Jones Jr., has 18 holes, is par 72 and 7,000 yards. Guests at Cabo Real hotels receive a discount on greens fees. **Cabo del Sol Golf Club** ((114) 58200 TOLL-FREE (800) 386-2465, in the Corridor, has 18 holes, is par 72 and 7,051 yards; some holes are right by the sea. The **Cabo San Lucas Country Club** ((114) 34653, on Highway 1, at Km 2 just north of Cabo San Lucas, was designed by Roy Dye and has 18 holes at par 72, 7,000 yards.

Horseback riding has become popular, thanks to a couple of first-rate ranches including **Cuadra San Francisco** ((114) 40160, in the Corridor across from the Meliá Real hotel. Several hotels also offer horseback riding; check at the Meliá San Lucas and the Hotel Finisterra.

Each time I return, I'm amazed at the improvement in **shopping** possibilities in Los Cabos. Thanks to the abundance of palatial private homes, interior designers have set up shop in both towns and offer some of the finest furnishings and household items to be found in Mexico. Most are happy to ship purchases anywhere in the world. The best selections can be found at **El Callejon, Cartes, Necri** and **Galería Gattamelata** in Cabo San Lucas and at **ADD** in San José. Mexican folk art, masks, hammocks and pottery of the highest quality, are available at **El Rancho, Zen Mar, Mama Eli's,** and **Galería Dorado** in Cabo San Lucas and **Huichol Collection** and **Copal** in San José.

WHERE TO STAY

Los Cabos is an incredibly expensive destination, with precious little accommodation for low-budget travelers. The least expensive places are in San José and the most expensive (charging upwards from $300 a night) are in the Corridor. Advance reservations are essential during the winter months and around United States and Mexican holidays.

Very Expensive

Sublime luxury and individual attention make **Las Ventanas al Paraíso** ((114) 40257 TOLL-FREE (888) 525-0483 FAX (114) 40255, in the Corridor, within Cabo Real, the most exclusive hotel in the area. The architecture is stunning, incorporating hand-laid stone walkways, woven wood ceilings, hand-carved wood doors and in-room telescopes and fireplaces. The 61 suites with private terraces and great views of the sea are so gorgeous one hates to leave the room; even the bathtubs are enormous. The hotel's spa, one of the first in the area, offers all sorts of soothing treatments and the restaurants are superb. The **Hotel Palmilla** ((114) 45000 TOLL-FREE (800) 637-2226 FAX (114) 45100, on Highway 1 south of San José del Cabo, is my favorite hideaway, thanks to its Mexican architecture, attentive service and traditional Mexican ambiance. Despite a complete renovation in the mid-1990s, the hotel remains hidden amid towering palms, its white walls, arches and domes framed with scarlet bougainvillea. The pool is one of the most-user friendly I've seen, with its water-spurting fountains, shallow shelves where one can lie in the water and read, and areas for swimming laps. The 72 rooms and 62 suites are decorated with Mexican textiles and folk art; most face the sea. The restaurants serve excellent traditional and nouvelle Mexican cuisine; the Sunday brunch is the best in the area. Stop by for a superb margarita in the open-air bar at sunset. **Casa del Mar** ((114) 40221 TOLL-FREE (800) 221-8808 FAX (114) 40034 in the Corridor within Cabo Real is also stunning, and looks like an overgrown country home. The hotel has 25 rooms and 31 suites, a spa and a good restaurant. Also recommended in this price range is the stark white, modernistic **Twin Dolphin** ((114) 30256 TOLL-FREE (800) 421-8925 FAX (114) 30496 on Highway 1 at Km 12 in the Corridor, with 44 rooms and six suites. The **Westin Regina** ((114) 29000 TOLL-FREE (800) 228-3000 FAX (114) 29010, on Highway 1 at Km 22.5 in the Corridor, is a dramatic complex with vivid yellow and pink walls in the lobby atop a seaside cliff. The 305 rooms are located closer to the hotel's man-made beach, amid free-form swimming pools.

Expensive

My favorite hotel in Cabo San Lucas is the **Solmar Suites** ((114) 33535 TOLL-FREE (800) 344-3349 FAX (114) 30410 (or write to PO Box 383, Pacific Palisades, CA 90272 ((310) 459-9861 FAX (310) 454-1686), on Camino Solmar, off Boulevard Marina. One of Cabo's oldest hotels, the Solmar sits against the rocks at land's end on the Pacific side of the tip. Waves crash mightily on the broad beach; swimming is not advised. But the hotel has a private, secluded feeling, with its 90 rooms housed in unobtrusive white buildings on the sand. Mariachis play at the poolside bar during sunset, and the restaurant hosts a weekly Mexican fiesta on Saturday nights. The **Hotel Finisterra** ((114) 33333 TOLL-FREE (800) 347-2252 FAX (114) 30590 (or write to 6 Jenner, Suite 120, Irvine, CA 92618), just up the beach on Boulevard Marina between Camino Solmar and Camino del Mar, is another older hotel completely renovated in the 1990s. An eight-story highrise towers from the beach to the top of the cliffs where the hotel's original buildings are located. The nicest of the 237 rooms are in the tower, though old-timers still prefer the mountain-lodge type accommodation in rock-walled buildings atop the cliff. Another traditional favorite is the **Hotel Hacienda** ((114) 32062 TOLL-FREE (800) 733-2226 FAX (114) 30666, on Camino al Hotel Hacienda, off Paseo del Pescador. The white-washed hotel sits on a spit of land facing the Cabo San Lucas marina; its 114 rooms are scattered through the heavily landscaped property. There is an excellent water-sports center here and a good swimming beach. The hottest ticket in town these days is the **Meliá San Lucas** ((114) 34444 TOLL-FREE (800) 336-3542 FAX (114) 30418, at Paseo del Pescador between Playa el Médano and Highway 1. The hotel sits above Cabo's most popular beach, Playa El Médano. Its swimming pool area may well be the most crowded gathering spot in town, and the restaurants and bars, though unexceptional, attract festive groups. The hotel's 150 rooms and suites are well maintained, and it's easy to walk into town from here. In the Corridor, the venerable **Hotel Cabo San Lucas** ((114) 40014 TOLL-FREE (800) 733-2226 FAX (114) 40015, on Highway 1 at Km 14, resembles a rustic lodge, set amid groves of mature palms. The 89 rooms have a cozy, comfortable feeling, and the massive rock-walled dining room and bar faces the sea. In San José, the **Presidente Inter-Continental Los Cabos** ((114) 20211 TOLL-FREE (800) 327-0200 FAX (114) 20232, on Paseo San José at the Estero de San José, was the first property on the hotel zone. Its sand-colored buildings blend nicely with cactus gardens and well-tended lawns; the best of the 250 rooms are on the first floor and have patios shaded with trellis covered with bougainvillea. The hotel now operates on an all-inclusive basis, which makes its rates appear somewhat high. But San José's restaurants are a long walk away, so the package is good for those without wheels.

Moderate

Though not on the beach, the **Tropicana Inn** ((114) 20907 (for reservations in the United States ((510) 939-2725) FAX (114) 21590, Boulevard Mijares No. 30, between Benito Juárez and Doblado in San José, is an ideal choice for travelers watching their pesos. The 40 rooms are constructed around a pool and *palapa*-covered bar, and the property is decorated with hand-painted tiles. **La Playita** ((114) 24166 FAX (114) 24166, at Pueblo La Playa two kilometers (just over a mile) south of San José is perfect for total escapists who want nothing more than a pleasant room, good food and a long empty beach. The 24 rooms are air-conditioned and have televisions; phone service is available at the front desk. The hotel sits at the edge of the Pueblo La Playa community of modest residences; a small fleet of *pangas* on the beach is available for fishing trips. In Cabo San Lucas, **The Bungalows** ((114) 30585 FAX (114) 35035 (or write to 9051-C Siempre Viva Road, Suite 40-497, San Diego, CA 92173), on Calle Libertad off Avenida Cabo San Lucas, is a great find in a residential neighborhood about 10 blocks from the beach. Some of the 16 units have separate bedrooms and kitchenettes; a lavish continental breakfast is served under a poolside *palapa*.

Sport fishing remains one of Baja's biggest attractions, though anglers now release much of their catch.

Baja California

Inexpensive

Always popular, the **Posada Terranova** ((114) 20534 FAX (114) 20902, on Calle Degollado at Zaragoza is San José, is a friendly, comfortable spot with 25 immaculately clean rooms and a good restaurant. In Cabo San Lucas, the **Mar de Cortez** ((114) 30032 TOLL-FREE (800) 347-8821 FAX (114) 30232 (or contact: 17561 Vierra Canyon Road 99, Salinas, CA 93907 ((408) 663-5803 FAX (408) 663-1904) on Lázaro Cárdenas between Matamoros and Guerrero, is favored by anglers who return annually to the familiar setting and friendly staff. The 72 rooms are often booked well in advance. The restaurant specializes in shrimp dishes and is usually a merry spot. The **Hotel Marina** ((114) 31499 FAX (114) 32484, on Boulevard Marina at Guerrero, suffers from its proximity to the noisy main drag, but the 27 rooms are well maintained and you can't get any closer to the action.

WHERE TO EAT

The chefs of Los Cabos are beginning to create a Baja cuisine based on the fruits of the land and sea. Fish now appears with mango and papaya sauces, salads benefit from a variety of vegetables grown around Todos Santos, and meats, cheeses, chilis and spices are being imported from the United States and mainland Mexico. Some of the finest restaurants are in the hotels; don't miss **The Restaurant** and the **Sea Grill** ((114) 40257 at Las Ventanas al Paraíso, and **La Paloma** ((114) 45000 at the Palmilla. Both are expensive and worth every *centavo*. Few restaurants take reservations and dress is casual everywhere.

Expensive

One of the few fancy restaurants set right by the beach, **Pitahayas** ((114) 32157, within Cabo del Sol in the Corridor, is both romantic and exciting.

The first local place to specialize in Pacific-rim cuisine, the restaurant (named for a locally grown fruit) offers Thai, Japanese and Polynesian preparations of local seafood, along with roasted duckling and quail. **Peacocks** ((114) 31558, on Paseo del Pescador between Playa El Médano and Highway 1 in Cabo San Lucas, offers fresh dorado with a pecan crust, shellfish with fresh pasta and herbs and wonderful desserts. At **Casa Rafael's** ((114) 30739, on Calle Médano at Camino Pescador in Cabo San Lucas, a chef from Hawaii prepares lobster with black bean sauce and smoked dorado. A handsome setting with heavy carved wood chairs and tables, and piano music in the background, makes dinner at **El Galeón** ((114) 30443 across from the marina in Cabo San Lucas, a pleasurable experience. Huge lobsters, steaks, fish platters and pastas are all well prepared.

Moderate

Romance reigns at **Damiana** ((114) 20499, off Boulevard Mijares between Zaragoza and Obregón in San José. The best tables are in the jungle-like courtyard where candlelight flickers. Try the imperial shrimp steak and the Damiana margarita, made with a local liqueur. The **Tropicana Bar & Grill** ((114) 21580, on Boulevard Mijares in front of the Tropicana Inn, also has a romantic courtyard along with a rowdy bar where sporting events are shown on several screens. The menu includes Mexican dishes and imported meats.

In Cabo San Lucas, **Mi Casa** ((114) 31933, on Avenida San Lucas on the west side of the plaza, specializes in regional Mexican cuisine; if you've caught any fish bring it here and have it prepared with *chipotle* chilis. **Pancho's** ((114) 30973, on Hidalgo between Zapata and Serdán in Cabo San Lucas, has a huge menu of Mexican specialties from Oaxaca, Puebla, Yucatán and other parts of the country. The bartender pours over 100 brands of tequila and the festive decor encourages diners to indulge in some fun. **Mama's Royal Café** ((114) 34290, at Hidalgo between Zapata and Serdán, serves the best breakfasts in the area.

Inexpensive

It's difficult to eat well on a slim budget in Los Cabos where a single margarita can cost as much as a *comida corrida* in a rural town. Both towns have taco stands by their bus stations and in their commercial districts. You can get by fairly cheaply at the moderate restaurants listed above if you stick with appetizers, tacos and soups.

NIGHTLIFE

San José is fairly quiet at night, while Cabo San Lucas rocks until dawn. The most popular night spots are rowdy, noisy places where canned music blares and the tanned patrons flirt and shout.

The most happening spot is **Squid Roe** ((114) 30655, on Lázaro Cárdenas between Morelos and Zaragoza, a classic example of the Carlos Anderson chain of touristy restaurants and bars. Also part of the chain are **Carlos 'n' Charlie's** ((114) 30973, on Boulevard Marina, and **El Shrimp Bucket** ((114) 32498 at Plaza Marina Fiesta. The **Giggling Marlin** ((114) 31182 on Boulevard Marina at Matamoros is a longtime favorite with the drink-and-be-merry crowd; **Cabo Wabo Bar & Grill** ((114) 31198, at Guerrero between Madero and Cárdenas, was the hit of the early 1990s. The **Hard Rock Café** and **Planet Hollywood** now loom over Boulevard Marina, which is beginning to contain too many franchise names for comfort.

HOW TO GET THERE

National and international flights arrive at the San José international airport, 11 kilometers (seven miles) north of San José del Cabo. Aeroméxico, Mexicana, Continental, Alaska, America West and United all fly here, though some only serve Los Cabos in the winter high season. *Colectivo* vans transport passengers to the hotels; expect the ride to last at least a half-hour if you're staying in Cabo San Lucas. Buses connect Los Cabos with towns north and Tijuana at the border; most buses departing Cabo San Lucas stop in San José.

TODOS SANTOS

Artists, entrepreneurs and escapists have found a haven in **Todos Santos** (All Saints), 80 km (50 miles) up the Pacific Coast from Cabo San Lucas. Highway 19 travels up the coast from Cabo, passing by gorgeous isolated beaches and a few campgrounds and private homes. Watch for cows grazing along the road and sudden dips, called *vados*, and don't drive this road after dark. The small town sits inland, with late nineteenth-century houses framing a small plaza and church. Some of the older buildings have been converted into shops and galleries. Residents of Los Cabos and La Paz often drive to Todos Santos to eat at **Café Santa Fe** ((114) 40340, on Calle Centenario by the plaza. Owners Paula and Ezio Colombo opened this lovely restaurant after many years in the business in Los Cabos. They grow their own herbs and some produce in their garden and it is here, at their patio tables, that diners linger over long lunches of fresh pasta, fish in light herb sauces, and wonderful salads made with vegetables from their own garden and the organic farms in the area. The most established hotel in town is the 16-room **Hotel California** (/FAX (114) 50020 on Calle Juárez. Others are sure to open as moneyed transplants refurbish the town's older homes.

Surfers peruse one of several prime surfing areas along Baja's northern Pacific Coast.

Travelers' Tips

ARRIVING

By Air

Airlines from North, Central and South America, Europe, and Asia fly into Mexico City's Aeropuerto Internacional Benito Juárez in the northeast section of city, a 30- to 60-minute drive, depending on traffic, from the Historic Center. Cancún and Guadalajara are also served by several international airlines, and are good jumping-off points for other destinations.

The national carriers Aeroméxico TOLL-FREE (800) 237-6639 and Mexicana Airlines TOLL-FREE (800) 531-7921, have direct flights from many American cities to major Mexican cities and resorts, including Acapulco, Cancún, Cozumel, Guadalajara, Ixtapa, Mazatlán, Mérida, Mexico City and Puerto Vallarta.

Aeroméxico has direct flights from Europe to Mexico City. To take Aeroméxico from other locations, it is necessary to make a connection through a United States city such as New York, Miami, Houston, Tucson, or Los Angeles, or when coming from Europe, through Madrid or Paris.

Once inside the country, Aeroméxico and Mexicana — and their subsidiary regional carriers — serve most destinations including Aguascalientes, Bahía de Huatulco, Campeche, Cancún, Chihuahua, Ciudad Juárez, Ciudad Obregón, Culiacán, Durango, Guaymas, Hermosillo, Los Mochis, Matamoros, Monterrey, Oaxaca, Puebla, Reynosa, Tapachula, Torreón, Villahermosa and Zihuatanejo. Domestic flights in Mexico are generally lower in price than domestic American and European ones. In fact, travelers departing from the southern United States often find it advantageous to cross the border and fly south from one of the Mexican border towns.

By Car

Hundreds of thousands of tourists visit Mexico by car or RV (camper van) from the United States every year with no problems. Others encounter nothing but trouble, usually because they are unaware of Mexican laws. Before bringing a vehicle into Mexico you must obtain a Temporary Car Importation Permit and purchase auto insurance from a Mexican company. You must also leave the country with your vehicle at the end of your stay.

Obtaining a Temporary Car Importation Permit can be a major hassle. To obtain a permit you must present the following: proof of ownership of the vehicle or a notarized letter from the bank or lender holding the car's papers allowing you to take the car into Mexico; a valid driver's license; a major credit card in the same name as the vehicle's ownership papers; proof of nationality such as a passport; a stamped Mexican Tourist Card; and Mexican auto insurance for the length of your stay. A strong dose of patience comes in handy as well. You must present all of these papers at the Mexican Customs office at the border and sign a credit card slip as a deposit to ensure you will leave the country with your car. You are then given a temporary permit, usually valid for up to six months. You must turn the permit back in when you leave the country. The easiest way to complete this process is through an American Automobile Association (AAA) office or through Sanborn's Mexico Insurance Company TOLL-FREE (800) 222-0158.

Mexican auto insurance is mandatory for all cars driven in the country. Travelers can expect

enormous hassles if they are in an accident and do not have insurance. The Napoleonic Code prevails in Mexico — get in an accident and you are guilty until proven innocent. Mexican insurance can be easily purchased at insurance stands on both sides of the border; be certain your insurer has a list of adjusters in the areas you will be visiting. It is best to deal with major companies such as Sanborn's or AAA (mentioned above).

You must take the same car out of Mexico that is identified on your permit. If an emergency calls you out of the country and you want to leave your vehicle behind, call your embassy in Mexico City or nearest consulate to request assistance. Leaving the country without your car for any reason is not easy.

Having said all this, I must admit that I've never had to get a vehicle permit to drive in Baja California, and have never been asked for one by a police officer. I do, however, have annual Mexican auto insurance. I have found that it is less expensive to purchase a yearly policy than to buy insurance by the day every time I cross the border to shop, dine, or fly from Tijuana to mainland

OPPOSITE: Dating from the eighth century, the spectacular ruins at Palenque reward the effort of the hour-and-a-half drive from Villahermosa, the nearest city. ABOVE: Olmec wrestler.

Mexico. If you plan to drive around Mexico for several months, you may find a yearly policy to be the best bargain.

By Bus

There is good bus service between Mexico, Guatemala and Belize, and the border crossings are not difficult as long as you have your passport and visas in order. Bus service between the border cities in the United States and Mexico is also available; once in Mexico you must switch to a Mexican bus.

By Sea

Mexico is the destination of several cruise lines departing from the east or west coast of the United States. Usually the cruises include several Mexican ports with optional day excursions. Travel agents in the United States and Europe can best provide you with schedules and prices, which often include reductions on return flights to the liners' home ports.

DEPARTURE TAXES

There is an airport departure tax of approximately $12 on international flights and $10 on domestic flights. This may already be included on your air ticket. If not, you must pay in pesos or United States dollars when you check-in for your flight.

VISAS

Travelers to Mexico need a Tourist Card, free at customs offices upon presentation of proof of citizenship in the form of passport, a birth certificate accompanied by a photo ID, or notarized affidavit of citizenship. A passport is the safest. Tourist Cards can be obtained at the border, or from Mexican embassies or consulates before departure. Most airlines and travel agents provide the forms to fill out before arrival and immigration officers will validate them before one passes through customs.

A Tourist Card is valid for 90 days, must be carried at all times, and is collected upon exiting Mexico. Anyone wishing to visit Belize or Guatemala while in Mexico should request a multiple entry card. It is best to apply in advance.

Minors must have proof of citizenship. If traveling with only one parent, they must have notarized authorization from the absent parent allowing the child to go into Mexico. Children over 10 years of age must obtain a Tourist Card. The authorities are strict about these regulations.

INFORMATION FOR TOURISTS

Mexico operates an information line for the United States and Canada: TOLL-FREE (800) 44-MEXICO.

Travelers can order faxes on destinations in Mexico by calling Fax Me Mexico ((541) 385-9282 in the United States.

The Mexican tourist offices are currently undergoing some reorganization, so if you live elsewhere in the world we suggest that you contact the above fax number, or Amtave, or the Mexico City Tourist Information Office (both listed below) or your nearest embassy or consulate.

You can subscribe to the Mexican Association of Adventure & Ecotourism, **Amtave** (Asociación Mexicana de Turismo de Aventura y Ecoturismo) ((5) 661-9121 FAX (5) 662-7354 E-MAIL ecomexico @compuserve.com.mx WEB SITE www.amtave .com.mx and receive their brochures.

Arriving at Benito Juárez Airport in Mexico, there is an information booth ((5) 762-6773 or ((5) 571-3600, as well as information points on the highways to the city. Plenty of information is available at the **Mexico City Tourist Information Office** ((5) 525-9380 and 533-4700 FAX (5) 525-9387 in the Zona Rosa at Amberes No. 54 at Londres; open daily from 9 AM to 6 PM. **LOCATEL** ((5) 658-1111 is a 24-hour information hotline.

To check airline arrivals or departures, call general information at Benito Juárez Airport ((5) 762-4011. There is also a security line ((5) 571-3600 should you have any problems.

GETTING AROUND

By Air

Aeroméxico and Mexicana are the major domestic carriers, and their service is excellent and reasonably priced. Other airlines, including AeroCalifornia, Aviacsa and Aerocaribe, serve specific regions. Several United States and European carriers also serve major destinations; check with American Airlines, British Airways, Continental, United, Delta and America West.

Travel between destinations within Mexico often involves flying through a major airport such as Guadalajara, Mexico City or Cancún, though these cities may be out of your way. You may find that it takes less time to travel by bus between two cities such as Mazatlán and Puerto Vallarta than to go through a series of flights. On the other hand, you can save a considerable amount of time by flying on routes that cover mountainous terrain. For example, it takes a half hour to fly between Huatulco and Oaxaca city; by bus, the trip takes eight to ten hours. Tickets can be purchased for most Mexican airlines at travel agencies throughout the world.

Tlaquepaque, a suburb of Guadalajara in the state of Jalisco, is famous for its ceramics, leather and wood furniture, textiles, glass and sculpture and its shops displaying the best of old and new Mexican art.

Airlines

Mexico City is the headquarters for the country's international airlines, Aeroméxico ((5) 133-4010 and Mexicana ((5) 448-0990. In addition, major foreign airlines also have their offices downtown and are open during normal office hours. For information on arrivals and departures at Benito Juárez International Airport, it is advisable to contact the information line ((5) 762-4011 at the airport itself.

Listed below are the contact numbers in Mexico City of the major airlines, both national and foreign:
AeroCalifornia ((5) 207-1392
Aeroméxico ((5) 133-4010
Air France ((5) 627-6060
American ((5) 209-1400
Aviacsa ((5) 566-8550
Aviateca TOLL-FREE IN MEXICO CITY 95-800-453-8123
British Airways ((5) 628-0500
Continental ((5) 283-5500
Delta ((5) 395-2300
Iberia ((5) 130-3030
Lacsa ((5) 546-8809
Lufthansa ((5) 230-0000
Mexicana Airlines ((5) 448-0990
Northwest ((5) 202-4444
Taesa ((5) 227-0700
United TOLL-FREE IN MEXICO CITY 91-800-00307

BY TRAIN

Train travel within Mexico has become a risky proposition in most areas, and downright dangerous in some. Robberies are common, and the trains are in dreadful condition after years of neglect. The federal government is attempting to privatize the rail system, without success. If you're determined to travel by train, stick with the routes closest to Mexico City. The *Ferrocarriles Nacionales de Mexico* (Mexican National Railways) has service from Mexico City to Guadalajara, Veracruz, Morelia and San Miguel Allende. Reservations can be made at the Buenavista station in Mexico City ((5) 547-6593 or through Mexico by Train TOLL-FREE (800) 321-1699 FAX (210) 725-3659 in the United States.

BY BUS

Buses go everywhere in Mexico and are often the most convenient mode of travel. New in the 1990s are deluxe first-class express buses with air-conditioning, restrooms, movies and reclining seats. Several such carriers have appeared serving popular routes including Cancún to Mérida, Acapulco to Ixtapa, and all major routes from big cities. First-class buses serve all major routes with some stops along the way. Second-class buses never have air-conditioning. They stop at every wide spot in the road, and may include chick-

ens, goats, or other livestock as passengers. These buses are available everywhere and may be the only transport in rural areas. As a rule, travel by bus is the most economical way to get around, and usually provides travelers the opportunity to mingle with locals, practice their Spanish and enjoy the scenery.

Not all cities have a central bus station serving all lines. In many places the station for one destination may be in a different part of town than that for another, and the first-class and second-class stations may be in different places. Tourist information offices and travel agencies usually have schedules and prices; always ask about your options regarding the types of service. First-class fares

are often just a few pesos more than second-class ones. I sometimes deliberately choose second-class buses in rural areas because the bus windows open. I've taken some of my best people photographs when shooting from the bus window at backcountry stops.

It may sound like a sensible idea to travel by bus at night in Mexico, but I strongly advise against it. After several close calls myself and some frightening conversations with other travelers, I have decided to use long-range buses only in daylight. Fatal crashes are all too common, especially on dark mountainous roads where drivers take entirely too many risks. There have been reports of holdups where travelers are relieved of all their possessions in remote areas of Campeche, Tabasco, and Chiapas. I tend to put all of my valuables, including my wedding ring, in a hidden money pouch when traveling by bus. Always carry water, snacks, toilet paper and a good book—you never know when you'll be stuck by the side of the road for hours during a breakdown.

BY CAR

The rules of the road in Mexico are much the same as in the United States and continental Europe, and are largely based on common courtesy and good sense. International road signs using pictures rather than words are becoming more prevalent on major roads; words to live by include *disminuya su velocidad* (reduce your speed), *precaución* (take precautions), *cuidado* (take care), *peligroso* (dangerous), and *camino sinuoso* (sinuous or winding

libre. Major highways are called *carreteras;* smaller roads are *caminos*. Road conditions can deteriorate suddenly, and are usually pretty bad in rural areas. The Mexican Ministry of Tourism has a fleet of green and white emergency trucks, known as Angeles Verdes (Green Angels) to help stranded motorists. Staffed by bilingual mechanics, they patrol the major highways from 8 AM to 8 PM. Motorists pay for gas, oil and spare parts, but the services are given free of charge. To summon assistance, pull off the side of the road and raise the hood of your car.

Speed limits are posted in kilometers per hour. If the driver behind you wants to pass, he will flash his lights. Anyone doing this is impatient;

road). Detours and road work are often marked by large rocks plopped in the middle of the pavement, a disconcerting sight to those driving merrily along at high speeds.

Mexico's roadways have improved considerably in the past few years. Several toll highways, called *autopistas*, have been built between major destinations, including Cancún and Mérida; Acapulco and Mexico City; Mexico City and Oaxaca, Puebla, Morelia and Guadalajara; and Nogales and Mazatlán. The tolls are usually prohibitively high for local drivers, but not so high as to discourage travelers on tight itineraries. You miss all the local color when traveling via these high-speed highways; if going round-trip I usually use the *autopista* one way and the back roads the other. Other toll roads such as the one from Tijuana to Ensenada are designated by the word *cuota* (toll) and usually parallel free roads, called

for your own safety slow down and let him go. When two cars approach a one-lane bridge (marked *un solo carril* or *puente angosto*) at the same time, whoever flashes his lights first has the right-of-way. Speeders are discouraged by *topes* and *vibradores* (speed bumps) in roads passing through small towns; hit one of these suddenly and you'll never do it again. Always slow down when entering a town, especially in remote areas. Children, dogs, chickens and cyclists will most likely be crossing the road. Mexican drivers use a system of signaling that can confound newcomers. Large trucks flashing their left-turn signal light may be turning or signaling those at their rear that it is safe to pass. There have been several accidents, particularly in the Yucatán, caused by drivers speeding around a car that is actually turning left.

Baja ferry at Mazatlán.

Travelers' Tips

Never drive at night in Mexico. Street lights are uncommon, and in rural areas many people drive without using their headlights. Darkness seems to bring out the machismo in Mexican drivers, who think nothing of trying to pass three cars on a curve. Workers returning home walk for miles along back roads; dogs, rabbits, cows and vultures all scavenge the pavement for their nightly meal. If you must drive at night, keep your speed low, your lights bright and all your senses alert.

BY TAXI

Cabs can be picked up at *sitios*, cab stands. Some cruise the streets; a *libre* sign in the front window

firms have stands at Mexico City International Airport as well as offices in the resorts and cities; locally operated agencies may be less expensive but not as reliable in dealing with insurance claims. Make sure the car is in good shape, drives well, and has an inflated spare tire; also be sure to check the list of dents it may have, as you are liable for any dents not inventoried. Be sure to take out insurance on your rental car.

FOREIGN CONSULATES AND EMBASSIES IN MEXICO CITY

Foreign consulates and embassies in Mexico City are open from Monday through Friday and are

usually means the cab is free. Radio cabs can be called at one of the numbers listed under *sitios de taxis* in the telephone directory. Tourist taxis line up outside hotels in major cities; some of the drivers speak English and charge by the hour. Always confirm the fare before the cab starts moving. Meters are used in some areas, while others rely on a zone system, which is usually posted at cab stands and in hotel lobbies. Taxi passengers are being robbed in Mexico City at an appalling rate; take strict precautions, never flag down a cab in the street and only use those with posted licenses.

CAR RENTAL

If you are 21 years or older, have a valid driver's license, and a major credit card, you can rent a car in Mexico. Although rates differ from city to city, rental cars are relatively expensive. All the major

closed both for official Mexican holidays as well as for their own national holidays. Some provide emergency numbers for nonbusiness hours.
Australia ((5) 531-5225
Austria ((5) 251-1606
Belgium ((5) 280-0758
Brazil ((5) 202-8737
Canada ((5) 724-7900
China ((5) 616-0509
Denmark ((5) 255-3405
Egypt ((5)281-0823
France ((5) 282-9700
Germany ((5) 280-5409
India ((5) 531-1002
Indonesia ((5) 280-6363
Israel ((5) 540-6340
Italy ((5) 596-3655
Japan ((5) 211-0028
Holland ((5) 202-8453

New Zealand ((5) 281-5486
Norway ((5) 540-5220
Pakistan ((5) 203-3636
Portugal ((5) 545-6213
Spain ((5) 282-2974
Sweden ((5) 540-6393
Switzerland ((5) 514-1727
Thailand ((5) 596-8446
Turkey ((5) 520-2346
United Kingdom ((5) 207-2809
United States ((5) 211-0012

MONEY

Mexico's unit of currency is the *peso nuevo*, or new peso, which was introduced in 1993. The bills come in 10-, 20-, 50-, 100-, 500- and 1,000-peso notes; coins of 1, 2, 5, 10 and 20 pesos look quite similar and are easily confused. The bills are different colors, but are similar enough to also be confusing. The peso has gone through two decades of wicked inflation and devaluation, and fell to half its value in 1995. At press time the **exchange rate** hovered around eight pesos to US$1.

Foreign currency and travelers checks can be changed at most banks and at *casas de cambio*, currency exchanges, whose rates are slightly less favorable than the banks. The lower rates are justified, however, by longer hours and quicker service. It can often take two hours to get the transaction done at a bank and five minutes at a *casa de cambio*. Large hotels will also change foreign dollars or travelers checks, but at even worse rates. In small towns there may not be change facilities, or if there are they may only take United States dollars. It is recommended that European and Australian travelers buy United States dollar travelers' checks for their trips.

Many establishments (hotels, restaurants and shops) will take payment in dollars or dollar travelers' checks, converted at the current or lower exchange rates. When short of Mexican cash it is better to negotiate payment in dollars. In the cities and resorts, the larger hotels and restaurants accept major credit cards. Many shops do also, but only for the full price of merchandise. That is to say, one cannot negotiate a reduction and then pay with a credit card. Automatic teller machines (ATMs) using international symbols are available in most major cities and resort areas.

TIPPING

Service charges are rarely added to the bill and most service people including waiters, waitresses, chambermaids, bellboys, and gas station attendants are paid less than $4 a day. Be generous. In some resorts, a service charge is added to room and restaurant bills; ask if the staff actually get this money and tip accordingly.

At restaurants give at least 15%. This is a habit that many Europeans find difficult to adopt. If Europeans find they are less warmly welcomed in restaurants than Americans, it is probably because other Europeans have not been leaving tips. Bellboys and porters should be given three or four pesos (less than 40 cents) per bag, and more for any special services. Chambermaids should get at least three pesos a day. Cab drivers don't expect tips, but a little extra is always welcome, particularly if the driver has helped with your bags or followed, patiently, a set of unclear directions.

When tipping — and all cases of handling money in public areas, especially in resorts and large cities — it is best not to show a lot of cash.

Guard your valuables carefully. There are many pickpockets, particularly in Mexico City and Guadalajara. In every congested area, foreigners are obvious targets.

ACCOMMODATION

A note on addresses: For all the monuments, hotels, inns, restaurants and cafés we mention in this book, we have tried to give addresses. However, addresses in Mexico are not standardized and so, where no fixed street number is accorded to a place, we have in many cases given cross streets, kilometer markers or landmarks, as references. A street name followed by "s/n", means *sin número*, without number. If in doubt, ask once, and ask again, to ensure you have the correct directions.

We have also included contact numbers, unless there are none. Where available, we have also included the toll-free number, available to subscribers in the United States. Obviously, this number is not obtainable from calls dialed in Europe or Australasia.

Accommodation ranges from the bare necessities of a bed or hammock to the opulence of plush suites with many more comforts than most homes.

Mexico's modern hotels invite relaxation.

The prices vary accordingly. Hotel rates are established by the Ministry of Tourism, but hoteliers have been given more flexibility in adjusting their rates to meet the demand. It is important to bear in mind that prices of hotels in the large cities and resorts will be considerably more expensive than those in smaller cities and towns. Special package tours are often available to these more expensive destinations that include airfare, hotel room and some extras, for little more than the normal airfare. Travel agents can best supply a full range of choices. Hotels in non-tourist towns in the interior generally have constant year-round rates, while those on the coasts reduce theirs by as much as 30% during the off-season or rainy months of June, July, and September into November. Rates jump back up, however, in August when Mexican nationals and Europeans take their long vacations.

As a guide to hotel costs, we have classified the prices for guestrooms with double occupancy, including 15% tax, into four broad categories. (Note, however, that Mexico's tourist industry is growing rapidly and many of its hotels are being upgraded, thus the rates quoted below may have increased since the time of research):

VERY EXPENSIVE: Over $150 (Mexico City and the resorts)
EXPENSIVE: $101 to $150
MODERATE: $50 to $100
INEXPENSIVE: Under $50

The VERY EXPENSIVE category features award-winning hotels with a degree of opulence geared at the most moneyed traveler who expects every conceivable comfort at the press of a button. Hotel facilities in these two categories range from comprehensive to outstanding, and their restaurants are among the best in the country. A hotel in the EXPENSIVE bracket are usually self-contained, so that guests need only leave the grounds to get to and from the airport. Guestrooms are large, very comfortable and air-conditioned and include many amenities. Hotels categorized as MODERATE vary greatly in the size of rooms and comforts they provide. This seems to depend on the area and the local competition. In all cases they have en-suite bathrooms and most have air-conditioning, restaurants and pools. Often, INEXPENSIVE hotels are as good or better than the moderate ones, but usually do not have a pool, restaurant or air-conditioning. Accommodations in this final category may have either private or shared bathrooms.

Some of the hotels in our inexpensive category cost as little as $20 to $30 a night for a double room. These rock-bottom budget hotels are available in most areas, though it may take some intensive searching to find ones that are clean, secure and comfortable. Low-end budget hotels typically don't have fax numbers, making it a little more difficult to make advance reservation. Flexibility

is an important asset when traveling off the beaten path in Mexico.

The National Youth Hostel Association, CREA, operates several hostels. They offer dormitory accommodation and vary in size from 20 beds to 100. For more information, contact the Agencia Nacional de Turismo Juvenil ((5) 525-2548, Glorieta Metro Insurgentes, Local CC-11, 06600 Mexico DF.

EATING OUT

The cuisine of Mexico is one of the greatest pleasures of visiting this extraordinary country (see GALLOPING GOURMETS, page 48). From the small casual family-run restaurant to the large, fancy

candlelit dining rooms, most take pride in the freshness and quality of their meals.

RESTAURANTS

The restaurants listed under each of the regional destinations have been chosen for their reliably good food and quality of service. The categories are based on the approximate price of a full-course meal, but do not include wine or other beverages, tips and taxes. They are classified into four categories:

VERY EXPENSIVE: Over $20
EXPENSIVE: $16 to $20
MODERATE: $5 to $15
INEXPENSIVE: Under $5

Cautious travelers prefer to stick to foods that have been cooked, and fruits and vegetables which have been peeled. Sanitary conditions have, however, improved considerably in Mexico, especially in the resort areas.

An increasing number of tourist hotels and restaurants post signs indicating that purified water is used in all food and drinks; I usually believe them unless something raises my suspicions. I'm more cautious in older cities and small towns, and stay away from most street and market food. It's good to get in the habit of always having at least a liter (a quart) or more of purified water on hand, more if you are traveling by car.

Many hotels with old water purification systems charge exorbitant prices for bottled water; its better to find the nearest market and stock up there. You can easily make your own meals by stocking up on produce at the public markets, breads at a *panadería*, and sealed, homogenized cheese and yogurt from a grocery store.

POPULAR DISHES AND SNACKS

Below is a list of some of the most frequently found Mexican dishes with a brief description of each:
aguas — fruit juices, watered down
antojitos — appetizers, also called *botanes*
burrito — a flour tortilla wrapped around beans, meat, fish or a combination of ingredients
carne — meat, usually beef, which can also served as *carne asada*
carne asada — grilled, marinated thin strips of beef
cerveza — beer
ceviche — raw fish or shellfish marinated in lime juice, onions, cilantro (coriander) and tomato.
chilaquiles — tortilla strip cooked in broth
chili relleno — a green chili stuffed with meat or fish, and covered with a corn batter
cilantro — coriander leaves
enchilada — a corn tortilla dipped in a spicy sauce, wrapped around a meat or cheese filling and baked
flan — caramel or fruit-flavored custard
guacamole — a dip or sauce of mashed avocado
licuado — cold drinks of fresh fruit mixed with water or milk
mole — a sauce of multiple pungent spices, sometimes including bitter chocolate
pan — bread
pan dulce — sweet breads similar to Danish pastries
pescado — fish
pollo — chicken
postre — pastry
pozole — a stew of hominy (similar to corn) and chicken or pork
quesadilla — a flour or corn tortilla folded over a filling of melted cheese
queso fundido — melted cheese similar to fondue
salsa — a sauce of tomatoes, onions, hot peppers, citrus juice and other seasonings; there are many kinds of salsa, and some are fiery hot
taco — a soft or deep-fried corn tortilla wrapped around a meat, bean or cheese filling

tamales — a wrapping of corn husks enclosing cornmeal and meat, fruit or cheese
torta — a sandwich of a soft roll (*bolillo*) and filling

BASICS

TIME

Mexico has four time zones and started observing Daylight Saving Time in 1997. The Yucatán Peninsula is six hours behind Europe and on the same time as United States Eastern Standard Time. The central states are one hour earlier, the same as United States Central Standard; the western states of Nayarit, Sinaloa, Sonora, and Baja California Sur are another hour earlier, the same as United States Mountain Standard Time; and Baja California Norte is the same as United States Pacific Standard Time.

ELECTRICITY

Electrical current is 110 volt 60 cycle AC, and outlets and plugs are the kind you find in the United States.

WATER

The basic longstanding rule is: *Don't drink the water!* You can ignore that rule in expensive, high-quality hotels in new resort areas such as Cancún and Huatulco when there are posted signs saying the hotel treats its own water.

WEIGHTS AND MEASURES

Travelers from the United States beware: Mexico is a metric country. A kilometer is shorter than a mile (0.625 miles, to be exact), and a kilogram weighs 2.2 pounds.

CLIMATE

Nothing regulates the Mexican way of life more than its weather. With the Tropic of Cancer bisecting the nation, Mexico's climate is hot. Only in the north or at the highest elevations in the mountains is there ever snow, and then not very often, though nearly half the country is more than 1,525 m (5,000 ft) above sea level. Both coasts and the lower altitudes of the interior can be quite hot, with average year-round temperatures of about 23°C (73°F). Average temperatures in the Sierra Madres and the mountains of the Valley of Mexico range from 12°C to 18°C (54°C to 64°F), and the valley floor is usually 4°C (10°F) warmer.

Rather than winter, spring, summer and fall, Mexico alternates between the dry season (late

Street musicians, such as this organ grinder, bring regional touches to quieter corners of Mexico City.

November through early June) and the rainy season (June through November). The "tourist season" usually refers to the dry season, and particularly the months of December, January, February and March, and will include April when Easter falls in this month. The "off season" or rainy season is not at all a bad time to travel in Mexico. The rains are not constant; instead they are typically heavy showers followed by bright sunshine. Temperatures are hot during this time of year, and hotel prices are greatly reduced. Living in this climate year-round, Mexicans work early and late, taking a three- to four-hour siesta during the peak of the day's heat — a practice which is soon appreciated by visiting northerners.

Area codes within Mexico change constantly, and may have one, two or three digits. This doesn't affect international calls but can be extremely frustrating when making long distance and local calls nationally. If you run into a series of wrong numbers, try using the last digit of the area code with the local number; most times the change in numbers follows this system. Numbers, too, can have anything from four to seven digits, and are written in a variety of ways. Standardization will arrive one day! The fax has been one of the greatest technological advances to hit Mexico. Most business now have a machine, though they may have only one phone line. In such cases you must ask for the fax tone by saying *Necesito enviar un fax,*

COMMUNICATIONS AND THE MEDIA

por favor or *Por favor darme el tono por fax.* Fax machines are often turned off after business hours.

TELEPHONES

Mexico's telephone system is fairly efficient, but extremely expensive. The easiest way to make long-distance telephone calls is with a prepaid telephone card from LADATEL, available at pharmacies and markets. When calling from Mexico to the United States or to Canada dial "001" before the area code and number; for other countries, dial "00" plus the country code before the number. In 1998, Mexico instituted a new system for calling long distance within the country. The old system, still in use as this goes to press, is to dial "91" before the area code and number. The new system is to dial "01" before the area code and number.

THE INTERNET

Mexico is not as advanced as some other countries in its use of e-mail and tourism web sites. The government does have a tourism web site at www.mexico-travel.com, but I have found it to be too basic for my needs. Tour companies and travel agencies are the most likely web site users; their addresses can be found in YOUR CHOICE, beginning on page 23, and in the regional chapters.

MAIL

The Mexican postal system is so bad that I have practically given up on sending letters or packages to friends living in Mexico. If you wish to take your chances, remember that postal codes should be placed before the name of the city in the address. Post offices are usually open from 8 AM to 5 PM on weekdays and 9 AM to 12 PM on Saturday mornings.

In Mexico City the main post office, **Dirección General de Correos** ((5) 521-7760, is on Ejército Central at Calle Tacuba. Hours are Monday through Saturday from 8 AM to midnight, Sunday from 8 AM to 4 PM.

NEWSPAPERS

Mexico has two English-language newspapers, *The News* and *Mexico City Times*, published daily in Mexico City. Only *The News* is available throughout the country; you'll find each day's edition after the first plane from the capital has arrived. *USA Today* and *The International Herald Tribune* are available in Mexico City and other major destinations. European newspapers appear in some upscale hotels in resort areas.

ETIQUETTE

Mexicans are unfailingly polite, amiable and kind to strangers unless treated rudely. Then they can be obstinate, cold and aloof. Formal greetings are immensely important. Always say *con mucho gusto* (with much pleasure) when introduced to someone, and greet everyone with a polite *buenas días, tardes* or *noche*. Mexicans hug, kiss and walk arm-in-arm regardless of gender; it's as common to see two businessmen heartily embrace and pat each others backs as it is to see two women kiss on the cheek. When conducting business always ask about a person's health, family or general mood, before launching into a question or pitch.

HEALTH AND EMERGENCIES

HEALTH CONCERNS

Montezuma's Revenge is real. Most tap water in Mexico is polluted, and all but the poorest families buy water by the jug for human consumption. To remain in good health, travelers are well advised to follow these guidelines:

Drink only bottled or sterilized water (*agua purificada*), or beer and soft drinks, and only use ice cubes made from purified water.

If cut **lime** is served with a meal, use it unsparingly on all your food.

Avoid cold salads except in tourist restaurants; for fruits, eat only those that you can peel.

If you get sick, don't panic. Nearly every one feels queasy for a day or two on a foreign trip. It can often pass in 24 hours with the help of purified water and mild antacids. Some doctors suggest

you take a spoonful of Pepto Bismal or some other stomach-coating medication before each meal.

Mexican pharmacists are like neighborhood doctors; explain your symptoms and they'll come up with a cure, or at least a temporary fix. They will dispense medications in small doses, so you can buy cards of 10 aspirin rather than large bottles of 20 or more.

Mexico has several excellent medical schools, and doctors in private hospitals and clinics are well trained. Most hospitals and clinics are well-equipped. The rates are surprisingly low for the quality of service.

Infectious diseases such as cholera, malaria, hepatitis and dengue fever do occur, especially

during long heavy rains and after hurricanes. Inoculations are not required, though it is a good idea to have your tetanus booster up-to-date. Sexually transmitted diseases, including AIDS, are a definite concern if you're sexually active during your travels. Carry and use condoms.

Snakes and Scorpions

Like most tropical countries, Mexico has its share of low-to-the-ground venomous creatures. With very few exceptions, they would rather go their own way untroubled and let you go yours. To avoid antagonizing them, follow these simple rules:

Don't walk in the jungle or tall grass at night. Most snakes hunt at night and get irritated if they're

OPPOSITE: Zaachilla market. ABOVE: There's a deal for every budget and taste in Mexico.

stepped on. In snake country, it's best to avoid tall grass even in the day. In the jungle during the day, stick to the paths, and watch where you step.

Don't put your hand where it doesn't belong! This means avoid putting it into any cracks in rocks, in ruins, or in any other small dark place. Coral snakes and scorpions enjoy inhabiting such locations; they are generally quite peaceful but resent intrusions. Scorpions and palm snakes also like the broad fronds of palm and other beach front trees.

If you're camping out (even in the desert or mountains) or sleeping on the beach, shake out your shoes in the morning before you put them on (scorpions love to sleep in shoes), and check any cloth, tarp, or other item left on the ground before you use it.

In the rare case of a snake or scorpion bite, remember the size and color of the snake, and get to a doctor. There are antitoxins available for nearly all such venoms.

Toilets

What vast improvements there have been in the past few decades when it comes to toilet facilities! Outhouses are common only in the most remote areas. Toilet seats, on the other hand, seem to be a precious commodity. One manager of a budget hotel told me he only provides a seat if the guest asks for one; seat thievery is apparently quite common. Toilets may or may not flush, and can be utterly horrid on long train and bus rides. Always carry toilet paper, another luxury.

HOSPITALS

In the case of serious emergencies in Mexico City, the following two hospitals can be of assistance: **American British Cowdry ℭ** (05) 230-8000 (ABC) Hospital, Avenida Observatorio at Calle 132 Sur **Hospital Angeles de Pedregal ℭ** (05) 652-1188, Camino a Santa Teresa.

SAFETY AND SECURITY

I have always felt far safer in Mexico than in most major United States cities. You never saw or heard of violent crime until a few years back, and even now most travelers never encounter rough treatment. Theft, however, is becoming more and more common as poverty reaches into the middle classes. Always use a money belt; never flash around money and jewelry, and keep your possessions close at hand at all times. Highway robbery has become more common, and can be quite frightening. It most often occurs on remote thoroughfares, such as the long highways in the far northern and southern parts of the country. The usual scenario involves a tree or rocks set across the road; when the driver stops, robbers

appear much like the *bandidos* in movies of old. There's not much you can do under such situations except hand over your belongings.

The *mordida* (bribe) is jokingly called a tip by those in the know, and though Mexican authorities are trying mightily to cut down on corruption among its police force, *mordidas* are still common. If stopped by the police you are supposed to ask to be taken to the police station and formally ticketed; many locals avoid this tedious process by offering to pay the fine on the spot.

It is unwise to carry drugs because Mexican narcotics laws are very strict and even large quantities of prescription drugs can bring suspicion. If you need to travel with a large medicine chest, bring copies of your prescriptions. Embassies avoid getting involved in drug charges and it has been wisely said that it is better to be caught with drugs by American authorities than Mexican ones. Possession of even a film canister of marijuana can entitle one to a 10-year sentence (with no parole) in a jail that would make Hell seem like a resort.

WHEN TO GO

Mexico's peak tourism season begins in mid-November and lasts until after Easter, with another rise in August. I prefer traveling in Mexico from September through October though hurricanes sometimes wreak havoc with my plans. The weather from May to September is hot, muggy and even miserable in most coastal areas. See CLIMATE, page 361.

WHAT TO TAKE

Pack light! Mexico is a casual country and one rarely has need for winter clothes. Comfortable, lightweight clothing is all that is needed, unless one is planning to climb Popocatépetl or one of the other peaks, or hike in the northern mountains and desert during winter. In winter months and at high elevations, early mornings and nights can be cool, thus a lightweight jacket is recommended. It is wise to bring at least one long-sleeved shirt or blouse, and one pair of long pants for protection from both the sun and mosquitoes (jogging gear is often quite acceptable).

If pre-Columbian ruins are in your plans, bring a pair of comfortable walking shoes. Sandals are not suitable for rambling around archaeological sites. For any destination, sun screen is a must. The sun is more intense as you get closer to the equator.

Photographers are advised to bring extra film because it is more costly in Mexico than in the United States or in Europe. In addition, film purchased in Mexico may have been subjected to improper storage at high temperatures.

MEXICAN SPANISH FOR TRAVELERS

From the delight with which most Mexicans welcome any attempt by visitors to speak Spanish, it would seem that nothing gives them greater pleasure than hearing their language mispronounced. That really isn't the case, but if you go beyond the veneer of social niceties with a waiter or bellboy, you'll most likely find a frustrated language teacher. You can usually get by quite comfortably with a mix of Spanish and English, called "Spanglish" in border cities. Still, a pocket phrase book and a pad and pencil are always a good idea.

Spanish doesn't present many pronunciation problems because most letters always retain the same sound.

a is pronounced as in "rather"
e as in "they"
i as the "d" in "we"
o as in "bold"
u as in "food"
h is always silent
b and **v** are both pronounced "b"
ñ is an "ny" combination
j is pronounced like the English "h"
g is pronounced like the English "h" when it comes before "e" and "i"; elsewhere it is hard, as in "gold"
z is pronounced like the English "s"
qu is pronounced as a "k"
x is pronounced as "s" (e.g., Xochimilco or Taxco), but in some cases is pronounced as an "h" (e.g., Xalapa), and when preceded by an "e" it is pronounced "ex" as in "extra."

r is the troublemaker. It's pronounced with the tip of the tongue on the palate of your mouth, behind the front teeth, and the "rr" is rolled. It's tricky, but just wait until you try to pronounce some of the Indian names, most of which are difficult, even for Mexicans.

Then, there's the matter of gender. Basically, all you have to remember is that words that end in "o" are usually masculine and preceded by the word "el", and words that end in "a" are usually feminine and preceded by the word "la". There are, naturally, exceptions: "la papa" means the potato; "el Papa" means the Pope.

POLITE PHRASES

Good morning. *Buenos días.*
Good afternoon. *Buenas tardes.*
Good evening. *Buenas noches.*
Yes *Sí*
No *No*
Good-bye. *Adiós.*
Excuse me. *Con permiso* (when trying to get to the back of the bus).

Excuse me. *Discúlpame* (when you bumped into someone or made a mistake).
Thank you very much. *Muchas gracias.*

COMMON QUESTIONS AND ANSWERS

Where are you from? *De donde es usted?*
I'm from___. *Soy de___.*
Do you like Mexico? *Le gusta México?*
Yes, very much. *Sí, mucho.*
How long will you be in Mexico? *Cuánto tiempo va a estar en México?*
I'll be here___days/___weeks. *Voy a estar___días/___semanas.*

RESTAURANTS

Menu please. *La carta, por favor.*
Check please. *La cuenta, por favor.*
Purified water, without ice, please.
Agua purificada sin hielo por favor.

SHOPPING

How much does it cost? *Cuánto cuesta?*
What is your lowest price?
Cual es su último precio?
It's very expensive. *Es muy caro.*
Do you have it in my size?
Tiene esto en mi talla?

LONG DISTANCE TELEPHONE CALLS

I want to call___. *Quiero hacer una llamada telefónica a___.*
Collect call *Llamada por cobrar*
The area code is___. *La ruta es___.*
The number is___. *El número es___.*

NUMBERS

one *uno*
two *dos*
three *tres*
four *cuatro*
five *cinco*
six *seis*
seven *siete*
eight *ocho*
nine *nueve*
ten *diez*

Recommended Reading

AMES, NEILL, *Dust on my Heart: Petticoat Vagabond in Mexico*, Scribners, 1946.

BEALES, CARLTON, *Mexican Maze*, Lippincot, 1931.

BERMUDEZ, FERNANDO, *Death and Resurrection in Guatemala*, Orbis Books, 1986.

BRENNER, ANITA, *Idols Behind Altars*, Harcourt and Brace, 1929.

COE, MICHAEL, *The Maya*, Thames and Hudson, 1987.

DEL CARMEN MILLAN, MARIA, *Antología de Cuentos Méxicanos*, Editorial Nueva Imagen, 1982.

DÍAZ, BERNAL, *The Conquest of New Spain*, Shoe String, 1988.

FUENTES, CARLOS, *The Old Gringo*, HarperCollins, 1986.

JENNINGS, GARY, *Aztec*, Avon, 1981.

LAWRENCE, D.H., *Mornings in Mexico*, Penguin Books, 1960.

LEWIS, OSCAR, *Children of Sanchez*, Random House, 1979.

LEWIS, OSCAR, *Five Families*, Basic Books, 1979.

LOWRY, MALCOLM, *Under the Volcano*, NAL-Dutton, 1984.

MACINTOSH, GRAHAM, *Into a Desert Place*, Graham Macintosh, 1988.

METROPOLITAN MUSEUM OF ART, *Mexico: Splendors of Thirty Centuries*, 1979.

MICHENER, JAMES A., *Mexico*, Random House, 1992.

MICHENER, JAMES A., *Caribbean*, Random House, 1989.

O'REILLY, JAMES AND HABEGGER, LARRY, *Travelers' Tales Mexico*, Travelers' Tales, 1994.

OSTER, PATRICK, *The Mexicans: A Personal Portrait of the Mexican People*, Harper & Roe, 1989.

REAVIS, DICK J., *Conversations with Moctezuma*, Quill, 1990.

RIDING, ALAN, *Distant Neighbors: A Portrait of the Mexicans*, Random House, 1984.

RYAN, ALAN, *The Reader's Companion to Mexico*, Harcourt Brace & Co., 1995.

SCHELE, LINDA AND FRIEDEL, DAVID, *A Forest of Kings*, William Morrow, 1990.

SMITH, JACK, *God and Mr. Gomez*, Watts, Franklin, 1982.

STEVENS, JOHN LLOYD, *Incidents of Travel in Yucatán*, Dover, 1843.

STREET-PORTER, TIM, *Casa Mexicana*, Tabori & Chang, 1986.

PAZ, OCTAVIO, *Libertad Bajo Palabra*, Fondo de Cultura Economica, 1960.

PAZ, OCTAVIO, *A Labyrinth of Solitude*, Grove Press, 1985.

Additional Photo Credits
Mexican Tourist Office: pages 183, 184, 185, 200, 275, 279.
Sofocles Fernandez: page 187
Buddy Mays/Travel Stock: page 306

Quick Reference A–Z Guide
to Places and Topics of Interest with
Listed Accommodation, Restaurants and
Useful Telephone Numbers